D1392395

Also by Susanna Gregory

The Matthew Bartholomew Series

A BONE OF CONTENTION
A DEADLY BREW
A WICKED DEED
A MASTERLY MURDER
AN ORDER FOR DEATH
A SUMMER OF DISCONTENT
A KILLER IN WINTER
THE HAND OF JUSTICE
THE MARK OF A MURDERER
THE TARNISHED CHALICE

The Thomas Chaloner Series:

A CONSPIRACY OF VIOLENCE
BLOOD ON THE STRAND

SUSANNA GREGORY OMNIBUS

A Plague on Both Your Houses

An Unholy Alliance

Susanna Gregory

sphere

SPHERE

A Plague on Both
Your Houses

To my husband for his
encouragement and
enthusiasm

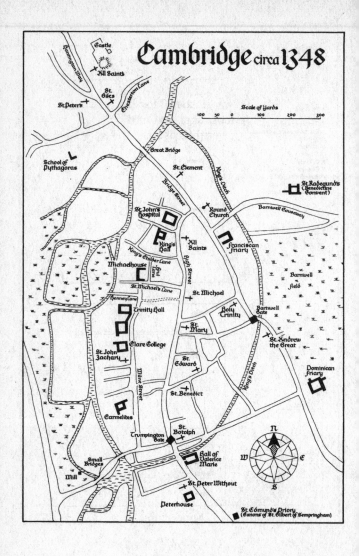

Cambridge circa 1348

Castle
All Saints
St. Giles
St. Peters
Huntingdon Road
Chesterton Lane

School of Pythagoras

Great Bridge

St. Clement

St. Radegund's (Benedictine Convent)

King's Ditch

Barnwell Causeway

St. John's Hospital

Round Church

Bridge Street

King's Hall

All Saints

Franciscan Friary

King's Childer Lane

Michaelhouse

Piron Lane

St. Michael's Lane

St. Michael

Barnwell Field

Henney Lane

Trinity Hall

Holy Trinity

Barnwell Gate

St. Mary

St. Andrew the Great

Clare College

St. John Zachary

St. Edward

Milne Street

Dominican Friary

St. Benedict

King's Ditch

Carmelites

Trumpington Gate

St. Botolph

N

Scale of Yards
100 50 0 100 200 300

Small Bridges

Mill

Hall of Valence Marie

W   E

S

St. Peter Without

Peterhouse

St. Edmund's Priory
(Canons of St. Gilbert of Sempringham)

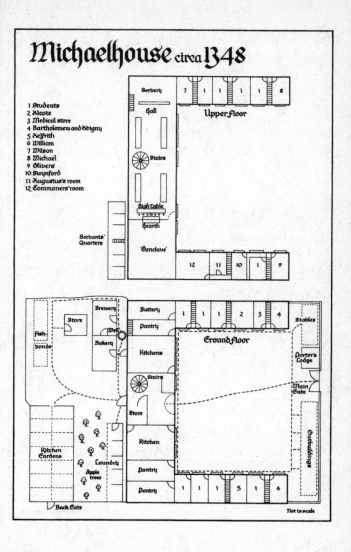

PROLOGUE

Cambridge, 1348

THE SCHOLAR WAITED IN THE BLACK SHADOWS OF the churchyard trees for the Sheriff's night patrol to pass by, trying to control his breathing. Two of the men stopped so close that he could have reached out and touched them. They stood for several minutes, leaning against the wall surrounding the churchyard, looking up and down the deserted road. The scholar held his breath until he thought he would choke. He could not be discovered now: there was so much to lose.

Eventually, the Sheriff's men left, and the scholar took several unsteady breaths, forcing himself to remain in the safety of the shadows until he was certain that they had gone. He jumped violently as a large cat stalked past his hiding place, glancing at him briefly with alert yellow eyes. He watched it sit for a moment in the middle of the road, before it disappeared up a dark alleyway.

The scholar gripped the voluminous folds of his cloak, so that he would not stumble on them, and slipped out of the trees into the road. The moon was almost full, and shed an eerie white light along the main street. He peered carefully both ways, and, satisfied that there was

1

no one to see him, he made his way stealthily down the street towards his home.

The main gates of the College were locked, but the scholar had ensured that the little-used back door was left open. He turned from the High Street into St Michael's Lane. He was almost there.

He froze in horror as he saw someone was already in the lane: another scholar, also disobeying College rules by being out at night, was walking towards him. Heart thumping, he ducked into a patch of tall nettles and weeds at the side of the road, in the hope that his stillness and dark cloak would keep him hidden. He heard the footsteps come closer and closer. Blood pounded in his ears, and he found he was trembling uncontrollably. The footsteps were almost level with him. Now he would be uncovered and dragged from his hiding place!

He almost cried in relief as the footfall passed him by, and faded as his colleague turned the corner into the High Street. He stood shakily, oblivious to the stinging of the nettles on his bare hands, and ran to the back gate. Once inside, he barred it with unsteady hands, and made his way to the kitchens. Faint with relief, he sank down next to the embers of the cooking fire and waited until his trembling had ceased. As he prepared to return to his room to sleep away what little remained of the night, he wondered how many more such trips he might make before he was seen.

Several hours later, the Bishop's Mill miller dragged himself from his bed, tugged on his boots, and set off to his work. The sky was beginning to turn from dark blue to silver in the east, and the miller shivered in the crispness of the early morning. He unlocked the door to the building and then went to feed the fat pony that he kept to carry flour to the town.

A short distance away, he could hear the rhythmic whine and swish of the water-wheel, powered by a fast-running channel diverted from the river. The miller had grown so familiar with its sound that he never noticed it unless there was something wrong. And there was something wrong this morning. There was an additional thump in the rhythm.

The miller sighed irritably. Only the previous week he had been forced to ask the help of his neighbours to free the branch of a tree that had entangled itself in the wheel, and he was loathe to impose on their good graces again so soon. He tossed some oats to the pony, and, wiping his hands on his tunic, he went to investigate. As he drew nearer, he frowned in puzzlement. It did not sound like a branch had been caught, but something soggier and less rigid. He rounded the corner and approached the great wheel, creaking and pounding as the water roared past it.

He felt his knees turn to jelly as he saw the wheel and what was caught in it, and sank onto the grass, unable to tear his eyes away. The body of a man was impaled there, black robes flapping wetly around him as the wheel dragged him under the water again and again. As the wheel lifted the body, one arm flopped loose in a ghostly parody of a wave, which continued until the body dived, feet first, back into the water for another cycle. The horrified miller watched the body salute him three times before he was able to scramble to his feet and race towards the town screaming for help.

1

THE DULL THUD OF HORSES' HOOVES AND THE gentle patter of rain on the wooden coffin were the only sounds to disturb the silence of the dawn. Black-gowned scholars walked slowly in single file along the High Street, following the funeral cart past the town gate to the fields beyond, where the body of their Master, Sir John Babington, would be laid in its final resting place. Somewhere behind him, Matthew Bartholomew heard one of the students stifle a giggle. He turned round and scowled in the general direction of the offending noise. Nerves, doubtless, he thought, for it was not every day that the College buried a Master who had taken his own life in such a bizarre manner.

The small procession was allowed through the gate by sleepy night-watchmen who came to the door of their guardroom to look. One of them furtively nudged the other and both smirked. Bartholomew took a step towards them, but felt Brother Michael's restraining hand on his shoulder. Michael was right; it would be wrong to turn Sir John's funeral into a brawl. Bartholomew brought his anger under control. Sir John had been one of the few men in the University who had been liked by the townspeople, but they had been quick to turn against him once the manner of his death became known. Had Sir John died a natural death, he would have been buried in the small churchyard of St Michael's, and been given a glorious funeral. Instead, church law decreed that, as a suicide, he should be buried in unconsecrated ground, and be denied any religious ceremony. So, in the first grey light of day, Sir John was escorted out of the city by the scholars of Michaelhouse, to be laid to rest in the waterlogged fields behind the church of St Peter-without-Trumpington Gate.

The horse pulling the cart bearing the coffin stumbled in the mud, causing the cart to lurch precariously. Bartholomew sprang forward to steady it, and was surprised to see Thomas Wilson, the man most likely to be Sir John's successor, do the same. The eyes of the two men met for an instant, and Wilson favoured Bartholomew with one of his small pious smiles. Bartholomew looked away. No love had been lost between the smug, self-satisfied Wilson and Sir John, and it galled Bartholomew to watch Wilson supervise Sir John's meagre funeral arrangements. He took a deep breath, and tried not to think how much he would miss Sir John's gentle humour and sensible rule.

Wilson gave an imperious wave of a flabby white hand, and Bartholomew's book-bearer, Cynric ap Huwydd, hurried forward to help the ostler lead the horse off the road and across the rough land to the grave site. The cart swayed and tipped, and the coffin bounced, landing with a hollow thump. Wilson seized Cynric's shoulder angrily, berating him for being careless in a loud, penetrating whisper.

Bartholomew had had enough. Motioning to the other Fellows, he edged Sir John's coffin from the cart, and together they lifted it onto their shoulders. They began the long walk across the fields to where the grave had been dug in a ring of sturdy oak trees. Bartholomew had chosen the spot because he knew Sir John had liked to read in the shade of the trees in the summer, but he began to doubt his choice as the heavy wood cut into his shoulder and his arms began to ache. After a few minutes, he felt himself being nudged aside, and smiled gratefully as the students came forward to take their turn.

Wilson walked ahead, and stood waiting at the graveside, head bowed and hands folded in his sleeves like a monk. The students lowered their burden to the ground and looked at Bartholomew expectantly. He arranged some ropes, and the coffin was lowered into the ground. He nodded to Cynric and the other book-bearers to start to fill in the grave, and, taking a last look, he turned to go home.

'Friends and colleagues,' began Wilson in his rich, self-important voice, 'we are gathered together to witness the burial of our esteemed Master, Sir John Babington.'

Bartholomew froze in his tracks. The Fellows had agreed the night before that no words would be spoken: it was felt that there were none needed – for what could be said about Sir John's extraordinary suicide? It had been decided that the Fellows and the students should escort Sir John to his resting place in silence, and return to the College still in silence, as a mark of respect. Sir John had done much to bring a relative peace to his College in a city where the scholars waged a constant war with each other and with the townsfolk. A few of his policies had made him unpopular with some University authorities, especially those who regarded learning to be the domain of the rich.

'Sir John,' Wilson intoned, 'was much loved by us all.' At this, Bartholomew gazed at Wilson in disbelief. Wilson had led the opposition to almost anything Sir John had tried to do, and on more than one occasion had left the hall at dinner red-faced with impotent fury because Sir John had easily defeated his arguments with his quiet logic.

'He will be sorely missed,' continued Wilson, looking down mournfully as Cynric shovelled earth.

'Not by you!' muttered Giles Abigny, the College's youthful teacher of philosophy, so that only Bartholomew could hear him. 'Not when you stand to gain so much.'

'May the Lord look upon his soul with mercy,' Wilson continued, 'and forgive him for his iniquitous ways.'

Bartholomew felt the anger boil inside him. He thrust his clenched fists under his scholar's tabard so that they should not betray his fury to the students, and looked to see the reaction of the other Fellows. Abigny was positively glowering at Wilson, while Brother Michael watched with a sardonic smile. The other theologians, Father William and Father Aelfrith, were more difficult to read. Bartholomew knew that Aelfrith did not like Wilson, but was too politic to allow it to show. William, who had backed Wilson on many occasions against Sir John, now stood listening impassively. The last two Fellows, Roger Alcote and Robert Swynford, who taught the subjects of the Quadrivium, nodded at Wilson's words.

The book-bearers had almost finished filling in the grave. A miserable drizzle-laden wind swished through the trees, and somewhere a lone blackbird was singing. Wilson's voice droned on with its platitudes for a man he had neither liked nor respected, and Bartholomew abruptly turned on his heel and strode away. He heard Wilson falter for an instant, but then continue louder than before so that the wind carried his words to Bartholomew as he walked away.

'May the Lord look kindly on the College, and guide her in all things.'

Bartholomew allowed himself a disgusted snort. Presumably, Wilson's idea of the Lord guiding the College was to make him, Wilson, the next Master. He heard footsteps hurrying behind him, and was not surprised that Giles Abigny had followed his lead and left the group.

'We will be in trouble, Matt,' he said with a sidelong grin at Bartholomew. 'Walking out on Master Wilson's carefully prepared speech.'

'Not Master yet,' said Bartholomew, 'although I imagine that will come within the week.'

They arrived back at the road and paused to scrape some of the clinging mud from their boots. It started to rain hard and Bartholomew felt water trickling down his back. He looked back across the field, and saw Wilson leading the procession back to the College. Abigny took his arm.

'I am cold and wet. Shall we see if Hugh Stapleton will give us breakfast at Bene't Hostel? What I need now is a roaring fire and some strong wine.' He leaned a little closer. 'Our lives at Michaelhouse will soon change beyond anything we can imagine – if we have a livelihood there at all. Let us make the best of our freedom while we still have it.'

He tugged at Bartholomew's sleeve, urging him back along the High Street towards Bene't Hostel. Bartholomew thought for a moment before following. Behind them, Wilson's procession filed through the town gate as he led the way back to Michaelhouse. Wilson's lips pursed as he saw Bartholomew and Abigny disappear through the hostel door; he was not a man to forget insults to his pride.

As Bartholomew had predicted, Wilson was installed as the new Master of Michaelhouse within a week of Sir John's funeral. The students, commoners, and servants watched as the eight Fellows filed into the hall to begin the process of electing a new Master. The College statutes ordered that a new Master should be chosen by the Chancellor from two candidates selected by the Fellows. Bartholomew sat at the long table, picking idly at a splinter of wood while his colleagues argued. Wilson had support from Alcote, Swynford and Father William. Bartholomew, Brother Michael and Abigny wanted Father Aelfrith to be the other candidate, but Bartholomew knew which of the two the Chancellor would select, and was reluctant to become too embroiled in a debate he could not win. Eventually, seeing that it would divide the College in a way that neither Wilson nor Aelfrith could heal, Aelfrith declined to allow his name to go forward. Alcote offered to take his place, a solution that met with little enthusiasm from either side.

The Chancellor selected Wilson, who immediately began in the way he intended to continue, by having three students 'sent down' for playing dice on a Sunday, sacking the brewer for drinking, and declaring that everyone –

Fellows, commoners and students – should wear only black on Sundays. Bartholomew had to lend several of his poorer students the money to purchase black leggings or tunics, since they only possessed garments made of cheap brown homespun wool, which were harder-wearing and more practical than the more elegant black.

The day of Wilson's installation dawned clear and blue, although judging from the clatter and raised voices from the kitchen, most of the servants had been up with their duties all night. Bartholomew rose as the sky began to lighten, and donned the ceremonial red gown that marked him as a Doctor of the University. He sat on the bed again and looked morosely through the window across the yard. Term had not yet begun, so there were only fifteen students in residence, but they made up for the deficit with excited shouting and a good deal of running. Through the delicate arched windows opposite, he could see Fathers William and Aelfrith trying to quieten them down. Reluctantly, Bartholomew walked across the dry packed earth of the yard for breakfast in the hall, a rushed affair that was clearly an inconvenience for the harried servants.

The installation itself was grand and sumptuous. Dressed in a splendid gown of deep purple velvet with fur trimmings, and wearing his black tabard over the top, Wilson processed triumphantly through Cambridge, scattering pennies to the townsfolk. A few grubby urchins followed the procession, jeering insults, and several of the citizens spat in disdain. Wilson ignored them all, and throughout the long Latin ceremony at Michaelhouse in which he made his vows to uphold the College statutes and rules, he could scarcely keep the smug satisfaction from his face.

Many influential people were present from the University and the town. The Bishop of Ely watched the proceedings with a bored detachment, while the Chancellor and the Sheriff exchanged occasional whispers. Some of the town's officials and merchants had been invited too. They stood together, displaying a magnificent collection of brilliant colours and expensive cloth. Bartholomew saw Thomas Exton, the town's leading physician, dressed in a gown of heavy blue silk, surrounded by his enormous brood of children. Near him was Bartholomew's brother-in-law, Sir Oswald Stanmore, who owned estates to the south of Cambridge, and had made a fortune in the wool trade. He was flanked by his younger brother, Stephen, and Bartholomew's sister Edith.

Giles Abigny had refused to attend, announcing that he had a disputation to organise with Hugh Stapleton, the Principal of Bene't Hostel. Brother Michael made his disapproval of Wilson known by muttering loudly throughout the proceedings, and by coughing, apparently uncontrollably, in those parts that should have been silent. Bartholomew did what was expected of him, but without enthusiasm, his thoughts constantly straying back to Sir John.

Bartholomew looked at Wilson in his finery seated in the huge wooden chair at the head of the high table in Michaelhouse's hall, and suddenly felt a surge of anger against Sir John. He had done so much to bring long-standing disputes between the University and the town to a halt, and, as a brilliant lawyer and stimulating teacher, had attracted many of the best students to the College. His lifelong ambition had been to write a book explaining the complexities of English law for students, a book that still lay unfinished in his rooms.

Everything had been going so well for Sir John and for the College under his care, so why had he killed himself?

Bartholomew, Father Aelfrith, and Robert Swynford had dined with Sir John the night before his death, and he had been in fine spirits then, full of enthusiasm for starting a new section of his book, and looking forward to a sermon he had been invited to give at the University Church. Bartholomew and the others had left Sir John around eight o'clock. Cynric had seen Sir John leave the College a short time later, the last to see him alive. The following morning, Sir John's body had been found in the water-wheel.

As a practising physician and the College's Master of Medicine, Bartholomew had been summoned to the river bank, where the white-faced miller stood as far away as he could from the corpse. Bartholomew shuddered as he thought about Sir John's body that morning. He tried to concentrate on Father William's rapid Latin in the ceremony that would install Thomas Wilson as the new Master of Michaelhouse.

Finally, Father William nodded to Cynric, who began to ring the bell to proclaim that the College ceremony was over. Noisily, the students began to clatter out of the hall, followed rather more sedately by the Fellows and commoners, all moving towards St Michael's Church, where the College would ask God's blessing on Wilson's appointment. Bartholomew paused to offer his arm to Augustus of Ely, one of the commoners, who had taught law at the University for almost forty years before old age made his mind begin to ramble, and he had been given permission by Sir John to spend the rest of his days housed and fed by the College. Michaelhouse had ten commoners. Six were old men, like Augustus, who had given a lifetime's service to the University; the others were visiting scholars who were using Michaelhouse's facilities for brief periods of study.

Augustus turned his milky blue eyes on Bartholomew and gave him a toothless grin as he was gently escorted out of the dim hall into the bright August sunshine.

'This is a sad day for the College,' he crowed to Bartholomew, drawing irritable looks from some of the other scholars.

'Hush, Augustus,' said Bartholomew, patting the veined old hand. 'What is done is done, and we must look to the future.'

'But such sin should not go unpunished,' the old man continued. 'Oh, no. It should not be forgotten.'

Bartholomew nodded patiently. Augustus's mind had become even more muddled after the death of Sir John. 'It will not be forgotten,' he said reassuringly. 'Everything will be well.'

'Fool!' Augustus wrenched his arm away from Bartholomew, who stared at him in surprise. 'Evil is afoot, and it will spread and corrupt us all, especially those who are unaware.' He took a step backwards, and tried to straighten his crooked limbs. 'Such sin must not go unpunished,' he repeated firmly. 'Sir John was going to see to that.'

'What do you mean?' asked Bartholomew, bewildered.

'Sir John had begun to guess,' said Augustus, his faded blue eyes boring into Bartholomew. 'And see what happened.'

'The man is senile.' Robert Swynford's booming voice close behind him made Bartholomew jump.

Augustus began to sway back and forth, chanting a hymn under his breath. 'See? He does not know what rubbish he speaks.' He put his arm over Augustus's shoulders and waved across for Alexander the Butler to come to take him back to his quarters. Augustus flinched away from his touch.

'I will take him,' said Bartholomew, noting the old man's distress. 'He has had enough for today. I will make a posset that will ease him.'

'Yes, all the pomp and ceremony has shaken his mind even more than usual,' said Swynford, eyeing Augustus with distaste. 'God preserve us from a mindless fool.'

'God preserve us from being one,' snapped Bartholomew, angered by Swynford's intolerance. He was surprised at his retort. He was not usually rude to his colleagues. Reluctantly, he admitted to himself that Wilson's installation and old Augustus's words had unsettled him.

'Come, Matt,' said Swynford, dropping his usual bluff manner. 'It has been a hard time for us all. Let us not allow the ramblings of a drooling old man to spoil our chances of a new beginning. The man's mind has become more unhinged since Sir John died. You said so yourself only yesterday.'

Bartholomew nodded. Two nights before, the entire College had been awakened by Augustus, who had locked himself in his room and was screaming that there were devils trying to burn him alive. He had the window shutters flung open, and was trying to crawl out. It had taken Bartholomew hours to calm him, and then he had had to promise to stay in Augustus's room for the rest of the night to ensure the devils did not return. In the morning, Bartholomew had been prodded awake by an irate Augustus demanding to know what he was doing uninvited in his quarters.

Augustus stopped swaying and looked at Bartholomew, a crafty smile on his face. 'Just remember, John Babington, hide it well.'

Swynford tutted in annoyance. 'Take him to his bed, Alexander, and see that one of the servants stays with him. The poor man has totally lost the few remaining wits he had.'

Alexander solicitously escorted Augustus towards the north wing of the College where the commoners lived. As they went, Bartholomew could hear Augustus telling Alexander that he would not need any supper as he had just eaten a large rat he had seen coming out of the hall.

Swynford put his hand on Bartholomew's shoulder and turned him towards St Michael's. 'Tend to him later, Matt. We should take our places in the church.'

Bartholomew assented, and together they walked up St Michael's Lane to the High Street. Throngs of people milled around outside the church, attracted no doubt by hopes of more scattered pennies.

They elbowed their way through the crowd, earning hostile glances from some people. The last fight between the scholars and the townspeople had been less than a month before, and two young apprentices had been hanged for stabbing a student to death. Feelings still ran high, and Bartholomew was glad when he reached the church doors.

Father William had already begun to celebrate the mass, gabbling through the words at a speed that never failed to impress Bartholomew. The friar glanced across at the late-comers as they took their places at the altar rail, but his face betrayed no sign of annoyance. Brother Michael, for all his mumblings during the College ceremony, had rehearsed his choir well, and even the clamour of the people waiting outside lessened as angelic voices soared through the church.

Bartholomew smiled. Sir John had loved the choir, and often gave the children extra pennies to sing while he dined in College. Bartholomew wondered whether Master Wilson would spare a few pennies for music to brighten the long winter evenings. He stole a glance at Wilson to see if there was any indication that he was appreciating the singing. Wilson's head was bowed as he knelt, but his eyes were open and fixed on his hands. Bartholomew looked closer, and almost laughed aloud. Wilson was calculating something, counting on his fat, bejewelled fingers. His mind was as far from Michael's music or William's mass as Augustus's would have been.

The church became stuffy from the large number of people packed into it, and an overwhelming number of smells began to pervade: strongly scented cloth, sweat, incense, feet, and, as always, the rank stink of the river underlying it all. Occasionally, a cooling breeze would waft in through one of the glassless windows, bringing a moment of relief to those inside. Despite Father William's speedy diction, the ceremonial mass was long, and, for those townspeople who did not know Latin, incomprehensible. Students and citizens alike became bored: first they shuffled, trying to ease legs aching from standing, and then, restlessly, they began to whisper to each other.

Finally, the mass ended, and Wilson led the way out of the church and back to College for the celebratory feast. The sky that had been a brilliant blue for most of the day had started to cloud over. Bartholomew shivered, finding the fresh air chilly after the closeness of the church.

Outside, the crowd of townspeople had grown, drawn by the pomp and splendour. Bartholomew could see that their mood was surly, resentful of the wealth that bespoke itself in the gowns of many of the scholars, and of their assumed superiority. As Wilson's procession filed out of the church, Bartholomew could hear whispered comments about idle scholars draining the town of its affluence, comments that became more than whispers as the crowd grew in confidence.

Aware that such an ostentatious display of Michaelhouse wealth might serve to alienate the townspeople, Wilson had ordered that coins be distributed among the poor to celebrate his new post. Cynric and the other book-bearers, who had been told to give out the small leather bags containing pennies, were almost mobbed as the crowd surged towards them. Immediately, any semblance of order was lost, as handfuls of money were grabbed by those strong enough to push their way to the front. Fists began to fly, and the book-bearers beat a hasty retreat, leaving the crowd to fight over the coins.

Bartholomew saw students begin to group together, some of them holding sticks and small knives. Hastily he ordered them back to their Colleges or hostels. It would take very little to spark off a town brawl. Even the sight of a group of students, armed and spoiling for a fight, could be enough to start a full scale riot.

Most of the students left, many looking disappointed, but Bartholomew saw two of Michaelhouse's students, the Oliver brothers, darting here and there. Within a few minutes they had assembled a group of at least thirty black-gowned scholars, some from Michaelhouse, but most from other Colleges and hostels.

He groaned to himself. He strongly suspected that the Oliver brothers had been involved in starting the last town brawl. And what better time for another than now? The townsfolk were already massed, many angry that they had not managed to grab any of Wilson's money, and resentment still festered regarding the hanging of the two apprentices. It would take only a shouted insult from a student to a townsperson, and all hell would break loose. Some would just use fists, but others, especially the Oliver brothers, would use knives and sharpened sticks, and the injuries, like last time, would be horrific. Why anyone would want to start such a scene was beyond Bartholomew's imagination, but there were the students, already furtively sharing out the illicit weapons they had concealed in their robes.

Cynric stood behind him. 'Cynric! Fetch the Proctor and warn him that there may be trouble,' Bartholomew said urgently.

'As quick as I can,' Cynric whispered, grabbing Bartholomew's sleeve, 'but watch out for yourself. This looks ugly.' When Bartholomew turned to look at him, he had already gone, moving quickly in and out of the lengthening shadows with all the stealth of a cat.

The light was failing quickly now, and it was difficult to distinguish faces. The Oliver brothers, however, could be identified in virtually any light. Well over six feet tall, they both sported long fair hair that fell to their shoulders and were renowned for their flamboyant clothes. Even in the gloom, Bartholomew could see gold thread glittering on the gown of Elias, the elder of the two.

'All Michaelhouse scholars have been invited to attend Master Wilson's feast,' said Bartholomew pleasantly to Elias. 'It should be a night to remember. I am sure you will enjoy it.'

Nephews of the influential Abbess of St Radegund's Convent, Michaelhouse had been enticed to accept the Olivers as students in exchange for a small house on Foul Lane. They were not noted for their dedication to learning: Elias could barely read and write, although his younger brother showed a natural quickness of mind that could have been trained in scholarly matters had he shown the slightest willingness to learn.

'We have promised to visit our aunt tonight.' Henry Oliver had approached unnoticed. The slow-witted Elias gave him a grateful look, and Bartholomew, not for the first time, had to admire young Oliver's cunning. How could a teacher of Michaelhouse forbid a devoted nephew from visiting the venerable Abbess of St Radegund's?

'This is a very special day for our new Master,' said Bartholomew. 'I know he would appreciate both of you being present to share it with him.'

Henry Oliver narrowed his eyes. 'But we have promised our aunt,' he said in a mock-pleading manner. 'I could not bear to have the noble lady disappointed.'

'I am sure she will not be,' insisted Bartholomew, 'when you explain why.' Hiding his irritation at Oliver's ploy – after all, the Abbess of St Radegund's was no frail old crone living solely for visits from her kin, but a healthy, strong-minded woman in early middle age – he took Oliver firmly by the arm and began walking towards St Michael's Lane. Behind them, the students muttered, but, deprived of their leader, reluctantly began to disperse, those from Michaelhouse falling in behind Bartholomew and Henry.

Bartholomew felt, rather than saw, the shower of small stones that followed them. Henry slowed, and tried to turn back, but Bartholomew dragged him round the corner into St Michael's Lane, and increased his speed as much as he could without actually breaking into a run. He stole a glance behind him, and saw that a good part of the crowd from outside the church had followed them, and Bartholomew and his students were outnumbered at least five to one.

'We should all have stayed together,' Henry Oliver hissed, squirming in Bartholomew's grasp. 'Now, what chance do we have!'

'Every chance if we do not retaliate,' Bartholomew returned, nevertheless unnerved by the continuing hail of small stones that rained down upon them.

They neared the College gates, and Bartholomew wondered whether the last of the students would be able to escape the crowd. He let go of Henry, and pushed him towards the College. 'Go quickly!' he said urgently, 'And make sure the gates are ready to be fastened once all the students are inside.'

Henry needed no second bidding; he was no fool and knew when courage in a fight became stupidity. He set off down the lane with his fellow students streaming behind him. Bartholomew saw that a group of four scholars, Elias Oliver included, had been slow to follow him, and were now being jostled and shoved by those at the front of the advancing crowd. A sturdy man in a blacksmith's apron gave Elias a hard push, almost sending him sprawling. Elias bunched his fists, his face a mask of anger. One of the other students pulled him forward as Bartholomew silently urged them not to fight back.

The first of the four broke into a run. He reached the College gates, and was hauled through them by those already safe inside. Bartholomew noticed that Henry had the sturdy oak gates all but closed already, just a crack remaining to allow the stragglers in before they would be slammed shut on the mob outside.

As Elias drew level with Bartholomew, the blacksmith drew a wicked-looking blade from his apron, and jabbed wildly with it. Bartholomew wrenched Elias out of the path of the slicing blade and, abandoning all further pretence of calm, yelled for the last three students to run for their lives. White-faced, they obeyed, only just staying ahead of the mob, which surged after them. Gasping for breath, the three, with Bartholomew at the rear, shot through the gates, which were slammed shut; heavy bars were shot across as the mob crashed into them.

Bartholomew heard screams and yells, and knew that the people in the front were being crushed against the gates and walls by those behind. A student slumped to the ground as a further barrage of stones flew over the high walls. Master Wilson came scurrying out of the hall, flanked by his Fellows and guests, to see what all the commotion was about, and stopped short as he saw the lethal volley of missiles raining over the walls.

'A fitting end to a miserable day.' Bartholomew turned, and saw Giles Abigny helping to hold the gate against the battering from outside. He winced as a particularly heavy thump jarred it. Leaving his post to be filled by the students that came pouring from the dormitories at the sound of the affray, most already in their cleanest gowns in anticipation of the feast to come, he motioned Bartholomew into a doorway where they could not be overheard, his fresh face unusually serious. 'We should pick our scholars more carefully, Matt. Young Henry Oliver was all set to slam the door before you were inside, and would have done had I not been there.'

Bartholomew looked at him in disbelief. 'You must be mistaken, he . . .'

'No mistake, Matt. I heard him say to that spotty student of yours, the one from Fen Ditton who always has a cold . . .'

'Francis Eltham?'

'Indeed. I heard him tell Eltham to make sure that the gate was closed before you reached it. I ensured it remained open, but Oliver was furious. Look at him now.'

Bartholomew easily spotted the Oliver brothers among the milling students – they stood a head taller than the rest. Now that the immediate danger was over, the scholars had regained their confidence, and were shouting taunts to the people outside. Henry Oliver did not join in. He stood glowering, his face distorted with anger. Bartholomew saw him raise a bunched fist, and Eltham shrank back. As if he felt their eyes on him, Oliver turned his head slowly and stared back. Bartholomew felt the hairs on the back of his neck rise as he felt the venom of his stare. Abruptly, Oliver turned away, and stalked off towards his room.

'What have you done to deserve that?' wondered Abigny, disconcerted at such raw hatred.

'Prevented him from starting a riot, I suppose,' said Bartholomew. 'I had no idea he was so dedicated to causing chaos.'

The shouting outside the gates increased, and then

22

faltered. Bartholomew heard horses' hooves, and knew that the Sheriff and his troops had arrived, and were beginning to disperse the crowd. The battering on the College gates stopped, and the only sounds were the Sheriff's men telling people they could either go home or spend the night in the Castle, and the groans of the people who had been crushed against the gates.

'Michaelhouse!' Bartholomew recognised the voice of the Sheriff, and went to help open the gates.

The Sheriff had been compelled to use his garrison to break up many a fight between the University and the townspeople, and was heartily sick of it. Since he was unlikely to be able to rid himself of the townspeople, he often felt he would like to rid himself of the University and all its bickering and warring factions. Students from Norfolk, Suffolk, and Huntingdonshire fought scholars from Yorkshire and the north, and they all fought the students from Wales and Ireland. Masters and scholars who were priests, friars, or monks were always at odds with those who were not. And there was even dispute between the different religious Orders, the large numbers of Franciscan, Dominican, Augustinian, and Carmelite friars, who begged their livings, at loggerheads with the rich Benedictines and the Austin Canons who ran the Hospital of St John.

As the gates opened, he glowered in at the assembly, making no attempt to enter. The Senior Proctor, the man who kept law and order in the University, stood next to the Sheriff, his beadles – men who were University constables – ranged behind him. Master Wilson hurried forward, his gorgeous purple gown billowing about him.

'My Lord Sheriff, Master Proctor,' he began, 'the townies have attacked us totally unprovoked!'

'I admire a man who takes such care to seek the truth before speaking,' Bartholomew said in an undertone to Abigny. Wilson's was also an imprudent remark, considering many of his guests were townspeople.

Abigny snorted in disgust. 'He should have known better than to try to distribute money today. He must have known what might happen.'

'I suggested he should let the priests give it out at mass on Sunday,' said Bartholomew, watching with distaste as Wilson regaled the Sheriff with claims that the townspeople had attacked the College out of pure malice.

'But that might have entailed some of the credit passing to the priests and not to him,' said Abigny nastily. He gestured outside. 'See to your patients, Physician.'

Bartholomew remembered the groans and shrieks as the crowd had surged against Michaelhouse's wall, chastened that he had not thought to see to the injured sooner. By the gate, a beadle stood by two prostrate forms, while more beadles bent over others further down the lane.

'Dead, Doctor,' said the beadle, recognising Bartholomew. Bartholomew knelt to examine the bodies. Both were young men, one wearing the short coat of an apprentice. He pressed down on the young man's chest, feeling the sogginess that meant his ribs were broken and the vital organs underneath crushed. The neck of the second man was broken, his head twisted at an obscene angle. Death would have come instantly to both of them. Bartholomew crossed himself, and paused at the gate to shout for Brother Michael to do what he could for their unshriven souls.

The other beadles moved aside to allow Bartholomew to examine the injured. Miraculously, there were only four of them, although Bartholomew was sure others had been helped home by friends. None of the four was in mortal danger. One middle-aged man had a superficial head wound that nevertheless bled copiously. Bartholomew gave him a clean piece of linen to stem the bleeding, and moved on to examine the next one. The woman seemed to have no injuries, but was deeply in shock, her eyes wide and dull, and her whole body shaking uncontrollably.

'Her son is over there.' Bartholomew saw that the speaker was the blacksmith, lying against the wall with his leg at an awkward angle. He followed the blacksmith's nod and saw that he meant one of the men who had died. He turned back to the woman and took her cold, clammy hands in his.

'Where is her husband? Can we send for someone to come to take her home?'

'Her husband died last winter of the ague. The lad was all she had. Doubtless she will starve now.'

'What is her name?' Bartholomew asked, feeling helpless.

'Rachel Atkin,' the blacksmith replied. 'What do you care?'

Bartholomew sighed. He saw cases like Rachel's almost every day, old people and women with children deprived of those who could provide for them. Even giving them money, which he did sometimes, did no more than relieve the problem temporarily. Poverty was one of the aspects of being a physician he found most difficult to deal with. Often, he would tend to an injury or an illness, only to find that his patient had died from want of good food or warmth.

He released the woman's hands, and went to

examine the blacksmith's leg. It was a clean break, with no punctured skin. It only needed to be set, and, given time and rest, would heal well enough. As he gently squeezed and probed the break, testing for splinters of bone, the blacksmith leaned towards him. Bartholomew realised that the ale fumes on his breath probably accounted for the fact that he did not scream, as many patients might, when his leg was examined. He should set it as soon as possible for the same reason.

'Why did you interfere?' the blacksmith slurred.

Bartholomew ignored him, and went to look at the last injury, a man complaining of pains in his back.

'It was under control,' the blacksmith continued. 'We knew what we were doing.'

'I am sure you did,' said Bartholomew absently, running his hands down the man's spine. He straightened up. 'Just bruised,' he said to the man, 'go home and rest, and in a few days it will feel better.' He turned to the blacksmith. 'I can set your leg now, or you can go to a surgeon. I do not care which you choose.'

The blacksmith looked dubious, and narrowed his eyes. 'I have heard of you, Physician. You tell the other doctors that they should not use leeches . . .'

There was a muted snigger from the listening beadles, and Bartholomew cut the blacksmith off abruptly by standing and preparing to leave. He had no desire to enter into a medical debate with the man. He knew his medical teaching was regarded with suspicion, even fear, by some people, but no one could deny that fewer patients died under his care than that of his colleagues. His success where they had failed often drove desperate people to him, and those he had healed usually rallied to his defence when others questioned or criticised his methods.

'And how much will it cost me?' sneered the blacksmith, seizing a corner of Bartholomew's gown to prevent him from walking away.

Bartholomew looked down at him. 'A shroud and a gravedigger for the woman's son.'

The blacksmith met his eyes, peering up to see if he could detect any trickery there. After a moment's thought, he nodded, and lifted his arms so that the beadles could help him into Michaelhouse, where Bartholomew had a small surgery.

Bartholomew quickly bandaged the first man's head, and sent him home. The woman still sat on the ground, staring into space. The beadles had lifted the bodies of the young men onto a cart to be taken to St Michael's Church, while Brother Michael had finished his prayers and was walking back into the College. Coming to a decision, Bartholomew reached down and took the woman by the hand, pulling her to her feet. He ignored the surprised looks of the porters at the gate, and made for the kitchens, Rachel Atkin in tow.

All the College servants were furiously busy preparing for Master Wilson's feast. Bartholomew pushed his way through the kitchens to the servants' living quarters beyond. Agatha, the enormous laundress, sat there, folding napkins in readiness for the feast. She looked up as he entered, her bushy grey eyebrows coming together as she saw the woman.

'Now what?' she demanded, struggling to heave her considerable bulk to her feet. 'What troubles have you brought me this time, you young scoundrel?'

Bartholomew smiled. Women were not generally

employed in the Colleges, but Agatha was quite an exception. Sir John had hired her when he first came to Michaelhouse, instantly recognising her abilities for organisation and efficiency. She had gradually established herself as undisputed leader of the College staff, and the College owed its smooth and generally conflict-free running to Agatha.

'You are always saying that you need an assistant,' he said, smiling at her. 'Could you take this one, just for a few days?'

'She is stark staring mad!' Agatha bellowed, peering suspiciously into Rachel Atkin's face.

'No, not mad, just grieving for her son,' said Bartholomew gently. Rachel began to look around her vacantly. 'Will you give her a chance? Not tonight – she should sleep. But maybe for a few days?'

'Are you insane?' Agatha shouted. 'What will Windbag Wilson say when he hears you have brought a woman into the College? He only tolerates me because he knows in his heart that I am twice the man that he will ever be. He will be after your blood, Master Matthew. I have heard that he is going to demand that all the Fellows take major holy orders like Michael and the Franciscans. He will have something to say about women in the College, you can be sure of that!'

'Just for a few days until I can think of something else. Please, Agatha?'

Agatha hid a smile, and put her hands on her ample hips. She had had a soft spot for the dark-haired physician ever since he had arrived at the College to teach medicine four years before and had cured her of a painful swelling on her foot. She had been dubious of accepting his help because he had abandoned the usual implements of his trade – leeches, star-charts, and urine examination – and had even been known to practise surgery, a task normally left to barbers. But Bartholomew's treatment of Agatha's foot had worked, and Agatha was not a woman to question something that improved the quality of her life so dramatically.

She eyed the woman impassively noting her old but clean dress, and the careful darns. 'Out of the question! You will be expecting me to share my own room with her next!'

'No, I . . .' began Bartholomew, but stopped as Agatha elbowed him out of the way, and steered Rachel towards one of the small rooms in which the servants slept. He needed to say no more. Rachel Atkin was in good hands for now, and he was sure he and Agatha could work out something between them later.

He dodged his way back through the frenetic activity of the kitchens and walked across the courtyard towards his room. The Sheriff and Wilson had gone, but students and servants were scurrying back and forth as the bell rang to announce that the feast was about to begin.

The blacksmith lay on the pallet in the tiny chamber Bartholomew used to store his medicines, and where the College's three precious medical books were kept chained to the wall. Engaging the help of two burly porters, Bartholomew pulled and heaved on the leg until he was certain the bones were in correct alignment. The porters exchanged grimaces of disgust as the sound of grating bone filled the room. But the blacksmith had apparently taken several healthy swigs from the jug of wine that stood on the table and was virtually unconscious by the time Bartholomew began: with the exception of one or two grunts, he lay motionless through the entire proceeding. Bartholomew bound the leg tightly between two sticks of wood, and checked his patient for signs of shock or fever.

The porters left, and Bartholomew covered the blacksmith with his cloak and left him to sleep. His family could collect him in the morning. He went into the room that he shared with Abigny, and slumped on his bed, suddenly feeling drained. What a day! He had sat through Wilson's interminable installation, narrowly averted a riot, almost been locked out of the College to face an enraged mob, attended four patients, and set a broken leg.

He leaned back against the wall and closed his eyes, feeling a warm lethargy creep over him. It would be pleasant to drift off to sleep. The courtyard outside was quiet now, and he could just hear the murmur of voices coming from the feast in the hall. His place at the high table would be empty and he would be missed. He should go or Wilson would take his absence as a personal insult, and would try to make life unbearable for him. He sat still for a few minutes, and then forced himself to stand up. He need only stay until the speeches were over. Speeches! He almost sat down again at the thought of listening to Master Wilson pontificate, but he had not eaten since breakfast, and the smells of cooking from the kitchen had been delicious.

He brushed hastily at the dust and mud that clung to his best gown, and straightened the black robe underneath. He walked across the courtyard, stopping on the way to look in on Augustus. The commoners shared a large dormitory on the upper floor of the southern wing, but because Augustus talked to himself and kept the others awake, he had been given a small room of his own, an unusual privilege for any College member, but especially a commoner. The commoners' room and Augustus's chamber were dark, but Bartholomew could make out Augustus lying on the bed, and could hear his slow, rhythmic breathing. In the main dormitory, Brother Paul, another commoner too frail to attend the feast, coughed wetly and muttered in his sleep.

Satisfied, Bartholomew made his way to the hall, and tried to slip as unobtrusively as possible into his seat at the high table at the raised end of the hall. Wilson leaned forward and shot him an unpleasant look. Next to Bartholomew, Giles Abigny had already had far too much to drink, and was regaling Brother Michael with a story of his experiences with a prostitute in London. For a monk, Michael was showing an unseemly interest. On Bartholomew's other side, the two Franciscan friars, Aelfrith and William, were already deep in some debate about the nature of original sin, while Wilson, Alcote and Swynford huddled together plotting God knew what. Bartholomew ate some of the spiced venison slowly, realising that he had grown so used to plain College fare, that the strongly flavoured meats and piquant sauces were too rich for him. He wondered how many scholars would over-indulge and make themselves sick. The ever-growing pile of gnawed bones and the grease-splattered table near Michael indicated that *he* had no such reservations.

A roar of laughter from the students jolted him from his thoughts. Members of the College usually spoke Latin, or occasionally court French, at the few meals where speaking was permitted, and the conversation was generally learned. But tonight, as a gesture of courtesy to his secular guests, Wilson had decreed that the conversation might be in any language. Bartholomew glanced around the hall, noting the brightly coloured tapestries, begged and borrowed from other Colleges for the occasion, that adorned the walls. The walls were normally bare so as not to distract scholars from their studies, and the benches, now draped with rich cloths, were plain wood. The guests from the town added splashes of colour among the students' black gowns. Servants scurried here and there bearing large jugs of wine and platters of food that left trails of spilled grease. In the gallery normally occupied by the Bible scholar, a small group of musicians fought to make their singing heard over the hubbub.

Down the table, Brother Michael chortled with unmonklike delight as he listened with rapt attention to Abigny. Fortunately for him, his imprudent laughter was screened from the austere Franciscan Fellows by another roar of laughter from the students.

The Oliver brothers were the centre of attention, a group of younger students gathering round them admiringly. Bartholomew heard Elias telling them how he had been the last one through the gates to make sure that all the others were safe inside. At that moment, Henry looked up towards the high table, and stared at Bartholomew, his blue eyes blazing with hatred. They held each other's gaze for a moment, before Henry, with a sneer, looked away.

Bartholomew was puzzled. He had had very little to do with the Oliver brothers – they were not his students, and he had never had to deal with them for any disciplinary breaches. He found it hard to believe that all the hatred that Henry had put into that look came from the incident outside the church. The mob had been in an ugly mood, and he had averted what might very easily have turned into a bloodbath. So what had he done to earn such emotions?

He tried to put it out of his mind. He was tired, and was probably reading far too much into Henry Oliver's looks. He sipped at the fine wine from France that Wilson had provided to toast his future success as Master, and leaned his elbows on the table. Abigny, his story completed, slapped Bartholomew on the back.

'I heard you have secreted a woman in the College . . .'

Abigny's voice was loud, and several students looked at him speculatively. Brother Michael's eyebrows shot up, his baggy green eyes glittering with amusement. The Franciscans paused in their debate and looked at Bartholomew disapprovingly.

'Hush!' Bartholomew chided Abigny. 'She is in the care of Agatha, and not secreted anywhere.'

Abigny laughed, and draped his arm round Bartholomew's shoulders. Bartholomew pulled away as wine fumes wafted into his face. 'I wish I were a physician and not a philosopher. What better excuse to be in a woman's boudoir than to be leeching her blood.'

'I do not leech the blood of my patients,' said Bartholomew irritably. They had been down this path before. Abigny loved to tease Bartholomew about his unorthodox methods. Bartholomew had learned medicine at the University in Paris from an Arab teacher who had taught him that bleeding was for charlatans too lazy to discover a cure.

Abigny laughed again, his cheeks flushed pink with wine, but then leaned closer to Bartholomew. 'But you and I may not be long for our free and easy lives if our new Master has anything to say. He will have us taking major orders as he and his two sycophants over there plan to do.'

'Have a care, Giles,' said Bartholomew nervously. He was acutely aware that the students' conversation at the nearest table had stopped, and Bartholomew knew that some of the scholars were not above telling tales to senior College members in return for a lenient disputation, or spoken exam.

'What will it be for you, Matt?' Abigny continued, ignoring his friend's appeal for discretion. 'Will you become an Austin Canon and go to work in St John's Hospital? Or would you rather become a rich, fat Benedictine, like Brother Michael here?'

Michael pursed his lips, but humour showed in his eyes. Like Bartholomew, being the butt of Abigny's jokes was nothing new to him.

Abigny blundered on. 'But, my dear friend, I would not want you to take orders with the Carmelites, like good Master Wilson. I would kill you before I would let that happen. I . . .'

'Enough, Giles!' Bartholomew said sharply. 'If you cannot keep your council, you should not drink so much. Pull yourself together.'

Abigny laughed at his friend's admonition, took a deep draught from his goblet, but said no more. Bartholomew sometimes wondered about the philosopher's behaviour. He was fair and fresh-faced, like a young country bumpkin. But his boyish looks belied a razor-like mind, and Bartholomew had no doubt that if he dedicated himself to learning he could become one of the foremost scholars in the University. But Abigny was too lazy and too fond of the pleasures of life.

Bartholomew thought about Abigny's claim. Most Cambridge masters, including Bartholomew, had taken minor holy orders so that they were ruled by church law rather than secular law. Some, like Brother Michael and the Franciscans, were monks or friars and had taken major orders. This meant that they could not marry or have relations with women, although not all monks and friars in the University kept these vows as assiduously as they might.

As a boy, Bartholomew had been educated at the great Benedictine Abbey at Peterborough, and, as one of their brightest students, had been expected to take his vows and become a monk. His sister and brother-in-law, acting *in loco parentis*, had other ideas, and a marriage was planned that would have benefited their cloth trade. Bartholomew, however, had defied them both, and had run away to Oxford and then Paris to study medicine. Since leaving Peterborough, Bartholomew had not given a monastic vocation another thought, other than taking the minor orders that would protect him from the rigours of secular law. Perhaps, a few months ago, the prospect of never having a relationship with a woman would not have mattered, but Bartholomew had met Philippa Abigny – Giles's sister – and was not at all sure that a vow of chastity was what he wanted.

The evening dragged on, speeches were made, and the candles gradually dipped lower in their silver holders. The guests began to leave. First the Bishop made his exit, sweeping out of the hall in his fine robes, followed as ever by his discreet chain of silent, black-robed clerics. The Chancellor and the Sheriff left together, and Bartholomew wondered what they had been plotting all evening. Edith, Bartholomew's sister, earned a nasty look from Wilson when she kissed her brother on the cheek and whispered an invitation to dine with her and Sir Oswald the following day.

The noise level in the hall rose as more wine was consumed, especially by the students and the commoners. Bartholomew began to grow drowsy, and wished Wilson would leave the feast so he could go to bed. It would be considered bad manners for a Fellow to leave the high table before the Master, and so Bartholomew waited, struggling to keep his eyes open and not to go face down in his food like Francis Eltham.

He watched expectantly as Alexander, the College Butler, made his way to Wilson, hoping that some urgent College business might draw him from the hall, so that the Fellows might leave. Wilson spun round in his chair to gaze at Alexander in shock. He then looked at Bartholomew, and whispered in the Butler's ear. Alexander nodded, and moved towards the physician.

'Begging your pardon, sir,' he began softly, 'but it is Master Augustus. I think he is dead.'

11

BARTHOLOMEW STARED UP AT ALEXANDER IN disbelief. He half suspected a practical joke by Abigny, but realised that even Abigny's sometimes outrageous sense of humour would not allow him to stoop to such a prank.

'What happened?' he asked hoarsely.

Alexander shrugged, his face pale. 'I went to take him and Brother Paul some wine, since Master Wilson thought they were too ill to attend the feast.' Bartholomew grimaced. Wilson did not want Augustus at the feast because he was afraid the old man's ramblings might embarrass him. 'I went to Brother Paul first, but he was already asleep. Then I went in to Augustus. He was lying on his bed, and I think he is dead.'

Bartholomew rose, motioning for Brother Michael to go with him. If Augustus were dead, then Michael would anoint the body and say prayers for his soul, as he had for the two men outside the College gates. Although Michael was a monk and not a friar – and would therefore not usually have been authorised to perform priestly duties – he had been granted special dispensation by the Bishop of Ely to give last rites and hear confessions. This was because, unlike the Franciscan

37

and Dominican friars, Benedictine monks were scarce in Cambridge, and the Bishop did not want his few monks confessing their sins to rival Orders.

'What is going on?' panted Michael, as he hurried to keep up with Bartholomew. Michael was a man who loved his food, and, despite Bartholomew's advice to moderate himself for the sake of his health, he was grossly overweight. A sheen of sweat glistened on his face and soaked into his lank brown hair just from the exertion of leaving the hall so quickly.

'Alexander says Augustus is dead,' Bartholomew replied tersely.

Michael stopped abruptly, and gripped Bartholomew's arm. 'But he cannot be!'

Bartholomew peered at Michael in the darkness of the courtyard. His face was so deathly white that it was almost luminous, and his eyes were round with horror.

'I went to see him after I had finished with those town lads,' Michael went on. 'He was rambling like he does, and I told him I would save him some wine from the feast.'

Bartholomew steered Michael towards Augustus's room. 'I saw him after you, on my way to the hall. He was sound asleep.'

Together they climbed the narrow wooden stairs to Augustus's tiny chamber. Alexander was waiting outside the door holding a lamp that he passed to Bartholomew. Michael followed the physician over to the bed where Augustus lay, the lamp and the flames from the small fire in the hearth casting strange shadows on the walls. Bartholomew had expected Augustus to have slipped away in his sleep, and was shocked to see the old man's eyes open and his lips drawn back over long yellow teeth in a grimace that bespoke of abject terror. Death had not crept up and claimed Augustus unnoticed. Bartholomew heard Michael take a sharp breath and his robes rustled as he crossed himself quickly.

Bartholomew put the lamp on the window-sill and sat on the edge of the bed, putting his cheek to Augustus's mouth to see if he still breathed – although he knew that he would not. He gently touched one of the staring eyes with his forefinger to test for a reaction. There was none. Brother Michael was kneeling behind him intoning the prayers for the dead in his precise Latin, his eyes closed so he would not have to look at Augustus's face. Alexander had been sent to fetch oil with which to anoint the dead man.

To Bartholomew it seemed as if Augustus had had some kind of seizure; perhaps he had frightened himself with some nightmare, or with some of his wild imaginings – as when he had tried to jump out of the window two nights before. Bartholomew felt sad that Augustus had died afraid: three generations of students had benefited from his patient teaching, and he had been kind to Bartholomew, too, when the younger man had first been appointed at Michaelhouse. When Sir John had arranged Bartholomew's fellowship, not all members of the College had been supportive. Yet Augustus, like Sir John, had seen in Bartholomew an opportunity to improve the strained relationship between the College and the town; Bartholomew had been given Sir John's blessing to work among the poor and not merely to pander to the minor complaints of the wealthy.

The gravelly sound of Michael clearing his throat jerked Bartholomew back to the present. Sir John was dead, and so, now, was Augustus. Michael had finished his prayers, and was stepping forward to anoint Augustus's eyes, mouth and hands with a small bottle of chrism that Alexander had fetched. He did so quickly, concentrating on his words so that he would not have to see Augustus's expression of horror. Bartholomew had seen many such expressions before: his Arab master had once taken him to the scene of a battle in France, where they had scoured the field looking for the wounded among the dead and dying, and so Augustus's face did not hold the same horror for him as it did for Michael.

While waiting for Michael, Bartholomew looked around the room. Since the commotion two nights before, Wilson had decreed that Augustus should not be allowed the fire he usually had during the night. Wilson said, with good reason, that it was not safe, and that he could not risk the lives of others by allowing a madman to be left alone with naked flames.

Bartholomew suspected that Wilson was also considering the cost, because he had questioned Sir John on several occasions about the necessity of the commoners having a fire in July and August. Michaelhouse was built of stone, and Bartholomew knew that Augustus was not the only old man to complain of being cold, even in the height of summer. That a small fire burned merrily in the hearth suggested that one kind-hearted servant had chosen to ignore Wilson's orders and let Augustus have his comfort.

'Matt, come away. We have done all we can here.'

Bartholomew glanced up at Michael. His face was shiny with sweat, and had an almost greenish hue. The chrism in the small bottle he held shook as his hands trembled, and he was looking everywhere except at Bartholomew and Augustus.

'What is the matter with you?' asked Bartholomew,

perplexed. Michael had often accompanied Bartholomew to pray for patients beyond his medicine and had seen death many times. He had not been especially close to Augustus, and so his behaviour could not be explained by grief.

Michael took a handful of Bartholomew's gown and pulled hard. 'Just come away. Leave him be, and come with me back to the hall.' Bartholomew resisted the tug, and the small bottle fell from Michael's hand and bounced onto the floor.

'Pull yourself together, man,' Bartholomew said, exasperated, and leaned down to retrieve the bottle, which had rolled under the bed. He picked it up to hand back to Michael, and was startled to see the hem of the monk's robes disappearing through the door. Michael had, quite literally, fled.

Bartholomew looked to Alexander, who appeared as bewildered as Bartholomew felt. 'Go back to the feast,' he said, seeing the steward's unease. 'You will be needed there. I will see to Augustus.'

Alexander left, shutting the door behind him, and Bartholomew heard his feet clattering down the stairs and the outside door slam shut. He chewed on his lower lip, bemused. What had been the matter with Michael? They had known each other since Bartholomew had been made a Fellow, and Bartholomew had never seen him in such a state before. Usually the obese monk was well in control of his emotions, and he rarely allowed himself to be so discomfited that he was unable to come up with a sardonic remark or cutting response.

As Bartholomew put the bottle of chrism down on the window-sill, he noticed that the lid had come off and that his hand was greasy with the highly scented oil. He wiped it on a napkin that lay on a desk under the window, and dropped to his hands and knees with the lamp to look for the bottle-top. It had rolled to the far side of the bed, and Bartholomew had to lie flat to reach it. As he stood up, he noticed that his clothes were covered with small flecks of black. Puzzled, he peered closely at some of the bits that clung to his sleeve. They looked like flakes of burned parchment. He brushed them off; they must have come from the fire in the hearth. He was about to leave when the edge of the bedclothes caught his eye. On the light green blanket was a pale scorch mark about the size of his hand. Curious, he inspected the rest of the covering, and found a similar spot at the corner.

Augustus's screams of two nights before came tearing into his mind. Augustus had claimed that devils had come to burn him alive! Bartholomew shook his head. He was being ridiculous. Agatha had probably burned the blanket while it was being laundered, although he would not wish to be the one to ask her. Nevertheless, he took the lamp, and, lying flat on his back, he inspected the wooden slats underneath the bed. He swallowed hard. The boards were singed, and one was even charred. Augustus had not been imagining things. There *had* been a fire under his bed.

Still lying on his back, he thought about the events of two days before. It had been deep in the night, perhaps one or two o' clock, when Augustus had started to yell. Bartholomew had thrown on his gown and run to the commoners' dormitory, which was diagonally opposite his own room across the courtyard. By the time he had arrived, Alcote, Alexander, and Father William were already there with Wilson's book-bearer, Gilbert, and the commoners from the next room. Alcote and William said that they had been working together in William's rooms on material for a public debate they were to hold the next day, and since William's room was directly below that of Augustus, had been the first to arrive. Gilbert, always ferreting information and gossip for Wilson, had materialised from nowhere, and Alexander never seemed to sleep.

Bartholomew screwed up his eyes. But one other person had also arrived before him. Brother Michael had been there. He had been dishevelled, as was Bartholomew, having been woken from his sleep, but Michael's room was above Bartholomew's, so he must have moved with uncharacteristic haste to have arrived first. Unless he had been there already. The thought came unbidden into Bartholomew's mind. Michael was dishevelled. Had he been involved in a tussle with Augustus and set a fire under the bed? Was Brother Michael the devil of Augustus's mind? But Augustus's door had been locked from the inside, and Michael had helped Bartholomew to break it down.

It made no sense. Why would Michael wish Augustus harm? Michael was a monk: a rarity in the University, where friars and priests abounded, but Benedictine monks were uncommon. Bartholomew reached for the damaged wood and scratched it with his fingernail. It was quite deeply burnt, not merely singed, so whoever had started the fire had meant business. Bartholomew thought again. The room had been horribly smoky, enough to make his eyes smart, but the windows were open, and the draught was sucking the smoke back down the chimney where it was billowing into the room. He remembered asking Alexander to douse the fire to allow some fresh air to circulate. Any evidence of smoke from under the bed would have been masked by the fire in the hearth.

He felt angry at himself. He had not believed for an instant that there could have been any degree of truth in Augustus's story. But what if his other ramblings held grains of truth? What of his statements today? What had he said? Something to the effect that evil was afoot and would corrupt them all, especially those who were unaware, and that Sir John had begun to guess and look what had happened to him.

Bartholomew felt his blood run cold. Sir John's sudden demise had taken everyone by surprise; he had certainly not seemed suicidal the night of his death as Bartholomew could attest. What if he had not committed suicide? What if there was truth in senile Augustus's mumblings, and Sir John had begun to guess something? But what? Michaelhouse had its petty rivalries and bids for power, as, no doubt, every other College and hostel in the University did. But Bartholomew found it hard to imagine that there could be anything so important as to warrant the taking of lives. And anyway, Michael and Bartholomew had seen Augustus alive before the feast, and none of the Fellows, commoners, or students had left the hall before Bartholomew had been summoned by Alexander.

He slid out from under the bed for a second time and dusted himself off. He looked down at Augustus's sprawled corpse, at the horrified look on the face. Sitting on the bed, he began a rigorous inspection of the body. He sniffed at the mouth to check for any signs of poison; he ran his fingers through Augustus's wispy hair to see if he had been struck on the head; he lifted the bed-gown to look for any small puncture marks or bruises; and, finally, he examined the hands. There was nothing, not even a fibre trapped under the fingernails. There was not a mark on the body, and not the merest hint of blood. Aware that the chrism may have masked the smell of poison, Bartholomew prised the dead man's mouth open again, and, holding the lamp close, looked carefully for any redness or swelling on the tongue or gums. Nothing.

He began to feel foolish. It had been a long day, and he was tired. Henry Oliver's attempt to leave him to the mercies of the town mob must have upset him more than he had thought, and it had not been pleasant to see the loathsome Wilson sit so smugly in Sir John's chair. I am as bad as old Augustus with his imaginings, Bartholomew thought irritably. The old commoner had most likely set the bed alight himself, not realising what he had done.

Bartholomew straightened Augustus's limbs, pulled the bed-gown down over the ancient knees, and covered him decently with the blanket. He kicked and poked at the fire until he was sure it was out, fastened the window-shutters, and, taking the lamp, left the room. He would ask Father Aelfrith to keep vigil over the body. It was getting late, and the feast should almost have run its course by now.

As he made his way down the stairs, he thought he saw a shadow flit across the doorway, and his heart almost missed a beat. But when he reached the courtyard, there was nothing to be seen.

The feast seemed to have degenerated somewhat since he had left, and the floor and tables were strewn with thrown food and spilt wine. Abigny was standing on one of the students' tables reciting ribald poetry to a chorus of catcalls and cheers, while the two Franciscans looked on disapprovingly. Brother Michael had returned to his place, and gave Bartholomew a wan smile. Alcote and Swynford were deep in their cups, and Wilson, too, was flushed, although with wine or the heat of the room Bartholomew could not tell.

'You have been a damned long time!' Wilson snapped at Bartholomew as he approached. 'What of old Augustus? How is he?'

'Dead,' Bartholomew said bluntly, watching for any reaction on the smug face. There was nothing, not even a flicker of emotion.

'Well, it is for the best. The man had lived his threescore years and ten. What kept you?'

Bartholomew suddenly found himself being examined closely by Wilson's heavily-lidded eyes. He stared back, hoping that the dislike he felt for the man did not show in his face. 'I had to make my examinations,' he responded.

The lazy hooded eyes were deceptive, and Wilson pounced like a cat. 'What examinations?' he said sharply. 'What are you saying? Michael returned ages ago. What were you doing?'

'Nothing that need concern you, Master Wilson,' replied Bartholomew coldly. He resented being questioned so. For all Wilson knew, he might have been visiting a patient, and that was none of his business.

'Everything in the College concerns me, Doctor Bartholomew. You may have had a loose rein under Babington, but you are under my authority now. I ask again: what examinations?'

Bartholomew felt like emptying a nearby pitcher of

wine over Wilson's head and walking out, but he had no wish to lose his fellowship over the likes of Wilson. He swallowed down several retorts of which the facetious Brother Michael would have been proud, and answered calmly, 'Augustus had not died in his sleep as I thought he might. His eyes were open and he looked terrified. It is my duty to make sure that the causes of death were natural.'

'"Causes of death were natural",' Wilson mimicked with a sneer. 'And? What did you find?'

'Nothing.'

'Of course you found nothing,' spat Wilson. 'Augustus probably frightened himself to death with one of his flights of imagination. What did you expect?' He turned to Swynford and gave one of his superior smiles, as if mocking the skills of medicine over his own common sense.

'There could be all manner of causes, Master Wilson,' said Bartholomew, masking his anger with cold politeness. 'What if he had died of the plague that is said to be sweeping towards us from the west? I am sure you would want to be the first to know such things.'

Bartholomew had the satisfaction of seeing Wilson blanch when he mentioned the plague. Good, he thought, with uncharacteristic malice, now I know how to get under the skin of this arrogant man.

Wilson recovered his composure quickly. 'I hope you are not so poor a doctor as to confuse plague with old age,' he said, putting his elbows on the table and placing together flabby hands shiny with grease from his dinner.

Bartholomew smiled. 'Let us hope not, for all our sakes,' he replied. 'And now, sirs, I bid you good-night,' and with a small bow took his leave of the new Master. If Wilson really did doubt his skills, Bartholomew hoped he would spend some restless nights wondering whether he was as safe as he might be from the plague that was rumoured to be devastating the West Country.

He paused to ask Aelfrith if he would keep vigil over Augustus. The friar looked straight ahead of him while Bartholomew imparted his news, and then rose and left the hall without a word.

Bartholomew walked back past Brother Michael and heard the monk follow him out into the cool night air.

'Are you well, Brother?' Bartholomew asked, trying to sound casual.

'Now, yes. I do not know what happened to me in there. Something about the old man's face. I am sorry I left in a rush, but I thought I was going to be sick.'

Michael had looked sick in the room. Perhaps he had over-eaten at the feast. It would not be the first time the monk had made himself ill with his greed for food and wine. 'I think some of the students will be sick in the morning, by the look of them now,' said Bartholomew, with a smile. 'I am willing to wager that none of them attend your lecture at six tomorrow morning.'

'And neither will I,' replied Michael. 'Our fine new Master has given all Michaelhouse scholars and masters tomorrow off. Is this the way he intends to continue the academic tradition of Michaelhouse?'

'Michael!' laughed Bartholomew. 'You are too incautious by far. Watch what you say, for shadows may have sharp hearing.'

Brother Michael's fat face suddenly became serious. 'More than we think, Matt. Heed your own words!' With that, he hurried over to the stairs that led up to his room, leaving Bartholomew standing in the courtyard alone.

Bartholomew rose with the first grey light of dawn the next morning to find that a small core of students were still enjoying Wilson's wine; he could hear them singing in the hall. Many had not been in their beds for more than two or three hours, Abigny among them. The philosopher lay sprawled on his back snoring loudly as Bartholomew went to find some breakfast.

As he walked across the courtyard, Bartholomew breathed in deeply. The air was cold and fresh, quite different from how it would be later when the hot sun would make the flies swarm over the putrid ditches that criss-crossed Cambridge.

He walked slowly along the cobbled footpath that ran around the courtyard, savouring the early morning, and admiring, as he often did, the fine building that was the centre of Michaelhouse. The north wing, in which Bartholomew lived, was the newest part, and was two storeys of dark yellow stone with slender arched windows. Regularly spaced along the front were three doorways leading to barrel-vaulted porches. Each porch contained doors leading to the two rooms on the lower floor, and a wooden staircase leading to two more rooms on the upper floor. The rooms were small, cramped, and in short supply, and Bartholomew felt himself fortunate that he shared his room with Abigny, and not three students, as did Father William.

The oldest part of Michaelhouse was the south wing, where the commoners, William, Swynford, and Aelfrith lived, and was, Bartholomew thought, the finest building.

It was also built around three staircases and contained twelve rooms of different sizes on two floors, but the original simple arched windows had been recently replaced by larger, wider ones that filled the scholars' rooms with light. Delicate traceries in stone had been carved at each window apex, each bearing the initials 'HS' in honour of Michaelhouse's founder, Hervey de Stanton, Edward II's Chancellor of the Exchequer. Unlike the north wing, the staircases in the south wing were built of stone, with brightly painted vaulted ceilings.

Joining the two wings was what had once been the house of a wealthy merchant, who had bequeathed it to the newly founded College. It was dominated by its handsome entrance, with the arms of Hervey de Stanton picked out in blue and gold above. The lower floor comprised a handsome reception room with a large spiral staircase leading to the hall on the upper storey, and the service rooms and kitchens, shielded from guests by a carved oak screen. The upper floor displayed a long line of arched windows that allowed light into the hall, and the little conclave, or combination room, at the far end. The hall was built of a pale, honey-coloured stone that changed with the light; at sunset it glowed a deep rose pink, while at noon it often appeared almost white.

Out of the corner of his eye, Bartholomew caught a flicker of light through the closed shutters on the upper floor of the south wing, and remembered Aelfrith and his vigil. He retraced his steps, thinking he would offer to relieve the friar for a while. He opened the door at the base of the stairs quietly, for he did not wish to awaken anyone who might have only recently retired to bed. Because the stairs were stone, Bartholomew found it easy to walk soundlessly. The stairway was dark and he kept one hand on the wall to feel his way upwards. Reaching Augustus's little chamber, he opened the door, and stopped dead.

Aelfrith, his back to Bartholomew, was squatting in the middle of the floor, vigorously scratching at the floorboards by the light of a single candle. Augustus's body lay next to him in a tangle of bedclothes and strewn pieces of parchment. In the dim light, Bartholomew could see that, here and there, parts of the plaster covering the walls had been chipped away.

Bartholomew took a step backwards, but shock made his movements clumsy, and he bumped into the door. Aelfrith jumped to his feet, spinning round to face him. Bartholomew was only aware of his dark robes, and the light was too weak to allow him to make out any expression on the face, enveloped as it was in a deep hood.

'Aelfrith!' Bartholomew exclaimed in a horrified whisper. 'What are you doing?'

Aelfrith turned to point at something, and then, before Bartholomew had time to react, dived forward, slamming him backwards into the door. Bartholomew felt all the breath rush out of him, and scrabbled at the billowing robes ineffectually as Aelfrith grabbed a handful of his hair. Bartholomew, numb with disbelief, saw the silhouette of something sharp in Aelfrith's free hand. The sight of it jolted him out of his shock, and he twisted out of Aelfrith's grip so that the knife screeched harmlessly against the wall.

Bartholomew grasped the hand holding the knife, and, for a few seconds, the struggle was at a stalemate. Then Aelfrith, perhaps made strong by panic, gave an almighty heave that sent Bartholomew sprawling backwards down the stairs. For a few moments, Bartholomew's world spun in all directions, until a sharp ache from a knee twisted in the fall brought everything back into focus. He was dimly aware of footsteps, although he had no idea from where they came. He picked himself up slowly, wincing at the pain in his leg. His fall had wedged him against the door, and so Aelfrith could not have left the building.

Cautiously, he hobbled up the stairs with as much silence as he could manage. The door to Augustus's room was still open, and the body still lay on the floor entangled in the blankets. Beyond, the door to the commoners' room was also ajar. Bartholomew swallowed, and began to inch forward. Aelfrith had to be in the commoners' room: there was no way out of this part of the building other than the door against which Bartholomew had fallen. He pushed the commoners' door so that it lay flat against the wall, and edged his way along it.

The commoners' room was lighter than Augustus's, because all the shutters had been thrown open to keep the room cool through the summer night. The commoners slept on pallets, simple mattresses of straw, that could be piled up on top of each other during the day to make more room. Bartholomew could see that all the commoners were there, and all asleep. He could see enough of their faces or bodies to know that none of them was Aelfrith, and there were no alcoves or garderobes in which to hide. Aelfrith was not there.

He backed out, and went to Augustus's room. He was totally mystified. There was nowhere for Aelfrith to hide, and he could not have left the building without passing Bartholomew on the stairs. Bartholomew leaned against the wall. Now that the first danger appeared to be over, he was beginning to shake with the shock, and his knee ached viciously. Legs trembling, he sank down onto the bed.

His heart leapt into his mouth as Augustus gave a long, low groan. Bartholomew stared at the body in horror. With a shaking hand, he reached out slowly, and grasped the bedcovers that had wrapped themselves around the corpse, easing them off the face.

He recoiled in confusion as the unmistakable bristly tonsure of Aelfrith emerged from under the tangle of blankets. For a few seconds, Bartholomew sat stupefied, just staring at the inert form on the floor. If this was Aelfrith, who was the man who had attacked him? And more to the point, where was Augustus? He crouched down beside the man on the floor. Gently, he eased him onto his side, noting the deep gash on the side of his head. Aelfrith's eyes fluttered open, and Bartholomew helped him to a sitting position. For a few minutes, all Aelfrith did was to hold his head in his hands and moan. Bartholomew limped to the table, and soaked a napkin in water from the nightstand to press against the swelling. Eventually, Aelfrith squinted up at him.

'What happened?' he croaked.

Bartholomew stared at him, trying to make sense out of the happenings of the last few minutes. 'You tell me,' he said finally, easing himself back down onto the bed. 'Where is Augustus?'

Aelfrith turned his head sharply to look at the bed, wincing at the quickness of the movement. He gazed at the empty bed, and then peered underneath it. He looked back at Bartholomew, his eyes wide with shock. 'Where is Augustus?' he repeated.

Bartholomew watched as Aelfrith hauled himself to

his feet and threw open the shutters. Both men looked around the small room in the better light. It was a mess. Augustus's few possessions had been scattered, his spare clothes pulled from the shelf and hurled to the ground, and a small box on the table ransacked so that odd bits of parchment lay everywhere. Bartholomew recalled that his attacker had been doing something in the middle of the floor, and leaned forward to see that the floorboards had been prised up in places. The sharp knife that had almost been the end of Bartholomew had evidently been used to scratch loose plaster from the walls, for small piles of dust and rubble lay all around the room.

'Tell me what happened,' said Bartholomew.

Aelfrith shook his head, and sank down onto the bed next to him. 'I do not know. I was kneeling, facing the crucifix next to the window, when I heard a sound. I thought it might be Brother Paul; he has taken a turn for the worse recently, so I went to make sure he was sleeping. He was curled up under his blanket fast asleep, so I came back here. I knelt down again, and that is all I can remember. The next thing I knew was that you were helping me up from the floor, and that Augustus was gone.' He turned suddenly, and gripped Bartholomew's arm. 'Matthew, are you sure that Augustus was . . .' he faltered.

Bartholomew nodded, remembering the extensive examination he had made. Not only was Augustus dead, but rigor mortis had begun to set in, and no drugs or poisons, however sophisticated, could mimic that.

'But who would do this?' Aelfrith blurted out. 'What could anyone want to gain from poor old Augustus? And where is the man who attacked me?'

Bartholomew leaned back against the wall and

closed his eyes. He thought about Augustus's previous claims and the burnt bed; about the unexpected death of Sir John; about Brother Michael's strange behaviour; and about the other Fellows' reactions – Wilson's lack of emotion when told that Augustus was dead, Swynford's dismissal of Augustus as a senile old man, and even Aelfrith's expressionless acceptance.

He began to feel sick in the pit of his stomach. All his suspicions of the night before came clamouring back to him. There were too many questions, and too many unexplained details. Suddenly, he had no doubts about the validity of Augustus's statements, and that, because of them, someone had wanted him out of the way. But who? And why? And even more urgent, where was Augustus's body? Why would anyone want to remove the body of an old man?

'Matthew?' Bartholomew opened his eyes. Father Aelfrith's austere face was regarding him sombrely, his normally neat grey hair sticking up in all directions around his tonsure. 'Look in the commoners' room to see if Augustus was moved there, then look down the stairs . . .'

Bartholomew sighed. 'Whoever attacked you also attacked me. I was knocked down the stairs, and I know Augustus is not there. I looked in the commoners' room and know that he is not there either. We will check again together, but whoever attacked us also seems to have taken Augustus.'

'That does not necessarily follow, my son,' said Aelfrith. 'You have no proof for such a statement.'

Bartholomew pulled a face. Aelfrith, one of the University's foremost teachers of logic, was right, but both attacks and the removal of Augustus had occurred in or near Augustus's room, and if the same person was not responsible, then at least both events must have been connected to the same cause.

'We should fetch Master Wilson,' he said. 'He should come to decide what should be done.'

'Yes. We will,' said Aelfrith. 'But first I want to find Augustus. He cannot be far. We will look together, and undoubtedly find that he has been moved for some perfectly logical reason.'

Aelfrith rose, looking under the bed a second time as he did so. In the interests of being thorough, Bartholomew also glanced under the bed, but there was nothing there, not even the black fragments of wood he had examined the night before. He looked closer. The dust that had collected under the bed had gone. It looked as though someone had carefully swept underneath it. He looked at the floor under the small table, and found that that too had been swept.

'You will not find him under there, Matthew,' said Aelfrith, a trifle testily, and began to walk to the commoners' room. Bartholomew followed, looking at the gouge in the wall where he had deflected the knife blade away from himself.

Both men stood in the doorway looking at the nine sleeping commoners. All along the far side of the long room were tiny carrels, or small workspaces, positioned to make use of the light from the windows. The carrels had high wooden sides so that, when seated, a scholar would not be able to see his neighbour; for most scholars in medieval Cambridge, privacy for studying was regarded as a far more valuable thing than privacy to sleep. All the carrels were empty, some with papers lying in them, one or two with a precious book from Michaelhouse's small library.

Bartholomew walked slowly round the room, checking each of the commoners. Five of them, including Paul, were old men, living out their lives on College hospitality as a reward for a lifetime of service. The man who had attacked Bartholomew had been strong, and of a height similar to his own. Bartholomew was above average height, and sturdily built. He was also fitter and stronger than the average scholar since a good part of his day involved walking to see patients, and he enjoyed taking exercise. The attacker could not have been any of the old men, which left four.

Of these, Roger Alyngton was Bartholomew's size, but had one arm that was withered and useless, and Bartholomew's attacker had two strong arms. So the number was down to three. Father Jerome was taller than Bartholomew by three inches or more, but was painfully thin and was constantly racked by a dry rattling cough. Bartholomew suspected a wasting disease, although Jerome refused all medicines, and would be far too weak to take on someone of Bartholomew's size. That left two. These were the Frenchman, Henri d'Evéne and the brusque Yorkshireman, Jocelyn of Ripon. D'Evéne was slight, and, although it was conceivable that he could have attacked Bartholomew, it was doubtful that he would have the strength to overcome him. Jocelyn was a recent visitor to Michaelhouse, and had come at the invitation of Swynford. He was a large man with a ruddy face and a shiny bald head. Bartholomew had not seen him sober since he had arrived, and he had been admonished several times by Sir John for his belligerent attitude when College members gathered in the conclave for company in the evenings. He certainly would have the strength to overpower Bartholomew.

Bartholomew stood looking down at him. Even in sleep, Jocelyn scowled. Could he be the assailant? Bartholomew bent close to him and caught the fumes of the previous evening's wine. His attacker had not had alcoholic fumes on his breath. Of course, this could be a ruse, and he could easily have downed a glass of wine as a cover for his actions. D'Evéne lay on the pallet next to him curled up like a child.

Bartholomew straightened, and tiptoed out of the dormitory, wincing at his sore knee. He joined Aelfrith who was still standing in the doorway, looking grey-faced and prodding cautiously at the gash on his head.

'How long was it before you were attacked?' Bartholomew asked of the friar.

Aelfrith thought carefully. 'I am not sure. The feast became very noisy after I left. I expect the other Fellows left shortly after us for it would not be seemly to continue to carouse when one of our number lay dead. The students, though, would have enjoyed their freedom and the wine. None of the commoners had returned, however,' he said suddenly. 'It is not every day that the commoners are treated to such food and wine, and, like the students, they intended to wring every drop of enjoyment out of it that they could.'

'So you, Paul, and Augustus were the only ones in this part of the building?' asked Bartholomew. 'And all the others were in the hall?'

'I do not know that they were in the hall,' replied the logician, 'but they were not here. The feast became noisy, as I said, and I found that it was distracting me from my prayers. I rose, perhaps shortly after midnight, to close the door to the room, and continued with my prayers. I may have nodded off for a while,' he admitted, 'but I would have woken if the commoners had returned.'

'Did you hear any sounds, other than the noise from the hall?'

'None,' said Aelfrith firmly. 'And what about you? How did you come to be in the commoners' room so early?'

'I rose at my usual time,' replied Bartholomew, 'and I saw a flicker of light coming from Augustus's room. I came because I thought you might like to be relieved for a while.'

Aelfrith acknowledged this with a bow of his head. 'Pray continue,' he said.

'I came as quietly as I could so as not to wake anyone, opened the door, and saw what I assumed to be you kneeling on the floor prising up the floorboards. What I thought was Augustus lay on the floor. As I entered, whoever it was that I thought was you leapt to his feet and came at me before I had the chance to react. He had a knife, and we grappled together. Then he pushed me down the stairs, and I heard footsteps. He did not come down the stairs because I fell against the door and he could not have opened it without moving me. I went back up the stairs, but could find no trace of him, either in Augustus's room or the dormitory. Then you came round and I realised that Augustus was missing.'

Aelfrith frowned. 'These commoners sleep very soundly,' he said. 'I am knocked on the head, and probably fell with quite a clatter. You have a fight on the landing virtually outside their room, and none of them wake. Now, we stand here speaking to each other, and not a soul stirs. Curious, would you not say?'

He strode into the centre of the commoners' dormitory, and clapped his hands loudly. Jocelyn's snores stopped for a second, but then resumed. Aelfrith picked up a pewter plate from a table, tipping off some wizened apples, and banged it as hard as he could against the wall, making an unholy row. Jocelyn groaned, and turned onto his side. D'Evéne and Jerome began to stir, but did not wake.

The cold feeling of unease that had earlier been in Bartholomew's stomach returned. He knelt down by Alyngton and felt his neck. His life beat was rapid and erratic. He pulled back his eyelids, noting how the pupils responded slowly to the light. He moved to one of the old men, and went through the same process.

He looked up at Aelfrith. 'They have been drugged,' he said. 'Of course! How else could an intruder hope to ransack a room and steal a body?'

Aelfrith stared back. 'My God, man,' he whispered. 'What evil is afoot in this College? What is going on to warrant such violence?'

Augustus's words of the previous day came back to Bartholomew: '"Evil is afoot, and will corrupt us all, especially those who are unaware."'

'What?' asked Aelfrith, and Bartholomew realised he had spoken aloud. He was about to explain, when something stopped him. He was confused. The events of the past few hours seemed totally inexplicable to him, and the brightness of the day seemed suddenly dulled, as suspicion and distrust settled upon his thoughts.

'Just quoting,' he mumbled dismissively, rising to check on the others.

'Here!' exclaimed Aelfrith. Bartholomew spun round. 'This must be it!' He held a large pewter jug in his hands, similar to the ones used to serve the wine at meals in the hall. Bartholomew took it gingerly. At the bottom were the dregs of the wine, and a few cloves. Evidently, Master Wilson's good wine had been replaced with inferior stuff that needed spicing when the feast had reached a certain point. But there was something else too. Swirling in the dregs and drying on the side of the jug were traces of a grey-white powder. Bartholomew smelled it carefully and detected a strong hint of laudanum. The commoners must have been drunk indeed not to have noticed it, and, at this strength, mixed with the effects of a night's drinking, would ensure that the commoners slept at least until midday.

He handed the jug back to Aelfrith. 'A sleeping draught,' he said, 'and a strong one too. I only hope it was not too strong for the old folks.' He continued his rounds, lying the torpid commoners on their sides so they would not choke, and testing for the strength of their pulses. He was concerned for one, a tiny man with a curved spine who was known simply as 'Montfitchet' after the castle in which he had been born. Montfitchet's pulse was far too rapid, and he felt clammy to the touch.

'I wonder whether it was consumed here, or in the hall,' said Aelfrith thoughtfully. 'We will find out when they awake. When will that be, do you think?'

'You can try to wake Jocelyn now,' said Bartholomew. 'I suspect he may be more resistant to strong drink than the others, and he almost woke when you banged the plate.'

Bartholomew reached Brother Paul. Paul had not attended the feast, and if he too had been drugged, the chances were that the wine had been sent to the commoners' dormitory to be consumed by them there. Bartholomew felt Paul's neck for a life beat, his mind on the mysteries that were unravelling all around him. He snapped into alertness, quickly dragged the thick covering from the pallet, and stared in horror. Aelfrith came to peer over his shoulder.

'Oh, sweet Jesus,' he breathed. He crossed himself and took a step backwards. 'My God, Matthew, what is happening here? The Devil walked in Michaelhouse last night!'

Bartholomew stared down at the blood-soaked sheet on which Paul lay. The knife that had caused his death still protruded from his stomach, and one of his hands was clasped loosely round the hilt. Bartholomew pulled at it, a long, wicked Welsh dagger similar to those that he had seen carried by Cynric and the soldiers at the Castle.

'Another suicide?' whispered Aelfrith, seeing Paul's hand on the hilt.

'I do not think so, Father. The knife was stabbed into Paul with such force that I think it is embedded in his spine. I cannot pull it out. Paul would never have had the strength for such a blow. And I do not think his death was instant. I think he died several minutes after the wound. Look, both hands are bloodstained, and blood is smeared over the sheet. I think he was trying to pull the knife out, and I think the murderer waited for him to die before arranging the bedclothes in such a way that no one would notice he was dead until the morning. And by then,' he said, turning to face Aelfrith, 'whatever business was going on last night would be completed.'

'Or would have been,' said Aelfrith, 'had you not

been an early riser and an abstemious drinker!' He shuddered, looking down at the pathetic body of Brother Paul. 'Poor man! I will say a mass for him and for Augustus this morning. But now, we must inform the Master. You stay here while I fetch him.'

While Aelfrith was gone, Bartholomew inspected Paul. He was cold, and the blood had congealed. Aelfrith had said that he had heard a sound and had gone to check Paul. Had he already been dead then? Was it the murderer Aelfrith had heard? Bartholomew had heard Paul cough when he had looked in on Augustus before he went to the feast, so he must have died later than that. Had Paul seen something and called out? Or had he just been dispatched as a caution to ensure the strange events of the previous evening were kept secret?

Bartholomew put his head in his hands. Two murders in his College. And what of Sir John? Bartholomew was beginning to have serious doubts that Sir John had committed suicide, and was inclined to believe that he had been murdered for something he knew or was about to find out. It seemed that Augustus was killed because he also knew, or someone thought he knew, something. And poor, gentle Brother Paul was murdered because he was too ill to attend Wilson's wretched feast! Bartholomew went to check on Montfitchet. Perhaps it would be four murders before the day was out, for the tiny man showed no signs of improving, and was beginning to turn blue around the mouth.

III

BARTHOLOMEW HEARD WILSON'S VOICE CARRYING across the courtyard. Wilson was due to move into Sir John's spacious room that day, and the College servants had been working furiously to prepare it to his fussy requirements. So the previous night, he had been in his old room, which he shared with Roger Alcote. Bartholomew looked out of the window and saw that Alcote was hurrying over the courtyard behind Wilson, and that Aelfrith had awakened Father William, too. Michael, a light sleeper, was peering out of his window to see what was going on, and Gilbert had evidently been dispatched to fetch Robert Swynford and Giles Abigny.

Wilson swept importantly past Bartholomew, paused briefly to look into Augustus's ransacked room and stopped as he saw Brother Paul's body. Bartholomew had left him as he had been found, the knife protruding from his stomach, and Wilson paled at the sight.

'Cover him up, damn you,' he snarled at Bartholomew. 'Leave the poor soul with some dignity!'

Bartholomew drew the bedcover over Paul's body, while Wilson looked around at the commoners in disdain.

'They are all drunk!' he proclaimed. 'We will not have such debauchery while I am Master!'

Bartholomew barely restrained himself from telling Wilson that if they were drunk, it was due to the copious amounts of wine he himself had supplied the night before, and that such 'debauchery' would most certainly not have been tolerated under Sir John's Mastership.

'Now,' Wilson said, sweeping some discarded clothes from a bench and sitting down, 'tell me what happened.'

Bartholomew looked at Aelfrith. As Senior Fellow, it was his prerogative to speak first. Aelfrith shook his head sorrowfully. 'I cannot begin to say what evil has walked in these rooms,' he began. Alcote and Swynford, in anticipation of a lengthy explanation, followed Wilson's lead and sat on the bench. Father William stood next to Aelfrith, silently offering his support, while Brother Michael, his black robes askew, leaned against the door. Abigny, less the worse for wear than Bartholomew would have expected, slipped into the dormitory noiselessly and stood next to him. All the Fellows were present.

Wilson folded his arms over his ample paunch and waited imperiously. 'Well?' he demanded.

'It is complex,' Aelfrith began. Bartholomew edged his way nearer to Montfitchet, partly so he could keep an eye on the old man, and partly so he would be able to see all the faces of the gathered Fellows. It was possible that one or more of them had committed some terrible acts, and he wanted to watch them all closely. He felt rather ashamed: these were his colleagues, and some of them, like Michael and Abigny, his friends whom he had known for years. None of them had any history of violence that he knew. He thought of Sir John, and his mangled body, and he looked across at the covered body of Paul, and steeled himself. They would be no friends of his if they had killed Sir John and Brother Paul!

'This is what I perceive to have happened,' Aelfrith continued. He looked over at Bartholomew. 'You must interrupt if you think I have left something out. Augustus died during the feast, and Matthew came to check the body at Master Wilson's request. He declared Augustus dead, and Brother Michael came to pray for his soul. Michael returned to the hall first, and Matthew came later.'

Wilson snorted, his eyes boring into Bartholomew. The physician had not realised that the Fellows had been so intrigued as to why he had taken so much longer than Michael. Well, he was certainly not going to reveal that he suspected Augustus had been murdered. Aelfrith continued.

'He made his report to the Master, and asked if I would keep vigil for Augustus. I went to Augustus's room, and kept vigil there until I was attacked from behind and knocked senseless. I have the wound to prove it. When I came round, Matthew was helping me to rise. Augustus's body was gone, and his room had been ransacked. I have no idea as to the reasons for either. Matthew and I made a quick search of this part of the building for Augustus and for the attacker. It was then that Matthew discovered that the commoners, who had been remarkably oblivious to all these goings-on, had been drugged. While examining them, he found that Brother Paul, God rest his soul, had been murdered. And that is all I know.' His story completed, he stood with head bowed and hands folded in front of him.

There was a silence among the Fellows, and then a

clamour of questions. Wilson tried to restore order, first by waving a pudgy hand in the air, and next by shouting. Bartholomew saw one or two of the drugged commoners stir, and bent down to examine Montfitchet.

'Well, Doctor Bartholomew,' said Wilson unpleasantly, 'what have you to say for yourself? You spend a considerable amount of time alone with Augustus before returning to the hall; you are standing over Father Aelfrith when he regains his senses after being knocked on the head by an unseen assailant; you discover the commoners have been drugged; and you uncover poor Brother Paul's body. What have you to say?'

Bartholomew looked at him in disbelief. The Master clearly thought that he had something to do with the sinister events of the night, an accusation not lost on the other Fellows who looked uneasy.

He took a deep breath, and recounted his story as he had done to Aelfrith, omitting nothing but his suspicions and speculations. When he mentioned his struggle at the top of the stairs, Alcote went to check the knife mark in the plaster.

Wilson watched Bartholomew closely as he gave his account of events. His unblinking eyes made Bartholomew uncomfortable, and he wondered whether this was a tactic employed by lawyers on their victims in court. The others listened with a mixture of horror and fascination, but Bartholomew could gauge nothing from their expressions other than shock.

When he had finished, Wilson stared at him for several long moments. 'Have you told us everything?' he asked. 'Is there anything you are keeping back?'

Bartholomew hoped his discomfiture did not show. 'I have told you everything I know. And everything I have told you is the truth,' he said. Bartholomew considered himself an appalling liar, but his statements to Wilson had been meticulously truthful. He had told the new Master only what he knew to have happened, and had omitted merely to speak of his growing suspicions. And how could he do otherwise? He had no real evidence, only a collection of strange coincidences and suppositions. But, he promised himself, he would have something more than unfounded suspicions soon.

'This is ludicrous!' exclaimed Abigny. 'Disappearing corpses, ransacked rooms of madmen, fights in the darkness! For heaven's sake, this is a College, not the London stews! Bodies do not just disappear. There must be some purely rational explanation.'

'Such as?' asked William.

'Such as,' said Abigny, exasperated, 'a secret exit! Some door unknown to us that allowed the murderer to escape, or to hide.' He began to look around him as though such a door would suddenly become apparent.

'Do not be ridiculous!' said Wilson aggressively. 'A secret door! Where? This is not a castle. The walls are less than a foot thick. Where could there possibly be such a door?'

'I do not know!' Abigny snapped back, his voice beginning to rise. 'It was only a suggestion. Maybe Augustus is not dead and is off wandering somewhere. Maybe some burglar came into the College, attacked Matt and Father Aelfrith and escaped out of a window.'

'You try jumping out of any of the windows here,' said Michael. 'You would need to be very agile, and,' he said looking ruefully down at his rotund form, 'very slender.

All the windows have stone mullions which would make them very difficult to squeeze through, and the drop is enough to break a leg. Perhaps Augustus or a burglar might have wriggled his way out, but he would not have landed undamaged.'

Wilson seized on Abigny's statement like a drowning man on a rope. 'Of course! Augustus was not dead and it was he who attacked Father Aelfrith and Doctor Bartholomew in the dark. That would explain everything.' He looked around triumphantly, considering the mystery to be solved. With an air of finality, he rose to leave.

'Augustus was dead!' said Bartholomew firmly. 'And he most certainly would not have had the strength to push me down the stairs. The man I fought with was a man of my size. And it also does not explain Paul's murder and the drugging of the commoners.'

'Yes, it does,' Wilson said. 'Augustus was mad, we all know that. He feigned his death to you, and then hit Father Aelfrith on the head when he came to keep vigil. He then, in his madness, went into the commoners' room and killed Paul – let us remember that he *was* insane,' he continued, looking around at each Fellow in turn. 'Perhaps he left the drugged wine for the others to drink when they returned, perhaps they are not drugged at all, but insensible after a night of debauchery.' At this he cast a scathing glance around at the comatose figures of the commoners still motionless on their pallets. 'But regardless, he returned to his room and began his foolish searching for the Lord knows what. When the Doctor surprised him, he attacked, made strong by insanity. Then, knowing his game was up, he jumped out of the window and escaped.'

'Escaped where?' asked Bartholomew. 'The gates are still locked.'

'Then he is hiding in the College,' said Wilson. 'I will order a thorough search to be made.' He looked behind him to where he knew Gilbert would be hovering, and raised his eyebrows. Gilbert disappeared immediately, and the Fellows could hear him summoning the College servants from their other duties. 'Do not worry,' he said to the Fellows, 'Augustus will be found and brought to justice. Paul's death will not go unavenged!' He turned to Bartholomew. 'I suppose *he* is dead, Physician?' he added with a sneer.

Bartholomew shrugged. 'Check for yourself,' he invited. 'And then check poor Montfitchet too.'

'What?' Wilson was momentarily thrown from his pomposity. The Fellows clustered around Montfitchet's pallet. His face had a bluish tinge to it and a small trickle of blood came from the corner of his mouth. Bartholomew gently closed the half-open eyes. Wilson elbowed him roughly out of the way to look for himself.

'Dead!' he proclaimed. 'Augustus has two murders to pay for!'

Outside, Bartholomew heard the servants clattering up the stairs and banging doors as they made their search of the College.

'Now,' began Wilson, taking matters in hand, 'Father Aelfrith, have your wound attended to – by our esteemed Master of Medicine if you trust him not to pronounce you dead. Of course, I will understand perfectly should you wish to consult another physician.'

Bartholomew raised his eyes heavenward. Now Wilson had his theory, he would hang onto it like a dog with a bone, and would take every opportunity to undermine Bartholomew's skills as a physician to give it more credence.

'Doctor Bartholomew will attend to me,' said Aelfrith quietly. 'I see no need to call upon the services of another physician.'

'That is your own choice, Father,' responded Wilson disparagingly, his tone making it clear that he would have no hesitation in taking his patronage elsewhere. Bartholomew studiously avoided Wilson's gaze, not trusting himself to speak civilly. He saw clearly that many of the objections that Wilson had raised to his appointment four years before would now be voiced; indeed, would be used against him at every opportunity, and perhaps Wilson would succeed in bringing about his dismissal from the College. Wilson gazed at Bartholomew in a hostile manner for several moments before continuing.

'Father William, would you arrange to have the bodies moved to the church? Then you and Brother Michael must do what is necessary for their souls. Master Alcote, I would like you to take the news to the Bishop, for we will need his services when our murderer is caught.' Since, like most scholars at the University, Augustus had taken minor orders, any crimes of which he might be accused would be dealt with by Church, rather than secular, law. 'Master Swynford, Master Abigny, perhaps you would oversee the search. Make sure that every nook and cranny is investigated. Augustus must be found!'

The Fellows scurried off to do his bidding. Bartholomew and Aelfrith made their way down the stairs together, heading for Bartholomew's room. As they reached the courtyard, Bartholomew went to look at the ground under Augustus's window. If anyone had managed to squeeze out of the first-floor window and jump, there would be some evidence, but there was nothing to be seen. There were a few tendrils of bindweed creeping up the wall: had someone leaped from the window, the plants would have been damaged or displaced. Bartholomew saw nothing that indicated anyone had made an escape from Augustus's window.

He stood up slowly, wincing at his stiffening knee. Wilson gave him a cold glance as he left, guessing what he was doing and disapproving of it. Bartholomew knew that Wilson would regard his action as a direct challenge to his authority, but was disturbed by Wilson's eagerness to accept the first excuse that came along and to dismiss any facts that confounded it.

Aelfrith waited, his hands folded in the voluminous sleeves of his monastic robes. 'Our new Master seems to dislike you, my son,' he said.

Bartholomew shrugged, and began to limp towards his room. Aelfrith caught up with him, and offered his arm for support. The tall friar was surprisingly strong, and Bartholomew was grateful for his help.

They arrived at the tiny chamber Bartholomew used to store his medicines. It had been used originally to store wood, but Sir John had ordered it cleaned for Bartholomew's use because he thought it was not healthy for him to sleep with the smell of his medicines.

The blacksmith still slept on the pallet bed, snoring noisily. Bartholomew had forgotten about him. He would have to send Cynric to ask his family to come to collect him. Aelfrith wrinkled his nose in disgust at the smell of stale wine fumes, and went to Bartholomew's own room next door. Abigny had thrown the shutters open before he had left, and the room was bright and sunny. Neither Bartholomew nor Abigny had many possessions – a few clothes, some writing equipment, and Bartholomew had a book he had been given by his Arab master when he had completed his training; all were stored out of sight in the large chest that stood at one end of the room.

Aelfrith looked around approvingly. The room was clean, with fresh rushes and herbs scattered on the floor, and a servant had already put the bedding out of the window to air. Bartholomew had been taught that dirt and disease went hand in hand – his insistence on cleanliness was another reason he was regarded as an oddity.

He sank down onto a stool. He had not realised what a wrench he had given his knee, and he knew it would slow him down for a few days. He made to stand again, remembering that he should be tending Aelfrith's head. Aelfrith pushed him back down firmly.

'Tell me what you need, Matthew, and I will get it. I am sure you can doctor me as well sitting as standing.'

As Aelfrith fetched water, linen, and some salves, Bartholomew thought about Augustus, Paul, and Mont-fitchet. He had been fond of Paul, and only now did the shock of his cruel death register. He took a shuddering breath, and blinked away tears.

Aelfrith drew a stool up next to him, and laid a hand on his shoulder comfortingly. Bartholomew smiled weakly, and began to tend to the wound in the friar's scalp. It was a nasty gash, and Bartholomew was not surprised that Aelfrith had been rendered unconscious. He could easily have been insensible for several hours. Aelfrith, like Bartholomew, was showing signs of delayed shock, with shaking hands and sudden tiredness.

Bartholomew inspected the ragged edges of the wound, and prodded gently to ensure no splinters were left that might fester. Satisfied that it was clean, he bathed it carefully, and tied a neat bandage around the tonsured head. Aelfrith rose to leave. He leaned out of the window, looked both ways, and closed the shutters and the door.

'I am too befuddled to think now,' he said in a low voice, 'but I am appalled at the wickedness that has been perpetrated in this house of learning. Our Master is mistaken in his explanation, and I, like you, know that Augustus was dead last night. I believe there is sinister work afoot, and I suspect that you think the same. Now, I will say no more, but you and I will meet later today to talk when we are both more ourselves. Trust no one, Matthew. Keep your counsel to yourself.'

His calm grey eyes looked steadily at Bartholomew. Bartholomew's blood ran cold and he suddenly felt inutterably tired. He was a physician, dedicated to healing, and here he was being sucked into some vile intrigue where the taking of life appeared to be of little consequence. Aelfrith seemed to detect Bartholomew's feelings, for he gave one of his rare smiles, his eyes kindly.

'Rest now, Matthew. We will deal with this together, you and I.'

He was gone before Bartholomew could respond. Bartholomew put cold wraps around his knee and hobbled over to his bed to lie down. It was gloomy in the room with the shutters closed, but he could not be bothered to get up to open them again. He thought of the drugged commoners. He should really go to see to them. And he should check the blacksmith's leg. And Agatha would be wondering what to do with the woman he left with her last night. And he had promised his sister he would visit today. With his thoughts tumbling around inside his head, Bartholomew fell into a restless doze.

Bartholomew awoke, the sun full on his face, to the sound of the bell ringing to announce that the meal was about to be served in the hall. Like most of the Colleges and hostels, the main meal at Michaelhouse was between ten and eleven o'clock in the morning, with a second, smaller meal around four, and bread and ale for those that wanted it later in the evening.

He was disoriented for a moment, since he seldom slept during the day. Then the events of the morning came flooding back to him, and some of the brightness went out of the sunshine. Abigny had returned and opened the shutters, and was sitting at the table writing. He turned when he heard Bartholomew moving, his face lined with concern.

'At last!' he said, 'I have never known you to sleep a day away before. Are you ill?'

Bartholomew shook his head. His knee felt better already from the rest. He sat quietly for a moment, listening to the scratching of Abigny's quill as he finished what he was writing, and Brother Michael's footsteps as he moved about in the room above. Brother Michael shared a room with Michaelhouse's two Benedictine students, but Michael's footsteps were distinct from the others' because of his weight. After a few moments, he came thundering down the stairs, bent on being the first to the meal. Bartholomew heard him puffing as he hurried across the courtyard.

Upstairs, the other brothers moved about much more quietly, their sandalled feet making little sound. Suddenly, something clicked in Bartholomew's memory.

As he had lain at the bottom of the stairs after being pushed, he had heard footsteps, presumably those of his attacker. He could not tell where they came from, but they had been very distinct. The south wing, where the commoners roomed, was better built than the north wing where Bartholomew lived – he had climbed the stairs that morning without making a sound, which was why he had taken his attacker by surprise. While Bartholomew could usually hear sounds from the upstairs rooms in the north wing, he had noticed that the south wing was very much quieter, and the ground-floor residents were seldom disturbed by the people above them.

So how was it that he had heard footsteps? Had he imagined it? Bartholomew had the feeling that if he could work out why hearing the footsteps bothered him, he would be much nearer to solving the mystery. For now, the answer eluded him, and he told himself that mysterious footsteps in the night were the least of his concerns compared to the murders of his colleagues.

He hauled himself up, splashed some water on his face, tried to restore some order to his unruly black hair, and made his way out. Abigny watched him.

'Well, you are in a mess,' he observed. 'No gallivanting off today, Physician. And I was going to ask you to come to St Radegund's with me to see my sister!'

Bartholomew glowered at him. Abigny's sister had been committed to the care of the nuns at St Radegund's following the death of her father a year before. It had not taken Abigny long to observe that his pretty, fair-haired sister and his scholarly chamber-mate seemed to find a lot to talk about. Philippa would give her brother no peace when he visited without Bartholomew in tow, though, for the life of him, Abigny could not imagine what his sister, who had spent the greater part of her life in convents, could ever have in common with the world-wise Bartholomew.

'Well, perhaps I should invite her to Michaelhouse,' he said playfully. 'You brought a woman here yesterday. I must tell Philippa about that; I am sure she would find it most amusing.'

Bartholomew shot him another withering glance.

'I am going,' Abigny said cheerfully, and waved a folded piece of parchment at Bartholomew. 'One advantage that a philosopher has over a physician is that he can write decent love poetry. So first, I am away to deliver this little work of genius to the woman of my dreams!'

'On which poor soul do you intend to prey this time?' asked Bartholomew drily. Abigny's innocent, boyish looks had cost many a girl her reputation, and Abigny seemed to move from relationship to relationship with staggering ease. He was playing with fire, for if Wilson had any inkling of what Abigny was doing, the philosopher would be forced to resign his fellowship and would have grave problems finding a teaching position elsewhere.

'That lovely creature from the Laughing Pig over in Trumpington,' replied Abigny, tapping Bartholomew on the shoulder gleefully. 'Now, do not look like that! I met her at the house of your very own sister, so she must be a woman of stainless reputation.'

'At Edith's?' queried Bartholomew. Edith's large household in the village of Trumpington, two miles away, was run with the style and elegance that befitted her husband's wealth and status. Bartholomew could not imagine how Abigny had met a tavern-maid there.

'Three weeks ago, at the farewell meal she had for young Richard going to Oxford,' said Abigny, seeing Bartholomew's confusion. 'I met her in the kitchens where she was delivering eggs. She has invited me to sample the fine ale that she has been brewing.'

'Giles, have a care! If you are caught frequenting drinking houses, Wilson will drop on you like a stone. He wishes himself rid of you only slightly less than he wishes himself rid of me.'

'Oh, come, Master Physician,' laughed Abigny, 'not so gloomy on such a wonderful day. The sun is shining, the birds are singing, and I am in love!'

Bartholomew looked dubiously at Abigny's piece of parchment. 'Can this barmaid read?' he asked.

Abigny laughed again. 'Of course not! So she will never know that the words here are actually a list of books I made for my students last term, now embellished with a few decorated capitals for appearance's sake. Parchment is expensive!'

Bartholomew noted that Abigny was wearing his best robe and hose, implying that his intentions towards the barmaid were serious, if not honourable. Abigny set off, jauntily waving his hat in the air before disappearing through the door. He put his head back a moment later. 'By the way,' he said, 'your smelly patient has gone. I sent Cynric to tell his family to come and remove him. I could not bear to have him lying about here all day! He said to tell you he would keep his side of the bargain whatever that might mean.'

He had disappeared a second time before Bartholomew had a chance to reply. Bartholomew saw that Alcote had emerged from his room on the next staircase, and, since his window shutters were open, had probably heard their entire conversation. Of all the Fellows, Alcote was the one who most strongly disapproved of women having anything to do with the College. Bartholomew wondered if he had once been married and the experience had driven him to extremes. Alcote was a small, fussy man who reminded him of a hen. He was impatient with his less-able scholars, and most of his students lived in fear of his scathing criticisms.

Bartholomew made his way slowly round the court-yard, Alcote walking silently next to him.

'Has Augustus's body been found?' Bartholomew asked.

Alcote looked sharply at him. 'Augustus has not been found yet,' he said. 'We are still searching and will bring him to justice, never fear. He could not possibly have left the College grounds, because the porters at the main gates were awake all night owing to the racket the students were making in the hall, and they are positive no one went past them. And your woman kept Mistress Agatha awake all night weeping, and she says no one went out of the back gate.'

'How are the commoners?'

Alcote smiled gloatingly. 'Waking with dreadful heads and sick stomachs, and it serves them right,' he said. 'Next time they will beware of the sin of gluttony.'

Bartholomew stopped and grasped Alcote's wrist. 'Are they really sick? Why did no one wake me? I may be able to give them something to relieve the symptoms.'

Alcote freed his wrist. 'There is nothing you can do. They will live.'

Aelfrith joined them. 'How is your head?' Bartholomew asked.

'My years of learning must have given me a tough skull,' said Aelfrith with a smile, 'for I feel no ill effects at all.'

They reached the main building and climbed the wide spiral stairs to the hall. The borrowed tapestries that had adorned the walls the night before had been removed, but evidence of the festivities was still apparent in the scraps of food that littered the rushes on the floor, and in the smell of spilled wine.

'Master Abigny?' asked Wilson, his voice loud in the otherwise silent hall.

'Visiting his sister,' replied Brother Michael. It had become a standard excuse. Sir John had not been too particular about whether his Fellows chose to eat in College or not, but, judging from the way Wilson's mouth set in a firm line of displeasure, from now on Fellows would be required to attend meals in hall.

Alcote whispered something to Wilson that made the master's eyes glitter with anger. Bartholomew had no doubt that Alcote was telling him about what he had overheard. Spiteful little man, he thought, and turned to see Michael raising his eyes heavenwards, much to the amusement of the students at the end of the table.

'Silence!' Wilson banged a pewter goblet on the table, making everyone jump, and the giggles of the students stopped instantly. Wilson glared around. 'Two of our members lie foully murdered,' he said. 'It is not a time for frivolous laughter.' Some of the students hung their heads. Gentle Paul would be missed. Throughout the summer he had sat in the sun in the courtyard and had been only too happy to while away the hours by debating with the students to help them develop their skills in disputation, and by patiently explaining points of grammar, rhetoric, and logic to those who had stayed on to try to catch up.

Wilson intoned the long Latin grace, and then nodded to the Bible scholar to begin the recital that would last throughout the meal. Sir John had encouraged academic debate, and had chaired some very lively discussions, all aimed to hone and refine the College's reputation of academic excellence. Wilson was more traditional in approach, and considered it fitting for scholars to listen to tracts from the Bible while they ate, so that they could improve their spiritual standing.

Bartholomew studied his colleagues. Brother Michael, on his right, hunched over his trencher, greedily cramming pieces of meat into his mouth. Bartholomew offered him the dish of vegetables seeped in butter, and received, as always, a look of disbelief. Michael firmly believed that vegetables would damage his digestion and lived almost entirely on large quantities of meat, fish, and bread. Bartholomew thought back to Michael's odd behaviour of the night before. Was it illness as he had claimed, or did he know something about Augustus's death? Bartholomew had never seen the fat monk in such a state, but whatever had upset him was obviously not affecting his appetite now.

Aelfrith sat between Bartholomew and Father William. When speaking was permitted at meals, the Franciscans would usually discuss theology in Latin. Bartholomew compared the two men. Aelfrith was tall and thin, with a sallow face and grey eyes that were often distant. Bartholomew did not find him a warm man, but he was compassionate, discreetly generous to many of Bartholomew's poorer patients, and devoted to his teaching. Father William was of a similar height, but much heavier. Like Aelfrith, he was in his late forties, but his hair was thick and brown. His eyes often burned with the passion of the fanatic, and Bartholomew could believe the rumours that he had been appointed to search out heresy by his Order, and had been sent to Cambridge because he was over-zealous.

Wilson was the oldest Fellow, probably just past fifty, and was a singularly unattractive individual. His dry brown hair released a constant dusting of dandruff that adorned all his gowns, and his complexion was florid with a smattering of spots that reached right down to his array of chins. Swynford leaned towards him and whispered. Swynford was distantly related to the powerful Dukes of Norfolk, and held considerable sway in University circles. In a place where a College depended on the seniority and authority of its Fellows and Master, Michaelhouse owed much of its influence to Swynford. Wilson would need to keep him happy. Swynford was a handsome man around the same age as the Franciscans, but his bearing was more military than monastic, his manner confident and assured. His hair was grey, thick, and neat, and his beard always well groomed. He was the only Fellow, other than the Master, to have the luxury of a room and a servant of his own, and he paid the College handsomely for the privilege. Beside his impressive figure, Alcote looked like a small bird.

Bartholomew speared a slice of turnip on his knife and chewed it thoughtfully. Alcote had said that the porters and Agatha were prepared to swear that no one had left the College, other than the guests, once the gates had been locked after the Oliver brothers had attempted to provoke the riot. This meant that, unless someone had entered the College early and stayed until after the gates were unlocked the following morning, the murderer was a College member. There were few places to hide in Michaelhouse: all the rooms were occupied by students, Fellows, commoners, or servants, and all, except Swynford, shared a room with at least one other person. It would be difficult to hide in a small room where two or more people slept. There had been students in the hall and the conclave all night, which meant that no one could have hidden there, and the servants would have noticed anything untoward in the kitchens and other service rooms.

The more Bartholomew thought about it, the more his instincts told him that the murderer was a College man, who knew the habits and routines of its members. Bartholomew glanced along the table at his colleagues. Which one, if any, had murdered Paul, Augustus and possibly Sir John, and attacked him and Aelfrith? From size alone it could not have been Alcote or Abigny – they were too small. Brother Michael was fat, and since he deplored exercise of any kind, Bartholomew thought it unlikely that Michael could best him in a tussle, although it was possible. That left William, Wilson, and Swynford, all of whom were tall and probably strong enough. Then there were the commoners, Henri d'Evéne and Jocelyn of Ripon.

The only way he could reduce the list would be by establishing who was where, when, and with whom. Michael and Bartholomew had seen Augustus alive before the beginning of the feast, which meant that he had died at some point between the time when Bartholomew left him and Alexander had found him. All the Fellows and commoners had been at the feast the entire time that Bartholomew had been there. There were privies between the hall and the conclave, so no one had needed to leave the hall for that reason.

Bartholomew rubbed his eyes. Had Augustus been murdered? He had spent a long time looking for evidence that he had been, and had found nothing. But it was all too coincidental – Augustus dying the night Paul was stabbed and the commoners drugged. And for what had Bartholomew's attacker been searching?

And what of Paul? When had he died? Assuming that Aelfrith was telling the truth, Paul had probably been killed about the same time that the Franciscan had been knocked on the head. Bartholomew remembered that Paul's blood had congealed slightly, and the body was cold and beginning to grow stiff. If all the Fellows had retired to their beds around the same time as had Bartholomew, any of them could have slipped over to the south wing, murdered Paul, and drugged the commoners' wine.

But why? What could be so important as to warrant murder? Why was Augustus's room ransacked? And where was his body? Why would anyone want to take it? And how did all this tie in with Sir John's death? The more Bartholomew thought about it, the more confused and inexplicable the possibilities became.

The meal took longer than usual because some of the servants were still employed in searching for Augustus. The Bible scholar droned on and Bartholomew grew restless. He should question the commoners about the drugged wine, and visit Agatha and Mistress Atkin. He had badgered a fellow physician, Gregory Colet, to lend him a scroll containing some of the writings of the great physician Dioscorides, and Bartholomew was anxious to begin reading it. Despite being a centre for learning, copies of books and scholarly writings were scarce in Cambridge, and each was jealously guarded. Colet would not wait too long before he wanted his scroll back. If the students were to pass their disputations, they had to know Dioscorides's lists of healing plants. But for Bartholomew merely knowing was not enough: he wanted his students to understand the properties of the potions they used, the harmful and beneficial effects these might have, and how they might affect the patient when they were taken over a long period of time. Before he began teaching them this, he wanted to refresh his memory.

At last the meal was over and the scholars rose for the final grace. Then the Fellows clustered around Wilson, who had just been listening to Gilbert.

'Still nothing,' he informed his colleagues. 'But I have alerted the porters to watch both gates for Augustus, and we will continue our search for the rest of the day if necessary. The man must be found. The Bishop will be here this evening, and I will turn this miserable business over to him, as is my duty. Doubtless he will want to see us all when he arrives.'

Bartholomew was glad to leave the hall and go out into the fresh air. It was not yet noon, but the sun was already scorching. He leaned against the wall for a minute, enjoying the warmth on his face, with his eyes closed. The air in the courtyard felt still and humid, and Bartholomew was acutely aware of the stench from the ditches west of the College. He thought of one of his patients, Tom Pike, who lived down by the wharves on the river and had a lung disease. This weather would make life unbearable for him. The smells and the insects were always worse by the river and the King's Ditch than elsewhere in the town. He wondered if bad smells and foul air were responsible for the spread of the plague that was ravaging Europe.

He saw the commoners, Jocelyn of Ripon and d'Evéne the Frenchman, coming out of the hall together and hailed them over.

'Are you better now?' he asked, looking closely at the rings under their eyes and the way they winced at the brightness of the sun.

'My head aches something rotten,' grumbled Jocelyn. 'Master Swynford told me the wine may have been tampered with, and I can tell you, Doctor Bartholomew, that it would come as no surprise to me if it were. I have not had a hangover like this since I was ten years old!'

Bartholomew could well believe it of this rough man who drank so much. D'Evéne coughed cautiously. 'That is the last time I drink French wine,' he said, a weak attempt at a joke.

'Do you recall which jug of wine it was that contained the drug?' asked Bartholomew.

Jocelyn looked at him in disbelief. 'Of course I do not!' he said. 'Do you think I would have drunk it if I thought it had been poisoned?'

Bartholomew smiled, acknowledging the absurdity of his question. D'Evéne interrupted. 'I remember,' he said. 'I have a natural aversion to wine – it brings on blinding headaches – so I avoid it whenever possible, and drink ale instead. Last night, a good while after you Fellows left, the commoners were all together enjoying the atmosphere, the food, the drink, when poor Montfitchet started to complain about feeling ill. We ignored him until he really was sick, which made us all begin to question the states of our own stomachs. We decided to leave, and went across to our room together. When we were there, before going to sleep, someone said it would be right and proper to toast Master Wilson and his new role with his best wine. Montfitchet and I declined the wine, but everyone else said we were being churlish, and that we should drink Master Wilson's health with his fine red wine. I had consumed a good deal of ale by then, and so I allowed myself to accept when I should have declined. So did Montfitchet. I have no idea how the wine came from the hall to our dormitory, but it was there.'

Jocelyn looked at him. 'Yes, by God!' he said. 'The wine in the jug. I poured it out. It was my idea to drink the Master's health. I do not recall how it arrived in our room. It was just there, and I saw it was fairly distributed among the lot of us.'

'When did you start to feel the effects?'

'It is difficult to say,' d'Evéne replied, with a shrug. 'Perhaps half an hour? The older folks had already dropped off to sleep, but Jerome, Roger Alyngton, Jocelyn and I were still chatting. We were already merry, and I do not think any of us felt that the sudden soporific feeling was anything more than too much strong drink. Although perhaps poor Montfitchet felt different.'

Bartholomew spoke to Alyngton, Father Jerome, and two of the old men. None of them could add to d'Evéne's story, although all claimed to have gone back to the dormitory together.

Bartholomew sat again, resting his back against the pale apricot stone, his head tipped back and his eyes closed against the brightness of the sun. A shadow fell across him, and he squinted up.

'We must talk, Matthew, but not here. Meet me

shortly, in the orchard.' Aelfrith, after a furtive glance round, glided off towards his room.

'Give me a hand up, Brother,' Bartholomew said to Michael, emerging last from the hall, his jaws still working on a scrap of food. Michael extended a hand and pulled. Bartholomew was momentarily taken aback by the strength of Michael's arm. He had always imagined the large monk to be flabby and weak, but Bartholomew was hauled to his feet with effortless ease.

'I am away to Barnwell Priory this afternoon,' Michael said, wiping his mouth on his sleeve. 'Want to come? We could stop off at St Radegund's on the way.' He gave a most unmonklike leer. Had Abigny told everyone of Bartholomew's interest in his sister?

'I cannot, Brother. I am going to talk to Aelfrith.'

Michael gave him an odd glance. 'What about?'

'This business about Augustus, I suppose,' said Bartholomew. 'Do you believe me, Michael? Do you think Augustus was dead last night?'

'Oh, yes,' said Michael fervently, 'Augustus was dead. I saw you do your usual checks, and I saw him myself. Look, Matt,' he said suddenly, seizing Bartholomew's wrist with a clammy hand, 'you must be cautious.' He glanced about him, as furtive as Aelfrith had been. 'I do not understand what is going on, but I am afraid. Afraid for me and afraid for you.'

'Afraid of what?' asked Bartholomew in a hushed voice.

'I do not know,' said Michael, exasperated, tightening his grip on Bartholomew's arm. 'Perhaps it is the work of the Devil. Augustus thought so, and now his body has disappeared.'

'Come now, Brother,' said Bartholomew reasonably.

'You cannot believe that. You have always told me that the only Devil is man himself. And what do you mean about Augustus and the Devil?'

Michael shook his head. 'I do not know. He spoke of it just before he died.'

'When exactly?'

Michael shook his head again and released Bartholomew's arm. 'I do not remember. But you must be cautious. Go to meet Aelfrith, but remember what I say.'

He scurried off and disappeared into the dark doorway of his staircase. Bartholomew watched him thoughtfully. What was bothering Michael? What was going on in the College?

IV

WHEN BARTHOLOMEW RETURNED TO HIS ROOM, there was a message from one of the wealthy cloth merchants in Milne Street asking him to visit. Bartholomew glanced up at the sun, trying to estimate whether he had sufficient time before he was due to meet Aelfrith. He hesitated for a moment, but then set off, swinging his heavy bag of potions and instruments over his shoulder, aware that he should walk slowly to avoid straining his knee. Since the merchant had never asked for him before, Bartholomew imagined that his brother-in-law must have recommended him.

He found the house, a rambling building gleaming under fresh whitewash, and knocked at the door. A servant directed him up the stairs and into a sumptuous room hung with cloth of blue and gold. There was even glass in the windows, and the sun filtered through it to make patterns on the wooden floor. Bartholomew introduced himself, and sat on the bed to listen to his new patient's problem. It did not take him long to discover that if Nathaniel the Fleming had been more abstemious with Master Wilson's wine at the Michaelhouse feast the night before, he would not have been lying in his bed complaining of pains in his head and stomach cramps. Bartholomew listened gravely to Nathaniel's list of ailments, and prescribed large quantities of watered ale and a cold compress for his head. Nathaniel looked aghast.

'But you have not consulted my stars. And should you not leech me?'

Bartholomew shook his head. 'There is no need for leeches, and I do not need to read your stars to understand the nature of your . . . affliction.' He rose to take his leave.

'Wait!' Nathaniel, with a burst of energy that made him wince, grabbed Bartholomew's arm. 'Oswald Stanmore told me you were the best physician in Cambridge. Is watered ale and wet cloths all that you prescribe? How do you know about the state of my humours?'

Bartholomew felt a flash of impatience. 'Of course, I could spend the afternoon consulting charts and learning of your humours. But at the end of the day, my advice to you would be the same: drink lots and apply a cool cloth to soothe your head. Time will heal the rest.'

Nathaniel half rose from his bed. 'But that is not enough! What kind of physician are you that you choose not to use the tools of your trade?'

'An honest one, Master Nathaniel,' retorted Bartholomew. 'I do not seek to charge you for services you do not need.'

'But how do you know?' argued Nathaniel. 'And I feel the need for leeches.'

'Then I cannot help you,' said Bartholomew, turning to leave.

'Then I will send for Master Colet,' said Nathaniel. 'He knows his leeches. You need not tend to me again.'

Bartholomew left, biting his tongue to prevent himself from telling Nathaniel he was a fool. As he clattered down Nathaniel's fine staircase, he heard the merchant ordering a servant to fetch Colet. Clenching his fists in frustration, he wondered whether he should have complied with Nathaniel's request – applied leeches to his arm to remove the excess of humours, and read his stars to see what other treatment they might suggest. But the man only had a hangover! Why should Bartholomew waste his time applying treatments that were unnecessary? And why should Nathaniel pay for them? As he walked home, his frustration and anger subsided. Once again, he had lost the chance of a wealthy patient because he tried to give him what he knew was best, rather than what the patient expected. Sir John had been wise when he encouraged Bartholomew to work among the poor – they seldom questioned his skills, even if they did not always follow his advice.

Bartholomew stopped at the kitchen for something to drink, and by the time he had limped to the orchard, Aelfrith was already waiting. It was pleasant in the shade of the trees, with the rich scent of ripe apples. Bartholomew made his way to the ancient tree-trunk that lay against the wall, and had been used by countless students to study in solitude or to enjoy a nap in the sun.

'I have made sure that we are the only ones here,' Aelfrith said. 'I want no one to overhear us.'

Bartholomew watched him warily, Michael's warnings ringing in his ears. Aelfrith took a deep breath. 'There is an evil loose in the College,' he said, 'and we must try to stamp it out.'

'What is the evil, and how do we stamp it out?' Bartholomew asked. 'And why all the secrecy?'

Aelfrith looked hard into Bartholomew's eyes, as if searching for something. 'I do not want to tell you what I am about to,' he said. 'Until last night I would have said you were better not knowing. But now things have changed, and I have been instructed to tell you for your own good.'

He paused and squinted up into the leafy branches of the apple trees, as if his mind was wrestling with itself. 'There is an evil afoot that threatens not only the College, but the whole University, and perhaps even all England,' he blurted out. Bartholomew studied him. He was deeply agitated about something, and perspiration beaded on his face. 'Satan is trying to destroy us.'

'Oh come, Father,' said Bartholomew, his patience beginning to wane. 'Surely you did not bring me here to tell me that. You sound just like Augustus!'

Aelfrith's head whipped round to look at him. 'Exactly,' he whispered. 'Augustus saw, but his wits were gone, and he was unable to keep his secret. Look what happened to him!'

'What happened to him, Father?' asked Bartholomew. He had spoken to no one about his suspicions that Augustus had been murdered. Perhaps now he would hear them confirmed.

'Augustus was taken by the Devil,' Aelfrith said in a whisper. Bartholomew tried not to show his irritation. He personally concurred with Michael that the only devils to exist were those within man himself, and he had considered Aelfrith beyond common superstitions about devils and demons.

'Is that all?' asked Bartholomew, beginning to rise. Aelfrith tugged him back down. 'No, that is not all,' he said coldly. 'You must be patient. This is most difficult for me.' He clasped his hands together, and muttered some prayer, trying hard to compose himself. Bartholomew picked up a fallen apple from the ground and began to eat it. It was sharp, and not quite ripe.

'It is a complex story, so you must be patient. You must remember that I am telling you this because it may be necessary for your own safety, and not because I wish to entertain you.'

Bartholomew nodded, intrigued, despite himself.

'A little more than a year ago, the master of King's Hall died. You probably remember. He is said to have hanged himself, although the official story is that he fell down the stairs and broke his neck.'

Bartholomew remembered the incident well, and had heard the rumours that his death had been suicide. Had that been true, then the Master of King's Hall would not have been buried in consecrated ground, as with Sir John. But he had died in the privacy of his own College, and his scholars had been able to hide the manner of his death from outside eyes. So he had been laid to rest in a fine alabaster tomb in All Saints' Church. Sir John had chosen a public place for his suicide, and, however much the Fellows wished the details of his death silenced, it had become public knowledge within a few hours.

'Within a few weeks, two more Fellows of King's Hall died, of summer ague. These three deaths disturbed the scholars of King's Hall, but a new Master was elected, and life returned to normal. About the same time, one of the Deans at Peterhouse was found dead in the fish-ponds. He was thought to have fallen in and drowned while in his cups.'

Bartholomew wondered where all this was leading.

Aelfrith continued, 'The Dean was a close friend, a Franciscan like myself. He did not like alcoholic beverages; he said they clouded his thoughts. I do not believe that he would have ever allowed himself to become drunk enough to drown in a fish-pond! A few days after the Dean, two Fellows at Clare lay dead from eating bad food.'

Bartholomew recalled the two deaths at Clare. He had been called to help by Gregory Colet, the teacher of medicine at Rudde's Hostel, who had been a guest of the Master of Clare that night. He and Colet had been mystified by the case. The two Fellows had eaten some oysters sent by the grateful parent of a successful student. Others, including Colet, had eaten the oysters, too, and although some complained of sickness, only the two young men had died. Colet and Bartholomew had stood by helplessly, and had watched them die.

'For several months there were no further deaths, but then, a few weeks ago, the Hall of Valence Marie, founded this most recent year, lost two Fellows to summer ague. Now, I know as well as you do that deaths from accidents and agues are not infrequent in Cambridge. But add these deaths to our four at Michaelhouse, and we have an unnaturally high figure: twelve in the Colleges in the last year.'

'So what exactly are you telling me?' Bartholomew asked, the unease that he had experienced in Augustus's room the previous night returning.

'That not all these deaths were natural, and that some of them are connected.'

The feeling of unease intensified. 'But why?'

'Not everyone wants the University to flourish,' Aelfrith said. 'There are those who wish to control it, or to stamp it out altogether. You know what happened to the University at Stamford in 1334. It was becoming a rival to Oxford and Cambridge, and the King suppressed it. He closed down all the hostels and forbade the masters to teach there. Many tried to go back to Oxford or Cambridge, but found that they were not granted licences to teach. If you remember your history, you will know that Henry III did the same to the University of Northampton in 1265. The University of Oxford is larger, older, and more powerful than Cambridge, but Cambridge is growing and is increasing its influence . . .'

'Are you saying that the University at Oxford is murdering our Fellows?' Bartholomew said incredulously. 'That is the most ridiculous thing I have ever heard! I am sorry, Father, but what kind of nonsense have you been listening to . . .?'

'It is not nonsense, and we have proof!' Aelfrith snapped back. 'Just listen to me! Every single Fellow who died had been an Oxford student before he came to Cambridge.'

'That is not proof, Father, that is coincidence. I went to Oxford first, and so did you!'

'Which is why I am telling you this,' replied Aelfrith, regaining his calm with difficulty. 'About thirty years ago, King Edward II founded King's Hall. He gave it money, buildings, and sent to it scholars and boys destined to be some of the most powerful men in England. Many scholars at Oxford considered this a great insult to them – the King should have endowed this great foundation in Oxford, not Cambridge. But the City of Oxford had refused to help Edward's – well, let us say "friend" – Piers Gaveston when he was imprisoned, and the man was later killed. Edward had no cause to love Oxford. The present

King has continued to give money and influence to King's Hall, and with its growing prestige and power, so grows the University of Cambridge. King's Hall is the largest and most influential of all the Colleges and hostels in Cambridge.

'There are many who believe that there is a secret group of Oxford men who have come to Cambridge to try to bring about the downfall of the Colleges, and when the Colleges fall, the University will crumble with them.'

'Come now, Father!' said Bartholomew, disbelievingly. 'The University would not crumble without the Colleges! Without the hostels, maybe, since there are more of them, and they house the majority of the masters and scholars.'

'Think, man!' said Aelfrith, his agitation rising again. 'The loudest and most frequently heard voices in the University are not from the hostels, they are from the Fellows of the five Colleges. The Colleges own their own buildings, their own land, and the hostels do not. The hostels rely on the good graces of the town – a landlord only need say he wants to reclaim the hostel because he wishes to live in it, then the hostel is finished, its scholars and masters no more than homeless vagrants. It is rumoured that Edmund Gonville will found another College soon, and so might the Bishop of Norwich. The Colleges are becoming powerful in the University – they are its future – and as the Colleges increase in power, so does the University.'

'But there are scholars enough for both Oxford and Cambridge, and we take them from different parts of the country anyway,' protested Bartholomew.

Aelfrith shook his head impatiently, and continued his narrative. 'You know the stories that a terrible pestilence is coming. For seven years it has been coming, from the lands in the Far East and across Europe. Many said it would not come across the waters that separate us from France, but it is already in the West Country. It is said that whole villages will be wiped out, and that it is a sign of God's wrath for the sin of man. It is said that God is especially angry with his priests and monks, and that many of us will perish for our sins.'

'With good reason,' muttered Bartholomew, thinking of the wealthy monasteries and the heavy Church taxes on the poor.

'You are failing to see the point!' said Aelfrith, exasperated. 'If there is a huge reduction in the clergy, then the two Universities *will* be competing for scholars. And who will teach them if we are to lose most of our masters? There are many, both in Oxford and Cambridge, who believe that the Universities will be fighting for their very existences before the year is out. Cambridge, being the smaller, is the more vulnerable. The weaker Cambridge is, the greater chance for survival Oxford will have. Ergo, some Oxford scholars are waging a secret war against us in anticipation of the events to come.'

'You really believe this, don't you?' said Bartholomew, incredulously.

'Yes, I do. And so should you. I spoke of evidence. We are not without our own spies, and we have documents from Oxford scholars stating their intentions very clearly.'

'You say "we",' said Bartholomew. 'Who else knows of this?'

'I cannot say,' said Aelfrith, 'because we do not know who is truthfully for Cambridge, and who may have been sent by Oxford. I can only tell you that seven of the Fellows whose deaths I mentioned earlier were of the same mind as me, including Sir John and the two young lads you tried to treat for food poisoning. This network of spies is nothing recent – there is nothing inherently wrong in watching the moves of the opposition, and we have had people who have traded information for as long as University records exist. But there has never been any violence, especially murder. Poor Augustus knew of the threat and he must have been killed because it was thought he might know something – someone believed he should not have done.'

'By whom? By Oxford people to strike at the Colleges, or by Cambridge people to keep him from spilling their secrets?'

'That is my problem, Matthew. I do not know.'

Bartholomew looked at him through narrowed eyes. 'Good company you keep, Priest, if you think them capable of murder.'

Aelfrith rose restlessly, and began to pace back and forth. Bartholomew caught a sparkle of tears in his eyes as he walked, and was sorry for his comment. Aelfrith was a virtuous man, and Bartholomew was sure that he had allowed himself to become embroiled in the murky world of University politics for the purest of reasons, and probably for what he considered to be the good of the College.

'You saw Augustus's room,' the friar said, after a moment. 'Someone was looking for something. Whoever attacked us had chipped loose plaster from the walls and had tried to prise up the floorboards. I have an idea of what the person may have been looking for.'

'What could possibly be worth the killing of two old men?'

Aelfrith smiled. 'You are a good man, Matthew, but you have been out into the world and you should know better than to ask a question like that. The lives of two old men are worth nothing to those that we are dealing with – on either side.' He stopped pacing and came to sit next to Bartholomew again. 'The spy system uses coded messages. We are dealing with some of the best minds in England here, so the codes have become very intricate and complex. All coded messages are affixed with a specific mark, or seal, so that their authenticity can be assured. Each time a message is sent, the seal is attached.

'You probably did not know that Sir John acted as an agent for the King for many years. Essentially, his task was to act as a link, passing information up and down the chain of communication. Each contact had a different sign that only he and Sir John knew, to ensure that only authentic information would be passed on. About a year ago – the same time as the first deaths in King's Hall – one of Sir John's contacts started to send messages about a group of scholars at the University of Oxford who are dedicated to bringing about the downfall of the University here.

'The sign Sir John used with this contact was an elaborate knot design carved into a gold signet ring – they had one each, exact duplicates in every detail. When a message came, Sir John only needed to match his seal with the one on the message to know that it was authentic. The design of the seals was very complex, and Sir John would have known if a message was marked with an imitation. Sir John carried this seal with him always, on a thick cord around his neck. After Sir John died, the seal he used to send his messages disappeared.'

Bartholomew nodded, a little impatient at the lengthy explanation. He had seen the ring Aelfrith was talking about. It always hung on a robust length of leather around Sir John's neck. Bartholomew had asked him about it once, and Sir John had given him the impression that it was a trinket of no inherent value, but of great personal significance. Bartholomew supposed, in the light of what Aelfrith had just told him, that Sir John had spoken the truth.

'On the night of his death Sir John visited Augustus, and may have hidden the seal in his room. I am sure Sir John was killed because someone wanted to steal the seal, but I am also confident that he was not wearing it when he died.'

'How can you be sure of that?'

'The manner of his death. He is said to have thrown himself into the mill race so that he would be either crushed or drowned by the water-wheel.'

Bartholomew swallowed hard and looked away. Aelfrith continued.

'There were two odd things about Sir John's death. The first is that when you, Swynford, and I dined with him on the night of his death, he did not seem like a man about to take his own life. Would you agree?'

Bartholomew assented. It was a fact that had played on his mind, increasing his sense of helplessness about Sir John's death. Had the Master seemed ill or depressed, Bartholomew could have offered his support and friendship.

'The second odd thing was the clothes he was wearing. Now,' Aelfrith held up his hand as Bartholomew began to protest, 'I am not going to say anything that will harm Sir John's reputation further. He was wearing the habit of a Benedictine nun. Correct?'

Bartholomew refused to look at Aelfrith. It had been the most disturbing aspect of Sir John's death. It was bad enough to imagine him being in a state of mind where he could hurl himself under the water-wheel. But that his own clothes were nowhere to be found, and that he was clad in the gown of a nun, drew much speculation on Sir John's sanity and personal life.

'I do not think Sir John was in disguise as has been suggested,' said Aelfrith. 'I believe his clothes were stolen so that they could be thoroughly searched for the seal. I think he was killed – perhaps by a knock on the head – and his clothes taken after he had died. The nun's habit was specifically chosen to bring Michaelhouse into disrepute. Its Master wearing nun's clothes to commit suicide at the mill! The plan succeeded: the town people still nudge each other and grin when Michaelhouse is mentioned, and scholars in Oxford claim that there, the masters are men in men's clothing.'

Bartholomew winced, but said nothing. Aelfrith saw his discomfiture, and hurriedly changed the subject.

'But whoever killed Sir John did not find the seal, and came to look for it in Augustus's room, assuming that Sir John had hidden it there because it was the only place he had been between dining with us and leaving the College. I was knocked on the head, Paul stabbed, and the commoners drugged to allow time to make a thorough search. You interrupted that search, and were attacked.'

Bartholomew was about to dismiss Aelfrith's explanation as inadequate, when he recalled Augustus's words on the afternoon of Wilson's installation. He had spoken of an evil in the College that would corrupt all, but there was something else, too. 'Just remember John Babington, hide it well.' Bartholomew's thoughts raced forward. Perhaps Aelfrith was right, and Sir John had hidden the seal with Augustus, and Augustus had watched him. So, did that mean that Augustus had been killed so that the discovery of the seal would remain a secret? Was he killed because he had refused to reveal where it was hidden? But Bartholomew had seen no marks on Augustus's body to support the possibility that he was forced to do anything.

'But this does not explain what happened to Augustus's body,' he said. He began to have hopes that the bizarre manner of Sir John's death might be explained, and his good reputation restored.

Aelfrith sighed. 'I know. But one of the last messages Sir John received from Oxford said that our protagonists are in league with witches and warlocks,' he said. 'I do not think we will see our Brother Augustus again.'

Bartholomew disagreed. 'Bodies do not just disappear, Father,' he said. 'His will be found, especially if it is hidden away in this heat!'

Aelfrith pursed his lips in disgust. 'This is the part that disturbs me most of all,' he said. 'I believe the disappearance of Augustus's body was the work of the Devil, and that the Devil has a servant in this College!'

Bartholomew was surprised that Aelfrith would so readily accept witchcraft as an answer. He had also been surprised with Brother Michael for the same reason. It was too convenient an answer.

'So who do you think attacked us and killed Paul and Montfitchet?' he asked, to move the discussion on. Bartholomew could believe that the Devil had a servant in the College easily enough – someone who was committing murder and stealing bodies – but the idea that the Devil was responsible he found too hard to accept. He sensed he would not agree with Aelfrith on this point, and that if he questioned it further they might end up in the orchard for hours discussing it as a point of theology.

'The Devil's servant,' replied Aelfrith in response to Bartholomew's questions. He turned to Bartholomew. 'I have told you all this because I wish you to be on your guard – for your own life and for the security of your University.'

'Do the other fellows know all this?' asked Bartholomew.

'Master Wilson does. He thinks you are a spy because you have a degree from Oxford, because your practice takes you out of College a lot, and because he was suspicious of your relationship with Sir John. He warned Sir John about you many times. He does not like you, and now he is Master, he will undoubtedly try to see that your days as a Fellow here are numbered.'

That Wilson thought the worst of him, and might attempt to rid Michaelhouse of him, did not come as any great shock to Bartholomew. 'Who else knows?' he asked.

'Michael seems to know some of it, although he did not learn it from me. William and Alcote know. It was William who told me to warn you. Alcote is in Wilson's pocket, and believes you are a spy. They both think you were looking for the seal when you took so long with Augustus.'

'And what do you think, Father?'

'That you are innocent in all this, and that you should

remain so. I also reason that you grieve too deeply for Sir John to have been involved in any way with his death, and that you have continued to be a good friend after most others have abandoned him.'

Bartholomew squinted up into the apple trees. He wished Sir John were with him now, to help him reason out all this subterfuge and plotting. 'What of the others? Swynford and Giles Abigny?'

'Swynford is aware of the Oxford plot, but declines to become involved. His family have lands near Oxford, and he says it is in his interests to remain neutral. Sir John's contact has already reported that Swynford declined Oxford when they tried to recruit him. Abigny would not find the time between his love affairs for matters of such seriousness, and in any case, I could not trust his judgement nor his discretion. He has no connections with Oxford anyway, and would make them a poor spy. He does not move in the right circles to be of interest to them, unless they are concerned with tavern gossip.'

Bartholomew smiled. The flighty Abigny was from a different world than the austere Franciscan friars, and they would never see eye to eye. But Aelfrith was right. Abigny was appallingly indiscreet, and would never manage to remain sober long enough to do spying of any value. Aelfrith stood to leave.

'If you think of anything, however small, that might throw light onto this wretched affair, will you let me know?'

Bartholomew nodded. 'I will, but I have thought it over many times, and have not deduced the tiniest shred of evidence that could be of value. I think I would be as much a loss as a spy as would Giles!'

Aelfrith reached out to touch Bartholomew on the

shoulder, a rare gesture of affection for the sombre friar, and walked out of the orchard.

Bartholomew sat for a while, pondering what Aelfrith had told him. He still found it difficult to believe that Oxford and Cambridge scholars would play such dangerous games, and he would not accept that Augustus's body had been stolen by the Devil. The sun was hot, and he thought back to what he had said to Aelfrith. Bodies did not just disappear, so Augustus's corpse must have been either hidden or buried. If it were hidden, the heat would soon give it away; if it were buried, perhaps it would never be found.

The bell began to ring for the afternoon service at St Michael's, and Bartholomew decided to go to pray for the souls of his dead friends.

Bartholomew made his way slowly back from the church down St Michael's Lane. A barge from the Low Countries had arrived at the wharf earlier that day, and all the small lanes and alleys leading from the river to the merchants' houses on Milne Street were full of activity.

At the river the bustle was even more frenzied. A Flemish captain stood on the bank roaring instructions in dreadful French to his motley collection of sailors who yelled back in a variety of languages. At least two were from the Mediterranean, judging from their black curly hair and beringed ears, and another wore an exotic turban swathed around his head. Further up-stream, fishermen were noisily unloading baskets of eels and the slow-moving water was littered with tails and heads that had been discarded. Overhead, the gulls swooped and screeched and fought, adding to the general racket.

Behind the wharves were the rivermen's houses, a dishevelled row of rickety wooden shacks that leaked when it rained, and often collapsed when it was windy. Bartholomew saw an enormous rat slink out of one house and disappear into the weeds at the edge of the river where some small children were splashing about.

'Matt!' Bartholomew turned with a smile at the sound of his brother-in-law's voice. Sir Oswald Stanmore strode up to him. 'We were worried about you. What has been happening at Michaelhouse?'

Bartholomew raised his hands in a shrug. 'I do not know. The clerics are mumbling about evil walking the College, but Wilson thinks it was only Augustus.'

Stanmore rolled his eyes. 'Wilson is a fool. You should have heard him pontificating to us last night, telling us everything we would ever need to know about the wool trade, and about French cloth. The man would not know French cloth from homespun. But we have heard terrible rumours about Michaelhouse! How much did you all drink last night?'

Ever practical, Stanmore had put everything down to drunkenness, not such an unreasonable assumption considering the amount of wine that had flowed.

'Nathaniel the Fleming seems to have had his share too,' said Bartholomew, turning as one of the swimming children emitted an especially piercing shriek.

Stanmore laughed. 'I told him last night he would need your services this morning. Did he call you?'

Bartholomew nodded, and told him what had happened. Stanmore threw up his hands in despair.

'Lord save us, Matt! I provide you with one of the wealthiest men in the town as a patient, and you cannot even subdue your unorthodox thoughts long enough to treat him. I know,' he said quickly, putting up a hand to quell the coming objection, 'what you believe, and I understand, even applaud, your motives. But for the love of God, could you not even try to placate Nathaniel? You need to be far more careful now Wilson is Master, Matt. Even a child can see that he loathes you. You no longer have the favoured protection of Sir John, and securing a patient such as Nathaniel might have served to keep his dislike at bay for a while.'

Bartholomew knew Stanmore was right. He gave a rueful smile.

'Edith told me to call on you today to make certain you were well,' Stanmore continued. 'What have you done to your leg? What debauchery did your feast degenerate into once the sobering effects of your town guests had gone?' He was smiling, but his eyes were serious.

'Tell Edith I am fine. But I do not understand what is happening at Michaelhouse. The Bishop is due to arrive today and will take matters in hand.'

Stanmore chewed his lower lip. 'I do not like it, Matt, and neither will Edith. Come to stay with us for a few days until all this dies down. Edith is missing Richard; if you came, it would take her mind off him for a while.'

Richard, their only son, had left a few days before to study at Oxford, and the house would be strangely empty without him. Bartholomew was fond of his sister and her husband, and it would be pleasant to spend a few days away from the tensions of the College. But he had work to do: there were students who had returned before the Michaelmas term so that they could be given extra tuition, and he had his patients to see. And anyway, if he left now, Wilson would probably see it as fleeing the scene of the crime, and accuse him of the murders. Regretfully he shook his head.

'I would love to, I really would. But I cannot. I should stay.' He grabbed Stanmore's arm. 'Please do not tell Edith all you hear. She will only worry.'

Stanmore smiled understandingly. 'Come to see us as soon as you can, and talk to her yourself.' He looked round as loud shouts came from a group of apprentices, followed by a splash as someone fell in the river. 'I must go before they start fighting again. Take care, Matt. I will tell Edith you will visit soon.'

As Bartholomew made his way back up the lane, he saw a small cavalcade of horses trot into Michaelhouse's yard, and knew that the Bishop had arrived. Servants hurried to stable the horses, while others brought chilled ale and offered to shake dust out of riding cloaks. Wilson hurried from his new room to meet the Bishop, soberly dressed in a simple, but expensive, black gown.

The two men stood talking for a while, while students, commoners, and Fellows watched out of the unglazed windows. Eventually, Wilson led the way into the main building, through the hall and into the smaller, more private conclave beyond. Alexander was sent to fetch wine and pastries, and the College waited.

First, the servants were sent for. Then it was the turn of the students, and then the commoners. It was nearing the time for the evening meal when the Fellows were summoned. The Bishop sat in the Master's chair, which had been brought from the hall, while his clerks and assistants were ranged along the benches on either side of him. Wilson sat directly opposite, and, judging from his pallor and sweaty jowls, had not had an easy time of it.

The Bishop stood as the Fellows entered and beckoned them forward to sit on the bench with Wilson. Bartholomew had met the Bishop before, a man who enjoyed his physical comforts, but who was able to combine a deep sense of justice with his equally deep sense of compassion. He was known to be impatient with fools, severe with those who told him lies, and had no time at all for those unwilling to help themselves. Although Bartholomew thought he probably would not enjoy an evening in the Bishop's company, he respected his judgement and integrity.

The Fellows sat on either side of Wilson, Bartholomew at the end so he could stretch his stiff knee. He felt as if he were on trial. The Bishop started to speak.

'Master Wilson and Fellows of Michaelhouse,' he began formally. 'It is my right, as Bishop of this parish, to investigate the strange happenings of last night. I must tell you now that I am far from satisfied with the explanation I have been given.' He paused, and studied the large ring on his finger that contained his official seal. 'These are difficult times for the Church and for the University. There is news that a terrible pestilence is sweeping the land, and may be here before Christmas, and relations between the Church and the people are far from ideal. Neither the University nor the College can afford to have scandals. Much damage was done to both following the unfortunate death of Master Babington. You cannot allow another unsavoury incident to occur if you wish your College to survive.

'Now, two College members have been murdered,

perhaps by another, although I do not care to guess who the perpetrator of the crime might be. The College has been searched, and has revealed nothing. All the commoners, students, and servants have alibis – assuming that Brother Paul was slain during or after the feast. The commoners were all together, and each can vouch for every one of the others. Since the regular term's lectures have not yet begun, there are only fifteen students in residence, and all, like the commoners, can give alibis for each other. The servants had a hard night of work, and one missing pair of hands would have been immediately noticed. After the feast, they all retired exhausted to bed, and the good Mistress Agatha, who was kept awake by a grieving woman, swears that none left the servants' quarters until woken by the Steward this morning.

'That leaves the Fellows. Please understand that I am accusing no one, but you will each tell me where you were last night, and with whom. Master Wilson, perhaps you would set the example and begin.'

'Me?' said Wilson, taken aback. 'But I am the Master, I . . .'

'Your movements, please, Master Wilson,' said the Bishop coldly.

Wilson blustered for a few moments, while the Bishop waited like a coiled snake for him to begin. 'After Doctor Bartholomew told us that Augustus was dead, I felt it inappropriate to continue at the feast. Father William, Master Alcote, and Master Swynford left with me. Bartholomew and Brother Michael had already retired, and Master Abigny stayed, although I did not condone this.' A glint of pleasure crossed his features at having expressed his disapproval of Abigny to the Bishop.

'On the contrary, Master Wilson,' the Bishop intervened smoothly, 'I hope you did condone it. After all, you were going to leave students in your hall with seemingly unlimited quantities of wine, and a riot narrowly averted earlier in the day. I would consider it an act of prudence to leave a Fellow to oversee affairs. Why did you not end the feast?'

Bartholomew hid a smile. He knew that many students disliked Wilson and he had been trying to win them round with his generosity with the wine. He would not have wished to negate any positive points he might have gained by ending the feast when the students were still enjoying themselves.

Wilson opened and shut his mouth a few times, before Swynford intervened. 'We discussed that, my Lord Bishop. We felt that Augustus would not wish such a joyous occasion to be brought to an early conclusion on his account.'

The Bishop looked at Swynford narrowly before returning his attention to Wilson. 'And what did you do after you left the hall, Master Wilson?' he continued.

'I walked with Master Alcote to our room. I only moved into the Master's room today; last night I was in my old room. We talked for a while about Augustus, and then we went to sleep.'

'Does this tally with your memory?' the Bishop asked Alcote.

The nervous little man nodded, looking even more like a hen than usual. 'Yes, we talked until the candle expired, and then went to sleep. Neither of us went out, or knew any more, until the next morning.'

'Father Aelfrith?'

'I left the hall and went straight to Augustus's room,

where I stayed all night. At some point, I heard a noise and went to check Brother Paul, who had been ill. He was asleep, and none of the other commoners had yet returned. I went back to my prayers, and was hit on the head from behind. I heard nothing and saw nothing. The next thing I recall was being helped up by Doctor Bartholomew.'

'Master Swynford?'

'I left the hall with Father William, and Masters Alcote and Wilson. I saw Brother Michael and Doctor Bartholomew walking together across the courtyard to their staircase. I went straight to my room and went to sleep. I am afraid that because I room alone, I have no alibi,' he said with an apologetic smile.

'Who else lives on your staircase?' the Bishop enquired.

'Father William lives downstairs from me.'

'Father, what were your movements?'

'I left the hall and went directly to my room. I saw Master Swynford go past moments later and disappear up the stairs. I share a room with three others of my Order, students, who left the feast when I did. All four of us prayed throughout the night for Augustus's soul, as did Father Aelfrith.'

'If Master Swynford had left his room during the night, would you have heard him?'

'I believe so, my Lord Bishop,' said William, after a moment's consideration. 'The night was humid. We did not want our voices to disturb others who were sleeping, and so the window shutters were closed, but the door was open to allow us some air. I am certain we would have heard if Master Swynford came down the stairs.'

'There is your alibi, Master Swynford,' said the Bishop. 'Doctor Bartholomew, where were you?'

'I went back to my room, checked on the blacksmith – he had had his leg broken in the skirmish outside the gates,' he added hastily, seeing the Bishop raise his eyebrows. 'I was tired and went to sleep straight away. I do not know when Giles returned. I rose while it was still quite dark, and, seeing the candle in Augustus's room, went to offer to relieve Father Aelfrith. I fought with someone and was pushed down the stairs. I could find no trace of him when I went to look, and then discovered that what I had assumed to be Augustus's body lying on the floor was actually Father Aelfrith, and Augustus had gone.'

'So you have no one who can confirm where you were all night?' asked the Bishop.

Bartholomew shook his head and saw Wilson exchange smug glances with Alcote.

'Brother Michael?' said the Bishop.

Michael shrugged. 'Like our physician, I have no alibi. We walked to our staircase together. I saw him check the disgusting man with the broken leg, and go into his own room. I went upstairs. My room-mates were enjoying Master Wilson's good wine in the hall, and were still enjoying it when dawn broke this morning. I was alone all night.'

'And finally you, Master Abigny. What have you to say?'

'I was in the company of Michael's two room-mates and the other students until I was too drunk to stay awake any longer,' Abigny announced cheerfully, ignoring Wilson's look of anger. 'The same two Benedictines took time from their roistering to help me to my room, where I remember nothing until woken by Alexander with stories of missing bodies and murder.' He sat back indolently, and Bartholomew knew that his entire demeanour was carefully calculated to annoy Wilson as much as possible.

'Let us summarise,' said the Bishop, ignoring Abigny's display. 'Everyone's movements can be vouched for except Bartholomew, Aelfrith, and Michael. Aelfrith could not have hit himself on the head from behind, and Bartholomew saw him lying on the floor before he engaged in his struggle.

'So, what we have left is a mystery. There is no doubt that evil deeds were committed, and that two men died. I find it difficult to believe that Doctor Bartholomew would mistake a living man for a corpse, but these things happen, especially after copious amounts of Master Wilson's good wine.' He raised his hand to stall the objection that Bartholomew was about to voice. He had had very little to drink the night before, chiefly because he did not feel Wilson's succession of Sir John good cause for celebration.

'Augustus, whether dead or alive, has gone. We may never know whether he was innocent or guilty of murder. It is imperative that this business is done with as quickly as possible. Neither your College nor the University can afford to have gossip about missing corpses and murders. You know what would happen – wealthy families would decline to send their sons here, and the University would eventually cease to exist altogether.'

Bartholomew shot a quick look at Aelfrith sitting next to him, echoes of their conversation coming back to him. Perhaps Aelfrith was right, and the whole affair was a plot by rivals to strike at the very foundations of the University.

The Bishop looked at each of the Fellows in turn before continuing. 'Neither you nor I has a choice in this matter. I have already spoken with the Chancellor and he agrees with me as to the course of action that must be taken. I repeat that you have no choice in this matter. There will be a funeral service for Augustus the day after tomorrow. It will be said that his body was discovered in the orchard, where he had been hiding. The excitement of the installation was too much for him, and had addled his wits. There are, I believe, medical conditions that make a living man appear as a corpse. Augustus was afflicted by this and was pronounced dead by the College physician. He later awoke from this trance, and struck Aelfrith from behind while he was praying. He ran down the stairs and slipped through the College buildings to the orchard, where he later died. Brother Paul, who had become depressed with his illness, took his own life. The other commoner . . .' The Bishop waved his hand impatiently.

'Montfitchet,' offered Wilson in a small voice, the enormity of what was being asked shaking him out of his usual smugness.

'Montfitchet, yes. Montfitchet died of his own excesses. The commoners have already attested to that. The man made a pig of himself all night, despite complaining of stomach pains caused by his gluttony. And that, Fellows of Michaelhouse, is what the world will be told happened here. There will be no rumours of evil in the College,' he said, looking hard at the Franciscans, 'and no tales of dead bodies walking in the night to murder their colleagues.'

He sat back to indicate that he had finished speaking. The conclave was totally silent, as the Fellows let his words sink in. The clerks, usually furiously scribbling when the Bishop spoke, sat ominously still. No record was being made of this meeting.

Bartholomew looked at the Bishop aghast. So, the Church and the University were prepared to cover the whole thing up, to smother the truth in a thick blanket of lies.

'No!' he cried, leaping to his feet, wincing as his injured knee took his weight. 'It would be wrong! Brother Paul was a good man, and you cannot condemn him to a grave in unconsecrated soil and allow his and Montfitchet's murderer to walk free!'

The Bishop rose, his eyes hard with anger, although his face remained calm. 'Brother Paul will be buried in the churchyard, Doctor,' he said. 'I will grant him a special dispensation in view of his age and state of mind.'

'But what of his murderer?' Bartholomew persisted, unappeased.

'There was no murderer,' said the Bishop softly. 'You heard what I said. One suicide, and two deaths by misadventure.'

'The servants already know Paul was murdered! They saw his body! And there are already rumours around the town.'

'Then you must make certain that no such rumours are given credence. You must prey on people's sympathies – a poor old man, lying alone listening to the celebrations in the hall. He decides to release his soul to the Lord so that he will no longer be an encumbrance to his College. Master Wilson tells me that there was a note saying as much found in Paul's hand.'

Bartholomew stared at Wilson in shock. The plan was becoming more and more elaborate with each passing moment. Wilson refused to meet Bartholomew's eyes and busied himself twisting the rings on his fat fingers.

'I agree with Bartholomew.' Swynford was also on his feet. 'This plan is not only foolhardy, but dangerous. If ever the truth were to be found out, we would all hang!'

'You will hang for treason if you do not comply,' said the Bishop casually, sitting down again. 'I have already informed you that the University cannot afford a scandal. There are many at King's Hall who enjoy the King's protection, who will consider any dissent in this matter to be a deliberate act of defiance towards the Crown.'

Swynford sat down hastily. He was well-enough connected with the University's power-brokers to know that this was not an idle threat. Bartholomew thought back to Aelfrith's words. The King, and his father before him, had invested money and power in King's Hall; any weakening of the University would injure their institution too, and no King liked to discover that he had made a poor choice in where he invested his authority.

'But what if Augustus's body is discovered after we "bury" it?' Bartholomew asked anxiously, his mind running through a wealth of possibilities in which the Michaelhouse Fellows would be discovered and exposed.

'Augustus will not be recovered, Doctor Bartholomew,' said the Bishop smoothly. 'I am sure I can rely on you all to see to that.'

Bartholomew swallowed. 'But this is against the laws of the Church and the State, and I will not do it,' he said quietly.

'Against the laws of the Church and the State?' said

the Bishop musingly. 'And who do you think makes these laws?' His voice became hard. 'The King makes the laws of the State, and the Bishops make the laws of the Church. You have no choice.'

'I will resign my fellowship,' persisted Bartholomew, 'rather than be a part of this.'

'There will be no resignations,' said the Bishop. 'We can afford no scandal. Now, we must come to some arrangement. Master Wilson informs me that you wish for a larger room for your medical consultations and an increase in your stipend . . .'

'And I will not be bribed!' retorted Bartholomew angrily.

The Bishop's face turned white with anger and Bartholomew knew that his protestations had touched a raw nerve. He stood again and advanced on Bartholomew.

'I see you have a bad leg, Doctor. Perhaps you would like to return with me to Ely so that my barber-surgeon can treat it? Perhaps there we can persuade you of your wisest course of action.' He gave Bartholomew one of the coldest smiles the physician had ever seen, and pushed him back down onto the bench.

William grabbed Bartholomew's arm as the Bishop walked back to his chair. 'For God's sake, man!' he hissed. 'The Bishop is being more than patient! He could hang you for treason right now, and if you force him to take you with him to Ely, you can be sure that you will not return the same man!'

Aelfrith nodded vigorously. 'Remember what I said to you,' he whispered. 'There are forces at work here of which you have no idea. Your life will not be worth a fig if you do not comply.'

'Now,' the Bishop began again, having controlled himself somewhat, 'I will require all here to take an oath that you will act as I have suggested. Master Wilson.'

The Bishop extended his hand, and Wilson stood slowly and knelt in front of the Bishop. He took the proffered hand.

'I swear, by all that I hold holy, that I will do everything in my power to save the College, the University, and the King's name from disrepute. I will tell no one of the events of last night other than as you suggest.' He kissed the seal on the Bishop's ring, bowed, and left the hall without looking back. For the first time since he had known him, Bartholomew felt sorry for Wilson. As Master, he had obviously been held responsible for the events of the night, and would have a formidable task in ensuring the Bishop's fabric of lies was accepted outside the College.

The Bishop eyed Swynford, who rose and swore the same oath. Bartholomew's thoughts were in turmoil. How could he make such a promise? It would be a betrayal of Sir John, Augustus, Paul, and Montfitchet. He would be saying that he, one of the most highly qualified physicians in the country, was unable to tell the difference between a living man and a dead one! He watched as Alcote scurried forward when Swynford left. What could he do? Perhaps he had already signed his death warrant with the Bishop, or with some of the forces about which Aelfrith had warned him.

Alcote left, and William stepped forward. Aelfrith seized his arm. 'You must take the oath! You will not live another day if you do not! Do it for the College, for Sir John.' He broke off as the Bishop gestured for him to approach. Michael slid along the bench towards Bartholomew, his eyes frightened in his flabby face.

'For God's sake, Matt! None of us like this, but you are putting us all in danger. Do you want to be hanged, drawn, and quartered at Smithfield? Just swear this wretched oath! You do not need to do anything else. You can always go away until all this dies down.'

Abigny stepped forward. Michael's grip became painful. 'Not to take the Bishop's oath will be treason, Matt. I understand the position you are taking, but it will cost you your life if you persist!' He stood as the Bishop gestured for him to advance, swore his promise, and left. Bartholomew reflected that his colleagues seemed very keen that he should take the Bishop's oath. Was this out of concern for him, or did they have other, more sinister reasons for wanting his silence concerning the deaths at Michaelhouse? The conclave was silent. The Bishop and Bartholomew regarded each other.

The Bishop suddenly snapped his fingers, and, in an instant, parchment was cleared away, inkhorns sealed, and pens packed. The clerks filed out in silence, leaving the Bishop alone with Bartholomew.

Bartholomew waited, and was surprised when the Bishop sat heavily at one of the tables and put his head in his hands. After a few moments, the Bishop looked up, his face lined and grey with worry, and gestured for Bartholomew to sit next to him.

'I have become so involved in the interests of the Church, and of upholding the law, that I have failed to see some things,' he said. 'I know what I am asking you to do is wrong on one level, and yet, on another it is absolutely right. This pestilence is at the centre of it. Have you heard the news? In Avignon, our Pope has had to consecrate the River Rhône because there were too many bodies for the graveyards. In Paris, the dead lie stinking in their houses and the streets because there are none left to bury them. All over Europe, villages lie silent. Many great abbeys and monasteries have lost more than half their brethren.

'Some say it is a visitation from God, and they may be right. The people will need their faith to deal with this terrible plague, and they will need their priests, friars, and monks to help them. If the same happens in England as has already happened in France, there will be a desperate shortage of clergy, and we will need every religious house and the universities to train more.

'Do you not see, Matthew? We must prepare ourselves, and gather our forces. We cannot allow the University to flounder now, just before the people will need it more than ever before. You may have been told that some scholars at Oxford would like very much to see Cambridge fall so that they will have a monopoly over students and masters. This may well be true, but I cannot allow that to happen. We must offer as many places of training as possible, so that we can produce learned clergy to serve the people.

'You made me angry earlier, and I am sorry. I had to threaten you because I could not allow your stand to cause the others to waver. I will not force you to take the oath, because you, of all the Fellows, would not want the people to suffer from a lack of spiritual comfort during this terrible plague and the years to follow. I have heard that you choose to work with the poor, when you could easily become rich by healing the wealthy. I know that you understand why I was forced to ask the others to protect the University.'

The Bishop was no longer the splendid figure in purple who had ridden in at the gates, but a man struggling to reconcile his actions with his conscience. Bartholomew's anger was still very much at the surface, and he had had too many dealings with crafty patients not to be aware that some people possessed powerful skills at lying.

'So where does this leave us?' he said suspiciously.

'It leaves us in your hands, Matthew,' said the Bishop. 'If you will not give outsiders the explanation I have offered, then say nothing. In a few weeks it may not matter anyway, and you and I could be dead.'

He sighed and stood up to leave. 'Go in peace, Matthew,' he said, sketching a benediction in the air above Bartholomew's head. 'You continue God's work in your way, and I will continue in mine, and may we both learn from each other.'

The Bishop walked out of the room, and by the time Bartholomew had limped over to the window to watch him leave Michaelhouse, he had regained his regal bearing. He sat upright in his saddle, and clattered out of the yard with his clerks and monks trailing behind him.

The door of the conclave burst open and Brother Michael shot in, his chest heaving with exertion. 'Oh, thank God!' he said, fervently crossing himself. 'I expected to find you here with a knife in your ribs!' His words brought back a memory of Brother Paul, and he visibly paled. 'Oh lord,' he groaned, flopping into Wilson's chair, 'we really are going to have to be careful!'

V

December 1348

BROTHER PAUL, AUGUSTUS, AND MONTFITCHET were laid to rest in the little cemetery behind St Michael's Church two days after the Bishop's visit. The official explanations for their deaths were given to any who asked, and, although speculation was rife for several weeks, the Fellows' consistent rendering of the same story began to pay off. Bartholomew, when asked specific questions, replied that he did not know the answer, although whenever possible he avoided the subject. Eventually, the excitement died down and the incident seemed to be forgotten. Term started at the beginning of October, and, although student numbers were low because of the fear of the impending plague, the Michaelhouse Fellows found themselves as busy as ever with lectures, disputations, and readings.

Bartholomew tried to forget about the events of August; even if he had discovered anything, what could he have done about it? He considered confiding his thoughts to his brother-in-law, but was afraid that if he involved Stanmore, he might endanger him somehow. For the same reason, he did not wish to involve any of his friends.

Rachel Atkin had regained her wits after the death of her son. As well as his manor in Trumpington, Sir Oswald Stanmore owned a large house at his business premises in Milne Street in which his brother Stephen lived with his family. Bartholomew persuaded Stephen to take Rachel as a laundress, and she seemed to settle well enough into his household.

The Oliver brothers remained a problem. They seldom attended lectures, and Wilson would have sent them down had not the College's acquisition of the property on Foul Lane depended on their academic success. Bartholomew occasionally saw Henry glowering at him, but it became so commonplace that eventually he came not to notice it.

Bartholomew spent many of the final days before term in the company of Philippa Abigny. They rode through the rich meadows to Grantchester, and watched the archery competitions in Barton, sometimes alone, but often in the company of her brother and one of his latest loves. Brother Michael or Gregory Colet occasionally acted as chaperons, prudently disappearing on business of their own once outside the sight of the nunnery, leaving Bartholomew and Philippa alone together. Edith also acted as chaperon, and was only too pleased to encourage her younger brother in his courting. She had been nagging him for years to find a wife and settle down. Bartholomew and Philippa often strolled together in the pleasant grounds of St Radegund's Priory, careful not to touch each other, for they knew that behind the delicate arches of the nunnery windows the Abbess watched with hawklike eyes.

On several days they attended the great Stourbridge Fair, which ran for most of September and drew huge crowds of people from the countryside for miles around. They saw fire-eaters from Spain, jugglers from the Low Countries, and jongleurs from France, who sang of deeds of daring. Men and women hawked pies, pastries, drinks of fermented apple, crudely made wooden flutes, and cloths and ribbons of all colours. The smell from roasting meat mingled with that of damp straw and horse manure. Animals bleated and squealed, children screamed in delight, jousting knights clashed their weapons, and here and there a lone voice shouted warnings of the terrible pestilence that swept over Europe and would soon claim all whom God deemed unholy.

The threat of the coming plague cast a grim shadow over their lives. Stories came to Cambridge of settlements like Tilgarsley in Oxfordshire where every inhabitant had died, leaving behind a ghost village. A third of the population of the city of Bristol was said to have perished, and in October the first cases began to appear in London. Bartholomew spent long hours consulting his fellow physicians and surgeons about how to deal with the pestilence when it came, although the truth of the matter was that they really did not know. The town officials tried to impose some sort of control on who was allowed into the town in an attempt to prevent the disease from spreading, but it was impossible to enforce, and those barred from entering merely crossed the ditches, swam the river, or hired a boat.

The first snows fell early, powdering the ground with white before the end of November, and Bartholomew saw an increasing number of elderly patients with chest troubles brought on by the cold. Then, just before term ended, he saw his first case of the plague.

* * *

It was a cold morning, with a raw wind howling from the fens, with the promise of more of the persistent drizzling rain that had been dogging Cambridge for the past three days. Bartholomew had risen at five, while it was still dark, and attended Father William's high-speed mass. Lectures started at six, and his students, perhaps sensing the role they might soon have to play, bombarded him with questions. Even Francis Eltham, whom Bartholomew doubted would ever make a physician, had joined in the lively discussion.

Lectures finished around nine, and the main meal of the day was at half-past ten. It was a Friday, and so the meal was fish, freshly baked bread, and vegetables. Bartholomew tuned out the reading of the Bible scholar and thought about the debate on contagion in which he had just led his students. He wondered how he could convince them that there was a pattern to whom infectious diseases affected, and they were not merely visitations from God. He had risked the wrath of the clerics by refusing to allow the students to consider 'struck down by God' as a determinant for contagious disease. They had to think for themselves. 'Struck down by God' was a convenient excuse for not working out the real causes.

After the meal, all members of College were obliged to attend the midday service in St Michael's Church. Bartholomew walked back to the College with Michael, who was grumbling about the cold.

'Right! I am away,' said Abigny, coming up behind them and slapping them both on the shoulders. 'It is too damned cold at that College. I am going over to St Radegund's, where they have warm fires to toast pretty little feet.' He raised an eyebrow at Bartholomew. 'Coming? Philippa specifically told me to ask you.'

Bartholomew smiled. 'Tell her I will come later. I have two patients to see first.'

Abigny tutted. 'But will she wait until later, Physician? I, for one, would not wish to embrace you after you had been in those shabby hovels you like to frequent.'

'Then it is just as well you will not get the chance, Philosopher,' retorted Bartholomew.

Michael nudged him. 'Just go, man. Your patients will wait; your love might not.'

Bartholomew ignored them and went to collect his leather sack of medicines and instruments. He was in good spirits as he set off towards the Trumpington Gate, despite the bitter wind and the promise of rain. His first call was to the family of tinkers that lived near the river; the other call was on Bridge Street, near the church of the Holy Trinity, to one of Agatha's numerous relatives. Afterwards, he could go straight to the Priory and visit Philippa while Abigny was still there, since the nuns would not allow Bartholomew to see Philippa unless she was chaperoned.

The first drops of rain were beginning to fall when he reached the tinker's house. A group of children waited for him, standing barefoot in the mud. He followed them to the ramshackle pile of wood and earthen bricks that was their home. It was cold inside, despite the fire that billowed smoke so that Bartholomew could barely see. He knelt down on the beaten earth floor next to a child who lay in a tangle of dirty blankets, and began his examination. The child was obviously frightened, and Bartholomew found himself chattering about all manner of inane subjects to distract her. The other children clustered round, giggling at his banter.

The child was about six years old, and, as

Bartholomew had thought, was suffering from dehydration resulting from severe diarrhoea. He showed the mother how to feed her with a mixture of boiled water and milk and gave her specific instructions about the amounts she should be given. He discovered that the child had fallen into the river two days earlier, and suspected that she had swallowed bad water.

The rain was falling persistently as he walked back along the High Street towards Shoemaker Row, and he was drenched by the time he reached Holy Trinity Church. It was the third time he had been soaked in a week, and he was running out of dry clothes. The only fires Wilson allowed in the College were in the kitchens and, on very cold days, in the conclave, and there was not enough room for all the scholars to dry their clothes. Bartholomew began to invent a plan to warm stones on the hearths so that they might be wrapped round wet clothes.

The house of Agatha's cousin, a Mistress Bowman, was a small half-timbered building, with whitewashed walls and clean rushes on the floors. Mistress Bowman ushered him in fearfully.

'It is my son, Doctor. I do not know what is wrong with him, but he is so feverish! He seems not to know me!' She bit back a sob.

'How long has he been ill?' asked Bartholomew, allowing her to take his wet cloak.

'Since yesterday. It came on so fast. He has been down in London, you know,' she said, a hint of pride in her voice. 'He is a fine arrow-maker, and he has been making arrows for the King's armies in France.'

'I see,' said Bartholomew, looking at her closely, 'and when did he return from London?'

'Two days ago,' said Mistress Bowman.

Bartholomew took a deep breath and climbed up the steep wooden stairs to the room above. He could hear the laboured breathing of the man before he was half-way up. Mistress Bowman followed him, bringing a candle because, there being no glass in the windows, the shutters were closed against the cold and it was dark. Bartholomew took the candle and bent down towards the man on the bed. At first, he thought his dreadful suspicions were unfounded, and that the man had a simple fever. Then he felt under the man's arms and detected the swollen lumps there like hard unripe apples.

He gazed down at the man in horror. So this was the plague! He swallowed hard. Did the fact that he had touched the man mean that he would now succumb to the disease himself? He fought down the almost overwhelming urge to move away and abandon him, to flee the house and return to Michaelhouse. But he had discussed this many times with his fellow physician, Gregory Colet, and both had come to the conclusion – based on what little fact they could distil from exaggeration or rumour – that their chances of contracting the plague were high regardless of whether they frequented the homes of the victims. Bartholomew understood that some people seemed to have a natural resistance to it – and those that did not would catch it whether they had the slightest contact with a victim, or whether they exposed themselves to it totally.

Would Bartholomew die now – merely from touching the man who writhed and groaned in his delirious fever? If so, the matter was out of his hands, and he could not, in all conscience, abandon the victims of the foul disease to their suffering. He and Colet had agreed. While, all over the land, physicians were fleeing towns and villages for secluded houses in the country, Bartholomew and Colet had decided to stand firm. Bartholomew had nowhere to flee in any case – and all his family and friends were in Cambridge.

Bartholomew braced himself and completed his examination. Besides the swellings in the arms, there were similar lumps, the size of small eggs, in the man's groin and smaller swellings on his neck. He was also burning with fever, and screamed and writhed when Bartholomew gently felt the buboes.

Bartholomew sat back on his heels. Behind him, Mistress Bowman hovered worriedly. 'What is it, Doctor?' she whispered. Bartholomew did not know how to tell her.

'Did he travel alone?' he asked.

'Oh, no! There were three of them. They all came back together.'

Bartholomew's heart sank. 'Where do the others live?' he asked.

Mistress Bowman stared at him. 'It is the pestilence,' she whispered, looking down at her son with a mixture of horror and pity. 'My son has brought the pestilence.'

Bartholomew had to be sure before an official pronouncement was made, and before people started to panic. He stood. 'I do not know, Mistress,' he said softly. 'I have never seen a case of the pestilence before, and we should check the other lads before we jump to conclusions.'

Mistress Bowman grabbed his sleeve. 'Will he die?' she cried, her voice rising. 'Will my boy die?'

Bartholomew disentangled his arm and took both her hands in his firmly. He stood that way until her shuddering panic had subsided. 'I do not know, Mistress. But you will do him no good by losing control of yourself. Now, you must fetch clean water and some linen, and sponge his face to bring his fever down.'

The woman nodded fearfully, and went off to do his bidding. Bartholomew examined the young man again. He seemed to be getting worse by the minute, and Bartholomew knew that he would soon see scores of cases of such suffering – perhaps even among those he loved – and be unable to do anything about it.

Mistress Bowman returned with her water and Bartholomew made her repeat his instructions. 'I do not wish to frighten you,' he said, 'but we must be careful. Do not allow anyone in the house, and do not go out until I return.' She had gathered her courage while she had been busy, and nodded firmly, reminding him suddenly of Agatha.

He left the house and went to Holy Trinity Church. He asked the priest if he could borrow a pen and a scrap of parchment, and hurriedly scribbled a note to Gregory Colet at Rudde's Hostel, telling him of his suspicions and asking him to meet him at the Round Church in an hour. Outside, he threw a street urchin a penny and told him to deliver the note to Colet, who would give him another penny when he received it. The lad sped off while Bartholomew trudged to the house of one of the other men who had travelled from London.

As he arrived, he knew that any attempt he might make to contain the disease would be futile. Wails and howls came from within and the house was thronged with people. He elbowed his way through them until he reached the man lying on the bed. A glance told Bartholomew that he was near his end. He could scarcely draw breath and his arms were stuck out because of the huge swellings in his armpits. One had burst, and emitted a smell so foul that some people in the room covered their mouths and noses with scraps of cloth.

'How long has he been ill?' he asked an old woman, who sat weeping in a corner. She refused to look at him, and went on with her wailing, rocking back and forth.

'God's anger is visited upon us!' she cried. 'It will take all those with black, sinful hearts!'

And a good many others besides, thought Bartholomew. He and Colet had listened carefully to all the stories about the plague that flooded into Cambridge in the hope of learning more. For months, people had spoken of little else. First, it was thought that the infection would never reach England. After all, how could the foul winds that carried the disease cross the waters of the Channel? But cross they did, and in August, a sailor died of the plague in the Dorset port of Melcombe, and within days, hundreds were dead.

When the disease reached Bristol, officials tried to cut the port off from the surrounding areas to prevent the disease from spreading. But the wave of death was relentless. It was soon in Oxford, and then in London. Bartholomew and his colleagues discussed it deep into the night. Was it carried by the wind? Was it true that a great earthquake had opened up graves and the pestilence came from the uncovered corpses? Was it a visitation from God? What were they to do if it came to Cambridge? Colet argued that people who had been in contact with plague victims should stay away from those who had not, but even as Colet's words of warning rang in his ears, Bartholomew saw that such a restriction was wholly impractical. Among the crowd was one of

Michaelhouse's servants – even if Bartholomew avoided contact with the scholars, the servant would be among them. And what of those who had already fled?

Thomas Exton, the town's leading physician, declared that none would die if everyone stayed in the churches and prayed. Colet had suggested that applying leeches to the black swellings that were purported to grow under the arms and in the groin might draw off the poisons within. He said he meant to use leeches until his fellow physicians discovered another treatment. Bartholomew argued that the leeches themselves might spread the infection, but agreed to try them if Colet could prove they worked.

Bartholomew pulled himself out of his thoughts and slammed the door, silencing wailing and whispering alike.

'How long has this man been ill?' he repeated.

There was a gabble of voices answering him, and Bartholomew bent towards a woman dressed in grey.

'He was ill when they came home the night before last,' she said. 'He had been drinking in the King's Head tavern on the High Street, and his friends brought him back when he began to shake with this fever.'

Bartholomew closed his eyes in despair. The King's Head was one of the busiest taverns in the town, and, if the rumours were true and infection spread on the wind, then those who had been in contact with the three young men were already in danger. A hammering on the door stilled the buzz of conversation, and a thickset man in a greasy apron forced his way in.

'Will and his mother are sick,' he yelled. 'And one of Mistress Barnet's babies has turned black!'

There was an immediate panic. People crossed

themselves, the window shutters were thrown open, and some began to climb out screaming that the plague was there. Rapidly, only the sick man, Bartholomew, and the woman in grey were left in the house. Bartholomew looked at her closely, noting a sheen of sweat on her face. He pulled her into the light and felt under her jaw. Sure enough, there were the beginnings of swellings in her neck; she was already infected.

He helped her up the stairs to a large bed, and covered her with blankets, leaving a pitcher of water near her, for she was complaining of a fierce thirst. He went to look at the young man downstairs on his way out, and saw that he was already dead, his face a dark purple and his eyes starting from his face. The white shirt under his arms was stained with blood and with black and yellow pus. The stench was terrible.

Bartholomew let himself out of the house. The street was unusually silent as he made his way to the Round Church of the Holy Sepulchre, where Gregory Colet was waiting anxiously.

'Matt?' he said, stepping towards him, his eyes fearful.

Bartholomew held up his hand, warning him to come no closer. 'It has come, Gregory,' he said softly. 'The plague has come to Cambridge.'

The next few weeks passed in a whirlwind for Bartholomew. At first, there were only a few cases, and one of them even recovered. After five days, Bartholomew began to hope that the pestilence had passed them by, and that the people of Cambridge might have escaped the worst of the fever, or that it had burned itself out. Then, without warning, four people became infected one day, seven the next day, and thirteen the day after that. People began to die and Bartholomew found himself with more requests for help than he could possibly answer.

Colet called an urgent meeting of the physicians and surgeons, and Bartholomew described the symptoms he had seen first-hand while he stood in the gallery of St Mary's Church, as far away from the others as possible. There was much to be done. Gravediggers needed to be found, and collectors of the dead. There were few who wanted such tasks, and there was an argument between the medics on the one hand and the Sheriff on the other about who should pay the high wages to entice people to do it.

The number of cases of the plague continued to rise dramatically. Some people died within a few hours of becoming ill, while others lasted for several days. Others still seemed to recover, but died as their relatives began to celebrate their deliverance. Bartholomew could see no pattern as to who lived and who died, and he began to doubt his fundamental belief that diseases had physical causes that could be identified and removed. He and Colet argued about it, Colet claiming that he had more success with his leeches than Bartholomew had with his insistence on clean water and bedding, and use of various herbs. To a certain extent that was true, but Colet's patients were wealthier than Bartholomew's, and suffered and died in warm rooms where lack of food was not a problem. Bartholomew did not consider the comparison a fair one. He discovered that in some cases he could ease the discomfort from the buboes by incising them to let the putrescence out, and that probably one in four of his patients might survive.

Term at the University was immediately suspended, and scholars who would usually have stayed in Cambridge for the Christmas break thronged the roads leading north, some taking the plague with them. Bartholomew was horrified that many physicians went too, leaving dozens of sick people to the care of a handful of doctors.

Colet told Bartholomew that the royal physician, Master Gaddesden, had also fled London, going with the King's family to Eltham Castle. The plague was not a disease that would profit the medical profession, for there seemed to be no cure and much risk. In Cambridge, three physicians had already perished, including the master of medicine from Peterhouse and Thomas Exton, who had proclaimed that praying in the churches would deliver people.

The plague seemed to bring with it unending rain. Bartholomew trudged through the muddy streets constantly wet and in a daze of exhaustion, going from house to house to watch people die. He sent a note to Philippa urging her to stay in St Radegund's, and it was advice that all the nuns seemed to take, for none were seen ministering to the sick. The monks and friars at Barnwell and St Edmund's did their duty by administering last rites, and they too began to fall ill.

College life changed dramatically. The remaining students and teachers gathered together in the church to attend masses for the dead and to pray for deliverance, but there were looks of suspicion everywhere. Who had been in contact with the sick? Who might be the next to be struck down? The regular assembling for meals began to break down, and food was left in the hall for scholars to take back to their rooms to eat alone.

Bartholomew wondered whether unchanged rushes on the floors and discarded scraps of food in the scholars' rooms might be responsible for the sudden increase in the number of rats he saw around the College. Master Wilson withdrew completely, and remained in his room, occasionally leaning out of his window to shout orders.

Swynford left to stay with a relative in the country, and Alcote followed Wilson's lead, although Bartholomew occasionally saw him scuttling about in the dead of night, when everyone else was asleep. The three clerics did not shirk from their religious duties, and were tireless in burying the dead and giving last rites.

Abigny made Bartholomew move out of their room and sleep on the pallet bed in his storeroom.

'Nothing personal, Matt,' he said, his face covered with the hem of his gown as he spoke, 'but you are a dangerous man to know since you frequent the homes of the sick. And anyway, you would not wish me to visit Philippa if I had been near the Death.'

Bartholomew was too tired to argue. Master Wilson had tried to isolate the College so that no one could enter. There were plenty of supplies in the storeroom, he had called to the assembled College members from his window, and clean water in the well. They would be safe.

As if to belie his words, one of the students suddenly pitched to the ground. Bartholomew ran over, and noted the symptoms with despair. Wilson's shutters slammed abruptly, and the plan was not mentioned again.

College members began to die. Oddly, the old commoners who Bartholomew thought would be the first to succumb, because they were the weakest, were the last to become infected. The Frenchman Henri d'Evéne died on the eve of his planned departure for France. He had been careful to touch nothing that might have been infected by plague bearers; he had drawn his own water from the well, and ate little from the kitchens. He bribed Alexander to let him use Swynford's room while he was gone, because the room faced north, and it was said that north-facing rooms were safe from the plague.

But, as the bell was ringing for Compline, Bartholomew heard a dreadful scream from d'Evéne's quarters. He ran up the stairs and hammered on the door.

D'Evéne opened it, his face white with terror. He was shirtless, and Bartholomew saw the swellings under his armpits, already turning black with the poisons within. He caught the young man as he swooned in his arms and laid him on the bed. D'Evéne tossed and turned with a terrible fever for two days, Bartholomew tending him as much as he could, and died as dawn broke, writhing in agony.

Bartholomew had noticed that the swellings took two forms. If they were hard and dry, and emitted little putrescence when lanced, the patient might survive if he could withstand the fever and the pain. If they were soft, and contained a lot of fluid, the patient would invariably die, regardless of whether the swelling was lanced or not.

Bartholomew and Colet not only had to tend the sick, they had to oversee the removal of bodies from houses and streets. Both knew that if these were not removed as quickly as possible, the streets would become so unhealthy that people would die from other diseases. The first few men who took on the unwholesome, but handsomely paid, task of removing the dead, quickly caught the plague and died, and it became more and more difficult to find people willing to take the risk. Bartholomew, walking along the wharves one night after tending people in the rivermen's homes, heard shuffling and muttering at one of the small piers. Going to investigate, he found two dead-collectors dumping their load into the river so that they would not have to go to the cemetery in the dark.

Bartholomew watched the pathetic corpses bob off downstream as they were caught in the current.

'You have committed them to an unhallowed grave,' he whispered. The dead-collectors shuffled uneasily. 'And now their bodies might carry the Death to villages down the river.'

'It is already there,' said one of the men defensively. 'It is at Ely already. At least fifteen monks have died so far.'

When they had gone he walked to the churchyard and peered into the pit. It would soon be full. He and Colet had asked that a larger pit be dug, just outside the Trumpington Gate, because the cemeteries of the parish churches were too small to cope with the dead, and there was not enough available labour to dig individual graves. Since no one knew how the plague spread, Bartholomew did not want bad humours seeping from the bodies into the river from where some people, despite his warnings, drew their drinking water. There were fields outside the Gate that were well away from the river and its ditches, and away from homes.

As he reached the gates at Michaelhouse, the porter greeted Bartholomew cautiously, a huge pomander stuffed with herbs over his mouth.

'Brother Michael asks if you will go to his room,' he said, backing away as far as possible.

Bartholomew nodded. He did not blame the man. Perhaps Bartholomew was doing more harm than good by visiting the sick in their homes. Perhaps he was aiding the spread of the Death by carrying it in his clothes or in the air around him.

Slowly he climbed the stairs to Michael's room and pushed open the door. Brother Michael knelt next to his bed giving last rites to Father Aelfrith.

'Oh, no!' Bartholomew sank down onto a stool and waited for Michael to finish. 'When?'

'He was well enough this morning, but collapsed in the yard just as I came home,' said Michael, his voice muffled.

Bartholomew went over to the bed, and rested his hand on Aelfrith's brow. He was barely breathing, but seemed to have been spared the terrible agony that some victims went through. It was a risk, visiting the sick and giving last rites, and physicians and clerics had all known that they too might be stricken. Seeing Aelfrith so near the end reminded Bartholomew, yet again, of his own mortality. His thoughts went to Philippa, hopefully secure in the convent, and of their brief spell of happiness at the end of summer.

'I will go again to see if I can find William,' said Michael, furtively rubbing a sleeve over his eyes.

Bartholomew tried to make Aelfrith more comfortable. He had found that stretching the arms out helped relieve pressure on the swellings, and so caused the patient less pain. He was surprised to find that Aelfrith had no swellings. He looked again more carefully, inspecting his neck and his groin. There was no trace of swelling anywhere, and none of the black spots that afflicted some victims, although there was evidence that he had been violently sick. Bartholomew hoped this was not some new variation of the plague.

Aelfrith's eyes fluttered open. He saw Bartholomew and tried to speak. Bartholomew bent closer to hear him, straining to hear the voice that was no more than a rustle of breath.

'Not plague,' he whispered. 'Poison. Wilson.'

He closed his eyes, exhausted. Bartholomew wondered whether the fever had made him delirious. Aelfrith waved his hand weakly in the air. Bartholomew took it and held it. It was cold and dry. Aelfrith's eyes pleaded with Bartholomew, who bent again to listen.

'Wilson,' he whispered again.

Bartholomew, his mind dull from tiredness and grief, was slow in understanding. 'Are you saying that Wilson poisoned you?' he asked.

Aelfrith's lips drew back from his teeth in an awful parody of a smile. And then he died. Bartholomew leaned close and smelled Aelfrith's mouth. He moved back sharply. There was an acrid odour of something vile, and he noticed that Aelfrith's tongue was blistered and swollen. He *had* been poisoned! By Wilson? Bartholomew could not see how, because the lawyer had not left his room for days. Bartholomew sometimes saw him watching the comings and goings in the courtyard through his window, although he would slam the shutter if Bartholomew or any of the clerics so much as glanced up at him.

Bartholomew felt all the energy drain out of him as the significance of Aelfrith's death dawned on him. Another murder! And now of all times! He thought that the plague would have superseded all the dangerous political games that had been played in the summer.

And what was Aelfrith doing in Michael's room anyway? Had Michael poisoned him? He began to look around for cups of wine or food that Michael may have enticed Aelfrith to take, but there was nothing.

He almost jumped out of his skin as the door flew open and Michael came back with Father William in tow.

'Sweet Jesus, we are too late,' groaned Michael, visibly sagging.

'Too late for what?' asked Bartholomew, his tone sharp from the fright he had just had.

'For Father William to give him the Host,' said Michael.

'I thought you had already done that,' said Bartholomew. Surely Michael would not have poisoned the Host? He would surely be damned if he had chosen that mode of execution for one of God's priests.

'I am a Benedictine, Matt,' said Michael patiently. 'He wanted to have the last rites from one of his own Order. I looked for William, but could not find him. I gave Aelfrith last rites because he was failing fast and I thought he might die before William was back.'

Bartholomew turned his attention back to Aelfrith. Was he being unfair to Michael? He thought back to Michael's reaction at the death of Augustus. Was Michael one of those scholars so dedicated to the future success of Cambridge that he would kill for it? Or was he one of those who wanted to see Cambridge fail and Oxford become the foremost place of learning in the land? Or had Wilson slipped out of his room in the dark and left poison for Aelfrith? Was Aelfrith telling him he should go and tell Wilson that he had been poisoned?

Bartholomew was just too tired to think properly.

Should he go to Wilson? Or would the wretched man think Bartholomew was trying to give him the plague? Bartholomew could not blame people like Wilson, Swynford, and Alcote who hid away to save themselves. Had he not been a physician, he might well have done the same thing. The College had divided down the middle, four Fellows going among the plague victims to do what they could, and four remaining isolated. In the other colleges, the division was much the same.

He felt his mind rambling. What should he do? Should he tell Michael and William that Father Aelfrith had been poisoned, and had not died of the plague at all? And then what? The Bishop had his hands too full with his dying monks to be able to investigate another murder. And he probably would not want to investigate it. He would order it covered up, like the others. Well, let us save the Bishop a journey, then, thought Bartholomew wearily. He would say nothing. He would try to see Wilson later, and he would try to question Michael. He wondered why someone had gone to the trouble of committing murder now of all times, when they could all be dead anyway by the following day.

Michael and William had wrapped Aelfrith in a sheet while Bartholomew had been thinking, and together they carried him down the stairs. Bartholomew followed them. What should he do about Aelfrith's burial? He had not died of the plague and so there was no reason why he should be put in the plague pit. He decided to ask Cynric to help him dig a grave in St Michael's churchyard.

The stable was being used as a temporary mortuary in which dead College members awaited collection by the plague carts. Bartholomew saw that there were already two others there, and closed his eyes in despair.

'Richard of Norwich and Francis Eltham,' said Michael in explanation.

'Not Francis!' exclaimed Bartholomew. 'He was so careful!' Eltham had been like Wilson and had shut himself in his room. His room-mates had left Cambridge, so he had been alone.

'Not careful enough,' Michael said. 'This Death has no rhyme nor reason to it.'

Father William sighed. 'I must go to Shoemaker Row. The sickness is in the home of Alexander's sister and they are waiting for me.'

He disappeared into the night, leaving Michael and Bartholomew alone. Bartholomew was too drained to be anxious about Michael's possible murderous inclinations, and too tired to talk to the fat monk about Aelfrith's dying words. Bartholomew wished he had spoken again to Aelfrith about his suspicions, but Aelfrith had taken his oath to the Bishop seriously and had never again mentioned the business to Bartholomew.

Next to him, Michael sniffed loudly, his face turned away from Bartholomew. They stood silently for a while, each wrapped in his own thoughts, until Michael gave a huge sigh.

'I have not eaten all day, Matt. Did you ever think I would allow that to happen?' he said in a frail attempt at humour. He took Bartholomew's arm, and guided him towards the kitchen. Michael lit a candle and they looked around. The big room was deserted, the great fireplace cold. Many of the staff had left the College to be with their families, or had run away northwards in an attempt to escape the relentless advance of the plague. Pots had been left unwashed and scraps of old food littered the stone-flagged floor. Bartholomew wrinkled his nose in disgust as a large rat wandered boldly into the middle of the floor.

As Michael and Bartholomew watched, it started to twitch and shudder. It emitted a few high-pitched squeals before collapsing in a welter of black blood that flowed from between its clenched teeth.

'Now even the rats have the plague,' said Michael, his enthusiasm for foraging for food in the kitchen wavering.

'Now why would God send a visitation down upon rats?' said Bartholomew mockingly. 'Why not eels or pigs or birds?'

Michael gave him a shove. 'Perhaps he has, Physician. When did you last have the time to watch birds and fish?'

Bartholomew gave him a weak smile, and sat at the large table while Michael rummaged in the storerooms. After a few minutes, he emerged with a bottle of wine, some apples, and some salted beef.

'This will do,' he said, settling himself next to Bartholomew. 'This is a bottle of Master Wilson's best claret. It is the first time I have been able to get near it without Gilbert peering over my shoulder.'

Bartholomew looked askance. 'Stealing the Master's wine? Whatever next, Brother!'

'Not stealing,' said Michael, uncorking the bottle and taking a hearty swig. 'Testing it for him. After all, how do we know that the plague is not spread by claret?'

And how do we know that it was not claret that poisoned Aelfrith? thought Bartholomew. He put his head in his hands. He liked Michael, and hoped he was not one of the fanatics of whom Aelfrith had warned him. He suddenly felt very lonely. He would have given anything for a few moments alone with Philippa.

'You must eat,' said Michael gently, 'or you will be no good to yourself or to your patients. Drink some wine, and then try some of this beef. I swear to you, Matt, it is no older than eight months, and only a little rancid.'

Bartholomew smiled. Michael was trying to cheer him up. He took the proffered piece of meat and choked some of it down. He rifled through the apples, looking for one that was not home to families of maggots. Finding one, he presented it solemnly to Michael, who took it with equal gravity and cut it in half.

'Never let it be said that Michaelhouse scholars do not share their good fortunes,' he said, presenting a piece to Bartholomew. 'When do you think this will be over?' he asked suddenly.

'The plague or the murders?' said Bartholomew. The strong wine on his empty stomach had made him answer without thinking.

Michael stared at him. 'Murders?' he asked, non-plussed. Understanding suddenly showed in his eyes. 'Oh no, Matt! Do not start on that! We swore an oath!'

Bartholomew nodded. He had told no one, not even his sister or Philippa, about the conversation he had had with the Bishop, despite probing of varying degrees of subtlety by Wilson, Alcote, and Michael.

'But we know the truth,' he said quietly.

Michael was horrified. 'No! No, we do not,' he insisted. 'We never will. We should not be talking of this!' He looked over his shoulder as if he expected the Bishop to be there.

Bartholomew stood up and walked over to the

window, where he stood staring out into the darkness of the yard.

'But murder is murder, Brother,' he said softly. He turned to look at Michael, whose fat face still wore an expression of disbelief.

'Perhaps so,' Michael said, nervously, 'but it is over and done.'

Bartholomew raised his eyebrows. 'Is it?' he asked gently, watching Michael for any slight reaction that might betray guilt.

'Of course!' Michael snapped. 'Over and done!'

Bartholomew turned back to the window. Michael had always loved the intricate affairs of the College, and took a strange delight in the petty plays for power. On occasions, Bartholomew and Abigny had found his persistent speculations tiresome, and had actively avoided his company. Bartholomew wondered whether his refusal to discuss them now meant that he took the Bishop's oath very seriously and really believed that the murders were over, or whether he had other reasons for maintaining his silence. Did he know that Aelfrith had been murdered? Bartholomew decided he would gain nothing by questioning Michael further, except perhaps to arouse his suspicions. If Michael did know more than he was telling, then Bartholomew would be foolish indeed to allow his suspicions to show.

Michael went to sit next to the fire in the large chair from which Agatha usually ran her domain. He shifted his bulk around until he was comfortable, stretching his feet out as if the fire were blazing. Bartholomew went back to the bench and lay flat, folding his hands over his stomach, looking up at the cobwebs on the ceiling. He would rest just a little while before going to his bed.

'Not only have I missed a good many meals,' said Michael, 'but I have been too busy to complain about my perpetually cold feet!'

'Missed meals will do you no harm, my fat monk,' said Bartholomew drowsily. It was freezing in the kitchen, and they were both wet from being out in the rain all day. They should not lie around in the cold, but should go back to their respective beds and sleep in the warm.

'When will it end?' asked Michael again, his voice distant, as if his thoughts were elsewhere.

Did he mean the plague or the murders in the College? wondered Bartholomew a second time, his thoughts beginning to tumble through his tired brain again. He asked himself why he was lying in a cold kitchen alone with someone whom he thought might know more than was safe about at least one murder.

'Why was Aelfrith in your room?' Bartholomew asked sleepily. Gradually, he was relaxing for the first time in days; it was a pleasant feeling, and he felt himself beginning to fall asleep.

'Mmm?' said Michael. 'Oh, I took him there. He collapsed in the yard. His room was locked, so I took him to mine.'

'Locked?' asked Bartholomew, now struggling to stay awake.

'Yes,' came Michael's voice from a long way off. 'I thought it was odd, too. But locked it was, and I could not get in. Perhaps one of his students saw him collapse and did not want him brought to their room.'

Bartholomew thought about that. It was possible, and he knew that Aelfrith's three Franciscan novices had been concerned that the work he was doing among the plague victims might bring the disease to them.

'When do you think this plague will end?' he asked in response, wriggling slightly to ease the ache in his back.

'When the Lord thinks we have learned,' said Michael.

'Learned what, for God's sake?' asked Bartholomew, settling down again. 'If this continues, perhaps there will be no one left to learn anything.'

'Perhaps not,' said Michael. 'But if He wanted us all to die, He would not have bothered to send the signs.'

'What signs?' Bartholomew felt his eyes begin to close, no matter how hard he struggled to keep them open. He tried to remember when he had last slept; a couple of hours two nights before?

'When the plague first started in the Far East, there were three signs,' began Michael. Bartholomew gave up on keeping his eyes open, and just listened.

'On the first day, it rained frogs and serpents. On the second day, there was thunder so loud that people hearing it were sent mad, and lightning that came as sheets of fire. On the third day a great pall of black smoke issued from the earth, blotting out the sun and all the light. On the fourth day, the plague came.

'There have been other signs too,' Michael continued after a moment. 'In France, a great pillar of fire was seen over the Palace of the Popes in Avignon. A ball of fire hung over Paris. In Italy, when the plague arrived, it came with a terrible earthquake that sent noxious fumes all over the surrounding country and killed all the crops. Many died from famine as well as the plague.'

'There have been no such signs here, Brother,' said Bartholomew, almost asleep. 'Perhaps we are not so evil as the French or the Italians.'

'Perhaps not,' said Michael. 'Or perhaps God does not want to waste His signs on the irredeemable.'

Bartholomew woke with a start. He was cold and very stiff, and still lying on the bench. Wincing, he eased himself up, wondering why he had not gone to bed to wake warm and rested. Daylight was flooding in through the window, and there was a crackle of burning wood. He looked behind him.

'Oh, you are awake, lazy-bones,' grunted Agatha. 'Sleeping in the kitchen indeed! Master Wilson will not be impressed.'

The kitchen had been cleaned since the previous night: the food swept away and the dead rat removed. One of the fireplaces had been cleared out and a warm blaze replaced the cold ashes. Stiffly, Bartholomew went to sit beside it on a stool, smelling the fresh oatcakes cooking on the circular oven next to the fire. Brother Michael still slept in Agatha's chair, black circles under his eyes and his mouth dangling open. Bartholomew's suspicions of the night before seemed unreasonable. Even if Michael had been connected with the death of Aelfrith in some way, he obviously meant Bartholomew no harm, when he could easily have dispatched him as he lay sleeping on the bench.

Bartholomew stretched himself and filched an oatcake when he thought Agatha was not looking. The sudden movement woke Michael, who sat looking around stupidly. 'What time is it?' he asked, blinking the sleep from his eyes and rubbing his cold hands together.

'A little before eight, I would say,' said Agatha. 'Now you sit down,' she continued, pushing Michael back in his chair. 'I have made you some oatcakes – if this greedy physician has not eaten them all.'

'But I have missed Prime,' said Michael, horrified. 'And I did not say Matins and Lauds last night.'

'Your stomach must still be asleep,' said Bartholomew, 'if you are considering prayers before breakfast.'

'I always say prayers before breakfast,' snapped Michael, and then relented. 'I am sorry, Matt. I cannot stick knives in boils and try to relieve fevers like you do. My way of fighting this monstrous pestilence is to keep my offices, no matter what happens. I hope it may make a difference.' He gave a rueful look. 'This will be the first time I have failed since this business began.'

'I was thinking yesterday that the clerics were doing more good than the physicians ever could,' said Bartholomew, startled by Michael's confession. 'Do not be too hard on yourself, Brother. Or, as you said to me last night, you will be no good to yourself or your patients,' he said in a very plausible imitation of Michael's pompous voice that made Agatha screech with laughter.

Michael laughed too, more at Agatha's reaction than at Bartholomew's feeble attempt at humour. 'Oh lord, Matthew,' he said. 'I never thought we would laugh again. Give me the oatcakes, Mistress Agatha. I had nothing but maggoty apples last night.'

Agatha pulled the oatcakes out of the oven and plumped herself down on a stool next to Bartholomew. 'I am gone for three days to tend to my relatives, and the College falls apart,' she said. 'Filth in the kitchens, rats in the rooms, and the food all gone.'

Michael coughed, his mouth overfull of fresh warm

oatcake. 'The servants have mostly left,' he said. 'That great lump of lard in the Master's room will not stir himself to take charge as he should, and the College is ruled by chaos.'

'Not any more,' said Agatha grandly, 'for I am back. And make no mistake, young sirs, no pestilence is going to get me! I have been three days going from house to house, seeing my relatives die, and I am still free from the pestilence. Some of us will not be taken!'

Bartholomew and Michael stared at her in astonishment. 'You may be right,' said Bartholomew. 'Gregory Colet and I wondered whether some people may have a natural resistance to the plague.'

'Not resistance, Master Bartholomew,' said Agatha proudly, 'I am one of God's chosen.' She shifted her ample skirts importantly. 'He strikes down those that anger him, and spares those he loves.'

'That cannot be, Mistress,' said Bartholomew. 'Why would God strike down children? And what of the monks and friars who risk themselves to give comfort to the people?'

'Monks and friars!' spat Agatha. 'I have seen the lives they lead: wealth, rich foods, women, and fine clothes! God will direct them to hell first!'

'Thank you for your kind words, Mistress,' said Michael, eyeing her dolefully. 'And how long would you say I have before God banishes me to hell?'

Agatha grinned sheepishly. 'I did not say he would take you all. But what other reason can there be that some die and some live? The physicians do not know. Gregory Colet told me I may be right, and the priests believe some are chosen to live and others to die.'

'Perhaps some people have a balance of humours

in their bodies that gives them a resistance to the plague,' mused Bartholomew, taking another oatcake.

'And have you compared the humours of those that live with those that die?' asked Michael.

Bartholomew nodded, frustrated. 'But I can see no pattern in it as yet.'

Michael patted his shoulder. 'Well, perhaps the balance is too fine to be easily seen,' he said. 'But if your theory is true, I do not want to know, for it would mean that I am doomed – to live or die – as my body directs, and that nothing I do – no matter how I pray or try to live a godly life, will make a difference. And then I would be without hope and without God.'

Bartholomew raised his hands. 'It would be no kind of answer anyway,' he said. 'I want to know how to cure this foul disease, not forecast for people whether they will live or die.'

Michael stood up, stuffing the rest of the oatcakes in his scrip for later. 'As much as I like your company, sitting here discussing the causes of the Death with two people who have no more idea why it has come than I have will benefit no one. I must say my prayers and visit the people.'

He marched out of the kitchen, and Bartholomew heard his strong baritone singing a psalm as he went to the porter's lodge. He also glimpsed Wilson's white face at his window, surveying the domain he dared not rule.

'You can stay a while, if you do not mind me clattering,' said Agatha. Bartholomew recognised this as a rare compliment, for Agatha did not approve of idle hands in the kitchen. She was already beginning to reimpose her order on the chaos, for the boys who worked in the scullery had been set to work washing floors, and Cynric and Alexander were collecting the bedclothes of those who had died to be taken to the laundry.

'Thank you, Mistress, but I must meet with Gregory Colet to see that the new pit is dug.'

He left Agatha to her work, and went to draw some water from the well. Back in the room where he stored his medicines, he washed quickly in the freezing water and changed his clothes. His clean ones were not quite dry, but it was going to rain again anyway, he thought. As he emerged from the storeroom, he saw Father William and hailed him over. He looked tired, and his eyes were red-rimmed.

'Nathaniel the Fleming has the plague,' he said. 'I have been called to give him last rites.'

'Not leeches?' asked Bartholomew, his own weariness making him obtuse.

William looked askance at him. 'Doctor Colet has already leeched him, but the poisons were too deep in his body to draw out.' He reached a meaty hand towards Bartholomew. 'What of Aelfrith? Will you see him taken to the plague pit?'

Bartholomew looked up at the pale blue sky. Did William know? Should he tell him? What if William and Wilson were in league, and had poisoned Aelfrith together? Bartholomew looked at the friar's face, grey with fatigue, and recalled also that Aelfrith and William had been close friends. 'Shall I bury him in the churchyard instead?' he asked, to buy himself more time to think.

William looked startled. 'Can we? Is it not safer for the living to bury him in lime in the plague pits?'

'I do not see why,' Bartholomew said, watching

William closely. 'Others were buried in the churchyard before the plague came in earnest.'

William pursed his lips. 'I have been thinking about that. Perhaps it is their corrupted flesh lying in hallowed ground that is causing the contagion to spread. Perhaps the way to stop the Death is to exhume them all and rebury them in the plague pits.'

Now it was Bartholomew's turn to be startled. Here was a theory he had not encountered before. He mulled it over in his mind briefly, reluctant to dismiss any chance of defeating the plague without due thought, no matter how unlikely a solution it might seem. But he shook his head. 'I suspect that would only serve to put those that perform the exhumation at risk, if not from the plague, then from other diseases. And I cannot see that they are a danger to the living.'

William looked at him dubiously. 'Will you bury Aelfrith, then? In the churchyard?'

Bartholomew nodded, and then hesitated. If William were involved in Aelfrith's murder, incautious questioning would only serve to endanger his own life, and if he were not, it would be yet another burden for the exhausted friar. 'Were you ... surprised that he was taken?' Bartholomew asked, before realising how clumsy the question was.

William looked taken aback. 'He was fit enough at the midday meal,' he replied. 'Just tired like us all, and saddened because he had heard the deathbed confession of the Principal of All Saints' Hostel. Now you mention it, poor Aelfrith was taken very quickly. It was fortunate that Brother Michael was near, or he might have died unshriven.'

He began to walk away, leaving Bartholomew less

certain than ever as to whether he was involved. Were his reactions, his words, those of a killer? And what of Wilson? What was his role in Aelfrith's death?

Before leaving, he decided to see Abigny briefly. He pushed the door open slowly, and a boot flew across the room and landed at his feet. Bartholomew pushed the door all the way open and peered in.

'Oh. It is you, Matt. I thought it was that damned rat again. Did you see it? It is as big as a dog!' Abigny untangled himself from his bed. 'What a time I had last night, Physician. What delights I sampled! None of the young ladies want to meet their maker without first knowing of love, and I have been only too happy to oblige. You should try it.'

'Giles, if you are sampling the delights of as many poor ladies as you say, I hope you do not plan to visit Philippa,' said Bartholomew anxiously. 'Please do not visit her if you are seeing people who may be infected.'

'Poppycock! She will die if it is her time,' said Abigny, pulling on some of his brightest clothes. Bartholomew knew only too well that this meant he was planning on impressing some female friends.

'And you will die before it is yours if you take the pestilence to her!' he said with quiet menace. He had always found Abigny rather shallow and selfish, although he could be an entertaining companion, but he had always believed the philosopher to be genuinely fond of his sister. Through the past few black weeks, it had been the thought of Philippa's face that had allowed Bartholomew to continue his bleak work. He could not bear to think of her falling prey to the filthy disease.

Abigny stopped dressing and looked at Bartholomew. 'Matthew, I am sorry,' he said with sincerity. 'You should know better than to think I would harm Philippa. No, I do not have the plague . . .' He raised his hand to stop Bartholomew from coming further into the room. 'Hugh Stapleton died last night.'

Bartholomew leaned against the door. Stapleton had run Bene't Hostel, and had been a close friend of Abigny's. Abigny spent more time at the Hostel than he did at Michaelhouse, and regularly took his meals there.

'I am sorry, Giles,' he said. He had seen so many die over the last several days, including Aelfrith, that it was difficult to sound convincing. He wondered whether he would be bereft of all compassion by the time the plague had run its course.

Abigny nodded. 'I am away to enjoy the pleasures of life, and I will not see Philippa,' he said. 'I was with Hugh when he died, and he told me to enjoy life while I had it. That is exactly what I am going to do.'

He flung his best red cloak over his shoulders and walked jauntily out of the yard. Bartholomew followed him as far as the stable where Father Aelfrith's body lay. While Abigny enjoyed life, Bartholomew had a colleague to bury. He glanced up and saw Wilson lingering at the window. Had he killed Aelfrith?

'Father Aelfrith is dead,' Bartholomew yelled up at him, drawing the attention of several students who were walking around the yard to the hall. 'Will you come to see him buried, Master Wilson?'

The shadowy shape disappeared. Bartholomew took a spade from the stable and walked to St Michael's churchyard.

VI

CHRISTMAS AT CAMBRIDGE WAS USUALLY A TIME for celebration and for a relaxing of the rules that governed scholars' lives. Fires would be lit in the conclave, and students and Fellows could gather round and tell each other stories, or even play cards. Since it was dark by four o'clock in the evening, a night by the fire in a candle-lit conclave was a pleasant change from the usual practice of retiring to dark, unheated rooms.

But the plague was still raging in Cambridge at Christmas, and few felt like celebrating. Bedraggled groups of children stood in the snow singing carols for pennies. Food was scarce because many of the farmers who grew the winter vegetables or tended the livestock were struck with the plague. Many who were fit did not wish to risk a journey into the town, where they might come into contact with infected people.

The cart patrolling the streets collecting the dead became a common sight. Old women who had lost entire families followed it around, offering prayers for the dead in return for money or food. Houses stood empty, and at night, after the curfew bell had rung and the depleted and exhausted patrols of University beadles and Sheriff's men slept, small bands of vagrants and thieves would loot the homes of the dead and the sick. The thieves soon became bolder, coming in from surrounding villages and even attacking during the daylight hours.

To make matters worse, it was a cold winter, with gales howling across the flat land, bringing with them driving snow. On clear days and nights, the temperature dropped so low that sick people had to go out foraging for sticks to build fires to melt ice for water to drink.

The monks at Barnwell Priory lost a third of their number, although St Radegund's fared better and only three nuns became ill. More than half of the monks at the great monasteries at Ely and Norwich perished, and Bartholomew began to appreciate the Bishop's point as he saw more and more people die without being given last rites. Some did not care, but only wished to end their agony; others died in terror of going straight to hell as a punishment for various petty sins. The church walls were full of paintings of the damned being devoured by demons in hell, so Bartholomew did not wonder that people were afraid.

It was impossible to tell how many members the University lost. At the first sign of the plague, some left the town and did not return. As the numbers of deaths rose, harried clerks began to lose count, and many people ended up in the plague pits without any record being made. By January, King's Hall lost ten of its scholars, and Michaelhouse lost eleven. Bartholomew had thought that perhaps the scholars might fare better than the townspeople because they were younger, fitter, and usually better fed. But the plague struck indiscriminately, and by Christmas the old commoners were still alive and well, but several healthy young students were dead.

However much Bartholomew thought and studied and worked, he could not understand why some people died and others recovered, or why, in the same household, some people caught the disease while others remained healthy, even after being in contact with the sick. He and Colet compared experiences regularly, and argued endlessly and without conclusion. Colet had given up leeching buboes, and incised them where he could, like Bartholomew. But he still believed that leeching after the incisions caused the recovery of his patients. Bartholomew believed the keys were rest, a warm bed, and clean water. Since neither had a better record of success than the other, each refused to adopt the other's methods. But Colet's patients were generally wealthy, with warm homes and clean bedding. Bartholomew's patients were poor, and warmth and cleanliness were not always easy to attain.

Bartholomew continued on his rounds, lancing the black swellings whenever he thought it might ease a patient's pain. Two more physicians died, and another two fled, so that only Bartholomew, Colet, and Simon Roper from Bene't Hostel were left. They found they could not trust the town officials to carry out their recommendations and had to supervise virtually everything, from the digging of the pits and the proper use of lime, to the cleaning of the streets of the dead rats and refuse that built up.

Bartholomew, arriving home at dawn after staying with a family that had five of seven children dying, was awoken within minutes by hammering on the door. Wearily, he struggled out of bed to answer it. A young man stood there, his long, unruly hair at odds with his neat scholar's tabard.

'I thought you would have been up by now,' said the man cheekily.

'What do you want?' Bartholomew asked thickly, so tired he could barely speak.

'I have been sent to fetch you to St Radegund's.'

Bartholomew's blood ran cold, and he was instantly awake. 'Why, what has happened?' he asked in a whisper, almost afraid to ask. 'Is it Philippa Abigny?'

'Oh, no,' said the student. 'A man wants you. But you had better hurry up or he said you will be too late.'

Bartholomew hastened back inside to dress. When he emerged, the tousle-haired man was leaning against the wall chatting to the porter. Bartholomew ignored him and made his way up St Michael's Lane at a steady trot. He heard footsteps behind him, and the young man caught him and tried to match his pace.

'If you want to travel quickly, why do you not take a horse?' he asked between gasps.

'I do not have a horse,' answered Bartholomew. 'Who has asked for me? Is it Giles Abigny?' The fear he felt earlier returned. He hoped Abigny had not become ill and gone to the convent for help. St Radegund's had escaped lightly until now, perhaps because the Prioress had determined on a policy of isolation, and no one was allowed in; money in a pot of vinegar was left outside the gates for all food that was delivered. Bartholomew hoped the Prioress had managed to continue so, not only because Philippa was inside, but also because he wanted to know if the plague could be averted in this way.

'You do not have a horse?' queried the student, losing his stride. 'A physician?'

'Who asked for me?' Bartholomew asked again. He was beginning to be annoyed.

'I do not know, just some man. I am only the messenger.'

Bartholomew increased his speed, and quickly left the student puffing and wheezing behind him. It was only a matter of moments before the walls of St Radegund's loomed up out of the early morning mist. He pounded on the door, leaning against the wall to get his breath, his legs unsteady from a brisk run on an empty stomach and anticipation of what was to come.

A small grille in the door snapped open. 'What do you want?' came a sharp voice.

'It is Matthew Bartholomew. I was sent for,' he gasped.

'Not by us,' and the grille slammed shut.

Bartholomew groaned and banged on the door again. There was no reply.

'You are unlikely to get an answer now.'

Bartholomew spun round, and the student found himself pinned against the wall by the throat. 'Hey! I am only the messenger!' he croaked, eyes wide in his face.

Bartholomew relented and loosened his grip, although not by much.

'Who sent for me?' he asked again, his voice dangerously quiet.

'I do not know his name. I will have to show you,' the student said, trying to prise Bartholomew's hands from his throat, some of his former cockiness gone.

He led the way around the walls towards the convent gardens. 'My name is Samuel Gray,' he said. Bartholomew ignored him. 'I am a medical student at Bene't Hostel.'

Bartholomew saw they were heading for a small shack where garden tools were kept. He and Philippa had sheltered there from a summer thunderstorm once as they had walked together among the fruit bushes. That had been only a few short months before, but to Bartholomew it seemed in another lifetime. Gray reached the hut first, and pushed open the door. Bartholomew took a step inside and peered into the gloom, trying to see what was inside.

'Philippa!' She was kneeling in a corner next to a figure lying on the floor.

'Matt!' She leapt to her feet, and before Bartholomew could prevent her, she had thrown herself into his arms. His first instinct was to force her away, lest he carried the contagion with him somehow in his clothes, but the shack was already rank with the smell of the plague, so there was little point. He allowed all else to be driven from his mind as he enjoyed the first contact he had had with Philippa since the plague began.

Suddenly she pushed him away. 'What are you doing here?' she said. 'Who asked you to come?'

Bartholomew gazed at her in confusion. He looked around at Gray, who stood at the door looking as surprised as Bartholomew.

'I do not know,' Gray said. 'It was a man. He told me to bring you here, and that he would be waiting to meet you.'

Bartholomew looked back at Philippa. 'I do not know of any man,' she said. 'I have been here since dawn. I had a message to come, and I found Sister Clement here. She has the plague.'

'But who told you to come? And how did you get out? I thought the convent was sealed.'

'I do not know, to answer your first question. A message came written on a scrap of parchment pushed under the door. I came here immediately. In answer to your other question, there is a small gate near the kitchens that is always open, although few know of it. Sister Clement has been using it regularly to slip out and go among the poor.' Her voice caught, and Bartholomew put his arms round her again.

He said nothing while she sobbed quietly, and Gray shuffled his feet in the doorway. On the floor, Sister Clement was near the end, her laboured breathing almost inaudible. Philippa looked at her, and raised her eyes pleadingly to Bartholomew. 'Can you help her?'

Bartholomew shook his head. He had seen so many similar cases during the last few weeks that he did not even need to examine her to know that there was nothing he could do. Even lancing the swellings at this point would do no more than cause unnecessary suffering.

'But you are a physician! You must be able to do something!'

Bartholomew flinched. These were words he heard every day, but they hurt nevertheless. He went over to look at the old lady, and arranged her arms so that the pressure on the swellings under them would be reduced. The buboes in her groin had burst, emitting the smell which Bartholomew had come to know well, but that still filled him with disgust. He sent Gray to find a priest to give her last rites, and sat back helplessly. Behind him, Philippa cried softly. He took her hand and led her outside into the clean morning air.

'Why did you come, Matt?' asked Philippa.

'That student came and said I was needed at St Radegund's. He does not seem to know by whom.'

'I receive a message to come here, sent by an unknown person, then you do. What is going on? Who wants us here together?' Philippa looked around her as if expecting the unknown person to emerge from the bushes.

'Friend or foe?' asked Bartholomew absently. He was horribly afraid that it was the latter, someone who wanted Philippa to come into contact with a plague victim, and Bartholomew to know it. He felt a sudden anger. Who would want to do such a thing? What had either of them done to harm anyone else?

'Now I am out of that horrid place, I will not go back,' said Philippa with a sudden fierce determination. 'I refuse. I can stay with you and Giles. I can sleep in your medicine room.'

'There is plague at the College, Philippa,' said Bartholomew. 'You would not be safe.'

'There is plague here!' said Philippa vehemently, gesturing to the shack behind them. 'And anyway,' she continued, 'I do not approve of the way the nuns skulk behind the convent walls. Sister Clement was the only one with any decency.'

'Do you want to die like that?' asked Bartholomew, gesturing back at the old lady.

'Do you?' countered Philippa. 'You see plague victims every day, and you are well. So is Gregory Colet. Not everyone who touches someone with the Death catches it.'

Bartholomew wondered what to do. It was out of the question to take Philippa to Michaelhouse. Even though Master Wilson was not in a position to do anything about it, the clerics would object. And she could not possibly sleep in the medicines room. The shutters did not close properly, and there were no separate privies that she would be able to use. He would have to take her to

Edith's house. Edith had not heeded his advice and locked herself away, and Stanmore was still trying to conduct his trade. Philippa would not be as protected there from the plague as she had been in the convent, but it was the best he could do.

Gray came back over the fields bringing with him an Austin Canon from Barnwell whom he had waylaid. They listened to his murmurings as he administered last rites to the old nun. After a few minutes he came out, told them that Sister Clement was dead, and went on his way. For him, it would be the first in a long day of such prayers, and who knew whether he would live to see another such day tomorrow?

Bartholomew took Philippa's hand, and together they began to make their way back to Barnwell Causeway. Gray tagged along behind.

Bartholomew decided to go to Edith's house in Trumpington immediately. They would have to walk because he knew of nowhere where he would be able to hire horses. All the usual places had been struck by the plague, and the horses turned to graze unattended in the fields. Bartholomew turned to Gray.

'Can you tell me anything else about this man who gave you the message? What did he look like?'

Gray shrugged. 'He was wearing a Dominican habit, and his cowl was over his face. He had ink on his fingers, though, and he tripped on the hem of his gown as he left.'

Ink on his fingers. He could be a clerk or a student, unfamiliar enough in the friar's long habit to fall over it when he walked. Were the fanatical scholars after him now? Was this a warning to him that he was vulnerable through Philippa, even though he had thought her safely tucked away in her convent? He wondered why on earth they were bothering. No one who watched the sun rise these days could be certain of seeing it set in the evening. All they had to do was wait. Why had they taken the trouble to poison Aelfrith? As Bartholomew's thoughts of murder came tumbling back, he clutched Philippa's hand tighter, glad to feel something warm and reassuring. She smiled at him, and they began to walk towards Trumpington.

Edith was delighted to see Bartholomew and surprised to see Philippa. She fussed over them both, and found Philippa a small room in the garret where she could have some privacy. Oswald Stanmore was just finishing a late breakfast in the parlour, and chatted to Bartholomew while Edith whisked Philippa away.

'She will be glad of some company,' he said, jerking his thumb towards the stairway where Edith had gone. 'She frets over Richard. We have had no word since the plague came. I keep telling her that she should look on this as a positive sign and that definite news might mean he has been buried.'

Bartholomew said nothing. He did not want to remind Stanmore of the dozens of unnamed bodies he saw tipped into the pits. People often died in the streets, were collected by the carts and their names were never discovered. He was sure that Stanmore must have seen this as he did his business around the town. He tried not to think about it; Bartholomew did not want to imagine Richard tipped into some pit in Oxford, never to be traced by his family.

'How are the figures?' asked Stanmore.

'Another fifteen died yesterday, including eight

children,' said Bartholomew. 'I have lost count of the total number, and the clerk who is supposed to note numbers of bodies going into the pits is drunk half the time. We will probably never know how many have died in Cambridge.'

'You look exhausted, Matt. Stay here for a few days and rest. You cannot keep going at this pace.'

'The plague will not last forever,' said Bartholomew. 'And how can I leave Colet and Roper to do everything?'

'Simon Roper died this morning,' said Stanmore. He noticed Bartholomew's shock. 'I am sorry, lad. I thought you would have known.'

Now Bartholomew and Colet were the only ones left, with Robin of Grantchester, the town surgeon, whose methods and hygiene Bartholomew did not trust. How would they manage? Because there had been cases where Bartholomew had lanced the black swellings and the patient had lived, he wanted to make sure that as many people as possible were given this tiny chance for life. If there were fewer physicians and surgeons, fewer people would be treated, and the plague would take those who might have been able to survive.

'Stay here with Philippa,' said Stanmore persuasively. 'She needs you, too.'

Bartholomew felt himself wavering. It would be wonderful to spend a few hours with Philippa and to forget all the foulness of the past weeks. But he knew that there were people who needed him, perhaps his friends, and he would not forgive himself if one of them died when he might have been able to help. He shook his head.

'I must go back to the College. Alexander was

unwell last night. I should check on him, and I must make sure that the pits are being properly limed, or we may never escape from this vile disease.' He stood up and stretched.

'Ride with me then,' said Stanmore, gathering scrolls of neat figures from the table and stuffing them in his bag. 'One of the apprentices can bring the horse back again tonight.'

Edith came in and told them that Philippa was resting. Apparently the death of the old nun had upset her more than Bartholomew had thought. He had become so inured to death that he had made the assumption that others had too, and had not considered that Philippa would be so grieved.

Edith gave Bartholomew a hug. 'Take care,' she whispered. 'Do not take too many chances. I could not bear to lose you.'

She turned away so that he would not see the tears in her eyes, and bustled around the fireplace. Bartholomew reached over and touched her lightly on the shoulder before following her husband into the yard. It was beginning to snow again, and the wind was bitterly cold. The muddy ruts in the track back to Cambridge had frozen, and the covering of snow made the travelling treacherous. Both horses stumbled several times, and the snow swirled about them so that they could barely see the way.

After a few minutes, Stanmore reined in. 'This is insane, Matt. We must go back. We can try again later.'

'You return. I have to go on,' said Bartholomew.

'Be sensible! We can barely see where we are going. Come home with me.'

'But I am worried about Alexander. And I promised the miller I would look in on his boy.'

'Go if you must, but I think you are mad. Take the horse. Please do not stable the poor beast at Michaelhouse, but take it to Stephen. He knows how to care for horses, unlike your dreadful porter.'

Bartholomew nodded and with a wave of his hand urged the horse on down the track, while Stanmore retraced his steps. The snow seemed to be coming horizontally, and Bartholomew was quickly enveloped in a soundless world of swirling white. Even the horse's hooves barely made a sound. Despite being cold and tired, he admired the beauty and tranquility of the countryside. The soft sheets of brilliant white stretching in all directions seemed a long way from the putrid black buboes and blood-laden vomit of the plague victims. He stopped the horse, so that he could appreciate the silence and peace.

He was startled to hear a twig snapping behind him. He twisted round in the saddle and saw a shadow flit between the trees. He hoped it was not robbers; he had no wish to be attacked for the few pennies in his pocket. He jabbed his heels into the horse's side to urge it forward, and it broke into a brisk trot. Glancing behind himself frequently, Bartholomew saw nothing but snow-laden trees and the hoof marks of his horse on the path.

He reached the Priory of St Edmund's, its buildings almost invisible in the swirling snow, and continued to Small Bridges Street. The miller was waiting for him, peering anxiously through the snow. As Bartholomew dismounted, he raced to meet him.

'He is well, Doctor, he lives! You saved him! You

said he had a chance, and you were right. He is awake now, asking for water.'

Bartholomew gave a brief smile and went to see his small patient. His mother had died of the plague three days before, followed by one of his sisters. The boy looked as though he would recover now, and the rest of the family seemed healthy enough. Leaving them with stern warnings not to drink the river water just because the well was frozen, he mounted and rode back to Michaelhouse, his spirits a little higher. As he turned to wave to the miller, he thought he saw a shadow dart into the long grass by the side of the stream, but it was no more than the merest flash of movement, and however hard he looked, he could see nothing else.

Bartholomew took the horse to Stephen Stanmore's house on Milne Street and stayed for a cup of mulled wine. Stephen looked tired and strained and told him that three of the apprentices had died. Rachel Atkin, whom Bartholomew had persuaded him to take, was proving invaluable in helping to nurse others with the sickness.

When Bartholomew returned to College, Alexander had already died, and Brother Michael was helping Agatha to sew him into a blanket. Cynric was also ill, shivering with fever, and muttering in Welsh. Bartholomew sat with him until the light began to fade, and went out to check on the plague pits.

Cynric was more friend than servant. They had first met in Oxford when they had been on opposing sides in one of the many town-and-gown brawls. Each had bloodied the other, but rather than continue, Bartholomew, who had had enough of his foray into such senseless behaviour, offered to buy the short Welshman some ale. Cynric had narrowed his eyes suspiciously, but had gone with Bartholomew, and the two had spent the rest of the day talking and watching their fellow brawlers being arrested. Bartholomew had arranged for the itinerant Cynric to work in the hostel where he studied, and, later, had invited him to Cambridge. Officially, Cynric was Bartholomew's book-bearer, although he did other tasks around the College and had a considerable degree of freedom.

Bartholomew walked back down the High Street to the scrap of land that had been hastily consecrated so that plague victims could be buried. He peered into the pit in the growing gloom, and ordered that the dead-collectors be told to use more lime.

It was still snowing heavily as he walked back to College. The snow was almost knee-deep in places, and walking was hard work. Bartholomew began to feel hot, and paused to wipe the sweat from his face. He also felt dizzy. Probably just tiredness, he thought impatiently, and he tried to hurry through the snow to return to Cynric. Walking became harder and harder, and Bartholomew was finding it difficult to catch his breath. He was relieved when he finally reached Michaelhouse, and staggered through the gates. He decided that he needed to lie down for a few moments before sitting with Cynric again.

He made his way over to his room, and pushed open the door. He stopped dead in his tracks as Samuel Gray rose languidly from his bed, where, judging from his half-closed eyes and rumpled hair, he had been sleeping.

Bartholomew desperately wanted to rest, and his

body felt stiff and sore. It must have been the unaccustomed riding. He took a step forwards, and Gray moved cautiously backwards.

'I have been waiting for you,' said Gray.

Bartholomew swallowed. His throat felt dry and sore. 'What for? Not more messages?'

'No, no, nothing like that,' said Gray.

Bartholomew felt his knees begin to give way. As he pitched forward into the surprised student's arms, he knew he had become a victim of the plague.

Epiphany came and went. Brother Michael, Father William, and a mere handful of students celebrated mass. Alcote slipped into the back of the church, and skittered nervously from pillar to pillar as a few parishioners straggled in. When one of them began to cough, he left and scuttled back to the safety of his room. Of Wilson, there was no sign.

Cynric had a burning fever for two days, and then woke on the third morning claiming he was well. Agatha, who had been nursing him, heaved a sigh of relief and went about her other duties, secure in her belief that she was immune. When a peddler came to the College selling crudely carved wooden lions covered in gold paint that he assured her would protect her from the plague, she sent him away with some ripe curses ringing in her ears.

The dead-collectors failed to come for Alexander, and so Agatha loaded him onto the College cart with the reluctant help of Gilbert, and took him to the plague pit herself. Agatha had heard that Gregory Colet, devastated by the death of Simon Roper and Bartholomew's sickness, had given up visiting new plague victims and no longer supervised the liming of the plague pits or the cleaning of the streets.

More of the dead-collectors died, and it became almost impossible to persuade people to take their places. Several friars and Canons from the Hospital offered their services, but these were not enough, and soon bodies lay for two or three days on the streets or in houses before they were taken away.

Many people believed that the end of the world was near, and that the plague was a punishment for human sin. It was said that entire villages were wiped out, and that in the cities, at least half the population had perished. Trade was virtually at a standstill, and civil disorder was rife in the cities and towns.

Bartholomew knew little about the days he was ill. Occasionally he was conscious enough to hear low voices, and he heard the College bell ringing for meals and for church services. The swellings on his neck, groin, and under his arms gave him intense pain, and he was usually aware of little else.

After five days, he saw a candle flickering on the shelf under the window. He watched it for a while, wondering why the shutters were closed and a candle burning when he could see daylight seeping under the door. As he tried to turn his head, a searing pain in his neck brought everything back to him. He remembered walking back from the plague pit and finding the obnoxious student sleeping on his bed, and recalled meeting Philippa in the shack in the convent grounds.

'Philippa!' he said, his voice no more than a whisper.

'She is well, but worried about you, as is your sister.' The student had appeared, and was leaning over him, dark rings under his eyes, and his hair even more rumpled than Bartholomew remembered.

'What are you doing here?' Bartholomew croaked.

'Tsk, man! The lad has been looking after you day and night! Show a little gratitude.'

Bartholomew gave a weak grin. 'Cynric! Thank God! I thought you might be gone.' He reached for Cynric's hand to assure himself his imagination was not playing tricks.

Cynric, touched, became brusque. 'Lie still, or those incisions will start bleeding again.'

'What incisions? Did Gregory Colet come?'

'Master Colet has given up on the world, and spends his days on his knees with the monks. It is young Samuel who has been looking after you.'

Bartholomew looked appalled, and winced as he tried to move his arms to check where the swellings on his neck would have been. 'I feel as though I have been savaged by a dog,' he groaned. 'What has he done to me?'

'He cut the swellings open to drain them. Just as you have been doing to others, Master Physician. Now you know how it feels,' said Cynric, ruefully rubbing his own lacerated neck.

Bartholomew looked at the student. 'Who are you?' he asked, wondering why a fit and healthy young man would opt to care for a plague victim he did not know.

'Samuel Gray,' said the student, promptly.

'Yes, from Bene't Hostel. But that is not what I meant. What do you want from me?'

Gray looked at the floor. 'I followed you to Trumpington, and then back in the snow. When you returned from seeing the miller's boy, I came here while you went off to see to Cynric. I was waiting for you, but you were such a long time, I fell asleep.' He looked up and met Bartholomew's eyes. 'I was Master Roper's student, and he is dead, so I would like to study under you.'

His speech over, he tried to look nonchalant, as if Bartholomew's response was not that important to him anyway, but in the silence that followed, his face grew anxious and he watched Bartholomew intently.

'I see.' Bartholomew was suddenly very tired, and could not stop his eyes from closing. Then he was shaken awake again. 'Will you have me?' the student asked insistently.

Bartholomew struggled to free himself from Gray's grip, but was as weak as a kitten. 'Why me? What have I done to deserve this?' he said, his voice heavy with sleepiness.

Gray looked at him narrowly, trying to assess whether there was a hidden insult in the question. 'There are not many of you left,' he said rudely.

Bartholomew heard Cynric laughing. He could feel himself drifting into a deep and restful slumber. Gray's voice brought him awake again.

'Will you have me? I have a good degree, you can ask Hugh Stapleton. Oh . . .' his voice trailed off. Stapleton was dead. 'Master Abigny!' he exclaimed jubilantly. 'You can ask him, he knows me!' He gave Bartholomew another gentle shake.

Bartholomew reached up and grabbed a handful of Gray's tunic, pulling him down towards the bed. 'You will never be a good physician unless you can learn when to let your patients rest,' he whispered, 'and you will never be a good student unless you learn not to manhandle your master.'

Releasing Gray's clothing, he closed his eyes and was instantly asleep. Gray looked at Cynric. 'Was that a yes or a no?' he asked.

Cynric, still smiling, shrugged and left the room, closing the door softly behind him. Gray stood looking down at Bartholomew for several minutes before tidying the bedclothes and blowing out the candle. He lay down on the pallet bed Cynric had given him and stared into the darkness. He knew that Bartholomew would live now, so long as he rested and regained his strength.

Bartholomew coughed in his sleep, and Gray raised himself on one elbow to peer over at him. He believed he had taken no risk in tending Bartholomew, for he was one of the plague's first victims in Cambridge and had survived. He did not think he would catch the disease a second time, and had been making a good deal of money by offering to tend plague victims in the houses of rich merchants. But that was nothing compared to what he may have earned by nursing Bartholomew. He had heard about Bartholomew's methods and ideas, and had longed to study with him when he was an undergraduate, but the physician already had as many students as he could manage.

Gray knew exactly what he wanted from life. He intended to become an excellent physician and have a large number of very wealthy patients. Perhaps he might even become the private physician of some nobleman. Regardless, he intended to find himself a position that would bring him wealth and enough free time to be able to enjoy it. He knew Bartholomew worked among the poor, but to Gray that meant he would gain far more experience of diseases than from a physician who tended the rich. He would be happy to work among the poor during his medical training, but then he would be off to make his fortune in York or Bristol, or perhaps even London.

Gray smiled to himself and lay back down, his arms behind his head. He and Cynric had been caring for Bartholomew continuously for five days and nights, and several times had thought their labours were in vain. Brother Michael had actually given Bartholomew last rites before the fever suddenly broke.

Once Bartholomew had slept almost twenty-four hours without waking, his recovery was rapid. He was out of his bed and taking his first unsteady steps around the College yard within a day, and felt ready to begin his work again within three days. Michael, Cynric, and Gray urged him to rest more, but Bartholomew insisted that tossing restlessly on his bed was more tiring than working. Bartholomew decided that all plague victims in the College should be in one room so that they could have constant attention. He set about converting the commoners' dormitory into a hospital ward, relocating the few surviving commoners elsewhere. Brother Michael's Benedictine room-mates willingly offered their services, and Bartholomew hoped that this arrangement might reduce the risks to others.

As soon as he could, Bartholomew went to see Gregory Colet. As he walked through the wet streets to Rudde's Hostel, he was shocked at the piles of rubbish and dead animals that littered them. There were three bodies, crudely wrapped in filthy rags, at the doors of St Michael's Church that Bartholomew judged to have been there for several days. Around them, several rats lay dead and dying, some half-buried in mud and refuse.

Brother Michael walked beside him, his cowl

pulled over his head in an attempt to mask the stench.

'What has happened here, Michael?' said Bartholomew in disbelief. He watched a ragged band of children playing on a huge pile of kitchen waste outside Garret Hostel, occasionally stopping to eat some morsel that they considered edible. On the opposite side of the street, two large pigs rooted happily among a similar pile of rubbish. He shook his head in despair at the filth and disorder.

Michael shrugged. 'There is no one left to do anything. Now that Colet has given up, you and Robin of Grantchester are the only medics here. All the others are dead or gone.'

'What about the priests? Can they not see that the streets need to be cleared and the bodies removed?'

Michael laughed without humour. 'We are in the business of saving souls,' he said, 'not bodies. And anyway, so many clerics have died that there are barely enough to give last rites. Did you know that there are only three Dominicans left here?'

Bartholomew gazed at him in shock. The large community of Dominicans had continued to work among the poor after the outbreak of the plague, and it seemed that their adherence to their way of life may have brought about their virtual demise.

Gregory Colet was not in his room at Rudde's, and the porter told them that he would be in one of the churches, usually St Botolph's. Bartholomew had always admired St Botolph's, with its slate-grey stone and windows faced with cream ashlar, but as Michael pushed open the great oak door and led the way inside it felt damp and cold. The stained glass that he had coveted for St Michael's Church no longer seemed to imbue it with soft colour, but served to make it dismal. The feeling of gloom was further enhanced by the sound of muted chanting. Candles were lit in the sanctuary and half a dozen monks and friars from various Orders knelt in a row at the altar. Colet sat to one side, his back against a pillar and his eyes fixed on the twinkling candles. One of the monks saw Bartholomew and Michael and came down the aisle to meet them.

Michael introduced him to Bartholomew as Brother Dunstan of Ely. Dunstan expressed pleasure to see Bartholomew well again.

'God knows we need you now,' he said, his eyes straying to Colet.

'What is wrong with him?' Bartholomew asked.

Dunstan tapped his temple. 'His mind has gone. He heard that Roper had died and that you had the sickness, and he gave up. He sits here, or in one of the other churches, all day and only goes home to sleep. I think he may be willing himself to die.'

Michael crossed himself quickly while Bartholomew looked at Dunstan in horror.

'No! Not when there are so many others that are being taken who want to live!'

Dunstan sighed. 'It is only what I think. Now I must go. We have so many masses to say for the dead, so much to do . . .'

Michael followed Dunstan to the altar rail, leaving Bartholomew looking at Colet, still gazing at the candles with vacant eyes. Bartholomew knelt down and touched Colet on the shoulder. Reluctantly Colet tore his eyes from the candles to his friend. He gave the faintest glimmer of a smile.

'Matt! You have escaped the Death!'

He began to look back towards the candles again, and Bartholomew gripped his shoulder.

'What is wrong, Gregory? I need your help.'

Colet shook his head. 'It is too late. You and I can do no more.' He became agitated. 'Give it up, Matthew, and go to the country. Cambridge will be a dead town soon.'

'No!' said Bartholomew vehemently. 'It is far from over. People have recovered and others have escaped infection. You cannot give up on them. They need you and so do I!'

Colet shook Bartholomew's hand away, his agitation quickly disappearing into a lethargic gloom. 'I can do no more,' he said, his voice barely audible.

'You must!' pleaded Bartholomew. 'The streets are filthy, and the bodies of the dead have not been collected in days. I cannot do it all alone, Gregory. Please!'

Colet's dull eyes looked blankly at Bartholomew before he turned away to look at the candles. 'Give it up,' he whispered. 'It is over.'

Bartholomew sat for a moment, overwhelmed by the task he now faced alone. Robin of Grantchester might help, but he would do nothing without being paid and Bartholomew had very little money to give him. He glanced up and saw Michael and Dunstan watching him.

'You can do nothing here,' said Dunstan softly, looking at Colet with pity. 'It is best you leave him be.'

Depressed at Colet's state of mind, Bartholomew ate a dreary meal in Michaelhouse's chilly hall, and then went to visit the building where Stanmore had his business.

Stephen greeted Bartholomew warmly, looking so like his older brother that Bartholomew almost mistook him. Bartholomew was urged inside and made to sit near a roaring fire while Stephen's wife prepared some spiced wine. Stephen reassured him that everyone was well at Trumpington, but there was a reservation in his voice that made Bartholomew uneasy.

'Are you sure everyone is well?' he persisted.

'Yes, yes, Matthew. Do not worry,' he said, swirling the wine in his cup, and assiduously refusing to look Bartholomew in the eye.

Bartholomew leaned over and gripped his wrist. 'Has anyone there had the plague? Did it come with Philippa?'

Stephen sighed. 'They told me not to tell you, because they did not want you to go rushing over there before you were well enough. Yes. The plague struck after you brought Philippa. She became ill before you were scarcely gone from the house. Then Edith was stricken, and three of the servants. The servants died, but Philippa and Edith recovered,' he said quickly as Bartholomew leapt to his feet. 'Sit down again and listen. They were not ill as long as you. They got those revolting swellings like everyone else, but they also got black spots over their bodies.'

He paused, and Bartholomew felt his heart sink. 'They are well now,' Stephen said again, 'but . . .' His voice trailed off.

'But what?' said Bartholomew. His voice was calm and steady, but he had to push his hands into the folds of his robe so that Stephen would not see them shaking.

'The spots on Edith healed well enough, but Mistress Philippa has scars.'

Bartholomew leaned back in his chair. Was that it? He looked perplexed, and Stephen tried to explain.

'There are scars on her face. She will not let anyone see them, and she refuses to speak to anyone. She wears a veil all the time, and they have to leave her food outside the door . . . where are you going?'

Bartholomew was already at the door, drawing his hood over his head. 'Can I borrow a horse?' he said.

Stephen grabbed his arm. 'This is difficult for me to say, Matt, but she specifically asked that you not be allowed to see her. She does not want to see anyone.'

Bartholomew shook him off. 'I am a physician. There may be something I can do.'

Stephen grabbed him again. 'She does not want you to go, Matt. She left a note saying that you were not to come. No one has seen her for the past week. Leave her. In time she will come round.'

'Can I borrow a horse?' Bartholomew asked again.

'No,' said Stephen, maintaining his grip.

'Then I will walk,' said Bartholomew, pushing him away and striding out into the yard. Stephen sighed, and shouted for an apprentice to saddle up his mare. Bartholomew waited in silence, while Stephen chattered nervously. 'Richard is back,' he said. Bartholomew relented a little, and smiled at Stephen.

'Thank God,' he said softly. 'Edith must be so happy.'

'As a monk in a brothel!' said Stephen grinning. The apprentice walked the horse over and Bartholomew swung himself up into the saddle. Stephen darted into his house and returned with a long blue cloak. 'Wear this, or you will freeze.'

Bartholomew accepted it gratefully. He leaned down

to touch Stephen lightly on the shoulder, and was gone, kicking the horse into a canter that was far from safe on the narrow streets.

Once out of the town, he had to slow down out of consideration for Stephen's horse. The road to Trumpington had been well travelled, and the snow had been churned into a deep slush. The weather was warmer than it had been before Christmas, and the frozen mud had thawed into a mass of cold, oozing sludge. The horse slipped and skidded, and had to be urged forward constantly. Bartholomew was beginning to think he would have to lead it, when the path became wider, and he was able to pick his way around the larger morasses.

He tried not to think about what he might encounter when he reached Edith's house. He thought, instead, of Gray's amazement when he discovered that Bartholomew did not own a horse. He wondered, not for the first time since his recovery, whether Gray was the kind of person he wanted to teach.

Bartholomew knew that he owed Gray his life. It was doubtful whether Bartholomew would have recovered without Gray's clumsy surgery and constant care. The student had taken quite a risk in lancing the swellings himself; he had not done it before, and had only seen Master Roper do it once. Bartholomew would bear the scars of Gray's inexperience for the rest of his life.

But Bartholomew remained unsure of Gray. He did not like the fact that it had been Gray who had been sent to bring him to meet Philippa, and did not like the feeling of being in debt to the flippant young man. In fact, he did not like Gray. He was confident to the point of arrogance, and was perpetually estimating how much each patient should pay as opposed to how much Bartholomew charged. Bartholomew's charges usually fell short of the cost of the medicines, and he was constantly aware of Gray's disapproving presence in the background. It was like having Wilson with him.

At last he reached the village and Edith's house. Richard came racing out to meet him, and Bartholomew was almost knocked off his feet with the force of the embrace. Richard was only seventeen, but was already almost as tall as Bartholomew. Richard chattered on in his excitement, forgetting the dignity, as befitting an under-graduate at Oxford, that he had been trying to cultivate. Bartholomew listened, Richard's descriptions bringing back vivid memories of his own time in Oxford.

Edith hurried out from the kitchen, wiping her hands on her apron before giving him a hug, and Stanmore came to slap him on the shoulders.

'Matt, you look thin and pale,' Edith said, holding him at arm's length. She hugged him again. 'It was horrible,' she whispered, so that only he could hear. 'We heard you were ill, and there was nothing we could do. I was so afraid for you.'

'Well, I am fine now. But you have been ill, too?'

Edith waved a hand dismissively. 'A couple of days in bed, that is all. But you should not have come.' Her face grew fearful, and she clung onto his arm. 'We told Stephen not to tell you,' she said.

'My lord, Matt! What on earth have you been doing with Stephen's horse?' Stanmore, for whom horses were a passion, was looking in horror at the bedraggled, mud-spattered mare.

Bartholomew groaned. He had not realised what a

state the horse was in. 'Stephen will have my hide. Can you clean it up?'

Richard went off with the stable boy to supervise, and Bartholomew followed his sister and her husband into the house. Once away from Richard, all three grew serious. Edith explained how she had gone to check on Philippa immediately after Bartholomew had left, and had found her feverish. Edith had become ill the same night, and the three servants by the following day. The fever had not seemed as intense as that of some of the plague victims, but had included a rash of black spots. Edith showed Bartholomew some faint pink marks on her arm.

Philippa's spots had been mainly on her face. She had asked Edith for a veil, and since then had locked herself in her room. That had been seven days before. Edith had spent many hours trying to get her to unlock the door, but she had eventually refused even to speak.

Bartholomew stood. 'She will not see you, Matt,' said Edith. 'She left a note that you specifically should not come to see her. Poor girl. I cannot imagine that she can be so badly scarred.'

Neither could Bartholomew. At least, not so badly scarred that he would not still want her. He thought of Colet. What terrible things this pestilence was doing to people's minds. He gave his sister the faintest of smiles before making his way up the stairs to Philippa's room. Edith did not try to stop him; she knew him too well. At the back of her mind lingered the hope that the sound of his voice might serve to pull Philippa out of her depression.

He stood outside the door for a few moments before

knocking. There was a rustle from inside the room, and then silence.

'Philippa?' he called softly. 'It is Matthew. Please open the door. There is no cause to be afraid.'

There was silence. He knocked again.

'Philippa. If you open the door and talk to me, I promise I will not try to touch you or look at you,' he called. 'Just give me a few moments with you.'

There was nothing. Bartholomew sat on the chest that was in the hallway and reflected. He would not have normally considered invading someone's privacy, but he wondered whether Philippa's mind, somehow affected by her illness, might mean that she was unable to look after herself properly. If this were the case, then she needed help, even though she might not know it herself.

Edith had married Stanmore when she was eighteen, and had come to live in Trumpington. Bartholomew had been eight, and whenever he had been permitted out of the abbey school in Peterborough, he had come to stay in Edith's rambling house. He knew every nook and cranny, and also knew that the lock on the door, behind which Philippa hid, was faulty. He knew that a sharp stick in the right place would open the door in an instant because he had played with the lock on many a wet afternoon as a boy.

He decided to try once more. 'Philippa. Why will you not answer me? Just let me talk to you for a few moments, and I promise to leave when you ask.'

There was no sound at all, not even a rustle. Bartholomew was worried, and was sure that there must be more wrong with her than a few scars. He took a sharpened piece of metal that was part of his medical equipment, and pushed it into the lock the way he had done so many years before with a stick. He had not lost his touch, and the door sprung open with ease.

Philippa jumped violently as he took a step towards her, and Bartholomew stopped. She huddled on the bed, swathed in the cloak he had given her when they had walked from the convent to Trumpington. It was still spotted with mud. Her face was turned towards him, but was covered by a long piece of gauze so that he could not make out any features. She was crouched over like an old hag, a piece of embroidery on her lap.

Bartholomew felt his breath catch as he looked at the embroidery. Philippa hated sewing and would do almost anything to avoid it. She most certainly would not be doing it voluntarily. He looked at her more closely. Her posture was wrong: something in the way she held herself was not right, and her feet were bigger than Bartholomew remembered.

'I asked you not to come.' The voice was the merest whisper, intended to deceive.

'Who are you? Where is Philippa?' Bartholomew demanded. Her head came up with a jerk when she realised she was found out, and Bartholomew caught the glint of eyes under the thick veil. He stepped forward to pull the veil off, but stopped short as she threw the embroidery from her lap and pointed a crossbow at his chest. Bartholomew took a step back. How ironic, he thought, to escape the plague and to die from a crossbow bolt.

The figure beckoned Bartholomew forward, waving the crossbow in a menacing gesture when he did not move.

'Who are you?' Bartholomew asked again. He wondered whether he would die before he found out, and whether the woman would have the courage to shoot him as he stood there.

'No questions, and turn around slowly,' she said in her dreadful whisper.

'Where is Philippa?' Bartholomew demanded, his concern making him desperate.

'One more question, and I will shoot you. Turn round.'

The whisper held a menace that was chilling, and Bartholomew had no doubt that this was not an idle threat. He turned round slowly, knowing what was coming next, and bracing himself for it.

He was not wrong. There was a sudden rustle of clothes and the crossbow came crashing down, aimed at his head. He half turned and was able to escape the full force of the blow, although it stunned him for vital seconds. The woman shot out of the door and tore down the stairs. Bartholomew staggered to his feet and lurched after her. She tore across the courtyard to where Richard was talking to the stable-boy, with Stephen's horse now clean and still saddled. Bartholomew could see what was going to happen.

'Stop her!' he yelled. He was too far behind to catch her, and ran instead towards the great oak gate, intending to close it so that she would not be able to escape.

Richard and the stable-boy gaped at the spectacle of Philippa racing across the yard clutching a crossbow, and Richard only pulled himself together at the last minute. He lunged at the would-be rider.

Meanwhile, Bartholomew was hauling at the gate with all his might. Stanmore seldom closed his gate by the look of the weeds that climbed about it, and it was stuck fast. He saw Richard hurled to the ground as the woman reached the horse. She was mounted in an instant, and wrenched the reins away from the stable-boy in a great heave that all but pulled the lad's arms out of their sockets. Bartholomew felt the gate budge, and heaved at it with every ounce of his strength. The woman wheeled the horse around, trying to control its frenzied rearing and aim it for the closing gate.

Bartholomew felt the gate move again, and was aware of blood pounding in his temples. The woman brought the horse under control, and began to urge it towards the gate. Bartholomew felt the gate shift another inch, but then he knew it would not be enough. The horse's iron-shod hooves clattered on the cobbled yard as it headed towards the gate.

Bartholomew suspended his efforts as the horse came thundering down on him. He made a futile attempt to grab at the rider, but was knocked from his feet into a pile of wet straw. The rider swayed slightly, and, as she glanced back, the wind lifted the veil, giving Bartholomew a clear view of her face. Richard shot through the gate after her, and raced down the track before realising a chase was hopeless. The rider turned the corner and was gone from sight.

'After her!' Stanmore cried, and his yard became a hive of activity as horses were saddled and reliable men hastily picked for pursuit. Bartholomew knew that by the time Stanmore was ready, their quarry would be long gone. Still, it was always possible that the horse might stumble and throw its rider, especially that miserable horse, he thought. Edith hurried up to him as he picked himself up.

'What happened? What did you say to her?' she cried.

'Are you all right, Uncle Matt? I am sorry. He was just too strong for me.' Richard looked forlorn at having failed. Bartholomew put a hand on his shoulder.

'For me too,' he said with a resigned smile.

Edith looked from one to the other. 'What are you saying?' she said. '*He?*'

Bartholomew looked at Richard. 'Did you see his face?' he asked.

Richard nodded. 'Yes, but why was he here? Where is Philippa?'

'Who was it, if not Philippa?' asked Edith, perplexed.

'Giles Abigny,' said Bartholomew and Richard together.

VII

BARTHOLOMEW LOOKED OUT OF THE WINDOW FOR at least the tenth time since Stanmore and his men had set off in pursuit of Abigny.

'Perhaps it was Giles all along, and you just thought it was Philippa you met outside the convent,' Richard said to him.

'I kissed her,' said Bartholomew. Seeing his nephew's eyebrows shoot up, he quickly added, 'And it *was* Philippa, believe me.'

Richard persisted in his theory. 'But you could have been mistaken, if you were tired, and . . .'

'Giles has a beard,' said Bartholomew, more patiently than he felt. 'Believe me, Richard, I would have noticed the difference.'

'Well, what do *you* think is going on?' demanded Richard. 'I have been sitting here racking my brain for answers, and all you have done is tell me they are wrong.'

'I do not know,' said Bartholomew, turning to stare into the fire. He saw Richard watching him and tried to pull himself together. He asked his nephew to tell him everything that had happened since he had left Philippa with the Stanmores ten days ago, partly to try to involve

Richard and partly to make sure that the sequence of events was clear in his own mind.

Philippa had become ill almost as soon as he had left, and either Edith or one of the servants had been with her through the two nights of her fever. On the morning of the third day, she seemed to have recovered, although she was, of course, exhausted. In the evening, she had asked for a veil and had closed her door to visitors, communicating by notes the day after that. Edith had not kept any of them, and so Bartholomew was unable to see whether the writing had been Philippa's or her brother's. No one could prove whether it had been Philippa or Giles who had been living in Edith's house for at least the last seven days.

Richard, with an adolescent's unabashed curiosity, had crouched behind the chest in the hallway to glimpse her as she emerged to collect the trays of food that had been left. Even with hindsight, he was unable to say whether the person who came from the room, heavily swathed in cloak and veil, was man or woman.

Bartholomew considered Richard's recital of events. What could be happening? Giles had behaved oddly ever since the death of Hugh Stapleton. Had he completely lost his mind and embarked on some fiendish plot to deprive Philippa of potential happiness because he had lost his? Had he secreted her away somewhere, either because he thought she would be safer with him, or because he meant her harm?

Richard and Bartholomew made a careful search of the garret room, but found nothing to provide them with clues to solve the mystery. There were some articles of clothing that Edith had lent her, and the embroidery, but virtually nothing else. The room had its own privy that emptied directly into the moat, but there was nothing to indicate how long Giles had been pretending to be Philippa.

Bartholomew thought carefully. There was not the slightest chance that Abigny would return to College if he thought Bartholomew might be there. He would hide elsewhere, so Bartholomew would need to visit all Abigny's old haunts – a daunting task given his dissolute lifestyle. Abigny had a good many friends and acquaintances, and was known in virtually every tavern in Cambridge, despite the fact that scholars were not permitted to frequent such places. Bartholomew grimaced. The company Abigny kept was not the kind he relished himself – whores and the rowdier elements of the town. Gray would probably know most of these places, Bartholomew thought uncharitably; after all, he had mentioned he knew Abigny.

A clatter in the yard brought Bartholomew to his feet again. Richard darted out of the door to meet his father, with Bartholomew and Edith close on his heels.

'Got clean away,' said Stanmore in disgust. 'We met a pardoner who had been on the road from Great Chesterford. He said he saw a grey mare and rider going like the Devil down towards the London road. We followed for several miles, but he will be well away by now. Even if the horse goes lame or tires, he will be able to hire another on the road. Sorry, Matt. He has gone.'

Bartholomew had expected as much, but was disappointed nevertheless. He clapped Stanmore on the shoulder. 'Thank you for trying anyway,' he said.

'Poor Stephen,' said Stanmore, handing his horse over to the stable-boy. 'He was attached to that mare.

And his best cloak gone with it! I suppose I must lend him one of mine until he can have another made.'

Bartholomew walked slowly back into the house. Stanmore was right. Given such a good start, Abigny was safely away. If he hired a fresh horse, reverted to another disguise, and joined a group of travellers as was the custom, it would be unlikely that Bartholomew would ever trace him. London was a huge sprawl of buildings and people, and it would be like looking for a needle in a haystack.

Edith put her hand on his arm. 'There is nothing you can do now,' she said. 'Stay here tonight, and Oswald will ride into town with you tomorrow.'

Bartholomew shook his head, trying not to compare Edith's warm and comfortable house with his chilly room at Michaelhouse. 'I must get back tonight. Colet has lost his mind, and there is much still to be done.'

'Then at least drink some warmed wine before you go,' said Stanmore. Before Bartholomew could object, Stanmore had taken his arm and was leading him up the flagged stairs to the solar. Richard followed. A fire burned steadily in the hearth, and the woollen rugs scattered on the floor muffled their footsteps. A sudden gust of wind rattled the shutters, and Bartholomew shivered.

'You will need help with the town,' said Stanmore. 'Stay here tonight and we will discuss what must be done.'

Bartholomew smiled at his brother-in-law's guile. They all knew he had overstretched himself on his first real day out. He would have been most disapproving had a patient done the same thing, and Edith was correct in that there was nothing he could do to help Philippa that night. He sat on a stool near the fire and picked up a stick to poke at the flames. Richard drew up a stool next to him, and Stanmore settled himself in a large oak chair covered in cushions and furs. For a while, no one spoke.

'How has Trumpington fared with the plague?' asked Bartholomew eventually, stretching outspread hands towards the fire.

'Twenty-three dead,' replied Stanmore, 'and another two likely to follow. Our priest died on Sunday, and one of the Gilbertine Canons is staying here until a replacement can be found.' He shook his head wearily. 'What is happening, Matt? The priests say this is a visitation from God, but they are dying just like those they accuse of sinning. The physicians can do nothing. I sent for Gregory Colet when Edith and Philippa became ill, since you, too, were stricken. He told me to put hot tongs in their mouths to draw the demons out. When I asked him to do it, because I was so concerned for Edith I would have tried anything, he refused because he said he was afraid the demon would enter him. What kind of medicine is that?'

Bartholomew stared into the fire. 'Colet has lost his mind. I suppose seeing so many die must have been too much for him to bear.'

'Colet?' exclaimed Richard in disbelief. 'Surely not! He always seemed so . . . cynical.'

'Perhaps that is why he has become so afflicted,' said Bartholomew glumly. 'I cannot understand it. And I do not understand the plague. Agatha walks among the victims daily and is fit and well; Francis Eltham and Henri d'Evéne hid themselves away and were taken. The old and sick cling to life, while the young and healthy die within hours. Some recover, some do not.'

'Then perhaps the priests are right,' said Stanmore. 'But why do they die too? Take Aelfrith. I heard he is dead, and he was as saintly a man as you could hope to meet.'

'The plague did not take him,' said Bartholomew, and then could have kicked himself for his thoughtless indiscretion. He drew breath to make amends, but it was too late.

'What do you mean?' asked Stanmore. 'Michael said the Death took him.'

Bartholomew hesitated. It would be a relief to tell Stanmore all he knew – about Sir John, Aelfrith, Augustus, Paul, and Montfitchet, and about the plot to suppress Cambridge University. But men had been killed, and it was likely that others would follow: the plague had not prevented Aelfrith from being murdered. Bartholomew could not risk Stanmore's safety merely to satisfy his own longing for someone with whom to share his thoughts. Edith entered the solar with a servant who carried a jug of steaming wine. She stood next to her husband, and Bartholomew's resolve strengthened. He had no right to put Stanmore's life or Edith's happiness at stake. After all, he had already lost five friends and colleagues to murder, many more to the plague, Colet to madness, and Giles and possibly Philippa to something he did not yet understand. There was only his family left. He changed the subject, asking Stanmore about his ideas for dealing with the plague in the town.

By the time Stanmore had finished outlining his plans for clearing the town of the plague dead, the day was too far advanced for Bartholomew to think of returning to Michaelhouse – as Stanmore had known it would be. Bartholomew spent the night in the solar, wrapped in thick, warm blankets, enjoying the rare luxury of the fire.

Bartholomew rose early the next day feeling much stronger. He rode into Cambridge with Stanmore, who offered to break the news of the stolen horse to Stephen. Bartholomew dismounted at St Botolph's and went to see Colet. He had to step over two bodies that had been dumped next to the door to await collection by the plague-cart. He buried his nose and mouth in his cloak against the smell and slipped into the dim church.

The monks were still there, different ones than last time, praying in a continuous vigil for deliverance from the plague and saying masses for the dead. Colet was there too. He sat on a bench wrapped in a blanket to protect himself from the damp chill of the church and playing idly with a carved golden lion that he wore on a long chain around his neck.

'Look at this, Matt,' he said, turning his face with its vacant grin to Bartholomew. 'Is it not pretty? It will protect me from the plague.'

Bartholomew sat beside him, and looked at the carving. He had seen others wearing similar icons, and had heard from Agatha that some rogue had been selling them in the town, claiming that anyone who wore one would be protected from the pestilence.

'It will not work, Gregory,' he said. 'We need to clean up the streets and bury the dead more quickly.'

Colet stared at him, and a thin drool of saliva slipped from his mouth onto the blanket. 'We should not do that. It is God's pestilence, and we should not try to fight His will by trying to reduce its effects.'

Bartholomew looked at him, aghast. 'Where on earth did you conceive that notion? You cannot believe that any more than I do.'

'But it is true, it is true,' Colet sang to himself, rocking back and forth.

'In that case,' Bartholomew said sharply, 'why are you hanging on to that ridiculous lion?'

He immediately regretted his words. Colet stopped rocking and began to cry. Bartholomew grabbed him firmly by the shoulders. 'Help me! I cannot do it all alone. Have you seen the streets? There are piles of rubbish everywhere, and the dead have not been collected in days.'

Colet snuffled into his blanket. 'If you stay with me, I will lend you my lion.'

Bartholomew closed his eyes and leaned back against the wall. Poor Colet. He had been one of the best physicians in Cambridge, and was now reduced to little more than a drooling idiot. He had acquired a large practice of rich patients, including some of the most influential men in the town, as well as teaching at Rudde's Hostel. Because of this, he was wealthy and had the ears of many powerful men. In short, he was at the beginning of what would have been a brilliant career.

Bartholomew made one last try. 'Come with me today. Help me with the sick.'

Colet shrank backwards against the pillar, fear stark on his face. 'No, Master Roper, I cannot go out there with you. I have heard there are people with the plague!' He began to twist the lion through his fingers again, staring unseeingly at the row of kneeling monks. He seemed to have forgotten Bartholomew was there at all.

*　　*　　*

Bartholomew went back to Michaelhouse. After a moment's hesitation, he opened the chest where Abigny kept his belongings and rummaged around. Nothing appeared to have gone: Abigny, it seemed, had not intended to flee Michaelhouse. Bartholomew stood for a moment looking out over the yard as he thought about what he should do first. His instinct told him to drop everything and go to the taverns and hostels in search of news of Abigny. Reluctantly, he put that aside; his first duty was to organise collection of the bodies and cleaning of the streets.

Stanmore had said already that he would put out a general message that good wages would be paid to anyone willing to rid the streets of rubbish. Since there were a number of people without employment because their masters had died, he anticipated that there would not be too much of a problem in attracting applicants. Even if it did not prevent the spread of the plague, it would reduce the spread of other, equally fatal, diseases.

Bartholomew's task was to arrange a better system of collecting the dead. Since he had been ill, the number of deaths seemed to have levelled off somewhat, although this did not mean that the plague had lessened its grip on the town. He walked to the Castle to see the Sheriff, who, pale-faced and grieving for his wife, was pliable to Bartholomew's demands. Bartholomew wondered if his mind had gone the same way as Colet's. He left the Sheriff morosely polishing his helmet and repeated his instructions to an able-looking sergeant-at-arms. The sergeant gave a hearty sigh.

'We cannot collect the dead,' he said. 'We have lost a third of the men already, and we do not have enough to patrol the town for these bloody robbers, let alone for collecting bodies. We cannot help you. Did you know that everyone in the little settlement near All Saints-next-the-Castle is dead? Not a soul has survived. The men are terrified of the place and believe that it is full of ghosts. Even if I did have the men to help, they would probably rather hang than collect the dead.'

Bartholomew left feeling depressed. He went to the settlement the sergeant had told him about and wandered through the pathetic little shacks that had been people's homes. The sergeant was right: there was not a living soul in the community. He left quickly, gagging on the smell of putrefaction.

There were more bodies in Bridge Street, although the area around St John's Hospital was relatively clean thanks to the Austin Canons. Bartholomew talked to the Canons and they agreed, albeit reluctantly, to pick up bodies they saw on the way to the plague pits when they took their own dead there. He walked on to St Edmund's Priory and obtained a similar agreement there, along with the promise of a lay-brother to supervise the filling of the plague pits.

Bartholomew's plans to keep the town free from plague-ridden bodies were beginning to come together. He still needed volunteers to drive the carts each day and collect up the piles of dead. He knew the risk of infection was great, but it was a job that had to be done.

He stood looking at the plague pit that he and Colet had organised almost two weeks before. It was so full that there was scarcely room to add the quicklime over the last layer of corpses, let alone cover it with earth afterwards. He shivered. It was a desolate spot, even though it lay only a short distance from the town gates. The wind seemed colder near the pit, and whistled softly through the scrubby trees and bushes that partially shielded it from the road. He went to a nearby tavern and offered to buy ale for any who would help him dig a new pit. At first, there was no response. Then a man stood, and said he would buy ale for any who could dig faster or deeper than he could. This met with catcalls and hoots, but the man strode out of the tavern rolling up his sleeves, and others followed.

In a short time, a new pit was dug, larger than the previous one and about twice as deep. Men competed with each other to show off their strength while, more sedately, women and even small children helped, ferrying stones from the pit to the ever-growing pile of earth to one side. Bartholomew took his turn in digging and heaving great stones out of the way. During a brief respite, Bartholomew went to speak to the man who had instigated the competitive spirit.

'Thank you, Master Blacksmith,' he said. 'I thought I might have to dig it alone.'

The blacksmith grinned, revealing the yellow-black teeth that Bartholomew remembered from the night of the riot. 'It will cost you in ale,' he said.

When the new pit had been dug, Bartholomew's helpers began to drift away. He handed over all the money he had to buy the promised ale and was pleasantly surprised to receive half of it back again with mutters that it was too much. He shovelled lime into the pit, and watched as it bubbled and seethed in the water at the bottom. The blacksmith helped him bury the first bodies, a pathetic line of ten crudely-wrapped shapes. Bartholomew covered them with more lime, and leaned on the spade wiping the sweat from his eyes.

The blacksmith came to stand beside him. 'I am

sorry,' he said, and pushed something into Bartholomew's hand. Bartholomew, bewildered, looked at the greasy black purse in his hand, and then back at the blacksmith. Abruptly the blacksmith turned away and began to walk back to the tavern. Bartholomew caught up with him, and swung him round.

'What is this?'

The blacksmith refused to meet Bartholomew's eyes. 'I did not want to do it. I told them it was wrong,' he mumbled, trying to head for the tavern. Bartholomew held him fast.

'What was wrong? What are you talking about? I do not want your money.'

The blacksmith looked up at the low clouds scudding overhead in the growing dusk. 'It is the money I got for the riot,' he said. 'I kept it all this time. I only spent enough to get some of my lads drunk enough to be brave on the night, and some to bury Mistress Atkin's son. It is Judas money and I do not want it.'

Bartholomew shook his head in bewilderment. 'What are you talking about?' he said. 'Did someone pay you to start the riot?'

The blacksmith looked Bartholomew full in the face, his eyes round. 'Yes, they paid me to get some of the lads excited. You know how it was that day – that pompous bastard throwing his wealth around while us poor folk stood and watched and waited for scraps like dogs.' He spat on the ground. 'They seemed to know how it would be, and they paid me to make sure there was a fight. Once the fight was started, I was to find you and warn you off.'

He paused, and searched Bartholomew's face, earnestly looking for some reaction to his confession.

Bartholomew thought back to the riot, of his last-minute dash into the College with the enraged mob behind him, and of Abigny telling him that Henry Oliver had ordered Francis Eltham to lock him out. Surely the whole thing had not been staged to get at him? Bartholomew shook his head in disbelief. What could he have done that people wanted him dead? He racked his brain for patients who might have died in his care, wondering whether his unorthodox treatment might have seemed to have killed when leeches might have saved, but he could think of none. Unbidden, Sir John's benign face came into his mind. But what had Sir John done, or Augustus and Aelfrith, to warrant their murders? He recalled Henry Oliver's looks of hatred at him since the riot every time they inadvertently met.

The blacksmith, watching Bartholomew's brows drawn down in thought, continued. 'It seemed like an easy way to earn some decent money at first, and trade had been poor, with the threat of the Death coming. I did a good job, getting people roused up against Michaelhouse. But it went wrong. It all got out of control before I could do anything, and the two lads died. Then you helped Rachel Atkin, and you set my leg. I have felt wrong ever since, which is why I have not spent the money. My broken leg was God's judgement on me for my actions. The men who gave me the money came to see me while my leg was mending, and I told them that I had warned you as they asked, just to get them out of my house.'

'Get who out?' asked Bartholomew, the whole mess slowly revolving in his mind, a confused jumble.

The blacksmith shook his head. 'I wish I knew, because I would tell you. These are evil men, and

I would wish you to be on your guard against them.'

'Where did they approach you?'

The blacksmith nodded over to the tavern. 'In there. I was having a quiet drink, and I got a message telling me that if I went outside, I could be a rich man. I went, and there were two men. They told me to cause a bit of a fight on the day of old fatso's ceremony, and to get you alone and warn you off.'

'What exactly did they say?'

The blacksmith closed his eyes and screwed up his face as he sought to recall the exact words. 'They said that I should just say to you "stay away". Those were their very words!' he said triumphantly, pleased at his feat of memory.

'What were these people like?'

'I could not say. Only one spoke, but I do not recall his voice. He was quite big, about your size, I would say. The other was smaller, but both of them wore thick cloaks with hoods, and I could not see their faces.'

Bartholomew and the blacksmith stood side by side in the darkness for several moments before the blacksmith spoke again. 'If I knew who they were, I would tell you. The only thing I can think of, and it is not much, is that the purse they gave me is nice. See?'

Bartholomew took a few steps to where he could see the purse in the faint light from the tavern windows. The purse had been fine in its time, but weeks in the blacksmith's grubby hands had begrimed its soft leather and all but worn away the insignia sewn in gold on the side. Bartholomew examined it more closely, turning it this way and that to try to make the gold thread catch the light. As he did so, the insignia suddenly stood out clearly. 'BH' – the initials of Bene't Hostel! He had seen Hugh Stapleton with a purse almost identical when he had been out with Abigny once.

He tipped the money out of the purse into his hand. About five marks, an enormous sum of money for a blacksmith. He turned round again. 'You keep this,' he said, pushing the money towards the blacksmith and slipping the empty purse into his belt. 'What is done is done. Thank you for telling me all this. I had no idea that I had such powerful enemies.'

The blacksmith gave a short laugh devoid of humour. 'Oh, they are powerful right enough. I could tell that just by the way they spoke to me. They are people used to ordering others about.' He put a mud-stained hand on Bartholomew's shoulder. 'I wish I had told you this before, but you seemed to be doing well enough. I do not want the money, though. I might go to hell if I take it knowing what it was for – and these days, a man cannot be sure of getting the chance to confess before he is taken.' He looked in distaste at the silver coins in his rough hand.

Before Bartholomew could stop him, he flung them all in the direction of the pit. Bartholomew saw some of them glitter as they plunged into its steaming depths. The blacksmith smiled. 'It is all right now,' he said quietly. 'The blood money is where it belongs.'

Bartholomew offered his thanks again, and made for home. He hoped that all the coins had disappeared into the quicklime. He did not want to think of people climbing into the pit to fetch them out.

He walked slowly, breathing in the cold night air in an attempt to clear his reeling mind. He was wholly confused. Someone had tried to warn him to stay away the same night that Augustus, Paul, and Montfitchet were murdered. But stay away from what? Had it been Hugh Stapleton who had issued the warning? Were there others with Bene't Hostel purses? Was it Abigny who had hired the blacksmith, since he was so often at Bene't Hostel and was apparently involved in something that had led him to pretend to be Philippa? But Michael had witnessed that it had been Abigny who had kept Francis Eltham from closing the gates until Bartholomew was safely inside. Gray had been at Bene't's too. Was he involved? It did not make sense. He wished Sir John or Aelfrith were alive so that he could tell them the whole insane muddle and they could help him to sort it out. He had already decided not to confide in his family, but who else could he trust? Michael? Bartholomew did not understand the monk's role in the death of Augustus, nor his position in the wretched Oxford plot. Abigny was clearly involved and, anyway, he had fled. The loathing he felt for Wilson was mutual, and how could he trust a man who skulked in his room and left the College to its own devices when it needed a strong Master? He considered the Chancellor and the Bishop, but what did he have to tell them? There was only his word that Aelfrith had been poisoned, and that Augustus had been dead when he disappeared. And the Chancellor and Bishop were unlikely to be impressed with him for producing the blacksmith as a witness, a self-confessed rabble-rouser and a man notorious for his drunkenness. With a heavy sigh, Bartholomew arrived at the same conclusion he had reached at Stanmore's house: that there was no one with whom he could speak, and he would have to reason through the muddle of facts alone.

Having reached St Michael's Church, he walked

across the churchyard and stood looking down at the pile of earth that marked Aelfrith's grave.

'Why?' he whispered into the night. 'I do not understand.'

He rethought the blacksmith's words as he crouched down in the long grass that grew over Aelfrith's mound. He had no reason to believe the man was lying. Were the mysterious men at the tavern ordering Bartholomew to stay away from Augustus? The blacksmith suggested that one of the men was educated and used to giving orders. Could it have been Wilson, suspecting that something might happen to Augustus and wishing to conceal the entire matter before it had occurred? He had certainly tried to hide the truth later.

Bartholomew stood, and stretched his aching limbs. It had been a long day, and the more he thought about it, the more loose ends there were and the murkier the matter became. He was tired and wanted to concentrate on finding Philippa. She might be in danger, and his feeble attempts at trying to unravel University business would not help her. Wearily he walked down the lane to Michaelhouse, intending to ask Gray to help him search the taverns for news of Abigny.

When he reached his room, there was no sign of Gray, and Bartholomew was uncertain how to begin questioning people in taverns. He knew that the wrong questions would not bring him the information he needed, and might even be dangerous. He heard a creak of floorboards in the room above, and an idea began forming in his mind. Philippa's disappearance was no secret, and it was only natural that he would want to find her. Why should he not enlist Michael's help for that? He would not need to reveal that he knew

anything of the alleged Oxford plot, only that he wished
to find Philippa.

Grateful that he had something positive to do, he
slipped out of his room and up the stairs to Michael's
chamber. He pushed open the door and saw that
Michael's bed was empty. The two Benedictines who
shared his room were sleeping, one of them twitching
as if disturbed by some nightmare. Disappointed, he
turned to leave.

As he closed the door, a scrap of parchment fluttered
to the floor from one of the high shelves, caught by a
sudden draught from the door downstairs. Bartholomew
picked it up, and strained to read the words in the
darkness. They were in Michael's bold, round hand,
the letters ill-formed and clumsy with haste. 'Seal must
still be in College. Will look with Wilson.'

Bartholomew stared at it. Michael had obviously
written this message and been unable to deliver it, or
had been disturbed while he was writing. Whatever the
reason, it proved beyond a shadow of a doubt that Michael
was embroiled in all this intrigue. Bartholomew felt his
hands shaking. Michael may have been the very one
who had paid the blacksmith to warn him away.

He gasped in shock as the note was snatched from
his hand. He had been so engrossed in his thoughts that
he had not heard Michael coming from the room opposite. He saw the monk's face in the gloom of the hallway.
It was contorted with rage, and he was controlling himself
with difficulty. Bartholomew could think of nothing to
say. He had not been prying in Michael's room, and had
not searched for the scrap of parchment, but there was
no reason for Michael to believe that.

Words would be meaningless now: what could be

said? Bartholomew pushed his way past Michael into the hallway. In the room opposite, he could hear the muffled voices of the three students that lived there. One of them must have become ill and called for help. Bartholomew poked his head round the door and saw the student writhing on his pallet bed, his room-mates staring at him fearfully in the light of a flickering tallow candle. Bartholomew felt the sick boy's head, and told the others to carry him to the commoners' dormitory.

He went back down the stairs to his own room and closed the door. His hands still shook from the fright he had had when Michael had snatched the note away. He should not be surprised by what he had learned, bearing in mind Michael's very odd behaviour on the night of Augustus's death. At the unpleasant interview with the Bishop, Michael had had no alibi for the night of the murders. Perhaps it was he who had struck down poor Paul and drugged the commoners after all.

So what should he do now? Should he tell Wilson? Or the Chancellor? But what could he tell them? He had not a single solid scrap of evidence to lay against Michael except the note, and that was doubtless a pile of ashes by now.

He froze as the door of his room swung slowly open and Brother Michael stood there holding a fluttering candle. The light threw strange shapes on the walls and made Michael look even larger than he was, as his voluminous robes swung about him. He stood in the doorway without saying a word for several moments. Bartholomew began to feel the first tendrils of fear uncoiling in his stomach.

Wordlessly, Michael closed the door, and advanced on Bartholomew, who stood, fists clenched, prepared for an attack. Michael gave an odd smile, and touched one of Bartholomew's hands with a soft, clammy finger. Bartholomew flinched and felt as though Michael must be able to hear his heart pounding in the silence of the room.

'I warned you to beware, Matthew,' he said in a low whisper that Bartholomew found unnerving.

Bartholomew swallowed. Was Michael's warning the one the blacksmith had been paid to give? Or was Michael merely referring to his words outside their staircase the night of Augustus's murder, and in the courtyard the following day?

'By prying you have put yourself in danger,' Michael continued in the same chilling tone.

'So what are you going to do?' Bartholomew was surprised at how calm his own voice sounded.

'What do you expect me to do?'

Bartholomew did not know how to answer this. He tried to get a grip on his fear. It was only Michael! The fat monk may have been bulkier and stronger, but Bartholomew was quicker and fitter, and since neither of them had a weapon, Bartholomew was sure he would be able to jump out the window before Michael could catch him. He decided an offensive stance might serve him to better advantage.

'What have you been meddling in?' he demanded. 'What have you done with Philippa?'

'Philippa?' Michael's sardonic face showed genuine astonishment. He regained his composure quickly. 'Now there, my friend, I have sinned only in my mind. The question is, what have *you* been meddling in?'

They stood facing each other, Bartholomew tensed

and ready to react should Michael make the slightest antagonistic move.

Suddenly the door flew open and Gray burst in, his face bright with excitement in the candlelight.

'Doctor Bartholomew! Thank God you are here! Brother Michael, too. You must come quickly. Something is going on in Master Wilson's room.'

He darted across the room, and grabbed Bartholomew by his sleeve to pull him out the door. Bartholomew and Michael had time to exchange glances, in which each reflected the other's confusion. They quickly followed Gray across the courtyard, and Brother Michael began to pant with the exertion.

'We will say no more of this,' he said in an undertone to Bartholomew. 'You will tell no one of what you read on the note, and I will tell no one that you read it.' He stopped and clutched Bartholomew's shirt. 'Do you agree, on your honour?'

Bartholomew felt as though his brain was going to explode, so fast were the questions pouring through it. 'Do you know anything about Philippa?' he asked. He watched Michael's flabby face wrinkle with annoyance at what he obviously perceived as an irrelevancy.

'I know nothing of her, nor of her wastrel brother,' he said. 'Do you swear?'

'I will swear, if you promise to me you know nothing of Philippa's disappearance, and if you hear anything, no matter how trivial it might seem, you will tell me.'

Gray bounded back to them. 'Come on! Hurry!' he cried.

'Oh, all right, I promise,' Michael said irritably. Bartholomew turned to go, but Michael held him fast. 'We are friends,' he said, 'and I have tried to keep you out of all this. You must forget what you saw, or your life and mine will be worth nothing.'

Bartholomew pushed the monk's sweaty hand away from his shirt. 'What dangerous games are you playing, Michael? If you live in such fear, why are you involved?'

'That is none of your business,' he hissed. 'Now swear!'

Bartholomew raised his hand in a mocking salute. 'I swear, o meddling monk,' he said sarcastically. Michael looked angry.

'You see? You think this is trivial! Well, you will learn all too soon what you are dealing with if you do not take care. Like the others!'

He turned and hurried to where Gray was fretting at the foot of Wilson's staircase, leaving Bartholomew wondering what the obese monk was involved in to have him scared almost out of his wits.

'Come on, come *on!*' called Gray, almost hopping from foot to foot in his impatience.

Bartholomew followed Michael and Gray up the stairs, and the three of them stood in the little hallway outside Wilson's room. Bartholomew moved away from Michael, not totally convinced that this was not some plot cooked up by Michael and Gray to harm him.

'What is it?' whispered Michael.

Gray motioned for him to be quiet. Bartholomew had not been up this staircase since Sir John had died, and he felt odd standing there like a thief in the dark. Gray put his ear to the door and indicated that the others should do likewise. At first, Bartholomew could hear nothing, and then he could make out low moaning noises, like those of an animal in pain. Then he heard some muttering, and the sound of something tearing. He moved away so that Michael could hear, almost ready to walk away and leave them there. He did not feel comfortable listening at the Master's door like this; what Wilson got up to in his own room, however nasty, was his own business, and Bartholomew wanted none of it.

All three leapt into the air as a tremendous crash came from inside the room. Michael leaned against the wall, his hand on his chest, gasping for breath. Gray stared at the door with wide eyes. Suddenly, Bartholomew became aware of something else. He crouched down near the bottom of the door and inspected it carefully. There was no mistake. Something was on fire in Wilson's room!

Yelling to the others, he pounded on the door, just as terrified screams started to come from within. Brother Michael shoved his bulk against the door, and the leather hinges gave with a great groan. It swung inwards, and Bartholomew rushed inside. He seized a pitcher of water from atop a chest, and dashed it over the figure writhing on the floor. He was aware of Michael and Gray tearing the coverings from the walls to beat out the flames that licked across the floor. Bartholomew used a rich woollen rug to smother the flames that continued to dance over Wilson.

It was all over in a few seconds. The fire, it seemed, had only just started and so had not gained a firm hold. Gray went round carefully pouring Wilson's stockpile of wine and ale over the parts that still smouldered. They had averted what could have been a terrible disaster.

Bartholomew carefully unrolled Wilson from the rug. One or two tendrils of smoke rose from his clothes, but the fire was out. Michael helped Bartholomew lift their Master onto the bed, where Bartholomew began to examine him. Michael wandered around the room picking up pieces of charred paper, watching them crumble in his hands, and muttering something about the College accounts.

The commotion had brought others running to see what had happened. Alcote was first; Jocelyn of Ripon, Father Jerome, Roger Alyngton, and the surviving commoners, were close on his heels. They stopped dead when they saw the Master lying on the bed in his burned gown and Bartholomew kneeling next to him.

'What have you done?' Alcote demanded.

Gray intervened, and Bartholomew admired his poise and confidence. 'I was just returning from Bene't's, and I saw flickering coming from the Master's room. I was worried there was a fire, so I went up the stairs and listened outside the door. I could not smell any smoke, but I could hear someone crying. He was crying with so much pain that it almost hurt to hear. I went to fetch Doctor Bartholomew, because I thought maybe the Master had lost his mind like poor Gregory Colet, and the Doctor might be able to help. Brother Michael was with him, so he came too.'

Michael took over. 'I heard no crying,' he said, 'but moaning. Then there was a crash, which must have been the Master knocking that table over, and the table had the lamp on it. We were just in time to put out the flames. It seems the Master was busy burning documents.' He held up a handful of charred remains for Alcote to see.

Alcote stepped dubiously inside the room. The floor was awash with spilled ale and wine, and cinders of Wilson's parchments lay everywhere. 'Why was he burning his documents?' he demanded. 'Why did he knock the table over? It is heavy. He could not knock it over with ease.'

'He probably fell against it,' said Bartholomew, looking up from his patient. 'He has the plague.'

Alcote gasped and shot back outside the room, fumbling for a piece of his robe with which to cover his mouth and nose. 'The plague? But that is not possible! He has been in his room since it started and no one has touched him!'

Bartholomew shrugged. 'He has it nevertheless. Come and look.'

Alcote shrank back further still, and disappeared into the group of students that had assembled outside. Bartholomew rose from Wilson's bed.

'It is all over,' he said to the onlookers. 'There was a fire, but it is out now. Go back to your beds.' He nodded to Gray, indicating that he should disperse them. Alyngton and Jerome stared in horror at one of Wilson's burned feet that stuck out of the end of the bed. Jocelyn bent down to pick up one of the pieces of burned paper.

'I have heard the plague turns people's minds. Poor man. He has burned the College accounts!' He took the arms of his fellow commoners, and led them away gently. Bartholomew wondered if Jocelyn had been a soldier, for he was remarkably unmoved by the ghoulish foot that poked out, red and blistered.

Michael closed the door and came to peer over Bartholomew's shoulder. 'How is he?' he asked.

Bartholomew bent to listen to Wilson's heart again. It still beat strongly, but his injuries were terrible. The fire had caught the edge of his gown, and had spread quickly up to his waist before Bartholomew had been able to put out the flames. Wilson's legs were a mass of blackened flesh and bleeding blisters, and even now his toes felt hot to Bartholomew's hand. As if that were not enough, Wilson had great festering buboes under his arms, on his neck, and in his groin. One had burst, and a trickle of pus and blood dripped onto his burned legs.

'Will he live?' asked Michael, deliberately not looking at Wilson's legs.

Bartholomew moved away, so that if some part of Wilson's brain were conscious, he would not be able to hear. 'No,' he said. 'He will die before the night is over.'

Michael looked over at Wilson's still figure. 'Why did he burn the College accounts?' he asked.

'Evidence of payments to people he wished kept secret?' mused Bartholomew, without really considering the implications.

'Such payments would not be written down,' Michael said scathingly. 'They would come out of a separate account, the records of which any sensible master would keep only in his head. These accounts,' he continued, waving a fistful of charred parchment in the air, scattering tiny cinders, 'are nothing. They are only records of the College's finances. There is nothing here to warrant burning!'

Bartholomew shrugged, and turned his attention to his patient. He guessed Michael had expected to find some documents relating to this miserable University business. Wilson lay quietly, and Bartholomew moistened his lips with the few drops of water remaining at the bottom of the pitcher. He placed a clean piece of linen over Wilson's burned legs, but saw no point in putting him through painful treatment when he was going to die in a few hours. If he regained consciousness,

Bartholomew could give him medicine that would dull his senses.

Since Gray was still busy dispersing the curious scholars, Bartholomew went to his storeroom to fetch the medicine himself. Recently, he had rarely needed to use such powerful potions – he did not use it for victims of the plague because it tended to make them vomit. He kept all such medicines in a small, locked chest at the back of the room and usually carried the key on his belt. He took it now, and leaned down impatiently when it would not fit. He turned the small chest to the light and looked in horror.

The lock on the chest was broken. Someone had prised it off completely. With a feeling of sick dread, Bartholomew opened the box and looked inside. He kept a very careful written record of these medicines, with dates, times, and amounts used. Most of the potions were still there, with one glaring exception. Bartholomew looked in shock at the near-empty bottle where the concentrated opiate had been. Was this what had been used to kill Aelfrith? There was certainly enough missing to kill.

Bartholomew leaned over the chest, feeling sick. Was all this never going to end? Had Wilson sneaked down to Bartholomew's room in the depths of some night to steal poison with which to kill Aelfrith? If Wilson were the murderer, he did not have long to wait before he was judged for it. Feeling appalled at the pointlessness of it all, he put a few grains of the remaining white powder in a spare bottle, marked it down in his record book, and returned to Wilson.

He told Gray to find another chest in which to lock the poisons and sat next to Wilson. Michael went to fetch the accoutrements he needed to give Wilson last rites.

Bartholomew dipped a corner of a cloth into some water, and wiped Wilson's face with it. He noted that even on his deathbed, Wilson still managed to look pompous. Bartholomew tried to stop himself thinking such uncharitable thoughts, and wiped Wilson's face again; to his shock, Wilson opened his eyes.

'Rest now, Master Wilson,' he said, trying not to think about whether the man had murdered Aelfrith. 'Try to sleep.'

'Soon, I will sleep all too much,' came the whispered reply. 'Do not try to fool me, Physician. I know I have only a short while left.'

Bartholomew did not argue. He rubbed the soaking end of the cloth over Wilson's parched lips, and reached for the medicine that might give him some relief. Wilson's white hand flapped about pathetically.

'No! I want none of your medicines!' he grated. 'I have things I must say.'

'Brother Michael will be here soon,' Bartholomew said, putting the stopper back on the bottle. 'You can make your confession to him.'

'I do not want to talk to him,' said Wilson, his voice growing stronger as he spoke. 'I have things I want to say to you alone.'

Bartholomew felt the hair on the back of his neck rise, and he wondered whether Wilson was about to confess to murder. Wilson's hand flapped again, and enveloped one of Bartholomew's. The Physician felt revulsion, but did not pull his hand away.

'It was me,' said Wilson. 'I fought with you in the

dark on the night of Augustus's death. It was me who pushed you down the stairs.'

Bartholomew snatched his hand back. 'Then it was also you who murdered Brother Paul!' he said. 'Poor Brother Paul! Murdered while he lay defenceless on his pallet bed!'

Wilson gave an awful grimace that Bartholomew took to be a smile. 'No! You have that wrong, Physician. You always were poor at logic. Listen to me and learn.'

Bartholomew gritted his teeth so that he would not allow his distaste for the lawyer to show.

Wilson continued wheezily. 'After I left the feast, I went back to the room I shared with Alcote. We talked for a while, and he went to sleep, as we told the Bishop the next day. But I did not sleep. Alcote was almost senseless with the amount of wine he had drunk. It was a simple thing to slip out of the room once it began to ring with his drunken snores. He woke only when Alexander came to fetch us when you had raised the alarm, and by then I was back in my bed. There was my alibi!'

He stopped speaking, and lay with his eyes closed, breathing heavily. After a few moments, Wilson opened his eyes again, and fixed Bartholomew with an unpleasant stare.

'I allowed quite some time to pass before I went to Augustus's room that night,' he continued, his voice weaker than before. 'I was going to send Aelfrith away and offer to pray for Augustus until dawn. I went up the stairs, but saw that Augustus's room had been ransacked, and that he was gone. Aelfrith was unconscious on the floor. The shutters were open, and in the light from outside, I could see that there was an irregularity in the wooden floor. It is doubtful I ever would have noticed it in ordinary light. I closed the shutters and had just prised up the board, when you came. We fought, and you lost.'

He paused, coughing weakly. Bartholomew wiped away a thin trail of blood that dribbled from his mouth and thought back to that struggle. Wilson, like Michael, was flabby, and was well-endowed with chins, but that did not mean to say he was also weak. If Wilson had been desperate and panic-stricken, Bartholomew believed he could have been overpowered by him.

'I assume your intention in going to Augustus's room was not to pray?' asked Bartholomew.

Wilson sneered. 'Damn right it was not to pray! I wanted to find the seal. I am certain that whoever murdered Sir John did not get it from his body.'

Bartholomew caught his breath. 'You say Sir John was murdered?'

Wilson sneered again. 'Of course he was! He was killed for the seal he always carried, and without which no further messages would come from his contact in Oxford. It was imperative I found that seal. I saw it round his neck as he went for dinner the night of his death. The way in which his body was dressed indicated that it had not been round his neck when he died, or his murderers would not have bothered taking his clothes – they would merely have thrown his body into the mill stream. No murderer stays too long at the site of his crime,' he said with a superior smile.

'The only place Sir John went between dinner and when he left College for the last time was to see Augustus,' Wilson continued. 'So, the seal had to be in Augustus's room. When you told me he had died, I decided to look for the seal before someone else did.'

'But you did not find it,' said Bartholomew. He thought of Augustus's senile ramblings the afternoon before the feast, exhorting John Babington to 'hide it well'. If Sir John had not hidden the wretched seal as well as he apparently had, Augustus, Paul, and Montfitchet might still be alive.

'I did not,' said Wilson. 'I had just felt about in the small hole in the floorboards when you came blundering in. But,' he continued, fastening a cold, but sweaty, hand round Bartholomew's wrist, 'I did not hit Aelfrith, I did not drug the wine, and I did not kill Paul.' He looked at Bartholomew. 'I also do not know what happened to Augustus, although I do not believe he was responsible for the happenings that night. The poor old fool was far too senile to have effected such a well-considered plan.'

'Well-considered?' said Bartholomew in disgust. 'You call the murder of Paul and Montfitchet well-considered?'

Wilson ignored him and lay silent for a while.

'So how did you escape?' asked Bartholomew after a while. 'You did not pass me on the stairs.'

'You are observant, Master Physician,' said Wilson facetiously. 'Had you looked up instead of down, you may have noticed where I was, although I doubt it, for it is very cunningly concealed. The south wing of Michaelhouse was designed with two trap-doors in the ceilings of the upper floor. It is a secret passed on from Master to Master should the need ever arise for him to listen to the plottings of his fellows.'

'Sir John died before you became Master. How did you find out about this?'

'The day the Chancellor told me I was to be Master, he gave me various documents locked in a small chest.

I had to return the box to him immediately after I had read the documents, lest I die without passing certain information to my successor. Reference to these secret doors was included with a stricture that only Masters should be informed of their presence. I immediately went to Augustus's room to look for one of them. He watched me, but did not understand what I was doing.'

'Who else knows about these trap-doors?'

'When you know that, you will know the murderer.'

Bartholomew's mind began to mull through this information. Wilson's callous dismissal of Augustus had probably brought about his death. Augustus had very possibly babbled to someone else, in one of his senile ramblings, about the trap-door he had watched Wilson uncover, and had thus endangered himself. So, who might he have told? Evidently not Aelfrith or he would have guessed where his attacker might have hidden himself, and would not have searched with Bartholomew. Was it Michael? Or another Fellow?

Wilson watched him trying to reason the muddle out, his expression smug, as if Bartholomew were one of his students trying to resolve some legal point for which there was no solution. He continued. 'All I had to do once I had pushed you down the stairs was to stand on the window-sill, and pull myself through the opening. I could hear you looking for me and knew you would never be able to spot the trap-door, especially in the poor light. Whoever killed Paul and took Augustus evidently also knew about the trap-doors.'

Bartholomew sat back and thought. It made sense. As Aelfrith had prayed over Augustus, the murderer had slipped through the trap-door – or perhaps even dropped something on the friar – and knocked him senseless. The wine was drugged, and Paul murdered so that the commoners would know nothing about what was going on. A search of the room was made, but, not finding the seal, and perhaps hearing Wilson coming, the murderer took Augustus's body through the trap-door to hide it.

'But why steal a body?' asked Bartholomew, still thwarted in his attempt to make sense of the new information.

Wilson sighed. 'You are intractable, Physician. It would not take long to search a corpse, and so the answer is obvious. Augustus was alive, and was taken so that he would reveal where the seal was hidden to the murderer!'

Bartholomew shook his head. 'Augustus was dead, Master Wilson. He was probably murdered too.'

'Rubbish,' said Wilson dismissively. 'He was alive. Why would anyone wish to steal a corpse? Think, man! Your supposition that Augustus was dead is not a reasonable one.'

He lay back on his pillow, his face red with effort. Bartholomew sponged it again while he let all Wilson's claims sink in. Wilson was right. It would make sense for the murderer to take a living person with him to be questioned later, but not a dead one. But Bartholomew knew Augustus had been dead! He had touched his eyes, and made a careful examination of the body. Nevertheless, apart from that, Wilson's story made matters a little clearer, and also explained why the Master had been prepared to put about the Bishop's lies. The Bishop had probably known exactly what Wilson had been doing in Augustus's room, and approved of it.

The door swung open on its broken hinges, and Michael entered, bringing the things he would need to give Wilson last rites and to hear his confession.

'Get out!' hissed Wilson, lifting his head from the pillow. 'Get out until I am ready!'

Michael looked annoyed, but left the room without arguing. Wilson waited until he heard his footsteps going down the wooden stairs.

'Why did you want this seal?' Bartholomew asked.

Wilson's eyes remained closed. The effort of sending Michael away had exhausted him. His voice was little more than a whisper when he finally spoke. 'Because the University is under threat from scholars at Oxford,' he said. 'Babington's seal would have enabled us to continue to receive reports on their activities from his contact there. Since the seal has gone missing, we have heard nothing, and we are missing out on vital information. I had to find it and could let nothing stop me!'

'Even murder?' asked Bartholomew softly.

'I assure you I did not murder anyone,' said Wilson tiredly. 'Although I did try to kill you when you found me in Augustus's room. I do not like you, Master Physician. I do not like the way you mix learning and dealing with those filthy thieves in the town you call your patients. I do not like the way your life and loyalties are divided between the College and the town. And I did not like the way Babington encouraged you to have it so.'

Bartholomew felt like telling Wilson that he did not like him either, but there was nothing to be gained from such comments at this point.

'Do you know anything about Aelfrith's death?' he asked instead. Wilson was fading fast, and he had many questions he wanted answered.

'No, why should I? The foolish man went out among plague victims. What did he expect?'

'He was murdered too. He was killed with medicines from my poisons chest. His last words were "poison" and "Wilson". What do you make of that?'

Wilson fixed bloodshot eyes on Bartholomew. 'Nonsense,' he said after a moment. 'You misheard him. Aelfrith was told about the seal, but he was an innocent, who should never have been allowed to know the secret. He was too . . . willing to believe good of people. Do not make up mysteries, Bartholomew. You have enough to do with those that already exist.'

'What were you doing when you set yourself alight?' asked Bartholomew. He remained uncertain whether Wilson really knew nothing of Aelfrith's murder and so was dismissing it out of hand, or whether he knew far too much but was refusing to say so. Bartholomew had to lean close to Wilson to hear his words, trying not to show repugnance at his fetid breath.

'I was burning the College records,' he said. 'My successor will probably be Swynford, and I will not make things easy for the likes of him by leaving nicely laid-out ledgers and figures. Oh, no! He can work it all out for himself! I was going to burn all the records, then send for you, but I was overcome with dizziness, and must have knocked the table over with the lamp on it.'

So, Wilson's motive for burning the ledgers had been spite, and Michael was wrong in assuming that it was anything more sinister or meaningful. Bartholomew looked down at Wilson with pity. How could a man, knowing he was going to die, perform such petty acts of meanness with his last strength? He thought of others he had seen die during the last weeks, and how many had died begging him to take care of a relative, or asking him to pass some little trinket to a friend who had not had the chance to say goodbye. Bartholomew felt sick of the University and its politics, and particularly sick of Wilson and his pathetic vengeance.

He moved away. He had one more question to ask, one that meant more to him than the others. He had to put it casually, because he sensed if Wilson knew it was important to him, he might not answer.

'Does any of this have anything to do with Giles or Philippa Abigny?' he asked, looking at where the door hung at an odd angle on its damaged hinges.

Wilson gave a nasty wheezing chuckle. 'Your lady love? It is possible. I have been thinking for some time now that Abigny might be one of the Oxford spies. He spends too much time away from the College, and I never know where he is. Perhaps it was he who found the seal. I heard that your lady has gone. She should have stayed in her convent. Probably ran off with some man who will make her richer and happier than you, Physician.'

Bartholomew fought down the urge to wrap his hands round the man's neck and squeeze as hard as he could. So, Abigny could be one of Oxford's spies. Was that why he had been hiding in disguise at Edith's house? But that did not explain where Philippa was. Bartholomew could see no option other than to become embroiled in this seething pit of intrigue and spies in order to find out about Abigny's possible role.

'Do you know for certain that Philippa ran away with a man?' asked Bartholomew as calmly as he could.

Wilson gave another breathy cackle. 'I am almost tempted to say yes because I would like to see the expression on your face,' he said. 'But the answer is no. I have no idea where your woman is, and I have no information whatsoever about her disappearance. I wish I had, because I want you to do two things for me, and I would like to make you feel obliged to do them by giving you information in return.'

Bartholomew grimaced. He wondered why Wilson had chosen him to do his bidding. 'What are they?'

Wilson's lips parted in his ghastly grin. 'First, I want you to find the seal.'

Bartholomew spread his hands helplessly. 'But how can I find it if you could not? And why me and not one of the others?'

'Swynford is gone, and I would not trust him anyway. Aelfrith is dead. Father William is too indiscreet, and would go about his task with so much fervour that he would surely fail. Brother Michael knows more than he is telling me, and I do not trust that he is on the right side. The same goes for Abigny, who has fled the nest anyway. Alcote is too stupid. That leaves only you, my clever Physician! You have the intelligence to solve the riddle, and Aelfrith assured me that you were uninvolved with all this before he died.'

Wilson lifted his head from the pillow and reached for Bartholomew's arm. 'You must find it, and pass it to the Chancellor. He will see you amply rewarded.' He released Bartholomew's arm, and sank back.

So Wilson thought that any of the surviving Fellows might be involved, although he thought it less likely of William or Alcote. Abigny and Michael were plainly embroiled. But the entire Oxford business seemed so far-fetched, especially now when towns and villages were being decimated with the plague. Why would Oxford scholars bother to waste their time and energy on subterfuge and plotting when they all might be dead in a matter of weeks anyway?

'It seems so futile,' he blurted out. 'Now of all times there are issues far more important to which scholars should devote their attention.'

Wilson sneered again. 'What is more important than the survival of the College and University? Even you must see that is paramount! You must have some love of learning, or you would not be here, exchanging comfort and wealth for the cramped, rigid life of a scholar. Your arrogance has not allowed you to see that there are others who love learning, and would do anything to see it protected. I sacrificed a glowing future as a cloth merchant to become a scholar, because I believe the University has a vital role to play in the future of our country. You are not the only one to sacrifice yourself for a love of knowledge and learning.'

Bartholomew watched the guttering candle. 'But the University at Oxford is stronger, bigger, and older than Cambridge. Why should they bother?'

Wilson made an impatient sound, and slowly shook his head. 'You will not be convinced, I see. Aelfrith said as much. But you will see in the end. Anyway, it matters not why you choose to seek the seal, only that you do so. Believe it will lead you to your woman if you wish. Believe it will avenge Babington's death. But find it.'

He closed his eyes, his face an ashen-grey.

'And the second thing?' Bartholomew asked. 'You said there were two things you wanted done.'

'I want you to see that I am not thrown into one of your filthy plague pits. I want to be buried in the church near the high altar, and I want an effigy carved in black marble. I am choosing you to do this because I know you are dealing with burials these days, and because you have already had the plague and might now survive the longest. Any of the others might catch it, and I cannot rely on them to carry out my wishes. You will find money for the tomb in my purse in the College chest.'

Bartholomew stared at him in disbelief, and almost laughed. Wilson was incorrigible! Even with so little time left, his mind was on pomp and ceremony. Bartholomew wanted to tell him that it would give him great pleasure to see his fat corpse dumped into the plague pit, but he was not Wilson, and so he merely said he would do what he could.

Wilson seemed to be fading fast, now he had completed his business. Sweat coursed down his face and over his jowls, and Bartholomew noticed that one of the swellings on his neck must have burst when he was moving his head. Thankfully, he did not seem to be in any pain. Perhaps the shock of the burns had taken the feeling from his body, or perhaps Wilson was able to put it to the back of his mind while he tied up the loose ends in his life.

'Tell Michael to come,' he whispered. 'I have done with you now.'

Bartholomew was peremptorily dismissed with the characteristic flap of the flabby hand that had been the cause of so much resentment among the College servants. He went to the door and called for Michael. Michael huffed up the stairs and spread out his accoutrements, obviously still indignant about his dismissal from the room earlier.

Bartholomew left so that Wilson could make his

confession in private, and went to examine the other plague cases in the commoners' room. He was summoned back by Michael after only a few minutes.

'The Master had little to confess,' said Michael in amused disbelief. 'He says he has lived a godly life, and has done no harm to anyone who did not deserve it. God's teeth, Matt.' Michael shook his head in wonder. 'It is as well he has asked you not to put him in the plague pit. In a tomb of his own, the Devil will be able to come to claim him that much quicker!'

VIII

WILSON DIED SHORTLY AFTER HE WAS ABSOLVED of his sins. Bartholomew helped Cynric stitch the body into one of the singed wall-hangings that Michael and Gray had used to put out the flames. Bartholomew did not want the body to stay in the College, nor did he want it lying in the church where it might infect others. The only solution was to dig a temporary grave so that it could be retrieved when the tomb was ready.

Gray went to purchase a coffin at an extortionate price – they had become a rare commodity – and at dawn that day, Cynric and Gray dug a deep grave at the back of the church. Agatha, Cynric and Gray watched from a distance as Bartholomew and Michael lowered the coffin, while William muttered a requiem mass at top speed.

When it was over, they went into the church for the morning service and then back to College for breakfast. The hall was cold and gloomy, and Bartholomew suggested that they all eat in the kitchen, where it was warm and Cynric would not have so far to carry the food. The other scholars had tended to prepare their own breakfasts in their rooms since the onset of the plague, to avoid unnecessary contact.

William gulped down some bread and watered wine, and went to take the news of Wilson's death to the Chancellor. Agatha watched him go.

'Would it be an unchristian thing to be thankful that that pompous old windbag was dead?' she asked Michael.

'Yes,' replied Michael, his hands full of chicken and his face covered in grease.

'Well, then,' she said, 'you have advance warning of what I will say in my confession. The College will be better without him. What will happen now?'

Michael swallowed a huge mouthful of food, and almost choked. Bartholomew pounded him on the back. 'The Fellows choose two names from their number, and the Chancellor picks one of them,' Michael said between coughs. As soon as he stopped coughing, he crammed as much food into his mouth as would fit, and went through the same process again.

'So, which two Fellows will you choose?' asked Agatha, beginning to clear away the table.

Michael swallowed hard, tears coursing down his cheeks. 'Dry, this chicken,' he remarked, making Bartholomew laugh. 'One nomination will have to be Swynford, I suppose. I would like you to be the other, Matt.'

'I am not doing it,' Bartholomew gasped in amazement. 'I do not have time.'

'Well, who else then?' asked Michael.

'You, Swynford, William, Alcote. Any of you would do well.' Bartholomew wondered which of them would promote the cause of the University, and which might be Oxford's spies. He rose and washed his hands in a bowl of water near the fire. Behind him, he could hear the cracking of bones as Michael savaged the remains of his chicken. Gray dabbled his hands quickly in the cold water, and wiped them on his robe. He did not see why Bartholomew was always washing his hands; they only became dirty again, especially in the shabby hovels that Bartholomew frequented.

Bartholomew's first duty of the day was to examine Alyngton and five students in the commoners' room. He lanced the swellings that looked as though they would drain, and left Michael's Benedictine room-mates with instructions on how to keep the sick scholars comfortable. That done, he visited three patients in the rivermen's houses down by the wharf.

Gray followed him from house to house carrying the heavy bag that contained Bartholomew's instruments and medicines. Bartholomew could feel the student's disapproval as he entered the single-roomed shacks that were home to families of a dozen. The only patient of which Gray did not disapprove was the wife of a merchant. She was one of the few cases with which Bartholomew had had success, and was lying in a bed draped with costly cloths, tired, but still living. The grateful merchant pressed some gold coins into Bartholomew's hand. Bartholomew wondered whether they would be sufficient to bribe people to drive the carts that collected the dead.

Once the urgent calls were over, Bartholomew turned to Gray.

'I need to discover what happened to Philippa,' he said. 'I am going to try to see if anyone knows Giles Abigny's whereabouts.'

Gray's face broke into a smile. 'You mean you plan to visit a few of his favourite spots?' he asked cheerfully.

'Oh, good. Beats traipsing around those dismal hovels. Where shall we begin?'

Bartholomew was thankful that Gray had so readily agreed to help. 'The King's Head,' he said, saying the first place that came into his head.

Gray frowned. 'Not a good place to start,' he said. 'We would be better going there later when it is busier. We should visit Bene't's first – that is where he spent most of his time outside Michaelhouse. Hugh Stapleton's brother, Cedric, is ill and now Master Roper is dead, they have no physician. We could see him first and then wheedle an invitation to eat there.'

Bartholomew saw he had a lot to learn in the sleazy ways of detection. He walked with Gray up the High Street to Bene't Street. Gray strolled nonchalantly into Bene't Hostel and a notion went through Bartholomew's mind that the scholars there might consider him to have poached Gray from them. The student had attached himself to Bartholomew with gay abandon, and Bartholomew had not asked whether he had sought permission from the Principal – whoever that was now that Hugh Stapleton had died.

The hostel was little more than a large house, with one room enlarged to make a hall. Bartholomew assumed that the hall would be used for communal meals as well as teaching. The hostel was far warmer than the chilly stone rooms of Michaelhouse, and the smell of boiled cabbage pervaded the whole house. Drying clothes hung everywhere, and the entire place had an aura of controlled, but friendly, chaos. No wonder Abigny had felt more at home here than in the strict orderliness of Michaelhouse.

Gray made for the small hall on the first floor of the

building. He stopped to speak to a small, silver-haired man, and then turned to Bartholomew. 'This is Master Burwell, the Sub-Principal,' he said. 'He is very grateful for your offer to attend Cedric Stapleton.'

Bartholomew followed Burwell up some narrow wooden steps into the eaves of the house. 'How long has Master Stapleton been ill?' he asked.

'Since yesterday morning. I am sure there is little you can do, Doctor, but we appreciate you offering to help.' Burwell glanced round to smile at Bartholomew, and opened the door into a pleasant, slant-sided room with two dormer windows. The windows were glazed, and a fire was lit, so the room was remarkably warm. Bartholomew stepped in and went to the man who lay on the bed. A Dominican lay-brother was kneeling by him, alternating muttered prayers with wiping his patient's face with a napkin. Bartholomew knelt next to him to peer at the all-too-familiar symptoms.

He took a knife and quickly made criss-cross incisions on the buboes in Stapleton's armpits and groin. Immediately, a foul smell filled the room, and the lay-brother jerked backwards with a cry of disgust. Bartholomew asked for hot water, and set about cleaning the swellings. It seemed that Bartholomew's simple operation had afforded Stapleton some relief, for his breathing became easier and his arms and legs relaxed into a more normal position.

Bartholomew sat for a while with Stapleton, then went in search of Gray. He found him holding court in the small hall, in the middle of some tale about how he had sold a pardoner some coloured water to cure him of his stomach gripes, and how the pardoner had returned a week later to tell him that the wonderful medicine had worked.

Bartholomew sat on the end of a bench next to Burwell. Burwell raised his eyebrows questioningly.

'It is too soon to tell,' Bartholomew said in response. 'You will know where you stand with Master Stapleton by nightfall.'

Burwell looked away. 'We have lost five masters and twelve students,' he said. 'How has Michaelhouse fared?'

'Sixteen students, three commoners, and two Fellows. The Master died last night.'

'Wilson?' asked Burwell incredulously. 'I thought he was keeping to his room so he would not be infected.'

'So he did,' said Bartholomew. 'But the pestilence claimed him all the same.' He was wondering how to breach the subject of Abigny without sounding too obvious, when Burwell did it for him.

'We heard about Giles Abigny,' he said. 'We heard from Stephen Stanmore that he had been hiding in your sister's attic, and then ran off with Stanmore's horse.'

'Do you have any ideas where Giles might be?' Bartholomew asked.

Burwell shook his head. 'I never understood what was going on in Giles's head. A strange combination of incredible shallowness mixed with a remarkable depth of learning. I do not know where he might be.'

'When was the last time you saw him?' asked Bartholomew.

Burwell thought carefully. 'He was very shocked at Hugh's death. After that he went wild, trying to squeeze every ounce of pleasure from what he thought might be a short life. He continued in that vein for perhaps a week. Then he seemed to quieten down, and we saw less of him. Then, about two weeks ago, after going to the King's Head, he regaled us with a dreadful tale about cheating at dice and stealing the wages of half the Castle garrison. He had an enormous purseful of money, so perhaps there was some truth in it. He went off quite late, and I have not seen him since.'

Bartholomew tried to hide his disappointment. A sighting two weeks ago did not really help. He stood to leave, and beckoned to Gray.

'Please send someone for me at Michaelhouse if I can be of any more help to Cedric,' he said to Burwell. 'And thank you for your assistance with Giles.'

Burwell smiled again, and escorted them to the door. He watched as they made their way down Bene't Street and the smile faded from his face. He beckoned to a student, and whispered in his ear. Within a few moments, the student was scurrying out of the hostel towards Milne Street, his cloak held tightly against the chill of the winter afternoon.

Bartholomew and Gray spent two fruitless hours enquiring after Abigny in the town's taverns. They came up with nothing more than Burwell had told them, except that Abigny's idiosyncrasies seemed to be notorious among the townspeople.

Bartholomew was ready to give up, and retire to bed, when Gray, with a display of energy that made Bartholomew wonder whether he had been at the medicine store, suggested they walk to Trumpington to visit the Laughing Pig.

'It is best we visit at night,' he said. 'More people

will be there, and they will have had longer for the ale to loosen their tongues.'

So the two set off for Trumpington. Although it was only two miles, Bartholomew felt he was walking to the ends of the Earth. A bitter wind blew directly into their faces and cut through their clothes. It was a clear night, and they could hear the crack and splinter of the water freezing in the ruts and puddles on the track as the temperature dropped.

Bartholomew breathed a sigh of relief when the Laughing Pig came into sight. Within a few minutes they were seated in the tavern's large whitewashed room with frothing tankards of ale in front of them. The tavern was busy, and a fire crackled in a hearth in the middle of the room, filling it with pungent smoke as well as warmth. The floor was simple beaten earth, which was easier to keep clean than rushes.

Bartholomew was well known in Trumpington, and several people nodded at him in a friendly fashion. He struck up a conversation with a large, florid-faced man who fished for eels in the spring and minded Stanmore's cows for the rest of the year. The man immediately began to gossip about the disappearance of Philippa. Bartholomew was dismayed, but not surprised, that her flight had become the subject of village chatter – doubtless by way of Stanmore's party of horsemen who had tried to catch up with the fleeing Abigny.

Overhearing the discussion, several others joined in, including the tavern maid with whom Abigny had claimed he was in love back in the summer. She perched on the edge of the table, casting nervous glances backwards to make sure the landlord did not catch her skiving.

'How long do you think Giles Abigny was pretending

to be his sister?' Bartholomew asked casually, in a rare moment of silence.

There was a hubbub of conflicting answers. Everyone, it seemed, had ideas and theories. But listening to them, Bartholomew knew that was all they were. He stopped paying attention and sipped at the sour ale.

'Giles was odd a long time before he did this,' whispered the tavern maid, who, as Abigny had said, was indeed pretty. She glanced towards the next table where the landlord was serving and pretended to clean up near Bartholomew. 'The last time I saw him was at the church two Fridays ago. He was hiding behind one of the pillars. I thought he was playing around, but when I grabbed him from behind, he was terrified! He ran out, and I have not seen him since.'

Two Fridays before. That was three days after Philippa had become ill. So Abigny had not been impersonating her at least until then.

'Do you know where he went?' Bartholomew asked.

The tavern maid shook her head. 'I ran after him, but he had gone.'

The landlord shouted for her to serve other customers, and she left. Bartholomew thought about what she had told him: Abigny had been in the church at Trumpington terrified of something.

He tried to bring the general conversation round to what Abigny's reasons could be, but the suggestions were so outrageous that he knew no one had any solid facts to add. Bartholomew and Gray talked with the locals for a while longer, and decided to stay with Edith for the night. Perhaps he would have more luck with his search tomorrow.

*   *   *

Gray was already up and admiring the horses in Stanmore's stable by the time Bartholomew awoke. He threw open the window-shutters and looked out over the neat vegetable patches to the village church. He could see the Gilbertine Canon, standing outside the porch talking to the early risers who had been to his morning mass. The weak winter sun was shining, glittering on the frost that lay over everything like a white sheet of gauze. Bartholomew took a deep breath, and the air was clean and fresh. He understood why Stanmore preferred not to live at the house in Milne Street so near the stinking ditches and waterways of Cambridge.

He went to the garderobes and broke the ice on a bowl of water. Shivering and swearing under his breath, he washed and shaved as fast as he could, and borrowed one of Stanmore's fresh shirts from the pile on the shelf in the corner. He went down to the kitchens, where a large fire blazed, and he and Edith sat on stools and discussed Philippa's disappearance. It seemed he could have saved himself a walk, because she had been busy on his behalf, collecting scraps of information from the Trumpington folk.

She, too, had spoken to the tavern girl, and had also questioned the Canon. He had told her that Abigny had frequented the church a great deal following Philippa's arrival. Abigny had seemed restless and agitated, and once the Canon had alarmed him by standing up suddenly from next to the altar where he had been meditating. Abigny had turned so white that the Canon had been genuinely concerned for his health. The day after, he had disappeared. The Canon had assumed that Abigny had been waiting while Philippa was ill, and as soon as she was well again, he had returned to Michaelhouse.

'So,' said Edith, 'Giles may have been in the house pretending to be Philippa as early as the day her fever broke, since that was when either of them was last seen. I do not understand why he did not just come here. He has stayed with us before.'

Bartholomew nodded in agreement.

'Of course,' she continued, 'since none of us actually saw Philippa once her fever had gone, there is no reason to assume that she was alone in the room.'

Bartholomew stared at her. 'What do you mean?' he asked.

'Perhaps as soon as Philippa was out of danger from the plague, he climbed up to her window to be with her. Perhaps there were two people in the room for some of the time, not just one. I thought she had rather a voracious appetite; she always ate everything we left on the trays outside the door, and we began leaving her larger and larger amounts. I thought it was just a reaction to the fever, or even boredom, making her eat so much.

'And you know what that means?' Edith continued, after a pause. 'It means that he probably nursed her himself for a time, before she left and he took her place. It means that she was not spirited away while she was still weak, but when she was stronger. So she probably went voluntarily.'

Bartholomew was not sure whether this was good or bad. 'But why was she spirited anywhere? Why did she not stay here? Why did Abigny feel obliged to keep up such a pretence? And why did Philippa and Giles not feel that they could trust us enough to tell us what was going on?'

Edith patted his hand. 'These are strange times, Matt,' she said. 'Oswald told me that one of his apprentices hanged himself two days ago, because he had accidentally touched a plague victim. He was so afraid he might catch it, he decided he would rather die by his own hand. Do not question too much. I am sure you will find Philippa eventually. And Giles.'

But even if he did, Bartholomew thought, things would never be the same. If Edith was right, and Philippa had gone from the house willingly, it meant that she had not trusted him enough to tell him her motives. The same was true of Giles.

Edith stood up. 'I must do some work,' she said. 'Did you know that we have the children from the village who have been orphaned in our stable loft? It is warm and dry there, and we can make sure they are fed properly. The bigger ones are helping to tend the vegetable plots, and I take care of the little ones here. Labour is becoming scarce, Matt. We will all starve if we do not continue to look after the fields.'

Bartholomew was not surprised at his sister's practicalities, nor of her carefully concealed charity. She would not offend the children's dignity by giving them meals and a place to stay for nothing, but provided them with small duties that would make them feel they were earning their keep.

Stanmore took a small cart into Cambridge so that Bartholomew and Gray would not have to walk. Richard went too, sitting in the back interrogating Gray about life as a student in Cambridge, and making comparisons with his own experiences in Oxford.

Bartholomew alighted at St Botolph's Church to see Colet, while the others went on to Milne Street.

The monks knelt in a line before the altar, although Bartholomew noted that there were fewer than there had been previously. Colet, however, was not there. Bartholomew went to Rudde's Hostel in search of him, but was told by the porter that he had gone out early that morning, and had not been seen since. Bartholomew's spirits rose a little. Did this mean that Colet had recovered and was visiting patients again?

The porter, seeing the hopeful look on Bartholomew's face, shook his head.

'No, he is as addled as ever. He had his hood pulled right over his face, and said he was going out to pick blackberries. At this time of year! He has been saying that every day recently. He will be back later to sit and dribble in the church.'

Bartholomew thanked him, and walked back to Michaelhouse. On the way, he met Master Burwell who asked if there was any news of Abigny. Bartholomew shook his head, and asked whether Giles had seemed afraid of anything on the last few occasions that Burwell had seen him. Burwell scratched his head.

'Yes. Now that you mention it. The hostel is a noisy place, and he was constantly jumping and looking round. I just assumed it was fear of the plague. Several of the students are in a similar state, and I have heard Master Colet is far from well in his mind.'

'Was there anything specific?'

Burwell thought again. 'Not that I can put a finger on. He was simply nervous.'

After Bartholomew had enquired after Cedric Stapleton, they parted, and Bartholomew returned to his room. He looked around carefully to see if Abigny had been there, but the minute fragments of rushes that he had secretly placed on Abigny's belongings were still in place. Gray burst in, full of enthusiasm, but he was less so when Bartholomew dispatched him to buy various herbs and potions from the town herb-seller, known locally as 'Jonas the Poisoner' following an incident involving several poorly-labelled bottles some years before.

Bartholomew went to examine his patients in the commoners' dormitory, to find that three students had died in the night. Roger Alyngton was no better, but no worse. That morning, the frail Father Jerome had complained of a fever, and was lying restlessly next to him. Bartholomew wondered whether Jerome would have the strength or the will to fight the sickness.

When the patients were all resting, Bartholomew slipped out and went into the room that had been Augustus's and that was now used to store clean blankets and linen. He carefully closed the door. The shutters were already fastened, but the wood had swollen and warped over many years, and were ill-fitting enough to allow sufficient light for Bartholomew to see what he was doing.

He crouched on the window-sill and peered up at the ceiling. He had never really noticed the ceilings in the south wing before. They were really quite beautiful, with elaborate designs carved into the fine dark oak. Looking carefully, Bartholomew could see no evidence whatsoever of a trap-door. He wondered if Wilson had been lying to him. He jumped down and lit one of the supply of candles he had appropriated from the hall for use in the sickroom. Climbing back onto the window-sill, he held the candle up and looked again. He could still see nothing.

He put the palm of his hand against the ceiling and

pushed gently, and he was startled to feel it move. He pushed again, and an entire section of the ceiling came loose. He had to drop the candle to catch the heavy wood and prevent it from crashing down onto his head. Carefully, he lowered the loose panel onto the floor, relit his candle, and cautiously poked his head into the space beyond.

At first he could make nothing out, but then gradually he saw that the trap-door, as Wilson had called it, did little more than conceal a way into the attic. He did not know what he had expected – a cramped secret passage, perhaps, with dusty doorways leading away from it. Still holding the candle he hauled himself up, bemused to think that Wilson had been fit enough to do the same.

There was not sufficient room for him to stand upright, so he walked hunched over. The candle was not bright enough to illuminate the whole of the attic, and it faded into deep shadows at the edges. There was an unpleasant smell too, as if generations of small animals had found their way in, but had become trapped and died. Bartholomew shook himself. He was being fanciful. The attic was basically bare, the wooden floor covered in thick dust, scuffed here and there by some recent disturbances. He walked carefully along the length of the south wing, his way lit by small holes in the floor, although whether these were for providing light or for spying on the people in the rooms below, he could not say. Over the commoners' room, he could clearly hear the Benedictine whispering comforting words to Alyngton, while over what had been Swynford's room – where d'Evéne had died – he could even read the words on a book that lay open on the table. At the very end of the attic, he found the second trap-door. It was marked by a large metal ring, and when Bartholomew pulled it up, he saw that it gave access to the last staircase. Wilson could easily have climbed into the attic, walked along to the second door, and slipped away down the stairs and back to his own room. So could the murderer of Paul, Montfitchet, and Augustus.

He lowered the door and retraced his steps, carefully examining the floor for any more entrances and exits. He found none, but at the far end, where the south wing abutted onto the hall, he found a tiny doorway. He squeezed through it, and down a cramped passageway that was so full of dust and still air that Bartholomew began to feel as though he could not breathe. The passageway turned a corner, and Bartholomew faced a blank wall. He scratched at the stones and mortar with his fingernail. It was old, and had evidently been sealed up many years before. He stooped to look for any signs that it had been tampered with in recent days, but there was nothing. The passageway must have run in the thickness of the west wall of the hall, and perhaps emerged in the gallery at the back. He vaguely recalled Sir John complaining that an old door had been made into the ugly window that was there now, so perhaps the secret passageway had been blocked up then. Regardless, it seemed that the sturdy wall blocking the passage was ancient, and would have no bearing on the current mysteries.

He turned round, and began to squeeze his way down the narrow passage again. As he reached the point where the passage turned the corner, he saw that one of the stones had been prised loose about the level of his knees, and that something had been stuffed into the space. Gingerly, he bent towards it, and eased it out. It was a very dirty green blanket that smelled so rank that Bartholomew obeyed his instinct, and hurled it away from him. As it lay on the floor, something caught his eye. It was a singe mark, about the size of his hand.

Heart thumping, he picked it up by the hem, and took it back into the attic where he spread it out on the floor. It was the blanket that Bartholomew had inspected on the night of Augustus's death. There were the singe marks that had made Bartholomew think that Augustus had not been imagining things when he had claimed someone had tried to burn him in his bed. And there were other marks too – thick, black, encrusted stains ran in a broad band from one end of the blanket to the middle. Bartholomew knew old blood-stains when he saw them, and their implication made him feel sick.

Augustus must have been taken from his room and hidden up in the attic before Wilson conducted his clandestine search below. Perhaps the murderer had watched Wilson through the spy-holes, or perhaps he had hidden Augustus's body in the small passageway, so that Wilson would not have seen it when he effected his own escape. If Wilson had already explored the attic as he claimed, he would have known the little passage was blocked, and would not have tried to use it to get away.

And then what? When Wilson had gone? Augustus had been dead, and no counter-claims from anyone would make Bartholomew disbelieve what he knew. Had the murderer believed Augustus was still alive, and battered him when he lay wrapped in the blanket? Had Wilson been lying, and it was he who had returned later and battered the poor body? And regardless of which solution was the right one, where was Augustus now?

Bartholomew retraced his steps, carefully exploring every last nook and cranny of the attic, half hoping and half afraid that he would find Augustus. There was nothing: Augustus was not there. Bartholomew went back to the passage. The dust had been disturbed, and not just by his own recent steps. It was highly likely that Augustus had been hidden here until the hue and cry of his death and disappearance had died down.

The candle was beginning to burn low, and Bartholomew felt as though he had gained as much information from the attic as he was going to. At the last minute, he stuffed the blanket back into the hole in the wall again, as he had found it. He did not want the murderer, were he to return, to know about the clues he had uncovered.

He lowered himself through the trap-door back into Augustus's room and replaced the wooden panel. As it slid into place, Bartholomew again admired the workmanship that had produced a secret opening that was basically invisible, even when he knew where to look. He brushed himself off carefully and even picked up the lumps of dust that dropped from his clothes. He did not want anyone to guess what he had been doing. He put his ear to the door, and then let himself out silently.

He glanced in at his patients, and went down the stairs. The sky had clouded over since the morning, and it was beginning to rain. Bartholomew stood in the porch for a moment, looking across the courtyard. It was here he had fallen when Wilson had pushed him down the stairs. He closed his eyes, and remembered the footsteps he had heard as he lay there. That must have been Wilson effecting his escape across the attic floor. In his haste to get away, he had obviously forgotten to move with stealth, and Bartholomew had been able to hear him running.

Bartholomew thought about the night that Augustus had claimed there were devils in his room wanting to burn him alive. It was clear now: someone had climbed through the trap-door into Augustus's room, locked the door, and tried to set the bed alight. Whoever it was had escaped the same way when Bartholomew and Michael had broken the door down. But that still did not mean that Michael was innocent. He could easily have let himself out of the attic through the other trap-door and run round to Augustus's staircase to be in time to help Bartholomew batter the door. It would even explain why Michael had been virtually fully dressed in the middle of the night.

Cynric was taking food from the kitchen to the hall for the main meal of the day. Bartholomew walked briskly across the yard, and went up the stairs to the hall. It was cold and gloomy. Cynric had lit some candles, but they only served to make the room seem colder and darker as they flickered and fluttered in the draughts from the windows.

Bartholomew took some leek soup from a cauldron and sat next to Jocelyn of Ripon, more for company than from any feeling of friendship. Jocelyn made room for him and began telling him how the landowners were having to pay high wages to labourers to make them work on the farms. Because so many labourers had died from the plague, those left were in great demand and were able to negotiate large payments.

Jocelyn rubbed his hands gleefully as he described the plight of the rich landowners. He then outlined his plans for gathering groups of people together and selling their labour *en masse*. This would mean that the labourers would have a good deal of sway over the landowners and could obtain better pay and working conditions. If one landowner treated them unfairly, they would go to another who would be willing to make them a better offer. Jocelyn saw himself in the position of negotiator for these groups of people. Bartholomew, uncharitably, wondered what percentage of the profits the avaricious Jocelyn would take for his efforts. He tried to change the subject.

'Do you have plans to travel back to Ripon?'

'Not while there is money to be made here,' Jocelyn said.

Bartholomew tried again. 'What made you come to Cambridge last year?' he asked, taking a piece of salted beef that had less of a green sheen to it than the others.

Jocelyn looked irritated at being sidetracked, and poured himself another generous cup of College wine. 'I contacted Master Swynford. We are distantly related by marriage, and I came here because I plan to start a grammar school in Ripon, and I wanted to learn how it might best be done. I have a house that I can use, and because it will be the only grammar school for miles around, I know it will be successful.'

Bartholomew nodded. He knew all this, because Swynford had talked about it when he had asked the other Fellows whether his relative could come to stay in Michaelhouse in return for teaching grammar. Jocelyn's plan had sounded noble, but, having met him, Bartholomew was convinced that the school would be founded strictly as an economic venture and would have little to do with promoting the ideals of education.

As the most senior member present, it was

Bartholomew's responsibility to say the Latin grace that ended all meals in College. This done, he escaped to his room.

Gray had not been able to buy all the medicines that Bartholomew needed, and there was no choice but to walk to Barnwell Priory to see what he could borrow from their infirmarian. Bartholomew waited for Gray to eat, and then set off for the Priory in the rain.

'You need not come,' said Bartholomew, when Gray started grumbling. 'You can stay in College and help in the sick-room.'

'I do not mind going to the Priory, and I want to learn about the medicines. I just do not like all this walking. Miles last night, and miles today. Why do you not get a horse?'

Bartholomew sighed. 'Not again, Samuel! I do not have a horse because I do not need one. By the time the thing was saddled and ready to go, I could have walked where I was going.'

'Well, what about when you go to Trumpington?' Gray demanded petulantly.

Bartholomew felt his exasperation turning to irritation. 'I usually borrow or hire one.'

'But you cannot hire them now, not with all the stable-men dead of the plague. And Stephen Stanmore will never lend you another after what happened to the last one.'

Bartholomew whipped round and grabbed Gray by the front of his gown. 'Look! You do not like walking. You do not like my patients. You do not approve of what I charge them. Perhaps you should find yourself another master under which to study if you find my affairs so disagreeable!'

He released the student, and walked on. After a few paces, he heard Gray following him again. He glanced round, and Gray looked back at him sullenly, like a spoilt child. Gray sulked all the way to the Priory, until listening to Bartholomew and the infirmarian discussing the plague took his mind away from his moodiness. Bartholomew regretted his outburst; the lad had saved his life after all. He made an effort to include Gray in the discussion, and tried to ensure that Gray understood which medicines he was taking from the infirmarian and what they were for.

Bartholomew and the infirmarian left Gray packing the herbs and potions into a bag, and walked out into the drizzle.

'How many monks have you lost?' asked Bartholomew.

The infirmarian bowed his head. 'More than half, and Father Prior died yesterday. Perhaps our communal way of life promotes the sickness in some way. You have heard that all the Dominicans are dead? But what else should we do? Forsake our Rule and live in isolation like hermits?'

There was no answer to his question.

When Gray was ready, they took their leave of the infirmarian, and walked back along the causeway to the town. Gray had recovered completely from his attack of the sulks, and chattered on about what he planned to do once he had completed his training. Bartholomew grew dispirited listening to him. Did people think of nothing other than making money?

Gray tugged at his cloak suddenly. 'We should go to St Radegund's!' he said.

'Whatever for? They will refuse us entry.'

'Maybe Philippa went back there after she left your sister's house.'

Bartholomew stared at him. Gray was right! Why had he not considered it earlier? Gray had already set off down the causeway, and was hammering at the convent door by the time Bartholomew caught up with him. While they waited for the door to be answered, Bartholomew fretted, wiping the rain from his face impatiently. Gray hopped from foot to foot in an attempt to keep warm. Bartholomew looked at the door, and, and, despite his preoccupation, saw that several tendrils of weed had begun to grow across it. The nuns were taking their isolation seriously.

The small grille in the door was snapped open. 'What?' came a sharp voice.

'I want to speak with the Abbess,' said Bartholomew. His voice sounded calm, but his thoughts were in turmoil. Perhaps he would find Philippa safe and sound back in the convent, and all his worrying would be over.

'Who are you?' snapped the voice again.

'Matthew Bartholomew from Michaelhouse.'

The air rang with the retort of the grille being slammed shut vigorously. They waited a few moments, but nothing happened.

Gray looked almost as disappointed as Bartholomew felt. 'Oh, well. That is that,' he said.

Abruptly, the grille shot open again, and Bartholomew could see that this time there were two people on the other side.

'Well?' came the first voice, impatient and aggressive.

Bartholomew was so surprised that the Abbess had

come to the door, that he was momentarily stuck for words.

'Is it Henry?' the Abbess's voice was deep for a woman, and she was tall enough that she had to bend her head slightly to look through the grille. Her reasons for coming to answer the door were suddenly clear to Bartholomew. She thought he was coming to bring her news of her nephews, the Oliver brothers.

'Henry is well, Mother,' Bartholomew replied. He moved nearer to the door so that he could see her more clearly.

'Come no closer!' she said, her voice hard and distant. 'I hear that you walk freely among the contagion. I do not want you to bring it here. What do you want of me?'

Bartholomew was taken aback by her hostility, but it was not the first time he had been repulsed because of his contact with plague victims, and doubtless it would not be the last.

'I came to ask whether you had news of Philippa Abigny,' he said, watching the beautiful, but cold, face of the Abbess carefully.

Bartholomew saw a flash of anger in the ice-blue eyes. 'How dare you come here to ask that when you stole her away from us! You have fouled her reputation by your actions.'

He had expected such a response, although he had not imagined it would be given with such venom. But he did not wish to get into an argument with the Abbess about whether he had sullied Philippa's reputation, and so he tried to remain courteous.

'I am sorry if you think that,' he said, 'but you have not answered my question.'

'Do you think I am so stupid as to answer?' The Abbess virtually spat the words out. 'You stole her away once. If I told you she was here, you would try to do the same again.'

Bartholomew shook his head. 'You misunderstand my intentions. She came with me of her own free will, although I wished her to go back to where she would be protected from the plague. I only want to know that she is safe.'

'Then you can continue in your agony of doubt,' said the Abbess. 'For I will not tell you of the news I have, nor of her whereabouts.'

'Then do you know where she is?' Bartholomew cried.

The Abbess stepped back from the grille and smiled at him with such coldness that Bartholomew felt himself shudder. He was suddenly reminded of the looks of hatred Henry used to throw at him. What a family, all consumed with hate and loathing! He saw a large shadow fall over the Abbess, and watched her turn towards it, the coldness evaporating from her smile in an instant. Bartholomew glimpsed the hem of a highly decorated black cloak, and knew that Elias Oliver was there.

'Where is she?' Bartholomew shouted. The Abbess began to walk away, tall and regal, smiling at the tall figure beside her and ignoring Bartholomew. Bartholomew rattled the door in frustration, but the grille was slammed shut, and no amount of shouting and battering would induce the nuns to open it again.

Bartholomew slumped against the wall in defeat. Gray sat down beside him.

'Do not fret so,' he said. 'I have an idea.'

Bartholomew fought to regain control of his temper.

Did the wretched woman know where Philippa was, or was she merely pretending in order to have revenge for his 'stealing' her? He had had very little to do with the nuns of St Radegund's. They lived secluded in their cloisters, and even when he had visited Philippa, he had seen little of the Priory or its inmates.

Gray stood up and set off round the Priory walls. Bartholomew followed, sharply reminded of what had happened when he had last followed Gray around the walls of the convent. Gray slipped in and out of trees until he reached a point where the walls were totally obscured by thick undergrowth. Without hesitating, he led the way down a tiny path until he reached a door in the wall. He knocked twice, softly.

Bartholomew watched in amazement as the door opened and a young woman in a nun's habit peeped out. Seeing Gray, she checked no one was looking, and stepped out, closing the door carefully behind her.

'This is my cousin, Sister Emelda,' said Gray, turning to Bartholomew.

The young woman smiled shyly at Bartholomew, and then looked at Gray. 'I knew you would come! I cannot stay long, though, or I will be missed.' She glanced around her, as if expecting the spectre of the Abbess to appear through the trees. Gray nodded, and passed her something wrapped in a cloth. Emelda took it quickly, and secreted it in her robes. She reached up and kissed him quickly on the cheek. 'Thank you,' she whispered.

Gray flushed. 'The doctor has something to ask you,' he said, to cover his embarrassment.

Emelda smiled at Bartholomew again. 'I know you from when you used to come to court Philippa. Poor

Philippa! She hated it here, especially in the winter months, and even more when you stopped coming.'

'Is she here now?' he asked.

Emelda quickly shook her head. 'No. She has not been seen since you took her away. If she were here, I would know, because I do the cooking, and food is very carefully rationed. I would know if there were another person hidden away.'

'Have you heard anything from her?'

Again, a shake of the head.

'Do you know if the Abbess has heard of her whereabouts?'

'She has not! And she is very angry about it.' Emelda giggled. 'It is hard to keep secrets in a small community like this, and I know that she has those beastly nephews of hers trying to find out where Philippa is. I hope you find her before they do.'

Inside the convent, a bell began to ring. 'Terce,' said Emelda. 'I must go.' She smiled at the two men and slipped quickly through the door again.

Gray led the way through the undergrowth and back to the road. Bartholomew was full of questions. 'That was the door Philippa spoke about, the door that Sister Clement used when she went out to work among the sick. How did you know about it?' he demanded. 'And you did not tell me you had a cousin in the convent! What was it you handed to her in that package?'

Gray raised his hand to slow the stream of questions, reminding Bartholomew unpleasantly of Wilson. 'Emelda has been at St Radegund's since we were children, and she told me about the gate. I never told you about her because you have never asked about my family. And what I gave her was my business.'

Gray knew he had overstepped his bounds before Bartholomew said a word. 'Sorry, sorry,' he muttered. 'I will tell you, but you have to promise not to fly into a temper.'

'I will promise no such thing,' said Bartholomew coldly.

Gray sighed. 'All right,' he said. 'It is medicine for my mother. She is in there too. She took orders when I was old enough to look after myself, but now she has a wasting sickness and every week I take her medicine to relieve her pain.'

He looked defiantly at Bartholomew before continuing. 'That was one of the reasons why I had to become apprenticed to you. I was making a lot of money nursing rich plague victims, but Jonas refused to sell me the medicine. I stole it from Roper when I was with him, and now I steal it from you.'

He stopped walking, and looked at Bartholomew belligerently, waiting. Bartholomew stopped too, and studied this strange young man. 'Why did you not just ask me?' he said gently.

'Because you are always too busy, and because my mother comes from a rich priory and I thought you might rather give the medicine to the poor.'

Bartholomew was shocked. Did he really appear so insensitive to Gray? 'I have never refused medicine to anyone, rich or poor,' he said.

Gray suddenly lost his belligerence, and looked at the ground. 'I know. I am sorry,' he said in a quavering voice. 'It just seemed easier to steal the medicine than to ask for it.'

Bartholomew realised that this was why Gray had persuaded him to go to St Radegund's – not to ask about Philippa, but to deliver medicine for his mother. Perhaps the strain of his mother's illness accounted for his dreadful behaviour earlier that day. 'Perhaps I could examine her . . .?' he suggested.

Gray grimaced. 'I wish you could, but that old bitch, the Abbess, will not let anyone in or out, and my mother is too ill to be moved now. The medicine is the only thing that helps.'

'Which medicine is it?' asked Bartholomew.

Gray told him. 'My God, man!' Bartholomew exploded. 'Concentrated opiates can be a powerful poison! No wonder Jonas refused to sell it to you! It does have pain-relieving powers, but if someone gives her too much, she could die!'

Gray winced and took a step back. 'I know,' he said defensively, 'but I know how much she can have. I watched Roper giving it out to one of his sons when he had a similar wasting disease. I measure it out and put it in little packets for Emelda to give her.'

'Oh, lord!' groaned Bartholomew. 'What have I done to deserve a student like this?' He looked at Gray. 'I suppose you knew my supply was running low, and that I have been wondering where it had gone, and that is why you have chosen now to tell me?'

The answer was in the way Gray hung his head and refused to meet his eyes.

Bartholomew began walking again. Gray followed. On the one hand Bartholomew was relieved that his medicines had not been the cause of Aelfrith's death; on the other hand, he was disturbed that Gray had stolen such a powerful drug from him and prescribed it to someone.

'You are a disreputable rascal, Gray. You lie and

steal, and I cannot trust you. We will go to Jonas now, together, and replenish my stocks of this wretched stuff. Then *I* will measure it out for your mother, and we will go together and discuss with Emelda what else we can do to make your mother's life more bearable. Medicine is not just giving out potions, you know. There are many other things that can be done to effect a cure or to relieve symptoms.'

Detecting that a lecture was about to begin, Gray skipped a little to catch up to him to listen properly. He would need to work hard to gain the trust of his teacher, but at least he knew Bartholomew was prepared to allow him to try.

Bartholomew, meanwhile, glanced at Gray walking beside him – a liar and a thief. He could not possibly confide in the student, and, excluding his family, there was not a single person left in the world whom he could trust.

It was dusk by the time Bartholomew and Gray arrived back at Michaelhouse. The rain had turned the beaten earth of the yard into a quagmire, and the honey-coloured stones of the buildings looked dismal and dirty in the fading light. Like a skull, Bartholomew thought suddenly, and the windows and doors were like eyeless sockets and broken teeth. He pinched himself hard, surprised at his morbid thoughts; he was becoming preoccupied with death.

As if to reinforce his thoughts, Father William emerged from the staircase leading to the plague room. He was dragging something behind him, a long shape sewn into a blanket. Bartholomew went to help.

'Who is it?' he asked, taking a corner of the

blanket and helping William to haul it through the mud. He wondered what he would have thought of this manhandling of the body of a colleague before the plague had struck and inured him to such things.

'Gilbert,' said William shortly, oblivious to the muddy puddles through which he dragged the body. 'Like his master, isolation did not keep him from the Death.'

The stables, used as a mortuary for College plague victims, smelled so strongly of death and corruption that William backed out so fast he fell. Bartholomew went to help him up.

'Holy Mother!' the friar exclaimed, clambering to his feet with his wide sleeve firmly pressed to his nose. 'Thank the Lord we have no horses! They would have died breathing that stench!' He walked away as quickly as he could, turning to shout at Bartholomew, 'Get rid of the corpses, Doctor. Do your job!'

Bartholomew went back into the stables, covering his nose and mouth with his cloak. William was right: the odour was terrible. The porter, hearing William's shouting, came over to say that the carts had not been for the bodies for several days, and so it was not surprising that they were beginning to smell. Bartholomew tipped rushes from a hand-cart so he could begin to load the bodies onto it. The scholars would have to take their colleagues to the plague pit themselves if the official carts did not come.

Gray came to help, but gagged and complained so much that Bartholomew told him to wait outside. Bartholomew hated what he was doing. These ungainly lumps sewn tightly into rough College blankets had been people he had known. There were five College students, two of the commoners, and now Gilbert. Eight College members who had been his friends and colleagues. But there were nine shrouded bodies. He frowned and counted again, running through the names of the dead scholars one by one. He must have forgotten someone.

He took a body by the feet, and began to drag it to where Gray waited outside by the empty cart.

'Who has died since we buried Wilson?' Bartholomew asked.

Gray looked taken aback. 'I thought you kept a note of all these things,' he said. Seeing a flash of annoyance pass across Bartholomew's face, he recited the names.

'Eight,' said Bartholomew. 'Who died just before Wilson?'

Gray named the others, nineteen in all. He thought he saw which way the conversation was leading, assumed he was being criticised, and began to object. 'You told me to take them to the plague pit, and I did. Ask Cynric. He helped. We took all of them!'

Bartholomew held up his hand to quell Gray's indignant objections. 'I believe you,' he said. 'But we seem to have an extra body here now.'

Gray looked at the one Bartholomew still held by the feet. 'One of the townspeople probably slipped it in here so that we would take it to the pits with the others,' he suggested.

'Unlikely,' said Bartholomew, 'unless they stole one of our blankets as well.'

Gray and Bartholomew looked at each other for a moment, and then back to the stables. Bartholomew began to drag the body back inside again.

'This had best be done out of sight,' he said over

his shoulder to Gray. 'I do not want anyone to see what I am going to do. Will you bring a lamp?'

Gray was gone only briefly, returning with a lamp and a needle and thread. He lit the lamp and closed the door against prying eyes. 'You cut the shrouds open, and I will sew them up,' he said, swallowing hard as he steeled himself for the grisly task.

Bartholomew clapped him on the shoulder, and made a small cut along the seam of the first body. It was Gilbert. He sat for a moment, looking at his face, more peaceful than most of his patients, but blackened with the plague nevertheless. Gray, kneeling next to him, nudged him with his elbow.

'Hurry up,' he urged, 'or someone will come and ask what we are doing.'

He began stitching the blanket back together while Bartholomew moved to the next one. It was one of the law students who had been studying under Wilson. He resisted the urge to think about the scholars as their faces appeared under the coarse blanket-shrouds, and tried to concentrate on the task in hand. The third was another student, and the fourth one of the old commoners. As he came to the fifth, he paused. The blanket was exactly the same as the others, but there was an odd quality about the body inside that he could not define. Instinctively, he knew it was the one that did not belong to Michaelhouse.

Carefully he slit the stitches down one side of the blanket, noting that they were less neat than the others he had cut. He peeled it back and cried out in horror, leaping backwards and almost knocking the lamp over.

'What? What is it?' Gray gasped, unnerved by Bartholomew's white face. He went to look at the body, but Bartholomew pulled him back so he should not see.

They went to the door for some fresh air, away from the stench of the bodies. After a few moments, Bartholomew began to lose the unreal feeling he had had when he looked into the decomposed face of Augustus, and rubbed his hands on his robe to get rid of their clamminess. Gray waited anxiously.

Taking a last deep breath of clean air, Bartholomew turned to Gray. 'It is Augustus,' he said. Gray looked puzzled for a moment, and then his face cleared.

'Ah! The commoner who disappeared after you had declared him dead!' He looked at the stables. 'He is dead now, is he?'

'He was dead then,' snapped Bartholomew, trying to control the shaking of his hands. 'And he is very dead now.'

Bartholomew led Gray back inside the stables again, noticing how the student's eyes kept edging fearfully over to the bundle that was Augustus. 'You must not tell anyone of this,' Bartholomew said. 'I do not understand what is happening, why his body has been put here now after all this time. But I think he was murdered, and his murderer must still be alive or Augustus's body would still be hidden. We must be very careful.'

Gray nodded, his usually cheerful face sombre. 'Just sew him back up again, and let us pretend to anyone who is watching that we have not noticed the extra one,' he said, going to the door and trying to peer out through the gaps in the wood.

It was possibly already too late for that, Bartholomew thought, if the murderer had seen them take Gilbert's body back inside again once they had realised that something was amiss. He collected his thoughts. Bartholomew could see why Augustus's body had reappeared. It had been no secret that Wilson had spent some time talking alone to Bartholomew before he died. The murderer had assumed, correctly, that Wilson would tell him about the trap-door to the attic – where Augustus had probably lain since his body had been taken. That would explain the unpleasant smell that Bartholomew had noticed there. If, as Bartholomew supposed, the body had been hidden in the passageway, Wilson would have been unlikely to have found it because he would have no reason to search a passageway he knew was blocked off. Unless, he thought, Wilson had known, and had deliberately told Bartholomew about the trap-door, knowing that he would find Augustus. What had Wilson said? Discover who in the College knew about the trap-door and he would find the murderer?

Bartholomew rubbed a hand over his face. He realised that once the murderer became aware that Bartholomew knew of the trap-door and would be likely to search the attic, he would have to dispose of the corpse that had lain there for several months. In many ways, it was an ideal time. When better to dispose of a body than when there were bodies of so many others to be taken away? Had William not complained, then Bartholomew might well have left the bodies to be collected by the dead-cart the following day, and no one would have known that one of them had not died of the plague at all.

So the person who had brought Augustus's body to the stables must also have been the person who had killed him. It could not have been Aelfrith, since he was long dead. It could not have been Wilson, because

Augustus's body had been placed in the stable after he had died – and Bartholomew was certain Gray was not lying to him about removing the previous corpses. Was it Abigny? Had he come back from wherever he was hiding when he had heard that Bartholomew knew about the trap-door? Could it have been Swynford, back from his plague-free haven? Was it Michael, who had reacted so oddly at Augustus's death? Was it William, who had prompted him to look at the bodies in the first place, or Alcote, skulking in his room?

Gray was handing him the needle and thread so he could sew up Augustus's shroud again. But Bartholomew had one more task he needed to do.

'Start taking the others out to the cart,' he said. 'I need to take a closer look.'

Gray's eyes widened in horror, but he began to drag the bodies outside to the cart as Bartholomew had instructed. Bartholomew knelt down by Augustus, and slit the shroud down the side, pulling it back to reveal the grey, desiccated body. Augustus was still dressed in the nightshirt he had been wearing when Bartholomew had last seen his body, but it was torn down the middle to reveal the terrible mutilations underneath. Bartholomew felt anger boil inside him. Whoever had taken the body had slashed it open, pulling out entrails, and slicing deeply into the neck and throat.

All Bartholomew could assume was that Augustus had led the murderer to believe he had swallowed that wretched ring of Sir John's, and the murderer had desecrated his body to find it. Bartholomew was beginning to feel sick. Augustus's blackened and dried entrails had been stuffed crudely back into his body with a total disregard for his dignity. The horrific mess made

Bartholomew wonder whether the murderer would ever have found the ring anyway.

He had seen enough. Hastily, he began to resew the bundle, hiding the terribly mangled body from his sight – and from Gray, who was becoming bolder and inching forward. Bartholomew looked at Augustus's face. The warmth of the attic in the top of the house in late summer must have sucked the moisture from the body, for the face was dry and wizened rather than rotten. The skin had peeled back from the lips, leaving the teeth exposed, and the eyes were sunken, but it was unmistakably Augustus.

As Bartholomew covered up the face, he whispered a farewell. His mind flashed back to Augustus's funeral back in September, when a coffin filled with bags of earth had been reverently laid to rest in the churchyard. He sat back on his heels, staring down at the shapeless bundle in front of him, and wondered if the requiem mass said for him by Aelfrith had truly laid his soul to rest. Bartholomew had often looked at the simple wooden cross in the churchyard, and wondered about the body that should have lain beneath it. At least in the plague pit the old man would rest in hallowed ground and no one would come again to desecrate his body.

IX

February 1349

JANUARY ENDED IN A SUCCESSION OF BLIZZARDS THAT coated everything in white. With February came wetter, warmer weather that turned the snow into icy brown muck that seeped into shoes and chilled the feet. Bartholomew still trudged around the houses of plague victims, incising buboes where he could, but mostly doing little more than watching people die. He and Gray had visited the last of Abigny's known haunts, and then revisited his favourite ones, but had learned nothing. Philippa and Abigny seemed to have vanished into thin air.

Bartholomew heard that Stanmore's older sister, her husband, and all seven of their children were dead, while at Michaelhouse he buried Roger Alyngton, two more students, and four of the servants. Colet still sat in St Botolph's Church and drooled his days away. Bartholomew had lain in wait for him one day, and dragged him along when he went to visit his patients – hoping to shock him back to rationality – but his patients had been disconcerted, and Colet had become so distressed that Bartholomew was forced to take him home.

It was mid-afternoon, but already growing dark because of the overcast skies, when Bartholomew and Gray were met on the way home by Master Burwell, who asked them to attend a student who was dying. Bartholomew did all he could, but the student died without regaining consciousness. Three other Bene't Hostel students were ill, and Bartholomew helped Burwell set up a separate room in which they could be cared for. It was a large room compared to the others, and Jacob Yaxley, Master of Law, who had had it to himself since the death of his room-mates, clearly resented being moved. He muttered and grumbled as his students helped him carry his books and papers to another chamber.

As they walked back to the College, Bartholomew thought he saw one body, all wrapped in its shroud, move, and went to investigate. He took his knife and slit open the crude sheet. The woman inside was still alive, although barely. Her neighbour shouted that the woman had sewn herself into the winding sheet when she knew she had the plague, because there was no one left to do it for her.

'What about you?' Bartholomew shouted.

The neighbour crossed himself quickly, and slammed the window shut. The woman muttered incoherently as Bartholomew carried her back inside. He had heard from Michael that some people, the last surviving members of their families, were preparing themselves for burial with their dying strength but he had dismissed it as yet another plague story intended to horrify. He sat back on his heels, patting the woman's hand abstractedly, unable to stop his mind running through the dreadful outcomes of such actions:

supposing the cart had come while she was still alive, and she had been smothered in earth or burned by the quicklime? He wondered if others had not already suffered that fate. The woman slipped away quietly while he was thinking, and he and Gray resewed the shroud and left her on her doorstep again.

It was dark by the time they arrived back at Michaelhouse. Bartholomew went to see his patients in the commoners' room. Jerome had recovered from the plague, but it had weakened him, and he was dying slowly from the wasting disease in his chest. As Bartholomew entered the room, he saw Father William was helping one of the Benedictine novices to sew someone into a blanket. A quick glance around the room told him it was Nicholas, at fifteen Michaelhouse's youngest student, who looked that morning as if he might recover. Bartholomew sat heavily on a stool.

'His end was so quick that there was no time to call you,' William said. The fanatical gleam that was usually in his eyes had dulled, and he looked exhausted. 'I have listened to so many dreadful confessions that hell will soon be running out of space.'

Bartholomew wondered if the Franciscan were making a joke, but there was no humour in his face. 'Then perhaps there will be an overspill into heaven,' he replied, standing up.

William grabbed at his sleeve and pulled him down again, whispering angrily in his ear. 'That is heresy, Doctor, and I advise you against such fanciful remarks!'

'So is your belief that hell has limited space,' Bartholomew retorted. He remembered the rumours when William had first arrived at Michaelhouse that he had been an inquisitor for the Church.

William let go of Bartholomew's sleeve. 'Do not worry,' he said, and Bartholomew saw the gleam come back into his eye as his mind ran over the implications of Bartholomew's reply. 'I will not entrap you in a theological debate. But I miss the company of Aelfrith. There was a man with a lively mind!'

Bartholomew agreed, and wished Aelfrith were alive, so that he could confide his thoughts and feelings to him at that moment. He could have trusted Aelfrith – unlike William or Alcote or Michael – with his concerns about the plague and the College. And thinking of Michael, Bartholomew had not seen him since the previous day. He asked if William had.

A curious expression passed over William's face. 'No,' he said. 'He has gone somewhere. He has left me with quite a burden, you know.'

Bartholomew thought it curious that Michael had told no one where he was going, but let it pass. He stood up from his stool, stretched his aching limbs, and helped William to carry Nicholas downstairs and across the courtyard to the stables. They placed the body near the door and left as quickly as possible. Bartholomew knew he would never enter the stables again without thinking about Augustus.

The following day, as he walked back along the High Street with Gray, Bartholomew felt the first huge drops of rain from a storm that had been threatening all morning. Gray hailed a student he knew, who invited them into Mary's Hostel to shelter from the worst of the rain. Like Bene't Hostel, Mary's was warm, steamy, and smelled of boiled vegetables. The student brought them spiced wine, and Bartholomew began to relax from the warmth of the fire and the effects of the wine.

He was virtually asleep when he became aware that Gary was introducing him to someone. Embarrassed, he jumped to his feet, and bowed to the scholar who was being presented to him. From Gray's words, he found it was the new Principal of Mary's, Neville Stayne. Bartholomew had known the previous Principal quite well, but he had died of the plague before Christmas. His successor was a man in his forties with a shock of oddly wiry black hair that seemed to want to be as far away from his scalp as possible.

Stayne gestured for him to sit again, and perched on a stool next to him, asking him about the progress of the plague in the town. After a while, Stayne brought the subject round to Giles Abigny, who, it seemed, had also spent a good deal of time at Mary's. The members of the hostel were anxious for his safety.

'Have you any idea where he might be?' asked Bartholomew, expecting the same range of speculation and unfounded rumour he had been given everywhere else.

The fire popped and crackled, and Stayne watched it for a moment before answering. 'I do not know where he is now, but I believe I saw him two nights ago in Cambridge.'

Bartholomew's stomach lurched. 'Where? What happened?'

'Well, I think I saw him coming out of the alehouse near the Dominican Friary the night before last. I had heard about him taking his sister off somewhere, and so seeing him stuck in my mind.' The Principal leaned back and closed his eyes as he tried to recall what he had seen. 'He was wearing a heavy cloak, and he turned when I called his name. Then he began to walk away from me quickly. He turned a corner, and I ran after him, but when I got there, the street was empty.' He shrugged. 'That is all, I am afraid. If asked to swear in a court of law, I would not be able to say it was definitely Giles. But it certainly looked like him, and he did turn and then run away when I called his name. Draw your own conclusions.'

Bartholomew and Gray took their leave as soon as the rain had eased. Stayne closed the door behind them and waited. From the small chamber to one side of the hallway, Burwell emerged. The two men spoke together in low tones for a short time, and then Burwell left, his face grim.

There were two alehouses near the Dominican Friary, but no one in either could remember Giles Abigny. When Bartholomew began to describe him, the fat landlord shook his head.

'We are on a main road, and our trade is excellent, even with this pestilence. I cannot remember everyone who buys ale from me. He may have been here, but I cannot be certain.'

The landlord at the other alehouse knew Abigny and was more helpful, but said Abigny had most definitely not been there two nights before. He smiled ruefully, and said that Abigny had once been caught cheating at a game of dice with two of the locals, and had not dared to show his face again for fear of what might happen to him.

They walked back to Michaelhouse, and, after a silent meal, Bartholomew went to the sick-room. The dim light of the grey winter afternoon made it feel gloomy, and Bartholomew stoked up the fire. He was sure that Wilson would have been appalled at the waste of fuel on dying men. He smiled to himself as a picture of Wilson in hell, telling the Devil not to waste wood on his fires, sprang into his mind. He felt someone touch him on the shoulder, and looked up to see William bending over him. He felt slightly uncomfortable. Was the ex-inquisitor reading his mind and seeing heretical thoughts within?

William beckoned him outside, and stood waiting in the chilly hallway outside Augustus's room.

'We have been sent a message from the Chancellor at last,' he said. 'He has chosen Robert Swynford to be our next Master.'

'No great surprise, and he will make a good Master,' Bartholomew said. 'Will he come back from the country?'

William shook his head. 'Robert also sent a message saying that there has been plague in the house of his relatives and most of the menfolk have died. He asks our indulgence that we allow him to remain away for a few weeks until he is sure the women will be properly cared for. He has asked Alcote to act as his deputy until then.'

Bartholomew wondered if leaving the College in the care of a man who had just been deprived of the position might not be a risky move. Then he thought of Robert Swynford's easy grace and confidence, and knew that he would have no problem whatsoever in wresting delegated power back from Alcote.

'But Alcote is hiding in his room like Wilson was,' said Bartholomew. 'How can he run the College?'

'I assume Swynford has not been told that,' said William. 'Alcote has asked for various documents to be sent to him, so it seems he will at least see to the administration.'

Bartholomew went outside for some air and to stretch limbs cramped from bending over his patients all afternoon. The rain had stopped, and the clouds were beginning to clear. The porter saw him and scuttled over, stopping a good ten feet from Bartholomew, a large pomander filled with powerful herbs pressed to his face. Bartholomew realised that he had not seen the porter's face since the day he had returned from the house of Agatha's cousin and announced to Michaelhouse that the plague had come. The man held a note that he placed on the ground so he would not have to go nearer to Bartholomew than necessary. When he saw Bartholomew pick it up, he scurried back into the safety of his lodge. Bartholomew watched as he slammed the door. Perhaps the porter was right, and Bartholomew did carry a dangerous miasma around with him. He felt well enough, but how did he know he did not carry the contagion with him, in his breath, his clothes? He sighed heavily and turned his attention to the scrap of parchment in his hand which, in almost illegible writing, said that he was needed at the tinker's house near the river.

Bartholomew collected his cloak and bag of medicines, and set off. A wind was getting up, and it seemed to be growing colder by the moment. Bartholomew wondered whether the river would freeze over, as it had done the year before. As first, he had welcomed this, because it had cut down the smell. But then people just threw rubbish onto the ice rather than into the water, and it was not long before the smell was worse than it had been when the river was running.

He reached the river, and turned to walk along the

row of shacks where the river people lived. He recalled that the last patient he had seen before the plague had been the tinker's little girl, and he remembered that he had seen her body buried in one of the first plague pits to be dug. The last house in the row belonged to the tinker, but only one child stood outside to greet him this time.

Entering the single room, he walked over to the pile of rags in one corner that served as a bed, and crouched down to look at the person huddled there. He was pleasantly surprised to see a healthy woman lying on the bed.

She appeared startled to see him, and exchanged a puzzled glance with the child who had followed him in.

'You sent for me,' said Bartholomew, kneeling on the earth floor. 'What can I do?'

The woman exchanged another look with the child, who shook her head. 'I would not send for you for this, Doctor,' the woman said. 'My baby is coming. The midwife is dead, and I had to send my lad to fetch a woman to help me. I do not need a physician.'

Bartholomew returned her puzzled look. 'But you sent me a note . . .'

He stopped as the woman tensed with a wave of contractions. When she relaxed again, she blurted out, 'I did no such thing. I cannot write, and nor can my children. I do not need a physician.'

And could not pay for one was the unspoken addendum. Bartholomew shrugged. 'But since I am here, and since your time is close, perhaps I can help. And I will require no payment,' he added quickly, seeing concern flitting across the woman's face.

Bartholomew sent the child to fetch some water and cloths, and not a minute too soon, for the top of the baby's head was already showing. Between gasps, the tinker's wife told him how the other women who lived nearby were either dead or had the pestilence, and she had sent her son to fetch her sister from Haslingfield. But since that was several miles, she had known help might come too late. Physicians usually left childbirth to the midwives, and Bartholomew was only ever called if there was a serious problem, usually when it was far too late for him to do much about it. He was not surprised to find that he was enjoying doing something other than dealing with plague victims. When the baby finally slid into his hands all slippery and bawling healthily, he was more enthusiastic over it than were the exhausted mother and her wide-eyed daughter.

'It is a beautiful girl,' he said, giving the baby to the mother to nurse, 'perfectly formed and very healthy.' He pulled back the cloth so he could look at her face, and exchanged grins with the mother. He took one of the tiny hands in his. 'Look at her fingernails!' he exclaimed.

The tinker's wife began to laugh. 'Why, Doctor, anyone would think a newborn baby was something special to hear you going on!' she said. 'You would not be like this if it was your ninth in twelve years!'

Bartholomew laughed with her. 'I would be happy to help with any more babies you might have, Mistress Tinker,' he said, 'and would consider it a privilege to be asked.'

Bartholomew left the house feeling happier than he had since the plague had started. He made his way back along the river, whistling softly to himself. As he turned the corner to go back to College, a figure stepped out

of the shadows in front of him, wielding what looked to
be a heavy stick.

Bartholomew stopped in his tracks and glanced
behind him, cursing himself for his foolishness. Another
two shadowy forms stood there similarly armed. The
note! It had been a trap! He swallowed hard, a vision of
Augustus's mutilated body coming to mind. His stomach
was a cold knot of fear. He had a small knife that he used
for medical purposes, but it would be useless against
three men armed with staves. He twisted the strap of
his bag around his hand, and suddenly raced forward,
swinging the bag at the figure in front of him as he did
so. He felt it hit the man, and heard him grunt as he
fell. Bartholomew kept going, hearing the footsteps of
the two behind him following.

He fell heavily to the ground as a fourth figure shot
out of some bushes in the lane and crashed into him. He
twisted round, and saw one of the men who had followed
raise his stick high into the air for a blow that would smash
his head like an egg. He kicked out at the man's legs, and
saw him lose his balance. Bartholomew tried to scramble
to his feet, but someone else had grabbed him by his
cloak and was trying to pull it tight around his throat.
Bartholomew struggled furiously, lashing out with fists
and feet, and hearing from the obscenities and yelps
that a good many of his blows were true.

He brought his knee up sharply into the groin of
one man, but he could not hold out for ever against
four. He looked up, and saw for the second time an
upraised stick silhouetted against the dark sky, but now
he was pinned down and unable to struggle free. He
closed his eyes, waiting for the blow that he was certain
would be the last thing he would know.

The blow never came. Instead, the man toppled onto him clutching his chest, and Bartholomew felt a warm spurt of blood gush over him. He squirmed out from underneath the inert body, and made a grab for the cloak of one of his attackers who was now trying to run away. The man kicked backwards viciously, and Bartholomew was forced to let go. He heard their footsteps growing fainter as they ran up the lane, while others came closer.

He drew his knife, knowing that he did not have the strength to run a second time, and prepared to sell his life dearly should he be attacked again. He squinted as a lamp was thrust into his face.

'Matt!' Bartholomew felt himself hauled to his feet, and looked into the anxious face of Oswald Stanmore.

'Matt!' Stanmore repeated, looking down the lane after Bartholomew's attackers. 'What happened? Who is this?' He pushed at the body of the man who had fallen with his foot.

Bartholomew saw that Stanmore's steward, Hugh, was with him, armed with a crossbow. Stanmore kept looking around, as if he expected the attackers to come again.

'I was sent a note to see a patient by the river,' Bartholomew said, still trying to recover his breath, 'and these men attacked me.'

'You should know better than to go to the river after dark,' said Stanmore. 'The Sheriff caught three of the robbers that have been menacing the town there only last week. Doubtless these are more of the same.' He glanced around. 'Who sent you the note? Surely you can tie note and attackers together?'

Bartholomew showed him the now-crumpled message. 'The tinker did not write this,' he said.

Stanmore took it from him and peered at it. 'The tinker most certainly did not,' he said, 'for he died last month. I heard that only two of his children live, and his wife is expecting her ninth, poor woman.'

Bartholomew bent to look at the man on the ground. He was dead, the crossbow bolt embedded deeply in his chest. Bartholomew rifled hurriedly through his clothes, hoping for something that would identify him. There was a plain purse, filled with silver coins, but nothing else.

Bartholomew shook the purse at Stanmore. 'He was paid this money to attack me,' he said. He thought about the tinker's baby: it would make a fine gift for her baptism.

Stanmore began to lead the way cautiously up the lane towards Michaelhouse. Bartholomew caught his sleeve as they walked. 'What were you doing here?' he asked, keeping a wary eye on the trees at the sides of the lane.

Stanmore raised the lamp to look into some deep shadows near the back of Michaelhouse. 'A barge came in today,' he said, 'and I have been sitting with the captain negotiating the price of the next shipment.' He nodded at his steward. 'When I am at the wharf after dark, I always tell Hugh to bring his crossbow. You never know who you might meet around here.'

Bartholomew clapped Stanmore on the shoulder. 'I did not say thank you,' he said. 'Had you been a second later, you would have been rescuing a corpse!'

They reached Michaelhouse, and Stanmore joined Bartholomew for a cup of spiced wine in the hall, while Hugh was despatched to take the news to the Sheriff.

Father William was there too, trying to read by the light from the candles, and several students talked in low voices in another corner.

Stanmore stretched out his legs in front of the small fire. 'These robbers are getting bold,' he said. 'They have only picked on the dead and dying up until now. This is the first time I have heard them attacking the healthy.'

Bartholomew put the purse on the table. He quickly told Stanmore about the blacksmith, and how he had been paid to do Bartholomew harm during the riot. Stanmore listened, his mouth agape in horror.

'For the love of God, Matt! What have you got yourself mixed up in? First this blacksmith business, then Philippa, and now this!'

Bartholomew could only look as mystified as his brother-in-law.

When Hugh returned, Stanmore rose to leave, declining Bartholomew's offer of a bed for the night. 'No thank you, Matt!' he said, looking round at the College. 'Why should I spend a night in this cold and wretched place when I can have roaring fires and bright, candle-lit rooms with Stephen?'

Bartholomew went back to his own room, and undressed ready for bed. He had to wash and hang up his clothes in the dark, because scholars were not usually given candles for their rooms. It was considered wasteful, when they could use the communal ones in the hall, or, more usually, the conclave. He tidied the room as best he could, and lay on the creaking bed, rubbing his feet together hard in a vain attempt to warm them up. Stanmore was right: Michaelhouse was cold and gloomy. He tried to get comfortable, wincing as the wooden board dug into a place where one of his attackers had kicked him.

So, who had tried to kill him? Both the blacksmith and the dead man had been paid about five marks in silver in leather purses. Were they connected? They had to be: surely there was not more than one group of people who would pay to have him killed! Bartholomew shifted uncomfortably. He could hear Michael's Benedictine room-mates chanting a psalm in the room above. Then, somewhere in the lane outside, a dog barked twice. A gust of wind rattled the shutters, and rain pattered against them. He curled up in a ball, and attempted to wrap the bedclothes round his frozen feet. He tried to concentrate, but his thoughts kept running together. Next he knew, it was morning.

It was overcast and wet. Bartholomew went to the church for mass, where he was the only one present other than Father William. The Franciscan babbled the Latin at such high speed that Bartholomew barely heard most of it. He wondered whether William could really be sincere at such a pace, or whether he believed God liked His masses fast so He could get on with other things. Bartholomew would have asked him had he not been reluctant to be drawn into a protracted debate.

Remembering his obligation to Wilson, Bartholomew went to look at the spot the lawyer had chosen for his glorious tomb. Bartholomew had already asked one of the Castle stonemasons to order a slab of black marble, although he wondered when he would be able to hire someone to carve it. The Master Mason had died of the plague, and the surviving masons were overwhelmed by the repair work necessary to maintain the Castle. As he gazed at Wilson's niche, he thought it unfair that good men like Augustus and Nicholas should lie in a mass grave, while Wilson should have a grand tomb to commemorate him.

Bartholomew left the church and stepped into the street, closing the door behind him. He pulled his hood up against the rain, and set off to check the plague pits. On his way, he met Burwell, who greeted him with a smile and told him that there had been no new cases of plague in Bene't Hostel for two days.

As they talked, a beggar with dreadful sores on his face approached, pleading for alms. Bartholomew knew the beggar prepared his 'sores' every morning with a mixture of chalk, mud, and pig's blood. The beggar suddenly recognised Bartholomew under his hood, and backed off in dismay, as Bartholomew grasped Burwell's hand to prevent him from giving his money away.

As Bartholomew turned to explain to Burwell, he saw the purse in the hand he held. It was made of fine leather, and had 'BH' embellished on it in gold thread. Bartholomew had one just like it in his pocket. He felt his stomach turn over, although there was no reason why the Sub-Principal of Bene't Hostel should not have one of its purses. Burwell looked at him curiously. 'Doctor?' he said.

'Sores painted on fresh every day,' mumbled Bartholomew, hoping Burwell had not noticed his reaction, and if he had, did not guess why.

Burwell looked up at the sky as the church bell rang out the hour, and drew his hood over his head. 'Well, I must be about my business, and I know you must be busy.' He started to walk away, and then stopped.

'When you next see that rascal, Samuel Gray, could you tell him that he still owes us money for his fees last term?'

Bartholomew was a little angry at Gray. He should have cleared his debts with the hostel before changing to a new teacher. It was just another example of the double life the student seemed to lead. Bartholomew wondered what else he kept hidden. Since he was passing, Bartholomew went into St Botolph's Church to look for Colet. The Physician sat in his usual place, staring at the candles and twisting the golden lion round his fingers again and again.

When Bartholomew tried to talk to him, Colet fixed him with a vacant stare, and Bartholomew was in no doubt that Colet no longer knew who he was. His beard was encrusted with dried saliva, and his clothes were filthy. Bartholomew wondered if he should try to do something for him, but Colet did not seem to be in any discomfort. He decided to wait for a day or so and reconsider it then.

He left the church and continued along the High Street. As he passed the King's Head, Henry Oliver emerged and gave him such a look of undisguised enmity that Bartholomew stopped dead in his tracks. Oliver began to walk towards him. Bartholomew waited, taking the small knife out of his bag and keeping it hidden under his cloak so that Oliver would not see it.

'Found your lady yet, Doctor?' he said, his voice little more than a hiss.

Bartholomew wanted to push him into the stone trough that was full of water for horses, just behind him. 'Why do you ask?' he said, his voice betraying none of the anger that welled up inside him.

Oliver shrugged nonchalantly and gave a cold little smile. 'Just curious to know whether she continues to hide from you.'

Bartholomew smiled back. 'She still hides from me,' he said, wondering what Oliver thought he was going to gain from this cat-and-mouse game. 'Now, if you will excuse me, pleasant though it is to talk with you, the plague pit calls.'

He walked away, wondering what on earth could be the matter with the young man, and decided to speak to Swynford about it when he returned to College. The unpleasantness had gone on quite long enough.

As he approached the plague pit, an urchin darted up to him and mumbled something before turning to race away. Bartholomew, quick as lightning, grabbed him and held him as he struggled frantically, kicking at Bartholomew with his small bare feet. Bartholomew waited until the child's frenzy was spent and spoke gently.

'I did not hear what you said. Say it again.'

'A well-wisher has sommat to tell you if you come here at ten tonight,' he stammered, looking up at Bartholomew with big frightened eyes. 'But you got to come alone.'

Bartholomew stared at him. Was this another ploy to get him into a place where he could be dispatched as he almost had been the night before?

'Who told you to tell me this?'

The brat struggled again. 'I don't know. It was a man all wrapped up. He asked if I knew you – you came to my ma when she was sick – so I said yes, and he told me to tell you that message and to run away after. He gave me a penny.' He thrust out his hand to show it. Bartholomew let the child go and watched him scamper down the muddy street.

Now what? he thought. As if the plague, the College and Philippa were not enough to worry about!

The rain had eased off during the day, and, as night fell, patches of blue began to appear in the sky. But by the time Bartholomew returned to Michaelhouse after attending his patients, it was so late that most of the scholars were already in bed.

He went to the kitchen where Cynric dozed in front of the dying fire, and rummaged in the pantry until he found the remains of a loaf of bread and some hard cheese. While he ate, Cynric stoked up the fire, and set some wine to mull for them both. Bartholomew considered whether he should go to meet his 'well-wisher' at the plague pit. It seemed an odd choice for a rendezvous, but it would certainly be private, for no one in his right mind would frequent that place of desolation and despair in the dead of night. He glanced at the hour candle. He would need to make up his mind fairly quickly, for the meeting was in less than an hour.

Perhaps the mysterious sender really did wish him well, and would have information about Philippa. He tried to consider it logically. The people who attacked him would hardly expect that he would accept a second invitation to meet an unknown person in the dark in some god-forsaken spot after what had happened to him the previous night. Therefore, his 'well-wisher' must be someone who did not know about the attack. Of course, his attackers might use the same line of reasoning as he had just done. He stared into the fire and tapped his fingers on the table as his mind wrestled with the problem.

Abruptly, he stood. He was going. He would arm himself this time, and would be alert to the possibility of danger, unlike the previous night. He had spent hours in taverns and hostels trying to learn something about the disappearance of Giles and Philippa: it was possible that his well-wisher might have the information he wanted, and he did not wish to miss out on such an opportunity by being overly cautious.

Cynric looked at him sleepily. 'You going out again?' he asked. His eyes snapped open as Bartholomew took a large double-edged butchery knife from its hook on the wall and slipped it under his cloak.

'Now what are you going to do with that?' he said. He sat up straight in Agatha's fireside chair, his interest quickened. 'Not roistering about the town?'

'I have a meeting,' said Bartholomew. He saw no reason why he should not tell Cynric where he was going. At least then, if he were attacked, Cynric could tell the Sheriff it had been planned, and was not some random skirmish by the robbers as Stanmore plainly believed had happened the previous evening.

Cynric grabbed his cloak from where it lay in a bundle on the floor. 'At this time of night? After what happened to you yesterday? I had better come too, to keep you from mischief.'

'No,' said Bartholomew, thinking about the message. It told him to come alone, and he did not want to run the risk of frightening off a potential informant.

Cynric threw his cloak around his shoulders, and stood next to Bartholomew. 'We have known each other for a long time,' he said quietly, 'and I have seen that there has been something amiss with you since Sir John died. Perhaps I can help. I know you are anxious about the Lady Philippa. Is that what this meeting is about?'

Bartholomew gave a reluctant smile. He had forgotten how astute the small Welshman could be. He nodded and said, 'But I have been told to come alone.'

Cynric dismissed this with a wave of his hand. 'The day someone sees Cynric ap Huwydd when he does not want to be seen will be the day he dies. Do not worry, boy, I will be there, but none will know it other than you. Now, where are we going?'

Bartholomew relented. He was nervous about the meeting, and it would be reassuring to have Cynric nearby. If nothing else, at least he could run for help if things took a nasty turn. 'But you must be cautious,' he said. 'I have no idea who we are meeting, or what they want. If there is trouble, run for help. Do not come yourself or you may get hurt.'

Cynric shot him a disbelieving look. 'What do you take me for, boy? You should know me better than that. I learned something of ambush tactics in the Welsh mountains, you know.'

'I am sorry. It is just that so many people have met untimely deaths in the College and I do not want to lose anyone else.'

'Like Augustus, Paul and Montfitchet, you mean?' asked Cynric. Bartholomew looked at him askance.

'Just because I have no degree, like you scholars, does not mean I have no sense,' said Cynric. 'I know they were murdered, despite the lies that fat Wilson put about. I will keep my mouth shut,' he added quickly, seeing Bartholomew's expression of concern. 'I have done until now. But you should know that you are not alone in this.'

It was a long speech for Cynric, who indicated that the subject was closed by pinching out the candles and selecting a knife of his own.

Bartholomew slipped out of the kitchen door and across the courtyard. He walked briskly up St Michael's Lane and turned into the High Street. It was not easy to walk in the dark. The night had turned foggy, blocking out any light the moon might have given, and it was almost impossible to see the pot-holes and rubbish until he had stepped into them. At one point, he stumbled into a hole full of stinking water that reached his knees. Grimacing with distaste at the smell of urine and offal that came from it, he picked himself up and continued. From Cynric there was not a sound, but Bartholomew knew he was there.

At last he reached the field where the plague pits had been dug. A crude wooden fence had been erected around the field to prevent dogs from entering and digging up the victims. Bartholomew climbed over it and looked around. The mounds from the two full pits rose from the trampled grass like ancient pagan barrows. The other pit gaped like a great black mouth, and Bartholomew could make out the paler layer at the bottom where the lime had been spread over the last bodies to be laid there.

He tried to detect whether there was anyone hiding in the hedges at the sides of the field, but he could see nothing moving. A sound behind him made him spin round and almost lose his balance. His heart beat wildly and he felt his knees turn to jelly. He grabbed at the fence with one hand, while the other groped for the long knife that he had tucked into his belt.

A figure stood outside the fence, heavily cloaked and hooded. It made no attempt to climb over, and when Bartholomew took a step forward, it held up its hand.

'Stay!'

It was a woman's voice. Bartholomew's heart leapt. 'Philippa!' he exclaimed.

The figure was still for a moment, and then shook her head. 'Not Philippa. I am sorry.'

Bartholomew's hopes sank. It was not Philippa's voice: it was deeper, older, and with an accent that suggested the speaker came from the Fens rather than the town.

The woman looked around her quickly. 'I am glad you came, but it is not safe for us to meet like this.'

She glanced around again, and leaned over the fence so she would not have to speak so loudly. 'There is a meeting tomorrow at Bene't Hostel. I cannot say what it is about, but you should try to find out because I think it will affect you. The best way would be for you to go to the back of the house and climb to the window in the room they use for the hall. There is a deep sill there, and you will be able to hear what is being said through the shutters. You must take utmost care, for these are dangerous men. But I think you will be safer knowing than not knowing what they say.'

Bartholomew was totally confused. 'Is this about Philippa?' he asked.

The figure took a step away. 'I cannot say. You will have to listen and work it out for yourself.'

'But who are you?' Bartholomew asked.

The woman took another step away. 'Please! I will

lose everything if anyone finds out I met with you tonight. Now I must go. Please do not follow me. I ask you this because I took a risk for you tonight.'

Bartholomew assented. 'Is there anything I can do for you?'

The woman stopped and he could feel her looking at him from the depths of her hood. 'You have done enough,' she said softly, and slipped away into the mist.

Bartholomew looked after her, totally mystified. What kind of meeting held at Bene't Hostel could possibly have any relevance to him? And how was he supposed to climb up the back of the building and eavesdrop like some spy? Was this a ploy to discredit him, to get him into some dreadfully compromising position so that he could be dismissed from the University? Were there Oxford scholars plotting against him? Wilson and Aelfrith would probably think so, but there was something about the Oxford plot that Bartholomew could not accept. He understood why Wilson and Aelfrith had believed in it, but he still felt that the entire business was far more important to Cambridge than Oxford, and that Oxford would not waste time on it.

Cynric materialised in front of him, making him jump almost as much as he had when the woman had appeared. Cynric put his hand on his shoulder.

'Easy, boy! Not so jumpy. Shall I follow her?'

Bartholomew dug his nails into the fence, taking deep breaths to calm himself down. The woman had taken a risk to give him information she considered to be important to him, and had asked him not to put her in further danger by following her home.

'No, Cynric,' he said. 'Let her go.'

'Who was it?' Cynric asked, sounding disappointed. Bartholomew had the feeling his book-bearer was enjoying this nocturnal escapade.

'I do not know, but I think she means us no harm,' he said, climbing slowly over the fence.

'What did she want?'

Bartholomew was silent for a moment before telling Cynric what she had said.

Cynric rubbed his hands together gleefully. 'Should not be too difficult to do,' he said. He screwed up his eyes as he thought. 'Yes. It is possible to climb up the back of Bene't Hostel. It is all covered with ivy that they have never bothered to cut. They throw their rubbish in the back yard, and one of the garderobe chutes empties there. No one bothers to go there because it is so filthy, so I think we should have no problems.'

'We?' queried Bartholomew nervously. 'I cannot drag you into this . . .'

'You cannot keep me out of it! And anyway, I am much better at this sort of thing than you are.'

Bartholomew had to acknowledge that he was right, but he did not feel comfortable with the notion of dragging Cynric into anything unsavoury or dangerous. He stared out into the mist in the direction in which the woman had gone. The fog thinned slightly for a few moments, and Bartholomew could see the King's Head opposite.

As he watched, a figure emerged. Bartholomew tensed. It looked like Oswald Stanmore. He blinked, and the figure had gone. He shook himself. He was imagining things. Stanmore would be tucked up safe and warm in his bed in Trumpington by now, and would never be seen frequenting a disreputable place like the King's Head. Bartholomew was obviously tired and prone to an overactive imagination. He took hold of Cynric's sleeve and tugged, indicating the way back down the High Street towards home.

Cynric was already making plans for entering Bene't's yard the next night, and Bartholomew, seeing his eyes gleam with excitement, did not have the heart to tell him he could not go. He was not even sure whether he wanted to go himself. The mist clung to their clothes as they walked, and seemed to muffle the usual sounds of the night. Distantly, Bartholomew heard wailing. Another plague death? Or a cat hunting among the piles of rubbish? He was glad when the walls of Michaelhouse loomed up out of the fog, and too tired to speculate any further on his well-wisher's intentions. He fell asleep in his clothes listening to the regular breathing of Gray in the other bed.

Early the next day, Bartholomew received a message from the barber-surgeon Robin of Grantchester saying that he had convened a meeting with representatives from the town to discuss what they were going to do about the settlement near All Saints-next-the-Castle, where all had lain dead for many weeks. Rumours abounded that the dead walked down into Cambridge at night, and were spreading the pestilence. The meeting was acrimonious, and the real issue about what should be done about the community beyond the Castle was sidestepped until Bartholomew rapped on the table with the hilt of Stanmore's dagger to make the voices subside.

'Everyone who lived in settlement beyond the Castle is either dead or has left,' he said. 'I have seen that there are bodies rotting in virtually every house. While I do not believe they walk in the town at night, the area should be cleared in the interests of health. I propose we burn it down.'

Horrified faces stared at him, open-mouthed.

'With the bodies still inside?' whispered Stephen Stanmore.

'Unless you would like to go and fetch them out,' said Bartholomew.

'But that is sacrilege!' said Father William, aghast. 'Those people must be buried decently.'

'So fetch them, and then we will burn the houses.'

There was a silence, and then mutterings of reluctant assent. Clerics and medics alike accepted that there was no other safe way to deal with the problem, but no one had wanted to be the one to suggest such an unpopular solution.

Bartholomew had a hasty meal with William, and set off for the settlement. Two lay-brothers had volunteered to help, and people came out of their houses to watch them pass. The burning did not take long: the houses were flimsy and, despite the rain that had drenched them during the past few weeks, fired easily.

When the flames died down, Bartholomew found he was shaking, and wondered if he had really condemned the spirits of the people to walk in perpetual torment as the rector of St Clement's had claimed. William scattered holy water about, and Bartholomew watched it hiss and evaporate as it touched the still-hot embers of the houses. Bartholomew knew he would never want to visit this part of the town again.

'That was a foul day's work,' William remarked as they returned to Michaelhouse. 'But it had to be done. The rector was wrong: the souls of those people will go wherever they were destined to be, and nothing you have done today will change that. Put it from your mind, and think of other things.'

Bartholomew smiled gratefully. William was most certainly not a person to give false assurances; if anything, he tended the other way, and his words made Bartholomew's mind easier.

'I heard you helped Mistress Tinker to give birth to another child,' said William.

Bartholomew thought back to his delight at seeing the baby born and remembered the purse he had taken to give her. He asked William if he would give it to the mother when he baptised the child the following day. William raised his eyebrows.

'Not your own child, is it?' he asked.

Bartholomew was taken aback. What twisted minds these University people had! What made them read sinister motives into even the most innocent of acts? William caught his look and changed the subject. 'Have you seen Brother Michael today?'

Bartholomew had not seen Brother Michael for some days and was growing anxious. He had even looked up in the attic that morning, to satisfy himself that the murderer had not been at work again. He was about to voice his concerns to William, when he saw Colet being escorted out of St Botolph's Church by two monks. Colet was laughing uncontrollably, and drooling even more than usual. His eyes, instead of being blank, were wild and starting from his head.

'What has happened?' Bartholomew watched in pity as Colet cackled to himself.

'He acts so around this time of day,' one of the monks said, 'and we have to take him home.

His mind has gone. There is nothing you can do, Doctor.'

Agatha would not let Bartholomew into the kitchen, saying he smelled of the 'fires of death'. She took his clothes away to be laundered, and made him wash thoroughly in water she had liberally peppered with herbs to take away the smell. Although the water was cold, Bartholomew felt better when the smell of burning had gone. He sat shivering next to the kitchen fire, eating stale marchpanes.

Cynric drew a stool up next to him. He glanced around to make sure Agatha could not hear, but she was busy trying to persuade William to go through the same process as Bartholomew, and was unlikely to be distracted from her purpose until William had bent to her will.

'I have been out and about,' he said in a low voice. 'The steward at Bene't's has been given the night off tonight, and told he can visit his mother. They are also short of candles, and the Sub-Principal has suggested that all lights be extinguished at eight o'clock until they can replenish their stocks. You know what all this means?'

Bartholomew could guess. The steward was being invited to leave the premises overnight, and the students, deprived of light, would probably go to bed early since there was little they could do in the dark. All this suggested that his well-wisher was right, and that there would be a clandestine meeting at Bene't Hostel that night. He had not given the matter much thought during the day since he had had so much else to think about, but now he needed to come to a decision.

He slipped out through the back of the kitchen and

made his way to the orchard, remembering that the last time he had done this was when Aelfrith had spoken to him. Now, it was bitterly cold, and the branches of the trees were grey-brown and bare. He sat for a while with his eyes closed, trying to concentrate on the silence of the orchard and not the roaring in his head from the fires. He began to think about whether he should go to Bene't Hostel to spy. Was it safe, or was it a trap? Who was this woman who claimed to wish him well? He rubbed a hand through his hair, and stood, hugging his arms around his body to keep warm. But when he thought about Philippa, he knew he would eavesdrop on the meeting. After all, Cynric would be there, and if anyone could enter and leave places unseen it was Cynric. He began to walk slowly back through the College heading for his room, but was intercepted by a breathless Cynric.

'There you are!' he said, his tone slightly accusatory. 'You had better come quick. Henry Oliver is here, and he is terrible sick of the plague.'

X

AS BARTHOLOMEW AND CYNRIC HURRIED through the College, they could hear Henry Oliver's enraged yells coming from the commoners' room. Cynric told Bartholomew that two students had found him lying outside the King's Head tavern, and had brought him back so he could be cared for in the plague ward. Oliver, it seemed, had other ideas, and had kicked and struggled as much as his weakened body would allow, demanding to be taken to his own room.

The Benedictines were having a difficult time trying to quieten him down, and his shouts and curses were disturbing the other patients. One of the monks was almost lying on top of him to keep him in the bed. When Oliver saw Bartholomew standing in the doorway, his struggles increased.

'Keep him away from me,' he screamed. 'He will kill me!'

Slowly Bartholomew approached the bed, and laid his hand gently on the sick student's head. Oliver shrank away, pushing himself as far back against the wall as he could.

'Come, now, Henry,' Bartholomew said softly. 'No

one is going to hurt you. You are ill and need help, and this is the best place for you to get it.'

'No!' Oliver yelled, his eyes darting frantically round the room. 'You will kill me here!'

'Now why would I do that?' asked Bartholomew, reaching out to turn Oliver's head gently, so he could inspect the swellings in his neck.

Oliver's breath came in short agonised gasps. 'The Master told me,' he whispered, flashing a terrified glance at Bartholomew.

'Swynford?' asked Bartholomew, astonished. 'Swynford told you I would kill you?'

Oliver shook his head. 'Master Wilson. Wilson said you would kill him. And you did!' He sank back against the wall, exhausted. Bartholomew looked at him thunderstruck, while the monk knelt to begin taking off Oliver's wet clothes.

The Benedictine smiled briefly at Bartholomew. 'Delirious,' he said. 'They claim all sorts of things, you know. Poor Jerome over there keeps saying he was responsible for the murder of Montfitchet!'

Bartholomew groaned. It was all happening too fast. Did this mean that Jerome, in his feverish delirium, was declaring that he was the murderer? And why had Wilson told Oliver that Bartholomew was going to kill him?

His energy spent, Oliver was unresisting while the monk and Bartholomew put him to bed. He began to squirm and struggle again when Bartholomew examined him, but not with the same intensity as before. The swellings were as soft as rotten apples in his armpits and groin, and Bartholomew knew that lancing them would bring no relief. While the monks tended to the other patients, Bartholomew tried to make Oliver drink some water.

Oliver spat the water from his mouth, and twisted away from Bartholomew.

'Poison!' he hissed, his eyes bright with fever.

Bartholomew took a sip from the water cup himself, and offered it again to Oliver, who took it reluctantly, but drank thirstily.

'Now,' said Bartholomew. 'You must rest.'

He stood to leave, but Oliver caught at the edge of his sleeve. 'Master Wilson said he was in fear of his life from you, Physician,' he said. 'My aunt believes you killed him.'

Bartholomew had had enough of Oliver and his unpleasant accusations. 'Well, she is wrong,' he said. 'And how would she know anyway, since Wilson never left his room to talk to anyone, and your aunt never leaves her Priory?'

Oliver sneered and spat onto the floor. '*He* went to see *her*,' he said.

'Wilson visited your aunt?'

'Of course!' Oliver said, his voice dripping contempt. 'Most days, between Compline and Matins.'

'In the middle of the night?' said Bartholomew, amazed. 'Wilson visited your aunt in the middle of the night?'

'They were lovers,' said Oliver, 'although what she ever saw in that fat pig I will never know.'

'He was going to take major orders,' said Bartholomew, bemused, 'vowing to abstain from physical relationships with women.'

Oliver gave a short bark of laughter. 'My aunt had already taken such a vow,' he said, 'but what did that matter?'

Bartholomew stared at the student. Oliver glowered

back at him spitefully, and once again, Bartholomew wondered what he had done to earn himself such an intense dislike. Oliver, however, was growing exhausted, and Bartholomew did not want to tire him further with more questions. He went to sit with Jerome, who was still fighting his illness with a spirit of defiance that Bartholomew never guessed he had. Jerome's skeletal hand gripped his.

'I did it,' he muttered. 'I killed Montfitchet. I made him drink the wine when he said he had already had enough. Jocelyn and I made him drink the Master's health, and he died. His death is on my head.'

'Did you know the wine was drugged?' asked Bartholomew.

The old man shook his head slowly, his eyes filling with tears. 'No, I did not. But that does not absolve me,' he whispered.

Bartholomew rose to leave. 'Father William will come to you,' he said. 'He will absolve you.' He felt a sudden urge just to leave Michaelhouse and Cambridge and go to York or Lincoln where he could practise medicine in peace, and escape from the vile intrigues and affairs of the University. Even Father Jerome, who had probably never harmed anyone in his life, had been drawn into its murky depths, and would die believing he had committed a crime in which he had played no knowing part.

As he left the commoners' room and made his way back to the kitchen, he thought about Oliver's words. Oliver had said that Wilson had left the College almost every night to visit his mistress, the Abbess. That certainly explained how he might have caught the plague when, in everyone's eyes, he had isolated himself from the outside world. Bartholomew and Cynric had slipped unnoticed in and out of College the night before, so there was no reason why Wilson could not have done the same.

But it still made no sense. Bartholomew had already established that Wilson could not have been the murderer, because Augustus's body had been dumped in the stables after Wilson had been buried. Did Wilson believe Bartholomew was the murderer? Did he talk to him on his deathbed so that Bartholomew would fall into some kind of trap and be exposed? But that made no sense either, because if Wilson believed Bartholomew to be capable of committing so grave a sin as murder, why did he ask him to ensure that his tomb was built? Why not Michael, or William?

He went to huddle near the kitchen fire, elbowing Cynric to one side so that they could share the warmth. They could not risk going too early in case they were seen, so Bartholomew dozed until Cynric announced it was time to leave. The Welshman made Bartholomew change his white shirt and dispensed with cloaks and scholar's robes because they were difficult in which to climb. Both wore two pairs of woollen leggings and two dark tunics to protect them against the cold. When he was satisfied that they were well prepared for a long chilly wait on a narrow window-sill, Cynric led the way out of the College.

Bartholomew was amazed at the way the nimble Welshman could blend into the shadows, and felt clumsy and graceless by comparison. When they reached Bene't Hostel, it was in total darkness, but Cynric insisted on waiting and watching for a long time before he decided it was safe. He slipped down a narrow passageway like a cat, Bartholomew following as quietly as he could. The passageway had originally led to the yard at the back of the hostel, but had been blocked off by a wall when the yard had become more of a refuse pit.

The wall had not been built of the best materials, and Bartholomew found it easy to gain hand- and footholds in the crumbling mortar, and climb to the top. Cynric pressed him back into the shadows, where they waited yet again to ensure it was safe to continue. At last Cynric motioned that they could drop over the wall into the yard below. Bartholomew was used to foul smells, but the stench that rose from the deep layer of slime on the floor of the yard made his eyes water. Cynric quickly led the way to a row of straggly shrubs that grew against the wall of the hostel.

Bartholomew cursed under his breath as he skidded on something slippery and almost fell. Cynric grabbed at his arm, and they waited in tense silence until they were certain that no one had heard. They reached the bushes where they could hide from anyone looking out of the windows, and Bartholomew smothered an exclamation of disgust as his outstretched hand touched a rotten slab of meat that had been thrown there.

Cynric pushed his way through the bushes until he reached the ivy that climbed the wall of the house. It was ancient and sturdy, and Bartholomew nodded that he could climb up it without difficulty. They had agreed that Bartholomew would climb to the window-sill, while Cynric would keep watch down the passageway from the top of the wall for any indication that the well-wisher had led them into a trap. If that were the case, they would effect an escape by climbing up the ivy, and over the roofs.

Gingerly, Bartholomew set his foot on the vine,

and began to climb. The slop drain was apparently directly above, for the ivy was treacherously slick, and all manner of kitchen waste was caught on its branches. Bartholomew tried not to think about it, and continued upwards. Glancing down, he could not see Cynric. He must already have slid into his vantage point in the shadows at the top of the wall.

The sound of soft singing came through the slop drain. Bartholomew prayed that it was not a scullery boy who would throw the kitchen waste down on his head. Cautiously, he climbed a little further, noting that the singer's words were slurred and his notes false. One of the scholars, objecting to an early night, must have slipped down to the pantry to avail himself of the wine and ale stored there. From his voice, it would take a thunderbolt to disturb him, not someone climbing stealthily outside.

He climbed higher, until he saw the lancet windows of the hall just above him. For an awful moment, he thought the woman had misinformed him, for there was no deep window-sill on which he could wait and listen, but then he realised that he was too far to one side, and needed to move to his right. This proved more difficult than he had anticipated, and he had to climb down past the kitchen drain before he could find a stem of the ivy large enough to bear his weight.

At last he saw the window-sill above him, and he was able to grasp its edge with both hands and haul himself up. The shutters were firmly closed, but he could just see the merest flicker of light underneath them, suggesting that someone was there. He almost fell when a branch he had been holding snapped sharply in his hand. He held his breath and waited for the shutters to be flung open and his hiding place discovered, but there was no sound from within, and gradually he relaxed.

He eased himself to one side of the sill, his back propped up against the carved stone window-frame. He learned that, by huddling down a little, he could see a fraction of the main table in the large hall through a split in the wood of the shutter. But, although one of the Sub-Principal's precious candles burned, there seemed to be no one there to appreciate it. The meeting was evidently not due to start for a while. Bartholomew tried to make himself more comfortable. A chill wind was beginning to blow, and, although the sky was clear and it seemed unlikely to rain, he knew that, despite Cynric's precautions, he was going to be very cold before he could go home.

He heard the church clock strike the hour twice before anything happened. He was beginning to wonder whether he had been sent on a wild-goose chase, and was considering giving up. It was freezing on the window-sill, and the bitter wind cut right through his clothes. He felt that if he did not climb down the vine soon, he would be too cold to do so at all.

Suddenly, he became aware that something was happening. Huddling down to peer through the split wood, he saw Master Burwell pacing around the hall, and heard him giving orders to Jacob Yaxley, who had been ousted from his room to make way for the plague ward. Yaxley was lighting more candles and sweeping the remains of the scholars' evening meal off the table onto the rushes. Burwell walked across Bartholomew's line of vision and seemed to be talking to someone else. The wind rattled one of the shutters, and Bartholomew swore softly. If this happened, he would not be able to hear what was going on in the meeting. Carefully, he broke off a piece of vine, and jammed it under the loose wood. The wind gusted again, and Bartholomew saw with satisfaction that he seemed to have solved that problem at least.

The clock struck the hour again, and the activity in the hall increased dramatically. There was a growing murmur of voices, and Bartholomew could see a number of people filing into the hall. He was surprised: he had been expecting a small gathering of perhaps four or five people, but there were at least fifteen men, with a promise of more to come.

He heard someone banging softly on the table to bring the meeting to order.

'Gentlemen. I would not have called you here in this manner unless there was an important reason,' Burwell began. 'I am afraid that our cause has suffered a grave setback.'

There was a mumble of concerned voices, and Burwell waited for them to die down before continuing.

'We have heard that the Acting Master of Michaelhouse has established contact with Oxford.'

The voices this time were louder, and held questions.

Burwell raised his hand. 'I do not need to spell out the implications of this to you, gentlemen. We have been uncertain of Master Alcote's loyalties, and this proves we were correct. Our spies have intercepted messages from him telling which hostels were the weakest and most likely to flounder under pressure. Oxford will now see that pressure will be brought to bear against these places, and the University will be undermined as they fall.'

The room erupted into confusion again, and Burwell had to bang on the table to bring the meeting back under control.

'What do you suggest we do?' asked one man. Although he had his back to Bartholomew, he recognised the wiry black hair as belonging to the Principal of Mary's Hostel, Neville Stayne.

Burwell sighed. 'We could take Alcote from the equation,' he said. Bartholomew saw Stayne nod his head in approval, but there were voices of dissent.

'Who would succeed him? We might end up in a worse state,' asked another voice that Bartholomew did not recognise.

'It is most likely that Swynford would return,' Burwell said. 'He is an unknown quantity to us: we do not know where his loyalties lie, but since he is not obviously for Oxford, like Alcote, it might be possible to talk to him and put forward our point of view.'

Bartholomew could see Stayne nodding again.

'But how would we rid ourselves of Alcote's mastership?' another person asked.

Burwell spread his hands. 'There are ways and means,' he said simply.

'I am concerned about the physician,' said Stayne, abruptly changing the subject. 'He has been asking questions at Mary's about Abigny.'

'We agreed that he would be left alone,' someone said firmly. Bartholomew felt physically sick as he recognised the voice of his brother-in-law, Oswald Stanmore. He struggled to get a better view of the men seated at the table, and saw the blue sleeve embroidered in silver thread that was unmistakably Stanmore's. Bartholomew's shock made him clumsy, and he fell back harder against the window-frame than he had intended.

'What was that?' said Stayne, coming to his feet and looking towards the window suspiciously. Burwell joined him, and together they approached the window. Bartholomew could see them standing only inches from it. He held his breath. Stanmore, too, came over, and to Bartholomew's horror, began to open the shutters. Now he would be discovered! He heard Stanmore swear as the shutter jammed. Bartholomew glanced down and saw that the twig of ivy he had used to stop the shutter from rattling was preventing Stanmore from opening the window.

'It is stuck,' Bartholomew heard him mutter. A sudden gust of wind rattled the other shutter.

'It is only the wind,' Burwell said, relief in his voice. 'We are all so nervous we are even afraid of the wind. Come and sit down again.'

Bartholomew saw him put a hand on Stanmore's shoulder to lead him back to his seat. He let out a shuddering breath, and tried to concentrate on what was being said.

'No harm comes to Bartholomew,' said Stanmore firmly, 'or we are out of this. Your University can go to the Devil.'

'Hush, hush,' said Burwell placatingly. 'We will leave it to you to keep him out of our way. But you must understand that we cannot allow him to jeopardise the social stability of this country, which is what his meddling might bring about if he exposes some of our actions and the University falls.'

'I will talk to him,' mumbled Stanmore. 'I can ask him to join us.'

Stayne tutted angrily. 'He will not! I believe he holds us responsible for the death of Babington. He will not join us, and even if he did, I would not trust him.'

'Let us not leap to conclusions,' said Burwell, intervening smoothly. 'Let Stanmore talk to Bartholomew, and we will leave it at that. For now,' he added ominously.

Bartholomew felt as though he was listening to arrangements for his own death and, despite the cold, felt beads of sweat break out on his face and prickling at the small of his back. Was it Burwell's group who had paid the blacksmith and the men in the lane to kill him? How had Stanmore become involved in all this? He had nothing to do with the University. Bartholomew fought to quell the cold, sick feeling in his stomach, and concentrate on the meeting.

'Bartholomew is not the main problem,' Burwell continued. 'Michaelhouse is. Something is afoot at Michaelhouse of which we know nothing. I heard that Wilson never left his room, so how did the plague take him? How was it that the Michaelhouse Fellows arranged for him to be buried in the churchyard, and not in the plague pit? What of the rumours about the commoners that died that were so firmly quashed last summer? And finally,' he said, 'I still do not accept that Babington killed himself. Neither did Father Aelfrith or Master Wilson when I questioned them. I think Michaelhouse is a rotten apple, and the quicker it folds in on itself and collapses, the better for us all.'

There were mutters of assent, and the meeting went on to discuss various scraps of information that had been gleaned via the spy networks: there had been a convening of anti-Cambridge scholars at Bernard Hall in Oxford; one of Cambridge's spies had been killed in a town brawl; and two new halls had been established in Oxford, but none in Cambridge.

'We must not allow them to become too much bigger than us,' said Yaxley. 'The bigger they become, the easier they will be able to crush us.'

'We are putting pressure on that widow who lives in the house near St Nicholas's Church to bequeath it to us,' said Burwell. 'That will become St Nicholas Hostel, and we are in the process of altering the house by Trumpington Gate. It should be ready for new scholars in a matter of weeks.'

Heads nodded, and murmurs of approval were given. Bartholomew saw Stayne glance at the hour candle. 'It is growing late,' he said, 'and we must end this meeting. So, we are all to keep a keen ear for potential houses that can be converted into hostels; Stanmore is to deal with his brother-in-law; and as for Michaelhouse, do we act, or let it drown in its own corruption?'

'I do not see what else we can do but watch,' said Burwell. 'We know Father William sympathises with us generally, and we know that Alcote and Bartholomew do not. We do not know where Swynford or the Benedictine stand, and that flighty boy – Abigny – has apparently vanished. I suggest we wait and watch. We especially watch Alcote and his dealings. I would like everyone here to make that a priority.'

The meeting began to break up. Bartholomew saw Stanmore clearly through the crack in the shutter, and watched him leave the hall, followed by Richard and Stephen. Stephen looked unhappy and fiddled with the silver clamp on the cloak Stanmore had lent him when Abigny had stolen his. Richard looked solemn, but Bartholomew could see the excitement in his eyes at being included in such a meeting.

Bartholomew closed his eyes in despair. He had battled to keep his problems from Stanmore and his family in the belief that it would keep them from harm, despite his increasing loneliness and desperation to talk to someone. Now it seemed he had made the right decision, but for entirely the wrong reasons. Everyone was involved, even his young nephew.

He watched Yaxley and Burwell through the crack in the shutter as they fussed about the hall hiding evidence that the meeting had taken place. The rushes were stamped down, furniture moved back into place, and wax from the candles scraped away. Eventually, they were satisfied, and went to their beds, leaving the hall in darkness. Bartholomew sighed in relief, and began to flex his frozen limbs. He was so cold and stiff, he wondered whether he would be able to climb down the ivy and back up over the wall without falling and giving himself away. He rubbed his arms and legs vigorously for a few moments to try to warm them, and then began his descent. He almost slipped twice, and discovered that it was much easier climbing up slime-covered vines than down them. He really did lose his footing when he was near the bottom, and landed with a crackle of dead, broken branches in the bushes.

Cynric was there to help him up. 'You will wake the dead!' he whispered irritably. 'Try to be quieter.'

Bartholomew followed him across the disgusting yard, even more slippery now that some of the filth had turned to ice in the night air. Getting over the wall proved difficult, for Bartholomew could not feel his cold fingers sufficiently to find handholds in the stones. They managed eventually, and Cynric retraced his silent steps back through the shadows into Michaelhouse. The front gates were closed, but Cynric, showing characteristic foresight, had left the back gate unlocked, and they made their way through the College vegetable gardens, past the laundry, and into the College itself. It occurred to Bartholomew that Wilson must have made the same journey when he returned from seeing his lover, the Abbess.

Bartholomew sank gratefully into Agatha's chair. His knees were still trembling from the shock of hearing that his family was involved in the University's business, and that there were people who obviously wanted him out of the way. How had he managed to manoeuver himself into the position where he stood virtually alone against his family and friends? He had no wish to see the country short of trained clergy and educated men who would be able to serve their people, and he had no wish to see the social order of England crumble because there was only one University from which these men could graduate. It was probably fair to say that he actually approved of the aims of this clandestine group. But there remained something odd about the whole business, a sinister edge to it that Bartholomew could not define.

Cynric began to prod some life into the embers, and they both stretched cold hands towards the meagre flames. Bartholomew went into a storeroom and emerged with one of Wilson's bottles of wine. Cynric took the bottle and pulled the cork out with his teeth. He took a hearty swig, and passed it to Bartholomew.

Bartholomew followed suit, grimacing at the strength of the wine. Cynric grinned at him, and took the bottle again. 'This was the one Gilbert said was the best,' he said, peering at the label in the firelight. 'This single bottle cost six marks; Wilson was saving it for when the Bishop came.'

Bartholomew took the bottle and studied it. The parchment wrapped round it said it came from the French Mediterranean, and so would be more expensive than English wine, or wine from the north of France. He took another sip. It had a tarry flavour that Bartholomew was already beginning to like. He took a third swallow and passed it back to Cynric, who raised it into the air in a salute.

'To Master Wilson, for leaving us his wine. And for leaving us.' He gave a short laugh, and drank. 'Now,' he said, 'what did you learn?'

Bartholomew began to relate what he had learned, embarrassed that his voice cracked when he mentioned the involvement of his family. Cynric sat quietly, not interrupting. Eventually, Bartholomew faltered and stopped. What more could he say? He started to tell Cynric that he would talk to Stanmore, and reason with him about the University business, but got no further than the first few words. Would Stanmore then be forced to kill him, as Sir John and Aelfrith had been killed because they had been in the way? Or would it be Stephen or Richard who would perform that duty?

He rubbed his eyes hard, feeling an aching tiredness underneath that made them burn. He was at his wits' end, and knew no more what to do than would the great rat that sat boldly washing its whiskers in the middle of the kitchen floor. He watched as it snapped into alertness, standing on hind legs and sniffing the air, before scampering away to disappear down a hole in the corner. At the same time, there was a chill draught as the door was opened.

'Matt?' said Philippa softly, walking towards him and dropping to her knees by his chair. She took one of his hands in hers. 'You look tired and miserable. Tell me what is wrong.'

Bartholomew looked in astonishment over her fair head to Abigny, who stood in the doorway.

'The last time we met, you were wearing a dress,' Bartholomew said coldly, trying to control the sick, churning feeling in his stomach.

'I was a damn fine woman!' Abigny said proudly. 'Fooled your family for almost four days. Would have done for longer if you had not been so ungentlemanly as to burst into a woman's boudoir unannounced.'

Bartholomew half rose, pulling his hand away from Philippa, but then sat back down again, uncertain what he had been intending to do. Abigny settled himself comfortably on one of the benches.

'We owe you an explanation,' he said.

Bartholomew looked at him warily. 'I should say you do,' he said, trying to keep his voice from wavering. When he dared to glance at Philippa again, she smiled at him lovingly, but without remorse. Chilled, he moved away so that no part of her touched him.

'Oh, Matt!' she said, giving him a playful push. 'Do not sulk! You knew why I went!'

'I know nothing!' he said with a sudden intensity. 'I left you with Edith, then there was some peculiar story about you refusing to see me, then Giles pretended to be you for God knows how long, and then you both disappeared!'

'What?' she said, her small face puckered. 'No! Giles explained it all to you. You know I would never give you cause for concern!' She turned to her brother. 'You did

316

tell him. You told me you did!' Her voice was accusing, and Abigny stood and backed away, his hands raised in front of him in a placatory gesture.

'I decided against it. I thought it was best. You do not know him like I do; he would have tried to see you, and then you both would have been in danger! I did what I thought was right.'

Philippa stopped from where she had been advancing on her brother, and looked back at Bartholomew with a curious mixture of shame and resignation. 'Well, then,' she said in a small voice. 'You do owe Matt an explanation.'

Cautiously, alert to every movement his sister made, Abigny perched on the edge of the table. Philippa stayed where she was, at a distance from either of them. Abigny took a deep breath, and began to speak.

'In order that you understand what I did, and why, I must start at the beginning. When Philippa was still a baby, she was married. The marriage was legal, although it was of course never consummated. Her husband died shortly after, and Philippa inherited a considerable amount of property in Lincoln. Before our father died, he arranged for Philippa to stay at St Radegund's until she chose either to marry, or to take the veil. The Abbess, of course, was keen that Philippa should take the veil, because then all her property would go to the convent.'

He shuffled on the table, while Philippa watched him, her face pale.

'The fact that you were paying her obvious attention was not likely to encourage her to a life of chastity, so the Abbess, God rot her soul, decided she would remove you: if you could be persuaded to give up your courting, she imagined that Philippa, in paroxysms of grief, would become a nun, and all her worldly wealth would go to the convent. Her plan was that her dreadful nephews, the Olivers, were to start a riot and the blacksmith was paid to deliver a warning – "stay away". It seems the warning was too obtuse for you, because you continued to visit Philippa. The blacksmith swore he had given you the message when pressed by the Olivers. Then the plague came, and the Abbess was able to imprison Philippa in the convent under her policy of isolation.

'Anyway, to take things in order, I managed to work out what the Abbess had done by listening at doors and chatting to the nuns, who told me that the Abbess was bringing great pressure on Philippa to take her vows.'

Philippa nodded her agreement. 'She told me it was my duty to take the veil because so many clerics were dying of the plague. She said there were not enough left to say masses for the dead, and that I could not, in all conscience, refuse to commit myself to a monastic life when there were the souls of so many at stake.'

Abigny watched her for a moment before continuing. 'I became afraid that the Abbess might use the Death to her own advantage, and that she might kill Philippa for the property and blame it on the plague. I decided I had to take Philippa away from her. So I sent you a message with that cocky medical student, and his cousin, Sister Emelda, agreed to pass a note to Philippa. You were supposed to meet each other in the shed, fall into each other's arms, marry, and live happily ever after. But poor Sister Clement chose that shed in which to die, and you, of course,' he said, bowing to Bartholomew, 'began to suspect all sorts of foul play, and took Philippa to your sister's home.'

He stopped for a minute, and chewed on one of

his nails. 'Philippa could not be safe there. The Abbess would work out where she was and take her back. And this time, I was certain she would kill Philippa. You had upset my plans horribly. Instead of taking her to the safety of matrimony, you took her to the very unsafety of Trumpington – and on top of that, she got the plague. I was furious with you,' he said to Bartholomew with a flash of defiance.

Bartholomew interrupted him, piecing together Abigny's story with what he had learned himself. 'So you hung around Trumpington until she began to recover, seen by the Gilbertine friar and the barmaid from the Laughing Pig,' he said, his voice hard. 'Then you stayed with Philippa for a few days, pretending Philippa was distressed because of her scars, so that poor Edith would not know there were two of you.'

The barmaid had told him Abigny seemed terrified of something. Could it have been the Abbess? Or was Abigny afraid of a more sinister foe – the Oxford scholars, or even the Cambridge men?

'More or less,' said Abigny, unperturbed by Bartholomew's hostility. He glanced at Philippa who stood motionless near the door. He continued. 'I took her to Hugh Stapleton's house in Fen Ditton, where she would be safe, and I took Philippa's place in Edith's house, waiting with my crossbow to see whether the Oliver brothers would come. It was a tense wait, I can tell you. I was almost relieved when you came and uncovered my disguise in that dramatic way, and I could get away from such a nerve-racking situation. We have both been at Fen Ditton ever since.'

'You used my sister!' said Bartholomew, his voice dangerously quiet. He stood abruptly and swung round to face Abigny, who blanched, but did not flinch. 'How did you know the Abbess or the Olivers would not harm her while you skulked in her house?'

'I reasoned it out. I made sure that news of my escape was common gossip. The Abbess would hardly go there if she knew Philippa was gone.'

'But you were there for almost a week!' exploded Bartholomew. 'They might have come then.'

'And who took Philippa there in the first place?' yelled Abigny, his temper snapping. 'If anything, this was all your fault!'

Cynric, anticipating violence, uncoiled himself from the fire and moved between them, but Philippa was there before him.

'Please,' she said. 'Hear Giles out.'

Abigny mastered his temper with an effort, and resumed his explanation. Bartholomew listened, his face white with fury. 'I assumed that the Abbess would not harm you. With Philippa gone, what possible importance could you be to her? Well, I misread her. She held you responsible for Philippa's flight, while Wilson, her lover, claimed that you meant him harm. Within days, Wilson lay dead, burned to death in his own room with you conveniently first at the scene. Sister Emelda told me that she had overheard the Abbess and Henry Oliver discussing how they sent hired thugs to kill you. The Abbess was furious that your brother-in-law made a timely intervention. Not only that, but the money she paid to the thug that was killed was stolen! She sent Elias Oliver to retrieve it from the body: he found the body but the purse had gone.'

Bartholomew gritted his teeth, trying to master the fury, mingled with relief, that welled up inside him. If the blacksmith had been given a clearer message to deliver, perhaps some of this might not have happened. Philippa came to stand next to him. 'Hugh Stapleton's son came a few hours ago to tell us that the Abbess was dead,' she said. 'Apparently Henry Oliver became ill in the convent, and passed the sickness to her. We went immediately to hear the truth from Sister Emelda. And the next thing we did was to come see you.'

Bartholomew let out a huge sigh and stared up at the ceiling, feeling the energy drain out of him. He flopped back into the chair, trying to make sense of what he had heard. He looked at Philippa, her face ashen, and at Abigny, eyeing him expectantly. Could he believe their story? It was certainly true that Henry Oliver had the plague, and may well have passed it to his beloved aunt. Henry had said that Wilson believed Bartholomew meant to kill him. And the essence of the story fitted in with the facts as he knew them. But was there something more? Could he trust Abigny's explanation? How could he be certain that they were not somehow tied up with the University business and the murder of his friends? It seemed pertinent to Bartholomew that Abigny fled to the house owned by Hugh Stapleton – the dead Principal of Bene't's Hostel – where he had so recently heard his death discussed by his own family.

Outside, the first streaks of dawn were lightening the sky. Philippa rose to leave.

'It seems there have been misunderstandings,' she said coolly, her gaze moving from Bartholomew to Abigny, 'and I am sorry that people have been hurt. But I am not sorry to be alive, and I doubt that I would be had not Giles acted as he did.' She turned to Abigny. 'I will never forgive you for lying to me, although I appreciate you felt it was in my best interests.'

She swept from the kitchen before Bartholomew could respond. Abigny darted after her, and Bartholomew heard the philosopher's voice echoing across the yard as he tried to reason with her. Bartholomew was overwhelmed with a barrage of emotions – anger, grief, hurt, relief. The whole business had gone far enough. He had spent weeks agonising over Philippa's safety, and had undergone all kinds of mental torment because he did not want to run the risk of endangering his family when he had been desperate to confide in someone. Now, within a few hours, his trust in his family and in Philippa had been shattered. Gradually, as he considered what he had learned, his confusion hardened into cold anger. He stood up abruptly and reached for his cloak. Cynric looked at him in alarm.

'I am going to see Oswald,' he said. 'Perhaps then I might learn the truth.'

'No!' exclaimed Cynric, starting forward. 'Do not act foolishly because a woman has upset you. You know Sir Oswald is involved in all this. What can be gained by a confrontation?'

Bartholomew's face lit in a savage smile that made Cynric step back. 'A confrontation is the only way I will gain any peace. This wretched business has taken my friends, my family, and now it seems it will destroy all I had with Philippa.'

He turned on his heel and stalked out, leaving Cynric uncertain as to what to do.

The gates to Stanmore's business premises were just being opened by a yawning apprentice. He told

Bartholomew no one else was awake, and suggested he wait in the kitchen. Bartholomew ignored him and made for the solar. This large room leading off the hall on the first floor served as Stanmore's office, and contained all his records of sale and purchase, as well as the petty cash. As Bartholomew expected, the door was locked, but he knew the spare key was kept in a hidden pocket in one of the tapestries that lined the wall of the hall. He found it, unlocked the door and entered.

Stanmore was meticulous in his business dealings, and records of all the transactions he had undertaken were stored neatly in numbered scrolls on the shelves. Bartholomew began to sort through them, knocking some onto the floor and piling others onto the table. He was not sure exactly what he was looking for, but he knew Stanmore well enough to know that if he had done business with the University men, there would be a record of it.

'Matt! What are you doing?' Stephen Stanmore stood in the doorway, still wearing his night clothes. Perhaps the apprentice had woken him up and told him Bartholomew was waiting. Bartholomew ignored him, and continued his search. He saw that, two years before, Bene't Hostel had bought a consignment of blankets from Stanmore, who had been paid handsomely. Stephen watched him for a few moments, and then disappeared. When he came back, Oswald Stanmore was with him, followed by a sleepy-eyed Richard, whose drowsiness disappeared in an instant when he saw his uncle ransacking his father's office. They must have declined to make the journey back to Trumpington in the dark and stayed the night with Stephen.

'Matt?' said Stanmore, watching Bartholomew in

bewilderment. 'What do you want? Perhaps I can find it for you?'

Bartholomew waved the document at him. 'I am looking for transactions you have had with the men of Bene't Hostel,' he said tightly. 'I am looking for evidence that shows that you were involved in the murders of my friends and colleagues.'

Bartholomew saw Stephen turn white, while Richard's mouth dropped open. Stanmore took a step towards him. 'Matt! What are you talking about?'

Bartholomew's eyes blazed. 'Enough lies! Where are they, Oswald? Where are the documents that show how much it cost to buy you?'

Stanmore froze in his tracks, and looked unsteadily at Bartholomew as realisation began to dawn on his face. 'I do not know what you mean,' he said, but his voice lacked conviction.

Bartholomew advanced towards him menacingly. 'I thought your rescue was timely two nights ago. You knew, because your Bene't Hostel associates planned it with the Abbess of St Radegund's! Why did you bother, Oswald? Or does your conscience balk at the murder of relatives?'

The door was flung open, and Hugh stood there, brandishing his crossbow. He saw Bartholomew moving threateningly towards Stanmore, saw his face dark with anger, and fired without a moment's hesitation. Simultaneously, Richard screamed and Stanmore lunged forward and knocked into Hugh so that the bolt thudded harmlessly into the ceiling. Hugh started to reload while Bartholomew gazed open-mouthed in shock. He had known Hugh since he was a child, and yet Hugh had not given a second thought to shooting him. Had the plague and the University business changed their lives so much?

'This is not necessary, Hugh,' said Stanmore in an attempt to sound in control. 'Please leave us.'

Hugh looked as if to demur, but Stephen took him roughly by the shoulder and pushed him from the room, closing the door behind him. Richard stared at the quarrel that was embedded, still quivering, in the wooden ceiling. Stanmore lost his usual, confident bearing, and slumped into a chair, where Richard and Stephen came to stand behind him. Bartholomew suddenly noticed the similarity between the three of them. Oswald and Stephen had always been alike, and Richard was beginning to look like a younger version, without the silver beard.

Bartholomew eyed Stanmore sitting in his chair with his head bowed, and moved cautiously to the other side of the room, where he could see all three of them at once.

It was Richard who broke the silence.

'You are wrong,' he said, his voice unsteady. 'My father would never let them harm you. He always made sure they understood that.'

Stanmore seemed to pull himself together. He gestured that Bartholomew should sit next to him. Bartholomew declined, and stood waiting, tense and wary. Stanmore took a deep breath and began to speak, his voice sometimes so low that Bartholomew had to strain to hear it.

'It started about a year ago,' he said. 'You know I maintain my own network of informants about the town? Well, word came to me that there were moves by Oxford scholars to try to undermine the University here, but I assumed that it was merely overpaid scholars with too much time on their hands playing games. Perhaps it started like that, but last year the business seemed to escalate. There were all sorts of rumours of spies, secret messages, and the like. Then people began to die: there were the two lads who had eaten bad oysters, and the Master of King's Hall, to name but three. Anyway, it became clear that there was a plot afoot to strike at the University through some of its most powerful members – the Fellows and Masters of the Colleges.'

He paused and studied his fingernails. Bartholomew waited impatiently.

'Last spring, Burwell came to me and told me that the hostels had set up a secret committee to look into the matter. Deaths were occurring in the Colleges, and there was speculation by the hostels that the Colleges were riddled with spies from Oxford. The hostel group believed that Oxford, by striking at the Colleges, might force prospective benefactors like the Bishop of Norwich and Edmund Gonville to withhold money from Cambridge, because the Colleges appeared to be rank with corruption. The hostel group did not include anyone from the Colleges because they could not be sure who was honest and who was a spy. Are you following me?'

Bartholomew nodded restlessly.

'The hostel group also decided to include some trustworthy citizens from the town. The hostels are poor, unlike the Colleges that have their endowments and support from the King, and it takes money to set up a system of spies. They included me and five others because we conduct a lot of business with the University, and it is in our interests to ensure that the University does not flounder. So, we provided them with money, and they ensured that we had custom. A harmless relationship.'

'It was not harmless for Augustus, Sir John, or Aelfrith,' said Bartholomew coldly.

Stanmore looked up sharply. 'Father Aelfrith? He died of the plague.'

'He was poisoned,' said Bartholomew bluntly.

Stanmore stared at Bartholomew in disbelief. 'I did not know,' he said eventually. 'But I have not finished, Matt. For a while, it seemed as if the hostels' system of spies was having some success, for the deaths ceased. Then, without warning, they started again. Two Fellows from the Hall of Valence Marie died, Sir John committed suicide, and then there were all those rumours about the commoners being killed for his seal. We have been meeting regularly and secretly to try to find out what is happening. In the last few months, most of the trouble has been at Michaelhouse. There is something going on there that none of us understand. Perhaps the entire conspiracy against the University is coming from Michaelhouse.'

He glanced up at Stephen, who nodded agreement. Bartholomew kept his expression neutral, although his mind was teeming. Aelfrith had told him that there were deaths at King's Hall, Clare, and Peterhouse, and then a long gap before those at Valence Marie and Michaelhouse. Bartholomew wondered, since Stanmore's information coincided with Aelfrith's, if Stanmore's motives were pure after all.

'The University buys cloth from me rather than from other merchants,' Stanmore continued. 'In turn, I give them money to help them maintain their network of informants. But I have most certainly not been involved in murder, and I have never done anything that would harm you. That was one of the conditions on which I joined the hostels' group – that if there was anything that would affect you, I would be told first so that I could keep you out of it.'

'And what about the plan to dispose of Alcote?' asked Bartholomew.

Stanmore looked at him in shock. 'How do you know about that?' He put his head back in his hands again. 'Oh, God, no! We have a spy in our midst, too! Do not tell me our group is known of in Michaelhouse. If that is so,' he said, looking up at Bartholomew, 'then all our lives could be in danger.' He turned to Richard. 'Why did I involve you in this?' he cried, suddenly desolate.

Richard met his eyes with a level stare. 'You did not, Father. I was approached independently of you.' He looked at Bartholomew. 'At Oxford, I can listen and learn, and I, too, can send back information that may help to put an end to this silly plot.'

Bartholomew ignored him. 'You did not answer my question,' he said to Stanmore. 'What about the plan . . . how was it put? . . . to take Alcote out of the equation?'

'It was you!' said Stephen suddenly. 'That noise we heard outside the window. It was you listening!'

Bartholomew continued to hold Stanmore's eyes. 'Well?' he said.

'Not what you think,' he said wearily. 'Our group does not condone murder. There are other ways. A word to the Chancellor to say that women have been seen coming out of his room early in the morning. Or even boys. A rumour that he has been drinking too much, or that his College has become riotous. It is not necessary to kill to remove a man from office. And if Alcote is a spy for Oxford, as our intelligence suggests, then he should not be in a position to run your College anyway, would you not agree?'

'But who are you to judge?' Bartholomew said quietly. He glanced round at the three men, and was suddenly sick of it all. He wanted to make for the door. Richard barred his way. Bartholomew did not want to manhandle him and stopped in his tracks.

'We have done nothing wrong,' Richard said with dignity, 'except to try to sort out this mess, to stop more people from dying. I would do the same again. And I also want you to know that Father has been using the hostels' spies to try to find out about Philippa for you. He has paid a good deal of money and spent a lot of his time following false leads and asking questions on your behalf. We all have. Father and I spent all of the night before last in that seedy King's Head because someone had told us that a traveller would be there who may have seen Abigny on the London Road.'

A memory flashed into Bartholomew's mind. He had thought he had seen Stanmore coming out of the King's Head after he had met his well-wisher by the plague pit. So, his eyes had not deceived him after all.

'I am sorry,' Stanmore said. 'We found the traveller, but he could tell us nothing about Abigny.'

Bartholomew suddenly felt ashamed and bewildered. He had become so confused by all the lies and deceit, and so accustomed to suspecting his colleagues of intrigues, that he had applied the same rules to his family. Perhaps he had also misjudged Philippa and Abigny. Stanmore's neat office was in total disarray, with scrolls scattered everywhere and a crossbow quarrel in the ceiling. Bartholomew sank down onto a stool, uncertain whether his weariness came from the fact that his family's apparent involvement appeared to be harmless after all, or from the battering his senses had taken in the past few hours.

In an unsteady voice, Stanmore said, 'I dread to think what Edith will say if she ever learns that her beloved brother was shot at in her husband's office.'

'Your steward seems somewhat trigger-happy,' said Bartholomew, also shakily, when he recalled how Stanmore's quick reaction had saved his life. 'Remind me never to haggle over cloth prices in your office.'

'It is a dangerous game we play, Matt,' Stanmore said. 'You were attacked by the river; Giles Abigny pursues some strange business of his own under my very roof; and Richard and I were ambushed by footpads the other night. Hugh saved our lives, as he saved yours down by the river, and doubtless the responsibility is beginning to tell on him. He had never, in thirty years of service, been called upon to use his crossbow, and then, in a matter of days, he is required to use it three times.'

Bartholomew looked from Richard to Stanmore, bewildered. 'Ambushed?'

Richard nodded vigorously. 'When we left the King's Head. Four men ambushed us just outside the gates here. Hugh shot one of them and captured another.'

'They were farmers from out Shelford way,' said Stanmore. 'They heard how easy it was to steal in Cambridge with so many dead of the plague, and thought to try it for themselves. Of course, it is easy to steal from the dead and dying, but these four fellows felt that was unethical, and decided to steal from the living instead.'

'The Sheriff should shoot anyone seen out after the curfew,' said Stephen. 'His laxity is the cause of all this villainy.'

'And what if he had seen you out last night as you returned from Bene't's?' retorted Bartholomew. 'I am often called out to patients at night, and would not relish being shot at before I had a chance to explain myself.'

'We would not have been able to explain our business last night, Stephen,' Stanmore agreed. 'We swore an oath of secrecy, and we could hardly tell the watch where we had been and what we had been discussing.'

Stephen acquiesced with a sideways tilt of his head, and there was silence. As if it were a magnet, the gaze of all four lit upon the crossbow bolt.

'What will mother say?' Richard said, echoing his father's words.

'Why would she find out?' asked Bartholomew with a weak smile.

'Well, thank the Lord we have resolved all that!' said Richard heartily, his natural cheerfulness bubbling to the surface again. 'I hated having secrets from you, Uncle Matt. We all wanted to tell you, but we were afraid it might put you in danger, being at Michaelhouse and all. We have tried hard to keep you away from it as much as we could, but I suppose it is your home.'

Bartholomew smiled at him. Richard was at an age where he could make astonishingly adult observations, but could still make things childishly simple. Bartholomew could see that Richard considered that no lasting damage had been done by the scene in his father's study, and was quite happy to continue his life in exactly the same way as before.

'I will tell the cook to make us some breakfast,' he said, marching out of the room.

'You really let him spy in Oxford?' asked Bartholomew, after he had gone.

Stanmore looked askance at him. 'Of course not, Matt. What do you think I am? He is a bright boy, and he is good at listening, but the information he sends us is nothing. It pleases him to think he is helping, and I would not hurt his feelings by telling him otherwise.'

'I believe I owe you an apology,' said Bartholomew.

'And we owe you one. We should have told you. We wanted to, but we honestly believed you would be safer not knowing. I had decided I would tell you everything if you ever asked, but you never mentioned anything to me. I also did not want to distress you by telling you I thought Sir John had been murdered. Especially since there was nothing you could have done, and I was afraid you would start on some investigation of your own that might lead you into danger.'

He laughed softly. 'We involve a child like Richard, and we keep you in the dark. How stupid we must seem to you!'

'I am sorry,' said Bartholomew. He rubbed his hand over his eyes. 'All this intrigue, with the plague on top of it, must be addling my mind, like Colet. I misjudged you.'

The Stanmores dismissed his words with impatient shakes of their heads. Stephen suddenly gave him a hard poke in the chest. 'You lose my best horse, and now you tear our offices apart. Just stay away from my hounds and my falcons,' he said, feigning severity. Bartholomew smiled and followed Stephen down the stairs, where Richard was shouting that breakfast was ready. Hugh

332

slouched in the inglenook in the fireplace, and looked uneasily at Bartholomew. Stanmore whispered in his ear, and he gave Bartholomew a grin before leaving the room.

'What did you say to him?' Bartholomew asked.

'Oh, I just told him you had spent the night sampling Master Wilson's best wine,' said Stanmore.

'You told him I was drunk?' asked Bartholomew incredulously.

Stanmore nodded casually. 'He loathed Wilson, and it will give him great pleasure to think you have been drinking his wine. His collection of fine wines is quite the envy of the town, you know.'

Bartholomew did not, and sat for a while, talking to the Stanmores before they were obliged to attend to their business. Bartholomew fell asleep in the parlour, and only awoke when a clatter of horses' hooves echoed in the yard. He sat up and stretched, scrubbing at his face with his hands, and thinking about what he should do that day. He glanced out of the window, and stared morosely at the raindrops that pattered in the mud. He wondered why he felt so gloomy when Philippa was safe, and his family had exonerated themselves from the evil doings of the University.

But the University was still at the heart of the matter. Despite all that he had learned over the last few hours, there were questions that remained unanswered. Such as who had killed Sir John. He knew why, but he was no further forward in discovering who. Did the same person murder Sir John, poison Aelfrith, and take Augustus's body? Bartholomew rubbed his chin. Whoever killed Sir John for the seal must also have killed Augustus and desecrated his body – also for the seal. But why had Aelfrith spoken Wilson's name on his deathbed? Bartholomew knew that Wilson had not killed Augustus, and if not Augustus, then probably not Sir John.

Could it have been Alcote? He was the spy in their midst, according to the hostels' information. Was he also the murderer? Wilson had said that Alcote had been so drunk that he had not known when Wilson had left their room to search Augustus's room for the seal. But supposing Alcote had not been drunk, and had been pretending? Then he too could have been up and sneaking around the College. But Wilson had said that Augustus had already gone from the room when he got there, and Wilson and Alcote had been together until then.

Of course, Bartholomew thought, all this was assuming everyone was telling the truth. Alcote and Wilson may have been in this together, each lying to protect the other. Bartholomew wondered if Alcote knew of Wilson's nocturnal visits to the Abbess, and whether he approved. He wondered whether he should warn Alcote that his information had been intercepted. Bartholomew had no doubt that the Stanmores believed that Alcote would merely be discredited to remove him from his position of power, but Bartholomew thought of Sir John, Augustus, Paul, Montfitchet, and Aelfrith, and was not so sure.

He thought of Alcote – small, fussy, and petty. Could he have had the strength to drive the knife so deeply into Paul's body? Could he have overpowered Sir John? Bartholomew thought of Wilson hauling himself through the trap-door, and of Michael's strong arm in hauling him to his feet once. Perhaps he spent too much time with the weak and dying, and no longer appreciated the strength of the healthy, strength that could be magnified by fear or desperation.

The more he thought about it, the less he understood. Despite all that he had learned from eavesdropping, Philippa and Abigny, and his confrontation with the Stanmores, he was as much in the dark as ever. Far from easing his mind, his conversation had made him even more concerned for the safety of his family. Abigny had thought nothing of endangering Edith when he was trying to help Philippa. Bartholomew thought about what Stanmore had told him of the Oxford plot, and wondered whether the survival of the University was enough of a reason for men like Yaxley, Stayne, and Burwell to become involved. Stanmore claimed he knew nothing of murder, and Bartholomew believed him. But Yaxley, Burwell, and Stayne might. So was the University's survival sufficient reason for which to commit murder? Wilson intimated on his deathbed that there were those who cared passionately about it, and might give their lives for it. Would they also take lives?

And so he came back to the same question yet again: who was the murderer in Michaelhouse? All the Fellows had alibis for Augustus's death, so was the killer an outsider after all? And where was Michael? Had he fled Cambridge to escape the plague like so many others, or was he, too, lying dead somewhere? Bartholomew stood watching the rain for a while longer, but his thoughts began to repeat themselves. He wondered what he should do next. He was too battered emotionally for a confrontation with Philippa, Abigny, or one of the hostel men, but he still had patients to see. Reluctantly, he left the warmth of Stephen's house, and prepared to trudge back to Michaelhouse.

XI

BARTHOLOMEW HAD BARELY RETURNED TO Michaelhouse when a messenger arrived with a note from Edith saying that she had hurt her arm. She said it was very painful, and asked that he come to tend it as soon as possible. A shout from the commoners' window made him look up.

'Father Jerome is dying,' the Benedictine called, 'and he is asking for you.'

Bartholomew was torn with indecision. Should he go to the dying man or his sister? As if in answer to his prayers, Gray came sauntering through the gates. Bartholomew strode over to him in relief. Gray could go to Edith; a sore arm did not sound too serious.

Gray listened attentively to Bartholomew's instructions, secretly gratified that Bartholomew was allowing him to attend his sister: he was not to try to set the arm if it was broken; he was to make sure that if there was a wound, it was clean before he bound it; he was only to use water that had been taken fresh from the spring; he was to check carefully for other injuries and fever; and he was to give her one measure only – and here Gray was subjected to a stern look from his teacher – of a sleeping draught if she complained of too much pain.

Proudly carrying Bartholomew's bag of medicines, Gray set off at a jaunty pace towards the High Street, while Bartholomew hurried back to the commoners' room.

Father Jerome was indeed dying. He had already been anointed, and his breath was little more than a reedy whisper. Bartholomew was surprised that, after his long and spirited struggle, his end should come so fast. Almost as fast as that of Henry Oliver, who had died several hours before.

William came and Jerome confessed to enticing Montfitchet to drink the wine that had been left in the commoners' room the night of Augustus's murder, even though Monfitchet had said he had drunk enough already. Without Jerome's encouragement to drink, Montfitchet might still be alive. Bartholomew thought it was more likely that Montfitchet would have been dispatched in the same way as Brother Paul, but held his silence. Finally, Jerome laid back, his face serene, and waited for death. He asked if Bartholomew would stay with him until he died. Bartholomew agreed, hoping that Edith was not seriously hurt, and that Gray would not attempt anything beyond his capabilities.

In less than two hours, it was over, and Bartholomew helped the monks to stitch Jerome into a blanket. Bartholomew was torn between grief and impotent anger that he had not been able to do anything other than sit at the sick man's bedside. He laid Jerome gently in the stable next to Henry Oliver, and stalked out of the College towards the church. Everything seemed grey to Bartholomew. The sky was a solid iron-colour, even though it was not raining, and the houses and streets seemed drab and shabby. The town stank, and the mud that formed the street was impregnated with bits of rotting food and human waste. He made his way through it to St Michael's, where he paced around the church for a while, trying to bring his emotions under control.

After a while, he grew calmer and began to think about Philippa. She was safe – something for which he had been hoping desperately ever since Abigny had fled from Edith's house. He wondered again whether he had perhaps been over-hasty the previous night, and whether he should have shown more understanding for Abigny's point of view. But he had been exhausted by his eavesdropping excursion in the cold, and still shocked to learn that the Stanmores had been involved. He wondered where Philippa had gone, and felt a sudden urge to talk with her, and to resolve the questions about her disappearance that still jangled in his mind. The best way to find her would be through her brother, who would be most likely to seek a temporary bed at Bene't's until he deemed it safe to return to his own room.

Bartholomew set off down the High Street, his mind filled with unanswered questions. As he approached Bene't's, he shuddered, thinking about the hours he had spent perched on the window-sill above the filthy yard. He had scarcely finished knocking on the door when it was answered by a student with greasy red hair. The student said that Abigny was out and he did not know when he was likely to return, but offered to let Bartholomew wait. Bartholomew assented reluctantly, not wanting to be inside Bene't's, but his desire to see Philippa was strong. He expected to be shown into the hall, but a glimpse through the half-closed door indicated that the students were engaged in an illicit game of dice, and would not want him peering over their shoulders. He was shown into a small, chilly room on an upper floor, and abandoned with cheerful assurances that Abigny would not be long.

He was beginning to consider leaving Abigny a note asking him to go to Michaelhouse, when he heard the door open and close again. He hurried from the chamber and peered down the stairwell.

But it was not Abigny climbing the stairs, it was Stephen, preceded by Burwell. Bartholomew was on the verge of announcing himself when he heard his name mentioned. He froze, leaning across the handrail, his whole body suddenly inexplicably tense.

'. . . he is too near the truth now,' Stephen was saying, 'and he does not believe in the Oxford plot. I could see in his face he was doubtful.'

'Damn,' said Burwell, pausing to look back at Stephen. 'Now what do we do?'

'Kill him,' came a third voice, oddly familiar to Bartholomew. 'It will not be difficult. Send him another note purporting to be from Edith and have him ambushed on the Trumpington road.'

Heart thumping, Bartholomew ducked back into his chilly chamber as Burwell reached the top of the stairs. There would be no need for an ambush: they could kill him now, in Bene't Hostel. Bartholomew felt his stomach churn and his hands were clammy with sweat as he stood in the semi-darkness. To his infinite relief, the three men entered the room next to his, closing the door firmly behind them. Leaning his sweat-drenched forehead on the cold wall for a moment to calm himself, Bartholomew eased out of his chamber, and slipped along the hallway to listen outside the other door. It was old and sturdily built, and he had to strain to hear what was being said.

'Another death at Michaelhouse might look suspicious,' Stephen was saying.

'On the contrary,' came the voice of the third man, smooth and convincing. 'It might improve our cause immeasurably. We have sown the seeds of an idea into the minds of these gullible people – that Michaelhouse is a rotten apple. What better way to have that idea confirmed than yet another untimely death there? What families will send their sons to Michaelhouse where the Fellows die with such appalling regularity? And then our Oxford plot will seem all the more real, and all the more terrifying.'

Bartholomew fought to control the weak feeling in his knees and tried to bring his jumbled thoughts into order. Had he been right all along in his uncertainty about the Oxford plot? He had never accepted the concept fully, as Aelfrith, Wilson, and even Sir John had done. Could there be a plot within a plot? The group of hostel men who had gone to Stanmore had fed him lies about a plan by Oxford scholars to bring down Cambridge. Or had they? What was Stephen doing there? And who was the third man whose voice was so familiar? It was not Stanmore or Richard. Was it a Fellow from Michaelhouse? He racked his brain, trying to identify the smooth intonation, but it eluded him.

'What about Oswald?' Stephen was saying.

'Now there is a real problem,' came the familiar voice. 'Neville Stayne was foolish to have mentioned Bartholomew in front of Oswald. Now if anything happens to him, it will immediately arouse his suspicions, and all we have worked for will have been for nothing.'

'We cannot allow that, not after all we have done!' Stephen said emphatically. 'Five Michaelhouse men have died for this, and we have carefully nurtured so many rumours. We have invested months in this!'

'Easy,' came the reassuring tones of Burwell. 'We will not allow your brother and his tenacious in-law to interfere in our business. Too much is at stake.'

Stephen appeared to have accepted Burwell's assurance, for he made no further comment. The third man continued to speak, outlining a plot that would have Bartholomew and Stanmore ambushed together. Bartholomew clenched his fists, his instincts screaming at him to throw open the door and choke the life from Stephen's miserable, lying throat. But that would serve no purpose other than to allow Burwell and the third man to kill Bartholomew. And then they would be able to slay Stanmore.

Bartholomew was so preoccupied with his feelings of loathing for Stephen that he almost missed the sound of footsteps coming towards the door. Startled, he bolted back into the other room, wincing as his haste made him careless and he knocked a candle from its holder. The three men did not hear, however, and stood in the doorway conversing in low tones.

'Tonight it is, then,' came the familiar voice. Bartholomew risked opening the door a crack to see his face, but he had already started off down the stairs, and all Bartholomew saw was the hem of a cloak.

Bartholomew itched to be away to warn Stanmore of the impending threat on their lives, but Stephen and Burwell lingered at the top of the stairs, discussing the possibility of increasing hostel rents. Bartholomew silently urged them to conclude their tedious conversation so that he could leave. A dreadful thought occurred to him. Supposing Abigny arrived and found him? Then his death would be immediate, for how could they let him go after what he had heard? And, Bartholomew thought, Abigny must be involved, for how could he spend so much time at Bene't's and be unaware of what was happening?

'Here.' Bartholomew heard the tinkle of coins as money was passed from Burwell to Stephen, followed by the rustle of cloth as Stephen secreted them in his cloak.

'This is important to you,' said Burwell suddenly. 'More than just wealth.'

Bartholomew risked looking at them through the crack in the door. He saw Stephen shrug, but noted that he was unable to meet Burwell's eyes. 'I have worked for my brother all my life,' he said, 'but it will not be me who will inherit the business when he dies. It will be Richard. And what then? What of my children? The Death has made it necessary for me to consider alternative sources of income.'

Burwell looked surprised. 'But I understand that young Richard is anxious to follow in his uncle's footsteps and become a leech.'

Stephen faltered for a moment. 'People change,' he said. 'And I do not, cannot, rely on my nephew's charity for the rest of my life. What if I were to be taken by the pestilence? I must leave some funds to safeguard my children. It is no longer viable to rely on relationships and friendships to secure a future. Only this works.' He held a gold coin between his thumb and forefinger and raised it for Burwell to see.

'And you would sacrifice your brother for this?' mused Burwell. In the shadows of his chamber,

Bartholomew closed his eyes and rested his head against the wall.

'Yes,' said Stephen softly, 'because by this time tomorrow I might be in the death pits. What if Oswald and I were to die, and Richard? How could the womenfolk maintain the business? Even if they were allowed to try, and that in itself is unlikely because the Guilds would not permit it, they would be easy prey for all manner of rogues. They would be gutter fodder within the month.' He turned to face Burwell. 'I do not relish what I am about to do, but my future and the future of my children is more important than Oswald.'

Bartholomew listened as their voices faded down the stairs. He was almost beside himself with anxiety. Where had the third man gone while Stephen and Burwell chattered? Was Oswald already in danger? The two men stopped to talk again by the front door before finally taking their leave of each other. Bartholomew forced himself to wait several moments before hurrying down the stairs. Looking down the High Street, he saw Abigny walking towards him. Bartholomew ignored him, and fled in the opposite direction towards Stanmore's shop.

He raced through the gates into Stanmore's yard, his feet skidding as he fought to keep his balance on the slippery mud. He was about to go into the house to seek Stanmore out when he saw him entering the stable with a tall figure that looked very familiar. It was Robert Swynford.

Bartholomew was relieved beyond measure. Good. Now Swynford was back, he could take over the College, and Alcote would be spared being discredited, or worse, at the hands of the hostels. Breathlessly, Bartholomew ran over to the stable, pushed the door open and staggered inside. Stanmore stood just inside the door with his back to Bartholomew, but turned when he crashed in. Bartholomew's stomach flipped over when he saw it was not Stanmore at all, but Stephen. Bartholomew cursed himself for a fool as he realised Stephen was still wearing Oswald's cloak. Stephen and Swynford seemed as disconcerted to see him as Bartholomew was to see Stephen, but Swynford recovered almost immediately and shook Bartholomew by the hand, saying how pleased he was to be back in the town and asking how the College was faring.

Bartholomew, smiling politely, began to back out of the stable, but Stephen was quicker. He made a sudden movement with his hand, and Bartholomew found a long-bladed dagger pointing at him. Bartholomew gazed in panic before trying to bluff it out: Stephen did not know Bartholomew had heard him speaking with Burwell and the other man at Bene't's. 'What are you doing? Where is Oswald?'

'At Trumpington seeing to Edith. Which is where you were supposed to be,' Stephen said coldly. 'Why did you not go?'

'I had to stay with Father Jerome. I sent Gray,' Bartholomew replied, bewildered.

Stephen laughed without humour. 'You have been a problem to us almost every step of the way. I tried hard to keep you out of all this, but you have been remarkably uncooperative!'

Bartholomew tried to move away as the knife waved menacingly close, but he was hemmed in by walls on one side, and Stephen and Swynford on the other.

'I thought we had agreed to be honest with each

344

other this morning,' Bartholomew said, looking from Swynford to Stephen.

The knife waved again, and Bartholomew felt it catch on his robe. He gazed at Stephen in horror.

'Was it you?' he whispered. 'Was it you who killed Sir John and the others?'

Stephen grinned nastily and looked at Swynford, who eyed Bartholomew impassively.

'We cannot allow him to interfere any more than he has already,' Swynford said. 'There is too much to lose.' Stephen nodded, and Bartholomew wondered whether they meant to kill him there and then in the stable. Stephen obviously thought so, for he took a step towards Bartholomew, tightening his grip on the knife.

'Not here!' snapped Swynford. 'What will your brother say if he finds blood in his stable and the physician missing? Put him downstairs.'

'Downstairs?' said Stephen, lunging at Bartholomew, who had made a slight move to one side. 'Are you serious?'

'There are rooms with stout doors,' said Swynford. 'We must plan his death carefully or the Bishop might discover some streak of courage in his yellow belly and order some kind of enquiry.'

Bartholomew was lost. Swynford the murderer? He looked desperately towards the stable door, but Stephen guessed what was in his mind, and prodded him hard with the knife. 'You should have gone to see Edith,' he said, edging Bartholomew towards the end of the stable. 'Oswald and Richard went, and they will be safely out of the way until our meeting has finished.'

Stephen shoved Bartholomew against the back wall, while Swynford cleared some straw from the floor, and indicated that Bartholomew should pull up the trap-door he had uncovered. Bartholomew did not move. Stephen moved towards him, brandishing the knife threateningly, but Bartholomew still did not move.

'Open it,' said Swynford impatiently.

'Open it yourself,' said Bartholomew. If they did not want Oswald Stanmore to find blood on his stable floor, what did he have to fear from Stephen's knife?

'I do not want to kill you here,' Swynford said, as his cold, hard eyes flashed, 'but I will if necessary. Blood can be cleaned away, and a knife wound can always be hidden with other injuries, as you have probably guessed was the case with Sir John. Now, unless you wish your death to be long and painful, open the door.'

Bartholomew slowly bent to pull open the trap-door. Stanmore had shown him the small storerooms and passages under the stables when he had been a boy. They had been built by a previous merchant to hide goods from the King's tax-collectors. As far as Bartholomew knew, Stanmore had never used the underground rooms, and they had lain empty for years.

The door was made of stone, and was heavy. Bartholomew hauled at it and stood back as he let it fall backwards with a crash that echoed all over the yard. Stephen and Swynford looked at each other.

'That was rash,' said Swynford. 'One more trick like that and I will kill you myself.'

Swynford took a lamp from a shelf, and lit it. He held out a hand for Bartholomew to precede him down the wooden stairs that disappeared into the darkness below. Bartholomew climbed down cautiously, wondering if this were to be his last journey. Swynford followed him, and Stephen brought up the rear.

Bartholomew was prodded along one of the musty corridors and told to open the door to the largest chamber. To his surprise, it was already lit with candles and filled with people. A hard shove in the small of his back sent him stumbling into the middle of the room.

'We have something of a problem, gentlemen,' said Swynford calmly.

'Why did you bring him here?' It was no surprise to Bartholomew to see Burwell and Yaxley there, standing shoulder to shoulder with Neville Stayne from Mary's Hostel. Jocelyn of Ripon, too, was present, his face creased into its perpetual scowl.

'What did you expect us to do?' snapped Stephen. 'Send him home? We did our best to make sure he was out of the way. It is not our fault he failed to answer a call of mercy from his own sister!'

'What do we do with him now?' asked Burwell.

'We will keep him here until I think of a way to get rid of him that cannot be traced back to us,' said Swynford. 'We have done it before, and we can do it again.'

'Then it was you who killed Sir John and poisoned Aelfrith!' exclaimed Bartholomew.

'No. That was me.' It was the voice he had heard at Bene't's but could not identify. Bartholomew spun round and looked into the face of Gregory Colet.

Bartholomew was rendered speechless, and could only gaze dumbly as Colet sauntered round the room and perched himself on the edge of the table. He saw Bartholomew's expression of disbelief, and laughed.

'I was convincing as the drooling fool, wasn't I?' he said, crossing his legs and looking at Bartholomew. 'You were quite a nuisance, though. You would insist on visiting me when I had a great many other things to do. And I had to keep wearing these,' he said, pulling distastefully at his filthy clothes. 'You were supposed to have given up on me and left me to my own devices.'

'Why?' whispered Bartholomew, looking at his friend. 'What brought you to this?'

Swynford snapped his fingers impatiently. 'Enough of this! We have better things to do than to satisfy the curiosity of this meddling fool.'

Bartholomew was bundled out of the room and into a long chamber down the corridor by Yaxley, Jocelyn, and a man he had seen at Garret Hostel. They made him sit down on the floor at the far end and backed out of the room, slamming the door behind them. Bartholomew heard bolts shooting across on the other side. He sat in the darkness trying to comprehend what had happened to him. Stephen and Colet, whom he had believed to be friends, were so deeply embroiled in whatever foul plans were afoot, that they were prepared to kill him for them. And Colet had killed Sir John and Aelfrith!

He leaned his head back against the wall, and tried to think rationally. But it would do him no good to speculate. What he needed to do was to think of a way out. There was no window in the chamber and it was pitch black. Bartholomew felt his way along the walls, searching for other possible exits or even a weapon. There was nothing. He discovered there were several large crates in the room, but other than that the room was empty. He pushed against the door with all his strength, but it was made of thick oak bound with iron, and he knew from his childhood visits to the cellars that there were two huge bolts and a stout bar on the outside.

He sat down again despondently. Unbidden, an image of Philippa came into his mind. Was she involved too? Would she be the one to offer to make his death look like an accident? He leaned back against the wall again and closed his eyes. He could hear raised voices from the room down the corridor. He was glad they were arguing with each other: such an unholy alliance should not be free from dissent and strife. The meeting did not last long, and it was no more than half an hour later when it finished and he could hear people leaving.

The heavy stone trap-door was dropped into place with a hollow thump, and Bartholomew's prison was as dark and silent as the grave. He found it strange at first, and then disconcerting. Michaelhouse was usually noisy during the day, with scholars coming and going, and at night there was always some sound – students debating in low voices, someone's snoring through open window shutters, or footsteps on cobbled paths leading to the kitchens or the latrines. Bartholomew was aware that he could not even hear the bells that called parishioners to church or scholars to lectures and meals. In a sudden panic, he crashed towards the door and hammered on it until his fists were bruised and his voice was hoarse from yelling.

He forced himself to pace out the room in an effort to calm himself, counting the number of steps, and then exploring every unevenness in the earthen walls. In one of the crates he found some bales of cloth and wrapped them round him against the chill of the room. When he felt as though he had mastered his panic, he perched on a chest, tucked his feet up underneath him, and began to review what he had learned. At least he would not go to his death confused and demanding answers.

He knew the men involved: Colet, Burwell, Yaxley, Stayne, Jocelyn, the man from Garret Hostel, Stephen, and Swynford. Swynford was clearly in charge: even Colet had obeyed his instructions. Jocelyn obviously had no intention of founding a grammar school in Ripon, but had been imported by his kinsman into Michaelhouse to help him in his plotting. Stephen's role was probably to encourage Stanmore and the other merchants to maintain their support of the bogus hostels group, while the money they invested was pocketed by Swynford. With a start he remembered Burwell telling him that he had heard of Philippa's flight from Stephen, although there was no reason why they should have known each other well enough to exchange gossip. And Colet? Colet, by his own admission, had been the one to murder Sir John and Aelfrith. Did he also kill Paul and Augustus, and drug the commoners? And how far was the Abbess of St Radegund's involved? While Abigny's story had a ring of truth to it, the blacksmith had been paid to warn Bartholomew in a purse from Bene't Hostel.

Bartholomew wrapped his arms around his body more tightly for warmth, and pressed on with his reasoning. It would probably have been easy to kill Sir John. Cynric had seen him leaving the College after he had eaten dinner with Aelfrith and Bartholomew, probably called to a meeting connected with the alleged Oxford plot. Bartholomew and Stanmore had received false messages from Swynford and his clan, and Colet had probably sent a similar one to Sir John. Sir John had suspected something was amiss, however, because he had taken the precaution of leaving the seal behind. He had gone to the meeting by the mill, a place where few went after dark, where he was murdered by Colet. Swynford had indicated that the fatal wound had been hidden by the injuries sustained when Sir John was crushed by the water-wheel. Colet had been unable to find the seal, and so had exchanged Sir John's clothes for another set – probably the ones he had worn himself as a disguise when he went to meet Sir John with the intention of killing him.

But if the Oxford plot was a sham, why did Colet want the seal? Bartholomew rubbed his arms hard, trying to force some warmth into them. He supposed it was to add credence to the Oxford plot, to show that the business was worth killing over. He wondered what the Oxford scholars thought about the business. He had no doubt that the rumours had reached them, and that they must be as mystified by the whole affair as were the Cambridge men. Perhaps they had even initiated their own investigation, word of which would filter back to Cambridge, where it would be used by Swynford to underline further still that something untoward was happening.

So when did it all start? Bartholomew thought back to what Aelfrith had told him about the uncannily high number of deaths of Fellows in the Colleges last year: Aelfrith's friend who had drowned in the Peterhouse fish-ponds, supposedly in his cups; the Master of King's Hall who was said to have fallen down the stairs; two deaths from food poisoning; and four cases of summer ague. So Aelfrith's assumptions had been correct, and the Fellows had been murdered by Swynford and his associates so they could start a rumour discrediting the Colleges and blaming Oxford for the deaths. Aelfrith's friend had been drowned, the Master of King's Hall hanged, and the others probably poisoned. He thought of the two young men he had attended as they lay dying from bad oysters. He closed his eyes in the darkness as he recalled who had been with him. Colet. Colet had been dining at Clare that night, and it had been Colet who had called Bartholomew so it would seem that he had made every effort to save their lives. Clever Colet, using Bartholomew as a shield so no blame for the deaths should ever fall on him. And of course, who better to have access to subtle poisons, and to know how to use them, than a physician?

These deaths, it seemed, had been sufficient to force the merchants into action. When the so-called hostels group was formed, Stanmore had said that the deaths had stopped. The merchants must have felt that their financial contributions were doing some good. But why kill Sir John and the others if the merchants had fallen for the ploy and were paying their money? Bartholomew rolled the possibilities through his mind. The merchants must have grown complacent, secure in the knowledge that they had done their bit for the town. Perhaps news of the plague took their minds away from the University. The deaths at Michaelhouse would serve to show them that the business was far from over.

But what of Augustus? Who had killed him? It was obvious why: Wilson had told him that Sir John had visited Augustus before attending the fatal meeting that Bartholomew now knew was with Colet, and half the world suspected that the seal had been hidden in his room. The first attempt on Augustus's life had failed, and the killer had returned three nights later. Bartholomew supposed that Augustus's room could hardly be searched with Augustus in it, and he had been murdered to secure his silence. Poor Augustus had given the killer reason to believe he had swallowed the seal. The killer must have hidden in the attic when Alexander came to bring Paul and Augustus some wine. He must have been watching Bartholomew from his hiding place, wondering what he had been doing when he examined Augustus's body and looked under the bed. When Aelfrith had come to keep vigil, it had been an easy thing to knock him on the head and drag Augustus into the attic. Wilson had come then to begin his own search for the seal, and he too had fled to the attic when disturbed, first knocking Bartholomew down the stairs. How crowded the attic had been at that point: the killer, Wilson, and Augustus's body.

But who had actually killed Augustus? And how? There had been no signs of poisoning or violence, but the expression of abject terror on his dead face confirmed that his death had not been natural. All the Fellows and commoners had alibis for the time Augustus had died, so it must have been an outsider. Could it have been Colet again? Bartholomew thought about it, and decided there was no other plausible possibility. Whoever had sliced Augustus apart to investigate his innards had possessed some degree of surgical skill. The incision was crude and brutal, but it would take a physician's knowledge to search the inside of a corpse, and perhaps a physician's nerve and stomach.

So Colet must have determined, with the help of Swynford and perhaps Jocelyn, to search Augustus's room for the elusive seal while Michaelhouse scholars were at Wilson's feast. Poor Brother Paul was too ill to attend, something that Colet had probably not anticipated. So, Paul was dispatched as a precaution against him crying out. Bartholomew screwed up his eyes in thought. When he had gone to check Augustus, he had heard Paul cough, but now he could not be sure that it had not been Colet, standing next to Paul's bed, and imitating the hack of an old man to prevent Bartholomew from checking on him too. But even if Bartholomew had looked at Paul, what then? He would have seen exactly what he had seen the following morning – Paul with his blanket tightly tucked around him hiding his face, the spilled blood, and the knife in his stomach.

Drugged wine was left in the commoners' room, lest they returned from the feast too early. And Jocelyn had told Bartholomew that it had been his idea to drink Wilson's health with the wine he had found on the table. He must have known it was drugged, and also that the others were too drunk to question how the wine had come to be there so conveniently. How Jocelyn must have gloated at the ease with which that part of the plan had gone. Montfitchet did not want to drink because he felt ill, but, luckily for Jocelyn, Father Jerome persuaded him, unwittingly bringing about his death. D'Evéne, who had a bad reaction to wine, had also been persuaded to drink.

Bartholomew stood and began jumping up and down on the spot, trying to force some warmth into his legs. As he considered the information he had, it was easy to see what Colet had done. He must have hidden in Swynford's room. Swynford was the only Fellow to have a room to himself, so no one would have seen Colet once he had slipped into the College in the commotion before the feast. He could then have used the second trap-door in the hallway outside Swynford's room to gain access to the attic, and gone from there to Augustus's room.

But how did Colet know about the doors to the attic? Wilson had said they were a secret passed from Master to Master. Wilson himself did not know about them until he read about them in the box from the Chancellor.

Try as he might, Bartholomew could come up with no reason why Swynford or Colet should know, and he felt his carefully constructed argument begin to crumble. He could not imagine that Sir John would have broken trust by telling Swynford, and Swynford had not been at Michaelhouse long enough to have known the previous Master. Exhausted by his thinking and the events of the day, Bartholomew finally slipped into a restless doze huddled in a corner.

Bartholomew lost track of the time he was kept in his underground tomb. Once the door opened briefly and some bread, salted beef, and watered ale were shoved inside, but it occurred so quickly that by the time Bartholomew realised what had happened, the door had been closed and he was alone again. He sniffed at the food suspiciously, wondering if Colet meant to poison him, but he was hungry and thirsty enough to throw caution to the wind.

He thought about what his death might mean. Colet had said in Bene't Hostel that it would fit nicely into their plan, and would reinforce the notion that something was sadly amiss at Michaelhouse. What of Stanmore then? He would never accept Bartholomew's murder, no matter how cunningly disguised. He would try to seek out Bartholomew's killer, would confront members of the hostel committee, and generally make problems until he, too, was dispatched. And then Richard would guess something untoward had happened, and perhaps start an inexperienced, clumsy investigation of his own. Where would it all end? Would Stanmore's colleagues be suspicious of three accidental deaths in one family? Would they, too, start to look into matters?

Bartholomew recalled with a pang why he had been captured in the first place – trying to warn Stanmore that Stephen and Burwell planned to kill him. He cursed himself again for his ineptitude. He had seen Stephen wearing that cloak before. But the more he thought about it, the more he came to believe that Stanmore would be safe until his own body was found. Stanmore had no reason to be suspicious of Bartholomew's disappearance – since the plague had come he had kept such irregular hours that no one knew for certain where he was – and the hostel group was unlikely to cut off a source of funding in Stanmore before it became absolutely necessary.

He was dozing in the corner when the room was suddenly filled with light that hurt his eyes. There was noise too – shouting and arguing. Through painfully narrowed eyes, Bartholomew saw Swynford outlined in the doorway, flanked by a burly porter from Rudde's Hostel who was armed with a loaded crossbow. Irrelevantly, Bartholomew remembered Colet telling him that the porter was a veteran of the King's wars in France before exchanging a soldier's career for a more sedentary life keeping law and order in one of the University's rowdier establishments.

Swynford held up the torch and the light fell on Bartholomew. Bartholomew squinted, wondering if they had come to murder him. He struggled to his feet, dazed and clumsy, but prepared to sell his life dearly. Swynford glanced at Bartholomew disinterestedly, and gestured to someone outside. Bartholomew had a fleeting glimpse of Brother Michael, firmly in the grasp of Jocelyn and Colet, before he was hurled into the room.

'Company for you, Physician,' said Swynford. 'Now you have someone with whom you can discuss what you think you know of us.' He turned to leave. Bartholomew, savouring the sound of voices after so long alone, was strangely reluctant to let them go. He thought quickly, wondering how he might detain them.

'Gregory!' he called, trying to disentangle himself from Michael who had stumbled into him. 'Did you kill Augustus and Paul?'

'Yes and no,' replied Colet smoothly, ignoring Swynford's look of disapproval. 'I killed Paul. He kept calling out for someone to bring him water. He was a nuisance, and had to be silenced. But I did not kill Augustus, he killed himself.'

'What do you mean?' said Bartholomew. 'There were no marks of violence on him.'

'So that was what you were doing with his body,' said Colet. 'I wondered what you were up to. I had planned to kill the old fool, and had my knife ready to slip between his ribs as he slept. But he was awake when I entered his room, and I saw him swallow something. I was wearing a black cloak and hood, and I really think he believed I was Death coming for him. He just keeled over and died of fright.'

Bartholomew remembered Wilson's dismissive words when Bartholomew told him he had been trying to discover the cause of Augustus's death. 'He probably frightened himself to death with his imagination,' Wilson had said, and he had been exactly right. But, even if no weapon were used, it was still murder to frighten an old man so much that his heart stopped. Colet seemed about to continue, and Bartholomew could tell from the tone of his voice that he was only too happy to talk about the deeds he had done and boast of his own cleverness in evading detection, but Swynford took him roughly by the arm and pulled him away. The door was slammed shut and firmly bolted and barred again from the outside. Once more the room was plunged into pitch blackness. Bartholomew heard Michael groping around in the darkness, and moved across to him. The fat monk was damp with sweat and trembling violently.

'How do you come to be here, Brother?' Bartholomew asked, leading him to a crate, the position of which he knew so well from his wanderings in the dark.

'How do you?' retorted Michael angrily, pulling away from Bartholomew and stumbling against the chest. 'The word is that you have gone to Peterborough on a mercy call from your old mentor the Abbott.'

Bartholomew immediately appreciated that it was a clever ploy on the part of Swynford to say that he had gone to Peterborough. It was very plausible that Bartholomew might answer a call of distress from the monks at the abbey where he had gone to school, and at any time other than while the plague raged in Cambridge, Bartholomew would have gone without hesitation. But Colet and Swynford did not know him as well as they thought.

'I would not leave,' said Bartholomew, 'when there is only me and Robin of Grantchester to help the sick. And the Abbott would know I would not desert my patients, and would never ask me to go.'

Michael gave a grunt. 'I suppose that seems reasonable. But you still have not explained how you come to be here.'

'Oswald!' said Bartholomew suddenly. 'How is he?'

'He was hale and hearty when I saw him this morning. Why do you ask?'

Bartholomew sagged in relief. His reasoning had been correct, and Stanmore was still safe. 'I overheard Colet plotting to kill him,' he said. 'I was coming to warn Oswald when I very stupidly ran into Stephen and Swynford, and I have been here since Wednesday.'

'Which was when you were said to have left for Peterborough,' said Michael. Bartholomew heard a metallic sound as Michael struck a flint, and helped him smash one of the crates so that they could kindle a splinter of wood. The light was feeble, and it gave off eye-watering smoke, but Bartholomew was grateful to be able to see, if only dimly.

Michael put the burning stick near Bartholomew's face and peered at him closely. 'Oh lord, Matt! You look terrible. You should never have involved yourself in all this. I warned you against it.'

'The same could be said for you,' retorted Bartholomew, 'for we both seem to be in the same predicament, regardless of our respective motives.'

'Never mind that,' said Michael. 'We need to get out. Come and help me look.'

'There is no way out,' said Bartholomew. 'Believe me, I have checked.'

He watched as Michael went through the same process that he had; how long before had it been? The monk hammered and heaved at the door, he banged at the ceiling with a stick, and he prodded at the walls. Finally, defeated, he came to sit next to Bartholomew again.

'I have been in Ely with my lord the Bishop,' Michael said. 'We have been going over all the information he has been sent during the past few months about the Oxford plot.'

Bartholomew shook his head. 'There is no plot,' he said.

Michael looked at him curiously. 'We also came to that conclusion,' he said. 'Is there anything to eat here? I missed dinner.'

Bartholomew indicated a few crusts of bread that he had been saving, and a dribble of water in the pitcher. Michael looked at them and shuddered. He continued with his story.

'I arrived back last night,' he said, 'and it is now Friday evening. You probably have no idea of time in this wretched hole.'

'Have you seen Philippa?' Bartholomew interrupted, thinking of the reason he had gone to Bene't's in the first place.

'No,' said Michael, 'but I have seen Giles Abigny, and he told me his tale. He is not mixed up in all this, you know. I imagine that while you were ferreting around for information about Philippa you inadvertently picked up clues about this Oxford business. But I can tell you with absolute certainty that the Abignys are wholly unconnected with it all.'

'Really? Do you not think it a coincidence that all this should happen at the same time, and that Bene't Hostel figures in the Oxford business and is also Giles's second home? And that the Principal of Bene't's – before he died – was Hugh Stapleton, in whose house Giles and Philippa hid?'

'No, I do not,' said Michael. 'I can see why you are suspicious, but the Oxford business has been rolling on for more than a year now. Philippa and Giles only executed their little plot over the past few weeks. And I would be as suspicious of Giles as you are, if I were not sure that Hugh and Cedric Stapleton were also innocent in all this. Hugh suspected something was fermenting in his hostel and contacted the Bishop about it. He sent reports on various comings and goings, and Cedric continued them after Hugh's death. Hugh and Cedric were fickle, frivolous men, like Giles, and quite the wrong kind of people to be recruited by Swynford. They were not even recruited for the bogus hostel group that your brother-in-law was mixed up with.'

'You know about that?' said Bartholomew, startled. 'What else do you know?'

'I was telling you,' said Michael with a superior expression, 'but you interrupted me with your question about Philippa. And while we are on that subject, she has taken your supposed journey to Peterborough very personally. Abigny tells me she fluctuates between anger and sorrow, and will think of nothing else. How can you doubt her, Matt?'

Bartholomew shook his head. So he had been wrong, and Philippa and Abigny were innocent after all. If Philippa were acting as Michael described, then she could not know that he was being kept prisoner in Stephen's dungeon. But it would not matter soon anyway if Swynford's plans came to fruition. Bartholomew's greatest regret would be that he would never have the opportunity to tell Philippa he was sorry, and she might hate him for it.

Michael kindled another piece of wood, coughing as it released a choking grey smoke. 'As I said before, I have been sifting through reports the Bishop has received during the last year in an attempt to understand this, and I believe I now know the truth.'

'Then how did you come to be taken by Swynford?' asked Bartholomew.

'I was rash,' said Michael. 'I reported my findings to the Bishop, and he told me to return to Michaelhouse and do nothing. But there were gaps in my knowledge, and I could not resist trying to fill them in. I undertook to question Burwell, and then Stayne. They obviously grew suspicious, and I received a message from Stanmore asking me to visit him. I went, and found not Stanmore, but his younger brother. I brazened it out, asking guileless questions and pretending to be convinced of the reality of the Oxford plot, but it was all to no avail. Colet and Swynford appeared out of nowhere, and I was hauled down here.'

'A note,' said Bartholomew, bitterly. 'How many times have Colet and Swynford used that device? They sent such a note to Sir John, enticing him to the meeting at which he was killed; they sent one to me saying I was needed by a patient, after which I was attacked; and they sent one to Oswald and me purporting to be from Edith, intending to get us out of the way so Swynford could have his meeting here.'

'It seems we are in a fix, Matt,' said Michael, his flabby face serious. 'Will they kill us?'

'They will try,' Bartholomew replied.

Michael gave him a weak smile. 'It will do them no good. The Bishop knows everything I do, except your role in all this, and Abigny's innocence, of which I have only recently learned.'

'What of rescue?' asked Bartholomew hopefully. 'Did you tell anyone where you were going?'

Michael smiled ruefully. 'The note purporting to be from Oswald asked me to keep our meeting a secret.'

'But what of the Bishop? Will he not grow suspicious of your disappearance?'

'Undoubtedly. But unless one of the hostel cabal reveals where we are, he is unlikely to stumble on us by accident.'

Bartholomew thought about the cunningly concealed entrance in the stable and concurred. Stanmore and Richard knew about the chambers, but they would never imagine that Stephen had used them to imprison him. They might not visit the underground storerooms for years to come.

'What about you?' asked Michael. 'Will Cynric wonder about your sudden disappearance?'

'I think I would have been rescued by now if he had,' said Bartholomew. 'And he probably thinks I have gone to Peterborough, as you did. Even if he is suspicious, he will blame Oswald, not Stephen.'

They were silent for a while, each wrapped in his own thoughts. Michael's piece of wood crackled and the flame went out.

'I thought you were involved in all this,' said Michael distantly, kindling another piece of wood. 'You talked to Aelfrith in the orchard, but would not tell me what you had discussed. You spent ages with Augustus after he died, and I thought you were looking for the seal. Wilson singled you out to talk to on his deathbed. You had no alibi for when Augustus and Paul were murdered. And how was I to know that you had not hurled yourself down the stairs that night to confound us? You also searched my room, and I found you reading my note to the Bishop.'

'The Bishop!' said Bartholomew. So that was to

whom Michael was writing. He reached forward to grab Michael's arm. 'I did not search your room. The note just fell on the floor when I opened the door to look for you.'

'Well,' said Michael, 'there were occasions when I was convinced you were the killer, while other times I was uncertain. I took a terrible risk for you when I agreed not to tell anyone you had read my note. I suppose I could not bring myself to think that you would harm Augustus and Paul, and I also believe you are a good physician and would not make mistakes about the quantity of whatever foul potion was used to drug the commoners. But even more, I know how close a friend Sir John was to you, and could not suppose that you would ever have done anything to harm him.'

'When I read the note I thought you might be the murderer,' said Bartholomew.

'Me?' said Michael aghast. 'On what grounds? I have never done anything the least bit suspicious!'

'You were one of the first to arrive when the initial attempt was made on Augustus's life. Aelfrith, who was poisoned, died in your room. And you acted most strangely over Augustus's corpse. You refused even to look at it.'

'Ah, yes,' said Michael, struggling to light another piece of wood. 'Augustus.' He shook his head sadly. Bartholomew waited for him to continue.

'He was murdered, you know, for Sir John's seal. You know about the seal?' Bartholomew nodded, and Michael continued. 'Before he died, Augustus claimed that devils were in his room. Remember? Well, before all that happened, he had told me that someone would try to kill him. He kept me up a long time that night with his

rantings. I thought I had calmed him down, and went off
to the kitchen for something to eat. Within a few minutes,
he started screaming again. I ran to his room where you
and I broke the door down together. It was full of smoke,
and he was insane with fear. I realised that I was not the
only person to have worked out that Augustus's room
was the only place Sir John could have hidden the seal
before he died. You arrived just after me.'

Bartholomew remembered well. He had wondered
at the time how Michael had managed to reach Augustus's
room before him. That he had been raiding the kitchen
made perfect sense.

'You offered to stay with Augustus for the rest of the
night, and so I knew he would be safe if anyone really had
been trying to kill him in order to search for the seal. I
kept a close eye on him for the next couple of days, and
went to check on him before Wilson's installation dinner.
I was absolutely horrified when I heard he had been killed
during the feast, especially after one attempt on the poor
man had already been made. Anyway, I had never seen a
murdered man before, and I am afraid it unnerved me
more than I would have thought. I was afraid to look
into his face, because I have heard that a picture of the
murderer is always burned into the victim's eyes. I have
also heard that a victim's body bleeds in the presence
of his murderer, and I felt that Augustus might bleed
for me because I was unable to save him when I knew
his life was in danger.'

He stopped, and looked at Bartholomew with a
weak smile. 'All silly nonsense, of course, and I would
not usually stoop to such superstition. But the whole
of that day was unreal – Wilson's endless ceremonies,
all that wine, town people in the College, the riot, the

Oliver brothers trying to lock you out, and then Augustus dead. It was all too much. I was deeply shocked, because I had seen him alive such a short time before. Does this explain my behaviour to you?'

Bartholomew shrugged. 'I suppose so, but you do not usually panic so easily.'

'Well, there was one other thing too,' he said. 'The Bishop spoke to me that day, and said that he wanted me to act as his agent in Michaelhouse. He told me about the deaths of Fellows in other Colleges, and said that Aelfrith was already acting as his spy. He said he wanted me to act totally independently of Aelfrith, so that if one line of communication were to fail, the other would remain intact. He gave me until the following day to decide whether I would take on the task. When Augustus died, I realised exactly what he was asking me to embroil myself in, and, frankly, it terrified me. But the next day, I spoke to the Bishop, and told him I would do it – for the College and for the University.'

He paused again. 'I have been acting on behalf of the Bishop ever since. I tried to warn you to keep out of it, Matt. I thought you did not realise what you might get into, and Augustus's murder showed me that it was no longer a silly game played by bored scholars with active minds and too much free time, but something far more deadly.'

Michael's lighted stick crackled and popped, and Bartholomew realised again how wrong he had been. He stood up, and stretched carefully. He sat again, and made up his mind. He began to tell Michael everything he knew and had surmised.

XII

ICHAEL GAVE UP LIGHTING HIS FRAG-
ments of wood, and most of Bartholomew's
tale was delivered in darkness. That he had
been alone and in darkness for so long occasionally made
him wonder whether Michael was really there at all, and
several times he reached out to touch him, or asked
him a needless question just to hear his voice. Michael
added scraps of his own evidence here and there, and by
the time he had finished, Bartholomew felt at last that
he understood most of what had happened. He heard
Michael give a sigh as his narrative was completed.

'The Colleges will be powerful forces in the University, Matt. There are five of them now, and there
are plans to found another two next year. That will
mean there will be seven institutions with Fellows and
their own property. The Fellows will be more secure in
their futures than the teachers in the hostels, and the
longer they remain at the Colleges, the more power
they will accrue. The hostels own no property, and are
therefore inherently unstable, and, in time, the Colleges
will take their power. As it is, the most powerful men in
the University now are Fellows of the Colleges, not men
from the hostels. Swynford must have determined that

the advance of the Colleges had to be stopped, because in time, they will become so powerful that they will become independent of the University, and they will crush the hostels.'

'But why?' said Bartholomew. 'Swynford is a Fellow with a powerful voice in the University, and he is now the Master of Michaelhouse.'

'The Bishop's records show that he owns many of the buildings that are used as hostels,' said Michael. 'The rents he charges have made him a rich man. He would not wish to lose this source of income.'

'Is that it?' asked Bartholomew incredulously. 'Is it about money? Like Stephen?'

Bartholomew heard Michael laugh softly in the dark. 'Matt! Have you spent your life asleep? Do you not know that nearly all crime in this country is committed with the intention to increase personal wealth? Of course, there is good old-fashioned lust, too; that often plays a part. But the overriding human emotion is greed.'

They sat in silence for a while, before Bartholomew started talking again, more to hear Michael's voice than to resume their discussion. 'I wonder why Swynford wants so much money. It is almost as if he is aiming for something specific.'

'Perhaps he is,' said Michael. 'Another hostel perhaps? A position?'

'A position?' queried Bartholomew. 'What sort of position would he need to buy?'

Michael shrugged. 'I do not know. Mayor? A position at court? A See?'

'A See?' exclaimed Bartholomew. 'You cannot pay to become a bishop!'

'Oh, but you can, Matt. Not direct payment perhaps,

but a sum of money forwarded to the King's coffers might ensure a position of some kind.' He suddenly slammed his first into his open palm. 'Of course! That is it! The Bishop of Lincoln grows old, and Swynford asked our Bishop about who might be next in line to succeed him at Wilson's feast. I heard him! Swynford was saving to become a bishop! And what a bishop he would make: he is learned, of noble birth, and highly respectable.'

'Respectable indeed,' said Bartholomew. 'Murder, corruption, fraud. All highly respectable talents.'

Michael said nothing, but Bartholomew could hear him shifting around, trying to get comfortable on his crate.

'So, let us summarise what we have reasoned,' said Michael. 'About a year ago Swynford decided to crush the Colleges to strengthen the hostels. He, and a band of selected helpers, put about rumours to blame it all on Oxford, and even killed Fellows in King's Hall, Peterhouse, and Clare to make it appear serious. Merchants were persuaded to give money on the grounds that were the University to collapse, they would lose a good deal of trade. Sir John unwittingly aided them in this because they took advantage of a spy system that had nothing to do with the Universities, but one in which Sir John played a minor role for the King. When Sir John became suspicious, he was murdered, and his death was made to look like suicide. Michaelhouse was discredited because his body was discovered . . . not wearing his own clothes.'

'Shortly afterwards, Colet and Swynford decided to add credence to the plot by undertaking to look for Sir John's seal. They killed Augustus and Paul, and Montfitchet died too. They failed to find the seal, even after tearing out Augustus's entrails. Wilson sneaked off into the night to search for it too, acting on behalf of the Chancellor, but he also failed. The damage was done to Michaelhouse, even though the seal remained hidden. The Bishop, realising that there was more at stake than Michaelhouse's reputation, forced the Fellows to deny the truth. Perhaps Colet and his friends realised they had gone far enough, or perhaps they were more concerned with the approaching Death, for they made no further attempts to find the seal. They poisoned Aelfrith when his enquiries brought him too close to the truth.'

'Of course!' exclaimed Bartholomew, leaping to his feet and pacing in the darkness. 'William, without knowing what he said, told me why Aelfrith was killed a long time ago, but I did not see it. He told me that before his death Aelfrith had seemed depressed because he had heard the deathbed confession of the Principal of All Saints' Hostel. That Principal must have been involved too! News must have got out that he had made a confession, and Aelfrith was killed in case he had been told something sensitive.'

'Aelfrith believed in the seal of confession,' said Michael. 'Even if the dying Principal had told him everything, Aelfrith would never have revealed it to another.'

'Stephen is prepared to kill his own brother for this,' said Bartholomew, 'and the others seem equally fanatical. Killing a friar as a safeguard would be nothing to them.'

'Sadly, I suspect you are right,' said Michael. 'But, to continue. Wilson told you about the attic, perhaps so that you might try to see justice done for the poor victims whose deaths he and the Bishop had ensured went unavenged. It was no secret Wilson spoke to you at length on his deathbed, and it would not take a genius to suppose that Wilson might have told you of the attic, where Augustus's body still lay. I imagine either Colet or Jocelyn carried the body to the stables, hoping that it would be taken away unnoticed by the plague cart.'

He paused again and sniffed. 'Lord, it is as cold as the grave in here.'

'Apt description,' muttered Bartholomew, his mind still on the web of intrigue he and Michael were unravelling.

Michael continued. 'The pestilence must have brought about the deaths of some of those involved in this affair – like the Principal of All Saints'. I suppose now is a good time to strike more blows at the Colleges, while we are weakened and unsuspecting. They have made moves against Alcote, an attack on whom will not reflect badly on Swynford, and might even enhance his reputation – he will be seen now as an honourable man returning from protecting his female kinsfolk in a vain, but noble attempt to save the College from corruption. You and I will also provide them with a godsent opportunity to kill us in a way that will bring Michaelhouse into further disrepute. What a fool I was to try to question them!'

'Do you think all the hostels are involved in this?' Bartholomew asked after a pause.

Michael sucked in his breath. 'I doubt they could have operated so efficiently and secretly for such a long time if all the hostels were implicated. The Bishop's records indicate that certain people are definitely involved: John Rede, Principal of Tunstede Hostel, but he is dead of the plague; Jocelyn and Swynford from Michaelhouse; Burwell and Yaxley from Bene't's; Stayne from Mary's; the Principals of Martin's and All Saints' Hostels, although the plague took them, too; Colet from Rudde's; and Caxton and Greene from Garret Hostel, but Greene is dead.'

Bartholomew leaned against the damp wall and folded his arms. 'And do you know which of the merchants were involved?'

'None,' said Michael. 'Only hostel men were allowed in on the real plot. But the merchants were an essential component in Swynford's plan. It would not have worked without them. He would not wish to spend his own money, nor that of his colleagues, on fighting the Colleges. The merchants contributed generously, thinking that they were saving the University from being crushed by Oxford, when the reality was that their money was used to undermine the Colleges.'

Lies, counter-lies, and more lies, thought Bartholomew. Good men had lost their lives because of this wretched business.

'What about the need to protect both Universities so that there will be two places in which to train new priests and clerics when we recover from the effects of the plague?' he asked.

'I am sure they endorse it fully. The more priests and clerics that can be encouraged to come to the University the better. They will live in the hostels Swynford owns, and their rents will swell his coffers. The Bishop believes that half our clergy will perish from the Death, and that the country will desperately need to train more if we are to retain our social order. Without priests among the people, there will soon be insurrection and bloodshed. Swynford's hostels will be offering England a vital service.'

At least Stanmore's money had not totally been squandered, thought Bartholomew, if it could help to achieve some degree of social stability once the plague had burned itself out.

'Why do you think Colet became involved?' asked Michael. 'I always understood he had a glorious future as a physician – far more so than you because he is less controversial.'

'I do not know. Perhaps because of the pestilence? First, a good many of his wealthy patients were likely to die, thus reducing his income. Second, the plague is not a good disease for physicians: the risk of infection is great, and the chances of success are low. We discussed it *ad nauseam* before it came, and he knew as well as I that physicians were likely to become social outcasts – shunned by people who were uninfected, and treated with scorn by those that were because we would be unable to cure them. His leeching for toothaches and hangovers would not stand him in good stead with the Death. He was probably taking precautions against an uncertain future, like Stephen.'

Bartholomew gazed into the darkness and thought about Colet. He had stopped treating his patients when Bartholomew became ill and Roper had died. But about the same time, the wealthy merchant Per Goldam had died, and he had been Colet's richest patient. Colet must have decided that helping Bartholomew in the slums and with the plague pits was not for him. What better way to escape from constant demands from people for help than to feign madness? In the church, he would be relatively safe from plague-bearing people, and would be in a place where his associates could easily drop in to see him. His ramblings around the churches and his trips for blackberries were merely excuses to go about his business.

Bartholomew was overcome with disgust. He had liked Colet. What an appalling judge of character he must be to misjudge Philippa, Stanmore, and Michael, and not to suspect Colet. There was nothing more to be said, and each became engrossed in his own thoughts.

Although time dragged in the dark room, it did not seem long before they heard the sound of the trap-door being opened again. Bartholomew heard Michael draw in his breath sharply, thinking, like himself, that their executioners might be coming. There was a crash as Michael, backing away, knocked a chest over. Bartholomew stationed himself near the door. The bolts were drawn back with agonising slowness, and Bartholomew felt sweat breaking out at the base of his neck.

The door swung open slowly, and light slanted into the room, dazzling him.

'Stand back,' said Colet. 'Master Jocelyn carries his crossbow and will not hesitate to use it if you attempt anything foolish.'

Slowly Bartholomew backed away, his eyes narrowed against what seemed like blinding light. He saw Jocelyn standing beyond the door, his crossbow aimed at Bartholomew's chest. The Rudde's porter was there too, holding a drawn sword. Colet was obviously taking no chances with his two prisoners.

'What do you want?' said Bartholomew with more bravado than he felt.

'You are an ingrate, Matt,' said Colet, and Bartholomew wondered why he had never detected the unpleasant smoothness in his friend's voice before. 'I have come to bring you food and wine. I thought you must be hungry by now, and your fat friend is always ravenous.'

He nodded his head, and the porter slid a tray into the room with his foot. On it there was bread, wizened apples, and something covered with a cloth. Red wine sloshed over the rim of the jug as the tray moved.

'So,' said Colet. 'You two must have had quite a conversation down here.'

When Bartholomew and Michael did not answer, Colet continued, his voice gloating, goading. 'So now you understand everything? What we have been doing, and why?'

Again, Bartholomew and Michael did not reply, and Colet's composure slipped a little. 'What? No questions? Surely we have not been so careless as to leave nothing that you have been unable to work out?'

Michael affected a nonchalant pose on the crate he had knocked over. 'Doctor Bartholomew lost his taste for questions when the answers proved so unpleasant,' he said. 'But I confess there are two things that puzzle me still. First, how did you kill Aelfrith? We know why and that you used poison. But we remain uncertain as to how you made him believe it was Wilson.'

'I do not wish to know,' said Bartholomew in disgust. 'That you murdered a good man, and that you used so low a weapon as poison to do it is more than enough for me.'

'Oh, surely not?' said Colet, laughing. 'What happened to your spirit of learning and discovery? I never thought that you, of all people, would refuse to learn after all our debates and experiments together.'

'We were different men then,' said Bartholomew, with undisguised loathing.

'Perhaps,' mused Colet. 'But Brother Michael asked me a question, and I feel duty-bound to answer it. Aelfrith was coming too close to the truth. I heard from the monks in St Botolph's that Aelfrith heard Wilson's confession every Friday. So, I sent Aelfrith a small bottle of mead with a signed message from Wilson saying he appreciated Aelfrith's understanding, and he should drink the mead to help him relax after his hard work in the town. The message, of course, was written by me, and the mead was poisoned. I retrieved the rest of the bottle the night he died, lest you should find it.'

He smiled absently. 'I was almost caught. The poison was slower-acting than I had imagined, and Aelfrith was still alive and staggering around when I came for the bottle. You, Brother, tried to take him back to his room, and I only just managed to lock the door before you came. You took Aelfrith elsewhere to die, but it was a narrow escape for me.'

Bartholomew remembered Michael telling him that Aelfrith's door had been locked, and recalled assuming Aelfrith's room-mates had shut it because they did not want a plague victim in the chamber with them. But Colet had been hiding there, with the murder weapon in his hands.

'So you kill by stealth,' said Bartholomew bitterly. 'As I am sure you did with Sir John, for you would never have overpowered him in a fair fight.'

'True enough,' said Colet, 'and I most certainly was not prepared to try. I had help that night. Masters Yaxley and Burwell accompanied me.'

'Why did you go to so much trouble for the seal?'

asked Michael. 'It would have been no use to you at all after the death of Sir John.'

'You are right, the seal is nothing,' said Colet. 'Once it was known by the King's spies that Sir John was dead, there would have been no value in his seal, and it could never have been used for the same purpose again. But it suited our plans to make believe that there were men desperate to retrieve the seal. If people thought the seal was important enough to kill for, they would also think that the information Sir John received from his spy – our messages – was of great significance.'

'Was it you or Swynford that tried to burn poor, sick Augustus in the middle of the night?' asked Michael.

'Neither, actually. We did not want to set Augustus's room on fire or burn him in his bed. That would have drawn attention to the room we were trying to search. Our notion was to make the fire smoke to asphyxiate him.'

'I see,' said Bartholomew sarcastically. 'And how could you possibly have made such a mess of this simple operation?'

Colet eyed Bartholomew malevolently for a moment. 'Jocelyn thought the fire was taking too long, and lit another under the bed to speed the process along. Instead of smoke, there were flames and the old man woke.' He looked in disgust at Jocelyn, who curled his lip in disdain at Colet. 'Fortunately he was too confused to identify Jocelyn, who managed to put out the fire and escape by the trap-door before you two came and broke down the door. When I returned to make amends for his bungling the night of the feast, I was careful to remove all evidence that there was ever a fire.'

Bartholomew recalled the cinders that had clung to his gown when he lay on the floor to retrieve the lid of the bottle Michael dropped. When he had looked for them the morning after, they had gone.

'You disgust me, Colet,' said Bartholomew softly. 'You are a physician, sworn to heal. Even if you did not use a weapon, it is still murder to frighten an old man to death.'

'You almost caught me, actually,' said Colet, and Bartholomew could see that the entire affair was little more than an intellectual game for him. 'I let myself out of the other trap-door and hid in Swynford's room, since I was uncertain whether you would know about the one in Augustus's room, and you might have come looking for me in the attic. But you did not and so I climbed back into the attic ready to continue my search.'

Bartholomew had a sudden, sharp memory of the shadow flitting across the door as he walked down the stairs after he had examined Augustus's body. If only he had looked harder, this whole thing may have ended there and then.

Colet smiled. 'It was no simple matter lifting a body through the trap-door. But even so, I had an easier time of it than when that fat slug Wilson tried to heave his bulk into the attic. You must have rattled him when you found him prising up Augustus's floorboards, Matt, because had he been himself, he would certainly have spotted the blood on the floor and one of Augustus's legs sticking out of the passageway. But he did not, and we both escaped.'

'Not only did you break your oath to heal, but you desecrated the dead too,' Bartholomew said accusingly.

'That was most disagreeable,' Colet agreed, 'but it had to be done. I was never as adept at surgery as you, Matt, and I am afraid I made rather a poor job of it. I told you I saw Augustus swallow something. What else could it have been but the seal? After I had completed my inspection of his innards, I wrapped him up and hid him in the blocked-off passageway.'

'I take it you found nothing,' said Bartholomew.

'On the contrary,' said Colet. 'I found this.' He held up an object for Bartholomew to see. There, glittering in the light from the candle was Colet's golden lion. Bartholomew felt sick. Colet must be an ill man indeed to have ripped out a man's entrails and to have kept a pathetic ornament he had discovered there.

'And this brings me to the second point I do not understand,' said Michael. 'How did you know about the trap-doors? They were meant to be a secret passed from Master to Master.'

'Poor, sick Augustus told Swynford about them. Augustus was Master of Michaelhouse once, if you remember,' said Colet. 'They made things easier, but we would have managed without them. We would have just planned differently.' He took the golden lion from his pocket and began to twist it through his fingers. He started suddenly as voices could be heard down the hallway. Swynford. Bartholomew recalled his disapproval of Colet speaking to him before, and was not surprised when Colet left abruptly.

In the darkness, Bartholomew heard Michael move towards the food that Colet had brought. 'I wonder what poison they have used,' he mused, smiling grimly as he heard Michael drop the plate.

'Damn you, Matt,' Michael grumbled. 'Do we starve here or die of poison?'

'The choice is probably yours, Brother,' replied Bartholomew.

Once again, time began to drag. Bartholomew and Michael talked more about what Colet had told them, but he had revealed little they did not already know, merely answering how Aelfrith had come to believe Wilson had killed him, and how Swynford had known about the trap-door in Augustus's room. Bartholomew presumed that Stanmore's underground rooms were used for secret meetings only at night, when Oswald Stanmore went home to Trumpington, and Stephen had the premises to himself.

When he heard the scratching noise outside the door, he first assumed it was his imagination, or Michael fidgeting in the darkness. But the sound persisted, and Bartholomew thought he could see the merest glimmer of light under the door. So, this is it, he thought. Swynford had conceived another diabolical plan, and he and Michael would be murdered just like the others who had threatened his objectives. He shook Michael awake, cautioning him to silence with a hand over his mouth.

The door swung open very slowly, and two figures slipped in, one shielding the light from the stub of a candle with his hand. The other closed the door behind them and they stood peering into the gloom.

'Michael! Matt!' came an urgent whisper.

Bartholomew was bracing himself to jump at one of the figures to see if he could overpower him when the candle flared and he found himself looking at Abigny, his youthful face tense and anxious.

'Thank God! You are unharmed!' he whispered, breaking into a smile, and clapping Bartholomew on the back.

'Giles!' exclaimed Bartholomew in amazement. 'How . . .?'

'Questions later,' said the philosopher. 'Come.'

The other figure at the door gestured urgently, and Abigny led the way out of the chamber and along the passageway. They quickly climbed the wooden stairs and Abigny closed the trap-door carefully, covering it with straw. The other person snuffed out the candle, leaving them in darkness and together they set off for the door at the far end of the stables.

They froze at the sound of someone in the yard. Hastily, Abigny bundled them into a stall with an ancient piebald nag, hoping that it would not give them away. Bartholomew saw Stephen come into the stable with a lamp, while outside, they could hear some of the men who worked for him chattering and laughing. Stephen set the lamp down, and went to a splendid black gelding, which he patted and caressed lovingly. Oswald had bought Stephen the horse to compensate for the one Abigny had stolen.

Bartholomew's legs were like jelly and, judging from Michael's shaking next to him, the fat monk felt the same. To his horror, Michael give a muffled sneeze. The straw! Michael frequently complained that straw made him cough. Bartholomew pinched Michael's nose to stop him from sneezing again. Stephen ceased crooning to the horse, and looked up.

'Who is there?' he asked. He picked up the lamp and shone it down the building. Next to them, the piebald horse stirred restlessly, its hooves rustling in the dry straw. Stephen tutted as he heard it, and went back to the black horse. He gave it one last pat on the nose, and left, carefully shutting the stable door behind him. Bartholomew heard the voices of Stephen and his men recede as they crossed the yard to the house.

'We must leave here as soon as we can,' said Abigny. 'Cynric is keeping watch outside.'

He opened the door a crack and peered out. 'They have gone into the house,' he whispered, 'and the candles are out. Come on.'

The night was clear, and the yard was lit brightly by the moon. Bartholomew hoped Stephen's dogs would not begin to bark, for anyone looking out of the windows of the house would surely see them in the yard. Cynric appeared out of nothing, and beckoned them to follow, moving like a cat through the shadows. To Bartholomew, he, Abigny, and Michael sounded like a herd of stampeding pigs compared to Cynric, and he kept glancing at the house, certain that he would see someone looking out because of the noise.

Finally, they reached the huge gates, where the smaller person stepped forward with a key to unlock the wicket gate. Cynric pushed it open, and all five of them slipped outside.

In the moonlight, Bartholomew saw the face of the small person as she turned to go back inside.

'Rachel Atkin!' he said in surprise.

'Shhh!' she said, glancing fearfully about her. 'Go now, quickly. I must get back to bed before anyone realises I am missing.'

'You were my well-wisher!' he said, light dawning suddenly. 'You must have overheard Stephen talking . . .'

She put her hand over his mouth. 'Go,' she said again. 'Master Abigny will explain.'

Before he could say anything else, she had slipped back through the wicket gate, and they could hear it being locked from the inside.

Cynric led the way through the dark streets and

into Michaelhouse, where Bartholomew sank gratefully into Agatha's chair.

Michael sat heavily on a stool next to him, wiping the sweat from his eyes, and snatched the bottle that Cynric was handing to Bartholomew.

'My need is greater than yours, Physician,' he said, downing a good quarter of the bottle in the first gulp.

Bartholomew sat back in the chair and asked Cynric for some water. Although he wanted to drain it in a single draught, he sipped it slowly, because he knew that the cold water would be likely to give him stomach cramps after so long without drinking.

He leaned forward and touched Abigny on the hand. 'Thank you,' he said. 'And Cynric, too. How did you know?'

Cynric closed the shutters on the windows, and sat near Bartholomew so he could poke at the fire. Michael took another hearty swig from his bottle – another of Master Wilson's, Bartholomew noted.

'Your friend told us,' said Abigny. 'Rachel.'

Bartholomew was amazed. Once he had arranged for Rachel to work for Stephen, he had not given her another thought. He had seen her around Stephen's house several times, and had been told that she was settling in well, but that was all.

Cynric took up the tale. 'She was grateful for what you did for her when her son was killed – she could not have paid for a decent funeral for him, and you saw to it, as well as finding her work and a place to live. She is a silent sort, who people come not to notice after a while.' Cynric paused, and Bartholomew wondered whether Cynric saw some of himself in Rachel Atkin.

'She overheard conversations between the Stanmores

organising a secret meeting, and she knew you were seeking information about Philippa. She heard them mention your name and so thought you might learn something to your advantage if you eavesdropped. She knew what the back of Bene't Hostel looked like because she and her son were sometimes hired to clean the yard when the smell got too unbearable. You know the rest: we met her by the plague pits and we listened in on the meeting.'

Abigny continued. 'Cynric grew worried about you when you did not return Wednesday night. He was still concerned that the Stanmores might be involved and felt that, in the light of what he had been through with you the night before, you would not have gone to Peterborough without telling him. He did the only thing he could think of and waylaid Mistress Atkin on her way to the market. She already knew that meetings took place in the rooms under the stables when Oswald was away, and so they considered it a possibility that you were being kept there.'

Cynric interrupted. 'I also saw Michael given a note on Thursday, and I followed him to Stanmore's business premises. He also did not return.'

'Cynric, in the absence of anyone else he could trust, asked me to help,' concluded Abigny.

'How long were we in that wretched place anyway?' said Bartholomew, leaning down to rub some warmth into his cold feet.

'It is now almost Saturday morning. When Gray came back with your brother-in-law and said that they had been sent on a wild goose chase regarding Edith's supposed sore arm, Cynric guessed that the hostel men had been up to something.'

Abigny was full of questions, and despite his tiredness, Bartholomew felt that he and Cynric were owed answers. Michael began the long, elaborate explanation that had Bartholomew dozing in the warmth of the fire, and Abigny and Cynric mesmerised. Eventually, Michael rose, and Bartholomew started awake.

'I am afraid we are going to have to go through all this again,' he said. 'The Bishop will arrive this morning.'

Bartholomew groaned. 'We have been talking for days.'

Michael waved a fat white finger at him. 'Which is far preferable to what Swynford and Colet had in mind for you.'

There was no disputing that Michael was right. They stood outside the kitchen for a while, Bartholomew enjoying the clear, crisp smell of night, and looking at the sky he had thought he might never see again.

Cynric yawned hugely. 'I had better get some sleep. The University Debate is due to start in a couple of hours, and I have been invited to earn a shilling by being a deputy beadle and keeping an eye out for pickpockets in the crowd. That is, unless you want me to stay with you,' he added suddenly, looking at Bartholomew anxiously.

Bartholomew smiled and shook his head. 'You will enjoy yourself at the Debate, so go,' he said. He looked up at the sky, and a thought occurred to him. 'I thought the Debate had been cancelled because of the plague.'

Michael sniffed. 'It is an important occasion with people coming for miles to listen. Why would the town cancel an event from which it can make money? What is the containment of the Death when there are goods to be sold, beds to be rented, and deals to be made?'

*   *   *

Bartholomew woke to darkness. At first he thought he was still in the cellar, but he was warm and comfortable and knew he was in his bed in Michaelhouse. He remembered leaving the window shutters open when he went to sleep – he had been in darkness so long that he felt shutting out any daylight would be a terrible sin. But the shutters were closed now. He snuggled further down under the bedclothes. Perhaps Abigny had closed them after he had gone to sleep; perhaps he had slept right through the day, and it was now night again.

He tensed suddenly. Someone was in the room with him.

'Giles? Michael?' he said, raising himself on one elbow.

There was a scraping noise, and a shutter was thrown open. Bartholomew gazed in horror at the victorious smiles of Swynford and Stephen, each holding an unsheathed sword.

'We have come for you,' said Swynford sweetly. 'We have decided upon the plan for your death and we have come to carry it out. Your escaping and returning here was no great problem, since we had decided to kill you here anyway. You merely saved us the bother of bringing you here ourselves.'

Bartholomew listened intently. It was daytime, but the College was strangely quiet. He could hear shouting, carried distantly on the wind. Swynford heard it, too, and cocked his head to one side.

'The University Debate at St Mary's Church,' he said. 'Always a lively affair. The entire College is there as usual, including your faithful Welsh servant. Giles Abigny is one of the leading participants this year – quite an honour for Michaelhouse; do you not think? Meanwhile, Brother

Michael has had a message asking him to meet the Bishop at the Carmelite Friary in Newnham, and, like a good lackey, he has gone scurrying off. When he arrives, he will find Master Yaxley waiting with a surprise for him. I had already suggested to Alcote that the servants be given the day off. After all, the scholars will be at the Debate, so why would servants be needed?'

Bartholomew was, once again, dazzled by the ruthless efficiency of these men.

'All the scholars and servants have gone,' said Swynford, re-emphasising his point. 'Except you, and the man who will kill you. The Bishop will arrive just in time to try to cover it all up with another tissue of lies. Of course, it will be much more difficult a second time, and questions will be asked in all kinds of circles.'

Bartholomew stared at him uncomprehendingly. 'Alcote!' said Swynford impatiently. 'Who has still not left his room, even though he is Acting Master. Two birds with one stone. A petty quarrel between two Fellows that erupts into a fight with knives. In the struggle, a lamp will be knocked over, and Michaelhouse will burn. Wilson gave me the idea for this,' he added conversationally. 'You and Alcote will die in the fire, as well as your patients in the plague ward and the monks caring for them.'

Bartholomew pushed the blankets back and climbed out of bed, keeping a wary eye on Swynford and Stephen.

'It is no good expecting a second rescue,' said Swynford. 'Jocelyn, out of kindness, took your patients a large jug of wine a while ago. He will ensure that they all drink some, including the Benedictines who are with them. By now, they should all be sleeping peacefully. It worked so well last time that we could not resist trying it again. In case they wake, he has locked the door of the room to make sure that none will come to cause us trouble.'

Bartholomew looked at them in disgust and reached for his gown. Swynford poked at his hand with the sword. 'You will not be needing that,' he said. 'Shirt and leggings are good enough.' He gave Bartholomew a sharp prod to make him leave the room and walk across the courtyard. Swynford was right. It was deserted.

Stephen took a grip on his arm to stop him from running away, and jabbed the point of the short sword into his side. 'I will use this willingly if you make more trouble,' he hissed. 'You have hindered our cause too much already.'

Bartholomew was marched across the yard and up the stairs to the hall. Colet was there already, pointing a crossbow at the petrified Alcote. A pathetic look of relief came over Alcote's face when he saw Swynford.

'This mad physician brought me here,' he began, and stopped short when he saw the sword Swynford held, and how it was pointed at Bartholomew. He put his hands over his face, and began to weep silently.

'It was Robert,' Bartholomew could hear him moan. 'Robert killed them all.'

Swynford set about preparing the room to make a convincing show of a struggle. He knocked benches over, threw plates and cups onto the floor, and ripped one or two wall-hangings down. When he was satisfied, he turned to his victims.

'Right,' he said, rubbing his hands together. 'Let me think.'

'Your plan is fatally flawed,' said Bartholomew.

The hand-rubbing stopped. 'Nonsense,' Swynford said, but there was hesitation in his voice.

'Alcote would never consider taking me on in a fight! Look at him! No one would believe that he would fight me.'

'True,' Swynford said. 'It would be an uneven match. He probably wounded you with a crossbow first,' he said, nodding to Colet, who raised the instrument and pointed it at Bartholomew.

'Even worse,' said Bartholomew. 'Everyone knows that Alcote cannot tell one end of such a weapon from another, and certainly would not be able to wind it and loose a quarrel at me before I could overpower him.'

'Well, perhaps he dashed your brains out with a heavy instrument,' said Swynford, growing exasperated.

'Like what?' said Bartholomew, gesturing round. 'A pewter cup? A piece of fish?'

'It really does not matter, Rob,' said Colet. 'So what if this all looks like the elaborate plot it is? Anyone working out what really happened will believe what we tell them – that the Oxford men are becoming bold again. What a formidable force they must be to sneak into the heart of a College and murder two of its Fellows in broad daylight.'

Swynford's face slowly broke into a smile, and he nodded.

'Come on, let us get it done so we can leave,' said Colet. He took a lamp from a table, lit it, and dashed it onto the floor. The rushes immediately caught fire, and Alcote screamed as the flames danced towards him. Bartholomew twisted suddenly and drove his elbow into Stephen's stomach with all his strength. Stephen gasped and dropped to his knees. Bartholomew kicked the sword away from him and leapt onto a table to escape a lunge from Swynford. Colet swung round and aimed the crossbow. Running along the table, Bartholomew felt the missile pluck at his shirt as it sped harmlessly by.

Colet began to reload, and Bartholomew dodged Swynford's sword, picked up one of Agatha's iron loaves of bread and hurled it as hard as he could at Colet. It hit him on the side of the head, stunning him sufficiently to make him drop the crossbow. Swynford stabbed at him again, entangling his sword in Bartholomew's legs.

Bartholomew, balance gone, toppled from the table, and landed heavily on the other side. Swynford leapt over the table and threw himself at Bartholomew, flailing wildly with the sword. The flames in the rushes licked nearer, but Swynford seemed to see nothing but Bartholomew. Bartholomew jerked his head away as the sword plunged down and heard the metal blade screech against the stone floor. He struggled violently, tipping Swynford off balance, and scrambled away under the table. He felt his leg gripped as Swynford seized him, and his fingernails scrabbled on the floor as he felt himself being dragged backwards.

Bartholomew twisted again and kicked backwards. Swynford's grip lessened for an instant, and Bartholomew scrambled under the table, clambering to his feet on the other side before Alcote crashed into him, knocking him down.

'What the hell are you doing?' he gasped, and then stopped as he saw Swynford totter forward holding his stomach.

'Damn!' Colet was already reloading the crossbow, ignoring Swynford's increasing bellows of pain as he concentrated on his task.

At the same moment, Stephen, seeing Swynford shot by Colet, bolted across the burning rushes towards the door. Right into the arms of Brother Michael.

'Watch Colet,' Bartholomew yelled. Colet had seen the flicker of movement out of the corner of his eye, and had heard Stephen's dismayed yell. He whipped round and pointed the crossbow at Michael. Bartholomew scrambled over Alcote and threw himself at Colet's legs. Colet toppled, and the crossbow fell to the ground. Colet desperately tried to reach it as Bartholomew fought to get a better grip on him.

Suddenly, Colet had a knife in his hand, and Bartholomew let him go as it swung down in a savage arc that would have pierced his eye had he not wrenched his head backwards. Colet shot away from Bartholomew and ran towards the servery door. Bartholomew raced after him, dimly aware that there were others entering the hall through the main entrance. Colet spun round, his face a mask of fury, and flung the knife at Bartholomew. It was a move born of desperation, and was nowhere near its mark. Bartholomew sprang at Colet, forcing him to the ground.

Almost immediately, he felt himself hauled up, and, thinking it was Swynford, lashed out with his fists as hard as he could.

'Easy! Easy!' Bartholomew became aware of his surroundings, and his intense anger faded as quickly as it had come. Colet, already in the custody of two burly beadles, looked fearfully at Bartholomew, his face battered and bleeding. Bartholomew was held in a similar grip by Michael and one of the Benedictines.

A loud snap dragged their attention away from Colet and Bartholomew.

'The fire!' yelled Michael, releasing Bartholomew's arm. 'Stop the fire!'

The flames had secured a good hold on the rushes on the floor and were licking up the wall-hangings. Bartholomew raced to drag them down before the flames reached the wooden ceiling. Outside, someone had started to ring the bell, and the hall filled with scholars using their black gowns to beat out the flames.

One of the students gave a shout, and, with a groan, the carved wooden screen behind the servery gave way, crashing onto the floor in an explosion of flames and sparks. More scholars poured into the hall, some from Michaelhouse, but many from other Colleges and hostels. Bartholomew and Michael quickly organised them into a human chain passing all manner of receptacles brimming with water from the well.

Bartholomew yelled to Alcote, flapping uselessly at some burning rushes with his gown, to evacuate the sick from the commoners' room. Bartholomew knew that once the fire reached the wooden ceiling of the hall it would quickly spread to the wings. Thick smoke billowed everywhere, and Bartholomew saw one student drop to the floor clutching at his throat. He hauled him down the stairs and out into the yard where he coughed and spluttered. Bartholomew glanced up. Flames leapt out of the windows and thick, black smoke drifted across the yard.

The plague victims were brought to lie near the stable where they were tended by Michael's Benedictine room-mates, one still reeling from the effects of the drugged wine. Alcote hauled on the College bell, and scholars and passers-by ran in to help.

Bartholomew darted back up the stairs to the hall.

William and Michael had affixed ropes to the wooden gallery and rows of people were hauling on them to pull it over. Bartholomew understood their plan. If the gallery were down, the fire would be less likely to reach the wooden ceiling and might yet be brought under control. He took an empty place on one of the ropes and heaved with the others.

The gallery, wrenched from the walls, tipped forward with a screech of tearing wood and smashed onto the stone floor of the hall. Men and women dashed forwards and began to beat out the flames. The hot wood hissed under a deluge of water, and gradually the crackle of flames began to relent. Eventually, all was silent, and the men and women who had answered the bell surveyed the mess.

'It was about time the rushes on the floor were changed anyway,' said Bartholomew. He had intended his remark for Michael's ears only, but in the silence of the hall it carried. The tense atmosphere evaporated, and people laughed. Disaster had been averted.

Agatha, who had worked as hard as anyone, sent people here and there with brushes, and ordered that burned rushes, tables, benches, and tapestries be thrown out of the windows. At Bartholomew's suggestion, Cynric fetched all that remained of Wilson's fine collection of wine, and scholars and townspeople alike fortified themselves for their work with wines that cost more money than most of them would earn in a year.

In the panic to control the fire, Bartholomew had almost forgotten Colet, Stephen, and Swynford. He made his way over to a small group of people who stood around a figure lying on the floor. William was kneeling next to Swynford anointing him with oil, and muttering the words of the absolution. Swynford's eyes were closed, and blood bubbled through his blue lips.

He opened his eyes when William's mutterings finished. 'The third Master to die in less than a year,' he said in a whisper. He looked around the group of people until he found Bartholomew.

'You are still alive,' he said. 'I was not sure whether Colet would get you. You have really confounded my plans this time. Another few months, and I would have been Bishop, and I would never have needed to step in this accursed town again.'

He closed his eyes then, and did not open them again.

Colet and Stephen had already been hustled away to the Castle when Oswald Stanmore, his face white with strain, sought out Bartholomew.

'Oh, God, Matt,' he said. 'What happened?'

Bartholomew could think of nothing to say, and made him sit on one of the benches that was not too singed and drink a cup of wine. Richard sat next to him, his face tear-streaked.

Stanmore sipped at the wine and then cradled the cup in shaking hands. 'He played me like a fool, Matt,' he said. 'He took my money, made me believe all Swynford's lies, and then tried to kill you. My own brother!'

Bartholomew rested his hand on his shoulder. 'What will happen to his wife and children?'

'Stephen and his wife had not been close for some time,' Stanmore said. 'She had been complaining about his absences during the night. I should have listened to her. Richard has offered to stay with her for a while at the house on Milne Street. There is plenty of room, so there is no reason she and the children should not stay. Also, Edith will help them as much as she can.'

'I will help, too,' said Bartholomew.

Stanmore nodded. 'I know you will. What will happen to him, Matt?'

Bartholomew did not know. He imagined there would be a trial, and there was enough evidence to hang them all. Michael told him that Stephen had started to confess everything before he was even out of the College gates, despite dire threats from Colet. On his evidence, the Sheriff and the Proctor would round up the others who had been involved.

'I am sorry, Matt,' sighed Stanmore. 'What a vile mess.'

'It is over now,' said Bartholomew. 'We both need to put it behind us and look to the future.'

'Yes, I suppose so,' Stanmore replied. Accompanied by Richard, he left to tend to his affairs. He was still not out of the woods, and there would be many questions to be answered and accounts to be examined before this business was over.

Brother Michael had been engaged in deep conversation with the Bishop in the solar. As Stanmore left, Michael poked his head round the door and beckoned Bartholomew over. The Bishop was wearing a plain brown robe, a far cry from his finery of the previous visit. He looked at Bartholomew's bruised hands. 'I hear you tried to give Master Colet his just deserts,' he said.

Bartholomew looked at Michael. 'I was stopped before I had really started.'

'Just as well,' said the Bishop. 'There has been enough murder in this College to last a century.'

'What happened?' Bartholomew asked Michael.

'How did you manage to arrive in the nick of time? How did you escape Yaxley?'

'I was sent a message, supposedly from the Bishop,' said Michael, 'asking me to meet him at the Carmelite Friary at Newnham. I saw nothing odd in this and assumed my lord the Bishop merely wanted me to provide him with the details of what I had learned before he arrived at Michaelhouse. As I walked, I heard St Mary's bell in the distance calling scholars to the Debate in the church and I suddenly realised I had made a dreadful mistake. We had already discussed Swynford's love of false messages, but I never thought he would dare to send me another.

'It became horribly clear. Me out of the way, perhaps heading into a trap, and all the scholars at the Debate. You are a heavy sleeper at the best of times, and I knew the bell would not wake you. Colet, who knows you well enough, would also guess you would sleep through the bell. I knew he was going to come for you, Matt, as you slept alone in the College. I ran back as fast as I could, stopping at St Mary's to raise the alarm on the way.'

'The Chancellor was none too pleased at being interrupted mid-argument by my yelling, but your Gray got the students mustered. When we came near the College, I saw smoke coming from one of the windows. I thought perhaps we were too late, and rushed up the stairs. I saw Colet kill Swynford by mistake, and then try to shoot me.'

He poked Bartholomew with his elbow. 'I saw what you did,' he said.

'What do you mean?' asked Bartholomew wearily.

'You saved me from Colet's crossbow. He could not have missed me from that range. I saw you knock him over.'

Bartholomew gave a soft laugh. 'Alcote did the same for me. The bolt that killed Swynford was meant for me, and he pushed me out of the way.'

The Bishop spread his hands. 'So, Michaelhouse Fellows risk their lives to save each other,' he said. 'Not all that has come of this is bad, and now you know whom you can trust.'

At last, thought Bartholomew, looking out of the window at the bright blue sky.

The Bishop stood to leave. 'These men have committed treason, and they will be taken to the Tower to stand trial. Stephen's willingness to confess in a vain attempt to save himself will ensure that they are all caught, and then the University – both hostels and Colleges – can begin again. I believe the Chancellor will need to make a visit to Oxford to explain what has happened, and to offer his abject apologies for blaming her for crimes of which she was wholly innocent.' He put his hand on Bartholomew's head. 'No secrets this time,' he said softly. 'Everything will be made known, from the murder of the Master of King's Hall fifteen months ago right up until the evil-doings of today.'

He went to the door, and then turned. 'Sir John Babington,' he said. 'He was no suicide, and can rightly be buried in the church. Shall I arrange that?'

Bartholomew thought about the revolting black effigy he had promised to have made for Wilson and shook his head. 'Sir John would prefer to be where he is, among the oak trees, and as far away from Wilson's glorious tomb as possible.'

The Bishop smiled. 'I believe you are right,' he said, and left.

Bartholomew and Michael sat in companionable

silence for a while, each rethinking the events of the past few days.

Michael went to look out of the window. 'The Death is still out there,' he said softly. 'Despite all that has happened, it is still there.'

Bartholomew stood next to him. 'And I still do not understand it,' he said. 'I still do not know why some live while others die, and I have no more idea how it spreads now than I did when it first came.'

'Perhaps there is nothing to understand,' said Michael, watching the Proctor organising his beadles in the yard for the arrest of the hostel men. 'Perhaps we are all doomed.'

'No, Brother. There are those that have remained healthy, like you and Agatha, and there are those who have recovered. We will survive it.' He shivered, and wondered whether he should ask Cynric to build a fire. He glanced through the open door where Gray and a few other industrious students were clearing the floor of debris, and decided that he had had enough of fires for one day.

'Matt!' Philippa exploded into the solar, followed more sedately by Abigny. 'Thank God you are safe! We saw the smoke coming from Michaelhouse, and I thought . . .'

Bartholomew rubbed his hands over his face, leaving smears of black. 'I owe you and Giles an apology,' he said. 'I misjudged you both, and Giles has saved my life.'

'Yes. I was there when Cynric came to him with his dilemma, and I told them the answer was quite simple,' said Philippa. 'I told them to enlist the help of Rachel Atkin and to go to see whether you and Michael were being held prisoner under Stephen's stables as she surmised. They were considering leaving it until tonight, but I said to go there and then. I would have gone myself, but I am not so foolish as to risk the success of such a mission merely to satisfy my own curiosity.'

Bartholomew stared at her wonderingly, and then hugged her, first gently, then harder. He could feel her laughing as she tried to catch her breath, and was reminded of how carefree they had been in the summer.

Abigny and Michael watched with obvious delight, and Bartholomew became embarrassed. Still with an arm across her shoulders, he spoke to Abigny.

'Thank you again for last night,' he said.

'Think nothing of it,' said Abigny cheerfully. 'All in a day's work for a philosopher.' He became serious again. 'I spoke to Elias Oliver on our way here. He is grief-stricken at the loss of his brother and aunt, and more than prepared to spill his heart. He says it was Henry who organised the riot, and Henry who tried to kill you in the lane. He also told me that both Wilson and Master Yaxley of Bene't Hostel were seeing the Abbess, although neither knew of the other.'

'Really?' said Brother Michael with gleeful fascination. 'Whatever next!'

So that explains how the blacksmith came to be paid with money in a Bene't Hostel purse, thought Bartholomew. It must have been Yaxley's, although it had been rash of Henry to pay the blacksmith with a marked purse. Perhaps he disapproved of his aunt's illicit relationships, and was hoping that Bartholomew would begin to suspect Yaxley. He remembered the blacksmith bearing down on Elias Oliver during the riot, and almost stabbing him in the process. No wonder the Olivers had glowered so, when they were almost victims of their own plotting.

'Elias also said that Wilson had been in quite a panic one night, saying that he feared the physician,' said Abigny. 'The Abbess and her two dear nephews thought he meant you, and that you were going to kill him. But by "the physician" Wilson must have meant Colet, not you at all.'

'And you had nothing to do with this University business?' asked Bartholomew.

Abigny looked at him as though he were mad. 'Me? Get mixed up with that crowd of calculating, power-hungry maniacs?' he said in disbelief. 'No fear! I have more sense, and frankly, Matt, I would have thought you had, too. I am appalled that you allowed yourself to become embroiled in such filthy matters.'

'One of the keys to the whole affair was the presence of the trap-door. If you think back to when we found Paul's body, it was you who suggested that there might be a secret door . . .'

Abigny laughed. 'That just goes to show, Physician, that you need a philosopher to sort out all your mysteries! So, I immediately lit upon the essence of the problem, did I? What an amazing mind I have.' He preened for a while. 'I do not even remember saying it,' he admitted. 'I was just throwing out ideas and trying to think through the thing logically. I had no idea the College was furnished with such devices, and if I did mention it, it was purely owing to my sense of logic.'

Bartholomew sighed. At last. All the loose ends had come together. One stupid error in all this was his assumption that Philippa's disappearance was connected to the University business, whereas the reality was that they were totally unrelated. There were tenuous links – Wilson and Yaxley sharing the Abbess's favours, Abigny's frequenting of Bene't Hostel – but that was all.

He held out his hand to Philippa, who took it and pressed it to her lips. He smiled at the black smudges that his hand left on her white skin, and tried to wipe them off. He only made them worse. Philippa began to giggle, and out of the corner of his eye, Bartholomew saw Abigny bundle a goggle-eyed Michael out of the room and close the door, leaving him alone with Philippa.

'Why did you not tell me you had been married as a child?' he said, recalling what Abigny had told him – some days ago, now.

'I thought you might not marry me if you thought I were a rich widow,' she said.

Bartholomew stared at her. 'Are you serious?'

She nodded. 'You told me so many times you did not want to treat rich patients for the money that I thought you might prefer a poor wife. The irony of all this silly mess was that I was thinking I would give all the property to the convent anyway,' she said. 'To please you.'

Bartholomew groaned. 'You will never believe the problems caused by my failing to understand what money means to people,' he said.

Philippa squeezed next to him on the window seat. 'So tell me,' she said.

EPILOGUE

I T WAS MARCH, AND ALTHOUGH THE PLAGUE STILL raged, and reports of enormous numbers of deaths remained common, Bartholomew felt that it was beginning to relinquish its hold on Cambridge. The death toll was lower than it had been in January and February, and, with the coming of spring, many felt a new hope.

Colet, Stephen, Jocelyn, Yaxley, Burwell, Stayne, and five others were taken for trial at the Tower of London. They were accused of treason for attempting to undermine the University, particularly King's Hall, which was endowed with royal money. All were executed at Smithfield, although the news of their deaths did not reach Cambridge until three weeks later. Oswald Stanmore was at London for the trial, and told Bartholomew that Stephen was fully repentant for his wrongdoings. Colet was less so, and sent Bartholomew a package. Inside was the golden lion. When Bartholomew explained its significance to Philippa, she dropped it in disgust, and walked away. Bartholomew looked at it for a moment and then followed her. The small child that found it lying in the mud in the High Street sold it to a passing traveller for a penny later that day.

The University began to settle back into the business of teaching. Although officially closed because of the plague, there were still students who wanted to learn, and scholars who wanted to teach. Bartholomew was as busy as ever, teaching, seeing his patients, trying to control Gray, and visiting Philippa, now living with Stephen's wife in Milne Street.

One bright day when the air was filled with the fresh smells of spring, masking even the stench of the river, Bartholomew and Michael walked to Newnham, Bartholomew to see to a wheezing cough, and Michael to persuade children to join his depleted choir. The sun shone, and the first lambs of the year gambolled about the fields. Michael and Bartholomew completed their business, and turned homeward. They walked in silence, enjoying the clean air and the feel of the sun through their clothes.

When they reached the small footbridge, Bartholomew stopped and looked down into the swirling waters underneath. Michael stood next to him, leaning his ample forearms on the handrail.

'Sir John's seal caused a lot of deaths, and it was basically worthless,' said Bartholomew.

Michael looked at him askance. 'What brought that up?' he said. After a while, watching Bartholomew drop blades of grass onto the water he said, 'The seal was nothing. It could only be used by Sir John for the King's business, and as soon as he was dead, the seal was defunct. It was given unwarranted significance by evil men for evil reasons. Sir John would have been horrified if he knew what trouble it would cause.'

Bartholomew reached into his pocket and handed something to Michael, whose eyes widened in shock.

'Where did you get this?' he asked in wonder, turning Sir John's intricate seal to the sun so he could look at it closely.

'Sir John gave it to me on the night he died,' said Bartholomew, 'although I did not realise it at the time.'

Michael gazed at Bartholomew in stupefaction. 'How?' he managed to ask.

'He must have slipped it into the sleeve of my gown,' said Bartholomew. 'You know how those sleeves are for us non-clerics? They are sewn up at the bottom, with slits for the arms half-way up. The ring was there for quite a while before I thought to look.'

'But what made you look?'

Bartholomew gazed over the meadows, edged with the pale yellow of primrose. 'Sir John did not leave it with Augustus, and it was not found on his body when he was killed. It *was* with him when we had dinner. I saw it on the cord around his neck. The only logical conclusion was that he must have given it to Swynford or Aelfrith when we parted after dinner. Sir John would not have given it to Aelfrith because Aelfrith was already involved and would be an obvious target, and I know he was always a little wary of Swynford. He often wondered why a man with Swynford's connections and wealth should deign to become a poor University teacher. Then I wondered whether Sir John had passed the seal to me. I searched through all my clothes, and there it was, lying in a corner at the bottom of my sleeve.'

'And Wilson accused you of being a poor logician!' said Michael, shaking his head and smiling. 'Now I think about it, it is the only obvious answer. Sir John trusted you above all the other Fellows, and would have been far more likely to give you the seal than anyone else. Thank God no one else thought the same, or you may have gone the same way as Augustus!'

'Sir John must have had some misgivings about his meeting that night, and decided to leave the seal behind.'

'Unfortunately, his misgivings were not strong enough,' said Michael sadly. 'If they were, he would never have gone to the meeting, and he most certainly would not have put you at risk by hiding the seal with you. And he would never have visited Augustus if he could have foreseen the consequences. I suppose he intended to recover it from you when he returned.'

Bartholomew scuffed some small stones from the bridge into the water with the toe of his boot and watched as they disappeared with tiny splashes. 'I think Sir John may have believed that the purpose of the meeting that night was to entice him out of the College so that his room could be searched, not so that he could be murdered. I think he knew that the person he was meeting would guess he would not wear the seal as usual because of the unusual circumstances of the rendezvous – during the night in a remote place. I expect he thought he would be able to retrieve it from my sleeve himself before anyone else had had the time to reason where he may have hidden it.'

'When did you work all this out?' asked Michael.

'When Wilson told me to find it,' said Bartholomew. 'I told no one, because I did not know whom I could trust, and I did not want anyone else to die for it. So, I kept my silence.'

Michael started to laugh, looking at the seal in wonder. 'You are a dark horse, Matt! So many people looked for this wretched thing, and all the time it was with you! Why have you chosen now to tell me about it?'

Bartholomew shrugged, watching the sunlight dance on the river. 'I have told no one else, not even Philippa.' He turned to Michael. 'I suppose I thought you would like to know.'

Michael held the ring between his thumb and forefinger and looked at it intently. 'Who would think that such a tiny thing would cause so much harm?'

'No,' said Bartholomew, 'the ring did not do the harm. The people who used it did.'

Michael was silent for a while, still looking at the small gold ring with its intricate knots and ties. 'So what are you going to do with it?' he asked.

Bartholomew sighed and turned his face up to the sun, his eyes closed. 'Give it to you, for your Bishop.'

'To me?' exclaimed Michael. He looked at it a little longer, then shook Bartholomew's arm to make him open his eyes.

'Watch,' he said. He pulled back his arm, and flung the ring as far as he could down the fast-flowing river. They saw it flash once in the sunlight before it dropped soundlessly midstream, and was gone from sight. They stood for a while, looking at the place where it had fallen, thinking about the people whose lives it had affected. Bartholomew gave another huge sigh and looked at Michael. Michael gazed back, the beginnings of a smile twitching the corners of his mouth and twinkling in his eyes.

'Come on, old friend,' he said, tugging Bartholomew's sleeve to make him move, 'or you will make me miss my dinner.'

An Unholy Alliance

For Peter Sage

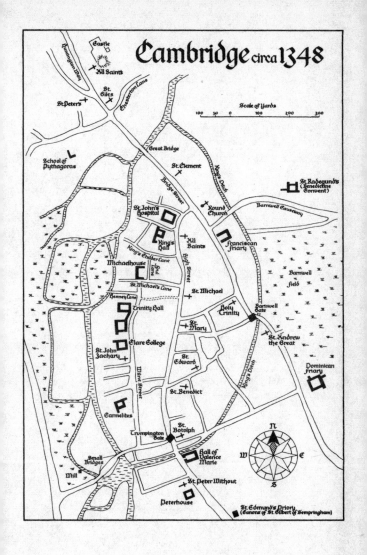

Cambridge circa **1348**

Castle

All Saints

St. Peters

St. Giles

Huntingdon Way

Greencroft Lane

School of Pythagoras

Great Bridge

St. Clement

Bridge Street

King's Ditch

St. John's Hospital

Round Church

St. Radegund's (Benedictine Convent)

Barnwell Causeway

King's Hall

All Saints

Franciscan Friary

King's Childer Lane

Pyll Lane

Michaelhouse

St. Michael's Lane

St. Michael

Barnwell field

Henney Lane

Trinity Hall

Holy Trinity

Barnwell Gate

St. Mary

St. Andrew the Great

Clare College

St. John Zachary

St. Edward

King's Ditch

Dominican Friary

Milne Street

St. Benedict

Carmelites

St. Botolph

Trumpington Gate

Hall of Valence Marie

Small Bridges

Mill

St. Peter Without

Peterhouse

St. Edmund's Priory (Canons of St. Gilbert of Sempringham)

Scale of Yards
100 50 0 100 200 300

N
W E
S

PROLOGUE

Cambridge, 1350

ISOBEL WATKINS GLANCED FEARFULLY BEHIND HER
for at least the fourth time since leaving the home
of the wealthy merchant on Milne Street. She was
sure she was being followed, but each time she stopped
and looked behind her, she could hear and see nothing
amiss. She slipped into a doorway and held her breath
to control her trembling as she peered down the dark
street behind her. There was nothing, not even a rat
scurrying from the mounds of rubbish that lined both
sides of the High Street.

She took a deep breath and leaned her head back
against the door. She was imagining things, and the
recent murder of two of her colleagues in the town had
unnerved her. She had never been afraid of walking
alone in the dark before: indeed, it was usually when
she met her best customers. She poked her head out
and looked down the street yet again. All was silence
and darkness. In the distance she heard the bell of St
Michael's chiming the hour: midnight.

Dismissing her fears, she slipped out of the doorway

1

and began walking quickly up the High Street towards her home near the town gate. It was only a short walk, and the night-watchmen on duty at the gate would be within hailing distance soon. She grimaced. It would not be the first time she had been forced to give her night's earnings to the guards in order not to be arrested for breaking the curfew. She caught her breath again as she heard the faintest of sounds behind her, and decided she would be happy to part with an entire week's earnings just to be safely in her own bed.

She saw the pinprick of light coming from the gate, and broke into a run, almost crying in relief. She was totally unprepared for the attack that came from the side. She felt herself hurled to the ground as someone dived out of the small trees around St Botolph's Church. She tried to scream as she felt herself dragged into the churchyard, but no sound would come. She felt a sudden burning pain in her throat and then a hot, sticky sensation on her chest. As her world slowly went black, she cursed herself for being so convinced that she was being followed that she had failed to consider whether it was safe ahead.

A short distance away, a man wearing the habit of a Dominican friar knelt in the silence of the tower of St Mary's Church. In front of him stood the great iron-bound box that held the University's most precious documents – deeds of property, records of accounts, scrolls containing promises of money and goods, and a stack of loose pages recording important occurrences in the University, carefully documented by the University clerks.

The University chest. The friar rubbed his hands and,

balancing the merest stub of a candle on the chest, began to work on one of the three great locks that kept the University's business from prying eyes. The only sounds in the tower were tiny clicks and metallic scrapes as he concentrated on his task. He felt safe. He had spent several days in the church, kneeling in different parts so he could become familiar with its layout and routine. That night he had hidden behind one of the pillars when the lay-brother had walked around the church, dousing candles and checking all the windows were secure. When the lay-brother had left, the friar had stood stock still behind his pillar for the best part of an hour to make certain that no one had followed him and was also hiding. Then he had spent another hour checking every last corner of the church to make doubly sure. He had climbed on benches to test that the locks on the window were secure and had taken the added precaution of slipping a thick bar across the door before climbing the spiral stairs to the tower.

He hummed to himself as he worked. The singing that evening had been spectacular, with boys' voices soaring like angels over the drone of the bass and tenor of the men. The friar had been unfamiliar with the music and had been told it had been written by a Franciscan called Simon Tunstede who was earning something of a reputation as a composer. He paused and stared into the darkness as he tried to recall how the Sanctus had gone. As it came back to him, he resumed his fiddling with the lock and sang a little louder.

The first lock snapped open, and the friar shuffled on his knees to the next one. Eventually, the second lock popped open and the friar moved onto the third. He

3

stopped singing and small beads of sweat broke out on his head. He paused to rub an arm over his face and continued scraping and poking with his slivers of metal. Suddenly, the last lock snapped open, and the friar stood up stiffly.

He stretched his shoulders, cramped from hunching over his work, and carefully lifted the lid of the great box. It groaned softly, the leather hinges protesting at the weight. The friar knelt again and began to sort carefully through the documents that lay within. He had been working for only a few moments when a sound behind him made him leap to his feet. He held his breath in terror, and then relaxed when he realised it was only a bird in the bell chamber above. He turned back to the chest again, and continued to rifle through the scrolls and papers.

He suddenly felt a great lurching pain. He tried to stand up, but his legs failed him. He put both hands to his chest and moaned softly, leaning against the great box as he did so. He was aware that the light from the candle was growing dimmer as the pain in his chest increased. With the tiniest of sighs, the friar collapsed over the open chest and died.

4

CHAPTER 1

DAWN WAS COOL AND CLEAN AS MATTHEW Bartholomew and Brother Michael walked together across the College yard to the great iron-studded doors that led to Foul Lane. As Michael removed the stout wooden bar from the wicket gate and chided the rumpled porter for sleeping when he should have been alert, Bartholomew looked up at the dark blue sky and savoured the freshness of the air. When the sun became hot, the small town would begin to stink from the refuse and sewage that were dumped in the myriad of waterways, ditches, and streams. But now the air was cool and smelt of the sea.

Michael opened the gate, and Bartholomew followed him into the lane. The large Benedictine tripped over a mangy dog that was lying in the street outside, and swore as it yelped and ran away towards the wharves on the river bank.

'There are far too many stray dogs in Cambridge,' he grumbled. 'Ever since the plague. Stray dogs and stray cats, with no one left to keep the wretched things off the streets. Now the Fair is here, there are more than ever. And I am certain I saw a monkey in the High Street last night!'

Bartholomew smiled at the monk's litany of complaints and began to walk up the lane towards St Michael's Church. It was his and Michael's turn to open the church and prepare it for the first service of the day. Before the plague had swept through England, all the religious offices were recited in the church by the scholars of Michaelhouse, but the shortage of friars and priests to perform these duties meant that the College's religious practices were curtailed. Brother Michael would pray alone, while Bartholomew prepared the church for Prime, which all the scholars would attend. After, they would go back to Michaelhouse for breakfast, and lectures would start at six.

The sky was beginning to lighten in the east, and although there were sounds – a dog barking, a bird singing in the distance, the clatter of an early cart to the market – the town was peaceful, and this was Bartholomew's favourite time of day. As Michael fumbled with the large church key, Bartholomew walked over the long grass of the churchyard to a small hump marked with a crude wooden cross. Bartholomew and Michael had buried Father Aelfrith here when, all over the city, others were being interred in huge pits at the height of the plague. He stared down at the cross, remembering the events of the winter of 1348, when the plague had raged and a murderer had struck at Michaelhouse.

Bartholomew had buried another colleague in the churchyard too. The smug Master Wilson lay in his temporary grave awaiting the day when Bartholomew fulfilled a deathbed promise and organised the construction of an extravagant tomb carved in black marble. Bartholomew felt a deep unease about the notion of removing Wilson's body from its grave in the churchyard to the church. Even after a year and a half of rethinking all he had learned, Bartholomew still did not understand how the plague spread, or why it struck some people and not others. Some physicians believed the stories from the East, that the pestilence had come because an earthquake had opened the graves of the dead. Bartholomew saw no evidence to prove this was true, but the plague was never far from his thoughts, and he was loathe to risk exhuming Wilson.

He heard Brother Michael begin to chant and dragged himself from his thoughts to go about his duty. Faint light filtered through the clear glass of the east window, although the church was still shades of grey and black. Later, when the sun rose, the light would fall on the vivid paintings on the walls that brought them alive with colour. Especially fine was the painting that depicted Judgement Day, showing souls being tossed into the pits of hell by a goat-devil. On the opposite side St Michael saved an occasional soul. Bartholomew often wondered what had driven the artist to clothe the Devil in a scholar's tabard.

As Michael continued to chant, Bartholomew opened the small sanctuary cupboard, took out chalice and paten, and turned the pages of the huge Bible to the reading for the day. When he had finished, he walked around the church lighting candles and setting out stools for those of the small congregation who were unable to stand.

As he checked the level of holy water in the stoup, he grimaced with distaste at the film of scum that had accumulated. Glancing quickly down the aisle to make sure Michael was not watching, he siphoned the old water off into a jug, gave the stoup a quick wipe round, and refilled it. Keeping his back to Michael, Bartholomew poured the old water away in the piscina next to the altar, careful not to spill any. There were increasing rumours that witchcraft was on the increase in England because of the shortage of clergy after the plague, and there was a danger of holy water being stolen for use in black magic rituals. The piscina ensured that the water drained into the church foundations and could not be collected and sold. But Bartholomew, as a practising physician, as well as Michaelhouse's teacher of medicine, was more concerned that scholars would touch the filthy water to their lips and become ill.

Michael finished his prayers and Bartholomew saw him sneak a gulp of wine from the jug intended for the mass. The monk yawned hugely, and began to relate a tale of how a pardoner had tried to sell him some of the Archangel Gabriel's hair at the Fair the previous day. Michael, outraged, had demanded proof that the hair had indeed belonged to Gabriel and had been informed that the angel himself had presented it to the pardoner in a dream. Michael proudly announced that he had tipped the scoundrel and his fake hair into the King's Ditch. Bartholomew winced. The Ditch was a foul affair, running thick with all kinds of filth and waste, and Michael's righteous anger might well have caused the unfortunate pardoner to contract a veritable host of diseases.

Before he could respond, the doors were pushed open and sleepy-eyed scholars began to file silently into church. Michael and Bartholomew shot to the altar rail and knelt quickly in the hope that they had not been seen chattering when they should have been praying. Bartholomew watched the Michaelhouse scholars take their places in the choir: the Fellows in a line to the right headed by the Master, and the students and commoners behind. Cynric ap Huwydd, Bartholomew's book-bearer, rang the bell to announce that the service was about to begin. The scholars of Physwick Hostel, who had begged use of St Michael's Church from Michaelhouse because their own church had been closed since the plague, processed in and stood in a neat line opposite the Michaelhouse scholars. The arrangement was an uneasy one: Physwick resented being forced to rely on Michaelhouse's good graces, and Michaelhouse was nervous at sharing the church after twenty-five years. Bartholomew saw Physwick's Principal, Richard Harling, exchange a smile far from warm with Michaelhouse's Senior Fellow, Roger Alcote.

In the main body of the church a few parishioners drifted in, yawning and rubbing the sleep from their eyes, and Michael began the service, his rich baritone filling the church as he chanted. Out of the corner of his eye, Bartholomew saw something fly through the air towards the Michaelhouse students. It landed harmlessly, but a stain on the floor attested that it was a ball of mud. Bartholomew scanned the congregation, and identified the culprits in the form of the blacksmith's sons. They stood, hands clasped in front of them, eyes raised to the carved wooden roof, as though nothing had happened. Bartholomew frowned. The University had a stormy relationship with the town, and, although the University brought prosperity to a number of townsfolk, it also brought gangs of arrogant, noisy students who despised the people of the town and rioted at the least provocation. Bartholomew saw one of the Physwick students bow his head in laughter at the mud-ball. The University was not even at peace with itself: students from the south loathed scholars from the north and from Scotland; they all hated students from Wales and Ireland; and there was even fierce rivalry between the different religious orders, the mendicant friars and priests at loggerheads with the rich Benedictines and the Austin Canons who ran the Hospital of St John.

Bartholomew turned his attention away from the blacksmith's loutish sons, and back to the service. Michael had finished reading, and the scholars began to chant a Psalm. Bartholomew joined in the singing, relishing how the chanting echoed through the church. As the Psalm finished, Bartholomew stepped forward to read the designated tract from the Old Testament.

He faltered as the door was flung open, and a man walked quickly down the aisle, gesturing urgently that he wanted to speak to the Master, Thomas Kenyngham. Kenyngham was a gentle Gilbertine friar whose rule of the College was tolerant to the point of laxity. He smiled benignly and waved the messenger forward. The man whispered in his ear, and Bartholomew saw Roger Alcote surreptitiously lean to one side to try to overhear. The Master favoured Alcote with a seraphic smile until Alcote had the grace to move away. Out of the corner of his eye, Bartholomew saw that one of the clerk's frenzied gestures was directed towards him, and wondered which of his patients needed him so urgently that mass could be interrupted.

Kenyngham left his place and walked towards the

altar, laying a hand on Bartholomew's arm to stop his reading.

'Gentlemen,' he began in his soft voice, 'there has been an incident in St Mary's Church. The Chancellor has requested that Brother Michael and Doctor Bartholomew attend as soon as possible. Father William and I will continue the mass.' Without further ado, he took up the reading where Bartholomew had stopped, leaving William to scramble to take his own place. Michael dropped his prayerful attitude with a speed that verged on the sacrilegious and made his way down the aisle, eyes gleaming with anticipation. Cynric followed, and Bartholomew went after them, aware of the curious looks from the other scholars. The Master of Physwick plucked at his sleeve as he passed.

'I am the University's Senior Proctor,' he said in a low whisper. 'If there has been an incident in the University church, I should come.'

Bartholomew shrugged, glancing briefly at him as he walked briskly down the aisle. He did not like Richard Harling, who, as the University's Senior Proctor, patrolled the streets at night looking for scholars who should be safely locked in their College or hostel, and fined them for unseemly or rowdy behaviour. Bartholomew sometimes needed to be out at night to see patients, and Harling had already fined him twice without even listening to his reasons. Harling had black hair that was always neatly slicked down with animal grease, and his scholar's tabard was immaculate.

The messenger was waiting for them outside. It was lighter than in the church, and Bartholomew recognised the neat, bearded features of the Chancellor's personal clerk, Gilbert.

'What has happened?' asked Michael, intrigued. 'What is so important that it could not wait until after mass?'

'A dead man has been found in the University chest,' Gilbert replied. Ignoring their looks of disbelief, he continued, 'The Chancellor ordered me to fetch Brother Michael, the Bishop's man, and Matthew Bartholomew, the physician.'

'Not the plague!' whispered Bartholomew in horror. He grabbed Gilbert's arm. 'How did this man die?'

Gilbert forced a smile. 'Not the plague. I do not know what killed him, but it was not the plague.'

Harling pursed his lips. 'This sounds like business for the Proctor.'

Gilbert raised his hands. 'The Junior Proctor is already there. He said you had been on duty last night, and you should not be disturbed until later.'

He turned, and set a lively pace towards St Mary's Church, so that the obese Michael was huffing and sweating within a few moments.

Bartholomew nudged the Benedictine monk in the ribs. ' "Brother Michael, the Bishop's man",' he repeated in an undertone. 'A fine reputation to have, my friend.'

Michael glowered at him. A year and a half before, he had agreed to become an agent of the Bishop of Ely, the churchman who had jurisdiction over the University since Cambridge had no cathedral of its own. Michael was to be alert to the interests of the Church in the town, and especially to the interests of the Benedictines, since Ely was a Benedictine monastery. There was a small hostel for Benedictines studying at the University, but the four monks that lived there were more concerned with their new-found freedom than the interests of their Order.

Bartholomew began to feel uncomfortable. The chest was where all the University's most important documents were stored, and the series of locks and bolts that protected it in the church tower was rumoured to be formidable. So who had broken through all that security? What sinister plot had the University embroiled itself in this time? And perhaps more to the point, how could Bartholomew prevent it from sucking him in, too?

The Church of St Mary the Great was an imposing building of creamy-white stone that dominated the High Street. Next to its delicate window tracery and soaring tower, St Michael's looked squat and grey. Yet, Bartholomew had heard that there were plans to rebuild the chancel and replace it with something grander and finer still.

Bartholomew had barely caught up with the clerk when they reached St Mary's. Standing to one side, wringing his hands and throwing fearful glances at the tower was St Mary's priest, Father Cuthbert, an enormously fat man whom Bartholomew treated for swollen ankles. A small group of clerks huddled around the door talking in low voices. The Chancellor, Richard de Wetherset, stood in the middle of them, a stocky man with iron-grey hair, who exuded an aura of power. He stepped forward as Bartholomew and Michael approached, allowing himself a brief smile at Michael's breathlessness.

'Thank you for being prompt, gentlemen.' He turned to Harling. 'Master Jonstan is already here, Richard. I was loathe to disturb you when you had been up all night.'

Harling inclined his head. 'But I am Senior Proctor, and should be present at a matter that sounds so grave.'

De Wetherset nodded his thanks, and beckoned Bartholomew, Michael, and Harling out of earshot of the gathered clerks. 'I am afraid someone has been murdered in the tower. Doctor, I would like you to tell me a little more about how and when he died, and you, Brother, must report this incident accurately to our Lord the Bishop.'

He began to walk through the churchyard, raising a hand to prevent the gaggle of clerks, and Cynric, from following them. Michael and Harling followed quickly, Father Cuthbert and Bartholomew a little more slowly. Bartholomew felt his stomach churn. At times, the University could be a seething pit of intrigue, and Bartholomew had no wish to become entangled in it. It would demand his time and his energies when he should be concentrating all his efforts on his teaching and his patients. The plague had left Cambridge depleted of physicians, and there was an urgent need to replace those who had died all over the country. Bartholomew considered the training of new physicians the most important duty in his life.

St Mary's was still dark inside, and the Chancellor took a torch from a sconce on the wall and led the way to the tower door at the back of the building. They followed him up the winding stairs into a small chamber about half-way up the tower. Bartholomew glanced around quickly, looking for the fabled chest, but the chamber was empty. Michael emerged from the stair-well, wheezing unhealthily, and Cuthbert's ponderous footsteps echoed until he too stood sweating and gasping in the chamber.

De Wetherset beckoned them close and shut the small wooden door so that they would not be overheard.

'I do not want the details of this incident to become common knowledge,' he said, 'and what I am about to tell you must remain a secret. You know that the University chest is kept in the tower here. To reach it, you must open three locked and bolted doors, and you must be able to open three locks on the chest itself. These locks were made in Italy and are, I am told, the finest locks in the world. Only I have the keys and either I, or my deputy, are always present when the chest is unlocked.'

He paused for a moment, and opened the door quickly to listen intently. He closed it again with a sigh and continued. 'You may consider all these precautions rather excessive to protect indentures and accounts, but the truth is that one of my best clerks, Nicholas of York, was writing a history of the University. He was quite frank, and recorded everything he uncovered, some of which could prove embarrassing if revealed in certain quarters. This book, you understand, will not be randomly distributed, but is intended to be a reliable, factual report of our doings and dealings. One day, people may be interested to know these things.'

He looked hard first at Michael and then at Bartholomew. 'The events of last year, when members of the University committed murder to make their fortunes, are recorded, along with your roles in the affair. And there are other incidents too, which need not concern you. The point is, a month ago Nicholas died of a fever, quite unexpectedly. I was uneasy at the suddenness of his death, and in the light of what has been discovered this morning, I am even more concerned.'

'What exactly has happened this morning?' asked Michael. Bartholomew began to feel increasingly uncomfortable as the Chancellor's revelations sank in.

'I came at first light this morning, as usual, to collect the documents from the chest I would need for the day's business. I was accompanied by my personal clerk, Gilbert. That group of scribes and secretaries you saw outside waited in the church below. Even in the half-light, we could see there was something wrong. The locks on the chest were askew and the lid was not closed properly. Gilbert opened the chest and inside was the body of a man.'

'Gilbert has already told us as much,' said Bartholomew. 'But how did the body come to be in the chest?'

The Chancellor gave the grimmest of smiles. 'That, gentlemen, is why I have asked you to come. I cannot imagine how anyone could have entered the tower, let alone open the locks on the chest. And I certainly have no idea how the corpse of a man could appear there.'

'Where is the chest?' asked Michael. 'Not up more stairs I hope.'

The Chancellor looked Michael up and down scathingly, and left the room. They heard his footsteps echoing further up the stairs, and Michael groaned.

The room on the next floor was more comfortable than the first. A table covered with writing equipment stood in the window, and several benches with cushions lined the walls. In the middle of the floor, standing on a once-splendid, but now shabby, woollen rug, was the

University chest. It was a long box made of ancient black oak and strengthened with iron bands, darkened with age. It reminded Bartholomew of the elaborate coffin he had seen the Bishop of Peterborough buried in years before. Guarding the chest and the room was the Junior Proctor, Alric Jonstan, standing with his sword drawn and his saucer-like blue eyes round with horror. Bartholomew smiled at him as they waited for the others. Jonstan was far more popular than Harling, and was seemingly a kinder man who, although he took his duties seriously, did not enforce them with the same kind of inflexible rigour as did Harling.

De Wetherset stood to one side as Michael and Cuthbert finally arrived, and then indicated that Bartholomew should approach the chest. Bartholomew bent to inspect the wool rug, but there was nothing there, no blood or other marks. He walked around the chest looking for signs of tampering, but the stout leather hinges were pristine and well-oiled, and there was no indication that the lid had been prised open.

Taking a deep, but silent, breath, he lifted the lid. He looked down at the body of a man in a Dominican habit, lying face down on the University's precious documents and scrolls. Jonstan took a hissing breath and crossed himself.

'Poor man!' he muttered. 'It is a friar. Poor man!'

'Have you touched him?' asked Bartholomew of the Chancellor.

De Wetherset shook his head. 'We opened the chest, as I told you, but, when I saw what was inside, I lowered the lid and sent Gilbert to fetch you.'

Bartholomew knelt and put his hand on the man's

neck. There was no life beat, and it was cold. He took the body by the shoulders while Michael grabbed the feet. Carefully, they lifted it out and laid it on the rug next to the chest. The Chancellor came to peer in at the documents. He heaved a sigh of relief.

'Well, at least they are not all covered in blood,' he announced fervently. He began searching among the papers and held up a sheaf triumphantly. 'The history! I think it is all here, although I will check, of course.' He began to rifle through the ream of parchments at the table in the window, muttering to himself.

Bartholomew turned his attention back to the body on the floor. It was a man in his fifties with a neatly cut tonsure. His friar's robe was threadbare and stained. Bartholomew began to try to establish why he had died. He could see no obvious signs, no blows to the head or stab wounds. He sat back perplexed. Had the man committed suicide somehow after lying in the chest?

'Do you know him?' he asked, looking around at the others.

Jonstan shook his head. 'No. We can check at the Friary, though. The poor devils were so decimated by the Death that one of their number missing will be very apparent.'

Bartholomew frowned. 'I do not think he was at the Friary,' he said. 'His appearance and robes are dirty, and the new Prior seems very particular about that. I think he may have been sleeping rough for a few days before he died.'

'Well, who is he then? And what did he want from the chest? And how did he die?' demanded the Chancellor from across the room.

Bartholomew shrugged. 'I have no idea. I need more time. Do you want me to examine him here or in the chapel? I will need to remove his robes.'

The Chancellor looked at Bartholomew in disgust. 'Will it make a mess?'

'No,' Bartholomew replied, startled. 'I do not believe so.'

'Then do it here, away from prying eyes. I will post Gilbert at the bottom of the stairs to make sure you are not disturbed. Father Cuthbert, perhaps you would assist him?' He turned to Bartholomew and Michael. 'If you have no objections, I will not stay to watch.' De Wetherset brandished the handful of documents. 'I must put these in another secure place.'

'*Another* secure place?' quizzed Michael under his breath to Bartholomew.

De Wetherset narrowed his eyes, detecting Michael's tone, if not his words. 'Please report to me the moment you have finished,' he said. He beckoned for Harling and Jonstan to follow him, and left, closing the door firmly behind him.

Bartholomew ran a hand through his unruly hair. 'Not again!' he said to Michael. 'I want to teach and to heal my patients. I do not want to become embroiled in University politics!'

Michael's face softened, and he patted his friend on the shoulder. 'You are the University's most senior physician since the Death. The fact that you have been asked here to help means no more than that. You are not being recruited into the University's secret service!'

'I should hope not,' said Bartholomew with feeling. 'If I thought that were the case, I would leave Cambridge immediately, and set up practice somewhere I would never be found. Come on. Help me get this over with. Then we can report to de Wetherset and that will be an end to it.'

He began to remove the dead man's robe. The stiffness meant that he was forced to cut it with a knife. Once the robe lay in a bundle on the floor, Bartholomew began to conduct a more rigorous examination of the body. There was no sign of violence, no bruises or cuts, and no puncture marks except for a cut on the left hand that was so small that Bartholomew almost missed it. He inspected the fingernails to see if there were any fibres trapped there, but there was only a layer of black dirt. The hands were soft, which implied that the man had been unused to physical labour, and a small ink-stain on his right thumb suggested that he could write. Bartholomew turned the hand to catch the light from the window, and the small callus on the thumb confirmed that the man had been a habitual scribe.

Bartholomew leaned close to the man's mouth and carefully smelled it, ignoring Michael's snort of disgust. There was nothing to suggest he had taken poison. He prised the man's mouth open and peered in, looking for discoloration of the tongue or gums, or other signs of damage. There was nothing. The man had several small ulcers on one side of his tongue, but Bartholomew thought that they were probably more likely caused by a period of poor nutrition than by any subtle poisons.

He turned his attention to the man's throat, but there was nothing to imply strangulation and no neck bones were broken. He looked at one of the man's hands again. If he had died because his heart had seized up, his fingernails, nose and mouth should show some blueness. The man's fingernails were an unhealthy waxy-white, but certainly not blue. His lips, too, were white.

Eventually, Bartholomew sat back on his heels. 'I have no idea why he died,' he said, perplexed. 'Perhaps he came here to steal and the excitement burst some vital organ. Perhaps he was already ill when he came here. Perhaps he was already dead.'

'What?' said Michael, his eyes wide with disbelief. 'Are you suggesting that someone brought a corpse up here in the middle of the night and left it?'

Bartholomew grinned at him. 'No. I am merely following the rules of the deceased Master Wilson and trying to solve the problem logically.'

'Well, that suggestion, my dear doctor, has less logic than Wilson's crumbling bones could present,' said Michael. 'How could someone smuggle a corpse into the church and leave it here? I can accept that someone might hide below and then sneak up here after all was secured for the night, but not someone carrying a corpse!'

'So, the friar hides in the church, picks three locks to reach this room, picks three locks to open the chest, lies face-down in it, and dies. Master Wilson would not have been impressed with your logic, either,' retorted Bartholomew.

'Perhaps the friar came up here as you suggested and died suddenly,' said Michael.

'And closed the lid afterwards?' asked Bartholomew, raising his eyebrows. 'De Wetherset said it was closed with the friar inside. I think it unlikely that he closed it himself.'

'You think another person was here?' asked Michael, gesturing round. 'What evidence do you have for such a claim?'

'None that I can see,' replied Bartholomew. He went to sit on one of the benches and Michael followed him, settling himself comfortably with his hands across his stomach.

'Let us think about what we do know,' the monk said. 'First. It is likely that this man hid in the church and then made his way up to the tower after the church had been secured. We can ask the sexton what his procedures are for locking up.'

'Second,' said Bartholomew, 'I think this man was a clerk or a friar, as he appears, and that he has been sleeping rough for a few nights as attested by his dirty clothes. Perhaps he had undertaken a journey of several days' duration, or perhaps he had spent some time watching the church in preparation for his burglary.'

'Third,' Michael continued, 'you say he appears to have suffered no violence. He may have died of natural causes, perhaps brought on by the stress of his nocturnal activities.'

Bartholomew nodded slowly. 'And fourth,' he concluded, 'the locks seem to have been picked with great skill.'

'But there are no tools,' said Michael. 'He must have needed a piece of wire at the very least to pick a lock.'

Bartholomew went to the chest and rummaged around, but there was nothing. 'So either he hid the tools before he died, or someone took them.'

'If there was another person here with him to take

the tools and close the lid, that person could have killed him,' said Michael.

'But there is no evidence he was murdered,' said Bartholomew.

They sat in silence for a while, mulling over what they had deduced.

'And there is the question of the Chancellor's scribe, Nicholas of York,' said Bartholomew. 'De Wetherset says he is now suspicious of his death – a death that appeared to be natural, but now seems too timely. Two deaths that seem natural, connected with the University chest?' He frowned and drummed on the bench with his fingers.

Michael looked at him hard. 'What do you mean?' he said.

'Although I can find nothing that caused the death of this man, I am reluctant to say it was natural. I suppose it is possible he could have suffered a fatal seizure, fell in the chest, and the lid slammed shut. But what of the missing tools? And anyway, people who have such seizures usually show some evidence of it, and I can see no such evidence here.'

'So what you are saying,' said Michael, beginning to be frustrated, 'is that the friar does not seem to have been killed, but he did not die naturally. Marvellous! Where does that leave us?'

Bartholomew shrugged. 'I have just never seen a man die of natural causes and his body look like the friar's.'

'So what do we tell the Chancellor?' said Michael.

Bartholomew leaned his head back against the white-washed wall and studied the ceiling. 'What we know,' he said. 'That the man was probably an itinerant friar, that he probably had some considerable skill as a picker of locks, that he died from causes unknown, and that there was probably another person here.'

'That will not satisfy de Wetherset,' said Michael, 'nor will it satisfy the Bishop.'

'Well, what would you have us do, Michael? Lie?' asked Bartholomew, also beginning to be frustrated. He closed his eyes and racked his brain for causes of death that would turn a man's skin waxy white.

'Of course we should not lie!' said Michael crossly. 'But the explanation we have now is inadequate.'

'Then what do you suggest we do?' demanded Bartholomew. He watched Michael gnaw at his thumbnail as he turned the problem over in his mind. It gave him an idea, and he went to look at the tiny cut on the friar's thumb. He sat cross-legged on the floor and inspected it closely. It was little more than a scratch, but it broke the skin nevertheless. He let the hand fall and sat pondering the chest. It suddenly took on a sinister air as his attention was drawn to the locks.

He reached across the body to the middle lock. Protruding from the top of it was a minuscule blade, less than the length of his little fingernail. He took one of his surgical knives and pressed gently on it. Under the pressure, it began to slide back into the lock. When he moved his knife, the small blade sprang back up again.

Michael watched him curiously, and stretched out a hand to touch it.

'No!' Bartholomew slapped Michael's hand away. 'I think the lock has its own precaution against intruders,' he said, looking down at the dead friar. 'I think it bears a poison.'

*　　*　　*

The Chancellor looked in horror at the lock that lay on his table, the little blade coated with its deadly poison protruding from the top.

'A true Italian lock,' he said in hushed tones. He picked up a quill and poked the lock further away from him, as though he was afraid that it might poison him from where he sat, and exchanged a look of revulsion with his clerk, who stood behind him.

'Did you know that the lock had the capacity to kill?' asked Bartholomew. Michael gave him a warning elbow in the ribs. The head of the University was not a man of whom to ask such a question.

De Wetherset looked aghast. 'I most certainly did not!' he said, standing and walking to the opposite side of the room, still eyeing the lock with deep suspicion. 'I unlocked it myself many times!' The thought of a possible narrow escape suddenly dawned on him and he turned paler still.

'Are you sure that the lock has not been changed since you last saw it?' said Michael.

The Chancellor thought for a moment, his eyes involuntarily swinging back to the lock on the table. 'Not really,' he said. 'It is the same size, the same colour, and has the same general appearance, but in a court of law I could not swear that this lock was the one that was there yesterday. It probably was, but I could not be certain. What would you say, Gilbert?'

'It looks the same to me,' said his clerk, leaning down and examining it minutely.

'Father Cuthbert?' asked Bartholomew of the fat priest.

Cuthbert put up his hands defensively. 'I am priest

25

only of the church. The tower is beyond my jurisdiction and belongs to the University. I know nothing of poisoned locks.'

'Who else might know?' said Bartholomew.

'My deputy, Evrard Buckley, is the only person other than me who is permitted access to the chest. Even Gilbert does not touch it,' said de Wetherset. 'And the only person other than me to have keys is the Bishop. He keeps a spare set in Ely Cathedral, but we have had no cause to use those for years.'

'Are you the only person actually to use the keys?' asked Bartholomew. 'Do you ever give them to a clerk or your deputy to open the locks?'

De Wetherset pulled on a cord tied around his neck. 'I keep my keys here and I only remove them when I hand them to Buckley to lock or unlock the chest. The keys are never out of my sight, and, outside the chamber where the chest is kept, I never remove them from round my neck.'

'Not even when you bathe?' pressed Bartholomew.

'Bathe? You mean swim in the river?' said the Chancellor with a look of horror.

'No, I mean take a bath,' said Bartholomew.

'A bath would mean that I had to remove all my clothes,' said the Chancellor distastefully, 'and I do not consider such an action healthy for a man in his fifties.' He held up a hand as if to quell any objection Bartholomew might make. 'I am aware of your odd beliefs in this area, Doctor,' he said, referring to Bartholomew's well-known insistence on cleanliness. 'I cannot think why Master Kenyngham allows you to entertain such peculiar notions, and while I suppose they may have a measure of success on the labourers you physic, I do not believe they will apply equally to me.'

'All men are equal before God, Chancellor,' said Bartholomew, taken aback by de Wetherset's statement. He ignored Michael's smirk. 'And all men are more likely to contract certain sicknesses if they do not keep themselves clean.'

De Wetherset looked sharply at him. 'Do not try to lure me into a debate on physic,' he said. 'The Bible does not say those who do not bathe will become ill. And it also does not recommend against drinking from God's rivers as I have heard you do. Now, we have more important matters to discuss.'

Bartholomew was startled into silence, wondering whether his teaching and practice were really as outlandish as many of his colleagues seemed to feel. Bartholomew had learned medicine at the University in Paris from an Arab doctor who had taught him that incidence of disease could be lessened by simple hygiene. Bartholomew fervently believed Ibn Ibrahim was right, a notion that brought him into conflict with many of his patients and colleagues. De Wetherset's arguments had tripped very lightly off his tongue, suggesting that he had debated this issue before. Michael, hiding his amusement, resumed the questioning of de Wetherset.

'So there is no time ever when you might remove the keys?'

'Never,' said de Wetherset. 'I even sleep with them.'

'What about Master Buckley?' said Michael. 'Where is he? We should really ask him the same questions.'

'He is unwell,' said de Wetherset. 'Did you not know that, Doctor? He is your patient.'

Master Buckley, the Vice-Chancellor, was a Fellow of King's Hall. He taught grammar, and, many years before, Bartholomew's older sister Edith had hired Master Buckley to coach him when the school at Peterborough Abbey broke for holidays. Bartholomew's knowledge of grammar had not improved, and Buckley's dull company had done a great deal to convince him that this subject made a very poor showing after arithmetic, geometry, and natural philosophy. Bartholomew had met Buckley again when he had been made Master of Medicine at Michaelhouse six years before, and had treated Buckley frequently for a skin complaint.

'Who usually opens the chest?' Bartholomew asked.

'Well, Master Buckley, actually,' said de Wetherset. 'Gilbert usually kindles the lamps, and I like to set out the table, ready to work on the documents locked in the chest.'

Bartholomew looked at Gilbert, who hastened to explain. 'Master de Wetherset hands Master Buckley his keys, he unlocks the chest and removes any documents we require, and then he locks it again immediately.' He looked down at the lock in renewed horror. 'You mean poor Master Buckley could have been killed like that poor friar just by unlocking the chest?'

Michael shrugged. 'Yes. Assuming the lock has not been changed.'

Bartholomew stood to leave. 'That is all we can tell you,' he said. 'I am sorry it is not more, but perhaps Masters Harling and Jonstan will uncover the truth when they begin to investigate.'

The Chancellor shook his head slowly, and indicated he should sit again. 'My Proctors cannot investigate this,' he said. 'They have their hands full trying to keep peace between students and the gangs of people gathered for the Stourbridge Fair. Also, there are scores of entertainers, mercenaries, and the Lord knows what manner of people wandering through the town gawking at our buildings and assessing our wealth. An increase in non-University folk around the town has always been a danger, but has been especially so since the Death, with lordless labourers strolling free.'

Bartholomew knew all this: the Fair was the largest in England, and merchants from all over England, France, and even Flanders came to trade. The Fair also attracted entertainers – singers, dancers, actors, fire-eaters, jongleurs, acrobats, and many more – and with the entertainers came pickpockets, thieves, rabble-rousers, and tricksters. The Proctors always struggled to keep the scholars out of trouble, but this year the situation was far more serious. The plague had taken landowners as well as those who worked for them, and many previously bonded men had found themselves free. A shortage of labour had forced wages up, and groups of people wandered the country selling their services to those that could pay the most. Compounding all this, the soldiers who had been fighting the King's wars in France had begun to return. It was easier to steal than to work, and robbers on the roads were increasingly common, especially given the number of carts that trundled along taking goods to and from the Fair. The Fair was only in its second week, but already there had been three deaths, and a riot had been only narrowly averted when a local tinker had stolen a student's purse.

'Because my Proctors are busy with the Fair,' the Chancellor continued, 'I will need to crave your indulgence a little longer, and ask that you might make some preliminary enquiries on my behalf. Of course, Harling and Jonstan will help wherever they can, but . . .'

'If you will forgive me, Master de Wetherset,' interrupted Bartholomew, 'I would rather not be a party to an extended investigation. I am a physician, and I think the events of two Christmases ago show clearly that I am not adept at this kind of thing. You would be better asking one of your clerks to do it. Perhaps Gilbert?'

'I require a physician to examine the body of my scribe Nicholas to see if he, too, was killed by this foul device,' said de Wetherset, gesturing to the lock on the table. 'Gilbert cannot tell me whether a man has been poisoned or not.'

'But Nicholas is buried!' said Michael, shocked. 'You said he died a month ago.'

'You mean to dig him up?' gasped Gilbert, his face white under his beard.

Cuthbert joined in. 'Nicholas has been laid to rest in hallowed ground! You cannot disturb him! It is contrary to the will of God!'

De Wetherset looked disapprovingly at them before addressing Michael and Bartholomew. 'Nicholas lies in the churchyard here. I will obtain the necessary permits from the Bishop and you will exhume the body this week. You will also report back to me regularly. I will speak with

Master Kenyngham and ask that you be excused lectures if they interfere with your investigation.'

Bartholomew felt a flash of anger at de Wetherset's presumption, followed by a feeling of sick dread. He had no wish to investigate murders or delve into the University's sordid affairs.

'But my students have their disputations soon,' he protested. 'I cannot abandon them!'

'I need a physician to examine the corpse,' repeated the Chancellor. 'You underestimate your abilities, Doctor. You are honest and discreet, and for these reasons alone I trust you more than most of my clerks. I think you – both of you,' he added, looking at Michael, 'are perfectly equipped to get to the bottom of this matter. I know you would both rather teach than investigate University affairs, but I must ask you to indulge me for a day or so, and do my bidding. I know the Bishop will support me in this.'

'But if your clerk has been dead for a month, I will be able to tell you nothing about his death,' Bartholomew protested. 'Even if there were once a small cut on his hand, like the one on the friar, the flesh will be corrupted, and I doubt I will be able to see it.'

De Wetherset winced in distaste. 'Perhaps. But you will not know until you look, and I require that you try.' He leaned towards Bartholomew, his expression earnest. 'This is important. I must know whether Nicholas came to harm because of the book I ordered he write about the University.'

Bartholomew held his gaze. 'You must be aware of the stories that say the plague came from the graves of the dead,' he said. 'It is a risk . . .'

'Nonsense,' snapped de Wetherset. 'You do not believe that story, Doctor, any more than I do. The plague is over. It will not come again.'

'How do you know that?' demanded Bartholomew, irritated at the man's complacency. 'How do you know someone at the Fair is not sickening from the plague at this very moment?'

'It has passed us over,' said de Wetherset, his voice rising in reply. 'It has gone north.'

'There are people at the Fair who have come from the north,' countered Bartholomew, becoming exasperated. 'How do you know they have not brought it back with them, in their clothes, or in the goods they hope to sell?'

'Well, which is it, Doctor?' said de Wetherset triumphantly, detecting a flaw in Bartholomew's argument. 'Is it carried by the living, or in the graves with the dead? You cannot have it both ways.'

'My point is that I do not know,' said Bartholomew, ignoring Michael's warning looks for arguing with the Chancellor. 'No one knows! How can we take such a risk by exhuming your clerk? Will you endanger the lives of the people of Cambridge, of England, over this?'

De Wetherset snorted impatiently. 'There is no risk! Nicholas died of a summer ague, not the plague. I saw his body in his coffin before he was buried. Your peculiar ideas about cleanliness are making you over-cautious. You will exhume the body in two or three days' time when I have the necessary licences. Now, what do you plan to do about this friar?'

Michael pulled thoughtfully at the thin whiskers on his flabby cheek, while Bartholomew threw up his hands in exasperation, and went to stand near the window to bring his anger under control.

'Can you test the lock to make certain it is poisoned?' Michael asked Bartholomew.

Bartholomew looked at him distastefully and stifled a sigh. 'Will one of your clerks do that?' he asked de Wetherset.

'How?' asked de Wetherset, looking at the lock in renewed revulsion.

'Test it on a rat or a bird. If the poison killed the friar through that tiny cut, then the poor animal, being considerably smaller, should die fairly quickly.'

Bartholomew felt a sudden, unreasonable anger towards the friar whose death was about to cause such upheaval in his life. What was the man doing in the tower anyway? He could only have been there to steal or to spy. Bartholomew watched de Wetherset issue instructions to Gilbert to test the lock on a rat, and gestured to Michael that they should go.

'Wait!' the Chancellor commanded, standing as they made to leave. 'I must ask that you observe utmost discretion over this business. That a man has died in the University chest cannot be denied, but I do not wish anyone to know about the University history that was being written.'

Michael nodded acquiescence, bowed, and walked out, while Bartholomew trailed after him, feeling dejected. He was going to become entangled in the unsavoury world of University politics a second time, and be forced to question the motives of his friends and family.

Outside, Michael rubbed his hands together and beamed. 'What shall we do first?' he asked, and

Bartholomew realised that the fat monk was relishing their enforced duties. Michael had always loved University affairs, and thrived on the petty politics and plots that were a part of College life. He saw Bartholomew's doleful expression and clapped him on the shoulder.

'Come, Matt,' he said reassuringly. 'This is not like the other business. There are no threats to those we love, and your Philippa is safely away visiting her brother. This has nothing to do with Michaelhouse. It is just some minor intrigue that has gone wrong.'

Bartholomew was unconvinced. 'I should have gone with Philippa,' he said bitterly, 'or followed her brother's lead and moved away from this vile pit of lies and deception to London.'

'You would hate London,' Michael laughed. 'You make enough fuss about the filth and dirt here. In London it would be ten times worse, and they say that the River Thames is the dirtiest river in England. You would hate it,' he said again, drawing his morose friend away from the shadows of the church and into the bright sunlight to where Cynric waited for them.

They began to walk down the High Street towards King's Hall to visit Master Buckley. The streets were busier than usual because of the Fair, and houses that had stood empty since the plague were bursting at the seams with travellers. A baker passed them, his tray brimming with pies and pastries, while two beggars watched him with hungry eyes.

With an effort, Bartholomew brought his mind back to what Michael was saying about the dead friar. Michael, strolling next to him, began to run through the possibilities surrounding the friar's death, for Cynric's benefit. They turned suddenly as they heard a wail. A woman tore towards them, her long, fair hair streaming behind her like a banner. Bartholomew recognised her as Sybilla, the ditcher's daughter, and one of the town's prostitutes. Her mother, brothers, and sisters had died in the plague, and her father had allowed her to follow any path she chose, while he took his own comfort from the bottles of wine she brought him. Bartholomew caught her as she made to run past.

'What has happened?' he said, alarmed by her tear-streaked face and wild, frightened eyes.

'Isobel!' she sobbed. 'Isobel!'

'Where?' asked Bartholomew, looking down the street. 'Has she been hurt?'

He exchanged glances with Brother Michael. They were both aware of the murder of two of the town's prostitutes during the last few weeks. Bartholomew had seen the body of one of them, her eyes staring sightlessly at the sky and her throat cut.

Sybilla was unable to answer and Bartholomew let her go, watching as she fled up the High Street, her wailing drawing people from their houses to see what was happening. Bartholomew and Michael, concerned for Isobel, continued in the direction from which Sybilla had come, until they saw people gathering in St Botolph's churchyard.

Two women bent over someone lying on the ground, and Bartholomew and Michael approached, the monk stifling a cry of horror as he saw the blood-splattered figure. Bartholomew knelt next to Isobel's body and gently eased her onto her back. Her throat was a mess of congealed blood, dark and sticky where it had flooded down her chest.

Michael squatted down next to him, his eyes tightly closed so he would not have to look. He began to mutter prayers for the dead, while Bartholomew wrapped her in her cloak. Cynric disappeared to report the news to the Sheriff and to locate the dead woman's family. When Michael had finished, Bartholomew picked up the body and carried it into the church. A friar, who had been in the crowd outside, helped put her into the parish coffin and cover her with a sheet. While the friar went to clear the churchyard of ghoulish onlookers and to await Isobel's family, Bartholomew looked again at the body, while Michael peered over his shoulder. The sheet was not long enough to cover the dead girl's feet and Bartholomew saw that someone had taken her shoes. Her feet were relatively clean, so she had not been walking barefoot. He looked a little more closely and caught his breath as he saw the small red circle painted in blood on her foot.

'What is wrong?' asked Michael, his face white in the dark church.

Bartholomew pointed to the dead girl's foot. 'That mark,' he said. 'I saw a circle like that on the foot of the last dead girl, Fritha. I thought it was just chance – there was so much blood – but Isobel has a mark that is identical.'

'Do you think it is the killer's personal signature?' asked Michael, with a shudder. 'I assume all three women were killed by the same person.'

Bartholomew frowned. 'Perhaps, yes, if there were a similar mark on the foot of the first victim. I did not see her body.'

'God's teeth, Matt,' said Michael, his voice unsteady. 'What monster would do this?' He clutched at one of the pillars, unable to tear his eyes away from the body in the coffin. He began to reel, and Bartholomew, fearing that the monk might faint, took him firmly by the arm and led him outside.

They sat together on one of the ancient tombstones in the shade of a yew tree. A woman's anguished cries suggested that Cynric had already found Isobel's family and that they were nearing the church. Next to Bartholomew, Michael was still shaking.

'Why, Matt?' he asked, looking to where a man led his wailing wife into the church, escorted solicitously by the friar.

Bartholomew stared across the churchyard at a row of young oak trees, their slender branches waving in the breeze. 'That is the third girl to be killed,' he said. 'Hilde, Fritha, and Isobel, and all of them murdered in churchyards.'

The Fair had resulted in a temporary increase in prostitution. The town burgesses had called for the Sheriff to rid the town of the women, but Bartholomew believed the prostitutes were providing a greater service to the town than the burgesses appreciated: as long as they were available, scholars and itinerant traders from the Fair did not pester the townsmen's wives and daughters. Bartholomew suspected Michael felt much the same, although such a position was hardly tenable publicly for a Benedictine Master of Theology.

They sat for a while until Michael regained some of his colour, and watched the crowd in the churchyard. When the Sheriff's men arrived, it became ominously silent.

Bartholomew frowned. 'What is all that about?'

They watched as the soldiers tried to disperse the crowd. 'There are rumours in the town that the Sheriff is not doing all he might to investigate the murders of Hilde and Fritha,' said Michael. 'As Sheriff, his duty is to try to prevent prostitution, and it is said that he considers the murderer to be doing him a favour by killing these women.'

'Oh, surely not, Brother!' said Bartholomew in disbelief. 'What Sheriff would want a killer in his town? It will do nothing to make it peaceful.'

'True enough,' said Michael. 'But it is said that the killer fled to St Mary's Church and claimed sanctuary. The Sheriff set a watch on the church, but the killer escaped, and now it looks as though he has struck again.'

'How is it known that this man was the killer?' asked Bartholomew curiously.

'He is supposed to have killed his wife before fleeing,' said Michael. 'It is rumoured that the Sheriff deliberately set a lax watch on the church so that the killer could continue his extermination of the prostitutes.'

'Do you think there is any truth in these stories?' asked Bartholomew, watching the soldiers, frustrated with the sullen crowd, draw their swords to threaten the people away.

'It is true that a man killed his wife and claimed sanctuary at St Mary's, and it is true that he escaped during the night despite the Sheriff's guards. Whether he is also the killer of Hilde, Fritha, and now Isobel, is open to debate.'

The crowd, faced with naked steel, reluctantly began to disperse, although there were dark mutterings.

Bartholomew was surprised that the crowd was sympathetic to the prostitutes. There were those who claimed that the plague had come because of women like them, and they faced a constant and very real danger from attack.

'Come on, Brother,' Bartholomew said, rising to his feet. 'We must pay a visit to the ailing Master Buckley. Perhaps he will explain everything, and this University chest business will be over and done with before more time is wasted.'

Michael assented and they walked in silence up the High Street, each wrapped in his own thoughts. Michael could not stop thinking about the face of the dead girl, while Bartholomew, more inured to violent death, was still angry that he was being dragged into the sordid world of University politics and intrigue.

Towards King's Hall the houses were larger than those near St Botolph's, some with small walled gardens. Many homes had been abandoned after the plague, and the whitewash was dirty and grey. Others were well maintained, and had been given new coats of whitewash in honour of the Fair, some tinged with pigs' blood or ochre to make them pleasing shades of pink, yellow, and orange. But all were in use now that the Fair had arrived.

The street itself was hard-packed mud, dangerously pot-holed and rutted. Parallel drains ran down each side of it, intended to act as sewers to take waste from homes. By leaning out of the upper storeys of the houses, residents could throw their waste directly into the drains, but not everyone's aim was accurate, and accidents were inevitable. Scholars especially needed to take care when walking past townspeople's houses in the early mornings. On one side of the street, Bartholomew saw a group of ragged children prodding at a blockage with sticks, paddling barefoot in the filth. One splashed another, and screams of delight followed as the spray flew. The physician in him longed to tell them to play elsewhere; the pragmatist told him that they would find somewhere equally, if not more, unwholesome.

King's Hall was an elegant establishment that had been founded by Edward II more than thirty years before. The present King had continued the royal patronage, and it was now the largest of the Cambridge Colleges. The centre of King's Hall was a substantial house with gardens that swept down to the river. Bartholomew and Michael asked for the Warden, who listened gravely to Michael's news, and took them to Master Buckley's room himself.

'Many of the masters have a room to themselves now,' the Warden said as they walked. 'Before the Death, we were cramped, but since that terrible pestilence claimed more than half our number, we rattle around in this draughty building. I suppose time will heal and we will have more scholars in due course. Master Kenyngham tells me that Michaelhouse has just been sent six Franciscans from Lincoln, which must be a welcome boost to your numbers.'

Bartholomew smiled politely, although he was not so certain that the arrival of the Franciscans was welcome. So far, all they had done was to try to get the other scholars into debates about heresy and to criticise the Master's tolerant rule.

The Warden led them up some stairs at the rear of

the Hall and knocked on a door on the upper floor.
There was no answer.

'Poor Master Buckley was most unwell last night,'
said the Warden in a whisper. 'I thought it might be
wise to allow him to sleep this morning and recover
his strength.'

'What was wrong with him?' asked Bartholomew,
exchanging a quick glance of concern with Michael.

The Warden shrugged. 'You know him, Doctor. He is
never very healthy and the summer heat has made him
worse. Last night, we had eels for supper, and he always
eats far more than his share, despite your warnings about
his diet. None of us were surprised when he said he felt
ill.' He knocked on the door again, a little louder.

With a growing fear of what he might find, Bartholomew
grasped the handle of the door and pushed it open. The
three men stood staring in astonishment. The room
was completely bare. Not a stick of furniture, a wall
hanging, or a scrap of parchment remained. And there
was certainly no sign of Master Buckley.

chapter 2

AFTER THEY TOOK THEIR LEAVE OF THE BEWIL-dered warden, Bartholomew and Michael walked back to Michaelhouse together.

'We still need to talk to the man who locked up the church,' said Bartholomew.

Michael pulled a face. 'Not until I have had something to eat,' he said. 'What a morning! We are dragged out of mass to look at a corpse in the University chest, we discover a nasty poisoning device, we see a murdered harlot, and we find that the Vice-Chancellor has run away carrying all his worldly goods and some of King's Hall's. And all before breakfast.'

'I am supposed to be teaching now,' said Bartholomew, glancing up at the sun, already high in the sky. 'These students will face their disputations soon and need all the teaching they can get, especially Robert Deynman.'

'They will have to wait a little longer,' said Michael, pointing across the yard to where the porter stood talking with a young woman. 'You have a patient.'

Seeing Bartholomew and Michael walk through the gate, the woman began to walk towards them, the porter's attentions forgotten. Bartholomew recognised her as Frances de Belem, the daughter of one of the wealthy merchants on Milne Street, who owned a house next to that of his brother-in-law Sir Oswald Stanmore. Years before, Stanmore and de Belem had started negotiations to marry Frances to Bartholomew, so that Stanmore's cloth trade could be linked to de Belem's dyeing business. At fourteen years of age, Bartholomew had no intentions of being married to a baby, nor of becoming a tradesman, and he had fled to study at Oxford. De Belem had promptly found another merchant's son, and Stanmore, fortunately for Bartholomew, was not a man to bear grudges when his errant kinsman returned fifteen years later to take up a position as Fellow of Medicine at Michaelhouse.

The rift between Stanmore and de Belem caused by Bartholomew's flight, however, had never completely healed, and Bartholomew was still occasionally subjected to doleful looks from his brother-in-law when de Belem overcharged him for dyes. But Frances bore Bartholomew no ill will and always seemed pleased to see him. Her marriage ended, as did many, when the plague took her husband the previous year.

As Bartholomew walked towards her, he noticed that her face was white and stained with tears. She almost broke into a run as he drew close, and was unable to prevent a huge sob as she clutched at his arm.

'Frances?' said Bartholomew gently. 'Whatever is the matter? Is your father ill?'

She shook her head miserably. 'I must talk to you, Doctor,' she said. 'I need help, and I do not know who else to ask.'

Bartholomew thought quickly. He could not take a

woman back to his room, especially with the Franciscans undoubtedly already watching with disapproval the presence of a woman on Michaelhouse soil. He could not take her to the hall or the conclave because they would be in use for teaching, and he was reluctant to send her away when she obviously needed his help. The only possible place for a consultation was the kitchen, where the hefty laundress Agatha could act as chaperon and preserve Frances's reputation and his own.

He ushered her across the yard towards the main building. Michaelhouse comprised several buildings, joined in a three-sided structure around a courtyard. The south and north wings, where the scholars lived, were two-storeyed buildings. The hall linked the two wings and was a handsome house built by a merchant. The house had been bought in 1324 by Hervey de Stanton, Edward II's Chancellor of the Exchequer, when he founded Michaelhouse, and was dominated by the elegant porch topped with de Stanton's coat of arms. A spiral staircase led from the porch to the hall on the upper floor, while a door below led to the kitchen.

Frances in tow, Bartholomew made his way through the servants scurrying to prepare the main meal of the day, to the small room where Agatha kept her linen. She sat in a chair, legs splayed in front of her, snoring loudly in the sunlight that flooded the room. Agatha was a huge woman, almost as big as Brother Michael. Women were not usually allowed to work in the University's Colleges and hostels, but Agatha was exempted since she was unlikely to attract the amorous attentions of even the most desperate scholar. As Bartholomew entered, she awoke, and looked balefully at him, and then at Frances behind. It was not the first time Bartholomew had used her services when female patients had arrived unannounced, and she said nothing as she scrubbed at her eyes and heaved her bulk into a less inelegant position.

'You can trust Agatha to be discreet with anything you might say,' he said, as Frances looked nervously at Agatha's formidable form.

Agatha smiled, revealing an array of strong yellow teeth. 'Never mind me,' she said to Frances. 'I have things to be doing, and nothing you can say to the Doctor will shock me.'

'I am with child!' Frances blurted out. Agatha's jaw immediately dropped, and the hand that was reaching for some sewing was arrested in mid air. Bartholomew was startled. Her father, who had allowed Frances a free rein since the death of her husband, would be furious; especially so since Stanmore had told Bartholomew that arrangements were already in hand to remarry Frances to a landowner in Saffron Walden, a village south-east of Cambridge.

Bartholomew collected his tumbling thoughts when he saw Frances was waiting for an answer with desperate eyes. 'I cannot help you,' he said gently. 'You must seek out a midwife to advise you about the birth. Physicians do not become involved in childbirth unless there is danger to the child or the mother.' He smiled at her reassuringly. 'And I am sure that you need have no worries on that score. You are young and healthy.'

'But I do not want it!' cried Frances. 'It will ruin me!'

Agatha, seeing the girl's tears, gave her a motherly hug.

Bartholomew looked at them helplessly. 'I can do nothing to help,' he said again. 'I can only advise you to see a midwife to secure the safe delivery of the child.'

'I want you to get rid of it for me,' said Frances, turning a tear-streaked face to Bartholomew. 'I do not want it.'

'I cannot do that,' said Bartholomew. 'Quite apart from the fact that I do not know how, it would be a terrible crime, and dangerous for you.'

'I care nothing for the danger,' cried Frances. 'My life will be worth nothing if I have it, so I have nothing to lose. You must be able to help me! I know there are medicines that can rid a woman of an unwanted child. Of all the physicians in the town, you are the one most likely to know them, since you learned your medicine in dark and distant lands from foreign teachers.'

Bartholomew wondered if that was how all his patients saw him, endowed with knowledge of mysterious cures alien to physicians who had studied in England. 'I do not know how to make potions for such purposes,' he said, looking away from Frances and out of the window, hoping that she would not see he was lying. He did know of such a potion, and it was indeed Ibn Ibrahim who had shown him writings by a woman physician called Trotula where such remedies could be found: equal portions of wormwood, betony, and pennyroyal, if taken early, might sometimes cause the foetus to abort. He had seen it used once, but that was because the mother was too exhausted from her last birthing to manage another. Even then, Bartholomew had been confused by the ethics of the case.

'You do know!' said Frances, desperation making her voice crack. 'You must.'

'Go to a midwife,' said Bartholomew gently. 'They understand, and will help with your baby.'

'Mistress Woodman killed Hilde's younger sister,' said Frances bitterly, meeting his eyes. 'Did you know that?'

'Hilde the prostitute?' asked Bartholomew. 'The one who was killed?'

Frances nodded. 'Her sister was three months with child, and she went to Mistress Woodman, the midwife, to rid herself of it. Mistress Woodman tried to pluck the child out with a piece of wire. Hilde's sister bled to death.'

Bartholomew knew such practices occurred – many dangerous poisons were used, and if these failed, operations were attempted that invariably left the mother either dead or suffering from infection. He turned away and looked out of the window. There was no disputing that it was wrong to kill, but what if Frances went to Mistress Woodman and died of her ministrations?

'What of the baby's father?' he asked. 'Will he marry you?'

Frances gave a short bark of laughter. 'He cannot,' she said, and would elaborate no further. Bartholomew assumed the father must already be married.

'Do you have money?' he asked. Frances nodded, hope flaring in her eyes, and she showed him a heavy purse. 'You have relatives in Lincoln. Tell your father you are going to stay with them. If you can trust them, have the baby there. If not, there are convents that will help you.'

The hope in Frances's eyes faded. 'You will not help?' she said.

Bartholomew swallowed. 'Think about going away to have the child. Come to talk to me again tomorrow, but do not go to Mistress Woodman for a solution.'

Frances sighed heavily, and turned to leave. 'I will give it thought,' she said, 'and I will come tomorrow. But my mind is already made up.'

As she left, Agatha sank down in her chair. 'Poor child,' she said. 'One rash act will cost her everything, while her paramour lives on to sully another.'

'That is not fair, Agatha,' said Bartholomew. 'Frances is twenty-four years old, and has been married. She is no green maiden taken unawares.'

'But the outcome is the same,' growled Agatha. 'The woman suffers, and may even die, while the man merely selects another for his attentions. Perhaps I will tell her how to rid herself of the baby.'

'How?' demanded Bartholomew disbelievingly. Agatha never ceased to amaze him with her assertions.

'You take two parts of wormwood to one part of crushed snails, add a generous pinch of red arsenic, and grind it into a poultice. You then insert the paste into the private regions, and the babe will sicken and die.'

'And so might the mother,' said Bartholomew, cringing. 'Where did you learn such a dangerous recipe?'

Agatha grinned suddenly and tapped the side of her nose. Bartholomew wondered whether she might have made it up, but the use of wormwood was common to effect cures of women's ailments, and crushed snails were also popular. The thought of medicines reminded him that he was supposed to be teaching. Thanking Agatha for her help, he walked quickly back through the kitchen, and up the wide spiral staircase that led to the hall on the upper floor. Father William, the dour Franciscan teacher of theology, was holding forth to a group of six or seven scholars on the doctrine of original sin, his voice booming through the hall to the distraction of the other Fellows who were also trying to teach there. Piers Hesselwell, Michaelhouse's Fellow of Law, was struggling valiantly to explain the basic principles of Gratian's *Decretum* to ten restless undergraduates, while Roger Alcote, probably tired of competing with William's voice, had ordered one of his scholars to read Aristotle's *Rhetoric* to his own class. As Bartholomew passed him on his way to the conclave at the far end of the hall, Alcote beckoned him over.

'What is the news?' he asked. 'Are these rumours true about dead friars in the chest?'

Bartholomew nodded, and tried to leave, reluctant to engage in gossip with the Senior Fellow. He was a tiny, bitter man who fussed like a hen and had a fanatical dislike of women that Bartholomew thought was abnormal.

'What House?' Alcote asked.

'Dominican,' answered Bartholomew, guessing what was coming next.

Alcote shot him a triumphant look. 'Dominican! A mendicant!' Bartholomew gave him a look of reproval. If the Fellows harboured such unyielding attitudes, what hope was there that the students would ever forget their differences and learn to study in peace? Alcote had recently taken major orders with the Cluniacs at Thetford, and had immediately engaged upon a bitter war of attrition with the mendicant Franciscans. Michaelhouse had been relatively free from inter-Order disputes until then; Brother Michael, the one Benedictine, picked no quarrel with the strong Franciscan contingent there, while those who had taken minor orders, like Bartholomew, had no quarrel with anyone.

Most scholars at the University took religious orders. This meant that they came under the jurisdiction of Church, rather than secular, law. This division between scholars and townspeople was yet another bone of contention, for secular law was notoriously harsher than Canon law: if Alcote or Bartholomew stole a sheep, they would be fined; if a townsman stole a sheep, he was likely to be hanged. Being in minor orders meant that Bartholomew had certain duties to perform, such as taking church services, but the protection it offered was indisputable. Other scholars, like William, Michael, and now Alcote, had taken major orders, which forbade marriage and relations with women.

Bartholomew left Alcote to his nasty musing, and made for the conclave. It was a pleasant room in the summer, when the light from the wide arched windows flooded in. The windows had no glass, and so a cool breeze wafted through them, tinged with the unmistakable aroma of river. The coolness was welcome in the summer, but in the winter, when the shutters had to be kept firmly closed against the weather, the conclave was dark and cold. The lime-washed walls were decorated with some fine wall-hangings, donated by a former student after a fire had damaged much of the hall two years before, and, at Bartholomew's insistence, there were always fresh rushes on the floor.

Bartholomew's students were engaged in a noisy

dispute that he felt certain was not medical, and they quietened when he strode in. He settled himself in one of the chairs near the empty fireplace and smiled round at his students, noting which ones smiled back and which ones studiously avoided his eye because they had failed to prepare for the discussion he had planned. Sam Gray was one of the ones looking everywhere but at his teacher. He was a young man in his early twenties with a shock of unruly, light-brown hair. He looked tired and Bartholomew wondered what nocturnal activities he had been pursuing. He was certain they would not have had much to do with trepanation, cutting the skull open to relieve pressure on the brain, the subject of the day.

Bartholomew had been taught how to perform a number of basic operations by Ibn Ibrahim, and was considered something of an oddity in the town for knowing both surgery and medicine. He believed that medicine and surgery could complement each other, and wanted his students to have knowledge of both, despite the fact that most physicians looked down on surgical techniques as the responsibilities of barbers. Another problem he faced was that those students who had taken major orders were forbidden to practise incision and cautery by an edict passed by the Fourth Lateran Council in 1215.

'What is trepanation?' he asked. He had described the operation the previous term, but was curious to know who had remembered and who had not.

There was a rustle in the room as some students shuffled their feet, and one or two hands went up. Bartholomew noted that the first belonged to Thomas Bulbeck, who was his brightest student.

'Master Gray?' Bartholomew asked maliciously, knowing that Gray would not have the faintest idea what trepanation was because he had missed the previous lecture.

Gray looked startled. 'Trepidation,' he began, his usual confident manner asserting itself quickly, 'is a morbid fear of having your head sawed off.'

Bartholomew fought down the urge to laugh. If these young men were to be successful in their disputations, there was no room for levity. He saw one or two of the students nodding sagely, and marvelled at Gray's abilities to make the most outrageous claims with such conviction. Secretly, he envied the skill: such brazen self-assurance in certain situations might give a patient the encouragement needed to recover. Bartholomew was a poor liar, and his Arab master had often criticised him for not telling a patient what he wanted to hear when it might make the difference between life and death.

'Anyone else?' he asked, standing and pacing back and forth in front of the fireplace. Bulbeck's hand shot up. Bartholomew motioned for him to answer.

'Trepanation,' he said, casting a mischievous glance at Gray, 'is the surgical practice of removing a part of the skull to relieve pressure on the brain.'

'Surgery!' spat one of the Franciscans in disgust. 'A tradesman's job!'

Bartholomew wandered over to him. 'A patient comes to you with severe headaches, spells of unconsciousness, and uncoordinated movements. What do you do, Brother Boniface?'

'Bleed him with leeches,' Brother Boniface replied promptly.

Bartholomew thrust his hands in the folds of his tabard and suppressed a sigh of resignation. Wherever he went, people saw bleeding as a panacea for all manner of ailments, when other, far more effective but less dramatic, methods were to hand. He had lost many a patient to other physicians because of his refusal to leech on demand, and some had not lived to regret it. 'And what will that do?'

'It will relieve the patient of an excess of bad humours and reduce the pressure in the brain. Without the use of surgery,' he concluded smugly.

'And what if that does not work, and the patient becomes worse?' asked Bartholomew, sauntering to the window and sitting on one of the stone window seats, hands still firmly in his gown to prevent himself from grabbing the arrogant friar and trying to shake some sense into him.

'Then it is God's will that he dies, and I give him last rites,' said Boniface.

Bartholomew was impressed at this reasoning. Would that all his cases were so simple. 'But anyone who becomes ill and who is not given the correct treatment may die,' he said, 'and any of you who are unprepared to apply the cure that will save the patient should not become physicians.'

There was a sheepish silence. Bartholomew continued. 'Under certain circumstances there may be a surgical technique that can be used to save a patient's life. If it were God's will that these people should die, He would not have made it possible to use the technique in the first place. But the point is that many people who might have died have been saved because a surgeon has known how to do it. You need not perform the operation yourselves, but you should be prepared to hire the services of a barber-surgeon who will do it for you. Your first duty as a physician is always to save life, or to relieve painful symptoms.'

'My first duty is to God!' exclaimed Boniface, attempting piety, but betrayed by the malice that glittered in his eyes.

'Physicians serve God through their patients,' said Bartholomew immediately, having had this debate many times with Father William. 'God has given you the gift of healing through knowledge, and the way in which you use it is how you serve Him. If you choose to ignore the knowledge He has made available to you without good reason, then your service to Him is flawed.'

'Do you believe you serve God without using the leeches He saw fit to provide for that purpose?' asked Boniface blithely.

'I try to save my patients' lives with the most effective method,' replied Bartholomew. 'If I was certain leeching a patient would secure his recovery, I would leech him. But when my own experience dictates that there are other, more effective, cures for certain ailments than leeches, it would be wrong of me not to use them.'

'Does trepanation hurt the patient?' asked Robert Deynman suddenly, causing stifled laughter among the other students, and effectively ending Bartholomew's debate with Boniface. Deynman was Bartholomew's least able student, who had been accepted by Michaelhouse because his father was rich. Bartholomew eyed him closely, wondering if the question was intended to needle him, but a glance into the boy's guileless eyes told him that this was just another of his unbelievably stupid questions. Bartholomew felt sorry for him. He tried hard to keep up with the others, but study was entirely beyond him. The thought of Deynman let loose on patients made Bartholomew shudder, and he hoped he would never pass his disputations.

'Yes,' he answered slowly. 'It can be painful.' He wanted to ask how Deynman thought having a hole sawn in his head would feel, but did not want to embarrass the student in front of the others, especially the Franciscans. 'But there are things we can do to alleviate some of the discomfort. What are they?'

He stood up again and went back to the fireplace, kicking at the rushes as Bulbeck recited a list of the drugs and potions that might be used to dull the senses. 'What about laudanum?' he snapped. They had discussed Dioscorides' recommendations for doses of laudanum the previous day, and Bulbeck had already forgotten it.

Bulbeck faltered, and then added it to his list.

'How much would you give to a child you were going to operate on?' he demanded.

Bulbeck faltered again and the others looked away.

'Three measures,' said Deynman.

'For a child?' said Bartholomew incredulously, his resolution not to embarrass Deynman forgotten in his frustration. 'Well, you would certainly solve the problem of pressure on the brain. You would kill it! Master Gray? Come on! Think!'

'One measure,' guessed Gray wildly.

Bartholomew closed his eyes and tipped his head back and then looked at his students in resignation. 'You will kill your patients with ignorance,' he said quietly. 'I have told you at least twice now how much laudanum is safe to give children and you still do not know. Tomorrow we will discuss Dioscorides's *De Materia Medica* and the medicinal properties of opiates. Bulbeck will read it here this afternoon, and I want everyone to attend. Anyone who does not know correct dosages need not come tomorrow.'

He turned on his heel and stalked out of the conclave, hoping he had frightened them into learning. He was frustrated that they did not learn faster when there was such a dire need for physicians, but he would not make their disputations easier. Badly-taught physicians could be worse than none at all.

The bell began to ring for dinner and Bartholomew went to wash his hands. Michael was already speeding across to the hall so he could grab a few mouthfuls before the others arrived. The Franciscans gathered together before processing silently across the beaten-earth of the yard. Father William, the fanatic whom, rumour had it, had been dismissed from the inquisition for over-zealousness, was their acknowledged leader.

Bartholomew took his place next to Michael at the table that stood on a raised dais at the south end of the hall where the Fellows sat in a row. The large monk had tell-tale crumbs on his face and there were obvious gaps in the bread-basket. To Bartholomew's left sat Father Aidan, another Franciscan. Aidan was prematurely bald with two prominent front teeth and small blue eyes that never changed expression. Bartholomew had been told that he was an outstanding theologian, although his few attempts at conversation had been painful.

Aidan sat next to William, while next to him sat Kenyngham, his wispy white hair standing almost at right angles to his scalp. Next to the Master was Roger Alcote, and Piers Hesselwell sat on the end. Hesselwell taught law, and always wore fine clothes under his scholar's tabard. It had been difficult to find a Master of Law, for life in post-plague England was sunny indeed for lawyers. The plague took many individuals who had not made wills, while many wills that had been made were contested bitterly, and there was work aplenty for the lawyers. Few were willing to exchange potentially meteoric careers as practising lawyers for poorly paid positions as University teachers.

The last students slipped into place at the two long trestle tables that ran at right angles to the high table in the main body of the hall, and the buzz of conversation and shuffling died away. After the meal, the tables would be stored along the walls so that the hall could be used for teaching.

The Master said grace and announced that conversation would be allowed that day, but it was to be exclusively in Latin. This was because some students had disputations the following day, and the Master thought academic debate during meals would allow them more practice. The Franciscans frowned disapprovingly and maintained their own silence. It was the usual custom for a Bible scholar to read during the silence of meals for the scholars' spiritual edification, and the new Master's occasional breaks from this tradition were causing friction between the friars and the others.

For Bartholomew and Michael, this afforded an

opportunity to discuss what they would ask the clerks at St Mary's that afternoon.

'How was your lecture?' asked Michael, leaning over Bartholomew to peer suspiciously at a dish of salted beef.

'Grim,' said Bartholomew. He looked down to where his students sat together at the far end of one of the tables. Gray shot him an unpleasant look, and Bartholomew knew his words had been taken seriously.

He picked up a piece of bread and inspected it dubiously. Since the plague, staple crops like barley, oats, and wheat had become scarce. College bread was made with whatever was cheapest and available, which sometimes included flour that was too old even for pig feed. Today, the bread was a grey colour and contained dark brown flecks. It tasted worse than it looked, ancient flour vying for dominance with rancid fat. The salted beef was hard and dry, and there was a large bowl containing lumps of something unidentifiable smeared with a blackish gravy.

Michael gulped down a large goblet of ale and crammed bread into his mouth. He gagged slightly, his eyes watering, and swallowed with difficulty.

'You will choke one day if you do not eat more slowly,' said Bartholomew, not for the first time during their friendship.

'You will be able to save me,' said Michael complacently, reaching for more meat.

Bartholomew chewed some of the hard College bread slowly. The ale, he noticed, was off again, and the salted beef should be thrown away before it poisoned everyone. The thought of poison brought his mind back to the business with the University chest. He had heard of such devices that were designed to kill unwanted meddlers, but never thought he would see one in action. He wondered who had put it there. A thought suddenly struck him and he almost choked on the bread in his eagerness to tell Michael.

Michael pounded on his back, and Bartholomew was reminded that the monk might look fat and unhealthy, but he was a physical force with which to be reckoned.

'It looks as if I will be the one to save you,' Michael said with malicious glee. 'Do not gobble your food, Doctor. You will choke.'

'Buckley,' gasped Bartholomew. 'His hands!'

Michael looked at him blankly. 'What about his hands?'

Bartholomew took a gulp of the bad ale, and resisted the urge to spit it out again. 'I treated Buckley for a skin complaint. He has weeping sores on his hands.'

'Please!' Michael looked disapproving at such matters mentioned at the table.

'He wears gloves, Michael! Not because the disease is infectious, but because the sores are unpleasant to see and he is embarrassed about them. Can you not see?' he cried, drawing the unwanted attention of the Franciscans. He lowered his voice. 'He probably wears his gloves when he unlocks the chest!'

Michael stared at him for a few moments, thinking. 'So,' he said slowly, 'we cannot be certain when this poisonous lock was placed on the chest, since de Wetherset says Buckley is the one who usually opened it, and he has been protected by his gloves. It may have been there for weeks or even months before it did its gruesome work.

Buckley may even have put it there himself knowing that he would be safe from it if he wore gloves.'

Bartholomew thought for a moment. 'Possibly,' he said, 'although I do not think so. First, that was a very small cut on the friar's hand. He may not even have noticed it, which suggests a very concentrated form of poison. It would be a brave man who would risk touching such a lock, even wearing gloves. Second, perhaps the poison was meant for Buckley, if it were known that he was the one who regularly opened the chest, and not the Chancellor.'

Michael rubbed his clean-shaven chin thoughtfully. 'But that would mean that someone so wants Buckley dead that he has been to some trouble to plant that poisonous lock on the chest. I have never bought one of those things, but I warrant they are not cheap.'

'So perhaps Buckley has fled, not because he planted the lock and was responsible for the death of the friar, but because he was in fear of his life. Although,' Bartholomew added practically, 'most men fleeing in fear of their lives do not take tables and chairs with them.'

The conversation was cut short as the Master rose to say grace at the end of the meal, and the Fellows filed in silence from the hall. As soon as they were out, Michael winked at Bartholomew and headed off towards the kitchens to scavenge left-overs. The students clattered noisily down the stairs into the yard, followed by the commoners. There had been ten commoners at Michaelhouse before the plague, but the numbers were now down to four, all old men who had devoted their lives to teaching for the College and were rewarded with board and lodging for the remainder of their lives. Bartholomew went to pay his customary call on one of them, a Cistercian in his seventies called Brother Alban. Alban grinned toothlessly at Bartholomew as the physician rubbed warmed oil into his arthritic elbow, and began to talk in graphic terms about the murder of the prostitutes. As always, Bartholomew was amazed at how the old man managed to acquire his information. He never left the College, yet always seemed to be the first to hear any news from outside. Occasionally, Bartholomew found his love of gossip offensive, but tried to be tolerant since the poor man had little else to do. Although he could still read, Alban's elbow prevented him from producing the splendid illustrated texts for which he had once been famous. Bartholomew occasionally saw the old man leafing wistfully through some of his magnificent work, and felt sorry for him.

'There will be yet more murders,' Alban said with salacious enjoyment. 'Just you see. The Sheriff is less than worthless at tracking this criminal down.'

'And I suppose you know who the murderer is,' asked Bartholomew drily, finding the discussion distasteful. He poured more oil into the palm of his hand, and continued to massage it into the swollen joint.

Alban scowled at him. 'Cheeky beggar,' he muttered. 'No, I do not know who the murderer is, but if I were your age, I would find out!'

'And how would you do that?' said Bartholomew, more to side-track Brother Alban from his lurid and fanciful descriptions of the killer's victims than to solicit a sensible answer.

'I would go to the churches of St John Zachary or All Saints'-next-the-Castle, and I would find out,' said

Alban, tipping his head back and fixing Bartholomew with alert black eyes.

'Why those churches?' said Bartholomew, nonplussed.

The old monk sighed heavily and looked at Bartholomew as he might an errant student. 'Because they have been decommissioned,' he said.

After the plague, the fall in the population meant that there were not enough people to make use of all existing churches, and many had been decommissioned. Some were pulled down, or used as a source of stone; others were locked up to await the day when they would be used again. Two such were St John Zachary and All Saints'-next-the-Castle. At the height of the plague, the entire population north of the river next to the Castle had died. Bartholomew had burned down the pathetic hovels there so that they would not become a continuing source of infection for the town. People claimed that the site of the settlement and All Saints' Church were haunted, and few people went there.

'So?' said Bartholomew, his attention to the conversation wavering as he concentrated on Alban's arm.

'Do you know nothing?' said Alban, more than a touch of gloating in his voice.

Bartholomew flexed the old man's elbow. 'I know that your arm is improving.' He was pleased. The old man could bend it further than he had been able to a week ago, and seemed to be in less pain. Typically, Alban was more interested in his gossip.

'There are works of the Devil performed in the churches,' he crowed, 'and I am willing to wager you will find out from them who is killing these whores.'

'Works of the Devil!' scoffed Bartholomew dismissively. 'Always the excuse for the crimes of people!'

'I mean witchcraft, Matthew,' said Alban primly. 'It goes on in those two churches, and a good many others too, I imagine. I do not need to tell you why. People are wondering why they should pray to a God that did not deliver them from the Death, and so they are turning to other sources of power. It is the same all over England. The murder of these harlots is symptomatic of a sickening society.'

Bartholomew finished his treatment of Alban's arm and left the old man's chatter with some relief. He had heard about the increase in witchcraft, but had given it little thought. Brother Michael had mentioned it once or twice, and it had sparked a fierce debate one night among the Franciscans, but Bartholomew had not imagined that it would occur in Cambridge. Perhaps Alban was right; he often was with his gossip. Bartholomew decided to ask whether Cynric knew anything about it, and, if he did, he would suggest to Sheriff Tulyet that he might consider asking questions about the murders in the churches of St John Zachary and All Saints'-next-the-Castle.

Michael was waiting for him in the yard and reluctantly Bartholomew followed him out of the gates to interview the clerks. The sun was hot and Bartholomew shed his black scholar's tabard and stuffed it in his bag. He knew he could be fined by the Proctors for not wearing it, but considered the comfort of wearing only leggings and a linen shirt worth the possible expense. Brother Michael watched enviously and pulled uncomfortably at the voluminous folds of his own heavy gown.

At St Mary's Church, they saw that the body of the dead friar had been laid out in the Lady Chapel. Bartholomew walked over to it and looked again at the small cut at the base of his thumb that had caused his death. Michael sought out the lay-brother who had locked the church the night before, a mouselike man with eyes that roved in different directions. He was clearly terrified. Bartholomew led him away to talk, but the man's eyes constantly strayed in the direction of the dead friar.

'What time did you lock the church last night?' asked Bartholomew gently.

The man audibly gulped and seemed unable to answer. Michael became impatient.

'Come on! We do not have all day!'

The man's knees gave out and he slid down the base of a pillar and crouched on the floor, casting petrified glances around him. Bartholomew knelt next to him.

'Please try to remember,' he said. 'It is important.'

The man reached out and grabbed his sleeve, pulling him close to whisper in his ear. 'At dusk,' he said, glancing up at the imposing figure of Michael with huge eyes. Michael raised his eyes heavenward, and went to gather together the other clerks with whom they would need to talk, leaving Bartholomew alone to question the lay-brother.

'At dusk,' the man repeated, watching Michael's retreating back with some relief. 'I doused the candles and went to see that the catches on the windows were secure. I put the bar over the sanctuary door as usual, and checked that the tower door was locked.'

'How did you do that?' asked Bartholomew.

The lay-brother made a motion with his hands that

indicated he had given it a good shake. 'Then I made sure the sanctuary light was burning and left. I locked the door behind me and gave the keys to Father Cuthbert.'

'Why did Father Cuthbert not lock the church himself?' asked Bartholomew.

'He does when he can. But he has pains in his ankles sometimes, so I lock up when he cannot walk.'

Bartholomew nodded. He had often treated Father Cuthbert for swollen ankles, partly caused by the great pressure put on them by his excess weight, and partly, Bartholomew suspected, caused by a serious affinity for fortified wines.

'Did you notice anything unusual?' he asked.

The man shook his head hesitantly, and Bartholomew was certain he was lying.

'It would be better if you told me what you know,' he said quietly. He saw sweat start to bead on the man's upper lip. Then, before he could do anything to stop him, the man dived out of Bartholomew's reach and scuttled out of the church. Bartholomew ran after him and saw him disappear into the bushes in the churchyard. He followed, ignoring the way the dense shrubs scratched at his arms. There seemed to be a small path through the undergrowth, faint from lack of use, but a distinct pathway nevertheless. Bartholomew crashed along it and suddenly found himself in one of the dismal alleys that lay between the church and the market-place, his feet skidding in the dust as he came to a halt.

This was one of the poorest areas of the town, a place where no one valuing his safety would consider entering after dark. The houses were no more than rows of wooden frames packed with dried mud. One or two of the better ones had ill-fitting doors to keep out the elements, but most only had a blanket or a piece of leather to serve as a door.

But it was not the homes that caught Bartholomew's eye. The lay-brother had disappeared, but others stood in the alley, a group of scruffy men who moved towards him with a menace that left Bartholomew in no doubt that he was not welcome there. He swallowed and began to back towards the pathway in the bushes, but two of the men moved quickly to block his way.

The alley was silent except for the shuffling of the advancing men. There were at least eight of them, with more joining their ranks by the moment, rough men wearing jerkins of boiled leather and an odd assortment of leggings and shirts. Bartholomew wondered whether he would be able to force his way through them if he took off as fast as he could and made for the market square. A look at the naked hostility on the men's faces told him he would not succeed. These men meant business. Fear mingled with confusion as he wondered why his blundering into the alley had resulted in such instant antagonism.

They moved closer, hemming Bartholomew against one of the shacks. He clenched his fists so that they would not see his hands were shaking; he was nearly overwhelmed with the rank smell of unwashed bodies and breath laden with ale fumes. One of the men made a lunge for his arm and Bartholomew ducked and swung out with his fists blindly. In surrounding him so closely, the men had given themselves little room for movement. Blows were aimed, but lacked force, although judging from several grunts of pain,

Bartholomew's own kicks and punches, wildly thrown, were more effective.

A leg hooked around the back of his knees and sent him sprawling backwards onto the ground, and he knew that it was all over. He twisted sideways to squirm out of the reach of a kick aimed at his head, but was unable to move fast enough to avoid the one to his stomach. The breath rushed out of him and his limbs turned to jelly so that he was unable to move.

'Stop!'

It was the deep voice of a woman that Bartholomew heard through a haze of dust and shuffling feet. The men moved back, and by the time Bartholomew had picked himself up and was steadying himself against a wall, the alleyway was deserted except for the woman.

He looked at her closely. She was dressed in a good quality, but old, woollen dress of faded blue, and her hair, as black as Bartholomew's own, fell in a luxurious shimmering sheet down her back and partly over her face. Her features were strong and bespoke of a formidable strength of character, and although she would not have been called pretty, there was a certain attraction in her clear eyes and steady gaze. As Bartholomew looked more closely, he saw two scars on each jaw, running parallel to each other. Not wishing to make her uncomfortable by staring, he looked away, wondering whether the scars marked her as a member of some religious sect. He had heard that self-mutilation had been common in Europe during the plague years, and it was possible that the scars had been made then.

'Who are you?' he asked.

She looked at him in disbelief and let out a burst of

laughter. 'I save your life, and what do you say? "Thank you"? "I am grateful"? Oh, no! "Who are you?"!' She laughed again, although Bartholomew was too shaken to find the situation amusing. That she obviously held some sway over the band of louts who had just tried to kill him he found of little comfort.

'I am sorry,' he said, contrite. 'Thank you. May I know your name?'

She raised black eyebrows, her blue eyes dancing in merriment. 'All right, then,' she said. 'My name is Janetta of Lincoln. Who are you and what were you doing in our lane?'

'Your lane?' he asked, surprised. 'Since when did the streets of Cambridge become private property?'

The laughter went out of her face. 'You have a careless tongue for a man who has just been delivered from an unpleasant fate. And you did not answer my question. What are you doing here?'

Bartholomew wondered what he could tell her. He thought of the terrified face of the lay-brother and was reluctant to mention him to this curious woman. He also wondered why he had been so foolish as to chase the man when he easily could have found out his address from Father Cuthbert.

'I must have taken a wrong turning,' he said. He looked around him and saw that his bag had gone, containing not only all his medical instruments and some medicines, but his best scholar's tabard too.

Janetta stared at him, her hands on her hips. 'You are an ingrate,' she said. 'I stop them from killing you, and you repay me with rudeness and lies.'

Bartholomew knew that she was right and was sorry.

But, despite the sunshine filtering down into the alley from the cloudless sky, Bartholomew felt something menacing and dark in the alley and longed to be gone. He straightened from where he had been leaning against the wall and took a deep breath.

'I saw a small path leading through the bushes in St Mary's churchyard,' he answered truthfully. 'I followed it and it finished here.'

She continued to stare at him for a few minutes. 'You were following it at quite a pace,' she said. 'I thought you were being pursued by the Devil himself.'

He grimaced and looked up and down the alley to see which way would be the best to leave. She followed his eyes.

'You will only be safe while you are with me,' she said. 'Would you like me to walk with you?'

Bartholomew ran a hand through his hair and gave her a crooked smile. 'Thank you,' he said. 'How is it that you seem to have so much control over these people?'

She gestured that he was to precede her down the alley. Although Bartholomew could see no one, he knew that they were being watched. The silence of the alley was a tangible thing. He glanced at Janetta walking behind him, striding purposefully.

She smiled at him, showing small, white teeth. 'I have taken it on myself to give them a community spirit, a sense of worth and belonging.'

Bartholomew was not sure he knew what she meant, but kept his silence. All he wanted to do was leave the filthy alley and go back to the relative peace and sanity of Michaelhouse. For some reason he could not place, the woman made him uncomfortable. He glanced behind them, and was alarmed to see that a crowd of people had gathered, and was following them down the alley, its silence far more menacing than words could ever be. Janetta also glanced round, but seemed amused.

'They wonder where you are taking me,' she said.

Then they were out of the alley and into the colour and cheerful cacophony of the market-place. Gaudy canopies sheltered the goods of the traders from the hot sun, and everywhere people were calling and shouting. Dogs barked and children howled with laughter at the antics of a juggler. Somewhere, a pig had escaped and was being chased by a number of people, its squeals and their yelling adding to the general chaos.

He turned to Janetta, who still smiled at him.

'Thank you,' he said again. 'And please tell whoever stole my bag that there are some medicines in it that might kill if given to the wrong person. If he or she does not want to give it back to me, the medicines would best be thrown into the river where they will do no harm.'

She nodded slowly, appraising him frankly. 'Do not come here uninvited again, Matthew Bartholomew,' she said.

Without waiting for a response, she turned and strode jauntily back down the alley, leaving Bartholomew staring after her, wondering how she had known his name when he had not told her.

'What happened to you?' exclaimed Michael in horror, looking at Bartholomew's torn and dirty clothes.

Bartholomew took his arm and led him back through the churchyard to the bushes where he had followed the lay-brother. But however hard he looked, he could not find the path. It simply was not there. He stood back, bewildered.

'What is going on, Matt?' asked Michael impatiently. 'What have you been doing? You look as though you have been in a fight.'

Bartholomew explained what had happened and sat on a tree-stump in the shade of the church while Michael conducted his own search of the bushes.

'Are you sure there was a path?' he asked doubtfully.

'Of course I am!' Bartholomew snapped. He leaned forward and rested his head in his hands. 'I am sorry, Michael. It was a nasty experience and it has made me irritable.'

Michael patted his shoulder. 'Tell me again about this woman. Pretty, you say?' He perched on the tree-stump next to the physician.

Bartholomew regarded him through narrowed eyes and wondered, not for the first time, whether Michael was really the kind of man who should have been allowed to take a vow of chastity.

'Tell me what you discovered from the clerks,' he said, to change the subject.

'They said they had noticed the friar praying in the church for the last three days. Some of them spoke to him, and he said he was travelling from London to Huntingdon and had stopped here for a few days to rest and pray. They did not ask why he was travelling. They also do not know exactly where he came from in London. He seemed pleasant, friendly and polite, and none of them thought it strange that he should spend so much time in this church.'

'Is that all?' asked Bartholomew. Michael nodded.

'Then we are really no further forward. We still do not know who he was or why he was in the tower, except that he probably travelled some distance to be there. And that poor lay-brother was terrified of something, and I did not like the atmosphere in that shabby alleyway.'

'You should not frequent such places, then,' said Michael. 'Although I would have imagined you would be used to them by now.'

'I thought I was,' said Bartholomew. He thought he knew most of the poorest parts of town through his patients, but had not been called to the alleys behind the market square since the plague. Like the little settlement by the castle, the people who lived in the hovels near the Market Square had either died or moved to occupy better homes when others died.

He and Michael sat in companionable silence for a few moments and then Michael stood. 'Stay here,' he said. 'I will send Cynric back with your spare tabard. If Alcote sees you dirty and dishevelled, he will fine you on the spot, and now you need to buy a new tabard you cannot afford it.'

He ambled off, and Bartholomew leaned back wearily. Now that the excitement had worn off, he felt tired and sick. He wondered whether everything fitted together – the dead friar, the poisoned lock, the disappearing lay-brother and Vice-Chancellor, the murdered women, and the sinister alley – or whether they were all independent incidents that just happened to have involved him. He felt more than a little angry at the Chancellor. He wanted to teach and to practise medicine, not to become involved in some nasty plot where women and friars were killed, and that forced him to exhume dead clerks.

He squinted up and watched the leaves blowing in the breeze, making changing pools of light over the tombstones in the graveyard. He could hear the distant racket from the market-place, while in the church some friars were chanting Terce.

'What are you thinking of, getting into all this trouble without me?' came a familiar voice. Bartholomew opened his eyes and smiled at the Welshman with Michael behind him. Cynric took a strange delight in the kind of cloak-and-dagger activity that Bartholomew deplored. He was more friend than servant, and had been with Bartholomew since he had been appointed to teach in Cambridge. As Bartholomew explained what had happened, Cynric made no attempt to conceal his disdain for Bartholomew's ineptitude in handling the situation.

While Bartholomew donned his tabard to hide his damaged clothes and Michael sat on the tree stump, Cynric·went to see if he could find the path. After a few minutes, he came back to sit next to Michael, eyes narrowed against the sun.

'The path is there sure enough,' said Cynric. 'Small twigs are broken and the grass is bruised. Someone must have come up the alley and arranged the bushes so that the path is hidden. I will come back later and explore it.'

'No, you will not,' said Bartholomew firmly. 'Whoever hid it did so for a reason, and I am not sure I want to know why. I have a feeling the lay-brother made a grave error in using that path and I was probably lucky not to have been killed for following him. Let it be, Cynric.'

Cynric looked disappointed, but nodded his agree-ment. 'But next time you go out, boy, make sure I go with you. Old Cynric is far better at these things than you are.'

It would not be too difficult to be better at 'these things' than he was, Bartholomew thought wryly, but Cynric was right. He would never have blundered blindly into the alley as Bartholomew had done.

Michael stood and rubbed his hands together. 'We have had a difficult day,' he announced. 'I propose we go and enjoy ourselves at the Fair.'

Barnwell Causeway, the road that led from the town to the fields in which the Fair was held, was thronged with people. Men with huge trays of pastries and pies competed with each other for trade, while water-sellers left damp patches on the road as the river-water they carried in their buckets slopped over the sides. Beggars lined the route, sitting at the sides of the road and displaying sores and wounds to any who would look. Some were soldiers from the wars in France, once England's heroes, now quietly ignored. The Sheriff's men elbowed their way through the crowd, asking if anyone had witnessed the murder of a potter the night before.

Michael shook his head to the sergeant's enquiry. 'The roads are becoming more and more dangerous after dark,' he remarked, as the sergeant repeated his enquiry to a group of noisy apprentices walking behind them. 'Safe enough now with all these folk, but deadly to any foolish enough to wander at night.'

Cynric made a darting movement, and there was a

yowl of pain from a scruffy man wearing a brown cloak.

'Not even safe in daylight,' said Cynric, handing Michael's purse back to him, and watching the pickpocket scamper away down the road clutching his arm.

Michael grimaced, and tucked the purse down the front of his habit. He brightened as the colourful canopies of the Fair booths came into sight, and stopped to look. War-horses pounded up and down a narrow strip near the river as their owners showed off their equestrian skills. Huge fires with whole pigs and sheep roasting over them sent delicious smells to mingle with the scent of manure and sweaty bodies. And everywhere there was noise: animals bleated and bellowed, vendors yelled about their wares, children shrieked and laughed, and musicians added their part to the general cacophony.

Bartholomew followed Michael and Cynric into the mêlée, shaking off an insistent baker who was trying to sell him apple pastries crawling with flies. Bartholomew smiled at the people he knew – rich merchants in their finery, black-garbed scholars, and the poorest of his patients who eyed the wealth around them with jealous eyes. He saw the Junior Proctor, Alric Jonstan, and two of his beadles talking together near a stall displaying neatly-stacked fruit.

Jonstan hailed him pleasantly, and sent his beadles to disperse a rowdy group of scholars who were watching a mystery play nearby. He rubbed a hand across his face, and beckoned Bartholomew and Michael behind the fruit stall to a quieter part of the Fair. He sat on a wooden bench, and summoned a brewer to bring them some ale.

'This is the finest ale in England,' he said, closing his eyes and taking a long draught with obvious pleasure. The brewer smiled, gratified, and set the remaining tankards on the table.

Jonstan held up his hand. 'As a Proctor, I should not be setting the example of sitting in an ale tent, but I have been working since I left St Mary's this morning, and even the most dedicated of men needs sustenance.'

'Excellent ale,' said Michael appraisingly, raising his empty tankard to be refilled, and wiping foam from his mouth. 'And we are all well-enough hidden here, I think.'

'Master Harling would not think so,' said Jonstan with a wry smile. Bartholomew could well-believe it of the dour Physwick Hostel scholar. 'But what did you discover about this friar?'

Michael set his tankard down, and rubbed his sleeve across his mouth. 'Nothing other than what we told you this morning. But if you have been here all day, perhaps you do not know that Master Buckley seems to have disappeared.'

'Disappeared?' echoed Jonstan, stunned. 'But he is coming to dine with me and my mother this evening.'

'I doubt he will come,' said Michael. 'But if he does, you might mention that the Chancellor would like to see him, and the Warden of King's Hall would like his tables back.'

Jonstan stared at him and shook his head slowly as Michael described Buckley's empty room.

'Where will you start to sort out this mess?' he asked, looking from Michael to Bartholomew.

'I would rather not start at all,' said Bartholomew fervently. 'I would sooner teach.'

Jonstan pulled a sympathetic face. 'I can understand that,' he said. 'I taught law before I became a Proctor, but have done no teaching since. I moved out of Physwick Hostel and bought a house in Shoemaker Row, so that my mother could keep house for me to allow more time for my duties. I wish Harling and I could help you with this business, but I think we will be too busy with the Fair. Hot weather, cheap ale, and gangs of students are a lethal combination, and we will be hard-pressed to keep the peace as it is.'

He stood suddenly as a student reeled towards him, arm-in-arm with a golden-haired woman from one of the taverns. The student saw the Proctor, released the woman and fled, all signs of drunkenness disappearing as quickly as if Jonstan had dashed a bucket of cold water over him. The woman looked around, bewildered, and Jonstan sat again with a smile.

'I wish all my duties were as easy as that,' he said.

'There was another prostitute murder,' said Bartholomew.

'I heard about that,' said Jonstan. He frowned. 'Does it seem to you that there are more prostitutes now than before the Death?'

'Inevitably,' said Bartholomew, sipping the cool ale. 'Some women lost their families in the plague, and it is one way in which they can make enough money to live.'

'There are other ways, Doctor,' said Jonstan primly. 'They could sew or cook.'

'Possibly,' said Bartholomew, watching an argument

develop into a fight between a buxom matron and a man selling rabbit furs. 'But all these travelling labourers mean that life as a prostitute is as well paid and secure as any occupation these days.'

'But it is sinful,' persisted Jonstan, his round blue eyes earnest. 'The plague was a sign from God that we should amend our wicked ways, and yet there are more prostitutes now than before. How can they fail to heed His warning?'

Bartholomew had heard these arguments before: the plague had been regarded as a punishment for all manner of wickedness – crime, the war with France, violation of the Sabbath, blasphemy, not fasting on Fridays, usury, adultery. Many people believed the plague was but a warning, and it was only a matter of time before it returned to kill all with evil in their hearts.

After a while, enjoying the ale and the warmth of the sun, he rose to leave. The others followed suit, and they parted from Jonstan. Moments later, Bartholomew felt a hand on his shoulder, and turned to see his brother-in-law, Oswald Stanmore, beaming at him.

Bartholomew returned his smile, and asked Stanmore how his business was faring.

'Excellent,' said Stanmore, his smile widening further still. 'I have sold almost all the cloth I had stored in my warehouse, and deposits have been made on the next shipment due to arrive within two days.'

'Has the Sheriff found the men who stole your cloth yet?' asked Bartholomew, referring to an incident in which two of Stanmore's carts were attacked and plundered on the London road.

Stanmore frowned. 'He has not. And I am unimpressed

with what he is doing to get to the bottom of the matter.'

Bartholomew raised his eyebrows. Sheriffs were seldom popular, but Richard Tulyet had recently excelled at making himself an object of dislike. First the townspeople complained about his lack of progress on the murders of the women, and now Stanmore about his stolen cloth.

Stanmore sighed. 'I know Tulyet has his hands full with the whore murders,' he said, 'but the town will suffer if he does not look into the attack on my goods: merchants will not come here if the roads are dangerous.'

'There was another murder this morning,' said Bartholomew, to divert Stanmore from the lecture on the importance of safe travel and trade he was about to give.

Stanmore nodded. 'It was all the talk at the Fair today,' he said. 'Some womenfolk are thinking of leaving early because of it.' He leaned towards Bartholomew so that he would not be overheard. 'I heard a rumour today that one of the guilds might look into this prostitute business, since Tulyet will not.'

'Which guild?' asked Bartholomew, concerned. 'Witch-hunters who will accuse any man out alone after curfew?'

'No, no,' said Stanmore. 'They call themselves the Guild of the Holy Trinity, and there are priests and monks among their number. It is nothing sinister, but a group of honest men who are concerned that sin and crime have increased since the Death.'

Bartholomew looked dubious, and Stanmore shrugged. 'There are many who feel as they do,' he said. 'These are not religious fanatics sniffing out heresy, like your Father

William, but plain folk who care about the changes that have occurred since the Death.' When Bartholomew failed to look convinced, Stanmore threw up his hands in despair. 'Look at the evidence in front of you! A tiny place like Cambridge, and we have a maniac who kills women in the dead of night, and it is not even safe for a cart of cloth to travel from London.'

'But the attack was miles away!' protested Bartholomew. 'You cannot blame Cambridge for what happened near London.'

'It was not near London, it was at Saffron Walden,' said Stanmore haughtily. 'A mere fifteen miles away.' He scratched at his chin. 'It is an odd business. I expected that the cloth would reappear at the Fair, sold by the thieves, but although I have had my apprentices scour the area, not so much as a thread of it has appeared.'

'Perhaps it was stolen for personal use,' said Bartholomew.

Stanmore looked impatient. 'This is finest quality worsted, Matt. You do not use such cloth to sew any old garment.'

Bartholomew shrugged. 'Perhaps the thieves anticipated you would look for it here, and plan to sell it elsewhere.'

'They must,' said Stanmore. 'But it is a wretched nuisance. I had to send that cloth to London to be dyed since de Belem's prices are so extortionate. So, not only do I lose the cloth, I have the expense of dyeing and transport. It is a bad time to be a merchant: labour prices are sky-high, fewer dyers and weavers mean that they can charge what they will because there is no competition, and, on top of all that, it is not safe to transport goods.'

'But most of that has always been true,' said Bartholomew, to placate the agitated draper.

'Not like this,' said Stanmore bitterly. 'English cloth and English wool are the finest in the world. But there are fewer shepherds to tend the sheep, less wool available for weaving, fewer weavers to weave it . . .'

'And fewer merchants to sell it,' interrupted Bartholomew, laughing. 'Come, Oswald! It is not all bad. You are not in the gutters yet!'

Stanmore smiled reluctantly. 'I suppose business at the Fair has been good,' he admitted. He turned to watch the antics of a small group of tumblers from Spain, who leapt, somersaulted, and cartwheeled in a flurry of red jackets and blue leggings. Bartholomew left him to admire the acrobats, and wandered off alone. He watched a troop of players perform the mystery play about Adam and Eve to a large and good-humoured crowd. Nearby, other players, with a far smaller audience, enacted scenes from the plague, claiming that the disease would come again unless wicked ways were mended. Bartholomew thought about the Guild of the Holy Trinity, and wondered if the few people watching and nodding sagely at the play's message were its members.

By the time Bartholomew met Michael and Cynric again, the daylight was fading, and traders were packing up. Many would stay, cooking stews on open fires, while others would leave an apprentice to guard their goods and walk back into Cambridge to sleep in taverns and brothels. The Fair was only half-way through, and already surrounding fields and coppices had been stripped of wood for the fires that provided warmth and hot food.

Bartholomew, Cynric, and Michael joined a group of

exhausted traders to walk the short distance back to Cambridge. By mutual consent, they waited until there were about twenty people. Many traders carried the day's takings to be deposited with a money-lender, or hidden in a secure place, and robberies along the dark stretch of road were not uncommon during the Fair. Stanmore and his steward Hugh, armed with a crossbow, joined the group, and they set off, some singing a bawdy tavern song despite their weariness.

Stanmore continued his dismal analysis on the safety of roads, which had Bartholomew glancing nervously over his shoulder. But despite Stanmore's gloom, they arrived at Michaelhouse without mishap, where Michael went to the kitchen for something to eat, and Bartholomew went straight to bed.

Early the next morning, he was awoken by an insistent knocking on his door, and Eli, the bow-legged College steward, burst in.

'Doctor Bartholomew!' he gasped. 'You must come! There is a girl dying in our orchard.'

CHAPTER 3

ELI LED THE WAY TO THE ORCHARD THAT LAY behind the kitchen. Agatha knelt in the long grass, leaning over someone lying on the ground. At a discreet distance, Master Kenyngham stood with Michael, Alcote, Cynric, and Piers Hesselwell.

As Bartholomew approached, he saw the bloodstained sheet that Agatha had used to cover the girl and knew what to expect. Yet another murder of a prostitute, except that this time the murder had not been in a churchyard, but on College property. As he knelt next to her, Agatha caught his wrist, her strong face unusually white. She glanced around to ensure she could not be overheard.

'Only you and I know about this, Matthew,' she said. 'We could keep it that way.'

He gazed at her, bewildered, but she would say no more, and Bartholomew turned his attention to the girl. He caught his breath in horror as he saw who lay beneath the sheet, and stared at Agatha in shock. She touched his arm and gestured at the figure on the ground, to bring his attention back to Frances de Belem. An attempt had been made to cut her throat, but, although there was a nasty wound there, it had failed to give her a quick

83

death. Bartholomew had no idea how long she had been in the orchard in this condition. Her body was cold, but he could not tell whether it was from the loss of blood, or from lying in the wet grass. Her eyes were closed and blood bubbled through her white lips as she breathed.

Bartholomew sent Cynric to fetch a sense-dulling potion that he kept in a locked chest in the chamber adjacent to his own room. While Cynric was gone, Kenyngham gave last rites. When he had finished, Bartholomew dripped some of the powerful syrup between her teeth, but hoped that she would not regain consciousness to need it. Frances's breathing grew more laboured, and Michael and Alcote knelt, and began intoning prayers of the dying.

Just when Bartholomew thought she would slip away, she opened her eyes and looked at him. Agatha took her hand and crooned comfortingly, while Bartholomew motioned to the clerics to keep their voices down. He leaned close to her to hear what she was trying to whisper.

'I am sorry for what I asked you to do,' she said, her voice little more than a breath.

'No harm was done,' Bartholomew said. 'But who did this to you?'

'It was not a man,' she said in a low voice, her eyes filling with tears. Her hand fluttered to a silver cross she wore around her neck.

When Bartholomew looked from the cross to her face, she was dead. He felt for a life beat, put his cheek close to her mouth to see if he could detect breathing, and covered her with the sheet.

Agatha leaned towards him. 'Will you condemn her

as a suicide? Or will you keep silent about what she told us yesterday?'

Before replying, Bartholomew pulled the sheet from her feet. She wore no shoes and there was the small circle on her left foot. Frances de Belem was too wealthy to go without shoes, so someone must have taken them. He covered her again, and glanced at Michael. Michael faltered in his prayers as he saw what Bartholomew was doing, and Bartholomew saw Piers Hesselwell look at them strangely as he noticed the exchange.

'She was no suicide, Agatha,' he said softly. 'She was murdered.'

'What?' queried Agatha loudly. 'Here in Michaelhouse? How do you know?'

'It is not easy to commit suicide by cutting your own throat,' said Bartholomew. And there were the circle on her foot and the missing shoes to consider, he thought.

Agatha hastily crossed herself. She let out a great sigh and muttered something about fetching the porters. Bartholomew watched her go, the usual aggressive buoyancy gone from her step. Kenyngham and the other Fellows came to form a circle around the dead girl.

'Does anyone know who she was?' Kenyngham asked.

'Frances de Belem,' said Bartholomew, looking up at him.

'The merchant's daughter?' queried Alcote, and then smirked. 'Ah, yes. I had forgotten how you would know that,' he added nastily.

The Master raised his eyebrows and Alcote continued, 'Matthew's sister married well, and her husband is Sir

Oswald Stanmore, who owns the large building next to Sir Reginald's house. That is how Matthew knows the daughters of wealthy merchants.'

Bartholomew saw Alcote exchange smug looks with Hesselwell. Was Alcote trying to curry favour with the new Master to advance his own career? If so, his tale-telling had failed to impress Kenyngham, who smiled benignly at Bartholomew and touched him lightly on the head.

'Then I am afraid, Matthew, that you are probably the best man to tell her family what has happened,' he said. 'Does anyone know how she came to be here?'

Vacant looks answered his question until Eli spoke up. 'Mistress Agatha found her here when she came to hang out the washing. She called for me, and I fetched you and the others.'

Bartholomew looked around at the grass. A trail of blood leading to a spot some distance away indicated that Frances had dragged herself from one place to another, perhaps in the hope of reaching Michaelhouse for help. It had dried, suggesting that she had probably been in the orchard for several hours, and perhaps even since the night before.

'Thank you, Eli,' said Kenyngham, 'but that does not explain how she came to be here in the first place. I doubt that she could have entered through the College, which means that she must have come in through the door that leads out to the lane.'

Cynric had already looked. 'The gate is open,' he said. 'I bar it myself at dusk each night, and so someone inside must have opened it between dusk last night and now.'

'Well,' said the Master, looking round at his Fellows, 'has anyone used the back gate this morning?'

There was silence as the Fellows shook their heads and looked at each other blankly.

'I will ask the students,' said Kenyngham. 'Now, I suggest we return to our duties. Eli and Cynric, take Mistress de Belem to the church with the porters. Master Hesselwell, take Brother Michael to his room: he looks ill. Master Alcote, I would like you to inform the Sheriff and the Chancellor.' As they scurried to do his bidding, he turned to Bartholomew.

'Matthew, I do not envy you your task. Would you like me to come with you?'

Bartholomew thanked him, but felt it was a duty he should perform alone. On his way to Milne Street, he met Stanmore, already heading for the Fair with his apprentices. His good humour evaporated when he learned Bartholomew's news.

'Heaven help us,' he said softly. He grabbed Bartholomew's arm. 'Let me come with you. Reginald and I have had our differences, but he may need me now.'

It was a long time before Bartholomew felt he could leave de Belem's house. Sir Reginald was working in the dim morning light in his solar. He stood when Bartholomew and Stanmore were shown in and came to greet them, surprised but courteous. He was a man in his early fifties, powerfully built, with thick hair that showed no trace of grey. Bartholomew had been with his wife when she had died during the plague a little over a year before.

De Belem stared in disbelief when Bartholomew told him why they had come, and then shook his head firmly.

'The killer takes whores,' he said. 'Frances was not a whore. You are mistaken: it is not her.'

Bartholomew, feeling wretched, met his eyes. 'I am not mistaken,' he said gently.

'But she is not a whore!' protested de Belem.

'The murderer did not know that,' said Stanmore, with quiet reason. 'It was probably dark, and he saw a girl in the streets alone. He must have jumped to the wrong conclusion.'

'How was she killed?' de Belem demanded suddenly, looking at Bartholomew. 'You were with her when she died, you say?'

'With a knife,' said Bartholomew, reluctant to go into detail while de Belem still dealt with the shock of his news.

'Her throat cut?' persisted de Belem.

Bartholomew nodded. There was no point in denying it if de Belem already knew from local gossip.

'Did she say anything?' said de Belem, ashen-faced. 'Was she aware of what had happened to her?'

Bartholomew raised his hands in a gesture of uncertainty. 'What she said made no sense,' he said. 'I had given her some syrup to dull her senses and she was probably delirious.'

'What did she say?' asked de Belem, his voice unsteady.

'That whoever killed her was not a man,' said Bartholomew reluctantly.

De Belem looked bewildered and shook his head slowly, as if trying to clear it. 'What does that mean?' he said. 'What was it? An animal? A devil?'

Bartholomew could think of nothing to say. The wound

on her throat had been inflicted by a knife, of that he was certain, and Frances's killer was unquestionably human. Was Brother Alban right, and were the murders of the women part of some satanic ritual?

'Do you have any ideas about why Frances may have been killed?' asked Bartholomew. 'Did she have any arguments with anyone recently?'

De Belem shook his head again, helplessly. 'We were not close,' he said, 'although I loved her dearly. Since my wife died, I have immersed myself in my work, and left her to her own devices. But I can think of no one who meant her harm.'

He paused and put his head in his hands. Stanmore reached out and patted his shoulder.

'Will you catch him for me?' de Belem asked suddenly, looking intently at Bartholomew. 'Will you catch the madman who killed my child?'

Bartholomew was startled. 'That is the Sheriff's duty,' he said.

De Belem stood abruptly and gazed down at him. 'The Sheriff is doing nothing to investigate the deaths of the other women. I know you are looking into the dead man found in the University chest. Give that up, and find out who murdered my Frances. I will pay you well.'

'I cannot,' said Bartholomew, disconcerted that his commission for the Chancellor seemed to be common knowledge. 'It is not only beyond my authority, it is beyond my capabilities.'

'You must,' said de Belem, seizing Bartholomew's shoulder with such force he winced. 'Or my daughter's death will go unavenged. The Sheriff will do nothing!'

'But how? It is not my affair!' protested Bartholomew.

'Please!' cried de Belem, grasping Bartholomew harder still. 'You and Brother Michael uncovered those murders last year. You will be my only hope!'

Bartholomew thought about Frances's unborn child, and was sorry that her last days had been tainted by unhappiness. She might have been his wife, had he not disobeyed Stanmore's wishes and chosen his own path.

'I will try,' he said finally. 'But anything I discover I will have to pass to the Sheriff.'

'No!' cried de Belem, virtually flinging Bartholomew away from him in his vehemence. 'Tell the Chancellor, or even the Bishop, if you must. But not the Sheriff! He would merely take your information and do nothing with it.'

Bartholomew made him sit down. 'There is no need to be arguing about whom we should inform when, as yet, we have nothing to tell,' he said soothingly.

De Belem relaxed a little, his hands dangling loosely between his knees.

'Why was Frances out alone?' said Bartholomew. 'She must have known that it is not safe at any time, but especially so with this killer at large.'

De Belem stared at him. 'She was a religious girl. She was probably going to mass.'

Bartholomew tried not to appear sceptical, and wondered if he had made a better job of it than Stanmore, who looked openly incredulous.

De Belem saw their expressions and sighed. 'She is gone,' he said to Stanmore. 'What good will come of questioning her actions now? Since her husband died, she has grown wild. I am too busy a man to be constantly chasing after an errant daughter.'

'Do you know why she might have been in Michaelhouse's grounds?' asked Bartholomew.

De Belem shook his head wearily. 'She must have been meeting someone.'

'Do you know who?' asked Bartholomew. He saw de Belem hesitate, but then seem to make up his mind.

'I do not want this to become common knowledge, but I think Frances had a lover. She did not stay out all night – even I could not countenance that – but she did leave early in the morning on occasions. Perhaps she had fallen for an apprentice somewhere, and joined him for his early morning chores.'

Or perhaps she had fallen in love with a scholar, thought Bartholomew, and met him as soon as the gates were opened to allow the academics out for church. He thought about the area where she died. There was Michaelhouse, of course, and opposite there was Physwick Hostel. King's Hall was a short distance to the north, while Garret Hostel, Clare College, Gonville Hall, and Trinity Hall were to the south. But Michaelhouse and Physwick Hostel were the closest.

It seemed de Belem could tell them no more, and they waited with him until the Sheriff's deputy arrived. De Belem agreed to speak to him only reluctantly. Bartholomew was nervous of leaving de Belem with the Sheriff's man in view of the merchant's evident contempt for the Sheriff's competence, but, as he pondered, de Belem's sister arrived full of concern and sympathy, and Bartholomew knew she would prevent any misunderstandings.

They stopped at Stanmore's business premises next door, before Stanmore left for the Fair and Bartholomew returned to his teaching duties at Michaelhouse. Stanmore ordered that a fire be built in the solar, for, despite the fact that it was summer, the day seemed chilly. He and Bartholomew sat in front of the flames and sipped some mulled ale.

'Have you heard about witchcraft being on the increase in Cambridge?' Bartholomew asked, partly to change the subject from Frances and partly for information. Stanmore had a network of informants who kept him up to date with the various happenings in the town.

'There have been rumours, yes,' said Stanmore. 'A religion where fornication, drunkenness, and violent acts are regarded as acceptable will have a certain appeal to people frustrated with being urged to practise moderation and told that the injustices of their lives are God's will.' He stared into the fire.

'What about in Cambridge?' Bartholomew tried to get comfortable on the wooden chair.

'I have heard that lights have been seen moving about All Saints' Church in the depths of the night. Many superstitious people think that part of the town is haunted. If you had not burned down those houses with the people still in them, the site of that settlement would not be so feared.'

'The people were dead, Oswald!' said Bartholomew, angry at the misrepresentation of fact. 'And no one wanted the task of taking the bodies to bury them in the plague pit! What would you have done? Left them there to rot and further infect the town?'

'Easy now,' said Stanmore, startled at his outburst. 'I am only telling you what people think, and you did ask. What is your interest in witchcraft?'

'None, really,' said Bartholomew, still annoyed. 'Old Brother Alban was rattling on about it and he thought it may have had something to do with the deaths of these women.'

Stanmore thought for a moment. 'It is possible, I suppose. I will ask my people to keep their ears open and will contact you if they hear anything.' He stood as Bartholomew rose to leave. 'Be careful, Matt. The rumours about these covens are unpleasant. In London, some fiend takes children from their cribs at night.'

'I am a little too old to be taken from my crib,' said Bartholomew, relenting from his irritation and laughing.

Stanmore laughed too. 'Your sister does not think so. You must visit her soon, Matt. She is lonely, and would like to see you.'

As Bartholomew walked back towards Michaelhouse, he thought about Frances. Was the father of her child the man who had killed her? And if so, did this mean that he was also the killer of the other women? Had they also been pregnant by him? He shook his head. That was absurd: the other women had been prostitutes who had probably known how to prevent pregnancy, as far as that was possible. Hilde's sister had not done very well, it seemed. But what had Frances's dying words – 'not a man' – meant? Was her death connected with the witchcraft that seemed to be on the increase all over the country? Why did so many people believe the Sheriff was reluctant to investigate? Bartholomew rubbed his chin thoughtfully. Was it possible he was involved in witchcraft too, and already knew the identity of the killer whom he had allowed to escape? Bartholomew ran a hand through his hair in frustration. The killer could be anyone! Hundreds of people had converged upon Cambridge for the Fair: any of them could be responsible. The more he thought about it, the more he realised he had set himself an impossible task by agreeing to help de Belem.

Bartholomew worked hard that morning, painstakingly discussing Dioscorides's text on opiates and how they might be used to ease a variety of ailments. After dinner he gave Gray and Bulbeck mock disputations to test their knowledge of Hippocrates and Galen, and then went to visit three different people who had contracted summer ague, a shivering fever that struck many people in the sweltering months of July and August. It was late by the time he had seen his last case, and the sun had already set.

He walked briskly through the dark streets towards Michaelhouse. Alcote, who had taken on unofficial duties as College policeman, saw to it that the gates were locked at dusk. Although Bartholomew had the Master's permission to answer summonses from patients after the curfew, he knew it was not an arrangement approved by the other Fellows, who considered that it set a bad example to the students. Bartholomew abused the privilege at times, despite knowing that it would take very little for the Fellows to exert sufficient pressure on Kenyngham to withdraw his limited freedom. Because of this, he usually used the back gate: if Cynric knew he was late, he left it unbarred.

As expected, the front gates were locked, and the porter on duty was the miserable Walter, who was paid a half-penny for every late scholar whose name he could report to Alcote. Bartholomew slipped off down the shadows in St Michael's Lane towards the back gate, to see if Cynric had left it open.

As he neared the gate, he saw a tiny movement, and instinctively melted further into the shadows at the side of the road. He strained his eyes in the darkness, trying to distinguish between the swaying of spindly bramble branches in the night breeze, and movements that might be more sinister.

A shadow glided silently from the shelter of one tree to another and he heard a soft, but unmistakable, cough. He pressed further into the shadows and cursed softly. The Master must have asked one of the Proctors to keep a watch on the gate. He stood for a moment and considered. He would have to retrace his steps, go along the High Street, and cut back through the Austin Canons' land that backed onto Michaelhouse. Cynric had shown him a portion of the wall that was in poor repair, where a desperate scholar might climb if both gates were locked.

Feeling absurd that he, a doctor of the University, should be sneaking around at night like some errant undergraduate, he made his way through the dark streets and prowled along the back of the College until he found the crumbling wall. He scrambled up it, wondering how many of his students had done the same, and hoping he would not meet any of them now.

Once on top of the wall, he walked along it until he came to a section where large compost heaps made the jump down the other side less hazardous. He crouched on the wall and let himself drop, landing in an undignified tumble that finished in a mound of cut grass. Swearing softly to himself, and trying in vain to brush the grass from his tabard, he made his way stealthily towards the kitchen door, keeping in the shadows as he had seen Cynric do. As he approached the bakery, he thought he saw something move. He froze and, for the second time that night, pressed further back into the shadows to watch.

Sure enough, someone was there. At first he thought it was Cynric, so soundlessly did the figure move, but it was a bigger person than Cynric. Bartholomew peered into the darkness, trying to gain some clue to the intruder's identity as he moved steadily towards the orchard to the place where Frances de Belem had died. A tiny light flared as a candle was lit. Leaving the shadows of the bakery wall, Bartholomew crept carefully towards the laundry, a long wooden building that housed the servants on its upper floor. The intruder appeared to be searching for something. Bartholomew's stomach tightened. Could it be the murderer, the monster whom Frances had said was not a man, searching for some vital clue to his identity that he had mislaid or lost as he killed her?

He leapt with fright as a hand was clapped over his mouth and held there firmly to prevent him from calling out. He struggled violently, stopping only when he felt the sharp prick of a knife against his throat.

'Hush!' came Cynric's voice. Bartholomew twisted round in disbelief. 'Sorry, boy,' the Welshman whispered, holding up the dagger. 'It was the only way I could get you to stop struggling long enough to let you know it was me.' He slipped his knife back into his belt and poked his head round the corner to watch the figure with the candle.

As Cynric observed, Bartholomew sank onto the grass to try to regain his composure.

'Hsst!' Cynric was off, gesturing for Bartholomew to follow. Still carrying the candle, the figure left the orchard and began to move down the path that led to the back gate. Cynric motioned for Bartholomew to watch from the wall that ran down one side of the vegetable gardens, while he moved like a ghost through the bulrushes that fringed the fish-ponds on the other side.

Bartholomew saw the figure reach out to open the door. He thought of Frances de Belem and the others with their throats cut by a maniac, and made his decision: the person must not be allowed to escape! He abandoned his hiding place and made for the gate at a run. The figure glanced round in shock, and began urgently to heave at the gate. It flung open just as Bartholomew reached the intruder and grabbed him. The figure span round with a cry of horror and drew a knife. Bartholomew knocked it from his hand, struggling to wrench the hood from the intruder's face.

At that moment the door was thrown inwards with such force that Cynric, who was closing it to prevent the intruder's escape, was knocked off his feet. At the same time, it burst into flames and a gigantic figure swathed in black leapt through it with an unearthly howl.

Bartholomew was aware of yellow teeth and glittering eyes as the huge shape swept towards where he still held the first intruder. His hands were wrenched from his captive as the enormous shape pounced on him, swinging him round so that he lost his footing and went sprawling onto the ground. He saw the first intruder disappear through the door, and tried to scramble after him, his feet slipping and sliding on the wet grass. He felt himself grabbed, and a great weight dropped onto his chest as massive hands clawed for his throat. The burning door crackled and blazed, and Bartholomew saw, in the light from the flames, that his attacker wore a red hood with holes for eyes and mouth.

As the huge hands tightened around his throat, Bartholomew was seized by panic. He tried to ram the heel of his hand under the man's nose and was horrified to feel teeth take a grip on his fingers and bite down hard. He jerked upwards with his knees as hard as he could and heard the man grunt with pain, but his teeth were still firmly clamped on Bartholomew's hand.

He was vaguely aware of Cynric leaping onto the man's back and thought he heard urgent shouting from the lane. The man shook Cynric away and headed towards the gate. Bartholomew struggled to his feet, hoping at least for a glimpse of the first intruder's face. Seeing him follow, the huge man turned to fight. Bartholomew picked up a handful of dusty soil and flung it into the man's face. The giant bellowed with rage and turned to stumble blindly towards the lane. Bartholomew followed, but the big man turned and thrust him away with such force that Bartholomew went tumbling head over heels backwards into the raspberry canes.

By the time Bartholomew's head had stopped spinning, the breeze in the trees and a small crackle from the burned gate were the only sounds to be heard. Bartholomew tensed as he saw a dark shape moving towards him, and then relaxed again as he saw it was Cynric.

'Are you hurt?' he whispered. Cynric shook his

head and went to look out of the still-smouldering gateway. After a few moments, he came back to sit with Bartholomew, who was trying to flex the fingers of his bitten hand.

'There is no one there, attacker or otherwise,' said Cynric unsteadily. 'What happened, exactly?'

'I am not sure,' Bartholomew replied, equally shaken. 'What were you doing in the orchard?'

'Coming to unbar the door for you. Then I heard you trampling like a herd of pigs along by the bakery and that figure in the orchard.'

Bartholomew ignored the unflattering reference to his attempt at stealth and Cynric continued. 'What was that thing that we fought? Did you see its face? It was bright red, like the Devil's.' He gripped Bartholomew's arm suddenly. 'Do you think it was the killer of Frances de Belem? She said the person who attacked her was not a man! Do you think it was the Devil?'

'Devil!' snorted Bartholomew. 'If that were the Devil, he would not have needed a gate to enter. That was a person, Cynric, wearing a red hood.'

'But how did a person make the gate burst into flames?'

'We will look tomorrow,' said Bartholomew, climbing wearily to his feet. 'It is too dark now. What shall we do about the gate?'

'I will slip out and inform the Proctor, and ask him to post a guard on the door.' Cynric looked at Bartholomew's hand. 'Did he bite you? Normal men do not bite, lad. That was no man. That was a fiend from hell itself!'

*   *   *

When Bartholomew awoke from a dream-filled sleep early the next morning, he was not surprised to find he was stiff and sore. As he was shaving and noting with annoyance a rip in a second shirt, Michael burst in.

'I was in the kitchen for something to eat before Lauds, and Cynric told me what happened last night!' he said excitedly. 'Why did you not come to wake me up? How will you explain what you were doing to the Master? How is your hand?'

Bartholomew went to the light of the window and inspected his hand where the man in the orchard had bitten him. There were clear teeth-marks but, oddly, while one row of teeth had scarcely made an impression, the others had made deep puncture marks surrounded by dark bruises.

'Do you think the man in the orchard was the murderer of Frances?' Michael asked. 'What about the man who bit you – Cynric's devil? Do you think he was the killer?'

'Why else would anyone be at the scene of a murder at that time of night with a candle?' Bartholomew asked with a shrug. 'Perhaps two people, rather than one, are responsible for the murders. It seemed to me that the smaller one was looking for something while the larger one kept watch outside. I saw and heard someone in the lane before I climbed over the wall. He came to his accomplice's rescue when I was on the very brink of pulling his mask away and revealing his face.'

'But what could they have been looking for?' asked Michael, frowning thoughtfully.

Bartholomew leaned back against the window-frame. 'Perhaps Frances struggled and tore something from his clothing that he only missed later.'

'That must be so,' said Michael, chewing on his lip. 'Why else would someone risk visiting the scene of a murder when, if he were caught, he would have much explaining to do? Do you think he found what they were looking for?'

Bartholomew thought carefully, tapping on the window-sill with his fingers. 'No. But I also think that what he was looking for was not there. Cynric and I did not frighten him into leaving: he had finished his search and was leaving anyway. I think he knew he would not find what he was looking for.'

Michael sat on Bartholomew's bed, his weight making the wood creak ominously. 'What was he like?' he asked. 'Was there anything familiar about him?'

Bartholomew shook his head. 'Nothing. He was swathed in a hooded gown. I think he was smaller than me, and he gave quite a yell when I seized him.'

'Could it have been a woman?' asked Michael.

'It sounded like a man's voice,' said Bartholomew. 'The large man was really enormous, but I could not see his face because of a red mask.'

'Well, someone of those dimensions should be easy to pick out in a crowd,' said Michael. 'What was the mask like?'

'Nothing more than a red hood, like an executioner's mask. Cynric thought he may have been what Frances saw when she said her killer was not a man.'

'He could well be right,' said Michael. 'I wish you had caught them, Matt. Now we have more information, but nothing tangible to lead us to the killer.'

Bartholomew looked around for his bag and remembered it had gone. 'Damn!'

'Father Aidan has a bag he never uses,' said Michael, guessing the cause of Bartholomew's annoyance. He glanced out of the window as he rose from the bed. 'Plenty of time before church,' he muttered. 'Come on.'

Bartholomew followed him across the yard, towards the orchard. The servants were already busy hauling water from the well, and starting fires in the kitchen. Bartholomew and Michael walked over the dew-laden grass to the back gate, and Michael whistled.

'Lord above,' he said. 'What a mess!'

Bartholomew pulled the door open so he could inspect it out of the shadows. He tugged at something and it gave way in his hand. He held it up to show Michael, who eyed it uncomprehendingly.

'The remains of a fire arrow,' Bartholomew explained. He rubbed his hand over the door and examined it closely. 'The Devil must be failing if he needs alchemy for his pyrotechnics.'

'I do not understand,' said Michael, taking the arrow from Bartholomew and examining it carefully. 'What alchemy?'

'The door was smeared with animal fat, soot, and something sticky. Some fats, when fermented, become volatile. I imagine it would not be safe to stand too close to ignite it, but an arrow dipped in pitch would burn. When the fire arrow hit the gate . . .' He raised his hands. 'Alchemy.'

'But why bother with all this?' asked Michael, scratching at the charred door with his fingernail. 'What was the point? They could have come and gone without us ever knowing they were there if they had not had the misfortune to run into you.'

'Perhaps it was intended for use at a later date, or perhaps it was meant as a warning to someone,' said Bartholomew. He sighed, exasperated. 'You are right, Michael. The more information we gain, the less it all makes sense.'

He wandered out into the lane, where one of the Proctor's beadles lounged against the wall, picking his teeth with a knife. He stood up straight when he saw Bartholomew and Michael, and pulled his greasy jerkin down over his shirt. Bartholomew heard him telling Michael that he had been at the door since instructed to be so by the Proctor the night before.

Opposite the gate, Bartholomew kicked around in the weeds at the side of the lane where he had seen the shadow, and stooped to pick up another arrow that had apparently been lit, but not used. He rolled it between his fingers and looked thoughtfully at Michael.

'Do you realise what this means?' he asked. Michael looked blankly at him. 'The gate burst into flames at almost the precise moment that the large man came through it, while I still had the smaller man in my grasp. There must have been three of them, Brother, not two: the large man, the smaller one, and the one who fired the arrow.'

Michael shook his head slowly. 'Three men to kill a woman? Lord save us, Matt! What is going on?'

As they emerged from the church after Prime, one of Stanmore's apprentices was waiting with a message for Bartholomew to meet his master at Milne Street. Michael, uninvited, went too, knowing that breakfast at Stanmore's house was likely to be far better than breakfast at Michaelhouse.

The streets were beginning to come to life, with apprentices hurrying to prepare for the day's trading at the Fair. The great gates of Stanmore's business premises were still locked, and Bartholomew hammered until someone came to let him in. Inside, the yard was a hive of activity. Huge vats of oatmeal were being carried steaming from the kitchens to the hall, and apprentices darted around trying to complete their chores before breakfast. Two horses were being harnessed in carts ready to carry bales of cloth to the Fair, and a cook was busy chasing a squawking chicken around the yard for Stanmore's dinner.

Stanmore was waiting for them, and escorted them from the frenetic activity in the yard to the pleasant solar on the upper floor. Bartholomew had always liked this room. Its walls were hung with thick tapestries, and the floor was strewn with an assortment of rugs of varying quality, age, and colours. Several comfortable chairs were ranged around the stone fireplace, and bales of cloth were stacked along one wall. Although the house on Milne Street was luxurious, especially compared to Michaelhouse, Stanmore preferred to live with his wife, Bartholomew's sister, at his manor in Trumpington, a village two miles distant.

Stanmore had arranged for breakfast to be brought to them, and several pans were being kept warm by the fire. Before Bartholomew could stop him, Michael had grabbed a loaf of freshly baked bread and a pan of sizzling bacon, and had settled himself comfortably in Stanmore's favourite chair to enjoy his booty. Stanmore looked askance at the greedy monk and sat opposite him, while Bartholomew sipped at a cup of watered ale.

'I went to work on those questions you asked about witchcraft,' said Stanmore.

Bartholomew understood that his brother-in-law had contacts in the most unusual places, but knew better than to ask questions.

'Your old monk was right,' continued the merchant, reaching across to take a slice of bacon before Michael could eat it all. 'The churches of All Saints' and St John Zachary are used for purposes not altogether religious. There are two active, but separate, covens in Cambridge, each illicitly based at one of the churches. I am told that although both covens worship fallen angels, there is rivalry between them and they do not like each other. I am also told that at least one of the groups is known to be connected to a guild, although I do not know which one. It is not mine,' he added hastily.

There were many guilds in Cambridge. Some, like Stanmore's Guild of Drapers, were formed to ensure a solidarity between traders and to establish good standards and training for apprentices. Other guilds were formed for charitable or religious purposes. Bartholomew remembered the complaints when Sir Richard Tulyet, the Sheriff's father, was elected Mayor of Cambridge. He had been a member of the Guild of the Annunciation and he had seen that members of his Guild were elected as bailiffs, burgesses, and to other prestigious positions. The current Mayor, Robert Brigham, was a clerk, and members of his Guild of St Peter and St Paul seemed to be doing well, although not as flagrantly as had Tulyet's friends.

The three men talked for a while, discussing which guilds might be a front for a coven, but were unable to come up with any convincing proof. Michael thought a group of pardoners might be responsible, but Bartholomew knew that Michael loathed pardoners and their trade, which took advantage of the gullible and the desperate. Stanmore thought the Guild of Dyers might be a coven in disguise, but Stanmore had always hated the dyers, at whose mercy he was if he wanted to sell coloured cloths. Bartholomew considered suggesting the Franciscans, for he thought there was something diabolical in their refusal to accept some of his teaching for reasons that were founded in ignorance. Seeing they had merely reached a stage where they were fuelling each other's personal bigotries, Bartholomew stood, stretched, and suggested they should be about their business.

As Stanmore stood with them at the gate, a breathless messenger staggered towards him, mud-splattered, his eyes red-rimmed from weariness.

'It has all gone!' he wailed.

'What has gone?' said Stanmore, nonplussed. 'Pull yourself together, man!'

The messenger took a gulping breath. 'The yellow silk from London. We were ambushed . . .'

'What?' snapped Stanmore. 'That cannot be. That cart was part of a huge convoy.'

'The silk has gone!' insisted the messenger. 'It happened as we were making a camp for the night. We chose a spot near the middle of the convoy, as you said we should, and we were cooking our supper. Men armed with great long bows sprung from nowhere. Will

Potter was shot as he reached for his sword, and so were two men who were guarding Master Morice's wines. The wolvesheads smashed the wine bottles, set fire to the silk, stole cheeses and dried meats, and escaped. Some of us gave chase, but the forests are dense, and what could we have done if we had caught them?'

'Damn!' said Stanmore, his lips pursed tightly together. He reached out and took the man by the shoulder. 'What of Will? Is he badly hurt?'

'He is dead,' said the messenger, shuffling his feet in the dust.

Stanmore paled. 'And the others? Where are they now? Are they injured?'

The messenger jerked his head back along Milne Street to where a dishevelled group of men shuffled towards them.

'Had you seen these outlaws before? Would you recognise them again?' Stanmore asked, taking a more secure hold on the man's arm as he reeled.

The messenger shook his head wearily, and Stanmore relented. 'Tell the others to get something to eat from the kitchens, and then come to my office,' he said. When the messenger had gone, Stanmore ordered an apprentice to take a message to the Castle, and sent for his steward to see to Will's body. He leaned against the door, and Bartholomew saw his hands were shaking. Bartholomew knew it was not only the loss of the valuable silk that distressed his brother-in-law; Stanmore was fond of the people who worked for him, and Will had been in his service for many years.

Michael looked grave. 'The roads are unsafe for decent people,' he said. 'We were even afraid to walk along

Barnwell Causeway from the Fair the night before last, and you can virtually see the town from there.'

'But why bother to attack if not to steal?' asked Bartholomew.

'They stole,' said Stanmore tightly. 'They took cheese and meat, and food is a valuable commodity when there is so little of it about.'

'But attacking is dangerous,' persisted Bartholomew. 'Why take the time to burn your cart and to smash the wine bottles, when it would be better to seize the food, and flee as quickly as possible?'

Stanmore sighed impatiently. 'Only a scholar would reason like that,' he said dismissively. 'These are louts, Matt, who gain pleasure from the crimes they commit. They probably enjoyed the damage they caused. You credit them with more thought than they are capable of.'

'Well, I am sorry for your loss,' said Bartholomew. 'For Will, too.'

'Oh, damn all this!' Stanmore exclaimed. 'I had already promised that silk to a merchant in Norwich. De Belem's prices for dyeing silk have become ridiculous, and I would pay more to him for dyeing than I would be able to charge for it. His wife's death during the plague must have damaged his mind. His prices will have to come down, or he will ruin us all. And if we fall, so will he.'

He turned as his men came through the gates, limping and travel-stained. Stanmore ran towards them, counting them like a mother hen. Bartholomew went to help, and spent the next hour bandaging and dispensing salves for grazes and bruises. He and Michael took their leave as Stanmore's steward arrived bearing the body of Will Potter.

'The friar is to be buried today,' said Bartholomew as they walked away. 'We do not even know his name. De Wetherset will want to know what we have done, and we have done nothing. Tomorrow we had better exhume the body of his clerk. We should invite him to be present to make sure we have the right corpse.'

Michael gave a snort of derision. 'De Wetherset will have nothing to do with that! What shall we do about this guild business?'

'I am not sure,' said Bartholomew. 'We should hand the information to the Sheriff, since he is supposed to be looking for the murderer of these women.' He turned to Michael. 'Do you think the two are connected? The murder of the women and the murder of the friar?'

'On what grounds?' asked Michael, surprised. 'Four victims with slit throats and one poisoned by a lock on the University chest; four ladies of ill-repute and one mendicant friar? No, Matt, I cannot see that they are connected.'

'Frances de Belem was not a lady of ill-repute,' said Bartholomew. 'She was the daughter of a respectable merchant.' He stopped suddenly. 'I wonder if de Belem belongs to a guild.'

Michael waved a dismissive hand. 'Now you are grasping at straws. Of course he is a member of a guild. The Honourable Guild of Dyers, probably.'

'But he might also be a member of another guild unrelated to his trade. Oswald is and so is Roger Alcote.'

'Are they?' said Michael, surprised. 'Your brother-in-law did not mention that when we were talking just now. And Alcote? Scholars are forbidden to join guilds.'

'Oswald is a member of the Guild of the Annunciation. Why do you think he became a burgess when Tulyet was Mayor? And Oswald once told me Alcote is also a member. Membership of these organisations is supposed to be secret, but if I wanted to know who is involved, all I would need to do would be to watch who went into the church on the day of their services. It would not be difficult to ascertain who was a member and who was not.'

'Good lord!' said Michael, his eyes gleaming. 'All this intrigue going on that I knew nothing about. This makes it all far more interesting.'

'Perhaps, but it does not help with the dead friar. The only way forward I can see is to find that lay-brother and see if we can make him tell us what he knows,' said Bartholomew. 'I do not feel inclined to go back to that alley again, so I suggest we ask de Wetherset to tell his clerks to trace him.'

'Do you think the lay-brother knows something?' asked Michael.

Bartholomew nodded slowly. 'Oh yes. I am certain of it. And we do not have the faintest idea what happened to Evrard Buckley,' he continued. 'Why did he disappear? And why did he take all his furniture with him?'

Michael raised his eyebrows thoughtfully. 'It could not have been easy moving all those belongings in the middle of the night from King's Hall,' he said.

'Maybe,' said Bartholomew. 'Buckley has roomed alone since the plague carried off his colleagues, and his window opens directly onto the garden that runs down to the river. The window is large, and, unless he had some really enormous pieces of furniture, I think there would have been no problem in lowering them down to the ground by rope.'

'He must have had help,' said Michael. 'Or it would have taken an age to do.'

'We should have something to report to de Wetherset,' said Bartholomew, 'and doubtless your Bishop will be wanting some news. We should walk round the back of King's Hall to see if we can see anything.'

Michael was not impressed with the idea, but went anyway. Bartholomew was right in saying that the Bishop would want answers, and it would be Michael's responsibility to give him some. They walked down to the river and along the towpath. A barge was being docked at the wharves, three exhausted horses having dragged it through the night to be ready to trade its wares at the Fair. The smell by the river was powerful. Stale eels that had not been sold the previous day lay in grey-black heaps on the bank, being squabbled over by gulls. All along the river people were dumping night waste into the water, while further downstream a group of children splashed and played in the shallows.

Bartholomew saw one of Stanmore's apprentices bartering for threads, and a small group of women were admiring a collection of coloured ribbons. Walking past them, and heading in his direction, was Janetta of Lincoln. Bartholomew saw the sun glint on her blue-black hair, and memories of his experience in the alleyway came flooding back to him. For a reason he could not immediately identify, he decided he did not want to speak to her.

Bartholomew pulled at Michael's sleeve. 'Come on,' he said, 'we do not have all day.'

'What is the matter with you?' grumbled Michael, objecting to this increase in his pace when the air was already beginning to grow thick and humid with the promise of heat to come.

It was too late. Janetta had seen him and came forward with the enigmatic smile he remembered from the day before, showing under her cascade of black hair. Michael stopped dead in his tracks and eyed her suspiciously.

'So, Matthew Bartholomew. Good morning to you.'

Bartholomew nodded to her, hiding his bitten hand under his scholar's robe. He instinctively knew that she would ask him about it, and he did not want to tell her about the incident in the orchard. In fact, he did not want to tell her anything at all.

Janetta laughed at his cautious response. 'I trust I find you well?' she said, looking him up and down and appraising him coolly.

Did she know about his skirmish last night? Was she surprised to see him intact? Or was she merely thinking about her rescue of him from the alleyway?

'Very well. And you?' he asked guardedly.

'In fine health,' she said. 'And now, Doctor, I have a great many things to do, and I cannot stand around gossiping all day like a scholar!'

She sauntered away, walking slowly, as if she were in no particular hurry to get back to her 'great many things'.

'And we cannot stroll around idly like harlots,' retorted Michael, nettled by her comment. She evidently heard his remark, for she turned around and wagged a finger at him, smiling, although Bartholomew thought he detected a flash of anger in her eyes.

'Who was that?' Michael asked, staring after her.

'Janetta of Lincoln,' Bartholomew answered, embarrassed by Michael's retort.

'Ah, yes,' said Michael. 'You did not tell me she was a convicted felon.'

'What?' said Bartholomew, startled. 'How do you know that?'

'Did you not notice those scars on her face? There was a judge at Lincoln who liked to sentence prostitutes to that punishment. He reasoned that it would force them to turn from prostitution because they would be unable to secure clients. He was only in office a short time, but he made a name for himself locally because of the sentences he gave to petty offenders.'

'Petty offenders?' said Bartholomew. 'Then perhaps she was convicted of a crime other than prostitution.'

Michael shook his head. 'He only scarred women like that for the crime of harlotry. She was a whore, Matt, and was convicted and punished for it. You mark my words.'

'What happened to the judge?' asked Bartholomew.

'Killed in a brothel,' said Michael, laughing. 'Full of women with scarred faces, I expect! I would say your Janetta of Lincoln was almost certainly one of his victims.'

'That might explain why she left Lincoln. If this judge's punishments are not common knowledge, perhaps she thought she might be able to live here without her past being known,' mused Bartholomew.

'The only reason I know is because I saw similar scars

on the face of a woman in a group of travelling singers,' said Michael. 'I asked her how she came by them, and she told me about the judge.'

Bartholomew looked doubtfully at him, wondering how the fat monk had managed to embark upon such an intimate conversation with a female travelling entertainer. Michael caught his glance and waggled his eyebrows before changing the subject. 'Let's go and look at this grass.'

As Bartholomew had predicted, the walls bore marks that Buckley's furniture had been passed out of the window. They also found the grass below it was trampled, and there were ruts made by a cart. But there was also something else.

'Michael, look,' said Bartholomew, bending to examine a small smear on the creamy stone.

'What is it?' asked Michael, looking, and not finding the brown mark especially enlightening.

'Blood,' said Bartholomew. He pointed to where the grass was less trampled to one side, and several blades of grass were stained. He straightened up and he and Michael exchanged a look of puzzlement.

'Well, at least we have something to report to the Chancellor,' said Michael.

CHAPTER 4

THE CHANCELLOR WAS NOT IMPRESSED WITH THE information they had gleaned, and he agreed only reluctantly to send one of his clerks to bring the lay-brother to them so that he could be questioned. He was also unsympathetic about Bartholomew's experience in the alleyway behind the church and denied that there was a short cut there through the shrubs in the churchyard.

'Why would there be such a thing?' he snapped. 'None of those people would deign to set foot in a church.'

Bartholomew wanted to tell him that it might be a short cut to the river that just happened to be through the churchyard, but could see no advantage in antagonising the Chancellor.

'Gilbert stuck that blade on the poisoned lock into a rat,' said de Wetherset. 'It died in moments. I also sent him to the Dominican Friary, but you were correct in your assumption that the dead man was not one of them. The Prior came to look at the body and said he had never seen the man before.'

Bartholomew felt guilty that the Chancellor had more to report to them than they had to him. He wished he would have a sudden insight to tie all the loose threads together, so that they could be done with it all and he could concentrate on his students' disputations.

'What do you plan to do next?' de Wetherset asked, picking up a piece of vellum covered with minute writing and studying it. Bartholomew rose to leave. The Chancellor clearly was not interested in how they went about getting the information, only in what they discovered. Michael remained seated.

'I would like to read Nicholas's book,' he said.

The Chancellor was momentarily taken off-guard. 'What for?' he asked suspiciously.

'When we first saw the body of the friar, you were more concerned with the book than anything else in the chest. Therefore, it is likely that the friar wanted to read or steal it more than any other document. If I were to read it, I might gain a better notion of why someone might want to kill for it,' he said, folding his large arms across his chest.

'Very well,' said de Wetherset, after a moment's deliberation. 'You have until Sext. Then I have business at Barnwell Priory and I want the book locked in the chest before I leave.'

Michael inclined his head, and the Chancellor conducted them to the small chamber in the tower of the church, where he donned thick leather gloves and undid the locks on the chest. Bartholomew saw that the three locks gleamed bright and new: the Chancellor was taking no chances.

As the last lock sprang open, de Wetherset straightened, and Bartholomew saw his face was beaded with perspiration.

'Poisoned locks!' he muttered. 'Whatever next? A puff of poison in the rugs to kill those who trample on them? Arsenic soaked into the documents themselves?'

Michael's hand had been half in the chest after the mysterious book, but now he withdrew it hastily. The Chancellor gave an unpleasant smile and tossed him his gloves.

'I will return before Sext. Please bar the door after I leave. I do not want anyone else in the chamber. Should anyone knock, tell them to go away.'

Bartholomew shot a sturdy bar across the door after he had gone and wandered around the small chamber restlessly. Michael took the book from the chest and placed it on the table. The leaves of the text were thick and there was no problem turning them while wearing the gloves.

'Can you get the spare set of keys from the Bishop?' Bartholomew asked suddenly.

Michael looked surprised. 'I could ask him. Why?'

'Because then we could try them on the old locks. If they do not fit the poisoned one, we would know that not only must a new lock have been put on the chest, but that someone had exchanged de Wetherset's keys. Since de Wetherset said the keys are never out of his sight, it would mean that Buckley, the only other person with access to them, must have exchanged them by some sleight of hand when he undid the chest. If the key does fit, then we know that either the lock was tampered with and the poisonous blade fitted, or that it was there all the time.'

Michael nodded slowly. 'The keys will be of no use to the Bishop now there are new locks on the chest. I see no reason why he should not let me have them.'

Bartholomew went to the window and looked across the High Street. By leaning out, he could see Michaelhouse, and remembered his students. He left the window and went to a wall cupboard, opening the wooden doors to peer inside. Michael shot him an irritable glance as he closed the doors again noisily. Bartholomew bent down to look at the rug on which the friar must have knelt when he picked the locks, but there was nothing to see.

'I should be with my students. Some of them have already failed their disputations once,' he said. 'And I should visit Mistress Bocher's baby. It gets colic.'

'I will never get through this if you keep distracting me,' said Michael, exasperated. 'Go and see your students. Come back for me before Sext.'

Bartholomew was apprehensive about leaving Michael alone in a room where the friar had died by such sinister means, but could see no benefit in wasting the day in idleness. He waited until he was certain that Michael had barred the door from the inside and began to walk down the stairs. When he was almost at the bottom, he stopped as a thought occurred to him, and turned to climb them again.

He passed the chest room and continued upwards. As he climbed higher, the stairs became dirty and were covered in feathers and dry pigeon-droppings, and Bartholomew guessed they were seldom used. There was an unpleasant smell, too, and Bartholomew noted the decaying corpses of several birds that had flown in and had been unable to get out.

He reached the bell chamber and walked in. The

bells stood silent among crooning pigeons and scraps of discarded rope and wood. The spiral stair ended, but a vertical wooden ladder led from the bell chamber to a trap-door in the ceiling above. Bartholomew tested it carefully, not trusting the cracked wood, nor the way in which the ladder leaned away from the wall as he prepared to climb.

The ladder was stronger than it looked, and he reached the trap-door without the rungs falling out or the ladder tearing away from the wall to deposit him on the bells below. He unbolted the trap-door and gingerly pushed it open, ducking as he disturbed a flurry of birds on the roof. The sunlight streamed down on his head, making him blink after the darkness of the tower. He hauled himself up and stood on the roof.

He surveyed the view in awe. The day was clear, not yet spoiled by the stinking mists that blew in from the Fens, and he thought he could see the distant towers of Ely Cathedral. He could certainly see the glitter of the maze of waterways snaking through the flat Fens, as they stretched off towards the sea. He leaned against one of the corner turrets and traced the silvery line of the river as far as he could, surprised that he could see a barge hauling in about two miles distant. He wondered that his brother-in-law did not post one of his informants on the roof permanently so he could have early warning of the arrival of trading vessels.

He peered directly down, intrigued at how the streets and buildings appeared from above. He saw the market stalls, looking brighter and prettier than they ever did in the market itself. Then he searched for the alley where he had been attacked the day before. He looked harder, leaning precariously over the edge as he screwed up his eyes to see. There was a gap between the rows of shacks, and following the line of it towards the church he saw a very distinct thinning of the undergrowth running towards the churchyard. There was his hidden pathway: he knew he would be able to see it from above!

He chose two prominent tombstones and a tree, quickly calculated angles and distances, and committed them to memory. He smiled grimly to himself. He would be able to find the entrance to it next time he looked, no matter how well hidden it was.

He stood for a few moments savouring the peace, and then made his way back down the ladder. As he was closing the trap-door, a tricky operation that involved wrapping one leg around the ladder and using both lands to heave the heavy wooden flap back into place, someone started to toll the bell for the friar's funeral. Bartholomew had heard that people were sent mad if they stayed too long in the chamber where bells were tolled, and that their ears would burst.

Another myth dispelled, he thought, as he climbed down the ladder. The bell's ringing was loud, but he did not feel it would send him mad or that his ears would burst. When he reached the bottom of the ladder, he put his hands over his ears to muffle the sound and watched the bell swing back and forth. His hands dropped to his side when he saw what had been concealed behind the bell, but what was exposed as the bell moved. He started towards it, but then stopped. While he did not believe the bell would damage his hearing within a short time, he did not relish the idea of being hit by the great mass of metal as it swept ponderously back and forth.

He went outside the chamber, closed the door, and sat on the stairs until the tolling had stopped. When the last vibrations had died away, and he could hear the first notes of the requiem mass drifting up the stairs, he opened the door again and edged his way towards the bell. There were four different-sized bells in the tower. It was the biggest one that had tolled for the friar and that concealed the body behind it. Even so, all that was visible was a white and bloated hand that dangled just below the bell frame.

The bells were supported in a wooden frame about three feet from the floor, and the easiest way to reach the body was to crawl on hands and knees beneath it. Bartholomew ignored the accumulated filth of decades and made his way to the other side of the chamber. Even as he neared the big bell, the sack that evidently held the body was all but invisible, and it was only the dead white hand that betrayed its presence. He used the bell to pull himself up onto the frame, and inspected the sack.

It had been jammed between the frame and the wall, quite deliberately positioned to hide it from prying eyes. Bartholomew, who had only spotted it when the bell was tolling, doubted if many people would choose to be in the chamber when the bells were ringing, and so the sack and its gruesome contents might have remained hidden for months or even years. He noted the debris that coated his clothes from his crawl across the filthy floor, and suspected that the cleaning of the bell chamber was not a high priority at St Mary's. He felt through the sack to the body inside. It was upside down: the legs were uppermost, while the head and torso were further down the bell frame.

He took a firm hold of the sack and pulled hard but it was securely wedged. He climbed further down the frame and tried to dislodge it sideways, but it was stuck fast. He leaned over to see if something was holding it in place and became aware of a rubbing sound behind him. For a moment, he could not imagine what it could be, and then he saw the great bell begin to tip. The requiem mass! Bartholomew could not believe his stupidity! When the mass was sung the bell ringer would chime the bell three times each for the Father, Son, and Holy Ghost. The ringer was beginning to haul on the bell rope, pulling hard to make the bell swing higher and higher until the clapper sounded against its side.

The bell swung upwards as Bartholomew flattened himself against the frame. It missed him by the merest fraction of an inch. The next time it swung up it would hit him. As soon as it began to drop, Bartholomew let himself fall to the floor, knowing that he would not have sufficient time to climb. He landed with a thump and flattened himself in the muck and feathers as the great mouth of the bell swished over him. He heard Brother Michael exclaim in the room below just before the bell spoke for the first time.

Bartholomew pressed his hands over his ears again, and tried to spit dusty old feathers from his mouth. The bell rang a second time and a third, and paused. Then came three more tolls and a pause, and then a final three and silence. Bartholomew did not wait for the last vibrations to fade before crawling away as fast as he could. He pounded on the door of the chest chamber.

'Go away!' shouted Michael, true to the Chancellor's instructions.

'Michael, it is me! Open the door!'

He fretted impatiently while Michael huffed noisily across the floor and fumbled with the bar. Bartholomew shot inside, leaving a trail of feathers and dried bird-droppings behind him. Michael looked at him, aghast.

'Have you been to that alley again?' he said, concern wrinkling his fat face.

'There is a body in a sack in the bell chamber,' said Bartholomew breathlessly. 'I tried to move it, but it is stuck fast.'

'I heard an almighty crash a minute ago. Was that you?' Michael stopped as the meaning of Bartholomew's words began to dawn on him. 'Who is the body?'

Bartholomew shook his head. 'I could not tell, but I saw the hand and it is that of an older man.' He ran an unsteady hand through his hair, oblivious to the feathers and cobwebs it deposited there. He looked at Michael. 'I have a terrible feeling we have just discovered the whereabouts of the Vice-Chancellor.'

Out of respect for the dead friar, they waited until he had been lowered into his grave in the cemetery before Michael approached the Chancellor and imparted the news. The Chancellor paled and gazed at Michael in shock.

'Another body in the tower? Do you know who it is?' he whispered.

'Not yet,' said Bartholomew. 'We will need help to get it out.'

De Wetherset closed his eyes and muttered something. When he opened them again, his eyes were hard and businesslike. He called for Gilbert and told him what had been discovered.

'What were you doing in the belfry to discover such a thing?' Gilbert asked, flashing the Chancellor a glance that indicated Bartholomew and Michael were not above suspicion themselves.

'Matt was looking to see if the friar had hidden his lock-picking tools there,' Michael lied easily.

Gilbert sighed. 'I should have thought of that myself,' he said. 'Although I would not have gone when the bells were ringing, and from what you say, I would probably not have seen this corpse.'

'We will recover the body ourselves before we spread the news abroad,' said de Wetherset. 'Who knows what we might uncover? Gilbert, please arrange that we will not be disturbed while I fetch Father Cuthbert. Brother, Doctor, please wait for me in the tower.'

While Michael and Bartholomew waited, Bartholomew slit the sack and tied some pieces of discarded rope around the legs of the body inside. They tried a few preliminary hauls, but to no avail. De Wetherset arrived wearing an old gown, while Gilbert and Cuthbert hovered anxiously behind him. Bartholomew wondered whether the portly de Wetherset, the fat Cuthbert, and the slight Gilbert would make much difference to their efforts.

While Bartholomew lay on the floor and pushed, the others heaved on the legs from the bell frame. They began to despair of ever getting it out, and de Wetherset had started to talk ominously of the skills of some physicians with knives, when they felt the body budge.

'Once more,' cried de Wetherset. 'Pull!'

The body moved a little further, and Bartholomew

joined Cuthbert to pull on one of the legs. With a puff of dust and a sharp crack from the bell frame, the body came loose, and Bartholomew and Michael hauled it across the bells and laid it on the floor by the door. De Wetherset, his face red from exertion, knelt next to it and slit the sack open with a knife. He gasped as the smell of putrefaction rose from the bundle, and then leapt up as the great swollen face looked out at him.

'God's teeth!' he whispered, staring at the face in horror. 'What is that? Is it a demon?'

'He has been hanging upside down for at least several days,' said Bartholomew gently. 'When that happens, the fluids of the body drain into the lowest part and cause the swelling you see here.'

'You were wrong, Matt. It is not Master Buckley,' said Michael, covering the lower half of his face with the sleeve of his gown.

Father Cuthbert coughed, his face pale. 'It is Marius Froissart,' he said. Bartholomew and Michael looked blankly at him and he explained. 'Froissart claimed sanctuary in the church about a week ago after he murdered his wife. You know it is the law that such criminals can claim sanctuary in a church, and he cannot be touched by officers of the law for forty days. The clerks locked him in that night, but by the next day he had escaped, despite the soldiers outside.'

'The whore killer whom the Sheriff was seeking!' exclaimed Michael. 'But dead himself!'

'But who killed him and put him here? And why?' asked de Wetherset, looking down at the body.

'Whoever hid his body here intended it to stay concealed for a long time,' said Bartholomew. He stretched out his hand to show the others what he had found. 'There was a reason it was so difficult to pull him free. He was nailed to the bell frame.'

De Wetherset stumbled down the stairs with his hand over his mouth. Gilbert followed him solicitously, while Bartholomew and Michael stayed with the dead man. Father Cuthbert hovered, uncertain whether to go or stay. When Bartholomew began to cut the sack to examine the body, Cuthbert looked away and gagged, and Bartholomew sent him with Michael to discover what de Wetherset wanted to do. He continued his examination alone. It looked as if Cuthbert's story of Marius Froissart's disappearance corresponded to the time that Bartholomew estimated him to have been dead. Which meant that Marius Froissart could not have killed Isobel or Frances.

Froissart's clothes were old, but neatly patched and mended. His beard and hair were unkempt, but, after a week in a sack, that was hardly surprising. Bartholomew tipped the head back and looked at the neck. Underneath the beard was a thin red line that circled his throat and was caked with blood. Bartholomew eased Froissart onto his back and inspected the dark marks at the nape of his neck. Garrotted. He felt the scalp under the matted hair, but there were no signs of a blow to the head. He prised the eyes and mouth open to look for signs of poison, and then looked at the rest of the body. There were no other injuries except for the marks on his shoulders and hips where he had been nailed to the bell frame.

Why would anyone go to such lengths? he wondered. He looked closely at the marks the nails had made.

There was very little bruising and no bleeding at all. Some of the wounds were torn, but that had happened when he had been pulled out, and there was nothing to suggest that he had been alive when they were first made. Bartholomew walked around the chamber and looked at the great bell from as many angles as possible. When the bell was stationary, there was no earthly chance that the body would be seen. Even if someone had come to tend the bells, the body might remain hidden as long as the bells were still. And the smell? Bartholomew looked at the dead birds he had noted earlier. Anyone noticing a strong odour would assume that it came from the dead birds, as he had done.

In the confines of the narrow spiral staircase, the stench of putrefaction became too much even for him. He walked down to the chest chamber and took some deep breaths through the window. He winced. The sun was beating down like a furnace, and the ditches that criss-crossed Cambridge stank. Even from the tower he could see a haze of insects over the river.

He turned as he heard footsteps and de Wetherset and Michael entered. De Wetherset was as white as a sheet, and Michael was unusually sombre. De Wetherset listened at the door for a moment before closing it firmly.

'Gilbert and Cuthbert are downstairs to ensure that we are not disturbed,' he said. 'What can you tell me about this man's death?'

'Froissart was garrotted. If his hand had not slipped loose, I doubt he would have been found until someone decided to clean the bell chamber.'

De Wetherset pursed his lips. 'Father Cuthbert has problems getting anyone to ring the things, let alone to clean them,' he said. 'It appears that our murderer knew this, and the body was intended to remain undiscovered for a very long time indeed.'

Bartholomew walked to the window and rubbed his chin. 'Froissart's death must be connected to the dead friar,' he said.

'Logic dictates that is so,' said Michael. 'It is improbable that two sudden deaths in the same place within days of each other will be unrelated.'

'But Froissart must have been killed the night he claimed sanctuary,' Bartholomew pointed out. 'That was last Tuesday. The clerks say the friar was here for about three days before he died. He was found dead the day before yesterday, and so he probably arrived here last Friday at the earliest, and Froissart had been dead for three days by then.' He picked up a quill from the table and examined it absently. 'The timing is such that Froissart and the friar could never have met.'

Michael sat on one of the benches and stretched his legs out in front of him. 'But perhaps the friar was here before. Perhaps he was in disguise and killed Froissart, and then came back to complete his business in the chest.'

Bartholomew thought for a moment and then shook his head. 'No. It does not ring true.' He saw the Chancellor wince at the mention of bells and continued quickly. 'The clerks were very observant about the friar. Had there been another person loitering in the church before him, they would have mentioned it. But more importantly, if the friar had been in disguise and had murdered Froissart, I think he would have been most unlikely to have returned to the church as himself, and there was nothing on the friar's body to suggest he was in disguise when he died.'

'But if he were responsible, what would he have to fear when he knew the body was so well hidden?' asked Michael.

Bartholomew thought for a moment. 'Master de Wetherset, you said Father Cuthbert has trouble finding people to ring the bells. Whoever put Froissart behind the bell frame knew that the chances of anyone going to the bell chamber to tend to the bells were remote. Why would the friar, a stranger to Cambridge, know that?'

De Wetherset grew exasperated. 'You two do not agree with each other,' he said. 'You, Brother, maintain that logic dictates that the two deaths are connected, while you, Doctor Bartholomew, confound any ideas we suggest to link them.'

Bartholomew smiled. 'Just because we cannot find the link here and now does not mean that it is not there. The evidence we have at the moment is just not sufficient to support any firm conclusions.'

De Wetherset sat heavily on the bench next to Michael and put his head in his hands. 'Tell me what we do have,' he said wearily.

Bartholomew sat on the chest before thinking better of it and moved to the window-seat. He quickly sorted out his jumbled thoughts and began to put them together.

'Last Tuesday, Froissart killed his wife and claimed sanctuary in the church. He was locked in Tuesday night, but had gone by Wednesday morning. It is most likely he was killed in the church on Tuesday night, and his body hidden at the same time. Three days later, on Friday, the itinerant friar arrived. He spent time, ostensibly praying and preparing himself to continue his journey, but more probably learning the routine of the church. Now that suggests to me that he had not been here before, and so was not the murderer of Froissart.'

De Wetherset nodded slowly. 'That is logical,' he said. 'Pray continue.'

Michael took up the analysis. 'We do not know why the friar was here, but we know he was a careful man. He spent three days watching and learning, and obviously possessed some skill in opening locks without keys. On Sunday night, he hid in the church while the lay-brother locked up, and then made his way to the tower. He picked the locks on the chest and began to go through its contents. The poison did not have an immediate effect, or he would not have been able to pick the third lock and open the lid. We do not know what happened next. He may have had a seizure brought on by the poison and fallen into the chest, closing the lid at the same time. Or he may have been put in the box by another person.'

'Perhaps the same person who killed Froissart,' said Bartholomew. 'I cannot imagine that the friar fell neatly into the chest and the lid closed of its own accord. I think it more likely that someone put him there.' He paused for a moment and continued. 'On the same night that the friar was preparing himself for his business in the tower, Evrard Buckley complained of stomach pains from a surfeit of eels, and retired early to bed. During the night, he removed the entire contents of his room through the window in King's Hall and loaded them onto a cart. At some point, he or another person, was wounded, perhaps fatally, as is attested by the blood on the ground outside his window.'

'We have forgotten Nicholas's book,' said Michael, gesturing to where the papers lay on the table near the window. 'He died a month ago, and no one thought much about it until the friar was found dead on top of his manuscript.'

'So, what we have left,' said de Wetherset somewhat testily, 'is a large number of unanswered questions. Who was the friar? What was he doing in the tower? Who put the poisoned lock on the chest? Was it intended to kill the friar or another? Who killed Froissart and why? Are the two deaths linked? Was Nicholas also murdered? Where is my Vice-Chancellor? And did he kill Nicholas, Froissart, and the friar?'

He stood with a sigh. 'I will have Froissart moved to the crypt. Gilbert will see to that. It might be most imprudent to let the murderer know his careful concealment has been uncovered, so I suggest we tell no one of this,' he said.

'But the Sheriff has a right to know,' said Bartholomew, startled. 'If Froissart is supposed to have murdered his wife, the Sheriff will be looking for him. We cannot keep such a matter to ourselves.'

'I said it would be most unwise to let the murderer know that we have discovered the body,' snapped de Wetherset. 'Supposing news of our discovery makes him kill again? The next victim might be one of us. The townspeople complain bitterly that the Sheriff is dragging his feet in tracking down the killer of the town prostitutes. There is little point in revealing this matter to such a man.'

'What if it were ever discovered that we kept such a matter secret?' said Bartholomew, unconvinced. 'The townspeople would have every right to be angry with the University, and relations between us and the town are strained as it is. There would be a riot!'

'The only way they would find out would be if you were to reveal it to them,' said de Wetherset coldly. 'And I am sure I need not worry on that score. Anyway, I imagine the killer would be more likely to strike at those who are seen to be investigating his crime if it were to become common knowledge Froissart has been found: you and Brother Michael.'

'Not if we turn the whole matter over to the Sheriff.' Bartholomew looked at Michael for support, but the monk looked studiously out of the window and would not meet his eye.

De Wetherset continued. 'I want you to question Froissart's family to see if they know anything, and I want you to examine Nicholas's body before dawn tomorrow. I have already obtained the necessary licences.'

He opened the door and left without another word. His footsteps were heavy and, despite his belligerence to Bartholomew, attested to his growing despondency about the events of the past few days. Bartholomew and Michael followed him, Bartholomew still angry, and they saw him giving instructions to Gilbert about the removal of Froissart.

'More lies and deceit,' said Bartholomew bitterly, watching de Wetherset walking away with an arm across Gilbert's shoulders. 'Why did you not come to my defence?'

'Because you were wrong,' said Michael. 'De Wetherset said that the Sheriff is conducting a less than competent investigation into the deaths of the women, and that is true. The townspeople are talking of little else. Why should we alert the murderer of Froissart that we have uncovered his carefully concealed victim by revealing it to the Sheriff? I do not see that it would do any good, and it might do a great deal of harm.'

'But perhaps one of the reasons the investigation is slow is because half the Sheriff's men are hunting Froissart, whom we know is dead. If we tell him that he need not look for Froissart, he will have more resources with which to hunt the killer of the prostitutes,' argued Bartholomew.

Michael shook his head. 'The Sheriff's problem is more deeply seated than manpower,' he said. He shook himself suddenly. 'Come, Matt! It is cold in here. You cannot reveal what you know to the Sheriff without contravening de Wetherset's orders, so do not even think about it. Let us put it from our minds and concentrate on the matter in hand.'

'So, what shall we do first?' said Bartholomew, walking with relief out of the cold church and into the hot sunshine outside. He brushed feathers from his gown and stretched stiffly.

'Back to College,' said Michael. 'You stink of that dead man, and it would not be tactful to question his family until you have changed. And anyway, I am hungry and you have students waiting for you.'

At Michaelhouse, Bartholomew washed and changed, giving his dirty clothes to the disapproving laundress.

'I cannot imagine what you have been up to these last few days,' Agatha grumbled. 'Filthy clothes, ripped shirts. You should know better at your age, Matthew.'

Bartholomew grinned at her as she pushed him out of the door. She watched him cross the yard towards the hall and allowed herself a rare smile. Agatha was fond of the physician, who had cured her of a painful foot that had been the bane of her life for years. She looked down at the dirty clothes and her smile faded: she hoped he was not doing anything dangerous.

She saw Gray and Deynman strolling across the yard and yelled at them in stentorian tones. 'Your master is waiting for you! He is a busy man and cannot be waiting around all day for you to wander into his lectures when you please!'

Gray and Deynman broke into a run and made for the conclave, where Bartholomew had already begun his lecture. He glanced at them, but said nothing as they hurriedly found seats and tried to bring their breathing under control. Bartholomew noted with satisfaction that the whole class was attentive, and when he sprung questions on them, they at least did not seem startled. Some even gave him the correct answers.

The time passed quickly, and soon the bell was ringing to announce lectures were over for the day. Bartholomew was surprised that the students listened to his final comments and did not immediately try to leave for the meal in the hall as they usually did. He stopped his pacing across the fireplace to address them.

'Tomorrow we must look again at diseases of the mouth. You may consider toothache to be an unimportant affliction, but it can make the patient's life a living hell. A toothache might be indicative of abscesses in the jaws, which can occasionally prove fatal to some people, by poisoning the blood. If I am late, I want you to consider dosages of different compounds that you might give to children who have painful swellings of the face, and what the possible causes of such swellings might be.'

He gave them an absent smile, his mind already busy making up such a list, and left. His students heaved a corporate sigh of relief.

'Another day survived!' said Gray, blowing out his cheeks and looking at the others.

'He is only trying to help us learn,' said Bulbeck defensively. 'He wants us to pass our disputations, and he wants us to become good physicians.'

Brother Boniface spat. 'He is teaching us contrary to the will of God. Why does he not teach us how to bleed patients? Why does he insist that we must always have a diagnosis? Some things are not meant to be known by man.'

'He does not believe that bleeding is beneficial,' said Gray. 'He told me that charlatans bleed patients when they do not know what else to do.'

Boniface snorted in derision. 'His teaching is heretical, and I do not like it. Give me a bottle of leeches and I could cure anything!'

Bulbeck laughed. 'Then tell Doctor Bartholomew that leeching is a cure for toothache in his lecture tomorrow,' he said.

Because Bartholomew had to see a patient, Michael went alone to hunt down the family of Marius Froissart. He asked the clerks in the church, but none of them knew where Froissart had lived. Somewhat irritably, he began to walk up Cambridge's only hill to the Castle to ask the Sheriff. The Sheriff had been called when Froissart had claimed sanctuary. Froissart could not, of course, be taken from the sanctuary of the church, but he had been questioned.

By the time Michael arrived, puffing and swearing at his enforced exercise, he was hot and crabby. He marched up to the Castle gate-house and pounded on the door. A lantern-jawed sergeant asked him his business, and Michael demanded an audience with the Sheriff. He was led across the bailey towards the round keep that stood on the motte. It was a grey, forbidding structure, and Michael felt hemmed in by the towering curtain walls and crenellated towers.

In the bailey a few soldiers practised sword-play in a half-hearted manner, while a larger group were gathered in the shade of the gate-house to play dice. Before the plague, the bailey had always seemed full of soldiers, but there were distinctly fewer now. Michael followed the sergeant up wide spiral stairs to the second floor. As he took a seat in an antechamber, raised voices drifted from the Sheriff's office.

'But when?' roared a voice that Michael recognised as Stanmore's. The sergeant glanced uneasily at Michael but said nothing. There was a mumble from within as the Sheriff answered.

'But that is simply unacceptable!' responded Stanmore. Michael stood and ambled closer to the door in an attempt to overhear the Sheriff's part of the conversation, but was almost knocked off his feet as the door was flung open and Stanmore stormed out. He saw Michael but was too furious to speak as he left. Before the sergeant could stop him, Michael strolled nonchalantly through the door Stanmore had left open.

The Sheriff stood behind a table, breathing heavily

and clenching his fists. He glared at Michael, who smiled back benevolently.

'Master Tulyet,' said Michael, sitting down. 'How is your father, the Mayor?'

'My father is no longer Mayor,' growled Tulyet. He was a small man with wispy fair hair and a beard that was so blond it was all but invisible.

'Then how are you? How is your investigation of the whore murders?' asked Michael, knowing instinctively he would touch a raw nerve.

'That is the King's business and none of yours,' Tulyet snapped. Michael saw the Sheriff's hands tremble when he picked up his cup to drink, and when he put it back down again, there were clammy fingerprints smeared on the pewter.

'Have you traced that other murderer yet? What was his name? Froissart,' probed Michael, leaning back in the creaking chair.

Tulyet glared at him. 'He escaped sanctuary,' he said through gritted teeth. 'I warned the guards that he might try, but they said they did not see him. I suppose they would not when they were asleep.'

'Who was it that he had killed?' asked Michael. 'A woman? And now a woman-killer stalks the night streets of Cambridge?'

'Marius Froissart is not the killer of the whores!' said Tulyet, exasperated. 'You believe that Froissart is the killer and that I lost him. Well, he is not the killer! Froissart did not even have the sense to confess to the murder of his wife, even though a witness saw him commit the crime! He could not have the intelligence to outwit me over the whore murders.'

'Oh? Who saw him commit the crime?' asked Michael with interest.

'His neighbour, a Mistress Janetta,' Tulyet said bitterly, 'although I am uncertain that her testimony is worth a great deal.'

Michael rose to leave. 'Thank you,' he said. 'You have been most helpful.'

Tulyet gaped at him. 'I have?' he said. 'You have not told me what you want.'

Michael beamed and clapped him on the shoulder. 'Keep up the good work,' he said, his comment designed to antagonise, and he swept out of the room and into the Castle bailey. He sauntered over to the soldiers playing dice.

'Gambling is a device of the Devil, my children,' he said cheerfully. 'Were you playing dice when you should have been watching St Mary's Church?'

The soldiers exchanged furtive glances. 'No,' one lied easily. 'Froissart did not leave. The only person to go in or out was the friar.'

'What friar?' asked Michael, feeling his interest quicken.

'The friar that visited Froissart in the church,' said the soldier with exaggerated patience.

'What time was this?' Michael asked.

The soldier squinted up at him. 'About an hour after the church was locked. It was dark by then, and we did not see him until he was almost on top of us.' He turned back to his game and threw his dice.

'Did you know him?'

The soldier shook his head, handing over a few pennies to one of his comrades, who laughed triumphantly. 'He said his name was Father Lucius, and when he shouted his name, Froissart opened the door and let him in.'

'What did he look like?'

The soldier shrugged. 'Like a friar! Mean-looking with a big nose, and a dirty grey robe with the cowl pulled up over his head.'

Michael nodded. If he were wearing a grey robe, he must have been a Franciscan. 'Did you see him leave?'

'Yes. After about an hour. He warned us about gambling, and left.' The soldier took the dice from his neighbour and threw them again. There was a series of catcalls as he lost a second time.

Michael sketched a quick benediction over them and strolled away. He had enjoyed making Tulyet give him the information he wanted by needling him into indiscretion. Michael had discovered not only where Froissart lived, but the identity of the neighbour who had witnessed his crime. From Tulyet's men, Michael had also discovered the identity of Froissart's murderer: the mysterious friar. He hummed a song from the taverns that he should not have known, and walked back down the hill a lot more happily than he had walked up it.

He saw Bartholomew talking to two Austin Canons outside the Hospital of St John the Evangelist as he turned from Bridge Street into the High Street. In fine humour he strolled across and greeted them. Bartholomew looked at him suspiciously and quickly concluded his conversation with the Canons.

'What have you been up to?' Bartholomew asked suspiciously. 'You are not usually so cheery after climbing Castle Hill.'

Michael told him, while Bartholomew listened thoughtfully. 'I know Richard Tulyet. He is not a bad man and, until recently, has been a good Sheriff. I hope you did not offend him. We might need his goodwill at some point.'

Michael hastily changed the subject to the Franciscan friar. 'How many do you know that are mean-looking and have big noses?' he said.

'Just about all of them,' said Bartholomew drily. 'We have at least five in Michaelhouse who match that description.'

Michael laughed. 'Shall we go and visit your Janetta, and Froissart's family?' he asked.

'We shall not!' said Bartholomew feelingly. 'It will be dark soon, and I have no desire to be there after curfew. De Wetherset's men can bring them to us tomorrow. I have had enough for today, and we have a very early start tomorrow when we exhume Nicholas.'

They began to walk back to Michaelhouse, stopping on the way for Michael to buy a large apple pie from a baker hastening to sell the last of his produce before trading ceased for the day. The sun was beginning to set, and weary tradesmen and apprentices were trailing in from the Fair.

'So Froissart knew his murderer,' said Michael, his mouth full.

'Possibly,' said Bartholomew. 'It is not absolutely certain that the Franciscan killed him. If Froissart allowed the Franciscan into the church, he may have let others in too while the soldiers were busy with their dice. And would one mean-looking friar have the strength to carry Froissart up to the tower and nail him to the bell frame?'

'I wonder whether Froissart fled up your path between the bushes from the scene of his crime to the church?' mused Michael. 'I wonder why Janetta of Lincoln went to such pains to hide it? Knowing what we do, I suspect that the only reason she intervened when the mob attacked you was because she is intelligent enough to know that two murders – yours and Froissart's wife – within a few days of each other might bring the unwanted attention of Tulyet's officers into her small domain. The death of Froissart's wife may have saved you, Matt.'

Bartholomew sighed. 'I want to read some Hippocrates tonight before the light fades completely. You could go to the Franciscan Friary and see if anyone there attended Froissart on the night of his death. The Franciscan's visit might be entirely innocent, and we should at least try to find out.'

Michael rubbed his hands. 'It is turning chilly,' he said, 'and not a red cloud to be seen. It will be raining when you dig up poor Nicholas tomorrow morning, Matt. You mark my words.'

CHAPTER 5

THE PORTER WAS ASLEEP IN HIS SMALL OFFICE when Bartholomew unbarred the wicket gate and stepped out into the lane long before dawn the following day. The night before, Kenyngham had enquired about the investigation concerning the body in the University chest, and Michael had given him a brief outline of what had happened, dutifully omitting any reference to Froissart and Nicholas's book. Kenyngham mentioned that the Chancellor had asked that they be relieved of teaching until further notice, a request of which he did not approve. It was relatively easy to find teachers of theology to take Michael's place, but there was no one who could teach medicine. Kenyngham instructed them to complete the business as soon as possible and to return to their obligations at the College.

'I am uncomfortable with the College becoming involved in this,' he had said. 'The relationship between town and University is unstable, and I do not want Michaelhouse to become a scapegoat. It is bad enough having to share St Michael's Church with Physwick Hostel – the Chancellor and both Proctors have connections there, and none but Jonstan are popular men.'

Bartholomew agreed. 'Perhaps relations may improve once the killer of these women is caught.'

'Ah, yes,' said Kenyngham. 'The man Tulyet allowed to escape.' Bartholomew and Michael exchanged a glance. 'That is not helping with University-town relations either. There is a rumour that he is being sheltered by one of the Colleges because the University does not approve of students visiting prostitutes.'

'That is an unreasonable assumption,' said Bartholomew. 'Women will always sell themselves so long as there is a demand.'

'I am not questioning the logic of the rumour, but of the damage it might do to us,' said Kenyngham, more impatiently than Bartholomew had heard him speak before. He must be concerned indeed, Bartholomew realised, for there was little that usually disturbed the gentle Gilbertine's equanimity.

Kenyngham continued. 'Michaelhouse is already the target for evil happenings. That business with the back gate worries me. We were lucky you and Cynric were to hand to save us all from being burned in our beds. Do you have any ideas as to why an attack should be aimed at us?'

Bartholomew and Michael shook their heads. 'It could only have been meant as some kind of warning,' said Michael. 'Perhaps it was not aimed at Michaelhouse at all, but at someone who uses the lane.'

'Really?' asked Kenyngham doubtfully. 'Like one of the merchants going to the wharves by the river?'

'It is possible,' said Michael. 'Such pyrotechnics need wood, and our gate is the only wood available.'

Kenyngham sighed. 'Well, I do not like it. I have asked that the Proctors set a beadle at the back gate until all this is resolved, and have stipulated that no one is allowed out of College after curfew for any reason except you two. The Bishop would not approve of me confining his best spy,' he said to Michael, 'and your work among the poor, Matthew, is very beneficial in maintaining good relations between us and the townspeople. So just remember that when you dispense some of your outlandish treatments. You might consider being more orthodox until this business is resolved.'

Bartholomew looked at him in bemusement, uncertain whether to be angry or amused that his work among the sick was being used as a political tool to placate the townspeople.

He mulled over Kenyngham's words as he waited for Michael and Cynric to join him, and glanced up at the low clouds that drenched the town with heavy rain. Michael's prediction had been right. Bartholomew pulled up the hood of his cloak and paced restlessly. The more he thought about what they were about to do, the more he felt it was terribly wrong. He was not averse to performing the exhumation in itself – he had seen far worse sights in his life – but he was afraid of the diseases the corpse might unleash. While he did not believe that supernatural powers opened the graves of the dead to bring the plague, he was reluctant to dismiss the rumour out of hand. When the consequences of an action might be as potentially devastating as a return of the plague, any risk, however small, was simply too great. He almost yelled out as a shadow glided up to him from behind.

'Easy, lad,' said Cynric, his teeth glinting white in a brief smile in the gloom.

'Do you have the lamp and rope?' Bartholomew asked, to hide his nervousness.

'And spades,' said Cynric. 'Stay here while I rouse that fat monk. He is probably still asleep.'

Bartholomew cursed softly as the first trickle of cold water coursed down the back of his neck. He closed his eyes against a sharp gust of wind that blew stinging rain into his face. What better conditions for an exhumation? he thought morosely. He remembered the murderer of the town prostitutes, the friar, and Froissart, and looked around uneasily. He hoped the night was sufficiently foul for murderers to want to be in their beds.

He almost cried out a second time as a heavy hand dropped onto his shoulder.

'Master Jonstan!' said Michael cheerfully, approaching and addressing the Junior Proctor who had given Bartholomew the fright. 'Were you told we have business tonight?'

Jonstan nodded. 'I have the licence here, signed by the Chancellor and the Bishop,' he said, waving a folded piece of vellum at them.

'Wonderful!' muttered Bartholomew irritably to Michael, his heart still thudding from the shock the Junior Proctor had given him. 'We may be about to risk the lives of hundreds of people by exhuming corpses, but all is well as long as we do so legally.'

'Believe me, Matt, I am as reluctant to do this as you are,' Michael replied. 'But the Chancellor has issued an order, and the Bishop's signature is confirmation that we have no alternative but to comply. Moaning about it will do no good at all.'

He took the bucket and a length of rope from Cynric, and set off up the lane towards St Mary's Church. Jonstan slipped away to instruct his beadles to stay at the College until he returned, while Bartholomew picked up a spade and trailed morosely after Michael, wishing the rain would stop. The single trickle of cold water down his back seemed to have developed into a deluge, and he was already shivering uncontrollably.

The others caught up with him, and they made their way silently to where St Mary's Church was a looming shadow against the dark sky. Father Cuthbert was waiting for them in the shelter of the porch, a huge black shape huddled up on a bench.

'Gilbert marked the grave with a rag on a stick,' he said, pulling a voluminous cloak around him against the cold. 'It is over there.'

'Are you certain it is the right one?' asked Bartholomew, aware of the priest's nervousness. He did not wish to dig up the wrong grave – especially since some of the first plague victims had been buried in the churchyard.

Cuthbert nodded quickly, and withdrew further into the shadows of the porch. He clearly had no intention of leaving his shelter to brave the elements, or to be directly involved in the unpleasant task that lay ahead. Bartholomew could not find it in his heart to condemn him for his attitude.

Cynric set up the lamp where it would be out of the rain, while Bartholomew took a spade and began to dig, grateful that Nicholas of York had not been considered important enough to have been given a tombstone that they would have had to move.

'No!' Father Cuthbert's voice was a hoarse cry. 'Not that one! The next one!'

Bartholomew peered at the mound Cuthbert indicated from the shelter of the porch. 'But this is the one that is marked.'

Cuthbert, reluctantly, left the porch, and came to stand next to the marker. 'It has been moved,' he said, surprised. 'Wretched children, I expect. I saw a group of them playing here late yesterday afternoon. That is the grave you need to dig, not this one.'

'How can you be sure?' asked Bartholomew, his resentment at the task imposed on him growing by the moment.

'Because when I said the funeral service for Nicholas, I stood under that tree, and water dripped down the back of my neck during the whole ceremony. I remember it clearly. I would not have stood so far away if he had been buried in this grave. I think this one is Mistress Archer's . . .'

'And she died of the plague,' Bartholomew finished for him, remembering her death vividly, one of the first he had witnessed. He shuddered. 'Really, Father, this affair is foolishness itself. Can we not merely assume the worst and say that Nicholas, too, was murdered? And then we can dispense with this distasteful business.'

Cuthbert gave a heavy sigh. 'Believe me, gentlemen, I tried as hard as you did to dissuade the Chancellor from this course of action, but he was immovable. I suspect the Bishop is behind it, and the Chancellor has little choice in the matter. Look,' he said, taking Bartholomew by the shoulder, 'you know what to expect, and you know how to avoid contamination. It is better that you do this than some of the beadles, who might well spread infection without realising what they are doing.'

Bartholomew nodded slowly. It was the first sense he had heard spoken since the business began. Cuthbert was right. Bartholomew had brought rags to wrap around their mouths and noses when they reached the coffin, and thick gloves to wear when he examined the body. Cynric had procured a bucket so that they could wash afterwards, and Bartholomew intended to burn any clothes that came in contact with the body. He doubted beadles would take such precautions.

He took up the spade a second time, and began to dig, while Cuthbert kicked around with his feet to hide the marks made on Mistress Archer's grave. Michael stood in the porch reading the licence, swearing to himself when he saw the ink had run in the rain, while Jonstan took the other spade and helped Bartholomew.

Despite the rain, digging was hard work. The last few weeks of hot, dry weather had baked the earth into a rock-like consistency. Bartholomew shed his cloak and tabard and dug in his shirt sleeves, grateful now for the rain that cooled him. Jonstan handed his spade to Cynric and went to sit in the porch next to Cuthbert to rest. When Bartholomew felt as though he had been digging for hours, the hole was still only thigh-deep. The rain sluiced down into the bottom of the grave as they worked, making their task even more difficult.

Michael relieved Bartholomew, who went to join Jonstan and Cuthbert in the porch. Cuthbert was telling Jonstan about the proposed rebuilding of the chancel, and both men were keen to discuss something other than the task in hand. Bartholomew glanced up at the sky. It was still dark, and dawn would come later because of the rain, but, even so, progress was slow. The law was quite clear that all exhumations should be carried out under cover of darkness, and they might have to come back the following night if they did not hurry.

Cynric looked exhausted, so Bartholomew went to take another turn. He bent to rest his hand on the ground and dropped lightly into the gaping hole. He was appalled to hear a loud splinter, and felt one foot break through wood. The water was too deep to see anything, and there was a horrified gasp from Jonstan, watching from above.

'I think we have reached the coffin,' Bartholomew said unnecessarily, looking up at the others. He poked and prodded with his spade and discovered that the coffin had been buried at an angle. When he dug further, he saw that a large boulder had blocked progress on one side, and so Nicholas of York's feet had been buried lower than his head. Bartholomew was able to clear the soil away from the top half of the coffin, and poked around under water until he felt the lower part was relatively free. Cynric dropped him a rope and he tied it around the crude wooden box.

Michael and Jonstan helped Bartholomew to climb out, and all five of them began to heave on the ropes. The coffin moved slightly, but it was immensely heavy. Bartholomew imagined it must be full of water.

After several minutes of straining and heaving to no avail, it became clear that they were not going to be able to get it out, and that Bartholomew would have to examine the body *in situ*. He tied one of the rags around his nose and mouth, donned the thick leather gloves and reluctantly climbed back into the grave, more carefully than he had the last time. The wood was slick in the rain, and it was difficult to stand upright. Until Cynric lay full length on the ground and held the lamp inside the grave, it was impossible to see what he was doing.

He inserted a chisel under the lid and tapped with a hammer. The lid eased up, and he got a good grip with his fingers and began to pull. The lid began to move with a great screech of wet wood, and came off so suddenly so that he almost fell backwards. He handed it up to Michael, and all five of them peered into the open coffin.

Bartholomew moved back, gagging, as the stench of putrefaction filled the confined space of the grave. His feet skidded and he scrabbled at the sides to try to prevent himself from falling over. Jonstan gave a cry of horror, and Cuthbert began to mutter prayers in an uneven, breathless whisper. Michael leaned down and grabbed at Bartholomew's shoulder, breathing through his mouth so as not to inhale the smell.

'Matt!' he gasped. 'Come out of there!'

He began to tug frantically at Bartholomew's shirt. Bartholomew needed no second bidding, and scrambled out of the grave with an agility that surprised even him. He sank to his knees and peered down at the thing in the coffin.

'What is it?' breathed Cynric.

Bartholomew cleared his throat to see if he could still speak, making Jonstan jump. 'It looks like a goat,' he said.

'A goat?' whispered Michael in disbelief. 'What is a goat doing there?'

Bartholomew swallowed hard. Two curved horns and a long pointed face stared up at him, dirty and stained from its weeks underground, but a goat's head nevertheless, atop a human body.

'Was Nicholas of York a devil?' breathed Jonstan. 'Was he not human, and reverted to his true form after death?' He raised his great round eyes to Cuthbert, who stared aghast down into the grave, his lips moving as he muttered his prayers.

'Men do not change into animals after they die,' said Michael, but his voice held no conviction, and Bartholomew saw Cuthbert and Jonstan exchange disbelieving glances.

'Perhaps he was not a man,' said Jonstan again, crossing himself.

'Nonsense,' said Bartholomew firmly, realising that if they did not get a grip on themselves soon, their imaginations would get the better of them. 'You knew Nicholas. Surely you would have noticed demonic qualities had he possessed them in life.'

He inhaled a deep breath of fresh air, thick with the scent of wet grass, took the lantern from Cynric, and leaned with it inside the grave. Shadows flickered eerily, but there was light enough to illuminate the peeling paint and the wood underneath.

'It is a mask!' he said, relief flooding through him. 'It is a wooden mask!'

'A mask? Why should Nicholas be wearing such a thing?' asked Cuthbert, his voice hoarse with horror.

For a few moments, no one said anything, and all five

stared into the gaping hole at the strange figure below. Bartholomew pulled himself together, and slid back into the grave to complete his examination. Anxious to finish as quickly as possible, he reached for the right hand to look for a tiny cut that might suggest Nicholas had died from the poison on the lock. Puzzled, he peered closer. The hand he held was small and dainty, with paint on the nails, but was too decomposed for him to be able to see whether there had been a cut there or not. He straddled the coffin precariously, grabbed the mask by its horns and pulled as hard as he could. The mask came off with an unpleasant sucking sound to reveal the face underneath.

'What is this?' cried Cuthbert. 'That is not Nicholas!'

'He *was* a devil!' whispered Jonstan, crossing himself vigorously. 'He *did* change his form after his death.'

'You have the wrong grave!' said Michael accusingly, looking at Cuthbert.

Cuthbert stared at him, his face white with shock. 'I do not!' he whispered. 'This is Nicholas's grave without question. I am absolutely certain.'

Michael and Bartholomew exchanged a look of bewilderment. The body whose face had been hidden by the mask was that of a young woman. Her eyes were sunken deep into her face, and the lips had stretched back to reveal fine, even teeth. That explained the delicate hand and painted nails, Bartholomew thought. He suddenly felt a great wave of compassion for her. Not only had she been brutally murdered, attested by the stab wound in her throat, but her body had been desecrated with the mask. But what was she doing there anyway? And where was Nicholas of York? Bartholomew took a deep breath and quickly looked under the woman to make sure there was not another corpse in the grave.

He was angry at the callousness of it all, and his anger brought him out of the sense of shock that had been dulling his wits. He bent to look at the woman. Assuming that the coffin had not been changed after Nicholas's funeral, she had been dead for a month. The state of decay confirmed this to Bartholomew, taking into account the fact that she had died during warm weather and that the earth had been baked dry for several weeks. The grave was only flooded now because of the sudden downpour. He looked at her feet, but they were wet, and even if the rain-water had not washed her feet clean, he would not have been able to identify a circle painted in blood on her rotting skin. The lamp above him fluttered in the wind and went out. Cynric swore and cursed in Welsh as he tried to re-light it, but the rain was coming down harder than ever and the wick was sodden.

Bartholomew waited in the dark, the water lapping about his ankles. The smell was overpowering, and it was becoming more and more difficult to resist the urge to turn around and scramble out.

'I cannot light it,' said Cynric from above him, his voice unsteady.

'What shall we do, Father?' asked Bartholomew. 'There is no point in examining this woman when she is not Nicholas. Shall we rebury her and leave her in peace?'

'We must bring the body out,' said Cuthbert. 'If not, the Chancellor will order that you bring her out another night so that she can be identified and the whole matter investigated.'

'She cannot be identified now,' said Bartholomew.

'She has been underground too long. And I can tell you now that she died because she was stabbed in the throat. It does not take a physician to see that.'

'Bring her out, Matt,' said Michael. 'Father Cuthbert is right in that the Chancellor will demand an investigation, and I for one do not want to go through all this again tomorrow.'

Cynric handed Bartholomew a chisel. 'Make a hole in the bottom of the coffin to let the water drain,' he said. 'Then it will be easier to lift.'

Michael fetched the rope, and Bartholomew fumbled about trying to tie the knots in the darkness while Jonstan attempted to light a second lamp under the shelter of the porch. Eventually, Bartholomew thought the knots were secure, and Michael and Cynric began to pull. With a slurp of mud, the coffin came free, sending water everywhere. Bartholomew steadied it until the others were able to heave it up and onto the ground.

Bartholomew found that his arms were too tired to allow him to climb out again, and he had a moment's panic until Michael offered his hand and hauled so hard that Bartholomew shot from the grave like a cork from a bottle. Cynric had put the lid back over the coffin and was enlarging the hole in the bottom to allow any water still remaining to drain away. Jonstan watched.

'It was that mask,' he said with a shudder. 'If it had just been the woman, it would not have been so bad. But that thing looks like something from hell.' He crossed himself yet again and backed away.

'I will unlock the church and we can put the body in the crypt out of sight,' said Cuthbert, clearly the more practical of the two. 'The goat mask can go in the charnel house until the Chancellor has seen it. Who would do such a thing to a corpse?'

But more to the point, who was she? Bartholomew thought. And where was Nicholas? Was he alive or dead? He wanted to rub his eyes, but glimpsed his filthy hands and thought better of it. He and Michael had gained nothing from this grisly business. They had answered no questions, but had raised many more.

The sky was brightening noticeably by the time they had removed the woman's body and filled in the grave. Michael, white-faced, went with Jonstan to give a complete report to the Chancellor, while Cuthbert remained in the church to say prayers for the dead woman. Bartholomew looked down at his wet and muddy clothes despondently. The rain was easing off with the onset of dawn, but the day seemed cold and gloomy.

He and Cynric walked home, where they hauled buckets of water from the well to wash, and Bartholomew threw the gloves and his old clothes onto the ever-smouldering fires behind the kitchen. Bartholomew was down to his last shirt, and he hoped he would have an uneventful day in order to give Agatha time to do the laundry. Shivering, they went to the kitchen, where Cynric warmed some potage left over from the day before. When the bell chimed for Prime, Bartholomew was fast asleep in Agatha's chair next to the fireplace, and she did not waken him.

Michael returned later, having spoken to de Wetherset, and said he planned to continue his reading of Nicholas's book. Bartholomew spent the rest of the morning teaching, and was pleased with the way some of his students were learning, although he was finding Brother Boniface difficult. The friar seemed to have been talking to the fanatic Father William, for he was obsessed with the notion of heresy. Boniface proclaimed that Bartholomew teaching them surgery was heretical, and sparked a bitter argument, with Bulbeck and Gray defending Bartholomew's position, and Boniface and his fellow Franciscans opposing it. It was not an argument based on logic and reason, but on ignorance and bigotry on both sides. Bartholomew did not take part, and listened with a growing sense of weariness.

Ibn Ibrahim had warned him that some of the techniques and cures he had been taught would meet with hostility and suspicion, but he was unprepared for such reactions from his own students. He thought about the difference between Arab and Christian medicine, and wondered whether he had made the right decision in choosing the former. Naïvely, he had assumed that his greater success with diseases and wounds than his more traditional colleagues would speak for itself, and that in time people would come to accept his methods. But Boniface claimed that Bartholomew's success was because he used methods devised by the Devil, while Gray and Bulbeck claimed he was blessed by God with a gift of healing, as though his painstakingly acquired skills were nothing.

As he listened to Boniface's raving, Bartholomew considered telling Kenyngham that he was impossible to teach. But all hostels and Colleges were finding it difficult to recruit students after the plague, with the exception of lawyers, and Michaelhouse could not afford to lose the Franciscans.

After the main meal of the day, eaten in silence, he went to St Mary's in search of Michael. The clerks told him they had been unable to find Janetta or Froissart's kinsmen. Bartholomew was relieved: he and Michael could not proceed until they had spoken to them, and the fact that they were unavailable would slow everything down and allow him to concentrate on his teaching duties.

He was about to return to Michaelhouse when he was hailed by de Wetherset, who wanted to know what could be discovered from the dead woman. Grimacing to register his reluctance, Bartholomew followed de Wetherset down into the small cellar under the altar. The door leading to the stairs was locked, and the Chancellor motioned the ever-solicitous Gilbert forward to open it and precede them down damp steps into the musty crypt. Gilbert held back, his eyes huge with fear. De Wetherset looked as though he would order Gilbert into the crypt, but he relented, and patted him on the shoulder.

'I have no taste for this either,' he said. 'Father Cuthbert!'

The priest waddled from where he had been scraping candle wax from the altar, took the keys from Gilbert, and puffed down the steps to the vault below. The crypt was little more than a passageway that ran under the altar from one side of the choir to the other. To the left was a small chamber protected by a stout door, where the church silver was kept. In the chamber, two coffins lay side by side on the ground: Froissart's and the woman's. Several large bowls of incense were dotted about, adding to the general overpowering odour.

'I am surprised you need to lock this,' said Bartholomew

hoarsely, his eyes watering. 'I would think the smell alone would be deterrent enough.'

De Wetherset ignored him and pulled the sheet off the coffin in which the woman lay. Bartholomew was again filled with compassion for her. He made a cursory examination of the wound on her throat he had seen that morning, and looked again in vain for a circle on the sole of her foot. Lifting the simple gown of pale blue, he inspected her body for other wounds, but found nothing. Her dress, home-made and like a hundred others in the town, would not help to identify her, and her face meant nothing to Bartholomew. He suggested giving a description of her to Richard Tulyet to see whether he had been told of some person missing over the last month.

'This makes five,' said de Wetherset, dismissing his suggestion with a contemptuous wave of his hand. 'Five prostitutes dead.'

'We do not know she was a prostitute,' said Bartholomew. 'And Frances de Belem was not a prostitute either.'

De Wetherset made an impatient gesture. 'They were all killed by wounds to the throat, and she, like the others, is barefoot. How much of a coincidence is that?'

Father Cuthbert peered over Bartholomew's shoulder. 'What happened to her hair?'

Bartholomew looked at the wispy strands attached to the woman's head and shrugged. 'I suppose hair falls out when the skin rots. Or perhaps she had an illness which made her hair thin.'

'Then she will be easy for Tulyet to identify,' said

de Wetherset. 'There cannot be many bald women in Cambridge.'

'I know some women who have used powerful caustics on their hair to dye it, and I have been called to treat the infections they cause,' said Bartholomew thoughtfully. 'Once the scalp has healed, the hair does not always grow again, and they need to wear veils and wimples.'

'Really?' queried de Wetherset with morbid fascination. 'How curious. The King's grandmother, Queen Isabella, always wears a wimple. I wonder if she is bald, too.'

Bartholomew stared at the woman in the coffin. Who was she? Had she been killed by the three men who had been in Michaelhouse's orchard two nights before? Or was there more than one group of maniacs in the town? Seven deaths – the five women, the friar and Froissart, plus Nicholas and Buckley missing. Were they dead too? Or were they the murderers?

'Did you see Nicholas dead?' asked Bartholomew.

De Wetherset looked momentarily taken aback by the question, and then understanding dawned in his eyes. 'Yes,' he said. 'I saw him here in the church, although I must confess I did not poke and prod at his body as I have watched you do to corpses. A vigil was kept for him by the other clerks the day before his funeral. Then his coffin was sealed and left in the church overnight, and he was buried the following morning.' He turned to Cuthbert, who nodded his agreement with de Wetherset's account.

'So, he must have been taken from his coffin that night,' said Bartholomew, 'and replaced with the dead woman wearing the mask.'

De Wetherset swallowed hard. 'Do you think Nicholas may not have been dead after all?' he said. 'That he might have killed the woman and put her in the coffin that was intended for him?'

Bartholomew shrugged non-committally. 'It is possible,' he said. 'But how? You say the coffin was sealed the night before his funeral, so how did he get out to kill a woman and put her in his coffin? And why was she wearing the mask?'

'Perhaps she came to let him out,' said de Wetherset, 'and he killed her so that there would be a body in his coffin the next day when we came to bury it.'

'That seems unlikely,' said Bartholomew. 'Why would a woman take such a risk? Was your clerk the kind of man to conceive such an elaborate plot, and then kill?'

De Wetherset shook his head firmly. 'No. Nicholas was a good man. He would never commit murder.'

Bartholomew remained doubtful, knowing that extreme events might drive the meekest of men to the most violent of acts. Perhaps one of the covens had come to the church to perform some diabolical ceremony over Nicholas's body and had exchanged his body for hers, although Bartholomew could think of nothing that might be gained from such an action. He drew the sheet over her, covering her from sight. Cuthbert shuddered.

'Now will you look at the mask?' asked de Wetherset.

Bartholomew looked at him in surprise. 'What can I tell you about that? You can see as well as I what it is.'

'You are always thorough when you look at corpses,' said de Wetherset, 'and if you are as thorough with the mask, you might uncover some clue I have overlooked.'

Bartholomew trailed reluctantly after him into the small charnel house in the churchyard and looked down at the mask. In the bright light of day, it was a miserable thing, poorly carved and cheaply painted. But the horns and the top of the skull were real, which Bartholomew had not realised before.

'The horns probably came from the butchers' market,' he said. 'And as for the mask, I have seen nothing like it before, and I cannot tell you where it came from. It must belong to one of the covens.'

'Covens?' said de Wetherset suspiciously. 'What do you mean?'

Bartholomew repeated the information Stanmore had given him, while de Wetherset narrowed his eyes.

'So you know about that,' he said. Bartholomew shot him an irritable glance. De Wetherset was not surprised by the information because he had known all along. What else was he keeping from them? 'Do you know about the Guild of the Holy Trinity too?'

'That is not a coven, is it?' asked Bartholomew, confused.

'Indeed not,' said de Wetherset. 'It is a group of people who are dedicated to stamping out sin and evil lest the plague come again. They are the antithesis of the Guild of the Coming and the Guild of Purification, or whatever blasphemous names these covens have chosen for themselves.'

'Could the Guild of the Holy Trinity be responsible for the murders?' asked Bartholomew. 'People who believe that prostitution is one of the sins that brought the plague? Do you know who is a member? What about Master Jonstan? He seems opposed to prostitution.'

'So am I,' said de Wetherset. 'But I am not a member of the Guild of the Holy Trinity, and neither is Jonstan. But Cuthbert is, and so was Nicholas.'

Bartholomew chewed on his lip, trying to understand. 'So Nicholas was in a guild that is known for its antagonism to the prostitutes. A month ago he died, but in his coffin is found not Nicholas, but a murdered woman.'

'Yes,' said de Wetherset, studying Bartholomew intently. 'Curious, is it not? I can see you are thinking that Nicholas might be the killer, freed from his coffin and stalking the town. But I am more inclined to believe that the disappearance of his body is the work of the covens, perhaps because he took an active stance against them. Perhaps they worked some sort of vile spell to bring him from his eternal rest.'

'I do not believe the dead can walk, Master de Wetherset,' said Bartholomew, 'and we should not allow that rumour to escape, or the town will revolt for certain if they think our dead clerks are killing their women. Perhaps Nicholas's body was stolen as you suggest. But the mask is the problem. Why go to the trouble of leaving this poor woman wearing the mask unless she was meant to be found – meant to be seen like this?'

De Wetherset looked appalled. 'Are you saying that someone knew we would exhume Nicholas?' he said.

Bartholomew spread his hands. 'Not necessarily. Perhaps the mask and the woman's body were meant to be found before he was buried, or even during the funeral service. I do not know. But why would anyone go to such trouble unless it was meant to be seen by others?'

'It could just be a person with a fevered brain,' said de Wetherset.

'Well, that goes without saying,' said Bartholomew drily, 'but I still think whoever did it intended his work to be found.'

De Wetherset shuddered again. 'I do not like being near this thing. Come with me back to my hostel and have something to eat. Have you ever been to Physwick Hostel?' Bartholomew shook his head and de Wetherset gave him a sidelong glance. 'I find it odd that Cambridge is small in some ways – one can never walk anywhere without seeing someone one knows – and yet you have never been inside Physwick, even though our gate lies almost opposite yours!'

Bartholomew smiled. It was not so odd. Hostels and Colleges were very competitive, and scholars were generally discouraged from wandering from one to the other. Less than a month before, students from one hostel had attacked those from another, and the result had been a violent fight. And only the previous week Alcote had tried to fine some unfortunate who had been caught dining in St Thomas's Hostel until the Master had intervened. He thought the Chancellor must know this, but perhaps he was making desultory conversation to take his mind away from the unpleasant events of the day.

'I must wash my hands first,' Bartholomew said, thinking of his examination of the woman's decomposing body.

'What for?' asked de Wetherset, perturbed. 'They look clean enough to me. Wipe them off on your tabard.'

Bartholomew gave him a bemused glance. He knew his insistence on washing his hands after seeing every patient was regarded with amusement in the town, but surely, even someone as adverse to washing as the Chancellor could see that hands needed to be cleaned after touching corpses! He hoped the Chancellor's standards of hygiene did not extend to the Physwick Hostel kitchens.

They walked outside into the sunshine, and Bartholomew saw the Chancellor glance to where Nicholas of York's grave had been. As they walked past, de Wetherset stopped and peered at something.

'What is that?' he muttered, inching closer.

'My bag!' exclaimed Bartholomew in delight. 'The one that was stolen in the alley the other day.'

He picked it up and looked inside. It appeared to be exactly as it had been before it had been stolen. His tabard was there, rolled up and stuffed on top of his medicines and instruments. His notebooks were there too, containing records of patients he had seen and what dosages of various potions he had given them. Nervously, he looked in the side pouch where the strong medicines were, and heaved a sigh of relief that they appeared unmolested.

'You know what this means?' said de Wetherset in a low whisper, his face solemn. 'It means that whoever stole your bag also knows that something went on at this grave this morning. Why else would they leave it here to be found?'

Bartholomew's elation at getting his precious bag back evaporated at the implications of de Wetherset's comments. He was probably right. Janetta of Lincoln must be involved in all this. She was linked to Froissart, and she was present when Bartholomew's bag had been stolen. Did she watch them exhume the grave that morning from her secret path? There was too much coincidence for it to be mere chance.

'I would discard any potions in that bag,' said de Wetherset, eyeing it suspiciously. 'Who knows what they might have been exchanged for? You might end up killing one of your patients. Are there any locks on it that may now have poisoned devices?' he asked.

Bartholomew turned the bag over in his hands. It looked the same, and he was pleased to have it back. The one Father Aidan had lent him did not have the same feel to it, and Bartholomew could never find what he wanted. Nevertheless, de Wetherset was right, and he decided not only to discard the medicines, but to test some of them too.

He and de Wetherset strolled the short distance to Physwick Hostel, a small, half-timbered building opposite Michaelhouse. Bartholomew saw Alcote watching him enter, but assumed the Senior Fellow could not object to Bartholomew accepting an invitation from the University's Chancellor, even if he were from another College.

Bartholomew's insistence on washing his hands was met with some amusement by de Wetherset's colleagues, which Bartholomew accepted with weary resignation. He knew most of the men of Physwick from standing opposite them in church. Richard Harling nodded coolly towards him, and continued a debate on canon law with another lawyer. Alric Jonstan was there, and greeted Bartholomew warmly. He seemed to have recovered from his morning excursion, although he was pale and his eyes seemed red and tired.

The ale at Physwick was far superior to that at Michaelhouse, and was clear and fresh. The bread, however, was the same: grainy and made with inferior flour. There was some cheese too, but that had been left in the sun and was hard and dry, and sat in a rancid yellow puddle.

They discussed the advantages and failings of the Cambridge examination system for a while, and then Jonstan began to chat to Bartholomew about his duties as Junior Proctor. Next to him, de Wetherset and Harling talked about a guild meeting that was to be held the following day. Bartholomew listened to them while appearing to be paying close attention to Jonstan's somewhat tedious account of the Proctor's statutory responsibilities. They were discussing a proposed meeting of the Guild of the Purification, and from what Harling was telling de Wetherset, trouble was expected.

'You recall what happened last time,' he said. 'The following day, St John Zachary's Church was full of spent torches and someone had drawn a sign on the altar in what looked to be blood.'

Bartholomew listened intently, strands of the mystery twining together in his mind. The goat mask on the woman in Nicholas's grave was clearly a demonic device, which might mean that the murders of the other women were also connected to witchcraft. The large man in the orchard who had bitten him had worn a red mask, obviously a satanic trapping.

Was this the clue he needed to tie it all together? Perhaps he would see whether Stanmore had learned anything else. Then they needed to find Froissart's family and Janetta of Lincoln. The reappearance of his bag told him that Janetta was most definitely in Cambridge, despite the claims of de Wetherset's clerks that they could not trace her. Should he try to seek for her himself? But she would know Bartholomew wanted to see her, and if she did not want to see him, nothing would be served by him risking his safety to go in search of her.

Of course, another thing he could do would be to talk to some of the friends of the women who had been killed. Some of them might have some indication of who the killer might be. Perhaps they were unwilling to talk to Tulyet, whose men were, after all, the ones who arrested them if they were caught touting for business on the town's streets. He decided he would ask Sybilla. She was the only prostitute he was aware he knew, and Sybilla had been the one to find Isobel.

And there was another thing: Frances de Belem had been killed in Michaelhouse grounds, but Physwick Hostel was a mere stone's throw away. He looked around at the men sitting with him at High Table – de Wetherset, Harling, and Jonstan. All high-ranking and well-respected University men, but was one of them the lover of Frances de Belem? Bartholomew reconsidered them: de Wetherset, stocky with pig-like features; Harling with his greased black hair and bad complexion; Jonstan with his odd tonsure and long teeth. Could she have fallen for any of these men? He would not have thought so, but Edith, his sister, frequently told him he did not understand women, and misjudged their likes and dislikes.

He became aware that Jonstan had asked him a question and was awaiting an answer, beaming affably, his large blue eyes curious. Bartholomew was embarrassed and reluctant to reveal to the pleasant Jonstan that he had not been listening to a word he had said.

'Oh, yes,' he said, smiling and hoping it was the expected response.

Jonstan looked puzzled, but shrugged. 'That is what my mother always told me,' he said, 'but I have never yet met a physician who agreed with her until now. I must encourage her to eat more of them.'

Oh lord! thought Bartholomew. I hope whatever it is does not make her sick!

After leaving Physwick Hostel, Bartholomew, on the Chancellor's orders, went to the Castle to talk to Richard Tulyet about discovering another victim of the killer. De Wetherset could not conceal two bodies from the Sheriff, and reluctantly conceded that he was obliged to tell him that the killer had claimed another. De Wetherset repeated his previous instruction that the death of Froissart should not be made known to the Sheriff, lest it should somehow lead the killer to strike again.

Bartholomew was shown into the same office in the keep that Michael had visited the previous day. At first, Tulyet refused to speak to Bartholomew, shouting angrily that he had better things to do than gossip with idle scholars. Bartholomew asked the sergeant to inform him that another victim had been found, and was escorted begrudgingly into Tulyet's office. Bartholomew could tell in an instant that Michael had antagonised Tulyet, and he was irritated with his friend. If the killer were to be tracked down, they would work a lot more efficiently by co-operating, than by bickering and playing power games.

He tried to begin the interview on a positive note by

asking Tulyet about his wife and baby. When Tulyet's baby was born, it was a strange yellow colour. The midwife sniffed imperiously and announced that it suffered from an excess of yellow bile and should be bled to relieve it of a dangerous imbalance of humours. Bleeding was usually the province of barber-surgeons, but, since the plague, there was only the unsavoury Robin of Grantchester, and Bartholomew had been called in his place.

Bartholomew had declined to bleed the baby, and had prescribed a wet nurse and a mild concoction of feverfew, comfrey, and camomile to relieve its fever and bring healing sleep. Employing a wet nurse allowed the mother to rest, and both child and mother began to recover rapidly, despite the midwife's dire predictions. But when Bartholomew examined the mother afterwards, he found a wound from the birth that would mean she was unlikely to have another child. The last time he saw them, both had been happy and healthy, and Bartholomew saw with pleasure that neither required his services any longer.

Tulyet sat behind a large table, writing, and looked up with open hostility when Bartholomew asked after his child.

'By what right do you ask about my family?' Tulyet demanded belligerently.

Bartholomew was nonplussed. People usually expected him to ask them how they were, and he wondered if Tulyet had had an argument with his wife. He changed the subject and began to tell him about finding the dead woman that morning. Tulyet leapt to his feet in dismay.

'Another woman, you say? Dead, like the others, with her throat cut?'

Bartholomew nodded and waited for the Sheriff to calm himself before continuing.

'She must have been killed and placed in Nicholas's coffin about a month ago. The Chancellor and his clerks saw the body in the chapel the night before his funeral. Father Cuthbert says the coffin was sealed before the church was locked for the night, because Nicholas was to be buried the next morning. His body must have been removed and the woman's put there instead.'

'But why?' said Tulyet, shaking his head slowly. 'I do not understand why.'

'Nor I,' said Bartholomew. 'I cannot believe that whoever put her there could have anticipated that Nicholas would be exhumed at a later stage. I think her body was intended to be found before the burial for some reason.'

'The murderer intended her to be found in Nicholas's coffin?' Tulyet rubbed at the sparse beard on his chin. 'That makes sense. His other victims have been left in places where they would be found – including your College, Doctor.'

'There was something else,' said Bartholomew. 'There was a goat mask on the body.'

Tulyet gaped at him. 'A goat mask? Are you jesting with me?'

Bartholomew shook his head. Tulyet stared out of the door across to where his men were practising sword drills half-heartedly in the fading daylight.

'Well,' he said, standing abruptly. 'I can think of no reason for that. It is odd, I suppose. But stranger things have happened.'

Not much stranger, thought Bartholomew, surprised

by Tulyet's dismissal of the desecration. He found himself wondering whether Tulyet was really as initially shocked by the revelation as he appeared to be. He changed the subject yet again.

'Have you noticed a common element to the deaths of these women?' he asked. 'Has a mark or a sign been left to identify their deaths as the work of one person?' He wanted to know whether the first victim, Hilde, had had a circle on her foot.

'Oh yes,' said Tulyet, bringing cold eyes to bear on him. 'Cut throats and no shoes. Signature enough, would you not say?'

'Have you noticed anything else?' persisted Bartholomew.

Tulyet regarded him suspiciously. 'What sort of thing did you have in mind, Doctor?' he asked softly, disconcerting Bartholomew with his icy stare.

'Nothing specific,' Bartholomew lied badly. He wished he had not attempted to question Tulyet. He should have left it to Michael, who was more skilled at investigative techniques than him. He recalled the rumours that Michael, de Belem and Stanmore had told him, that the Sheriff was not investigating the deaths as carefully as he might, and began to wonder whether there might be a more sinister reason for his inactivity.

Tulyet moved closer to him, fingering a small dagger he wore at his belt. 'Are you hiding information from us, Doctor?' he asked menacingly. 'Have you learned something about this while you have been after the Chancellor's business?'

Bartholomew inwardly cursed both de Wetherset for sending him on this errand when the clerks seemed to have been spreading news of their investigation all over the town, and his own inabilities to mislead people convincingly. Michael would not be experiencing difficulties now, and neither would de Wetherset. He shook his head and rose to leave. Tulyet forced him to sit back down again. Bartholomew glanced out of the open door. He could overpower Tulyet as easily as he could a child, for the man was slight and Bartholomew was far stronger, but he would never be able to escape across the bailey and through the gate-house without being stopped by Tulyet's men. Tulyet had been watching him, and shouted for two guards to stand by the door.

'You are right, Doctor,' he said, drawing his dagger and playing with it. 'If you were to run, you would never leave the Castle alive. I could arrest you now and question you until you tell me what I want to know, or you can volunteer the information. Which is it to be?'

Bartholomew thought quickly. He had come to Tulyet with the intention of telling him the little he knew about the murders of the women – the circle on their feet and its possible link to the guilds, the link between the goat in the coffin and witchcraft, and the fact that the murders of the women might somehow be related to Nicholas of York. But now he had doubts. How could he be sure that Tulyet was not a member of one of the guilds that dabbled in black magic? His reaction to the goat had been odd, to say the least. Perhaps he already knew who the killer was, but his hands were tied because of his membership of a guild. From what Bartholomew understood of guilds, Tulyet would be unlikely and unwilling to arrest a fellow member.

'I know nothing more than what I have told you,

except,' Bartholomew said, trying to quell his tumbling thoughts, 'that I wondered whether the other dead women might have been marked in some way. Perhaps with something from a goat, like the mask on the woman we found this morning.' He convinced himself he was telling Tulyet the truth. He knew very little, and was merely guessing at the tenuous links between the murders, witchcraft, the guilds, and the University.

'What nonsense are you speaking?' said Tulyet angrily. 'You saw four of the victims yourself! Did you notice a goat attached to them?'

'I did not say it would be a whole goat,' said Bartholomew testily, 'and you asked me what I knew, and I am telling you. I am only trying to ascertain whether there was something common to all victims that might give some clue as to the murderer's identity.'

'Well, your suggestion is ludicrous,' said Tulyet. He replaced his dagger in its sheath and leaned close to Bartholomew. 'I will let you go this time, Doctor. But you will report to me anything that you discover about the deaths of the whores while you investigate the body in the chest. If I think for a moment that you are withholding information from me, I will issue a warrant for your immediate arrest, and no amount of protesting and whining from your University will be able to help you.'

Bartholomew rose, not particularly unsettled by Tulyet's threat. The Sheriff was underestimating the combined power of the University and the Church. His arrest would be considered a flouting of the University's rights to be dealt with under Canon law, and the Sheriff would have no option but to release him once University and Church swung into operation. This protection was exactly the reason why most University scholars took minor orders.

Tulyet shadowed him out of the Castle, and Bartholomew was aware that he was watched until he was out of sight. He deliberately dawdled, stopping on the Great Bridge to see how much more of its stone had been stolen since the last time he looked. If the Sheriff had time to waste on trying to make him feel uncomfortable, let him waste it, he thought, leaning his elbows on the handrail and peering down at the swirling water below.

Later, back at Michaelhouse, he told Michael what had happened.

'I will tell de Wetherset and the Bishop,' said the fat monk. 'They will not countenance your arrest. Tulyet must either have a very inflated idea of his own powers, or what you said must have rattled him.'

'But why?' said Bartholomew. 'Is he connected? Is that why he has made so little progress in catching the killer?'

Michael thought for a while. 'It is possible,' he said, 'and I am even more prepared to think so because I do not like the man. I wonder why he reacted so oddly at the mention of the goat mask.'

'Perhaps he is a member of one of the guilds that is connected to witchcraft,' said Bartholomew. 'I have been told that the Devil is supposed to appear in the form of a goat.'

'Yes. Cloven feet and horns,' said Michael. 'Like the painting of the Devil devouring souls on the wall of our church.'

Bartholomew thought about the painting. Depictions

of hell and purgatory were common in all the town's churches. No wonder people like Father Cuthbert and Nicholas joined guilds that denounced sin so vehemently, if they thought they would end up like some of the characters in the paintings. But equally, why would others risk that to become members of covens?

'I am going to Ely tomorrow,' said Michael. 'I want that spare set of keys, and I must report what we have discovered to my Lord the Bishop.'

'Ask him about witchcraft,' said Bartholomew.

Michael looked amused. 'Now why do you think a Benedictine bishop would know such things?' he said, humour twinkling in his green eyes.

'Because any Bishop that did not make himself familiar with potential threats to his peace would be a fool,' said Bartholomew. 'I am sure your Bishop will have clerks who will be able to furnish you with a good deal of information if you were to ask.'

Michael stood and cracked his knuckles. 'Time for something to eat before bed,' he said. 'I may be in Ely for several days, so be careful. I will warn de Wetherset of Tulyet's threat to you. You can talk to Froissart's family, or Janetta of Lincoln, if they deign to appear. Otherwise, do nothing until I return with orders from the Bishop.'

Bartholomew watched him amble across the court-yard to the kitchen. He heard an angry screech as he was evidently caught raiding by Agatha, and then the College was silent. Only the richest fellows and students of Michaelhouse could afford to buy candles in the summer, and so once the sun had set and the light became too poor for reading, most scholars usually slept or talked. Here and there groups of students sat or stood chatting in the dark, and the sound of raised voices from the conclave indicated that the Franciscans were engaged in one of their endless debates about the nature of heresy.

One of the groups outside comprised Gray, Bulbeck, and Deynman, and Bartholomew smiled as he heard Bulbeck, in exasperated tones, repeating the essence of Bartholomew's lecture on Dioscorides. Deynman mumbled outrageous answers to Bulbeck's testing questions, which made Gray laugh. The light was fading fast, and Bartholomew turned to go to his own room before it became too dark to see what he was doing. He undressed and lay on the hard bed, kicking off the rough woollen blanket because the night was humid.

He closed his eyes and then opened them again as he heard a sound outside the open shutters of his window. A lamp was shining through it, but it was the monstrous shape on the far wall that made him start from the bed with a cry of horror. A great horned head was silhouetted there: the head of a goat. He swallowed hard and crept to the window, trying not to look at the foul shadow on the wall as it swayed back and forth.

He stared in disbelief at the sight of Michael and Cynric kneeling on the ground shaking with suppressed mirth. Michael held a lamp, while Cynric made figures on the wall with his hands. They saw Bartholomew and stood up, roaring with laughter.

'Agatha showed us how to do it,' Michael said, gasping for breath. 'Oh, Matt! You should see your face!'

'Agatha told you to do that to me?' said Bartholomew incredulously.

'Oh, lord, no!' said Michael. 'She would rip our heads off if she thought we had dared to play a practical joke on her favourite Fellow. She has a fire lit to cook the potage for tomorrow's breakfast, and she was showing Cynric how to make the shapes of different animals with his hands. She showed him a goat, and I could not resist the temptation to try it on you,' he said.

Cynric grinned. 'It worked wonderfully, eh lad?' he said, beginning to laugh again.

Bartholomew leaned his elbows on the window-sill, and shook his head at them, beginning to see the humour of it, despite his still-pounding heart. 'That was a rotten thing to do,' he said, but without rancour. 'Now I will never get to sleep.'

Still chuckling, Cynric took the lamp back to the kitchen, watched curiously by Bartholomew's students still talking in the courtyard. Michael reached through the window and punched Bartholomew playfully before returning to his own room on the floor above. Bartholomew could hear his heavy footsteps moving about, and his voice as he related his prank to his two Benedictine room-mates. He heard them laugh and smiled despite himself. He would think of some way to pay Michael back, and Cynric too. He went to lie back down on his bed, and after a moment got up and closed the shutters, disregarding the stuffiness. Satisfied, he felt himself sliding off into sleep. At the fringes of his mind, he was aware that the meeting of the coven at St John Zachary was planned for that night and that he had intended to ask Stanmore about it. But it was late, Bartholomew's day had been a long and trying one, and he was already falling into a deep sleep.

chapter 6

FTER THE FRENZIED EVENTS OF THE LAST THREE days, Bartholomew was grateful for a respite while Michael went to Ely. He drilled his students relentlessly, and when at noon on Friday the College bell chimed to indicate the end of lectures for the day, his students heaved a corporate sigh of relief and prepared to spend the rest of the day recuperating from the shock of being made to work so hard.

The porter had a message asking him to visit the miller at Newnham village half a mile away. He had a hasty meal of thin barley soup flavoured with bacon rinds and some unripe pears, and set off. He walked upstream along the river path, muddy and slippery from the rain of the day before. The river itself ran fast and grey-brown, and Bartholomew saw a drowned sheep that had obviously strayed too close to the edge and fallen in. He crossed the river at Small Bridges Street, paying a fee of one penny to use the two wooden bridges that spanned different branches of the meandering river. Once out of the town, peace prevailed. Larks twittered in the huge sky above him, and fields, neatly divided into ribbons, were rich with oats and barley. A man emerged from where he had been tending one field, and wielded a hoe at Bartholomew. Such was the shortage of crops that any farmer would need to guard his property well if he wished to feed his family or grow rich on the proceeds.

The miller and his family sat outside the mill sharing some baked fish. The three children – of ten – who had survived the plague looked thin and hungry, while their father's mill stood silent. There were three mills in Cambridge, and the one at Newnham was by far the smallest and the most isolated. Business was poor for all of them, for the lack of crops meant that there was little for mills to grind. Bartholomew had seen the miller at the Fair offering ridiculously low prices for his labour.

The family saw him coming and waved him over. The miller's wife held a child on her lap. Bartholomew, careful not to waken him, saw painfully thin limbs and a distended stomach that was full of nothing. The miller's wife said her milk had dried up, and the baby was unable to eat fish. She wanted him to bleed the baby, thinking that an excess of black bile might be making him sick from the fish, and offered him her last three pennies to do so.

Why people believed bleeding would cure so much was beyond Bartholomew's understanding. He sent one of the older children to buy bread and milk from a nearby farmer with the three pennies, and showed the mother how to feed the baby milk sops in small amounts so as not to make him sick. But what would happen when the bread and milk ran out next time? And what about the rest of the family, looking at the milk sops with envious eyes? Bartholomew vowed he would never complain about College bread again.

Since it was a pleasant evening for a walk, and he was

not expected back at Michaelhouse, he decided to visit his sister in Trumpington. He walked slowly, enjoying the warmth of the sun and the fresh, clean air of the countryside. Birds flitted from tree to tree, and at one point a deer trotted from the undergrowth across the path. Bartholomew stood still and watched as it nibbled delicately at a patch of grass. It suddenly became aware of him and stared intently until, unconcerned, it took a final mouthful of grass and disappeared unhurriedly into the dark scrub to the side of the path.

As Bartholomew strolled through the gates to Edith's house, she came running to meet him, delighted at his unexpected visit. He followed her into the kitchen and sat at the great oak table while she fetched him cool ale and freshly baked pastries, which made him think guiltily of the miller's child. Oswald Stanmore heard his wife's greetings from where he had been working in the solar, and came to join them. The kitchen was full of delicious smells, as meats roasted on spits in the fireplace. Edith had been picking rhubarb, and great mounds of it sat at one end of the kitchen table ready to be bottled.

Edith, with many interludes for helpless laughter, told him about how the ploughman's geese had escaped and trapped the rector in his church for an entire afternoon. He told her about Michael's prank the night before, and she laughed until the tears rolled down her face.

'Oh, Matt! To think you were frightened by such a trick! I used to make those shadows for you when you were a boy. Do you not remember?'

Bartholomew had not told her about finding the goat mask in the coffin with the murdered woman, and was sure that she would not have been so dismissive of his gullibility had she known. She ruffled his hair as she had done when he was young and went to tend to her rhubarb, still smiling.

He played a game of chess with Stanmore, which Stanmore won easily because Bartholomew became impatient and failed to concentrate, and then he strummed Edith's lute in the solar until the daylight began to fade. Stanmore offered to walk part of the way back with him, and they set off as the shadows lay long and dark across the Cambridge road, and the last red glow of the sun disappeared beyond the horizon.

'Any news of who killed Will?' asked Bartholomew.

Stanmore shook his head angrily. 'Nothing! And Tulyet is worse than useless. I discovered that the attack was being discussed by men in the King's Head and, like a good citizen, I passed my information to Tulyet, who has refused to investigate.'

'Refused?' said Bartholomew. 'Or merely did not initiate enquiries.'

Stanmore shrugged. 'Pedant,' he said. 'He said he would consider the information, but my man in the King's Head said there have been no soldiers asking questions. For Will's sake, I regret bitterly sending the silk to London for dyeing. Now I have little choice but to use de Belem. Since his wife died of the plague, his work has become shoddy.'

'I suppose lately Master de Belem has had other things to worry about,' said Bartholomew.

'Has anything further been discovered about the killer of his daughter?' asked Stanmore, picking up a stone and tossing it at a tree stump that rose out of a boggy meadow at the side of the road.

Bartholomew told him about the dead woman in the grave of Nicholas of York, and that she had been wearing a mask depicting the head of a goat.

Stanmore looked appalled, and shook his head slowly. 'Since the Death ravaged the land, many have turned from God,' he said. 'Who knows what evil stalks the land!'

'I wish I knew why Frances was killed at Michaelhouse,' said Bartholomew.

'Did you follow up on that information I gave you about the guilds?'

'I am not sure I know where to begin,' said Bartholomew. He told his brother-in-law what he had overheard Harling telling de Wetherset. Stanmore frowned and pulled at his neat grey beard thoughtfully.

'I asked one of my men to make enquiries about which two covens were using the decommissioned churches that Brother Alban told you about. They are the Guild of Purification, which uses St John Zachary, and the Guild of the Coming, which uses All Saints'. "Purification" apparently means purification from God, rather than by Him, while the "Coming" refers to the coming of Lucifer, not the Messiah. The Guild of Purification met last night at St John Zachary's Church, as you heard Harling say it would, and my man posted a guard outside. As the guild members came out of the church, he saw each one make the sign of a small circle on the ground with their forefingers.'

'A circle?' said Bartholomew, staring at Stanmore and thinking of the feet of the dead girls.

Stanmore nodded. 'So, it does mean something to you. My man could not be absolutely certain because he, rather sensibly, had placed himself a good distance away. He also said that people wore black hoods, and did not linger to be recognised. What does the circle mean to you?'

Bartholomew rubbed a hand through his hair. 'A small circle was drawn on the sole of the foot of three of the dead women I saw. I do not know if Tulyet saw the marks or not. He reacted oddly when I tried to ask him whether there was a similar mark on the foot of the first victim.'

'What do you mean, "acted oddly"?'

'He became angry and then dismissive. It was after I mentioned the possibility of all the victims bearing a similar mark that he threatened to arrest me.'

'Arrest you?' said Stanmore, horrified. 'Be careful, Matt! Even though Richard Tulyet the elder is no longer Mayor, he is still an influential man. If you anger the son, you will also anger the father.'

'Do you think the older Tulyet is in a guild other than the Guild of the Annunciation?' asked Bartholomew.

'He is certainly in his trade guild, the Tailors,' answered Stanmore. 'I suppose it is possible that he could also be in one of these covens, although he would be hard pushed if ever his loyalty to one were tested over the others.'

'I think there could be some connection between the dead women and the Tulyets,' said Bartholomew, 'based on the Sheriff's reaction to me, and the fact that he seems to be doing nothing to investigate their deaths.'

Stanmore frowned. 'If there were, it would have to be through one of these covens. The Guild of the Coming probably has the edge over the Guild of Purification in terms of power. I suspect that some highly influential person might be a member of the Coming. It is possible that person could be one of the Tulyet clan.'

Bartholomew sighed. It was all becoming very complicated.

Stanmore slapped him on the back. 'I will put a man on it and see what I can find out for you.'

Bartholomew gave him a brief smile. 'Thank you. How many people were there at this coven at St John Zachary?' he asked.

'My man counted five people, but I suspect there are more members than this.'

'Do you know the name of anyone who is in one of these covens?'

Stanmore screwed up his face and looked away. 'Not for certain,' he said.

'Who?' persisted Bartholomew, studying Stanmore closely.

'I do not know for certain,' Stanmore repeated. He stared back at Bartholomew. 'But I think de Belem might be a member of the Guild of the Purification.'

'De Belem?' said Bartholomew incredulously. 'Reginald de Belem?'

Stanmore nodded, and grabbed Bartholomew by his tabard. 'I am not certain, so please be careful how you use that information. Sir Reginald has been through enough with the death of his daughter, and I would not want to be the cause of further grief should I be mistaken.'

Bartholomew looked away and stared down the darkening path, his mind working fast. If there was rivalry between the two covens as Stanmore suggested, did this mean that someone in the Guild of the Coming was killing the women and leaving the secret sign of the rival coven on the bodies as some kind of insult? Or was it simply the work of the Guild of Purification? He thought about the incident in the orchard where at least three people had trespassed in Michaelhouse. Was an entire guild involved? Was he taking on dozens of people in this business? Was de Belem's daughter killed by the Guild of the Coming and marked as a warning to him, or had she been murdered by his own guild as punishment for some perceived misdemeanour?

He chewed absently on a stalk of grass. The woman in Nicholas's tomb had been wearing the goat mask. Was a goat the symbol of the Guild of the Coming? He knew goats were associated with the Devil, as attested by the painting in the church. Was the woman killed by the Guild of the Coming and buried with a goat mask to claim the murder as their work? It seemed rather extreme. And how was Nicholas of York involved? Bartholomew thought about de Belem's insistence that he investigate Frances's murder. Did he suspect that Tulyet might be involved with the Guild of the Coming, his rival guild, and would therefore do nothing to help? And what of the third guild, the Guild of the Holy Trinity, which de Wetherset had told him about, and of which Nicholas was a member? Were they involved in this? Were they using the sacred symbol of one of the covens so that it would be blamed for the murders?

'Matt.' Stanmore's voice cut across his thoughts. 'I do not like any of this, and I do not like the idea of you becoming involved in the doings of evil men. You must take care!'

Bartholomew turned to Stanmore and seized his arm. 'Do not bring Edith into the town until all this is over.'

'You can have no fear on that score,' said Stanmore fervently. 'And tomorrow I will bring my brother's widow and her children here, too. That will keep her safe and Edith busy.'

Bartholomew left Stanmore and began to walk home alone. He should not have spent so much time talking, for it was now dark and he began to feel uneasy. Walking along the Trumpington road to Cambridge alone in the dark was foolish in the extreme, especially carrying his medical bag. Anyone who did not know him would assume it was full of valuables, or even food, and he would be dead before they realised it contained little of worth to anyone but another physician. And perhaps not even then, he thought wryly, wondering how many physicians would be remotely interested in the surgical instruments he carried, or in some of the more exotic of his salves and potions.

He froze as something darted across his path, and forced himself to relax when he saw it was only a deer, perhaps even the same one that he had admired that afternoon. Somewhere behind him, a twig snapped, and he spun round scanning the pathway, but he saw only an owl swooping silently towards a frantically running rodent. He thought of how he had waited to join a large group of people before walking from the Fair into Cambridge at dusk, and now here he was, on a far more remote road, in the dark and totally alone. Something scrabbled in the bushes at the side of the road, and Bartholomew glimpsed two luminous eyes watching him balefully before slinking off into the undergrowth. A feral cat. He had had no idea there was so much wildlife on the Trumpington road at night which could frighten him out of his wits.

Swallowing hard, he took a few steps forward, wondering whether it would be better to go back to Stanmore and

Edith for the night. Distantly, he heard the sound of hoof beats, no casual travellers, but moving quickly along the track. Were they outlaws bent on earning a quick fortune by raiding travellers on the road? Uneasily, he left the path to hide among the bushes until they passed.

The hoof beats grew nearer, coming from the Trumpington side. He pressed back further, feeling cold water from a boggy puddle seep into his shoes. Suddenly the horses were on him, and Bartholomew felt faint with relief as he recognised the ugly piebald war-horse that belonged to Stanmore. He left his hiding place and hailed him.

'Matt!' said Stanmore, looking as relieved as Bartholomew felt. 'It was only when I was home that I realised how dangerous it was for you to walk home alone. A man was almost killed here only last week.'

Bartholomew climbed clumsily onto the spare horse Stanmore had brought, still trying to quell his jangling nerves.

'Thank you,' he said. 'I was beginning to become nervous.'

'Looks scared half to death to me,' Bartholomew heard Stanmore's steward mutter, and one or two of the men with him laughed.

'We should all be cautious,' said Stanmore. 'Especially after what happened to Will and my cart,' he added, with a look that silenced all humour. 'We live in dangerous times,' Stanmore continued, 'when a man cannot walk the roads alone. People say the Death is over, and that it has passed us by. But perhaps the wrath of God is still with us in a different way: people falling into witchcraft, masterless bandits roaming the highways, starvation and poverty increasing, the strong taking from the weak because there is no one to stop them, prostitutes brazenly flaunting their wares, murders in the town and the Sheriff doing nothing . . .'

'We should be on our way, sir,' said Stanmore's steward politely.

Stanmore, his mouth still open to continue his diatribe, relented. 'Of course. Hugh and Ned will ride with you, Matt, and will spend the night in Milne Street. The rest of you, home with me.'

Bartholomew parted from Stanmore for the second time that night, and cantered towards Cambridge after Hugh and Ned. After an uneventful, but uncomfortable, ride along the rutted road, he arrived safely back at Michaelhouse and was allowed in by the surly Walter, who clearly disapproved of the privileges of free exit and entry afforded to Bartholomew by the Master. A few minutes later, Bartholomew saw the porter leave his post and slip across to Alcote's room to inform him that he had been late.

He crept up to Michael's room to see if he had returned from Ely but the monk's bed was still empty. His room-mates slumbered on and Bartholomew went to his own bed and fell asleep almost immediately.

He was wakened after what seemed to be only a few moments by someone roughly shaking his shoulder. He opened his eyes and blinked as he saw Michael hanging over him, holding a candle. He winced as hot wax fell on his arm, and pushed Michael away.

'What is the matter?' he said drowsily. 'What has happened?'

'I thought we were friends,' Michael hissed in the

darkness. Bartholomew raised himself on one elbow, and looked at Michael in astonishment. The fat monk was agitated, and Bartholomew flinched a second time as Michael's shaking hands deposited more hot wax on his bare skin.

'Whatever is the matter with you?' he said, pushing Michael firmly away a second time and sitting up.

'I do not consider what you did was funny,' Michael said, his voice rising in anger.

'Shhh. You will wake the whole College. What are you talking about?'

Bartholomew jumped as Michael dropped something on his bed, and kicked it off in distaste.

'You left that in my bed,' said Michael in quiet fury. 'That is a far cry from shadows on the wall.'

Light began to dawn in Bartholomew's confused mind as he stared down at the severed head of a young goat that now lay on the floor. 'You found this in your bed?' he said, looking up at the furious monk.

'You put it there as revenge for my trick with the shadows,' stated Michael, his voice hard and accusing.

Bartholomew looked back down at the head. It had probably been taken from one of the butchers' stalls in Petty Cury. Bartholomew knew that Agatha often bought heads cheaply from butchers to boil up for soups and broths. The head in itself was not an object for disgust; but the fact that it had been dumped on Michael while he slept gave it a sinister connotation.

'When did you get back?' he asked Michael.

'About an hour ago. You were already fast asleep, or at least pretending to be, when I called out to you. That thing was not in my bed when I went to sleep, so you must have sneaked upstairs and put it on top of me while I slept. The smell woke me.' Michael still glowered at him, the light flickering eerily in the room as the hand that held the candle shook.

Bartholomew glanced up at Michael and saw the hurt in his eyes. He caught his breath as the implications dawned on him. Since the College was locked and guarded, who but a Michaelhouse scholar could have put it there? 'Oh, no! Please do not tell me that the College is going to become mixed up in all this,' he groaned.

'Someone from the College did put it there,' said Michael angrily. 'You.'

'You should know me better than that, Brother,' said Bartholomew. 'Dead animals can carry disease. Do you honestly believe I would put something in your bed that might make you ill?'

'Are you telling me you did not do it?' said Michael, sinking down on Bartholomew's bed, his anger evaporating like a puff of smoke.

'Of course I did not,' said Bartholomew firmly. 'And I doubt that Cynric would either, before you think to blame him. I suspect that this bearer of gifts had something far more sinister in mind than practical jokes.'

Michael shuddered. 'So someone came into my room while I slept and put that thing on me?' he asked, his anger now horror.

Bartholomew nodded. 'So it would seem,' he said. 'I saw Walter slope off to Alcote's room to tell him I had returned late. I suppose if he did the same when you returned, it is possible that someone entered the College while he was away, and that the culprit need not necessarily be a member of College.'

'But how would whoever it was know which was my room?' asked Michael.

'Perhaps it was intended for someone else,' said Bartholomew. 'Perhaps there are secret members of those covens in Michaelhouse.'

He thought back to the conversation he had had with Stanmore earlier, and his assumption that while the circle was the symbol of the Guild of Purification, a goat might be the sign of the Guild of the Coming. He told Michael, and they regarded each other sombrely as they considered the possibilities.

'But what does it mean?' asked Michael, white-faced.

'Was there a note or a message with it?' Bartholomew asked.

Michael shrugged helplessly. 'Just the head. Do you think the Guild of the Coming is warning me to stay away from them?'

'It must be,' said Bartholomew, rubbing his chin thoughtfully. 'And their message is clear. If they can leave a dead animal on you in your own College in the middle of the night, they can harm you in other ways.' He stood and looked down at Michael. 'Perhaps they chose you and not me because it is you who went to see the Bishop, and you who is reading Nicholas's book.'

'The book!' exclaimed Michael, snapping his fingers. 'There must be something in the book! But the only person who knows I am reading it, other than you, is de Wetherset.'

He met Bartholomew's eyes, and they exchanged a look of horror.

'Surely not!' breathed Michael.

'Does this book record anything about these unholy

guilds?' asked Bartholomew, refusing to dismiss too glibly the possibility that de Wetherset might be involved.

Michael shook his head. 'There is very little incriminating in any of it. I do not understand why de Wetherset was so relieved to discover it had not been stolen.'

'Unless he has not given all of it to you to read,' said Bartholomew.

Michael's green eyes were huge as he considered Bartholomew's words. 'Oh, lord, Matt! What have we been dragged into? You are right, of course. What I have read is nothing: de Wetherset had no reason to be concerned about the documents he has given me to read. He has only given me the parts he considers harmless! What a fool I have been! Do you think he is a member of a coven? Do you think he told them what I was doing?'

Bartholomew shook his head. 'If he knows you have access to only those parts of the book he considers innocuous, there is no reason for him to warn you away with dead animals. No, Brother. The warning is either from someone who has seen you at the church and who has guessed what you are reading, or it is unrelated to the book at all. I think de Wetherset has been less than honest with us, but I do not see why he would need to send you the head.'

Michael, appalled, stared at the head on the floor. 'I wish it had been you who left that thing on me after all,' he said fervently. 'If anyone had to dump dead animals on me in the night, I would rather it were you than anyone else! A practical joke, however vile, would be preferable to this sinister business.'

Bartholomew started to laugh and poked the monk with his elbow. 'Go back to bed,' he said. 'I will get rid of this thing. We can do no more tonight, and you should rest.'

Michael stood with a sigh. 'I am sorry, Matt,' he said. 'I was hasty in my accusation. Had I stopped to consider, I would have known that you, of all people, would do nothing that might endanger my health.' He left and went back to his own room while Bartholomew looked for a cloth in which to put the animal's head. He wrapped it up, and slipped out along the side of the north wing to the porch door. He unlatched it and went into the darkened building, first glancing across the courtyard to see if Walter were watching, but could see no moving shadows in the Porter's Lodge.

He walked through the kitchen to the gardens at the back. He tossed his grisly bundle, still in its cloth, onto the refuse fires that smouldered continuously behind the kitchen, and retraced his steps. He felt angry at Walter for being more interested in his half-pennies from Alcote for tale-telling than in doing his job of watching the College. He walked quickly around the courtyard to the small stone building that served as the Porter's Lodge, intending to berate him for being negligent in his duties.

He pushed open the door and called out. There was no reply. Perhaps Walter was off checking some other part of the College. The small room where the porters usually sat was empty. Curious, Bartholomew went through to the back room where they ate their meals, relaxed and, occasionally, slept. Walter was sprawled out on the straw pallet that served as a makeshift bed. Bartholomew was about to shout at him, to wake him with the fright he deserved, when he saw the man's face was unusually white in the light from the open window.

Bartholomew knelt by him and felt a cold and clammy forehead. He put a hand against Walter's neck and felt the slow life beat. Walter moaned softly, and murmured something incomprehensible. On the table, Bartholomew saw the remains of a large pie, and some of it was on the floor. Walter had evidently been eating it when he was stricken.

'Poisoned!' muttered Bartholomew into the darkness. He grabbed Walter by the shoulders and hoisted him onto his knees, forcing fingers down his throat. Walter gagged painfully, and the remains of the pie came up. He began to cry softly. Bartholomew made him sick a second time. The porter slipped sideways and keeled onto the floor.

Bartholomew left him and raced to the room that Gray shared with Bulbeck and Deynman, snatching the startled student out of bed by his shirt collar.

'Fetch me some raw eggs mixed with vinegar and ground mustard,' he said urgently. 'As fast as you can!'

Gray scuttled off towards the kitchens, unquestioning, while Deynman and Bulbeck scrambled from their beds and followed Bartholomew. Walter lay where he had fallen, and Bartholomew heaved him into a sitting position, helped by Bulbeck, while Deynman watched with his mouth agape. Bulbeck kindled a lamp, while Bartholomew heaved the porter onto his feet and tried to force him to stand.

'What is wrong with him?' said Bulbeck, staring in shock at the ghastly white face of the porter as the room flared into light from the lamp.

'Poison,' said Bartholomew. 'We must force him to walk. If he loses consciousness he might die. Help me to hold him up.'

'But who poisoned him?' said Deynman, staring with wide eyes at Walter.

Bartholomew began gently slapping Walter's face. The porter looked at him blearily before his eyes began to close.

'Walter! Wake up!' Bartholomew shouted.

At that moment, Gray appeared with a large bowl of eggs and vinegar.

'I did not know how much mustard you wanted,' he said, 'so I brought it all.'

Bartholomew grabbed the small bottle and emptied the entire contents into the slippery egg-mixture. Gray and Bulbeck exchanged a look of disgust. Bartholomew shook Walter until his eyes opened and forced him to drink some. He was immediately sick again, sinking onto his knees. Remorselessly, Bartholomew forced more of the repulsive liquid down his throat until the entire bowl had been swallowed and regurgitated. Walter began to complain.

'No more!' he whispered. 'My stomach hurts, Doctor. Leave me be.'

Bartholomew grabbed his arm and dragged him out of the door. 'Walk with me,' he said. Bulbeck ran to grab Walter's other arm, and they began to march him around the courtyard.

'Will he die?' asked Bulbeck fearfully.

Bartholomew shook his head. 'I think most of the poison must be out of his stomach. We need to keep him awake for several hours, though, just to make sure.'

'I never sleep on duty,' muttered Walter thickly.

Bartholomew smiled. The porter was regaining his faculties. Bartholomew had arrived just in time. The poison he suspected had been used was a slow-acting one that was virtually tasteless, and could easily be concealed in food or drink. It brought on a slow unconsciousness, and Walter probably just felt pleasantly drowsy, until he fell into the sleep that might have been his last.

'Who did this to him?' asked Bulbeck. Bartholomew had been wondering the same thing. It stood to reason it was the same person who had put the kid's head on Michael's bed. The noise they were making began to wake the other scholars, and soon the courtyard was full of curious and sleepy students and Fellows. The Master arrived breathlessly, followed by Alcote, who exclaimed in horror when he saw the state of his informant.

Bartholomew quickly explained what had happened, and instructed Gray and Bulbeck to walk Walter around the courtyard until he could manage on his own. The students hurried to do his bidding, proud to be the centre of attention as the other students clustered round them with questions.

Kenyngham watched them with his lips pursed. 'Where are the beadles? They are supposed to be watching the gates.'

'They are watching the back gate, Master,' said Alcote. 'The front gate is locked after dark, and with a porter on duty is always secure. It is the back gate that is vulnerable.'

'Cynric.' Kenyngham looked around for the small Welshman whom he knew would not be far away. 'Find out where the beadles are, and then come back to me. Matthew? Have you any idea what prompted all this?'

Bartholomew told him about Michael finding the goat's head on his bed, while the other Fellows exclaimed in horror. Michael paled as he considered the implications of Walter's poisoning – that someone had wanted him to receive the goat's head sufficiently to kill for it.

Bartholomew went to examine Walter again, and came back satisfied that he was recovering. The Fellows stood in a small group around Kenyngham, confused and fearful. Father William muttered prayers to himself, while Father Aidan and Hesselwell looked on in shock.

Kenyngham ordered the students back to their rooms and Cynric returned from the back gate with Jonstan.

'I saw and heard nothing!' said Jonstan, appalled. 'I have been patrolling the lane and keeping a permanent watch on the back gate since dusk. We saw nothing!'

'Do not worry, Master Jonstan,' said Kenyngham, seeing the alarm in the jovial Proctor's face. 'You did your best. I suspect we are dealing with clever and committed people.'

'But I am committed,' said Jonstan, stung. 'I have been overseeing my men and ensuring that the lane is checked constantly since dark. I saw Doctor Bartholomew and Brother Michael return, and I am willing to wager that they did not see me!'

The surprise on Bartholomew and Michael's faces told the watching Fellows that Jonstan's claims were true.

'I set up a regular patrol once the night became quiet,' Jonstan continued.

'How regular?' asked Bartholomew.

'Every quarter of an hour,' said Jonstan, his eyes still wide with shock.

'Then that is probably why you did not see the intruder,' said Bartholomew. 'If you were working to an established pattern, it would not take much to work it out and slip into the College when you were furthest away.'

Jonstan's face fell. Kenyngham rubbed at his eyes wearily. 'This cannot go on,' he said. 'I will not have the lives of College members threatened, and poisoners breaking in. Come, Master Jonstan. We must discuss what more can be done.'

He held out his arm to indicate that Jonstan was to precede him to his room.

'Poor man,' said Hesselwell, watching the dejected Jonstan leave. 'He thought he was being rigorous by establishing a regular pattern in his checks, while all the time he was achieving quite the reverse.'

Bartholomew nodded absently. He watched Gray and Bulbeck with Walter, although the porter was now able to walk on his own. Bartholomew was pleased at his students' diligence, and knew they would remain with Walter until he gave them leave to stop.

'Who is doing this?' asked Aidan, his prominent front teeth gleaming in the candle-light. 'Why would anyone mean Michaelhouse harm?'

'I cannot imagine,' said Hesselwell. 'I wondered whether it might be a commoner, or perhaps one of the students, but that is unlikely. It must be an outsider.'

'What makes you so sure?' asked Bartholomew, surprised at Hesselwell's quick deduction.

'Because everyone in College knows that Walter sleeps all night when he should be on duty, and would know there would be no need to use poison in order to sneak unseen into the building.'

'But the gate is locked and barred,' said Bartholomew, gesturing to where the huge oak plank was firmly in place. 'Even if Walter were asleep, it would be difficult to break in.'

'There are places where the wall is easily breached, as you know very well, Bartholomew,' said Hesselwell. 'And before you ask me how I know, I occasionally have problems sleeping, and sometimes walk in the orchard at night. I have seen students using it, and I imagine you have used it yourself while out on your nocturnal ramblings.'

His tone was unpleasant, and Bartholomew resented the accusation in his voice. He had only ever climbed across the wall once, and would not need to do so again now he had the Master's permission to be out to visit patients. Alcote looked on with malicious enjoyment.

'And how would this intruder present Walter with the poison and be sure he took it?' Bartholomew demanded. 'Would you eat something that appeared miraculously in the middle of the night?'

Hesselwell smiled smugly. 'I would not. But Walter might. He is not intelligent, and his greed might well get the better of his suspicion.'

Bartholomew realised that Hesselwell was right, although it galled him to admit it. It did seem more likely that the person who poisoned Walter and left the grisly warning for Michael was from outside Michaelhouse, for exactly the reason Hesselwell suggested: that everyone inside knew Walter slept, and that it would not be necessary to kill him to move about the College unnoticed.

'Where is Deynman?' said Bartholomew suddenly, looking around him.

Gray and Bulbeck looked round briefly, and shrugged, more interested in Walter than in Deynman's absence. When Bartholomew had hauled Walter out into the yard,

Deynman had stayed in the porters' lodge. Bartholomew began to walk across to the lodge, and then broke into a run. He shot into the small room, staggering as he slipped in the mess on the floor, and gazed at Deynman who was kneeling in front of the table, chopping the remains of the pie into ever smaller pieces. He grinned cheerfully at Bartholomew.

'I am looking for the poison,' he said.

Bartholomew leaned against the door in relief at seeing Deynman unharmed. He had been afraid that Deynman might have eaten the pie to see whether it had been poisoned. His eye was caught by a goblet on the table. He picked it up and looked at it before taking a cautious sip. It was slightly bitter and there was a grainy residue at the bottom of the vessel. He spat it out and looked at the bottle. It was not a kind that was kept in College. He inspected the chopped remains of Walter's pie: it was covered with some of Agatha's hard, heavy pastry and had, without doubt, been made in Michaelhouse.

'The poison was in the wine, Robert,' he said, and explained why. Deynman looked at the mess he had made, and his face fell as he realised that his initiative had failed.

Bartholomew relented at Deynman's crestfallen attitude. 'I will show you how to test for certain poisons,' he said, trying not to sound weary. 'But you are unlikely to find any of them by chopping something into tiny pieces. Go and help Sam and Thomas. I am trusting you to make sure that tonight Walter rests, but does not sleep. If he loses consciousness, fetch me immediately.'

Deynman's face brightened at being given such responsibility, and he scampered off to do as he was told.

'Is that wise?' asked Michael, looming in the doorway and watching him go. 'The boy is a half-wit.'

'Oh, hardly that,' said Bartholomew. 'He tries hard. I will give the others the same instructions before I retire. It is about time they had some practical training. With any luck it might put them off. They might choose a monkish vocation instead.'

'Heaven forbid!' said Michael. He became serious. 'Did you learn anything from Walter? Who poisoned him and when?'

Bartholomew rubbed a hand through his hair. Now the initial excitement had worn off, he felt exhausted. 'Walter had a close call. Whoever left that head was determined that you would get it.'

Michael shuddered. 'We should talk to Walter,' he said.

Out in the yard, Walter had recovered to the point of grumpiness. He glared at Bartholomew. 'My throat hurts,' he said aggressively, 'and I can still taste mustard.'

Bartholomew raised his eyebrows. 'Would you like some of that wine you were drinking in the lodge, to wash away the taste?'

Walter spat. 'I thought it had an odd taste about it. I should have known that no one gives gifts for nothing.'

'Who gave it to you?' asked Michael.

'The Master,' said Walter.

Michael and Bartholomew exchanged glances. 'How do you know it was from the Master?' asked Bartholomew. 'Did he give it to you in person?'

'He left it for me, and I knew it was from him, because

who but the Master has fine wines to give away? You two do not,' he added rudely. 'Why should I question the Master when he was offering good wine?' He paused for a moment in thought. 'I should have done, though.'

'You should indeed,' said Michael.

Deynman hauled Walter away for another turn around the yard, and Bartholomew watched him thoughtfully. 'So, because it seemed a good wine, Walter assumed it was from the Master,' he said.

'Can we be sure it was not?' Michael asked.

Bartholomew shrugged. 'I doubt Kenyngham would leave poisoned wine for Walter when he would be such an obvious culprit,' he said. 'And anyway, Hesselwell is right. The poisoner must be an outsider, because Kenyngham would know Walter sleeps most of the night.'

They talked for a while longer, and went back to their beds. Bartholomew repeated his instructions that the students should wake him immediately if Walter went to sleep or became ill, and left the surly porter in their less than tender, but hawklike, care. He smiled, remembering that Walter had landed Gray in trouble two weeks ago when he had stayed out all night and Walter had informed Alcote. Now the student could have his revenge, and Walter would find himself walked off his feet by the morning.

As Bartholomew lay on his bed to sleep, questions tumbled endlessly through his tired brain. Who had left the goat for Michael? What was in the book that was so incriminating that the Chancellor had censored it? How were the guilds connected to the deaths of the friar and Froissart? Who had killed them, and was the killer also the murderer of the women? Was Frances de

Belem killed because of her father's involvement with the Guild of Purification? He turned the questions over and over, searching for a common theme, but could think of nothing except the mysterious covens.

He lay on his bed, watching the clouds drift across the night sky through the open window shutters. Eventually he got up and closed them securely. He locked the door, too, something he had not felt obliged to do in Michaelhouse for a long time, and, when the bell chimed for Prime the following morning, he wondered whether he had slept at all.

Walter was back to his miserable self by dawn, complaining bitterly that his throat and stomach hurt from the enforced vomiting, and that his feet were sore from walking all night. Convinced that he was suffering no long-term ill-effects from his narrow escape, Bartholomew ordered that he rest, and he then returned to his teaching.

His students, having seen medical practice at work in their own College the night before, were full of questions, and Deynman proudly gave the class a description, reasonably accurate, of the treatment for a person with suspected poisoning. Bartholomew then described treatments for different kinds of poisons, and Deynman's face fell when he realised that, yet again, medicine was more complex that he had believed. Brother Boniface was sullen and uncooperative, refusing to answer questions, and Bartholomew wondered what was brewing behind the Franciscan's resentful eyes.

After the main meal, Bartholomew gave Gray and Bulbeck a mock disputation, and was pleased with their progress. He took them with him to treat Brother Alban's elbow. The old monk was delighted to have an audience of three whom he could regale with his gossip. He began talking about the increase in witchcraft in the town.

'More and more of the common people are flocking to evil ways,' he crowed gleefully.

'Oh, not you too,' said Gray disrespectfully. 'We have to listen to Boniface droning on about heresy and witchcraft all day.'

Bulbeck nodded in agreement. 'He sees heresy in everything,' he said. 'He thinks Doctor Bartholomew is a heretic for saving Walter last night. He says God called him and Doctor Bartholomew snatched him back.'

So that was it, thought Bartholomew. He was sure Walter would not agree with Brother Boniface's opinion, and wondered how Boniface proposed to be a physician with these odd ideas rattling around in his head.

Alban ignored them and chattered about the desecration of several churches in the town after one of the guild meetings two nights ago. He crossed himself frequently in horror, but his gleaming eyes made it obvious that he found the whole thing of great interest, and was eagerly waiting to hear what happened next.

'Have you found the killer of the whores yet?' he asked Bartholomew, beady black eyes glittering with malicious delight.

'They were not all whores,' said Bartholomew patiently, concentrating on his task.

'They were,' said Alban firmly. 'And you cannot try to defend that de Belem girl. She was worse than the rest.'

Bartholomew looked at him, startled, and seeing the

pleasure in the old man's face at having surprised him, he shook his head and continued with his treatment. Alban really was a nasty old man, he thought, for taking such delight in the downfall of others.

'She was out in the dark seeing her man,' Alban continued. 'After her husband died in the Death, her father could not control her lust.'

'Who was her man?' asked Gray, interested.

The old monk beamed at him, pleased to have secured a positive reaction at last. He tapped the side of his nose. 'A scholar,' he said. 'That is all I can say.' He sat back, his lips pursed.

'That is enough, Brother,' said Bartholomew, standing up as the treatment was done. 'No good can come of such talk, and much harm.'

' "No good and much harm",' mimicked Alban unpleasantly, beginning to sulk. Bartholomew was relieved to escape from the old man's gossip, although he could see that Gray would have been happy to stay longer.

When his bag had been returned to him the day before, Bartholomew had emptied all the potions and powders out, and exchanged them for new ones from his store. He did not want to harm any of his patients because someone had altered the labels, or substituted one compound for another. It would not be possible to tell whether some had been tampered with, and these he had carefully burned on the refuse fires behind the kitchen. But there were tests that could be performed on the others that would tell him whether they had been changed.

He left Gray, Deynman, and Bulbeck in his small

medical store carrying out the tests while he went to St John's Hospital to see a patient with a wasting disease. He stayed for a while talking to the Canons about the increase in cases of summer ague, and then went to the home of a pardoner with a broken arm on Bridge Street.

Since he was near the Castle, he decided to try to see Sybilla. She lived in a tiny wattle and daub house on the fertile land by the river. Although the land provided the families that lived on it ample reward in terms of rich crops of vegetables, their homes were vulnerable when the river flooded. It had burst its banks only a few weeks ago in the spring rains, and Sybilla and others had been forced to flee to the higher ground near the Castle for safety.

He knocked on the rough wooden door of Sybilla's house. There was a shuffle from within and the door was opened slowly. Sybilla, her face grey with strain, peered out at him. He was shocked at her appearance. There were dark smudges under her eyes, and her hair hung in greasy ropes around her face.

'Sybilla!' he exclaimed. 'Are you ill?'

She cast a terrified glance outside before reaching out a hand and hauling him into the house, slamming the door closed behind him. The inside of the house was suffering from the same lack of care as its owner. Dirty pots were strewn about the floor, and the large bed in the corner was piled with smelly blankets. Bartholomew had been told by Michael that Sybilla was renowned for offering a clean bed and a clean body to her clients, although how the monk came by such information Bartholomew did not care to ask.

He turned to her in concern. 'What is wrong? Do you have a fever? Are you in trouble?'

She rubbed a dirty hand over her face and tears began to roll. He saw a half-empty bottle on a table in the middle of the room, and poured some of its contents into a drinking vessel that had not been washed for days. He handed it to her and then made her sit on one of the stools. He sat opposite, and patted her hand comfortingly, feeling ineffectual.

Eventually she looked up at him, her eyes swollen and red. 'I am sorry,' she sniffed.

'What is wrong?' Bartholomew said helplessly. 'Please tell me. I may be able to help.'

She shook her head. 'You are a kind man, Doctor,' she said, 'but there is nothing you can do to help me. I am doomed.'

Bartholomew was nonplussed. 'Doomed? But why?'

Sybilla sniffed loudly and scrubbed her nose across her arm. 'I saw him,' she said, her eyes full of terror, and began to cry again. Bartholomew waited until the new wave of sobbing had subsided, and made her drink more of the cheap wine from the clay goblet.

'Tell me what happened,' he said. 'And then we will decide what to do.'

She looked at him, her eyes burning with a sudden hope in her white face. Just then, the door swung open and a woman entered. Bartholomew rose politely to his feet. She stopped dead as she saw him, and looked from him to Sybilla, her face breaking into a wide smile.

'Oh, Sybilla!' she said. 'I am glad you have decided to go back to work. I told you it would do you good. You look better already. I will leave you in peace.'

She turned to leave. Bartholomew was half embarrassed and half amused at her assumption.

'You misunderstand, Mistress,' he said. 'I am only a physician.'

The woman beamed at Sybilla. 'Better than that stonemason you had! You are doing well.'

Sybilla rose unsteadily and grasped the woman's arm. 'He is not a customer,' she said.

The other's attitude changed. 'Well, what do you want then?' she demanded of Bartholomew. 'Can you not see she is unwell?'

'Yes, I can,' said Bartholomew. 'That is why I am trying to help.'

'Help?' asked the woman suspiciously. 'How do you think you can help?'

'I cannot know that,' said Bartholomew, his patience fraying slightly, 'until I know what ails her. She was about to tell me when you came in.'

'Have you told him?' she asked Sybilla. Sybilla shook her head. 'Then do not. How do you know this is not him, or someone sent by him to find out what you know?'

Sybilla shrank back against the wall, and more tears began to roll down her face.

'If I were "him",' said Bartholomew testily, 'you have just told me that Sybilla knows something, and you have put her life in danger.'

The woman looked at him aghast. 'God's blood,' she swore in horror. She turned her gaze on Sybilla. 'What have I done?' She pulled herself together suddenly, seized a rusty knife from the table, and brandished it at Bartholomew. 'Who are you, and what do you want from us?' she demanded, steel in her voice.

Bartholomew calmly took the knife from her hands, and placed it back on the table. The woman glanced at Sybilla, stricken.

'I am no one who means Sybilla any harm,' he said calmly. 'My name is Matthew Bartholomew, and I came because I saw her running from St Botolph's churchyard the day that Isobel died.'

The woman gazed at him. 'You are the University physician?' she said.

'One of them,' he said, sitting down on the stool and gesturing for the women also to sit. Sybilla sank down gratefully, but the other woman was wary. Bartholomew studied her. She was tall, graceful, and wore a simple dress of blue that accentuated her slender figure. But it was her voice that most intrigued Bartholomew; she did not have a local accent, but one that bespoke of some education. Her mannerisms, too, suggested that she had not learned them in the town's brothels, as Sybilla had done.

Her eyes met his even gaze, and she stared back. 'Agatha told me about you,' she said.

Bartholomew was not surprised. Agatha had so many relatives and friends in the town that he could go nowhere where she had no links.

'My name is Matilde,' said the woman.

Bartholomew smiled. So that explained her accent. 'Agatha has told me about you, too,' he said.

Matilde inclined her head, accepting without false modesty that she might be an appropriate topic of conversation in the town. Agatha had told him about a year ago that one of her innumerable cousins had taken a lodger who was said to have been a lady-in-waiting to the wife of the Earl of Oxford. Rumour had it that this woman had been caught once too often entertaining men of the court in her private quarters, and had been dismissed. She had come to Cambridge to ply her trade in peace and was known locally as 'Lady Matilde' for her gentle manners and refined speech.

'Matilde is my friend,' Sybilla blurted out. 'She has been bringing me food since . . .' She trailed off miserably and gazed unseeingly at her bitten fingernails.

'Since Isobel was murdered,' finished Matilde, looking coolly at Bartholomew.

'Tell me what you saw,' said Bartholomew to Sybilla. 'Do you know the man who killed Isobel?'

Sybilla shook her head. 'I did not recognise him, but I saw him,' she whispered.

Matilde seized Bartholomew's wrist with surprising strength. 'Now you know, you carry a secret that could bring about her death,' she said, her eyes holding his.

Bartholomew gazed back, his black eyes as unwavering as her blue ones. 'I know that,' he said, firmly pulling his wrist away. 'But so might anyone else who saw her run screaming from Isobel's body on Monday.'

Matilde winced, and looked at Sybilla, who hung her head. 'I was so frightened, I do not remember what I did,' she said, beginning to weep again. Matilde took matters in hand.

'You must pull yourself together,' she said firmly to Sybilla. 'You told me no one knew that you had seen Isobel's killer. Now it looks as though half the town might know. I think it would be best if you told the doctor what you saw. He might be able to use his influence to catch this evil monster who is killing our sisters, since the Sheriff is unwilling to act.'

Sybilla took a great shuddering breath and controlled herself with difficulty. 'I was just finishing with one of the baker's apprentices in St Botolph's churchyard, when we heard the University Proctor and his patrol going past. The apprentice was able to slip off the other way, but I had to hide until they had gone. The Proctor's men usually leave us alone unless we are with scholars, but it is always best to avoid being seen when you can. It looks bad if you are seen about too often after the curfew.

'I decided to stay where I was, hidden in the bushes. The Proctor and his beadles were discussing that fight between two hostels last month, arguing about whether it could have been stopped if they had arrived earlier. I must have fallen asleep. When I woke, the Proctor and his men had gone. I was about to climb out of the bush when I heard a noise. At first I thought it was just a rat or a bird, but then I saw him.'

She stopped and turned great fearful eyes on Bartholomew. 'Go on,' prompted Matilde.

Sybilla swallowed loudly, wiped her nose on the hem of her dress and continued. 'He was skulking about in the bushes by the road. Then I saw Isobel coming back from one of her regulars. She kept looking behind her, and I saw that horrible black cat that the Austin Canons feed. It was following her, and she kept looking round as if she could hear it. If that vile cat had not been distracting her and making her look behind, she might have seen the monster in the bushes waiting for her. I wanted to call out, but I was too frightened.'

She stopped again and Matilde took one of her hands

to encourage her to finish. 'He leapt at her, and I saw the flash of his knife as he cut her throat. I think I must have fainted,' she said, and was silent for a moment. 'When I came round, Isobel was lying on the ground and the man had gone. I stayed in the bush for ages, trying to bring myself to go to her. When I did finally, she was covered in blood, and I ran. I do not remember going home. I only remember Matilde talking to me later.'

Her story finished, she wiped away fresh tears and blew her nose on a rag that Matilde handed her.

'You saw only one man?' asked Bartholomew, thinking about the three he had encountered in the orchard. 'Are you sure there were not others?'

'There was only him,' said Sybilla firmly. 'I am certain of that. Had there been others, I would have seen them. There was only him.'

'I was worried,' said Matilde. 'I usually see Sybilla at the market. I thought she might be ill, and so came to see her. She has not left her home since then. I bring her food, but she cannot stay like this for ever.'

'Did you see his face?' asked Bartholomew.

Sybilla rubbed her sore, red eyes. 'It was dark, and I was quite a distance away. I did not see his face long enough to recognise him. He was wearing a dark cloak or gown, and he had the hood pulled up. All I can say is that he was not young: he was a man and not a youth. He had no beard or moustache, and he was just average.'

'Average?' said Bartholomew, not understanding.

'Just like anyone else,' Sybilla said. 'Just average. Not tall, not short, not fat, not thin. He had two arms, he did not limp. He did not have great scars on him, or teeth that stick out. He was just normal.'

'Would you recognise him if you saw him again?' asked Bartholomew.

Sybilla swallowed. 'I do not think so, which is why I am frightened to leave the house.'

Bartholomew stood and went to look out of the hole in the wall that served as a window. The sky had clouded over and a light drizzle had begun to fall. He watched the river flowing past a few feet away, all kinds of refuse bobbing and turning slowly in the currents.

What should he do now? He was aware of the two women waiting for him to come up with an answer that would solve their problems. Sybilla was right to be frightened, he thought. If the killer had any inclination she had seen him murder Isobel, he would be foolish not to come to ensure her silence. But Sybilla had provided little to elucidate the muddle of information that Bartholomew had acquired over the past few days. All she could tell him was that the man was average. He could be anyone.

She could not stay in her home, that much was clear. It was probably only a matter of time before the killer heard that Sybilla had run screaming from the scene of Isobel's murder, and had refused to leave her home ever since, before he took action to ensure his identity could never be revealed. Even if he remained unaware that Sybilla had seen him, she had to be moved. She would become seriously ill if left by herself much longer.

He could not take her to Michaelhouse. Even for the best reasons, the Master would not allow him to bring a young prostitute to the College. He could give her money to find other lodgings in the town, but Cambridge was a small town and it was almost impossible to hide in it.

There was only one thing for it. He would have to impose upon Oswald Stanmore. He had done it before, when Rachel Atkin's son had been killed in a town riot, and Stanmore had benefited by gaining a very talented seamstress. However, Bartholomew thought wryly, Stanmore would not benefit from Sybilla unless he intended to open a brothel.

He told Sybilla to gather up what she would need for a stay at Stanmore's premises, and went outside to wait. Matilde followed him to the river bank, oblivious to the drizzle that fell like gauze upon her luxurious hair.

'It is kind of you to do this,' she said.

'I need not tell you that you must inform no one where she is,' he said. 'And you must not visit her until the killer is found, lest he follow you there. And do not come back here yourself. The killer may mistake you for Sybilla if he comes.'

Matilde gave him a smile. 'Agatha said you were a good man. There are not many who would take such trouble over a couple of whores,' she said. He looked away, embarrassed.

'There are quite a number of women like us,' she continued, 'and we talk a lot. It is imperative that we do: we need to know who might be rough, who might refuse to pay, who might be diseased. We hear other things, too, through our lines of communication. I heard that you blundered into Primrose Alley a few days ago.'

'Primrose Alley?' Bartholomew had never heard of it.

'Behind St Mary's,' said Matilde. 'Not an appropriate name for such a place, but I imagine that is why it got it. Anyway, I heard that you were escorted out by Janetta of Lincoln.'

Bartholomew was amazed. He seemed to be the only person in Cambridge without vast arrays of informants to tap into when he needed to know something. Stanmore had his own legion of spies; the Chancellor and the Bishop seemed to do well for information when they needed it; and even the town prostitutes appeared to know his every move.

Matilde touched his arm, seeing his reaction. 'It was Janetta we were interested in, not you,' she said. 'She arrived in Cambridge about a month ago and immediately assumed a good deal of influence in Primrose Alley with the rough men who have lived there since the Death. We did not know how much power she had accrued, until we heard that she was able to call off the louts that were attacking you, with a single word. We believe she was one of us in Lincoln, but she denies it to any who ask, and does not practise here. We do not usually share our information with outsiders, but you are helping us, and I would like to help you with a warning: have nothing to do with that woman.'

'I need to talk to her,' Bartholomew said. 'She may be able to give me information that might lead to the killer.'

'I would not trust any information gained from her,' said Matilde, 'although it would not surprise me to know that she had some to give. Who is she to have such command over those rough men within a month? She is a living lie from her fake smile to her false hair.'

'False hair?' said Bartholomew, surprised, thinking of Janetta's thick cascade of raven black hair.

'Yes,' said Matilde firmly. 'That black hair that you doubtless admired is none of her own. Perhaps she is grey and wants to retain the appearance of youth. Who knows her reason? But I know a wig when I see one.'

Bartholomew lent Sybilla his tabard and cloak, and pulled the hood up over her head to hide her face. He gave her his bag to carry, hoping that in the failing light she would pass for one of his students.

She trailed behind him, giving an occasional sniff. Matilde had already slipped away after giving him a final warning about Janetta of Lincoln. Bartholomew thought about her advice. He had thought it odd at the time that Janetta had such control over what seemed to be an unruly gang of men. She had arrived a month ago. Nicholas of York had died or disappeared a month ago, and the unknown woman buried in his place. The woman with no hair. He frowned. Had the woman's hair fallen out after she died, had she worn a wig like Janetta, or did Janetta's wig belong to the woman in Nicholas's coffin?

Bartholomew concentrated, barely aware of Sybilla behind him. Were the events related? Was the arrival of Janetta connected to the death, or disappearance, of the man who was writing the controversial book? He rethought Sybilla's story and Matilde's warning, but, try as he might, he could make no sense of them, nor tie them in with the information he already had.

When they arrived at Stanmore's business premises, most of the buildings were already in darkness and Stanmore had returned to Trumpington. Bartholomew bundled Sybilla into the small chambers behind the main storerooms, the place where Rachel Atkin worked, before anyone could see her. As he burst in unannounced, he stopped in astonishment. Cynric stood up, from where he had been sitting by Rachel on the hearth. He put down his goblet of wine and grinned sheepishly, caught in the act of his courting. It was late, and the other women had gone home, leaving Cynric to enjoy the company of Rachel alone.

Bartholomew was ashamed of himself for not knocking and giving the poor woman a chance to compose herself, but Rachel was unabashed. She looked curiously at Sybilla, still wearing Bartholomew's gown. Bartholomew found his tongue.

'Can Sybilla stay with you for a few days?' he asked, suddenly feeling awkward. 'I promise I will clear it with Oswald as soon as I can see him.'

'As you please,' Rachel said in her pleasant low voice. She helped Sybilla remove the heavy tabard and cloak. 'It appears Sybilla is in trouble, and she will not be turned away.'

At the kindness in her voice, Sybilla began to weep again, and Bartholomew took the opportunity to leave. Sybilla could tell Rachel her story and Rachel would have the sense and the discretion to deal with her accordingly. Bartholomew felt Cynric slip up behind him as he left.

'Sorry, Cynric. I should have knocked,' he said.

Cynric grinned at him. 'No matter, lad. We were just talking.' He became serious. 'Your brother-in-law saw me as I was going to Rachel's room, and told me to tell you that the Guild of the Coming are meeting tomorrow night at All Saints'.' He rubbed his hands gleefully, oblivious to Bartholomew's expression of dismay. 'Another night expedition, eh boy? You and I will get to the bottom of all this yet.'

chapter 7

AWN THE NEXT DAY WAS DULL AND GREY, THE hot weather of the past few weeks replaced by a chill dampness. It was the turn of the Franciscan Fellows, William and Aidan, to prepare the church, and Bartholomew was able to stay in bed longer than he had the previous week. He thought about Sybilla, hidden away in fear of her life, and the dead women, especially Frances de Belem, and he felt depressed by the fact that he even had a witness to one murder, but was still no further forward with uncovering the killer's identity. He considered de Wetherset too, concealing documents from Michael that might help them to reason out some of the jumble of information that they had accumulated.

When he heard the Benedictines moving about in the room above, he reluctantly climbed out of bed to wash and shave in the cold water left for him by Cynric the night before, hopping about on the stone floor in his bare feet. He groped around in the gloom for his shirt, shivering in the cool air. The bell was already ringing by the time he was ready, and he had to run to catch up with the others. Michael told him in an undertone that they had been asked to meet with the Chancellor that morning. Bartholomew groaned, his scanty morning humour evaporating.

Michael jangled some keys at him. 'We can try these out,' he said. 'The Bishop gave them to me yesterday.'

Bartholomew took them from him. There were three large keys and three small ones, all on a rusting metal ring. 'Why are there six keys?' he asked. 'There are only three locks.'

Michael shrugged. 'The Bishop said they had been deposited with his predecessor. There is another University chest at the Carmelite Friary containing duplicates of all documents. Did you know that? I thought not. I suspect that is a secret few other than de Wetherset know. Anyway, the scroll with the keys was dated November 1331. They have lain untouched at the bottom of one of the Abbey strong-boxes for almost twenty years! Can you believe that?'

Bartholomew wondered whether they were the right keys.

No such doubts assailed Michael, who cracked his knuckles cheerfully. 'Now we will get some answers. If they fit, it means that the lock was tampered with and the poison device installed recently; if they do not fit, it means the lock was changed completely.'

'And what does that tell us?' grumbled Bartholomew.

Michael shrugged. 'We will know whether someone planted that device deliberately to kill.'

'But if it were changed, it tells us only that it was done at some point between November 1331 and last Monday,' said Bartholomew, ignoring warning glowers from Alcote for talking in the procession.

'And that provides us with little information that will be of use.'

'It was your idea to check the Bishop's keys,' said Michael, crestfallen by Bartholomew's negative attitude. 'And if the lock has been changed, it must mean that de Wetherset's key must also have been changed – the key that only leaves the chain around his neck when it is given to the mysteriously absent Buckley.'

'So de Wetherset says,' said Bartholomew. 'But how do we prove that the poisoned blade was not put onto the lock only the day before the friar was killed?'

'Because Buckley locked the chest and the tower at dusk just a few minutes before the lay-brother locked the church. If the device was put there during the day, then Buckley would have been poisoned by it.'

'He wore gloves, remember?' said Bartholomew. He shook his head. 'Have you noticed that everyone we want to talk to, who might be able to help us, has disappeared? The lay-brother, Janetta, Froissart's family, Master Buckley. Even Nicholas, and he is supposed to be dead!'

Michael studied him in the gloom. 'What is wrong, Matt?' he asked. 'You are not usually so morose. Are you worried about de Wetherset?'

'No. I expect he is merely trying to safeguard the University's secrets by deceiving you over the book. But I am fed up with all this. The more I try to fathom it all out, the less I understand. It is something to do with those damn covens, I am sure. One of them is meeting tonight, and Cynric thinks I am going with him to spy. Meanwhile this killer is still free, and Tulyet seems to be doing nothing to catch him.'

Michael sighed. 'One thing at a time, Matt. We will

go to see the Chancellor, and then we will try to reason all this out. We are supposed to have some of the finest minds in the country. We must be able to solve this riddle.'

Bartholomew was not so sure. He tried to put it out of his mind during Prime, but found he could not. He thought about Sybilla and wondered if she would be safe at Stanmore's premises. He found himself looking at the wall painting where the goat-devil tossed people into the burning pit, and wondered whether Wilson's tomb, when he finally had it built, would hide it.

Father William was noted for the speed of his masses, but he was not matched by Aidan, who stammered and stuttered, and lost his place as he read. At one point he knocked the paten off the altar and the pieces of bread intended for communion scattered over the floor. Bartholomew saw Gray and Deynman start to laugh, making Alcote look at them sharply. As William and Aidan scrabbled to recover the bread, Bartholomew saw that Hesselwell was asleep. He watched, fascinated, as the lawyer slipped further and further down his seat until it tipped with a loud bang that echoed like thunder through the church.

Hesselwell looked startled, but returned the Master's deprecating look with a guileless smile that made it look as if the clatter had been caused by someone else. Gray and Deynman were having serious trouble in containing their laughter, and Bartholomew could see that if they did not control themselves, Alcote would fine them. Opposite, Harling watched in icy disapproval, making it clear that he regarded the students' behaviour as typical of Michaelhouse scholars. Kenyngham was blissfully oblivious to it all, his hands clasped in the sleeves of his monastic gown and his eyes fixed on the ceiling as he chanted. Jonstan, standing next to Harling, looked from the students to Kenyngham, and smothered a smile.

Finally, order was restored and mass continued, but it was late by the time they finished. Since it was Sunday, there were no lectures, and the scholars were expected to read or spend time in silent contemplation. Bartholomew saw no reason why his students should not read something medical. He hailed Gray and Bulbeck and told them to read specific sections of Galen's *Prognostica* until midday, at which point they were free to spend their time as they pleased. He gave Gray the keys so that he could unlock the valuable tome from where it was chained to a wall in Bartholomew's storeroom, and read it aloud to the others in a corner of the hall.

Boniface regarded him aghast. 'It is the Lord's day!' he exclaimed. 'We cannot work!'

'Reading is permitted,' said Bartholomew. 'But no one is obliged to attend if they feel themselves unable.'

'Working on the Lord's day is a sin!' said Boniface, looking down his long nose at his teacher. 'It is because of evil men like you that the Death was visited upon us.'

'That is true, Doctor.' Bartholomew turned to see Father William standing behind him, tall, immovable, and with a fanatical gleam in his eye that forewarned Bartholomew he was spoiling for a good theological debate.

'Perhaps it is,' said Bartholomew. 'But I do not consider listening to medical texts work.'

'But you hold a book, you turn its pages, and you use your voice to speak the words,' said William. 'That is work.'

'In which case you are working now,' said Bartholomew. 'You are trying to engage me in a theological debate – and theology is your trade, quite apart from your vocation, since you are paid to teach it – and you are using your voice to speak the words.'

William nodded, appreciating the logic. 'True,' he countered. 'Yet I do not consider it work.'

'And I do not consider reading medical texts work,' said Bartholomew. 'So we have reached a stalemate.'

Before William could respond, Bartholomew gave a small bow and began to walk away. Boniface ran after him and seized his sleeve.

'I will not read your heretical texts,' he hissed. 'And I will not commit the sin of working on the Sabbath. I will go to the conclave and listen to readings from the Bible with Father Aidan.'

'Do so, Brother,' said Bartholomew wearily. He had neither the energy nor the inclination to ask Boniface what he thought the difference was in listening to one text or another. He disengaged himself from his obnoxious student, and made for his room. This time he was accosted by Gray and Bulbeck.

'All those potions we tested yesterday seemed to be what you said they should be,' said Gray. 'Except for the white arsenic. That was sugar.'

'Sugar? How did you know it was sugar?' asked Bartholomew, startled. 'I gave you no tests to prove that!'

'Deynman ate it,' said Gray.

'He what?' cried Bartholomew, looking in horror at Deynman skulking nearby, waiting for his friends. He grinned nervously at Bartholomew.

'We thought the arsenic looked like that fine white sugar that we had at the feast last year. Deynman ate it, and said it was indeed sugar.'

Bartholomew put his hand over his eyes. He wondered what he had done to deserve students like Boniface and Deynman, one unable to see past the dogma of his vocation, and the other unable to see much of anything. 'Deynman!' he yelled suddenly, making the others jump and several scholars look over to see what was happening. He strode to where the student stood and grabbed him by the front of his tabard.

'What are you thinking of?' he said fiercely. Deynman shrugged and tried to wriggle free. Bartholomew held him tighter. 'You might have been poisoned – like Walter!'

'Sam and Thomas would have fetched eggs and vinegar to make me sick!' Deynman protested, struggling feebly. 'Like Walter.'

'The chances that eggs and vinegar would have saved you from arsenic poisoning are remote,' said Bartholomew. 'It would have been a horrible death, and I doubt I would have been able to help you.' He released Deynman, and stood looking down at him, torn between wonder and anger at the young man's ineptitude.

'But it was not arsenic, it was sugar,' protested Deynman. 'The poison that made Walter ill must have been stolen from your bag and replaced with sugar.'

'Oh, Rob!' exclaimed Bartholomew in despair. 'How can that be possible? I have just told you that arsenic produces a violent death, not a peaceful slipping away into sleep like Walter. Walter was poisoned with a strong opiate used for dulling pain. The arsenic missing from my bag was not the poison used on Walter.'

'But who would exchange arsenic for sugar?' cried Deynman, confused.

'I do not know,' said Bartholomew. 'And anyway,' he added severely, 'that is none of your concern. But if you ever taste any of my medicines again without asking me first, I will make sure that you are sent home the same day. Do I make myself clear?'

Deynman nodded, frightened by his teacher's rare display of anger. Bartholomew gave him a long hard look and sent him off before Alcote, hurrying across the courtyard towards them, could catch him. Alcote watched Deynman run to Bartholomew's storeroom to fetch the book with Gray and Bulbeck.

'What was all that about?' he asked.

'Alchemy!' snapped Bartholomew, still angry at Deynman's stupidity, but reluctant to tell the nosy Alcote anything that would get him into more trouble.

'Your students are a disgrace,' sniffed Alcote. 'When I catch them, I will fine them for laughing in church.'

He headed towards Bartholomew's store, head tilted to one side, looking more like a hen than ever. As he entered, Bartholomew saw the shutters fly open and the students clamber out of the window. Alcote emerged to see them running across to the hall with the book tucked under Gray's arm. Bartholomew laughed despite himself, and wondered how long they could keep a step ahead of the vindictive Senior Fellow.

He went to close the shutters, wondering why Janetta's friends had exchanged sugar for white arsenic. Arsenic was an unusual item for a physician to carry, but Bartholomew found it useful for eliminating some of the vermin that he believed spread diseases to some of his poorer patients. Despite his words to Deynman, Bartholomew did not carry enough of the white powder to kill a person, and he was not unduly worried about the amount that was stolen.

Michael was waiting for him by the porter's lodge, and together they walked to see the Chancellor.

'Why were you yelling at Deynman?' Michael asked curiously. He had seldom seen the physician angry enough to shout.

Bartholomew did not want to think about it, and avoided Michael's question. Cynric had already been dispatched to ask de Wetherset if they could try the keys on the locks, and when they arrived at his office, the Chancellor and Harling, recently promoted from Senior Proctor to Vice Chancellor to replace Buckley, were waiting for them. De Wetherset reported that his clerks had still been unable to trace Froissart's family, and suggested he be buried in St Mary's churchyard as soon as possible.

'I have made some enquiries,' said Harling. 'One of the two covens in Cambridge, the Guild of the Coming, uses goats in its rituals. I can only conclude that members of this guild must have left the head on Brother Michael's bed, perhaps as a warning?'

'A warning of what?' demanded Bartholomew. 'We cannot be a danger to them. We have made little headway in our investigation: we do not know who the friar was, or what he wanted from the chest, and we do not know who killed Froissart.' He stood abruptly and began to pace.

'We know that the Guild of the Coming must be connected to the woman in Nicholas's grave,' said Harling, trying to be placatory.

'Why?' snapped Bartholomew. 'How do you know it

was not one coven trying to desecrate the sacred symbol of its rivals, or trying to implicate it in a murder of which it is innocent? And what of the Guild of the Holy Trinity? That may be leaving satanic symbols to bring the covens into disrepute.'

Harling spread his hands. 'The Guild of the Holy Trinity is dedicated to stamping out sin, not to committing murder and desecration. But regardless, how would anyone guess that Nicholas's grave would be exhumed and we would find the mask?'

'As I said to Master de Wetherset,' said Bartholomew, still pacing, 'I suspect Nicholas's coffin was meant to be opened before his burial, not after.'

De Wetherset sighed. 'You are right – we know nothing to be a danger to anyone. Unless we know something that may seem unimportant to us that means a great deal to them.'

He had a point, and Bartholomew stopped wandering for a moment to consider it. After a few moments, he resumed his pacing, frustrated.

'I can think of nothing,' he said. 'The only way forward that I can see is to look into the murders of the town women. We know their deaths involve the University now that we have discovered the woman's body in Nicholas's coffin. There are no witnesses that can identify the killer. Rumours are spreading that the murderer is Froissart, but we know that cannot be so.'

De Wetherset watched Bartholomew pace, and turned to Michael. 'I understand you visited Ely,' he said. 'Do you have the keys?'

Michael produced them and de Wetherset fetched the old locks from a cupboard in the wall. He carried them carefully and placed them on the table on top of a piece of cloth. Michael selected a key, donned the heavy gloves, carefully inserted it into the lock, and waggled it about.

'It always was a bit sticky,' said the Chancellor, watching from a distance.

Michael jiggled the key a little more, and stepped back in alarm as the tiny blade popped further out, revealing jagged edges. Michael, his hands a little unsteady, took a grip on the key again and twisted it back and forth, but nothing happened. 'It does not fit,' he said. 'The lock must have been exchanged.'

'Wait!' said Bartholomew, moving towards the table from the window-seat where he had been watching. The others looked at him. 'How do you know it was sticky?' he asked de Wetherset. 'You said Buckley usually opened it.'

'Well, he did, usually,' said de Wetherset. 'But he was sometimes ill, so I would open it. I always struggled with the damn thing, although Buckley never had a problem.'

'When was the last time you opened it personally?' asked Bartholomew.

De Wetherset blew out his cheeks. 'Heavens,' he said. 'I cannot recall ... perhaps during spring. Why do you ask?'

Bartholomew's mind began to whirl. 'Open it now,' he demanded.

'Why?' said de Wetherset. 'Brother Michael has already shown the key does not fit.'

Bartholomew snatched the key from the table and handed it to de Wetherset. 'You try.'

The Chancellor looked puzzled, but donned the gloves

and inserted the key in the lock gingerly. Unlike Michael, de Wetherset steadied the lock with his other hand, and after a few moments of jiggling, there was a loud snap and the lock sprung open.

De Wetherset and Harling stared at it, while Michael looked at Bartholomew, a sardonic smile tugging the corners of his mouth.

'Tell us what flash of inspiration suddenly occurred to make you suggest that,' he said.

Bartholomew sat on a stool next to the table and peered at the lock. 'It is old,' he said, 'and the tower is damp. I suspect that the lock's insides are rusty. Buckley opened it almost every day, and was probably used to the way it sticks; so familiar, in fact, that he did not need to fiddle like you did just now, Master de Wetherset. Similarly, you know better how to manipulate the thing than Michael, who was unable to open it at all. I think the small blade that killed the friar has been hidden in the lock for years. Over time, the mechanism has become faulty and rusty. I suspect it would have killed you, Master de Wetherset, had you opened it more recently.'

Harling looked puzzled. 'So you are saying that this nasty device has been in place since the locks were bought from Italy twenty years ago, and that it has become faulty over the last few months because it has become worn.'

De Wetherset looked at the lock in horror. 'Are you telling me that if Buckley had not been available to unlock the chest recently with his gloved hands and his familiarity with the thing, I might have suffered the same fate as the friar?'

Bartholomew nodded. 'That is exactly what I am telling you,' he said. 'And I think if you were to show a locksmith the other two locks, you would find similar mechanisms not far behind this one in terms of increasing unreliability.'

De Wetherset looked sick, but went to the door and called for Gilbert whom he dispatched to send for Haralda the Dane, the town's leading locksmith.

Harling tried to stop him. 'I must caution you to keep this matter a secret. Bartholomew's explanation seems a plausible one. Why can we not leave it at that? And anyway, it is Sunday, and you cannot encourage the locksmith to work on the Lord's day.'

'I want to be certain,' said de Wetherset. 'If Matthew is wrong, we may draw the wrong conclusions from this wretched business and a murderer may walk free. I am quite sure the Lord will overlook Haralda's sin if it is to prevent the more heinous crime of murder.'

Harling opened his mouth to argue, but de Wetherset eyed him coldly, and nothing was said. Harling turned away in anger, and went to the window. Bartholomew was surprised at Harling's objections. So what if the town got to know the University had discovered three poisoned locks? It might act as a deterrent to anyone considering burgling the chest a second time. It seemed to Bartholomew that Harling's other objection – that Haralda would be working on the Sabbath – was a second thought grasped at in desperation. After all, by his very presence in his office on a Sunday, it might be considered that Harling was working, too. Perhaps he had other reasons for wanting the presence of the poisoned locks kept a secret.

While they waited for Haralda, Bartholomew sat on the damp cushions in the window-seat and watched Harling more closely. He was certainly agitated, and paced up and down as Bartholomew had done earlier. Bartholomew saw Michael observing too, and knew that he was not the only one to note Harling's tension.

It was not long before Gilbert ushered the tall Dane into the Chancellor's office. Haralda's eyes immediately lit on the locks on the table, and he let out an exclamation of delight.

'Ah! Padua locks!' he said. 'I have not seen one of these in many a year. May I?'

'They are poisoned!' cried Michael, springing forward to stop him from touching them.

Haralda looked at him pityingly. 'Of course they are poisoned,' he said. 'They are Padua locks. Clever devices. I assume these are the reasons you have invited me here?'

De Wetherset nodded, while Harling began to gnaw on his fingernails. Bartholomew was impressed at the Dane's command of English. When he had arrived six or seven years ago, he had conducted his business almost exclusively in French. Now, he not only spoke perfect English, but had acquired a gentleman's accent, not a local one. Bartholomew commented on it as he watched the locksmith work.

'I was taught by a lady,' he said proudly.

Bartholomew was puzzled, unable to imagine what kind of lady would be willing to coach a rough man like Haralda the Dane. Then the answer came to him. 'The Lady Matilde?' he asked.

The Dane grinned at him conspiratorially. 'The very same,' he said.

Cambridge was indeed a small town, thought Bartholomew. De Wetherset apparently did not agree.

'Lady Matilde?' he said, frowning as he thought. 'I do not believe I know her. Is she the wife of one of the knights at the Castle?'

'She does not live at the Castle,' said Bartholomew, and changed the subject before it got him into trouble. 'What can you tell us about the locks, Master Haralda?'

'They are old,' said the Dane. He slipped on a pair of thin but strong gloves and unrolled a piece of cloth containing some tiny tools. He carefully picked up one of the locks in his paw-like hands. 'Yes, this one is broken, see?' He pointed to the blade and waggled it with his finger, laughing at the exclamations of horror from Gilbert and de Wetherset.

He selected a minute pair of tweezers and removed the blade completely. It was a third of the length of Bartholomew's little finger and yet it had already killed one man. Haralda deftly unscrewed the lock to reveal its innards. Bartholomew peered over his shoulder.

Haralda tutted and shook his head. 'You do not know how to treat a lock, my lords,' he said reprovingly. 'This poor thing has not seen a drop of oil since the day it was made. You are lucky it has not killed someone.'

Harling glared at Bartholomew and Michael in turn, daring them to say anything. Haralda did not notice.

'This is an especially fine model,' he said. 'It became popular in Italy about twenty or thirty years ago, although few are made these days. It was one of the best locks ever to be produced. They are expensive, but worth the cost if you have something worth protecting.'

He looked up, and Harling eyed him coldly. 'Just documents,' he said. 'Nothing that would interest a thief.'

Haralda picked up the second lock and poked at it.

232

'Yes. This one is different. The blade comes through the back, not the top. It is in better condition than the other one, but not by much.'

He turned his attention to the third one, and wagged its finger at it as it gave a sharp click when he started prodding. 'Look at that! You are lucky, my lords. If any of you had tried to open this, you would be dead. The mechanism is so worn, it is almost smooth. I would say it would have released its blade within three attempts at opening it at most. You were right to have called me.'

'I do not understand why they have suddenly become so unreliable,' said de Wetherset. 'We have been using them for years without trouble.'

'But you have not cared for them as you should have done. They are rusty, and they have become dangerous. You could have had many years' service from them if you had treated them properly, but now I would recommend that you dispense with them.'

'How has the poison stayed for so long in so potent a form?' asked Bartholomew.

Haralda beamed at him, pleased that someone was expressing an interest, rather than disgust, at the locks. 'The blade has its own chamber here, see? It is sealed with lead, so no poison can leak and cause damage. If I were to open this chamber, which I would only do under the special conditions at my workshop, you would find the poison mixed with various mixtures, including quicksilver, to keep it fluid. Thus the poison is always ready. I saw a lock like this kill a dog in under ten minutes in Rome, although I would think perhaps, judging from the age of this lock, that the poison may have lost some of its potency. If you meant business, you would need to change the poison regularly to ensure its continued efficacy.'

Bartholomew nodded, staring down at the rusting insides of the three locks on the table. He picked up Michael's keys and played with them idly. Haralda took them from him.

'These smaller keys,' he said, holding them up, 'are to turn the poison mechanism on and off. In this way, the lock can be used normally.'

He inserted the smaller key into one of the parallel vertical slits on the back of one of the locks to show them. Bartholomew studied it closely and admired its ingenuity. The slit did not look like another keyhole, and anyone who did not know what it was, would never guess.

'I would assume,' said Haralda, 'that whoever last knew about this left the mechanism turned off. Once again, I say you are very lucky none of them slipped on while you were using them.'

'Which is why Buckley was safe, even without his gloves,' murmured Michael to Bartholomew. 'It must have broken as the friar poked about with it in a way that Buckley never had.'

Haralda stood up. 'Dispense with these, my lords. They are no longer safe.'

'Will you take them?' asked de Wetherset. 'I would feel more secure knowing that a professional man had disposed of them in a proper manner.'

Haralda bowed to him, flattered, and collected the pieces of the locks in the cloth. De Wetherset went to see him out of the church. Harling paced restlessly.

'It was a mistake bringing in another,' he said. 'He told us nothing we did not know or could not guess.'

'But now we are certain,' said Michael. 'We know the lock was not changed by Buckley, or by someone wanting to kill members of the University. We know that the locks are just old and worn, and that the friar was not murdered. I suppose it could be called accidental death.'

'But we still do not know what he wanted in the chest,' said Bartholomew. 'In fact, we are not much further forward at all.'

'Yes, we are,' said Michael. 'We are no longer looking for the murderer of the friar.'

'But we still want the murderer of Froissart,' said Harling. He chewed nervously at his fingers. 'If you will excuse me, gentlemen, I have much to be doing.'

He bowed and left the room. Bartholomew leaned out of the window, and saw de Wetherset still talking to Haralda below.

'Harling was unaccountably nervous,' said Michael, opening one of de Wetherset's wall cupboards and peering inside. 'Even if it is a Sunday, I feel he had another reason why he did not want us to fetch the locksmith.'

Bartholomew sighed and made for the door. 'Come on, Brother. Harling is not the only one with much to be doing,' he said.

They stepped outside and began to walk home. There was a flicker in the sky, followed by a low rumble, and then rain began to fall heavily. Bartholomew and Michael joined several others who ran to St Mary's Church to wait the thunderstorm out. Inside, the church was dark from the grey clouds that hung low overhead, lit brilliantly by occasional flashes of lightning. Bartholomew had never been in a church during a thunderstorm before, and the way the wall-paintings suddenly lit up reminded him of passages from Revelations about the end of the world.

He wandered around aimlessly, listening to the rain drumming on the roof. The tombs in the choir reminded him of his promise to Master Wilson to attend to the building of his sepulchre. Some tombs were plain, while others were vulgar. A plain one in black marble would not be too bad, thought Bartholomew, but, in his heart of hearts, he knew that Wilson would have wanted a vulgar one. Not for the first time, Bartholomew was disgusted. Wilson should have arranged to be buried in a fairground with the kind of tomb he had had in mind, not a church!

A sharp tug on his sleeve pulled him from his thoughts. One of the clerks was there, hiding behind a pillar. He looked frightened, and Bartholomew pretended to be reading an inscription on a nearby tomb, so that no one watching him would know he was speaking with a man in the shadows.

The lightning flickered again, making the man wince and press further back, but the storm was moving away.

'The day after the friar's death,' said the clerk, glancing furtively around him, 'I saw that the bar on the front door had been moved.'

'What does that imply?' asked Bartholomew softly, rubbing the brass on the tomb with his sleeve and pretending to look closer.

'Everyone here thinks that the friar hid in the church before it was locked up. He then went upstairs and died. But the bar on the door was in a different place in the morning than it was the night before,' whispered the clerk hoarsely. 'What I am saying is that I think the friar barred the door after the church was locked, which means that someone must have unbarred it from the inside, or we would not have been able to get in the next morning.'

Bartholomew's heart sank. He had just proved, rather ingeniously he thought, that the poisoned lock had been a cruel twist of fate that had killed the friar, and now this clerk was telling him the friar had not been alone in the church on the night of his death, which threw the whole thing back under suspicion.

'Are you certain?' he asked heavily, still careful not to look at the man and give him away.

The clerk nodded quickly. 'I think I may be putting myself at risk by talking to you, but if I do not tell you what I know, how will you be able to solve this mystery and let us get back to normal?'

Bartholomew was taken aback by the man's confidence in his abilities as a detective, and not particularly pleased at the pressure he felt it put on him to draw this matter to an acceptable conclusion. 'Do you know anything else?' he asked. 'Like the whereabouts of the man who locked the church that night?'

The man huddled further back behind his pillar. 'He has not been seen since you chased him. He has not been home, and his family have had no word from him.'

'Did you know Nicholas of York?' Bartholomew whispered, watching as a second clerk walked past him, carrying a pile of dirty-white tallow candles.

He felt the man's confusion. 'Yes. He died more than a month ago,' he said.

'Did you see his body or attend his funeral? Did you notice anything untoward?'

The clerk looked at him as though he were insane. 'I saw his body in his coffin the night before we buried him, but I fail to see why you ask.' He sank back into the shadows as the other clerk returned from depositing his candles. 'The friar died a few days ago, and Nicholas has been in his grave for weeks.'

Bartholomew sighed. 'Then do you know anything about the Guild of the Coming or the Guild of the Purification?'

The man crossed himself so violently that Bartholomew could hear his hand thumping hollowly against his ribs. 'You should not speak those names in this holy church!' he hissed. 'And do not try to find out about them. They are powerful and would kill you like a fly if they thought you were asking questions.'

'But they are small organisations with only a few members,' said Bartholomew, quoting Stanmore's information, and trying to allay the clerk's fears.

'But they have the power of the Devil behind them! They do his work as we do God's.'

Bartholomew already knew the two guilds might harm him or Michael if they thought they were coming too close to their secrets. When he glanced up again, the man had melted away into the shadows. He thought about what the clerk had said. Either two people were locked in the church that night, or the friar had let someone else in. But what was even more apparent was that the second person must have had a set of keys to the church, or how would the doors have been locked the following morning?

Bartholomew rubbed his chin thoughtfully. Buckley had to be involved. Perhaps he had not murdered the friar, as Bartholomew had considered possible, but did he lock the doors to the tower after the friar had died and he had put him in the chest? And then did he leave the church, lock it behind him, and flee the town with all his property? And was he also responsible for putting the murdered woman in Nicholas of York's coffin? In which case, he might also be the killer of the other women.

Even stranger was the case of Nicholas of York. The clerk and de Wetherset claimed they had seen Nicholas dead, which implied that someone must have made off with his body, first replacing it with the woman's. But what reason might anyone, even a coven, have for such an action? Bartholomew closed his eyes and leaned back against the tomb. But what if Nicholas were not dead? Perhaps he had feigned death, spending the day lying in his coffin while his colleagues kept vigil, and then broke out during the night. Perhaps the woman had helped him. Had Nicholas then repaid her by killing her and putting her in his place? Had she come to snatch his body away for some diabolical purpose and been foiled in the attempt? Perhaps Nicholas was the killer, a man assumed to be dead, and so not an obvious suspect.

And what of Tulyet's role in all this? The townspeople believed Froissart was the killer, but deaths had occurred after he was murdered and hidden in the belfry. Perhaps Tulyet was the murderer. He had reacted oddly to the mention of goats, and was doing nothing to catch the killer, although he could not know Froissart was dead. Perhaps it had been Tulyet who had snatched Nicholas's body for some satanic ritual.

Bartholomew opened his eyes and saw that the rain had eased. Michael was singing a Kyrie with another monk, their voices echoing through the church, Michael's rich baritone a complement to the monk's tenor. Bartholomew let their music wash over him, savouring the way their voices rose and fell together, growing louder and then softer in perfect harmony with each other. The faint smell of wet earth began to drift in through the open windows, momentarily masking the all-pervasive aroma of river. All was peace and stillness until a cart broke a wheel outside, and angry voices began to intrude.

'I am hungry,' announced Michael as they walked back to College in the light rain following the thunderstorm. 'Cynric foolishly told Agatha about that trick we played on you with the shadows, and she is refusing to allow me into the kitchen. We could sit in the garden behind the Brazen George and have something to eat while we talk.'

Bartholomew looked askance. 'What are you thinking of, monk? First, it is a Sunday, and second, you are well aware that scholars are not permitted in the town taverns.'

'What better day than a Sunday to celebrate the Lord's gift of excellent wine?' asked Michael cheerily. 'And I did not suggest entering a tavern, physician, merely the garden.'

'Michael, it is raining,' said Bartholomew, laughing. 'We cannot sit in a tavern garden in the rain. People would think we had had too much to drink! And the Brazen George will be closed because it is Sunday.'

'Not true,' said Michael. 'The town has given a special dispensation for the taverns to open on Sundays during the Fair. Otherwise what do you think all these visiting merchants, traders, and itinerants will do, wandering the streets with nowhere to go? If the taverns were closed, they would form gangs and roam the streets looking for trouble. The town council was wise when it ignored the pious whinings of the clerics and granted licences for the taverns to open on Sundays until the Fair is over.'

Bartholomew glanced up and saw a figure coming towards them, his head bowed against the spitting rain. Michael saw him too, and hailed him.

'Master de Belem!'

The merchant looked up, his eyes glazed and his face sallow. His thick, dark hair was straggly and he looked thinner and older than when Bartholomew had last seen him. He glanced up and down the street carefully, and then back at the scholars.

'I must talk to you, but not here. Where can we meet?'

'The garden at the rear of the Brazen George,' said Michael before Bartholomew could stop him. 'It is secluded and the landlord will respect our privacy.'

The merchant nodded quickly. 'Go there now and I will follow in a few minutes. I do not want anyone to know that we have been together.'

Michael gave Bartholomew a triumphant look and led the way to the tavern. He stopped at the small stable next door to it, pretending to admire the horses. When he was certain no beadles were watching, he shot down a small passageway and let himself into a tiny garden. The bower would be pleasant on a sunny day: it had high lime-washed walls over which vines crept, and two or three small tables were set among rambling roses. But it was raining, and as the wind blew, great drops of water splattered down from the leaves.

Bartholomew sighed and pulled his hood further over his head, looking for a spot that might be more sheltered.

Within moments, the landlord came out, wiping his hands on a stained apron, and not at all surprised to see them.

'Brother Michael! Welcome! What can I fetch for you?'

'Two goblets of your excellent French wine, some chicken, some of that fine white bread, cinnamon toast, and the use of your garden for some private business.'

The landlord spread his hands. 'If only I could, Brother, but white flour is not to be had at any cost, and we have no bread. But there is chicken and wine, and you are welcome to the garden for your private business.'

Michael looked disappointed, but nodded his agreement. The landlord hurried away to do his bidding. Bartholomew was surprised that the monk would break the University's rules so flagrantly. 'From that, I assume this is not your first visit?'

Michael beamed and led him over to a table under some trees where they were at least sheltered from the wind, if not the rain. De Belem slipped through the door, latching it carefully behind him.

'I am sorry for the secrecy, but it is for your own safety. I am a marked man, and it would do you no good to be seen with me,' he said, as he came to join them at the wet table.

'Marked by whom?' asked Bartholomew.

'I do not know,' he said, putting his elbows on the table and resting his face in his hands. 'But they have already killed my daughter.'

'How do you know that?' asked Bartholomew curiously.

De Belem raised his head. 'Allow me to explain. After my wife was taken by the Death, I lost my faith. Half the monks and priests in the land were taken, and I thought if God would not protect His own, why would He bother with me? I said as much to one of my colleagues, and a few days later I received an invitation to attend a meeting of the Guild of Purification. I did not know what it entailed, but I went because I was disillusioned and lonely. The Honourable Guild of Dyers was full of bickering because of a shift in the balance of power after the plague, and I felt I would have nothing to lose by joining another organisation.'

He paused and looked up into the swaying branches above. Bartholomew said nothing. Stanmore had already told him that de Belem was a member of the Guild of Purification.

'The guild pays allegiance to Satan,' de Belem continued. 'You are scholars, so you know Lucifer's story. He was an angel and was cast out of Heaven. His halo fell to his feet, and so our symbol is a circle – his fallen halo.'

Michael pursed his lips, and the three men were silent while the landlord brought the chicken and wine. De Belem huddled inside his hood. Discreetly, the landlord kept his eyes fixed on the food, and did not attempt to look at de Belem, leaving Bartholomew to wonder how many other such meetings Michael had conducted on his premises.

De Belem continued when the landlord had left. 'The religious, or,' he said, casting a rueful glance at Michael, 'the irreligious side of it held little appeal for me. But these people were united in a common bond of friendship and belief. It is difficult to explain, but I felt a fellowship with them that I had not felt since before the Death. I was even made the Grand Master.'

'You are the Grand Master of the Guild of Purification?' said Bartholomew, stunned. Michael looked at him with round, doleful eyes, as though he found the mere mention of satanic dealings offensive to his vocation.

'I was,' continued de Belem. 'Not now. In fact, I am no longer even a member, although it is too late to make a difference.'

He paused before continuing.

'I imagine you might think that someone from the Guild of Purification might have killed Frances, but I know that it is not so. Whatever you might believe about us, we do not kill or make sacrifices of living things. Like any other guilds, we join together for fellowship. The difference, perhaps, is that we speak as we feel, and have no priests to warn us of the fires of hell and to look ever for heresy.'

Bartholomew thought about the Franciscans at Michaelhouse, and their obsession with heresy, and did not wonder that some people were attracted to such an organisation. Michael appeared shocked.

De Belem continued. 'We met in disused churches, but did them no harm. The Guild of the Coming is perhaps a little more ritualistic than the Guild of Purification, but we do not kill: the deaths of those women and Frances were nothing to do with us. Someone else is responsible.'

'Like who?' asked Michael.

'Like the fanatics in the Guild of the Holy Trinity,' said de Belem. 'They are always railing about how the Death was brought by sinners like prostitutes and greedy merchants.'

'What makes you think they killed Frances?' asked Bartholomew.

'Because I was sent a note telling me that Frances would be murdered because I was a member of a coven,' said de Belem in a whisper.

'Do you still have it?' asked Michael.

De Belem shook his head. 'It so distressed me, I threw it in the fire. I was foolish. If I had kept it, we might have been able to glean clues as to the identity of her killer.'

'But why did you not tell me of this note before?' asked Bartholomew. 'Such as when you asked me to investigate Frances's murder.'

De Belem closed his eyes. 'I simply did not think of it until after you left. You must recall you had brought devastating news, and I was not thinking clearly.'

'Do you think notes were sent to the families of the other women?' asked Bartholomew. He had been assuming that the murders of the women were random killings, but de Belem's information suggested there might be a pattern to them. If there were a pattern, they might yet be able to solve the mystery.

'I do not know. Frances and Isobel were the only ones who meant something to me.'

'Isobel?' said Michael, through a mouthful of chicken. 'The whore?'

Bartholomew kicked him under the table. De Belem

turned sad eyes on Michael. 'A whore, yes, if you would. She came to my house twice every week and left before first light so Frances would not know. I should have insisted that she stayed until it was light that day. Isobel's life should have been worth more to me than my reputation with a wild daughter.'

Bartholomew leaned his folded arms on the table and studied the wet wood, thinking about what de Belem had told them. He was saying that at least two of the murders had been attacks against the satanists, deliberate assassinations intended to strike at specific people. He thought back to what Stanmore had told him the night he had gone to Trumpington: that he thought Richard Tulyet the elder might be a member of the Guild of the Coming.

'Did you tell the Sheriff about the note you received?' he asked.

De Belem nodded. 'He said he would look into it, but of course he found nothing.'

'Will you tell us the names of the other members of the guild so we might question them?'

A faint smile crossed de Belem's face. 'I cannot. It might put them at risk. The two guilds are innocent of the murders, and this maniac must be brought to justice. Tulyet is worthless, and you are my only hope of seeing Frances and Isobel avenged. If the guilds were the murderers, Frances and Isobel would be here now, and we would not be talking.'

The rain became heavier, and de Belem glanced up at the iron-grey clouds.

'I must go. I have been here too long already.' He stood slowly, rain dripping from his hair where it was not covered by his hood. He knelt quickly and awkwardly for Michael's benediction, slipped across the tiny garden, unlatched the gate, and was gone.

'Oh, Lord, Michael,' said Bartholomew, when the door had been closed again. 'Now what? Do you believe him?'

Michael, who had been sufficiently interested by de Belem's words to stop eating, wiped the grease from his mouth with his sleeve. 'His claims are possible,' he answered. 'I am inclined to believe de Belem that his guild is not responsible. After all, he lost his daughter and his woman.'

'But who was in the orchard the night after Frances's murder?' asked Bartholomew.

Michael scratched his head. 'It all makes little sense,' he said.

'Unless,' said Bartholomew, watching a bird swoop onto the table to peck up crumbs from Michael's food, 'de Belem speaks only for the Guild of Purification, of which he was a member. Oswald told me the two guilds were rivals. I think de Belem is underestimating the power of the Guild of the Coming, especially if the Tulyets are involved. I also think his grief might be influencing his reasoning. Perhaps he feels guilty that his loved ones have died because he is a satanist, and is trying to convince himself it is not his fault. If the Guild of the Holy Trinity is antagonistic enough towards satanism to murder, they would not be leaving satanic regalia on people's beds. I still believe the Guild of the Coming left the goat mask in Nicholas's coffin and the head for you.'

Michael rubbed some crumbs across the table idly as he thought. 'You could be right,' he said. 'It would be too easy to dismiss the covens from our enquiries. And de Belem can only have knowledge of his own guild, not that of his rivals. I suggest we treat Master de Belem's information with scepticism.'

He turned back to the remains of his meal, and Bartholomew, chewing on a bacon rind that flavoured the chicken, began to mull over the evidence yet again.

If Isobel made regular visits to de Belem at night, it would have been simple for the murderer to lie in wait for her. Did Frances also have a regular time when she slipped out of the house to meet her lover? But why Michaelhouse? Was she meeting her lover there, the scholar, as Brother Alban had claimed? Perhaps it was her lover who had killed her.

And what had Frances meant when she had said her killer was not a man? He drew circles on the wet table with his finger, lost in thought. She must have glimpsed her killer wearing a mask – either a red hood like the man in the orchard, or one of a goat's head like the dead woman in Nicholas's coffin. He wondered whether the killer was from Michaelhouse, but reasoned that was unlikely. The three people he had seen in the orchard were leaving after their search, not returning to their rooms, and he and Michael had already established that an insider would not have needed to drug Walter to go about his business at night because he would have known Walter slept on duty. What had the murderer lost in the orchard? If it were the Guild of the Coming who were committing the murders, then it must have been they who had attacked him and set the College gate afire. But Sybilla was certain that one man had killed Isobel.

And was Nicholas of York still alive somewhere as the

mastermind behind all this? It was odd that the first murder coincided with his death. Was it he who left the goat's head in Michael's room to warn him away? And what of the friar? Was he a member of the Guild of Purification killed by the Guild of the Coming, or perhaps a member of the fanatic Guild of the Holy Trinity rifling through the University history seeking out details of the covens? But Bartholomew and Michael had already shown that he was a stranger to the town and was unfamiliar with the daily rituals of St Mary's Church. Perhaps they should go back to the chest, and see whether there were any other documents there that related to these guilds which might explain why the deaths in St Mary's Church seemed to be connected to the murders of the women.

And where was Buckley? And why had Janetta and Froissart's family gone to ground? Bartholomew felt his head begin to reel. As soon as he felt he was beginning to make some progress, he merely raised more questions. He wondered suddenly how his students were proceeding. He should be with them, helping to train them to be good physicians, not sitting in beer gardens in the rain being warned against becoming involved in something that seemed to grow more sinister with each passing moment. He stood abruptly.

'I can see only one way forward,' said Michael, following him out. 'We must spy on the Guild of the Coming at All Saints' tonight and see what we can discover.'

Bartholomew turned his face to the falling rain, feeling it cool his face. 'I am tempted to go to the Chancellor and turn everything over to him. We are scholars, not witch-hunters. And anyway,' he added wryly, 'it is Sunday.'

Michael looked sharply at him. 'Are you giving up? Are you going to let evil men tell us what we can and cannot do in our own town?'

Bartholomew closed his eyes. 'How did we become embroiled in all this, Michael?' he asked softly. 'I can make no sense at all of the information we have, and the more we learn, the less clear everything becomes. I do not mind telling you that I find the whole business frightening.'

'I share your fears, but I also think that we will be in danger whether we continue to investigate or not. Everything we do will be held suspect from now on, and whoever left the head for me knows what we are doing. I believe the only way we will ever be safe is to unravel this mystery and unmask its villains. And you owe it to Frances de Belem, who might have been your wife had you not chosen another path.' Michael saw his friend's hesitation and added firmly, 'Tonight we will go to watch this coven meet at All Saints'.'

'Is there no other way?' groaned Bartholomew, shifting uncomfortably in his sopping cloak. 'Perhaps we should just go straight to Tulyet.'

'And say what?' demanded Michael. 'Ask him which member of his guild is murdering the town's whores? Is it his father or just one of his friends? Come on, Matt! We would get nowhere there, and the last time we took him on, I ended up in bed with a dead animal, and you were threatened with imprisonment in the Castle dungeons.'

'Will you tell de Wetherset what we intend to do?' said Bartholomew. 'Then at least someone will know the truth if we are caught and disappear, like Buckley and Nicholas. And ask him if Master Jonstan will come too. This is more in his line of duty than ours.'

'We will not be caught,' said Michael. 'Not with Cynric with us. Asking for Jonstan is a good idea, although I think I will request that the Chancellor does not reveal his plans to Harling. I do not trust that man.'

As Bartholomew and Michael walked home together, the rain became harder, the wind blowing it horizontally in hazy sheets. Bartholomew shivered and pulled his cloak closer round him. The High Street became a river of mud, and water oozed out of the drains and collected in the pot-holes and ruts. The streets were deserted, everyone either at home or in the noisy taverns. Passing St Mary's churchyard, Bartholomew saw something move out of the corner of his eye. He stopped and peered forward, clutching at Michael's sleeve.

'There is someone at Nicholas's grave,' he whispered. Michael stiffened, and together they crept forward.

'Who is it?' breathed Michael. Bartholomew peered through the rain. It was a man of medium height dressed in a priest's robe that was too large. As they inched forward, the man spun round, and seeing them coming, turned and fled. Bartholomew tore after him, leaping over the tombstones and mounds of grass. The man skidded in the mud and almost fell. Bartholomew lunged forward and grabbed a handful of his gown, but lost his balance as the man knocked his hand away. As he scrabbled to regain his footing, the man rushed past him, heading diagonally away from where Michael stood.

As Bartholomew scrambled to his feet, he saw Michael dive full-length towards the fleeing man and gain a hold on the hem of his gown. The man was stopped dead in mid-stride. In an effort made great by terror, he tried to run again, tearing free from Michael. Bartholomew saw him reach the High Street and turn left towards the Trumpington Gate.

Robes billowing, the man began to gain speed down the empty street, Bartholomew in hot pursuit. Bartholomew began to gain on him. And then disaster struck. A heavy cart carrying kegs of beer pulled ponderously out of Bene't Street. The man skipped to one side, skidded in the mud, regained his balance and ran on. But Bartholomew collided heavily with the cart. The horse, panicked by the sudden movement, reared and kicked. One of the kegs fell from the cart and smashed, and Bartholomew went sprawling into the mud.

He covered his head with his hands, hearing the horse's hooves thudding into the ground next to him, and tried to scramble away, but the mud was too slippery. Just as he was certain his head would be smashed by the horse's flailing hooves, one of his arms was seized, and he was hauled away with such force that he thought it had been yanked from its socket. Hooves pounded the spot where he had been moments earlier.

Next to him, Michael leaned up against the wall of a house and gasped for breath; while the carter began to regain control of his horse. Bartholomew sat shakily on the ground and watched the man he had been chasing disappear up the High Street.

'Why don't you watch where you are going!' the carter shouted furiously at Bartholomew.

Michael raised himself up to his full height and pointed a meaty finger at the carter. 'You should not be trading on a Sunday!' he admonished severely. 'You are committing a grave sin.'

The carter was sheepish but unrepentant. 'Well, why was he in such a hurry on a Sunday?' he countered, pointing at Bartholomew.

'He is a physician,' said Michael. 'Physicians attend patients all days of the week.'

'But they do not usually chase them!' the carter retorted, tossing his head in the direction the man had fled. Michael took a step towards him, and the carter, wary of the formidable strength he had witnessed when the monk hauled his colleague from under the horse, backed down. He raised his hand in a rude gesture and urged his horse to move on, yelling abuse when he felt he was far enough away to be safe.

'Thank you,' said Bartholomew, climbing unsteadily to his feet and rubbing his shoulder. He looked at the fat monk and wondered where his strength came from. He seldom took exercise and ate far more than was healthy, but the fat monk's strength of arm was prodigious.

Michael nodded absently. 'A pity you did not catch him,' he said. 'You would have done had that wretched carter not been in the way.'

Bartholomew flexed his arm to ensure it was still attached. 'I had him in my grasp in the churchyard, and so did you.'

Michael shook his head slowly. 'A great pity,' he said again. 'That man could have answered many questions. That was Nicholas of York.'

CHAPTER 8

I T WAS STILL RAINING WHEN DARKNESS FELL THAT
night and Bartholomew was more reluctant to go
out than ever. He waited in the kitchen with Cynric
and Michael until Michaelhouse grew silent, and followed
them resentfully through the orchard to the back gate.
He saw shadows flit across the lane as he eased open the
new gate and Jonstan materialised out of the darkness,
flanked by two heavy-set beadles.

'Two of my best men,' he whispered. 'We will station
them within hailing distance of All Saints' as a safeguard,
although the Chancellor has advised that we do nothing
but watch.'

'I have a bad feeling about this, Brother,' muttered
Bartholomew to Michael. 'We should not be sneaking
off in the night to spy on satanic rituals.'

'According to Brother Boniface, most of the medicine
you teach him involves satanic rituals,' Michael whispered
back with a chuckle.

'He said that?' said Bartholomew loudly, and dropped
his voice as the others glared at him. 'Did he tell
you that?'

Michael nodded, still laughing under his breath.

Cynric was elbowing him so he could close the door and Bartholomew was forced to let the matter drop. They made their way up the High Street and into Bridge Street. Once they met a group of beadles, but were allowed past without question when Jonstan spoke. They tried to keep out of sight as they neared the Great Bridge, lest any members of the guild were keeping a watch on it. Three soldiers guarded the bridge, talking in low voices. Bartholomew caught the glint of metal and saw that they were armed. Jonstan stopped to consider.

'It is likely that these satanists will cross the bridge,' he whispered, 'and must have done so for previous meetings. Therefore they must have bribed the guards. If we cross the bridge, the guards might tell them that others have already crossed.'

Cynric glanced at the river. 'We can wade across,' he whispered.

Bartholomew eyed the black, swirling waters dubiously. 'But the rain has swollen it,' he said. 'And besides, it is filthy.'

'You will not notice the filth in the dark,' whispered Jonstan consolingly.

Bartholomew stared at him in the dim light cast by the soldiers' lamps. 'Just because we cannot see it does not mean that it cannot do us harm,' he began.

The others made impatient sounds, and Michael pushed him towards the river bank. 'Now is not the time for a lecture on hygiene, Matt,' he hissed. 'Do not be so fastidious!'

Cynric led the way along the bank, well away from the bridge, and entered the water without a sound. The others followed more noisily, causing the Welshman to glare at them. Jonstan's amiable face was taut with concentration as he waded carefully through the water, swearing to himself when he slipped on the slick river bed. Jonstan was taking his duties seriously. Bartholomew gritted his teeth against the aching cold of the water that lapped around his knees, and then suddenly reached his waist. He tried not to think of Trinity Hall, Gonville Hall, Clare College, Michaelhouse, the Carmelite Friary, and St John's Hospital, all of which discharged their waste directly into the river upstream from where they were crossing. Next to him, Michael hoisted his habit higher and higher as the water rose, displaying startlingly white, fat legs.

They kept to one side of the road as they neared All Saints' Church. Overgrown land marked where a pathetic line of shacks had been burned to the ground during the plague. Few people ventured near the charred posts protruding from the tangle of weeds now: most claimed the area was haunted. While Bartholomew did not believe it was haunted, he felt it held an undeniable atmosphere of desolation. The Guild of the Coming had indeed chosen an apt spot for its demonic meetings.

The church itself was little more than four stone walls with gaping holes for windows. Although it had been decommissioned, it had not been made secure like the others. A wind was picking up, and it made a low hissing sound through the aisle. Cautiously, Bartholomew pushed open the door and stepped inside, while Cynric and Jonstan checked the churchyard, and Michael tried to wring water out of his sodden habit. Bartholomew looked down the small aisle with its peeling wall-paintings and stone altar. He had wondered whether it would hold an evil aura from the demonic ceremonies performed there, but All Saints' Church felt just like any other old and abandoned building: it smelled of damp wood, and a carpet of saturated leaves and a litter of twigs and moss was soft under his feet. He heard the distant chime of a bell. Not long to go now, if the Guild of the Coming intended to begin their unholy antics at midnight.

Jonstan returned to say that there was nothing untoward at the church or the grounds, and that Cynric had already secured himself a good vantage point in a tree. He suggested that Michael hid in the bushes to watch the entrance. Michael's habit was black and he was virtually invisible once he had secreted himself and the leaves had stopped rustling and twitching.

'I imagine that most of their ceremony will take place at the altar-end of the church,' said Jonstan to Bartholomew. 'We can either look through a window as Cynric is doing, or climb into the roof.'

'It will be rotten,' said Bartholomew, looking doubtfully at the roof timbers. 'We might fall through.'

'We stand a far greater chance of being discovered down here,' reasoned Jonstan.

Bartholomew peered up at the roof. He could see sky in patches, and a decaying piece of wood swung back and forth in the wind with a creaking sound.

'We could try,' he said, without conviction. Jonstan smiled and slapped him on the back. At the back of the church, a small spiral stair led up to the bell that had once hung there. The steps were crumbling, slick with wet leaves, and uneven, and Bartholomew was forced to steady himself by bracing both hands against walls that ran with green slime. Ahead of him, Jonstan suddenly lost his footing as a step gave way under his weight. Flailing with his arms, he tumbled backwards, falling heavily against Bartholomew. Both men were saved from falling further only because Bartholomew's cloak snagged on a jagged piece of metal that protruded from the wall.

'Are you all right?' whispered Bartholomew, when he had regained his balance.

'I think I have twisted my ankle,' replied Jonstan, sinking down onto the stairs and rubbing his foot, his face grey with pain. Bartholomew removed the Proctor's shoe and inspected the joint. In the dark, he could not tell whether it was broken or not, but at the very least, it was sprained. It already felt hot under his gently probing fingers.

'We should abandon this business,' he said. 'We should go home while we still can. It was a stupid idea to come here.'

'No!' Jonstan's grip on his arm was strong. 'We must get to the bottom of all this, or more people will die. We cannot leave now!'

'But you should rest your foot,' protested Bartholomew. 'It is already beginning to swell.'

'I will find somewhere I can take the weight off it,' said Jonstan. 'Putting an end to this evil is more important.'

Bartholomew looked up the stairs spiralling away into darkness. 'I suppose you might find somewhere to sit. But you will be in trouble if we need to run.'

'My mother is always telling me I am too old for things like this,' said Jonstan, trying to make light of their predicament. He stood unsteadily, and gave

Bartholomew a weak smile. 'Perhaps I should take her advice and become a clerk!'

Bartholomew helped him hop up the stairs until they reached a doorway that afforded access to the inside of the roof. It was lit only by the gaps where the roof was open to the sky, and, looking down, Bartholomew could see that entire sections had fallen into the aisle below. But the main rafters seemed to be sound enough, and if he did not step on the weaker timbers to the side, he should be relatively safe.

'I think I will be able to see from over there,' said Jonstan, pointing. To one side, a large part of the roof had fallen, but there were sturdy timbers on which Jonstan would be able to lean. Bartholomew helped him move, and, although the timbers creaked ominously under their weight, they held. Jonstan wedged himself between two posts where he could take the weight off his ankle and still be able to look down.

Bartholomew made his way back, and looked through the rafters at the floor a long way below. He wondered how he had let himself become involved in such business, but a picture of Frances de Belem came into his mind, so he gritted his teeth and moved forward. At one point, his foot went through a particularly rotten part, shedding shards of flaky wood into the darkness beneath. Bartholomew closed his eyes and clutched a post until he had recovered his nerve. He edged forward again, feeling as though at any moment the whole roof would give way, and he would be sent crashing to the floor.

After what seemed like an age, he reached the end, and looked for a place from which to watch. There was a crown post just above the altar with strong timbers, but Bartholomew knew he would see only the tops of people's heads. He climbed to the far side, and found that, by lying full length along one wide timber, he could see the altar and most of the choir.

Once the fear of being so high up had receded, Bartholomew found he was quite comfortable on his timber, and was sheltered from the wind and rain. Although his legs were wet from wading through the river, the rest of him was dry, and his position was infinitely preferable to those of Michael and Cynric watching from outside. He pulled his cloak tighter round him for warmth, and felt his eyes close. The church below was in darkness and the only sound was the soft patter of rain on the broken roof above him. He heard the gentle hiss of trees in the wind, and, despite his misgivings about their mission, began to feel drowsy.

He awoke with a start wondering where he was, gripping the timber desperately as he felt himself tip. He took a deep, shuddering breath and raised his head to see if he could see Jonstan. The Proctor was almost beside himself, virtually out of his hiding place and gesturing frantically. Even at that distance, Jonstan's face was pale with tension. Bartholomew looked to where he was pointing, and almost fell off the timber in fright.

A few feet from him, another person was climbing over the rafters as he had done. He felt his heart begin to pound. Now they would be uncovered! He glanced at Jonstan, but the Proctor had slipped back into his shadows. Bartholomew did not know what to do. Should he stay where he was and hope he was not seen? Should he attack the person crawling towards him before he was attacked himself? But then they would both fall through the roof, and Bartholomew had no weapon in any case.

As the person inched closer, Bartholomew held his breath and huddled into his cloak. He tried to quell his panic by telling himself that if someone was not expecting him to be there, he was hidden well enough. He was wrapped from head to foot in a black cloak and underneath he wore his black scholar's tabard. As long as he kept his face covered and the person carried no lamp, there was every chance Bartholomew might remain undetected. The person reached the crown post and turned to wave. Bartholomew felt sick as he saw a second man begin to make his way along the rafters.

Meanwhile, in the church itself, people were starting to gather. At first, there were just black shapes moving around in silence. Then pitch torches were lit and the church flared into light. The people wore black gowns with hoods that came over their heads and hid their faces. Bartholomew counted. Twelve standing around the altar, plus the two in the roof. Fourteen. Bartholomew looked down, watching their movements. Each time someone spoke, the others jumped, and several looked around them anxiously. One man was shaking so badly he could barely stand, while another gnawed agitatedly at his fingernails. For an evening in pleasant company, which was how de Belem had described them, the congregation appeared unaccountably nervous.

The second person had reached the first, and was watching the people below. He carried a large bundle that the first man began to unwrap. Bartholomew cringed as the beam on which he lay gave a creak, causing the smaller of the two men to look up. He held his breath, expecting at any moment to feel a dagger at his throat, or the beam tipped so he would fall to his death. But nothing happened, and after a few agonising moments, Bartholomew risked a glance up. The attention of the two men was again fixed on the scene below, for the ceremony was beginning.

The voices were low at first, but began to rise as a figure standing at the altar climbed on top of it. Bartholomew recoiled in shock as he saw a red mask. The chanting continued as the man began to speak. Bartholomew, keeping a wary eye on the two people in the roof, strained to hear his words, but the language was unfamiliar to him. But one word kept occurring – *caper* – the Latin for a male goat.

The chanting grew louder, and one or two people dropped to their knees, while the high priest began to dance in time with the chanting. He suddenly stopped and gave a great yell, throwing up his hands and raising his face to look straight at Bartholomew. Bartholomew felt his stomach turn over and tightened his grip on the rafters in anticipation of being revealed. But nothing of the sort happened, and although Bartholomew saw the glint of the high priest's eyes through the red mask, he apparently was not seen.

One of the two people in the roof moved, and Bartholomew saw a great black crow swoop down towards the altar. It circled twice and then flapped out of one of the windows, cawing loudly. Several of the worshippers screamed and covered their faces, while others shakily resumed their chanting and the high priest began dancing again. It took Bartholomew a moment to realise that the bird had been released by the person in the roof. So, that was why they were there: they were part of an act! He could well understand that to the people standing below the black bird would have appeared to have materialised out of thin air.

The whole process was repeated again with more urgency, the high priest drumming his feet wildly on the stone. When the chanting reached fever pitch, the high priest flung himself onto the floor and began to writhe. Bartholomew saw immediately it was to attract attention away from the roof, and watched closely. It took both people this time to lever something through the hole. The chanting faltered as the church filled with swooping silent bats. There must have been at least seven of them, enormous ones, bundled in the sack ready to be released. They soared uncertainly before fluttering out of the windows into the dark night beyond. One of the worshippers screamed and tried to run away, but was prevented by the others.

The high priest lurched to his feet and began the chanting again. The ceremony was apparently reaching its climax for the high priest cavorted and writhed, uttering the most incomprehensible gibberish. The worshippers edged closer together, casting terrified looks around them. As the chanting grew faster, one of them dropped to his knees and put his forehead to the ground. One by one the others followed. While all heads were conveniently averted, the two in the roof became busy again, and the head of a goat was lowered through the hole on a thin rope.

The high priest, still gibbering, quickly untied the knot so the rope could be pulled back up. That done, he gave a monstrous shriek and hurled himself backwards. The church became silent. Nervously, the worshippers began to look up. The high priest hauled himself to his feet and lifted the head into the air by the horns. His people cowered in front of him.

'Our lord has spoken to me in the language of the dark angels,' he began in English. Several of the worshippers began to whimper. 'He says you, his children, should obey your high priest in all things. Before the new moon, he will claim another for his own, as a sign that he is near.'

He lowered the head to the altar, bowed to it and covered it reverently with a black cloth. The ceremony was over. Or so Bartholomew thought. The two people in the roof were busy, and as the worshippers began to leave, they found themselves splattered with blood that rained through the broken roof above the altar. Bartholomew saw the upturned face of the older Richard Tulyet before he fled, wailing as he went. One old lady stood frozen with fright, her eyes fixed on the black cloth. It was Mistress Tulyet, abandoned by her husband and left to fend for herself. The high priest helped her from the church, where she fled with the rest of her unholy brethren.

Bartholomew watched as the two people in the roof gathered their belongings, and crawled back along the rafters. They were thorough: the smaller of the two even braved a treacherous section of the roof to retrieve a black feather. Jonstan was invisible, and the two left the roof in silence.

The high priest was waiting for them, and he and the smaller man stood for a moment talking in low voices, while the other kept a respectful distance. Bartholomew strained to see their faces, but they wore gowns with deep cowls and were taking no chances that one of the others might come back and recognise them. The high priest ushered them out and began to tidy up. After what seemed like hours, he doused the last torch, and removed his mask, dropping it into a bag with his other belongings. He drew his hood over his head and left. Bartholomew swore softly. He had not been able to see his face, and hoped one of the others had.

Stiffly, Bartholomew eased himself up and stretched. He had no idea how long the ceremony had taken, but his shoulders ached with tension. As he made the treacherous journey back across the rotten rafters he glimpsed the aisle floor a long way down. For an instant he felt dizzy, and had to stand still until the feeling passed.

Jonstan was waiting for him by the stairs, a sheen of sweat on his white face.

'Hell's teeth, Matthew!' he said. 'I have never been so frightened in my life! We must get away from this foul place as quickly as possible!'

Bartholomew helped him down the stairs. Jonstan started violently as Cynric materialised behind him, and clutched at his chest.

'They have all gone,' said Cynric in a low voice. 'I tried to follow the last one, but he was away over the Fens before I could get close enough.' He refused to meet Bartholomew's eye, and Bartholomew wondered whether he had been as assiduous in his trailing as usual.

Michael joined them, his flabby face pallid. 'We should not stay here,' he said and grabbed Bartholomew's arm. 'De Belem was wrong. This was nothing harmless: it was evil and terrifying. I have no doubt those vile people are behind much that is wrong in the town.'

Cynric led the way, scouting ahead to make certain none of the worshippers still lurked. Bartholomew and Michael followed, almost carrying Jonstan between them. They forded the river as before, wading waist-deep through the cold water. Jonstan leaned on them heavily, making their progress slower than Bartholomew would have wished. It was with considerable relief that they finally reached the back gate at Michaelhouse and slipped through the orchard to the kitchen. While Cynric went to explain to Jonstan's beadles that he had sprained his ankle, Bartholomew kindled a fire. It was cold for summer, and while he and Jonstan had stayed relatively dry, Michael and Cynric were soaked to the skin.

He set some wine to mull and inspected Jonstan's foot. It was twice its normal size, and already turning dark with bruising. Deftly, he wrapped it in wet bandages and placed it on a stool, cushioned with his cloak. He looked around at the others. They were all pale and subdued, and Michael was shivering uncontrollably. Bartholomew poured the wine and Michael gulped his and Bartholomew's down at an impressive rate, even for him, and held his cup out for more.

Jonstan took a deep breath. 'Did anyone see the face of that cavorting leader?'

The others shook their heads. 'Damn,' said Bartholomew. 'I thought you might, Michael.'

Michael shook his head. 'He was too far away, and he had his hood pulled over his head. I am surprised he could see where he was walking. I saw Richard Tulyet, though.'

'The Sheriff?' gasped Jonstan.

'No, his father, the merchant. Perhaps the Sheriff was there, but I did not see him.'

'I saw his mother,' said Bartholomew. 'Her husband abandoned her when the blood started raining down.'

'That was disgusting,' said Cynric with a shudder. 'I thought it was just some dye at first, but I had a good look and it really was blood.'

'Probably from the goat,' said Bartholomew.

'Of course,' said Jonstan, looking relieved. 'From the goat.'

'I was scared out of my wits,' said Michael in a low voice. 'Did you see that bird appear out of nowhere? And that head just lowered itself from the sky. I will never again mock powers I do not understand.'

Cynric nodded vigorously, while Jonstan closed his eyes and crossed himself. 'What were that pair up to near you, Matthew?' he asked weakly. 'I could not see.'

Bartholomew suddenly realised that he had been the only one able to see how the hoax was enacted. Cynric and Michael were outside, and Jonstan was too far away. They had been duped in the same way that the worshippers had. No wonder they were subdued.

'They were proving what you have always held, Michael,' he said, smiling. 'That the Devil's worst crimes are the handiwork of people.'

Jonstan slept on the pallet bed in Bartholomew's store-room for the few remaining hours of the night and was helped home by his two beadles at first light.

'You must rest your foot for a few days,' Bartholomew advised. 'Do you have someone who can care for you?'

'My mother will attend to me,' said Jonstan, smiling weakly. 'Although she will tell me that it is my own fault for climbing around old buildings in the dark.'

Bartholomew watched him hobble out of the yard, and turned his thoughts to what they had learned. The high priest and his two helpers could not have been the same three Bartholomew had encountered in the orchard, because the man who had bitten him had been huge, and none of the three satanists were above average size. Could one of them be Sybilla's 'average man'? Bartholomew supposed that must be likely, since the high priest had forecast that another murder would occur before the new moon, and how else would he know unless he or one of his associates was planning to commit the crime?

Perhaps the high priest was Nicholas of York, newly returned from the dead to frighten the living daylights out of his coven. The more Bartholomew thought about it, and the other tricks used to keep the congregation in a state of terror, the more he became convinced it was plausible. What better trick than to rise from the grave? Especially since so many people had seen him dead.

'We must do something to stop another murder being committed,' said Bartholomew to Michael, who had poked his head around the door of Bartholomew's room.

'I agree,' said Michael, moving to sit on the bed. 'But what do you suggest? Shall we entertain the town's prostitutes in College to keep them off the streets for the next few nights?'

'No, but I know something we might do,' said

Bartholomew, making for the door. Michael scrambled to follow, grumbling.

Bartholomew went to the kitchen and asked Agatha where he might find the Lady Matilde. The large laundress offered to show him, leaving through the back gate and cutting across the fields so that no one would ask why they were missing church. She took them to a small timber-framed house in the area near St John's Hospital known as The Jewry, dating from the time when it had been the home of Jewish merchants before their expulsion from England in 1290. Despite the fact that it was barely light, the town was already busy, and people ran here and there preparing for the day's business.

'Matilde,' Agatha yelled at the top of her voice, drawing the attention of several passers-by. 'Customers!'

Bartholomew cringed, while Michael looked furtive. Agatha gave them a knowing wink and marched into the house next door, calling loudly for yet another cousin. Bartholomew saw one or two people nudging each other at the sight of a physician and a monk outside the door of a well-known prostitute. Michael pulled his cowl over his head as if he imagined it might make him anonymous, and succeeded in making himself look more furtive than ever.

Matilde answered the door and ushered them inside, smiling at their obvious discomfort. She brought them cups of cool white wine and saw that they were comfortably seated before sitting herself. The room was impeccably clean, with fine wool rugs scattered about the floor, and tapestries on the walls. The furniture was exquisitely carved, and the chairs were adorned with embroidered cushions. A table with quills and parchment stood next to the window, suggesting that Lady Matilde could write as well as speak Court French.

'How may I help you?' she said. She gave Michael a sidelong glance that oozed mischief. 'I assume you have not come for my professional attentions?'

Michael, his composure regained now that he was away from public view, winked at her, and grinned.

'We have come to give you some information,' said Bartholomew quickly, before Michael could side-track them by flirting. 'We cannot reveal our sources, but we have reason to believe that there will be another murder in the town before the new moon.'

She looked at him intently, all humour gone from her face. 'The new moon is due in four days. When one is out at night, one knows these things,' she added, seeing Michael's surprise. She stood and went to look out of the small window, drumming her long, slender fingers on the sill as she thought.

Bartholomew watched her. She was indeed an attractive woman, with long, honey-coloured hair twisted into a braid that hung heavily down her back. She was tall, and carried herself with a grace that he had seen in few women other than Philippa, his betrothed. The thought of Philippa made him look away from Matilde guiltily: he had scarcely given her a thought since the business with the University chest had begun, and he realised he had not even remembered to write to her the day before – the first Sunday he had not sent her a letter since she had left for London two months previously.

'Thank you for telling me this,' said Matilde, turning to them, her voice breaking across Bartholomew's thoughts.

'I will ensure the word gets around to my sisters that they take extra care.'

'Sisters?' queried Michael, his green eyes dancing merrily.

'Fellow whores, Brother,' she said, with a gaze that would have discomfited most men.

Michael stared back unabashed, favouring her with what Bartholomew could only describe as a leer. 'Sisters mean something different to us holy men,' he said.

She smiled at him. 'Well, now you know what it means to us prostitutes,' she said.

Bartholomew had trouble dragging Michael away, and wondered yet again how someone with Michael's obvious interest in women could have chosen a vocation that demanded chastity. Bartholomew knew that Michael regularly broke other rules of his Order – he nearly always started eating before grace, he did not keep his offices, and his lifestyle was far from simple. Bartholomew wondered which other rules the large monk might bend or break.

They finally took their leave of Matilde, and walked home as early morning sun bathed the town. The High Street seethed with carts heading to the Fair, loaded way beyond safety limits with clothes, cheeses, meats, animals, furniture, and pots and pans. The drains at the side of the street were overflowing from the rain the night before, and great puddles of brown ooze forced Bartholomew and Michael to make some spectacular leaps to avoid them. In one, a sheep bleated pitifully as it stood up to its neck in mire, while a farmer tried to coax it out with a handful of grass.

Since they had missed breakfast, they bought hot

oatcakes from a baker. Bartholomew winced as the coarse grain and particles of stone grated against his teeth. When he had finished, he was still hungry, but the few pennies in his pocket were not enough to buy one of the delicious pies carried on a baker's tray, nor the soft white bread carried in the basket of another. He saw some children jostle the man with the bread, and one of them escaped with a loaf. Two of the children were the tinker's daughters, and Bartholomew wondered if their younger brother were still alive.

Michael stopped off to report to de Wetherset, while Bartholomew walked back to Michaelhouse to test his students on the Galen that they were supposed to have read. He was not pleased to discover that they had become side-tracked before finishing the first paragraph.

'Brother Boniface says that predicting the outcome of a disease is tantamount to predicting the will of God, and that is heresy,' said Gray in explanation.

Bartholomew ran a hand through his hair in exasperation. Surely Boniface could not claim Galen's works were heretical? They had been standard, uncontroversial texts for physicians for hundreds of years. In fact, they were so old that newer discoveries were beginning to throw some of Galen's theories into question.

He picked up a cup from the table and held it in the air. 'Brother Boniface. If I allow this to fall from my hand, what will happen?'

Boniface eyed him warily. 'It will drop to the floor,' he said.

'And if I drop a lighted candle into these dry rushes, what will happen?'

'They will burn.'

'You are making predictions about events. Why is predicting the outcome of a disease any different?'

'It is not heresy to predict the obvious,' said Boniface coldly. 'It is heresy to predict whether a man lives or dies.'

'But there are some injuries and wasting diseases from which it is clear a man will never recover, no matter what a physician might do,' said Bartholomew, frustrated. 'Is that knowledge heresy?'

'But those cases are obvious!' said Boniface, becoming angry.

'And at what point does the outcome become obvious, exactly?' said Bartholomew. 'And what is the difference between you deciding which cases are obvious and which are not, and predicting whether a patient lives or dies?'

Boniface glared at him, but was silent. Bartholomew could have taken the argument further, but he had made his point. He instructed that Gray was to read the passages from Galen that they should have read earlier with others from the *Tegni*. The students groaned. They would be busy until nightfall, but since they had already wasted time on meaningless debate, they had no choice if they wanted to pass their disputations.

'That was a neat argument,' said Michael, who had been listening. 'It put that beggarly Franciscan in his place. He is disruptive in my theology classes. I would not mind if he stimulated lively debate, but his arguments are based on ignorance and bigotry.'

Bartholomew frowned. 'Except for Deynman, the others will pass if Boniface lets them study. But I do not want to waste the day talking about Boniface. I have been invited to Gonville Hall for a debate on contagion with two physicians from Paris.'

He smiled enthusiastically, and ducked into his room for his bag. Michael waited outside. 'We have to go to see Sir Richard Tulyet,' he called.

'Tulyet?' said Bartholomew, looking out of his window at Michael. 'Is that not rather rash, considering what we saw yesterday?'

'We have been discreet for days, and it has got us nowhere,' said Michael. 'De Wetherset believes it is time for a more direct approach.'

'Easy for him to say, sitting safely next to his wretched chest,' grumbled Bartholomew.

Michael smiled grimly. 'De Wetherset wants us to go immediately.'

Bartholomew emerged from his room. 'Immediately? But what about my debate?'

'We will hurry. You will not miss much of it,' said Michael.

Bartholomew sighed. 'Damn this business!' he said. 'Come on, then. But no lagging on the way.'

The home of Richard Tulyet the elder was a gracious building near the Church of the Holy Sepulchre. It was half-timbered, rather than stone, but was sturdily built. There were expensive rugs on the polished floors, and the monotony of white walls was broken with fine tapestries. Bartholomew and Michael were shown into a sunny room overlooking a garden at the rear of the house.

Tulyet did not hurry to see them, and Bartholomew began to pace irritably. Even Michael, helping himself to several exotic pastries from a dish on the table, considered that Tulyet had exceeded the limit of courtesy for which visitors might be expected to wait. Eventually, Tulyet puffed into the room, spreading his hands in apology, although the expression on his face suggested anything but repentance. He was a small man with the same fluffy beige hair as his son.

'I have had a most busy morning,' he said, seating himself at the table and stretching his hand towards the pastry dish before realising that it was empty.

'We have not,' said Michael, pointedly.

Tulyet ignored his comment, and studied the monk over his steepled fingers. 'How might I help you?'

'How long have you been a member of the Guild of the Coming?' asked Michael bluntly.

Tulyet stared at him, the smile fading from his face. 'I do not know what you are talking about.'

'You were seen last night leaving All Saints' Church after a less than religious ceremony was conducted there,' said Michael. 'How is your wife, by the way?'

Bartholomew cringed. He realised that Michael was aiming to needle Tulyet into indiscretion, but suspected that this was not the way to gain the information they needed. Tulyet had been a burgess and Lord Mayor, and was unlikely to be goaded into revealing matters he wished to remain secret. Bartholomew stepped forward to intervene.

'Perhaps we might talk to Mistress Tulyet too,' he said politely.

'You may not,' Tulyet snapped. 'She is unwell. And before you tell me you are a physician, she has already seen one, and he advised her to rest after he finished bleeding her. Not that this is any of your affair. Good morning.'

He made to sweep past them. Bartholomew blocked his way. 'Who is it in the Guild of the Coming that you hold in such fear?' he asked softly.

Tulyet stopped abruptly and Bartholomew saw the uncertainty in his eyes.

'This must be stopped,' Bartholomew said gently. 'If you help us, we might be able to make an end to it.'

Hope flared on Tulyet's face, and he took a step forward.

'I do not believe my father wishes to talk to you.'

Bartholomew looked behind him and saw Tulyet's youngest son standing in the doorway with two of his sergeants from the Castle. 'We are trying to help,' said Bartholomew.

'You are trying to interfere, and succeeding very well,' snapped the Sheriff. 'My father's affairs are none of your business. Now, please leave our house.'

'Why will you not let your father answer for himself?' asked Michael.

'Get out!' yelled Tulyet the elder. 'I will not tolerate this in my own home. Leave now, or these men will throw you out.'

He spun on his heel and stormed out, all trace of his momentary weakness gone. Bartholomew was frustrated. The old man had almost told them what they needed to know, and he was clearly terrified by it. He had obviously sent to the Castle for his son while he kept him and Michael waiting, which meant that he must have felt he needed protection. Perhaps he had joined the Guild of the Coming for similar reasons to de Belem, and had become too deeply embroiled to back out.

The Sheriff leaned back against the door frame and

sneered at them. 'You heard my father,' he said. 'Leave, or be thrown out by my men.'

'Are you not man enough to do it yourself?' asked Michael. 'The father unable to answer questions himself, and the son needing others to fight his battles. Come, Matt. This is no place for men.'

Bartholomew was impressed by Michael's nerve, but uncertain that such fieriness was prudent, and followed him out into the street half expecting to feel a knife between his shoulder-blades. Sheriff Tulyet followed.

'If I discover that either of you are interfering with my investigation again, or that you are intimidating my family, I will arrest you,' he said loudly. 'I will put you in the Castle prison, and your Chancellor and Bishop will not be able to do anything to help you. How could they in matters of treason?'

He slammed the door and stalked back towards the Castle, his men following.

'Treason?' said Michael, simultaneously startled and angry. 'On what grounds? This has nothing to do with treason!'

'It is not unknown for officers of the law to fabricate evidence to fit a case, or for them to force false confessions,' said Bartholomew drily, taking the monk's arm and leading him away from Tulyet's house. Justice was swift and harsh in England, and often men accused of crimes were not given time to prove their innocence. 'You should watch your tongue, Brother. It would not take much for Sheriff Tulyet to follow such a path. He seems unbalanced.'

'Me hanged for treason, and you burned for heresy,'

said Michael with a flicker of a smile. 'What a pair the Chancellor has chosen for his agents.'

Bartholomew walked quickly from Tulyet's house down Milne Street to Gonville Hall, to which its Master of Medicine, Father Philius, had invited two physicians from Paris, Bono and Matthieu.

'Ah yes, Doctor Bartholomew,' said Bono, standing to bow to him as he was shown into the conclave by a porter. 'I know your old master in Paris, Ibn Ibrahim.'

Bartholomew was delighted, but not surprised. Paris was not so large that a man of his master's standing could remain hidden. 'How does he fare?'

'Well enough,' said Bono, 'although I cannot imagine that he will remain so if he does not amend his beliefs. During the Death he suggested that the contagion was carried by animals! Can you credit such a foolish notion?'

'Animals?' queried Philius, startled. 'On what premise?'

'That he conducted certain tests to show it was not spread by the wind. He concluded that it must have been carried by animals.'

Bartholomew frowned. It was possible, he supposed, but he had not been in contact with animals during the dreadful winter months of 1348 and 1349, and he had been a victim of the plague. He wished Ibn Ibrahim was with them now that he might question him closer. The Arab usually had well-founded reasons for making such claims.

'The man is a heretic,' said Matthieu. 'I would keep your apprenticeship with him quiet if I were you. Do you know he practises more surgery than ever now?'

Bartholomew was silent. He too was using a greater number of surgical techniques, and the more he used them, the more he found them useful. He listened to the others discussing how surgery was an abomination that should be left to the inferior barber-surgeons. As the discussion evolved, Bartholomew began to feel a growing concern that his own teaching and beliefs would be considered as heretical as those of Ibn Ibrahim, and that he soon might have to answer for them.

The discussion moved from surgery to contagion, and Bartholomew found himself attacked again because of his insistence that a physician might spread contagion if he did not wash his hands. Bono shook his head in disbelief, while Matthieu merely laughed. Father Philius said nothing, for he and Bartholomew had debated this many times, and had never found common ground.

By the time the daylight began to fade and Gonville Hall's bell rang to announce the evening meal was ready, Bartholomew felt drained. He declined the invitation to stay to eat, and walked back along Milne Street towards Michaelhouse. As he reached the gates, the porter told him he was needed at the Castle. Wearily he set off, wondering why Tulyet should have summoned him so near the curfew, and whether he would have the strength to deal with the hostile Sheriff.

As he climbed Castle Hill, a sergeant hurried towards him with evident relief.

'You came!' he said, taking Bartholomew's arm and setting a vigorous pace towards the Castle. 'I thought you might not – under the circumstances.'

'What do you mean?' asked Bartholomew, disengaging his arm.

'The de Belem girl was a friend of yours, and the Sheriff is doing little to search out her killer,' he said, glancing around nervously. He added more firmly, 'He was a good Sheriff, but these last few weeks he has changed.'

'How?' asked Bartholomew.

The sergeant shrugged. 'Family problems, we think. But none of us know for certain. Here we are.'

They arrived at the gate-house, and Bartholomew was escorted inside. Torches hung in sconces along the walls so that the entire courtyard was filled with a dim, flickering light. The towers and crenellated curtain walls were great black masses against the darkening sky.

The soldier steered Bartholomew to the Great Hall against the north wall. In a small chamber off the stairs a man lay on a dirty straw pallet, groaning and swearing. Other soldiers stood around him, but moved aside as Bartholomew entered.

'A stupid accident,' said the sergeant in response to Bartholomew's unasked question. 'I told him to take down the archery targets, and Rufus here did not hear me shout that practice was over.'

Rufus slunk back into the shadows, aware that the eyes of all his colleagues were on him accusingly. 'It was an accident!' he insisted.

Bartholomew knelt and inspected the wound in the injured man's upper arm. The arrowhead that was embedded there was barbed, and Bartholomew hesitated. Two options were open to him: he could force the arrowhead through the arm and out the other side, or he could cut the flesh and pull the barbs free. The second option was clearly the better one for the injured man, since the arrowhead was not embedded sufficiently deeply to warrant forcing it through the arm. But it would involve surgery, and Bartholomew had just spent an entire day hearing how physicians that stooped to use methods suited to barbers were heretics. The injured man opened pleading eyes.

Bartholomew took one of the powerful sense-dulling potions he carried, mixed it into a cup of wine near the bed and gave it to the man to drink. When he saw the man begin to drowse, he indicated to the others that they should hold his patient down. He took a small knife and, ignoring the man's increasingly agonised screams, quickly cut the flesh away from the arrowhead and eased it out. The man slumped in relief as Bartholomew held the arrow for him to see. Bartholomew bound the arm with a poultice of healing herbs, gave him a sleeping potion, and said he would return later to ensure no infection had crept in.

Bartholomew was escorted to the gate by the sergeant. 'Thank you,' he said, handing Bartholomew an odd assortment of coins. 'Will he live, do you think? Will he keep the arm?'

Bartholomew was surprised by the question. 'It is not a very serious wound, and there seems to be no damage to the main blood-vessels. There should be no problem if it does not become infected.'

'Father Philius came this morning. He said he could do nothing, and that we needed Robin of Grantchester, the barber-surgeon. Robin offered to saw the arm off at the shoulder for five silver pennies payable in advance, but we could not raise one between us and he refused to give credit. We decided to ask you to come when the Sheriff left for the night.' He smiled suddenly, revealing an impressive collection of long, brown teeth. 'Agatha, your College laundress, is a cousin of mine, and she told me you are flexible about payments for your services.'

Bartholomew smiled back, and shook the sergeant's proffered hand before taking his leave. Agatha was right: although Bartholomew kept careful records about the medicines he dispensed, he kept no notes of payments due, and more often than not, he forgot what he was owed. It was a bone of contention between Bartholomew and Gray, who argued that there were those who would take advantage of such carelessness. Master Kenyngham, however, saw that Bartholomew was popular among his patients, and encouraged Bartholomew's casual attitude towards remuneration on the grounds that it made for favourable relations between Michaelhouse and the town.

As he walked back to Michaelhouse, Bartholomew's doubts about his methods began to recede. Few patients who underwent amputations survived, especially amputations performed by the unsavoury Robin, who was so slow that many of his patients died from bleeding or shock before he had finished. He always demanded advance payments, because so few patients survived his ministrations and he had learned that it was difficult to extract payments from grieving relatives. In the young soldier's case, there had been no cause to amputate anyway, when all that was needed were a few careful incisions.

As he walked down Castle Hill, he was accosted by a breathless urchin.

'I was sent for you,' he gasped. 'There has been an accident. You are needed, Doctor. You must come with me!'

Bartholomew followed the lad, wondering what else would happen before he could go home. The boy trotted along the High Street and cut behind St Mary's Church. The first inclination Bartholomew had that something was not right was when the lad suddenly darted off to one side. Bartholomew watched in surprise as he disappeared between the bushes. Realising that he had been led into a trap, he turned and began to run back towards the main road.

A line of men emerged, cutting off his escape. Bartholomew put his head down and pounded towards them. They faltered, and for a moment he thought he would be able to force his way through them. Then he felt something akin to a brewer's cart slam into him and he went sprawling onto the wet grass. Something landed on top of him with such force that all the breath was driven from his body. He struggled frantically and uselessly.

Just as he was beginning to turn dizzy from lack of air, the weight lifted and he was dragged to his feet. As he leaned over, gasping for breath, he saw something large move through the undergrowth away from him, but when he looked a second time, there was nothing except two or three waving branches that indicated something had passed between them.

'Matthew Bartholomew! You go where you are uninvited and you run away from where you are welcome!' said Janetta, thick black hair falling like gauze around her face. She nodded to the two men holding him, and his arms were released. 'I thought you wanted to talk to me.'

Bartholomew, still trying to catch his breath, looked wildly around him. The men were withdrawing silently, although he knew they would reappear rapidly if she called for them. Within seconds, they were alone, although he knew they were being watched closely.

'Well?' she said, still smiling at him. 'What do you want?'

He thought of Matilde's words of warning, and tried to collect his confused thoughts.

'Master Tulyet told us that you were a witness to the murder of Froissart's wife,' he said. 'I wanted to ask you about that.'

'He told you what?' she said, her eyes opening wide with shock.

Bartholomew sat on a tombstone and watched Janetta suspiciously.

'I have never spoken to this Tulyet,' protested Janetta. 'I know of him by reputation, of course. But I have never spoken to him.'

'But why would he lie?' asked Bartholomew, his thoughts whirling.

Janetta sat on the tombstone next to him, although she was careful to maintain a good distance between them. 'I have no idea. I do not know how he would even know my name.'

'Did you know Froissart?'

'I know him,' she said. She shuddered suddenly. 'Do you know what people are saying? That Froissart is the one who is killing the whores.'

'Tulyet does not believe that,' said Bartholomew.

'That is because Tulyet almost had Froissart in his hands when he claimed sanctuary in the church, and his men allowed him to escape. What does that tell you about Tulyet?' Janetta spat.

'Do you believe Froissart is the killer?'

Janetta let out a deep breath and looked up at the darkening sky. 'I think that is likely.'

'On what grounds?'

Janetta turned to him with her slow smile. 'Questions! You are like the inquisition!' She leaned down, and picked a stem of grass that she began to chew. 'Froissart is a rough man who drinks heavily and is violent to his wife and sister. You are lucky he was not one of the ones who caught you in our alley last week.'

'Why did he flee to the church for sanctuary if there was no murder?' asked Bartholomew. In the darkening gloom, the scars on her jaw were almost invisible, and he wondered why she did not make an attempt to hide them with the powders she used on her cheeks.

'I did not say there was no murder. I said I did not witness it, and I did not speak to Tulyet. Marius Froissart's wife was murdered about two weeks ago.'

'So did Froissart kill her?' asked Bartholomew. This woman was worse than Boniface with her twisting and turning of words.

'I could not say. I did not witness it, as I have just said.'

Bartholomew was becoming exasperated. He forced himself not to show his impatience, knowing it would probably amuse her. He smiled. 'But what do you think?' he insisted as pleasantly as he could.

'I imagine he killed her,' she said, turning to face him.

'Where are the rest of his family?'

'They have fled the town because people believe Froissart is the killer. His family will not be safe here until Froissart is caught. People believed they were hiding him, and they left at my suggestion.'

'Where are they?' he asked.

'I do not know, and if I did, it would remain my secret,' she said, her smile not reaching her eyes. 'They have suffered enough.'

Bartholomew thought for a moment. 'Do you know a Father Lucius?'

Janetta looked amazed. 'A priest? Priests do not come to Primrose Alley!'

'What about high priests?' said Bartholomew, watching her carefully.

'High priests? You mean bishops?' she asked.

'I mean priests of satanism,' said Bartholomew, still eyeing her intently.

'Satanism?' She made an exasperated sound and flashed him a quick smile. 'You must think I am without wits: I keep repeating everything you say. Now, satanism. It is certainly practised in the town. But the poor only mumble the odd blasphemy and steal holy water to feed to their pigs. The rich summon great demons from hell. If you are wanting high priests, Doctor, do not look to our community, look to the merchants and the lawyers. And even the wealthier of the scholars.'

She mused for a moment. 'Why are you involved in all this? You are not a Proctor. Can you not see that this business is dangerous? Powerful men are involved who would kill you without a second thought. Leave this business for others to sort out.'

Bartholomew looked at her as she sat, her face shadowed. Another warning to stay away?

'Do you know where I might find the lay-brother who locked the church on the night of the friar's death?' he asked finally.

She sighed. 'So you will not heed my warning?'

Bartholomew did not reply, but waited for her to answer his question. She sighed again. 'The lay-brother you were chasing in our lane? No. That was the last any of us saw of him. You frightened him clean off the face of the earth.'

Bartholomew stood to leave. It was dark, and, although he would not have admitted it to Janetta, he did not feel safe with her in the churchyard. He wondered why she had picked this time and place to meet him, and felt uneasy. Was she watching his every move? Had she taken the arsenic from his bag and substituted it with white sugar? Was it Janetta who had left the goat's head on Michael's bed to warn him as she was warning Bartholomew now?

'You have been most helpful, Mistress Janetta,' he said. 'But please remember next time that it should not be necessary for your friends to sit on me to make me stay.'

A spark of anger glinted in her eyes so fast that Bartholomew thought he had imagined it, before it was masked by her enigmatic smile. He smiled, bowed, and walked purposefully away. His nerves tingled as he waited for figures looming out of the bushes that would block his escape. But there was nothing. He walked unmolested to the High Street and home to Michaelhouse.

When the sturdy gates of the College were barred behind him, he went straight to find Michael. The monk had just gone to bed, but was uncomplaining when Bartholomew dragged him from his sleep. They went to Bartholomew's room, where they would not disturb Michael's room-mates. Once Michael had settled himself comfortably on a stool, Bartholomew related the details of his meeting with Janetta.

'Oh Lord, Matt! I do not like that woman.'

He listened without further interruption until Bartholomew had finished his story and then sat thinking in silence.

'I think your other whore friend is right. I feel this Janetta is untrustworthy. Why did you not ask her about her scars?'

'That would not have been polite,' said Bartholomew. 'Why should I question her about a crime for which she had already paid?'

'You are too gentle,' said Michael. 'I suppose that and your curly black hair are the reasons you seem to have half the whores in Cambridge demanding your company. Janetta, Sybilla, "Lady" Matilde. What would the Franciscans say if they were to find out?'

'Michael, please,' said Bartholomew irritably. 'Think about what Janetta told me instead of troubling your monkish brain with unmonkish thoughts of prostitutes. Tulyet said Janetta was a witness to murder; she says she is not and has never spoken to him. It is black and white. They both cannot be right, so one of them is lying. Which? Is it Tulyet, who seems to be dragging his feet over the investigation, perhaps because of his family's involvement with the Guild of the Coming? Or is it Janetta, who holds sway over ruffians, and appears and disappears at will?'

'Or are they both lying?' asked Michael. 'Janetta saw the murder, but Tulyet never asked her. What about Froissart? You say you gave her no reason to assume that Froissart was dead? She has no idea he lies cold and stinking in St Mary's crypt?'

'Tulyet does not know of Froissart's death either. Janetta says the townspeople believe that Froissart is the killer and that Tulyet lost him. Tulyet says that Froissart does not have the intelligence to carry out the murders. Janetta says Froissart was violent.'

'They do not sound like the same man to me,' said Michael. 'Either Froissart was a clever and vicious killer or he did not have the intelligence to plan such things. Which Froissart was the real one?'

'I suppose it does not matter much,' said Bartholomew, leaning back with a yawn, 'since we know he is not in a position to do much about anything.'

Michael yawned too. 'I cannot make any sense out of this tonight. The Chancellor is burying Froissart and the woman tomorrow. Let us see what their funerals might bring to light.'

They both started suddenly, aware that someone else had entered the room and was standing silently in the shadows.

'Boniface!' said Bartholomew, leaning back against the wall again. 'You made me jump!'

'I am leaving, Master Bartholomew,' he said.

Bartholomew twisted around to look at him. 'Leaving?

But your disputation is in two days. I have already told you that if you can put heresy to the back of your mind for a couple of hours, you should pass.'

'I do not want to become a physician,' said Boniface. He stood stiffly in the doorway. 'And I do not want to be a friar.'

'Boniface!' said Michael kindly. 'Think about what you are saying. You have taken vows. At least talk to Father William first.'

'I have,' said Boniface. 'He told me I should take some time to consider before I act.'

'That is good advice,' said Bartholomew gently. 'But do not consider tonight. It is late. Come to see me tomorrow and we will talk when our minds are fresh.'

Boniface was silent.

'Frances de Belem!' he blurted out suddenly. 'She was coming to see me the day she died. We usually met before dawn under the willows by the fish-ponds. I unbarred the gate and waited, but she did not come. All the time she was dying in the orchard.'

Bartholomew remembered Alban claiming that Frances had a lover, and even her father had known she was meeting someone at dawn. Poor Boniface! A murdered lover was hardly something for which a young friar could claim sympathy from his fellows.

'I thought you might have killed her,' he said, swallowing and looking at Bartholomew.

'Me?' said Bartholomew, appalled. 'What on earth could have given you that idea?'

'Well, you are often out of the College at night, and I thought you must have seen her and killed her to keep your comings and goings secret,' said Boniface, 'especially if you were involved in all this business with witchcraft that Brother Alban was telling us about.'

'Brother Alban is a dangerous old gossip,' said Michael firmly. 'And Matt is not the only one to slip in and out of College at night. I do, I have seen Hesselwell and Aidan do so, and now you say you did.'

'I know,' said Boniface, 'but I was distraught, and I had no one to tell. I did not know what to do. She told me she had something important to tell me, and I waited but she never came.'

Bartholomew could not meet his eyes. If Boniface was Frances's lover, then he must have been the father of her child. No wonder Frances had said that the father could not marry her. He decided nothing would be gained by telling Boniface that Frances was carrying his child when she died. The student was in enough turmoil already.

'She was almost hysterical,' Boniface reflected. 'I asked her to tell me then, but she said she needed to tell me privately. Against my better judgement, I agreed to meet her in the orchard.'

'Did you not wait at the gate for her?' asked Michael.

Boniface shot him a bitter look. 'I waited for her by the fish-ponds. I was afraid of being seen, and there are reeds and willows in which to hide around the ponds.'

Bartholomew could think of nothing to say. He tried to remember the times he had broken the rules to meet a woman in the night while a student in Oxford, but the memories were dim, and he could not recall his feelings. Boniface hurried on.

'When I heard she had been dying while I hid among the reeds, I felt wretched. I took the arsenic from your bag, and put the sugar in its place because I was going to swallow it. Then you gave your lecture on dosages and I realised there was not enough to kill me. Here.' He pushed a packet at Bartholomew.

'I never carry enough to kill in case anyone steals it, or it falls from my bag by accident,' said Bartholomew, staring at the small packet in his hands.

'I am glad you are cautious,' said Boniface with a faint smile. 'At least now I have not compounded one sin with another by committing suicide.' He stood to leave.

Bartholomew rummaged in his bag and handed him a twist of cloth. 'This is camomile,' he said. 'Mix it with some wine, and it will help you sleep. Tomorrow we can talk again.'

Boniface looked as if he would refuse, but then leaned forward and snatched it from him. He gave a sudden smile that lightened his sullen features and made him almost handsome. Michael sketched a benediction at him, and the friar disappeared. Bartholomew looked out of the window to make sure he returned to his own room. When he saw Boniface pour himself a drink and lie down on his bed through the open window opposite, he sat again.

'I wonder what she wanted to tell him,' said Michael.

'Nothing that is of import to us,' said Bartholomew.

'You know?' said the astute Michael immediately. 'She told you!' Bartholomew tried to change the subject, but Michael was tenacious. 'She carried his child!' he exclaimed, watching Bartholomew intently. 'They were lovers, and he made her pregnant! That is why you know and he does not. She must have asked you for a cure.'

'Michael . . .' began Bartholomew.

Michael raised his hands. 'No one will hear of this from me. I will say a mass for the child since no one else ever will, and there will be an end to it.' He paused. 'So that explains why she was in Michaelhouse. But not who killed her. Is it a scholar here, do you think?'

Bartholomew shook his head slowly. 'It is possible,' he said, 'but if Frances could get into Michaelhouse, so could another. Tulyet, perhaps, since his night patrols mean that he is sometimes out at night. Or Nicholas – dead, but seen alive at his own graveside. Or Buckley, who conveniently disappeared the night the friar died in the chest containing the controversial University history. Or perhaps even Boniface, to free himself from a romance that was destroying his peace of mind and threatening his vocation.'

Michael stretched. 'It is beyond me,' he said. 'Like Boniface, I need to sleep, and we will talk again in the morning.'

CHAPTER 9

THE FOLLOWING MORNING, BARTHOLOMEW FOUND
that his students had managed to work their way
through the first set of texts he had set the day
before, but not the second. He instructed that they
finish it that afternoon and attend Master Kenyngham's
astronomy lectures in the morning. The students would
be tested on their knowledge of astronomy, and hearing
lectures would refresh their memories.

Boniface, looking more rested and relaxed than
Bartholomew had ever seen him, approached Bartholomew shyly. He said he intended to spend the day praying
in the church. Bartholomew gave him leave gladly,
thinking uncharitably that his other students would be
able to study better without him. Bartholomew decided
to attend Kenyngham's lectures too, partly to ensure none
of his students played truant, and partly because he found
Kenyngham's knowledge fascinating, and liked to hear
the enthusiasm in his voice as he spoke.

When the bell rang for dinner, Cynric was waiting to
tell him that the Chancellor had arranged for Froissart
and the unknown woman to be buried that afternoon.
The ceremony would not be an open one, and Gilbert

had told Cynric that the coffins had already been sealed to keep their contents from prying eyes.

Dinner was eaten in silence, apart from the voice of the Bible scholar who read a tract from Proverbs. His Latin was poor, and Bartholomew was not the only one of the Fellows to glance up at him in puzzlement when his pronunciation or missed lines made what he was saying incomprehensible. Beside him, Michael grumbled under his breath about the food, tossing a piece of pickled eel away in disgust when he found it rotten. Bartholomew felt little inclination to eat the fish and watery oatmeal, but he was hungry and ate it all. He noted that there was barely enough to go round, and many scholars left complaining they were still hungry.

'Damn the plague,' Michael muttered. 'The sickness has gone, but now we will starve to death.'

By mutual consent, Bartholomew and Michael resumed their discussion of the night before in the deserted conclave. The sun streamed through the windows, and Michael reclined drowsily among the cushions of the window seats. Bartholomew paced restlessly, trying to make sense of everything.

'I am certain that Janetta is involved in all this,' he said. 'Perhaps she killed the women.'

'Janetta?' said Michael in disbelief. 'That is not possible, Matt. She is not strong enough.'

'How strong do you need to be to cut someone's throat?' said Bartholomew. 'Perhaps she had help from one of those louts that always surround her. Perhaps it was her I saw in the orchard after Frances's murder.'

'But Sybilla saw the killer, and she said it was an average man, remember? There is no earthly chance that Janetta could be mistaken for an average man. Even wearing a man's clothes she would be too small.' He mused. 'But Nicholas is of average size.'

'So is Buckley. We have failed to find him, and it cannot be coincidence that he disappeared the night the friar died.'

'I think the killer might be Tulyet,' said Michael.

Bartholomew stopped pacing. 'He has good reason to be out at night while he keeps the Sheriff's peace, and he and his father are obviously involved with this Guild of the Coming.'

'If we knew the identity of the high priest, we would probably have the solution to all this in our hands,' said Michael. 'Did you see nothing at all that might give us a clue? A limp, a distinctive walk?'

Bartholomew shook his head. 'All I know is that he wore a similar mask to the one I saw on the man in the orchard. We should have raided All Saints' Church and had Jonstan arrest the lot of them.'

'That would have been outside Jonstan's power,' said Michael. 'He only has jurisdiction over University affairs, and there is not a shred of evidence that anyone from the University is involved. And we could hardly ask Tulyet to do it!'

Bartholomew rubbed his forehead, becoming exasperated with their lack of progress. He switched to another avenue of thought. 'So if you think Tulyet is the killer, it is likely that Tulyet is also the high priest, otherwise how would he be able to predict that there would be another victim before the new moon?'

Michael pulled at some stray whiskers at the side of

his face. 'Yes,' he said slowly. 'Before the new moon, when it is especially dark.'

After a while, they realised that they were getting nowhere with their discussion. They could generate as many theories as they wanted, but progressed no further as long as they lacked the evidence to prove or disprove their ideas. Eventually, they left Michaelhouse to attend the funerals in St Mary's Church. The afternoon sun was blazing in a clear blue sky and the air buzzed with flies. They made their way to the crypt where Gilbert waited restlessly for de Wetherset and Father Cuthbert to arrive so that the ceremony could begin. There was a buzz of flies there, too, hovering over the coffin in which Froissart's remains were sealed.

Bartholomew wandered over to look at the coffins, and wondered how secret their presence could be. He saw that both had been securely nailed down, and frowned. He ran his fingers over the rough wood of the woman's coffin and leaned to inspect a join where the wood did not meet properly. Gilbert and Michael watched him in distaste.

'Who ordered the coffins sealed?' he asked Gilbert.

'No one,' said Gilbert. 'But I have been given the duty of ensuring that their presence is kept secret. I do not need to tell you how difficult that has been in this warm weather. I sealed them myself. If anyone had managed to gain entry to the crypt, a sealed coffin presents a far more formidable obstacle than an open one.'

Bartholomew looked up as de Wetherset arrived, ushering Cuthbert in front of him, and pulling the gate closed.

'I have four clerks to help,' he said, rubbing his

hands together in a businesslike fashion to conceal his nervousness. 'They have been told we are burying two beggars. We will carry the coffins out of the crypt ourselves so that no one will detect how long they have been here.'

The others moved towards the coffins, but Bartholomew held back. 'This is perhaps an odd request,' he began, 'but they have been lying here for some time. I would like them opened to make certain that we know whom we are burying this time.'

De Wetherset looked at the coffins in distaste, while Gilbert was visibly angry. 'What for? Can we not just get this foul business over and done with? I am tired of all this death and corruption!'

The Chancellor patted the arm of his distraught clerk sympathetically. 'I am sorry, Gilbert. What I have asked you to do over the past week has been beyond your clerkly duties. I will see that you are well rewarded.'

Gilbert shook his head. 'You do not need to pay me for my loyalty. I want an end to this business with corpses and coffins. Let us just put these poor people in their graves and leave them in peace.'

De Wetherset nodded. 'You are right.' He bent to lift one of the coffins, and gestured to Bartholomew to pick up the other end.

Bartholomew stayed where he was. 'It will not take a moment,' he said. 'Wait outside if it distresses you, and I will do it alone.'

'What are your reasons for this?' asked de Wetherset, setting the coffin back down and eyeing Bartholomew with resignation.

Bartholomew pointed to the woman's coffin. 'When

we exhumed the body of the lady, she was in an advanced state of decay. The coffin is flimsy, and the lid does not fit properly. If the woman was in there, Master de Wetherset, you would need more than a few bowls of incense to keep her presence from being known. She would be smelt from the porch.'

De Wetherset let out an exclamation of dismissal. 'Rubbish! The shock of the exhumation has addled your brain, and now you are suspicious of everything. Gilbert is right. Let us just get this done.'

Bartholomew looked at Michael for help. Michael raised his eyes to the ceiling, but rallied to his side. 'It will take only a few moments. What harm can it do?'

'Why can we not just let the poor souls rest in peace?' muttered Cuthbert. 'Both murdered, and now, even in death, they are not safe from desecration!'

De Wetherset was torn. He looked at Gilbert's pleading eyes and grey, exhausted face, and then back to Bartholomew. He sighed. 'In the interests of thoroughness, and to satisfy the Doctor's unpleasant curiosity, I suppose the coffins may be opened. Do it if you must.'

Gilbert backed out of the door. 'I want to see no more decaying corpses. I will wait in the church.'

'I will wait with you,' said de Wetherset. 'I too have had my fill of sights from beyond the grave.'

Cuthbert followed them out, his fat features set in a mask of sorrow.

When they had gone, Michael turned to Bartholomew irritably. 'Is this really necessary? De Wetherset will be furious if you are wrong, and poor Gilbert is at the end of his tether!'

'Then wait outside,' said Bartholomew, losing patience. 'It is for your Bishop that we are investigating this.'

Michael went to sit on the steps as Bartholomew took a knife from his bag and levered up the lid of the woman's coffin. The cheap wood splintered, but the lid came off easily. He stared in shock, unprepared for the sight that faced him. He took a deep breath and stood back.

'Well?' said Michael.

Wordlessly, Bartholomew went to perform the same operation on Froissart's coffin, while Michael went to look in the woman's. Michael stared down at the corpse in the coffin in mystification and, hesitantly, went to look at Froissart's too. Bartholomew shut it before he could see.

'Look if you will,' he said, 'but it is only Froissart, alone and unmolested.'

Michael gazed in horror at the woman's coffin. 'Where is she?' He began a fruitless search of the crypt, hunting for a body that was not there.

Bartholomew scratched his head. 'Who knows? We should tell de Wetherset.'

Michael went to fetch him while Bartholomew re-nailed Froissart's lid. De Wetherset peered cautiously into the woman's coffin.

'Nicholas of York!' he breathed. He raised a white face to Bartholomew. 'How?'

Bartholomew inspected Nicholas's body. There was some stiffness, but Bartholomew imagined he had not been dead for more than a day. Like Froissart, a deep purple mark on his neck indicated that he had been garrotted.

He told de Wetherset, who looked at him blankly.

'But how could this have happened? And where is the body of the woman?'

'Someone must have stolen her,' said Michael. 'But Gilbert said he had been guarding the crypt, and that it is always locked. How could anyone have gone in without him seeing?'

'Where is Gilbert?' said Bartholomew. The small clerk had not followed de Wetherset back into the crypt.

'He is unwell. I have told him to wait in the church with Father Cuthbert,' said de Wetherset. 'All this has proved too much for him. But how could anyone take a body from here while the gate was locked?'

'Perhaps the gate was not locked,' said Bartholomew quietly.

De Wetherset looked blank for a moment. 'What?' he said sharply. 'What are you saying? Gilbert has been my personal clerk for the past ten years. I trust him implicitly.'

'Gilbert always came with you and Buckley when you opened the University chest,' said Bartholomew slowly. 'He knew about Nicholas of York's book. He was with you when you found the friar, and he helped us remove Froissart from the tower. Now we find he is the person to have the only key to the crypt during the time the woman's body disappeared.'

'That is preposterous!' de Wetherset almost snarled. 'Gilbert is my trusted clerk. How do I know that one of you is not behind all this?'

'There is nothing to be gained from this line of thought,' Michael intervened smoothly, giving Bartholomew a sharp glance. 'All we need to do is to talk to Gilbert. Come.'

He led the way out of the gloomy crypt and the others followed.

De Wetherset walked to the Lady Chapel where he had left Gilbert, but his clerk was not there, and neither was Cuthbert. The Chancellor walked outside.

'He has probably gone for some fresh air,' he said.

There was no sign of Gilbert outside either. De Wetherset hailed a lay-brother who was sweeping the path. The lay-brother strolled over to them.

'Poor Gilbert,' he said in response to de Wetherset's question. 'He came tearing out of the church as if it were on fire. Then he ran straight to the bushes there and disappeared. He ate at the Cardinal's Cap last night, and I have warned him about the food there.'

De Wetherset glared at Bartholomew. 'You have made him sick!' he exclaimed.

Bartholomew was looking over at the bushes where the lay-brother had pointed. 'Oh, I do not think so,' he said. He found the two tombstones and the tree he had used to calculate the entrance of the pathway to Primrose Alley from the church tower, ran through the angles and formulae in his mind, and headed for the spot where the entrance was concealed. De Wetherset and Michael watched him dubiously as he poked around the bushes before giving a triumphant shout.

They hurried over and he pointed out the path to them, almost invisible in the dense foliage, but an unmistakable pathway nevertheless.

'That proves nothing!' snapped de Wetherset. 'Gilbert? Are you there?'

He began to force his way through the undergrowth, while Michael followed. Bartholomew, recalling vividly the last time he had taken the path, grabbed at Michael's habit.

'Wait! We should fetch the Proctors,' he said urgently. He forced his way past Michael and seized de Wetherset. 'Wait!' he repeated.

There was a slight whistling sound followed by a thud, and de Wetherset gazed in disbelief at the arrow that trembled in the tree-trunk only inches from his head. Wordlessly, he turned and fled, thrusting Bartholomew out of the way in his haste to escape. Bartholomew followed more slowly. He knew that had Janetta's men meant to kill, the arrow would be in de Wetherset, and not in a tree. Perhaps Gilbert's loyalty to his Chancellor was worth something after all.

When he emerged into the sunshine, de Wetherset was white with fright, while Michael was bewildered.

'Gilbert might be dead in there,' de Wetherset gasped. 'He might be injured.'

'He might have set the archer there,' said Bartholomew.

De Wetherset strode over to him and grabbed him roughly by the shoulder. 'One more allegation like that, and you will be looking for a new teaching position!' he snapped angrily.

He thrust Bartholomew away from him with a glare, and strode back to the church, calling for a clerk to send for one of the Proctors. Michael watched de Wetherset go.

'Do you really think Gilbert is our man?' he asked.

Bartholomew shifted his bag into a more comfortable position. 'He is most certainly involved, would you not think? For a man who helped retrieve a corpse that had been nailed to a bellframe, he reacted very strongly over the mere opening of a coffin. Unless he already knew what we would find.'

'You are right,' said Michael, thinking carefully. 'I have been wondering whether one of the clerks has been acting as a spy. Who better than Gilbert, who is privy to all the Chancellor's secrets? That is why we have had so little success with our investigation. The perpetrators of these crimes have known exactly what we have been thinking and planning!'

Bartholomew rubbed his chin. 'Remember when we almost dug up Mistress Archer's grave because the marker Gilbert left was on the wrong tomb?'

Michael stared at him. 'Cuthbert said children must have moved it. But what if it had never been moved at all, and it was exactly where Gilbert had set it?'

'And he must have known precisely where to find the path,' said Bartholomew, looking back at where the bushes once again hid it from sight. 'He went there without hesitation. His arrival in Primrose Lane must have alerted them to the possibility of pursuit, and so the archer was set there.'

'I wonder what goes on in Primrose Lane that warrants such security?' mused Michael.

Bartholomew considered. Was that it? Did the seedy shacks and hovels behind the church hold the secret that would explain the deaths of the friar, Froissart, Nicholas, and the disappearance of Buckley?

'What can we do?' he said helplessly. 'We cannot ask Tulyet to raid it, because he is probably involved; it is beyond the Proctor's powers, because Gilbert disappearing down that path is insufficient to prove that it is University business; and if there are archers and crowds of ruffians on guard, we can do nothing ourselves.'

He turned as a large figure lurched out of the church. As Bartholomew and Michael waited for Cuthbert to reach them they saw tears glittering on his cheeks.

'Is it true?' he said. 'Does Nicholas lie dead in the crypt?'

Michael nodded, eyeing him suspiciously.

'He has been with me this past week. I confess it was a shock to see him out of his grave, but he told me he had needed to escape.'

'Escape what?' asked Bartholomew, bewildered.

Cuthbert shrugged, giving a huge sniff, and rubbing his face with his sleeve. 'He would not say, but he was clearly terrified. He said I would be safer not knowing.'

'Why did you not tell us?' cried Michael, exasperated.

'Because he said if I told anyone he was still alive, I would place him in mortal danger, and myself, too,' said Cuthbert, his voice rising. 'I am certain he told me the truth. I have never seen him so frightened or angry.' He looked up suddenly. 'That lay-brother who locked the church for me saw him once. He came to me and said he had seen Nicholas risen from the dead. I advised him to keep silent, and the next thing I knew was that he had fled the town.'

'Cuthbert!' exclaimed Bartholomew in disgust. 'Nicholas may have been the man who killed those women! How could you keep silent?'

'He was not!' cried Cuthbert vehemently. 'He would never kill,' he added more gently.

'But a dead woman was found in his coffin,' said Bartholomew. 'How can you explain that?'

'When we exhumed the grave, Nicholas had already come to me,' said Cuthbert. 'It was no surprise to me that he was not in the grave we dug up, but I was not expecting another corpse! When I returned home, I told him what we had found, and he became frantic with grief. He believed she was the woman he had been seeing before he escaped.'

'But why did you not tell us all this?' cried Michael in despair. 'Did you not recognise her?'

Cuthbert shook his head. 'She had thick black hair, and the woman in the coffin was bald. I told Nicholas it could not be his lover, but he said she had a disease whereby her hair fell out and she always wore a wig.'

'That is not proof that he did not kill her,' said Michael.

'He loved her,' said Cuthbert earnestly. 'I met her, and it is clear that they made each other very happy. He would not have harmed her. And we were members of the Guild of the Holy Trinity, a group dedicated to opposing sin. We do not kill!'

Bartholomew looked at him disbelievingly, while Michael walked with the distraught priest to his small house nearby. Bartholomew waited restlessly until Michael returned.

'Now what?' he said, exasperated. 'What a mess!'

'We must think,' said Michael, sitting down on the low wall surrounding the churchyard. 'Cuthbert claims that Nicholas returned a week ago in a state of terror.'

'We should start with his death,' said Bartholomew.

'He clearly feigned it, and if Cuthbert can be believed, he did so because he was afraid of something.'

'Yes,' said Michael. 'And what better way to escape danger than to pretend you are dead? Who ever hunts a corpse?'

'If the woman was Nicholas's lover, then she must have helped him feign his death, perhaps with potions and powders. Then she went to help him out of the coffin the night before he was due to be buried.'

'And then what?' asked Michael. 'We can prove nothing else. Did he kill her then to ensure her silence so that he would be safe? And why was she wearing that hideous mask?'

'Whatever happened, Nicholas fled, and then returned a week ago,' said Bartholomew. 'When Cuthbert told him that a bald woman was found in his coffin, he realised who it was, and took to roaming the streets.'

'But what could be so terrifying that he was forced to such measures?' mused Michael. 'It must be something to do with the book. Perhaps he was being threatened into revealing its contents.'

Bartholomew considered. 'You must be right,' he said. 'After Nicholas "died", whoever was terrifying him realised that alternative methods were needed to get at it. The friar was employed to steal the book, but was accidentally killed by the poisoned lock.'

'Which must mean that, as far as we know, whatever deadly secret led to all this is still there,' said Michael. 'Because de Wetherset seemed to have checked it all very carefully to ensure nothing was missing.'

'So did the person behind all this kill Nicholas?' asked Bartholomew.

Michael shrugged. 'It must be the same person who killed Froissart because they were both garrotted. It must be Gilbert.'

'Of course it must!' said Bartholomew suddenly. 'Gilbert has the only key to the crypt. It can only have been him who took the woman's body away and put Nicholas there.'

'It does not tell us why,' said Michael. 'But it does throw light on how the friar ended up inside the chest, dead, with the lid down. Gilbert must have used his keys to hide in the crypt, unbeknownst to the friar, before the lay-brother locked up, and emerged after the friar had gone to the tower to begin opening the chest. He probably had no intention other than to ensure his plan went smoothly. He must have become worried when the friar took so long, and went to see what had happened. He found the friar dead, and, in a panic, he pushed him into the chest and closed the lid.'

'De Wetherset said no pages were missing,' said Bartholomew. 'If Gilbert had gone to all this trouble, surely he must have stolen the part he wanted?'

Michael scratched his head thoughtfully. 'I am sure he did,' he said. 'When we lifted the friar from the chest, de Wetherset was only concerned about the book. He immediately went to check that certain sections were unmolested. The part Gilbert probably took must have been so unimportant to the Chancellor, he failed to notice it was missing. So there are at least two parts of this book that are important: the part that de Wetherset was so concerned with, and the part Gilbert took.'

Bartholomew thought again. 'Gilbert was not unduly worried about the friar's sudden death: after all, there was nothing to connect him with the dead man. He left the church, first removing the bar that the friar had put across the door for added security. One of the clerks mentioned to me later that the bar had been moved, proving that there had been two people in the church when the friar had died, not one.'

'Who was this Father Lucius who was allowed into the church by Froissart?' said Michael. 'Could that have been Gilbert?'

'No,' said Bartholomew. 'Froissart would have been a fool to allow anyone into the church. I suspect Gilbert, with his keys, hid himself in the crypt, and it was he who let this Father Lucius into the church, not Froissart. Froissart was probably already garrotted, and Father Lucius was necessary to help Gilbert haul his body into the belfry and secure it there.'

'Froissart garrotted, Nicholas garrotted,' said Michael. 'Gilbert must have killed them both. It almost fits, but we still do not know why all this happened.'

'And we never will so long as de Wetherset plays his own games and is less than honest with us about this book,' said Bartholomew.

Michael's shoulders sagged in defeat. 'Cynric is coming for you,' he said, seeing the small Welshman walking towards them. 'I will go to try to placate the Chancellor, and persuade him to send the Proctors after Gilbert.'

Bartholomew went to meet Cynric, who had a request that he visit the wounded soldier at the Castle. Cynric accompanied him, shyly confiding that he had an hour to spare before he was expected to meet Rachel Atkin at Stanmore's business premises.

The sergeant Bartholomew had met the night before

was waiting for him, and he was conducted across the bailey to the hall. The small chamber was flooded with light, the window shutters thrown open, and it was thronging with men. They parted to let him through.

The injured soldier sat up in bed and held up his arm where he had removed the bandage Bartholomew had tied, showing a neat wound with no trace of infection.

Bartholomew bent to inspect it. 'It is healing well,' he said, as he tied another cloth around it. 'But you must give it time, or it will break open again.'

'It is a miracle!' proclaimed the soldier. 'Father Philius pronounced I would die, and Robin of Grantchester wanted to saw off my arm. But you came and I am healed!'

'It is no miracle,' said Bartholomew nervously. One thing he dreaded were rumours of miraculous cures. First, he would have half the country coming to him pleading for help, and, second, his colleagues would believe none of it, and he would likely find himself proclaimed a heretic.

The soldier smiled at him. 'Well, miraculous then,' he said. 'You saved my life, and you saved my arm. I will yet be as good an archer as my father.' He smiled up at the sergeant. Bartholomew, pleased at the young man's rapid recovery, left, with instructions not to overtax his strength too quickly. The sergeant followed him out across the courtyard.

'You looked sorrowful last night,' he said, 'and I thought you might like some happy news.' He seized Bartholomew firmly on the shoulders. 'You saved my son. I wish we could do something for you, and catch this killer.'

'Do you know anything that might help?' asked Bartholomew.

The sergeant shook his head. 'Nothing. And believe me, I would tell you if I knew. The Sheriff had discovered virtually nothing before he stopped investigating. He is not even looking into these stolen carts now.'

'Oswald Stanmore's carts?' asked Bartholomew.

The soldier inclined his head. 'There is a strange business. Those were not random attacks, but carefully planned manoeuvres. I know the work of soldiers when I see it, and there were soldiers involved in those robberies right enough. Good ones too.'

Bartholomew was startled. Did that mean that Tulyet was using part of his garrison to strike at the traders and steal their goods? Was that why he was failing to investigate the crimes in his town?

As they left, Bartholomew almost collided with Tulyet himself.

'You!' the Sheriff snarled. 'What do you want here?'

'I am just leaving, Master Tulyet,' Bartholomew replied politely, not wishing to become embroiled in an argument that might prompt Tulyet to arrest him.

'Then leave!' Tulyet shouted. 'And do not return here without my permission.'

Bartholomew studied him. Tulyet was younger than Bartholomew, but looked ten years older at that moment. His face was sallow and there were dark smears under his eyes. His eyes held a wild look that made Bartholomew wonder whether the man was losing his faculties. Was he the murderer, knowing he would have to commit another crime because he had been so ordered at the ceremony at All Saints'? As a physician, Bartholomew could see signs that the man was losing his sanity and reason.

Without a word, Bartholomew left, Cynric following. When they were out of the Castle, Cynric heaved a sigh of relief.

'I have heard around town that he is losing his mind. They say it is because he cannot catch Froissart. I thought he might order us locked up for some spurious reason. He has arrested several others and accused them of being Froissart.'

Bartholomew reflected for a moment. Perhaps they should tell Tulyet that Froissart was dead after all, to save innocent people from being arrested. But then, Bartholomew reasoned, what good would that do? And if Tulyet were the real killer, Bartholomew might be signing his own death warrant by telling him that Froissart was dead.

Engrossed in his thoughts, he jumped when Cynric seized his arm in excitement. He looked around. They were near All Saints' Church, which stood half-hidden by the tangle of bushes and low trees that were untended around it.

'Someone is in the church!' exclaimed Cynric.

Before Bartholomew could stop him, Cynric had disappeared into the swathe of green. Bartholomew followed cautiously, making his way to the broken door and peering round it. Cynric was right. A person was there, bending to inspect the dark patches on the floor – a figure in a scholar's tabard like his own. Bartholomew looked around quickly. The man appeared to be alone, so he slipped through the door and made his way towards him, ducking from pillar to pillar up the aisle.

Was this the high priest, visiting the church to make certain he had left nothing, even after his careful removal of his accoutrements before he departed? He stopped as he trod on a piece of wood that had fallen from the roof, and a sharp crack echoed around the derelict church. The man looked up, startled at the loud noise.

'Hesselwell!' Bartholomew exclaimed.

On hearing his name, Hesselwell turned and fled, without waiting to see who had spoken. Bartholomew raced after him, throwing caution to the wind. Hesselwell reached the altar and stumbled as he reached the steps. Behind the altar was a large window and Hesselwell grabbed the sill with both hands to haul himself through. Bartholomew lunged at him as he was about to drop down the other side, and pulled as hard as he could. Both fell backwards, Hesselwell kicking and struggling like a madman.

Bartholomew gripped the flailing wrists and leaned down with all his weight. Pinned to the floor, Hesselwell was helpless.

'You!' he said to Bartholomew, his eyes wide with terror. 'It was you!'

Bartholomew was taken aback. Hesselwell began to struggle again, his face white with terror, but stopped when he saw Cynric come to stand over them, and sagged in resignation.

'What are you talking about?' said Bartholomew. 'What was me?'

'I should have guessed!'

'Guessed what?' Bartholomew was becoming exasperated. He released Hesselwell and watched as Cynric pulled the terrified scholar to his feet, keeping a firm grip on his arm. Hesselwell stood with his shoulders bowed and his tabard covered in dirt and flakes of rotten wood from the floor.

'What were you doing here?' asked Bartholomew, brushing off his own tabard. 'What were you looking for?'

Hesselwell tried to pull himself together, his eyes flicking over Bartholomew as though assessing whether he was armed. 'I wanted to know if the blood was real,' Hesselwell said. 'Or if it was dye.'

'You are a member of the Guild of the Coming?' asked Bartholomew, Hesselwell's actions suddenly making sense to him.

Hesselwell looked at him askance. 'You know I am,' he said.

'Why would I know?' asked Bartholomew, confused again. His flash of illumination was to be short-lived, it seemed.

'Because you are the high priest!' Hesselwell said, taking a deep breath and meeting Bartholomew's eyes. 'It makes sense to me now. You are always out at night; you dabble with poisons and potions; and your students say you are a heretic. You are the high priest,' he repeated. 'You gave me this,' he said, holding up a small glass phial. 'And even then I did not guess.'

Speechless, Bartholomew tore his gaze away from Hesselwell to look at the phial. It was, without question, one of the ones he used to dispense medicines, and it even had a small scrap of parchment wrapped around it with instructions for its use in his handwriting. Trying to bring his whirling thoughts into order, he reached out for the bottle.

Hesselwell misunderstood Bartholomew's expression of bewilderment for one of indecision, and the hand with the phial whipped behind his back. 'I could be of help to you,' he said slyly. 'No one else need know of this. After all, I have served you well, why should I not continue?'

'What are you talking about?' said Bartholomew, his skin beginning to crawl. If Hesselwell thought he was the high priest, did others too? Hesselwell leaned towards him and lowered his voice.

'I was successful in my warning of Brother Michael,' he said.

Bartholomew circled the altar to try to give himself time to bring his thoughts into order. So Hesselwell had put the goat's head on Michael's bed: it had been a Michaelhouse scholar all along. It explained how the intruder had known which room Michael slept in, and how he had known when the monk had returned from Ely. Michael was usually a light sleeper, but his long ride had probably tired him, which was why he had not woken when Hesselwell had entered his room.

He continued to edge around the altar as he tried to recall Hesselwell's reaction to Walter's poisoning. He had been standing with Father Aidan, and Bartholomew distinctly remembered their shocked faces. Unless he was possessed of an outstanding talent for deception, Hesselwell had been as horrified by Walter's brush with death as had the other Fellows.

'You almost killed the porter,' said Bartholomew carefully, watching him.

'That was not my fault,' said Hesselwell, his eyes desperate in his pale face. 'You left me the bottle of wine with instructions to give it to Walter without drawing suspicion to myself. You did not tell me it contained a virulent poison, only that it would make Walter sleep.'

'I am no high priest,' Bartholomew said to Hesselwell wearily. 'Your reasoning is flawed, Master Hesselwell. I am out at night usually because I am seeing patients; I dabble with poisons and potions because I am a physician and they are the tools of my trade; and some of my students think I am a heretic because they do not understand what I teach them. Not only that, but I know Walter sleeps on duty, and would have had no need to send him into a drugged slumber.'

Hesselwell gazed at him, nonplussed. 'Well, what are you then? Are you from the Guild of Purification?'

Bartholomew shook his head and Hesselwell sagged in Cynric's grip.

'What are you going to do? Who will you tell?' His eyes were pleading.

'I will tell the Master about your unholy alliance, and it will be up to him to decide what to do,' said Bartholomew.

'They will kill me!' cried Hesselwell. 'Please! You do not know their strength!' He looked so frightened that Bartholomew almost felt sorry for him. 'Will you tell him after sunset?' Hesselwell pleaded, wringing his hands together. Bartholomew squinted at the sky. Sunset was perhaps two hours away. 'It will give me a chance to collect my belongings, and hire a fast horse.'

He looked desperately from Bartholomew to Cynric. Bartholomew recalled the scholar's fright when he had first been apprehended in the church, and judged that he probably had very real grounds for his fear.

Bartholomew nodded after a moment's thought. 'But you must tell me all you know.'

Hesselwell looked wretched. 'They will kill me if I do.'

'They will kill you if I tell,' said Bartholomew. 'The choice is yours.'

Hesselwell glanced around him with furtive movements of his eyes. 'All right then,' he conceded wearily. 'But you will give me until sunset?'

Bartholomew nodded.

'How do I know I can trust you?' asked Hesselwell.

'You do not,' said Bartholomew. 'But you are not in a position to bargain.'

Hesselwell thought again, and then started to speak. 'I joined the Guild of the Coming when I first arrived in Cambridge. I was in a similar organisation in London because it brought me business – members of guilds tend to use the services of other members. I made enquiries, and was invited to join the Guild of the Coming.'

So that explained the lawyer's rich clothes, thought Bartholomew, when everyone else's gowns were either cheap, torn, old, or all three.

Hesselwell continued. 'All was well at first. There were occasional ceremonies and midnight meetings. Then, a month ago, our high priest disappeared, and another came to take his place. Things changed. There were more ceremonies, and they became frightening.'

'What can you tell me about this new high priest?'

Hesselwell shrugged. 'He, or one of his assistants, instructed me to perform certain duties for him, but

I never saw his face. On one occasion, the smaller of his assistants told me to rub some mixture on the back gate of Michaelhouse so that it would burn. Another time, the high priest himself ordered me to keep watch for him while he went into our College the night after the de Belem girl died.'

He hit his head suddenly with an open palm. 'Of course you could not be the high priest. It was you he fought in the orchard, and who almost unmasked him! He told us not to intervene, no matter what happened, but when I saw he was about to be unmasked, I shot one of the fire arrows at the gate to allow him to escape. If he were unmasked, I felt certain he would betray me, and so it was imperative I helped him, regardless of his order.'

'Who was the other?' asked Cynric. 'The Devil?'

Hesselwell shrugged again. 'I have never seen him – or any of the high priest's assistants – without a mask, and I do not know who any of them are, or where they come from.'

'What else?' asked Bartholomew as Hesselwell lapsed into silence.

'I almost killed Walter, and it was me who left the goat's head on Michael's bed.'

'Why did he ask you to do that?' asked Cynric.

'I do not know. He merely gave orders, and I followed without question. He terrifies me. And I do not know what he had in mind with the back gate either, and that black sticky solution. I wish to God I had not become embroiled in all this evil!'

'What else did you do?' asked Bartholomew.

'Just two things,' said Hesselwell. 'He wanted me to

prowl the streets at night to look for the whore killer. I thought the high priest was the killer because he predicted their deaths: I can only assume he was taking precautions to protect himself, so that he could say he was not the killer by virtue of the fact that he sent members of the coven to look for the real murderer.'

'And the second thing?' asked Bartholomew, recalling vividly how Hesselwell had almost fallen asleep in the church. He was not surprised Hesselwell was sleepy, if he were teaching all day, and out in the streets at night.

'With one of his assistants, I hid in the roof of the church and helped throw birds and bats down at the congregation. I had begun to be suspicious of some of the devices, and I think he decided to take me into his trust. He would know that once I was involved, I could never tell, for this makes me as guilty of the crimes as he is. And if I became a risk, he would simply kill me.'

'But why do you go along with all this if you know it is a hoax?' asked Bartholomew.

'Because I am afraid,' said Hesselwell. 'One member did question him, and was found a week later in the King's Ditch with his throat cut. And I believe the covens are not the ends in all this, but the means. They are aiming towards something bigger and more terrifying than I can imagine.'

Bartholomew was inclined to believe he was right, and that the elaborate hoax of the covens was simply a front for something infinitely more sinister. Some aspects of the affair had been made clearer by Hesselwell's information, and others less so. Bartholomew understood now what had happened on the night that Walter was poisoned:

Hesselwell had merely been following orders, and had not known why the bottle was to be given to Walter. Bartholomew's reasoning that the poisoning had been carried out by an outsider was, in effect, true, since it had come from the high priest.

Hesselwell glanced up at the sun nervously.

'One last question,' said Bartholomew. 'Why did the high priest give you that phial of medicine?'

'I was nervous about opening the gate to him after Frances de Belem's death. I knew there were Proctors and beadles prowling. I was so nervous that he gave me the phial and said it would calm me and allow me to carry out his instructions. I was to give it back to him the same night, but in all the excitement, I forgot to give it, and he forgot to ask.' He smiled ruefully. 'And he was right to have given it to me, because I would not have had the presence of mind to shoot the fire arrow without its calming effects.'

'Is that all?' asked Bartholomew.

Hesselwell nodded. 'He asked about College gossip, but that is all. May I go?' Bartholomew nodded, and Hesselwell looked so relieved he reeled slightly.

'One more thing,' he said as he followed them out of the church. Bartholomew looked at him. 'When I first came, I heard there were two guilds which were covens. No matter how hard I tried, I have never been able to find out about the Guild of Purification. People told me rumours about it – how it was powerful, and a rival to the Guild of the Coming – but I have never met a member of it, and to be honest, I am uncertain that it exists at all.'

*   *   *

Cynric was disapproving that Bartholomew had allowed Hesselwell to make good his escape, and so was Michael when they told him.

'He might come back and wreak all manner of havoc,' said the monk crossly. 'A self-confessed satanist and you let him go!'

'He was terrified, Brother, and his escape will make no difference. What if he had been right and he was murdered? How would you feel then?'

'He might have been able to tell us more about this high priest,' said Michael. 'He might have known what he was looking for in the orchard!'

'He told us all he knew,' said Bartholomew wearily, scrubbing at his face. 'He was used by the high priest, and told virtually nothing in return.'

'But he left that thing on my bed and you allowed him to go just like that!' said Michael, bristling with the injustice of the situation. 'He tried to murder Walter!'

'He did not know the bottle was poisoned. He was told it contained a sleeping draught,' said Bartholomew. He held up the phial Hesselwell had given him. 'This is perhaps the most important clue we have. When we know what it is, I will know to which of my patients I gave it, and we will know the high priest.'

Michael eyed it dubiously. 'But what if it is one of those common concoctions you give out to dozens of people, like betony and ginger oil?'

Bartholomew shook his head. 'I use these phials for more powerful potions.' He took out the stopper and sniffed cautiously. He recognised the compound immediately: there was only one patient to whom he had recently prescribed this medicine! Stunned, he turned to Michael.

'Master Buckley!' he exclaimed. 'He needs this strong draught when the hot weather makes his skin condition unbearable!'

'Buckley the high priest?' said Michael, frowning in concentration. 'It is beginning to come together. But it is well past sunset. Go and tell the Master about Hesselwell and his evil doings. Do not give him more time than you have already promised to make good his escape.'

Bartholomew began to walk across the courtyard to the Master's room when a man walked through the gate. He stopped dead in his tracks as Richard Tulyet the elder strode purposefully towards him. Bartholomew glanced up at the darkening sky as he did so. It seemed Hesselwell was to have more time still.

'Doctor,' said Tulyet quietly. 'Is there somewhere I can talk with you and Brother Michael alone?'

Cynric led the way to the conclave, and lit some candles, stolen from Alcole's personal supply that was secreted behind one of the wall hangings. Tulyet would say nothing until the Welshman had left, closing the door behind him.

'I should have come to see you before now,' said Tulyet, facing Bartholomew and Michael in the flickering light, 'but I did not know whom I could trust.'

Bartholomew knew exactly how he felt, but said nothing.

'You were right when you said I was a member of the Guild of the Coming, and you were right when you said I had been at All Saints' Church two nights ago.' He shuddered. 'I joined the Guild because the Death took my three daughters and all my grandchildren. The

Church said that only those who sinned would die, but I lived and the children died. I realised the Church had lied to me, and I wanted nothing more to do with it. The Guild of the Coming offered answers that made much more sense than the mumblings of drunken priests safe in their pulpits. Sorry, Brother, but that is how it seemed.'

His story was similar to de Belem's, and it seemed that the fears the Bishop had voiced to Bartholomew before the plague were realised: that the people would turn from the Church after the Death struck, and there would be insufficient priests and friars to prevent it. Tulyet continued.

'All was well at first, and I even introduced my family to the guild. But a month ago things began to change. A new high priest came to us, very different from Nicholas.'

'Nicholas?' said Michael in astonishment. 'Nicholas of York, the clerk at St Mary's?'

Tulyet nodded. 'Only I knew his identity, but he died this last month, and it cannot matter that I tell you now. After he died, we thought to elect one of our members as our leader, but even as we raised our hands to vote, the new high priest arrived in a puff of thick black smoke. He said he had been sent by the Devil to lead us.'

Thick black smoke, thought Bartholomew. Smouldering grass mixed with tar, perhaps, and blown around the high priest by bellows operated by his accomplices?

'Then the guild changed. Our ceremonies became frightening, full of blood and evil conjurings. I wanted to take my family away, but I was told that if I did, they would die. The high priest said the murders in the town were the Devil claiming his own. My wife is old, and I sometimes visited a certain young lady. Fritha. She was the second girl to die.'

He put his head in his hands while Michael and Bartholomew exchanged glances.

'The new high priest asked questions, too,' Tulyet continued. 'He wanted to know about town politics, my business as a tailor, and with whom I traded.'

The high priest had questioned Hesselwell too, thought Bartholomew, about Michaelhouse.

'Do you know who the high priest is?' asked Bartholomew gently.

Tulyet raised his head, his eyes haunted. 'No. None of us do. But I have a terrible fear of who it might be.'

'Is that why you have come?' asked Bartholomew. 'To tell us who you think it is?'

Tulyet nodded. 'I do not know who else I can tell, and I must do something. He is going to claim another victim!' He took a deep breath. 'The high priest is Sir Reginald de Belem.'

'De Belem!' exclaimed Michael. 'But that cannot be. Frances was his daughter. He would not have killed his own daughter!' Or Isobel, the woman who visited him on certain nights, was his clearly unspoken thought.

And de Belem was the high priest of the Guild of Purification anyway, Bartholomew thought, or so he claimed. Hesselwell had said he did not believe the Guild of Purification existed – but it would have been an easy matter to put about rumours of meetings, and to splash blood on the altar of St John Zachary's Church occasionally. And Stanmore had said there were only five people at the last meeting – perhaps the high priest of the Guild of the Coming and a few trusted helpers attending a meeting, the only purpose of which was to maintain the illusion that the Guild of Purification existed.

Bartholomew rubbed a hand through his hair. But they had already surmised that it was Gilbert who had killed Nicholas, so how did all this tie together? And the medicine the high priest gave to Hesselwell belonged to Buckley. Was there more than one high priest in all this business, just as there might be more than one killer of the women? Was it Buckley, Gilbert, or de Belem in the orchard with Hesselwell and the big man? Who was in the roof with Hesselwell, throwing birds and bats down at the coven? And why had de Belem told Bartholomew he was grand master of the Guild of Purification if no such organisation existed?

Tulyet gnawed at his lip. 'I have been over this again and again, but all the evidence points to de Belem. I am certain he is the high priest.'

'We thought it might be your son,' said Michael bluntly.

'Richard?' said Tulyet, aghast. 'Why would you think that?'

'Because he has made no attempt to catch the killer of these women, and because he has thwarted the efforts of others to do so,' said Michael.

Tulyet leaned back in his chair wearily. 'My son is not in a position to do anything,' he said.

'Why not?' said Michael. 'He is the Sheriff.'

'Because de Belem has Richard's son,' said Tulyet, putting his head in his hands. 'If he makes any moves against the guild, de Belem will kill him.'

'You mean his baby?' asked Bartholomew, horrified. 'The one born last year?'

Tulyet nodded. 'My only grandchild born after the Death. The only child Richard will ever have, as you told him yourself, Doctor.'

'But how do you know it is de Belem?' insisted Michael.

Tulyet took a deep breath, and composed himself before starting. 'Shortly after Richard's baby was snatched, he had a note warning him that his son would be killed if his investigations into the guilds did not cease immediately. Because Richard thought the guilds were connected with the killer of the women, he had to stop looking into that too. Richard is the only member of my family who refused to join the Guild of the Coming, because he did not want to be put in a position where his loyalty to members of the guild might conflict with his office as Sheriff.'

So that explained Tulyet's behaviour, thought Bartholomew, and why he was so vocal in threatening him and Michael. He was not threatening them so much as telling the spies of the high priest that he was not co-operating. It also explained his increasing agitation.

'Does Richard believe de Belem is committing these murders?' asked Bartholomew.

Tulyet nodded. 'He told me that the victims had circles on the soles of their feet. He assumed it was the killer claiming that the murders were committed by members of the Guild of Purification. When he began to investigate, his baby was snatched.'

Bartholomew frowned. But if de Belem were the killer, why did he encourage Bartholomew to investigate the death of Frances? He shook his head impatiently. It made no sense.

'The only clue Richard had as to his son's kidnappers was the note,' continued Tulyet. 'He noticed there were traces of yellow dye on the parchment.'

'And because de Belem is a dyer, you think he wrote it?' asked Michael incredulously. 'There are other dyers in the town, too!'

'No, there are not,' said Bartholomew. Stanmore had become tedious on the subject since the plague: de Belem held a monopoly on dyes. He was not only the sole dyer in the town, he was the only one for miles.

'But that is not sufficient evidence,' said Michael, shrugging his shoulders.

'I have not finished,' said Tulyet, tiredness in his voice. 'The day before her death, Isobel Watkins came to see Richard. She was de Belem's whore, and she told Richard that she had wandered where she should not have in de Belem's house and had discovered a dead goat and caged birds and bats. But what frightened her most was that she thought she had heard the cry of a baby.'

'Birds and bats?' said Bartholomew, thinking about the ceremony in All Saints'.

Tulyet met his eyes. 'Crows and big black bats, she said. And a dead goat. As you know, the goat is the symbol of our guild. Two nights ago at the ceremony you appear to have observed, birds, bats, and a dead goat made their appearance. I did not connect the contents of de Belem's house with the horrible ceremony in All Saints' until yesterday. It terrified me to the point where I simply forced it from my mind, and I did not think properly.'

'But why did Richard not demand to search de Belem's house for his baby?' asked Bartholomew. 'Once he had his son back, de Belem would be powerless to blackmail him, and Richard could pursue his investigation of the murderer and the guilds.'

'I said he should, but his wife was against it. She was afraid the baby would be killed as soon as Richard entered the house,' said Tulyet. 'Richard delayed, Isobel died, and, despite the fact that Richard has been watching the house, no baby has been heard since.'

Bartholomew leaned back against the wall and rubbed his chin. De Belem was a dyer, which meant that he would have ready access to certain chemicals, and would know which ones would explode, burn, or give off smoke. Added to the bats and birds, the evidence was powerful. He thought of the high priest's performance in All Saints'. He had been of a height and build similar to de Belem's. It could have been a good many other people too, however. But what about Frances? Bartholomew recalled his grief when he had broken the news of her death. Surely he had not killed her himself? What had she said on the night she died? That it was 'not a man'. Was it because de Belem had been wearing his red mask as he had in the church, perhaps the same red mask that Bartholomew had seen in the Michaelhouse orchard?

'So what do we do now?' Michael asked Tulyet.

Tulyet's face fell. 'I hoped you would know,' he said. He looked out of the window. 'It is getting dark and the high priest promised another murder. Richard's anguish has made him increasingly unstable over the last few days. I cannot allow him to be involved any further until he has the baby back. You are my last hope,' he said with sudden despair.

'How long has the baby been gone?' asked Bartholomew.

'Almost four weeks,' said Tulyet. 'He is a bonny babe, strong and healthy. Not like the yellow weakling you saw when he was born. But he still needs his mother.'

Bartholomew mused. About a month. The same time that Nicholas feigned his death, and the woman had been placed in his coffin; the same time that de Belem had made himself the new high priest of the Guild of the Coming; and about the same time that Janetta had been in town.

'We should question de Belem,' said Michael. 'Discreetly.'

'But if you go to de Belem, and he has even the slightest inkling of what you know, he might harm my grandchild,' said Tulyet.

'He asked us if we would investigate the death of his daughter,' said Bartholomew reasonably. 'He cannot be suspicious of us. We will go to him tonight. The longer we wait, the more likely it is that the child will come to harm.'

'But what of the risk?' cried Tulyet. 'What if you make a mistake?'

'What if the child dies because he is in the care of a man who does not know about children?' asked Bartholomew.

'Do you think he might die from neglect?' asked Tulyet anxiously.

Bartholomew raised his hands. 'It is in de Belem's interest to keep the child alive, but he will not be as well cared for as if he were at home.'

Tulyet sat in an agony of indecision, looking from Michael to Bartholomew with a stricken expression.

'This cannot go on,' said Michael gently. 'A child

needs its mother. And we cannot allow another murder to happen when we know what we do. Think of Fritha.'

Tulyet nodded miserably. 'But please be careful for the child,' he said. 'Many people are guilty of vile crimes in this business, but he is wholly innocent.'

Tulyet stood, white faced, and Michael clapped him reassuringly on the shoulder. 'Do not go home. Your anxiety might alert your son, and he may interfere and do harm. Wait with Master Kenyngham until we return. Tell him what you have told us, and we will inform you of what we have learned as soon as we can.'

Tulyet nodded again. Bartholomew called for Cynric to escort the merchant to Kenyngham's room.

'What made you come to us now?' asked Michael as he left.

Tulyet gave a weak smile. 'The town has failed since the Sheriff is helpless, and my own information has revealed nothing. The Church will not help me now I have sold my soul to the Devil. What else is there but the University? I came close to telling you the other day. Now I feel you are our only hope.'

They watched him walk across the yard, his shoulders stooped.

'What shall we do first?' asked Michael.

'I have an idea,' said Bartholomew.

CHAPTER 10

ICHAEL PUFFED ALONG NEXT TO BAR-tholomew on their way to Milne Street, while on his other side, Cynric glided through the shadows like a cat.

Bartholomew hoped Stanmore had not already gone home, and he was relieved when he saw lights burning in one of the storerooms. He led the way through Stanmore's yard, and found his brother-in-law supervising two exhausted labourers with the last bales of cloth from a consignment that had arrived from the Low Countries. Stanmore smiled at his unexpected visitors, waved his men home for the night, and wiped his hands on his gown.

'Dyed cloth from Flanders,' he said, patting one of the bales in satisfaction. 'Excellent quality. It goes to show that it is better to use the barges than the roads these days.'

'Do you have anything in black?' asked Bartholomew, looking around.

'I have black wool. What do you want it for?' asked Stanmore.

'A Benedictine habit,' said Bartholomew.

Stanmore frowned and looked at Michael's habit. 'I

have nothing in stock that would be appropriate. I would need to have something dyed. When do you need it?'

'Two days,' said Bartholomew. Michael looked from one to the other in confusion.

'I do not need another habit,' he said. 'I have two already.'

Bartholomew wandered to where Stanmore kept his tools and a small bucket of red dye used for marking bales of cloth as they arrived. He took a brush from the bucket and flicked it at Michael, who gazed in disbelief at the trail of red drops down the front of his black robe. Stanmore looked at Bartholomew as if he had gone mad, and edged nearer the door.

'Now you have only one,' said Bartholomew. 'But it is not good enough for you to attend your students' disputations in two days' time. The Bishop will be there, and you know how vain Benedictines like to look their best. It is a shame you were careless in Oswald's workshop when he had just told you he had no black cloth in stock.'

Michael looked up slowly, his green eyes gleaming as he understood Bartholomew's plan. 'It is essential we get the cloth tonight,' he said, 'or the habit will not be ready in time.'

It was Stanmore's turn to look from one to the other in bewilderment. 'I can buy some from Reginald de Belem,' he said. 'He always has plenty of black cloth dyed ready to sell me.'

'I bet he does,' said Bartholomew, drily. 'What do you think he would do if we wanted him to give us some tonight?'

'Like any good merchant, I imagine he would try to accommodate a customer.' Stanmore looked at him suspiciously. 'This is about the guild business, isn't it?' he said.

Bartholomew nodded. 'De Belem appears to be playing a bigger part in this than we thought. We need to enter his house. Once in, we will distract him while Cynric looks around.'

Cynric's dark face was alight with excitement, but Bartholomew felt a twinge of guilt for once again involving his book-bearer in something dangerous. He hoped Tulyet's information was accurate. It was only Isobel's claim that she had heard a baby that drove him on – since Isobel had been killed only a few days ago, the baby might yet be alive. That he had not been heard since might merely mean that he had been moved to a different room in de Belem's sizeable house. But at the back of his mind doubts nagged where facts did not fit together: de Belem's daughter had been murdered; the nerve-calming medicine the high priest of the Guild of the Coming had given to Hesselwell was Buckley's; and de Belem had been desperate that Bartholomew should investigate the murders. Yet other facts pointed clearly to de Belem's guilt: the birds and bats in his home; Isobel murdered after she had discovered them, albeit too late to ensure her silence; the baby crying in his house; and the dye staining the blackmail note. It was clear de Belem had some role in the affair, but Bartholomew remained uncertain whether it was that of high priest.

'This is not illegal, is it?' said Stanmore nervously.

'De Belem has already broken the law,' said Michael. 'We are trying to ensure that he does not do so again.'

He explained briefly what they had learned from Tulyet, and added one or two speculations of his own.

Stanmore picked up his cloak from where it lay on a bale of cloth. 'Well, let us see if Master de Belem will sell us what we need,' he said. He saw Bartholomew hesitate. 'Your excuse will appear more convincing if I am there also. And another man present will do no harm.'

They left Stanmore's premises and knocked at the door of de Belem's house. The house was in silent darkness, and all the window shutters were closed. For a moment, Bartholomew thought he may have ruined Michael's habit for nothing and that de Belem was not home, but eventually there were footsteps and de Belem himself opened the door. When he saw Bartholomew, Michael, and Stanmore, hope flared in his eyes.

'You know?' he said. 'You know who killed Frances?'

Stanmore shook his head. 'Not yet,' he said. 'We have come on another matter.'

He stood back to indicate Michael with his hand. De Belem's puzzled frown faded into a smile when he saw the red stains on the front of Michael's habit.

He leaned forward and inspected it. 'I can re-dye this and those marks will not show,' he said. 'That way, you can avoid buying new cloth from Master Stanmore and the cost of a tailor to sew it. Bring it to me tomorrow.' He ignored Stanmore's indignant look, and prepared to close the door.

'I need it dyed tonight,' said Michael quickly. 'This is my best habit and I want to wear it to my students' disputations.'

'I cannot dye it tonight, Brother,' said de Belem reasonably. 'All the apprentices have gone home, and the fires under the dyeing vats have been doused. Come back tomorrow at dawn. I will make it my first priority.'

'I will light the fires myself,' said Michael, inserting a foot into the door, 'if you dye it tonight.'

De Belem, despite his reluctance to refuse a customer, was beginning to lose patience. 'Sir Oswald, tell the Brother that it is not an easy matter to light the fires under the vats, and that if we were to start the process now, we would be here all night. I cannot help you, Brother.'

'Do you have any black cloth, then?' asked Michael.

Bartholomew was impressed at the monk's tenacity. De Belem sighed in resignation. 'Yes. I have black cloth dyed for the abbey at Ely. It will be a more expensive option for you, but if it will satisfy your desire to have something done tonight, I will sell you some now.'

They followed him into his house.

'He is exceeding himself in this!' Stanmore hissed to Bartholomew. 'He is not authorised to sell cloth, only to dye it. And he even has the gall to sell it with me present!'

Bartholomew shrugged off his arm impatiently and followed Michael inside, careful not to shut the door so that Cynric could slip in. Stanmore followed, still grumbling.

'If there were other dyers in the town this would never happen. The man thinks he can do what he likes now he has this monopoly. No wonder the cloth trade is poor if we are constantly being undercut by de Belem.'

Bartholomew silenced him with a glance, and Stanmore, still bristling with indignation, said no more. They followed de Belem down a long corridor where a door led directly into the yard. Two wooden buildings had been raised there. The smaller one, judging from the smell and the stained ground outside, was the dyeing shed, while the other was for drying and storage. De Belem took some keys from his belt and unlocked the door to the storeroom. A torch stood ready near the door, and he kindled it so he could find the correct cloth. The room smelled so strongly of the plants and compounds used for dyes that it was overpowering.

Bartholomew stayed outside, looking over at the house on the other side of the yard. It was in darkness except for lights flickering at one window, and Bartholomew saw a figure walk across it. He wondered who it might be. De Belem lived alone now his daughter was dead. Perhaps de Belem had found himself another prostitute. He felt his stomach churn. He hoped not, for that might mean that she was in very serious danger.

Bartholomew edged away from the storeroom when he heard Stanmore begin an argument with de Belem, first about the price and then about which cloth was best for the purpose. De Belem was becoming exasperated with his late customers and Bartholomew knew he would not tolerate them much longer. He had a sudden fear that they would not be able to distract him long enough for Cynric to conduct his search of the house, or worse, that Cynric would still be inside when they left.

Taking a hasty decision, he ran back across the court-yard to the house and began to climb up some large crates that were piled up against the outside wall. The house was not as well built at the back as it was in the front, and he was able to climb higher on ill-fitting timbers that jutted from the plaster. He made his way towards the lighted window, wincing as his feet slipped and scraped against the wall. Grasping the window-sill, he hauled himself up and peered through the open window just as Janetta of Lincoln looked out to see what had made the noise.

For a second, they regarded each other in silence, and then Janetta tipped her head back and yelled as loudly as she could. Someone who had been sitting with his back to the window leapt to his feet and spun around, and Bartholomew had his second shock as he recognised the missing Evrard Buckley. Bartholomew heard a shout from the storeroom and glanced back to see de Belem race out, pulling the door closed behind him. Something crashed against it from the other side just as de Belem got a stout bar into place.

De Belem saw Bartholomew and began to run towards him. Bartholomew cursed in frustration. How had Michael and Stanmore managed to let de Belem lock them in the storeroom? Janetta tried to prise his fingers from the window-frame, and at the same time, he felt de Belem make a grab for his feet.

'Michael!' he yelled, kicking out so hard he almost dislodged himself from the wall. Janetta picked up a heavy jug from the table and began clumsily to swing it at Bartholomew's head. As Bartholomew ducked, and tried to keep his feet out of de Belem's reach, he was vaguely aware of Buckley grabbing something from the bed. He heard a small whimper and knew Buckley had Tulyet's baby. Janetta gave a yell of anger and hurled the jug at Bartholomew, spinning round to follow Buckley to the door. Even as Buckley reached for the lock, the door flew open, and Cynric stood there, breathing hard.

'Cynric! The baby!' Bartholomew gasped.

De Belem had a good grip on Bartholomew's leg and was pulling with all his might, and Bartholomew found he could hold on no longer. As his fingers began to slip, he saw Janetta and Cynric engaged in their own furious struggle. And then he finally lost his grip on the window-sill, and was tumbling through the air.

His fall was broken by de Belem. For a moment, they both lay dazed until Janetta cried out, 'They have the baby!'

Abandoning Bartholomew, de Belem struggled to his feet and began to run towards the door of the house. Bartholomew dived after him and, grabbing him around the knees, brought him down again. De Belem twisted onto his back and lashed out, catching Bartholomew hard on the side of the head with his clenched fist. Stunned, Bartholomew released him, and heard de Belem scramble away. Vaguely he heard Stanmore and Michael shouting in the storeroom and de Belem yelling orders. He tried to stand to release Michael and Stanmore, but he was dizzy, and his legs would not hold him up.

The clatter of hooves brought him to his senses, and he saw horses being taken from the stable. He pulled himself into a sitting position and saw de Belem haul open the gates, leap onto a horse, and urge it into the street. Janetta followed and Bartholomew heard the thudding of hooves fading away. Someone slumped down beside him, and Bartholomew saw it was Buckley, awkwardly holding Tulyet's baby.

'Thank God!' Buckley said unsteadily. As Bartholomew took the baby from him, he saw the Vice-Chancellor's gloved hands were tied in front of him. 'I thought it would never end.'

Bartholomew turned his attention to the baby. It was feverish, but alive. He suspected it had not been given enough to drink and it was weak. That probably explained why it had not been heard crying. It was dirty too. He felt it carefully to ascertain that it was not more seriously hurt, while Cynric emerged from the house unsteadily and made his way to the storeroom. He heaved the bar up, and Michael and Stanmore exploded into the yard, looking about them.

'Master Buckley!' exclaimed Michael, hurrying across to them. 'And you have the baby!'

Cynric took a knife and sawed through the ropes on Buckley's hands.

'He had my cloth!' shouted Stanmore, beside himself with anger. 'Those were no random attacks on my cart. It was de Belem! He must have wanted to discourage me from sending cloth elsewhere to be dyed, and so he arranged to steal it from my carts! He must have killed Will, too!'

'To buy more time, I pretended to stumble and knock some bales down,' explained Michael. 'Hidden behind them was Oswald's stolen cloth. While we were witless with surprise, he dashed out and locked us in.'

'They have fled,' said Bartholomew, his voice jangling in his aching head. 'They took horses and left.'

Stanmore looked at the open gates. 'We might still catch them,' he said. 'Michael, Cynric! Help me with the horses!'

As they ran from the yard, Bartholomew turned to Buckley.

'Are you hurt?' he asked.

Buckley shook his head, his face grey with strain. 'They cut my arm when they came for me in the middle of the night. But that is healing. And they took my medicine. But that was perhaps as well since I did not want to sleep too deeply with de Belem and that woman prowling around. And there was that poor whimpering child that needed me.'

So that explained the blood they had seen on the ground outside his window at King's Hall. 'What happened?' Bartholomew asked.

'A noise awoke me one night, and the next thing I knew was that de Belem was in my room with some of his hired thugs. They made me climb out of the window and wait in a cart while they took everything from my room. I later assumed he meant he wanted it to look as if I had done something dreadful and fled with all my belongings.'

The baby gave a strangled cry, and Bartholomew rocked it.

Buckley swallowed hard. 'Will the child live? I have been trying to look after him, but he was becoming weaker. They told me he is Richard Tulyet's child, and that Tulyet would never come to rescue me as long as the baby was here. They were going to kill him if Tulyet so much as set foot in the yard.'

'I think he will recover once he is fed properly. Is there anything you can tell us that might help us catch de Belem and Janetta?' Bartholomew asked.

Buckley shook his head slowly. 'Only that the woman is here rarely, and that de Belem's men are mercenaries who are beginning to waver in their loyalties. I heard a savage argument last night between de Belem and one of the sergeants. Some have already gone. He had about thirty, half were garrisoned in Primrose Alley and half are elsewhere. Of the ones in Primrose Alley, he probably has fewer than five left. There are other things, too, but they are supposition, and I have little to substantiate them.'

He continued talking quickly, while Bartholomew listened, pieces of the puzzle falling into place with the scraps of information he had already gathered. He was still sitting on the ground, holding the baby, and listening to Buckley, when Michael and Stanmore returned with Cynric and two of Stanmore's men, all mounted and armed. Behind Cynric were Rachel Atkin and Sybilla.

'Matt! Come on, we must catch them!' said Michael, leaning down and grabbing at Bartholomew's tabard. Bartholomew climbed unsteadily to his feet and handed the baby to Rachel.

'Take him to Richard Tulyet's wife,' he said. 'You must tell her to feed him immediately. He is unharmed, but weak.'

'Matt, come on, or we will lose them!' cried Stanmore, already mounted.

'Tell her if she cannot feed him herself she must find a wet-nurse at once,' Bartholomew continued, glancing at Stanmore irritably.

Rachel nodded and wrapped the baby more warmly in her own cloak.

'Matt!' yelled Michael, wheeling round on his impatient horse.

'He is to be fed in small amounts. Too much at once and he will get colic. Master Buckley, will you go to the Sheriff? If you are too weak, call at Michaelhouse and they will send a student.' He gave one last look at the baby, and ran to the horse Stanmore was holding for him.

He climbed clumsily into the saddle, and closed his eyes as the ground appeared to tip and sway beneath him. The feeling passed, and he grabbed at the horse's reins in an attempt to stop it from skittering.

'They took the Trumpington Road,' said Stanmore. 'I heard them.'

Bartholomew jabbed his heels into the horse's side and followed the others as they clattered out of the yard, along Milne Street, and towards the High Street. They slowed as they neared the Trumpington Gate, and he saw the guards milling around. One of them was sitting on the ground holding a hand to his head.

'They ran him down!' the sergeant from the Castle shouted indignantly to Stanmore. 'There were two of them. Rufus stood to stop them and they just ran him down.'

Bartholomew moved to dismount to attend to the man, but the sergeant stopped him. 'Rufus will be fine, Doctor. They took the Trumpington Road, probably off to London. Go after them and bring them back to me. I will send to the Castle.'

'If Tulyet does not know yet, tell him his baby is safe,' Bartholomew yelled back at him as his horse, fired with the chase in the night, began to gallop after the others with no encouragement from him. 'You will find him more than willing to take action this time.'

The night was cloudy and dark. The new moon was not due for two nights and so there was nothing to light their way. They were forced to reduce their speed for fear of being thrown, since the Trumpington Road was, as usual, deeply rutted with cart tracks and pot-holes so deep that Bartholomew had seen a drowned sheep in one during the spring.

They reached Trumpington and Stanmore slowed,

yelling at the top of his voice. Several people emerged from their dark cottages and told him that other horses had passed moments earlier and had taken the path to Saffron Walden.

'Good thing we stopped,' Michael muttered, turning his horse down the smaller of the two roads. 'I would have bet my dinner they would make for London.'

'Wait for the Sheriff's men,' Stanmore shouted to the villagers. 'Tell them which way we have gone.'

He wheeled his horse round and started off down the Saffron Walden road, the others streaming behind him. Another piece of the jigsaw clicked into place in Bartholomew's mind. Saffron Walden. He thought about the two people he had seen in the roof of All Saints': one small and sure-footed, the other larger and less adept, but stronger. Janetta and Hesselwell, the high priest's assistants, throwing the birds and bats down into the church to frighten the congregation, with Hesselwell not knowing the identity of the other.

His horse stumbled, and Bartholomew was forced to abandon his analysis and concentrate on riding. He was not a good horseman, and was finding it difficult to stay in the saddle, let alone direct the horse. He was grateful Stanmore had thought to give him one that seemed able to look after itself. Michael was an excellent rider, having learned on the fine mounts kept in the Bishop's stables, while Cynric was inelegant, but efficient.

He strained his eyes, trying to see if he could detect any movement that they were drawing closer to their quarry, but could see nothing. He swore as a dangling twig clawed at his face, and leaned further down against his horse's neck. The beast was beginning to glisten with sweat and Bartholomew could see foam oozing from its mouth. Behind him, he heard Michael curse loudly as his own mount staggered, and only his skill kept him in the saddle.

'Slow down!' Michael yelled to Stanmore. 'You will ruin the horses!'

The pace dropped, and then was forced to drop further still when the road degenerated into a morass of thick cloying mud and great puddles. Spray flew and Bartholomew blinked muddy water from his eyes.

'There!' he yelled, glimpsing two shadowy figures far ahead, silhouetted against the skyline.

Stanmore stood in his stirrups and peered forward. He began to urge his huge piebald forward again, faster than before. Bartholomew clung on for dear life, feeling his legs begin to ache, and hoped they would catch de Belem soon. Saffron Walden was perhaps fifteen miles on the winding track from Cambridge, and they had travelled at least two thirds of that already. The track became better as they neared the small settlement at Great Chesterford and they thundered forward. Janetta and de Belem had also made good time through the village, and when they emerged at the other end, they were out of sight.

The road split again after Great Chesterford. A man materialised out of the darkness and pointed to the right fork.

'Horsemen went that way,' he said. 'The road is a better and faster route to London than the road from Trumpington at the moment.'

'No! They went left,' cried Bartholomew, clinging on to his horse as it skittered restlessly.

Stanmore hesitated, so Bartholomew urged his mount down the road on the left to lead the way. The horses were beginning to tire, and as soon as the track degenerated again, they were forced to slow to a trot. Michael swore and muttered, leaning forward to squint into the darkness to see if he could spot de Belem again. At a wider part, he drew level with Bartholomew, while Stanmore pushed past them.

'I do not understand this,' he said breathlessly. 'Why Saffron Walden? Why not London where they could easily disappear?'

'De Belem is a dyer,' said Bartholomew.

Michael looked blankly at him. 'So?'

'Saffron Walden is where crocuses are grown for saffron.' Bartholomew was surprised at Michael's slowness. 'Saffron is used for dye. De Belem is a dyer. He probably owns fields there. The plague left land vacant all over the country, and I am sure that the crocus fields could be bought relatively cheaply. I cannot imagine that an astute merchant like de Belem would miss an opportunity for that kind of business investment.'

'Stanmore's carts!' said Michael, urging his horse round a deep puddle. 'They were attacked at Saffron Walden, and Will was killed near there!'

'And de Belem was planning to marry Frances to some lord of the manor there,' said Bartholomew.

The track became narrow again, and Bartholomew was forced to drop back so Michael could ride ahead. Stanmore, now in the lead, saw a flash of movement ahead and urged them on.

'What do they think will happen when they reach Saffron Walden?' Michael yelled. 'We are still in pursuit.'

'They must have somewhere to hide,' Stanmore yelled back.

Bartholomew thought about Buckley's information. Fifteen mercenaries elsewhere. De Belem and Janetta would not ride so wildly just to be taken at Saffron Walden, hiding place or no. They must have had a plan!

'Stop!' he shouted. 'Wait!'

But Michael and Stanmore did not hear him. He kicked at his horse to try to catch up with them. As they reached the brow of a hill, he could see the dark regular shapes of buildings in the hollow below. They were almost there.

'Michael!' he yelled at the top of his voice, but the monk did not hear.

The track narrowed further so that trees slapped past the horses on both sides. Bartholomew's horse reared suddenly, panicked by some shadow that flicked across the path. Bartholomew fought to control it, drawing the reins tight and clinging with his knees to prevent himself from falling off. Branches tore at him, forcing him to raise one arm to protect his face against being blinded. His horse snorted with fear and thrashed with its hooves, and Bartholomew felt himself begin to slide off.

Stanmore's men, who had been behind, were past him before he could stop them, further panicking his horse. It turned and tried to bolt, but stumbled in the rutted track. Horse and rider fell together into the undergrowth. The horse staggered to its feet and was away, crashing blindly along the path the way it had come. Bartholomew heard its hooves drumming off into the distance and then there was silence.

The thick undergrowth had broken his fall, and

Bartholomew was unharmed. Cautiously he began to inch his way along the track towards the small settlement of Saffron Walden. He became aware of shouts ahead and slowed, wishing he could move as silently as Cynric. Peering through the undergrowth, he watched in horror as he saw Stanmore and Michael engaged in a violent skirmish with several rough-looking men wearing boiled-leather jerkins. Bartholomew had seen men dressed like this before: twice, when he had spoken to Janetta. These were the other half of de Belem's mercenaries, men who had fought with the King at the glorious victory at Crécy, but came back to roam restlessly around the country waiting for another war and selling their services to the highest bidder.

The highest bidder was apparently de Belem, who advanced as the skirmish ended, watching Stanmore and the others drop their weapons in surrender. Bartholomew was furious at himself. It had been obvious that de Belem was riding at such a pace for a reason, and they had fallen right into his trap.

'The Sheriff's men will be here soon,' said Stanmore boldly. 'You will only make matters worse for yourself if you do not surrender.'

De Belem laughed and his men joined in. 'The Sheriff's men will find nothing here,' he said. 'They will be told you must have taken the London road at Great Chesterford, for no horsemen came this way tonight.'

'You did not fool us. Why would you fool them?' asked Michael.

'My man at Great Chesterford will do a better job next time,' said de Belem. 'Because he knows what will happen to him if he does not.'

'Tulyet will hunt you down now that you no longer have his child,' said Michael.

De Belem sighed. 'There are many ways to skin a cat; I will think of something else.'

He motioned with his hand that they were to dismount and rounded them into a small group to be escorted into the village. Janetta suddenly appeared.

'Where is Bartholomew?' she said, looking around. 'Search for him,' she ordered two of the mercenaries.

'He stayed with the baby,' said Michael. 'We came without him.'

'Search for him,' said Janetta again, casting a disdainful look at Michael. 'Do not let him escape.'

Bartholomew fought down panic as the two mercenaries began to move towards him. He ducked back into the undergrowth, and wondered if he should try to run or try to stay hidden. One of the mercenaries carried a crossbow, already wound. Bartholomew crouched on the ground covering his face with his arms. If he stayed perfectly still, wrapped in his dark cloak, he might yet escape detection. He did not know the area well enough to escape through the woods, and would probably run into thicker undergrowth and make an easy target for the mercenaries.

He almost leapt up as he heard crashing behind him. He saw a figure dart across the path and plunge into the woods on the opposite side of the track. With howls of success, the mercenaries dived after him. Cynric, Bartholomew thought, unsurprised. He had obviously anticipated the ambush, even if the others had not.

Bartholomew stayed where he was until the sounds of Cynric leading the men away from him had faded.

Looking both ways, he set off down the track towards the village, stopping frequently to listen as he had seen Cynric do on occasions. The village comprised parallel rows of houses, most of them simple wooden frames packed with dried mud and straw. One or two gleamed with limewash, but most were plain. The dark mass of the castle crouched at the far end, looming over the village with empty malice since it had not been garrisoned since the plague. The large church, built on profits from the saffron trade, stood at the other end of the village.

He paused at the outskirts and listened. He heard de Belem speaking. Keeping to the shadows, he slunk along one side of the street towards the church, where Michael and the others had apparently been taken. He crept over grassy graves, and climbed on a tombstone to look through one of the windows.

De Belem was wearing his red mask, and white-faced villagers were trickling into the church, drawn by the noise and the torches that lit the inside of the church. Michael, Stanmore and his men were clustered together near the altar, under the guard of several heavily-armed mercenaries. More villagers began to arrive as someone rang the church bell, and a figure swathed in a black robe, that Bartholomew knew was Janetta, began to organise the church in preparation for a ceremony. She took a long knife from one of the mercenaries and laid it reverently on the altar in front of de Belem, and rearranged the torches so that most of the church was in shadow.

Bartholomew felt sick and crouched down on the tombstone so he would not have to watch. De Belem was about to perform some dreadful ceremony in which Michael and Stanmore would be murdered in front of the entire village. The sight of what would happen to those who did not comply with his wishes would doubtless be enough to ensure their co-operation for whatever other nasty plans de Belem had in mind. Bartholomew stood shakily and looked at the villagers. They were sullen and frightened, and some wore a dazed expression that suggested no such ceremony would be necessary to terrify them further. De Belem was holding an entire village to ransom.

He spun round as he heard a noise behind him and found himself staring down at a priest. He braced himself. He could not be caught now, not when he was the only one who could help his friends! Although the priest was tall, he was thin and looked frail. Bartholomew's only hope was that the priest would not cry out a warning when Bartholomew launched himself at him. As Bartholomew prepared to dive, the priest raised both hands to show that he was unarmed, and then very deliberately drew a cross in the air in front of him. Bartholomew watched in confusion. The priest put his fingers to his lips and motioned that Bartholomew should follow.

Bartholomew looked around him desperately. What should he do? The priest seemed to be telling him he was not a part of de Belem's satanic following by drawing the cross in the air. Perhaps he could persuade him to help. With a last agonised glance through the window, he jumped from the tomb and followed the priest.

'I am Father Lucius,' the man said when they were a safe distance from the church.

Bartholomew leapt away from him. He had been tricked! It was the man who had last been seen visiting Froissart before he died! But the soldiers said that Father

Lucius was a Franciscan, and this man was wearing the habit of a Dominican friar. Holding his breath, every fibre in his body tense, Bartholomew waited.

'These people have taken my church and I can do nothing about it. They say they will kill five of my parishioners if I send to the Bishop for help, and that I will be unable to prove anything anyway. I saw the horsemen being taken into the church. Are they your friends?'

Bartholomew nodded, still not trusting the man.

Lucius sighed. 'The high priest will kill them. He has done so before.' He shook his head in despair. 'More blood in my church.'

'Well, we have to stop him,' said Bartholomew. He chewed on his lip, scarcely able to think, let alone come up with a plan. He took a deep breath and forced himself to calm down. 'What is de Belem's business here?'

Lucius shrugged. 'Saffron. That is all we have here, and he owns all of it now.'

'All of it?' Bartholomew was amazed. Saffron was a valuable commodity. It could be used for medicine and in cooking as well as a high-quality dye for delicate fabrics like silk. Thousands of flowers were needed to produce even small amounts of the yellow-orange spice, and so it was expensive to buy. Anyone with a monopoly over saffron would be a rich man indeed. More pieces of the mystery fell into place in Bartholomew's mind, but he ignored them. Now was not the time for logical analysis. He needed to do something to help Michael and Stanmore.

'Is the saffron picked yet?' he asked, the germ of an idea beginning to unfold in his mind.

Lucius looked at him. 'The crocuses are picked, yes. The high priest has been withholding the saffron from the market to force up the price. It is stored in his warehouses.'

Bartholomew pushed him forward. 'Show me,' he said. 'Quickly.'

'They will be guarded,' said Lucius. 'They always are.'

He led the way through the churchyard to where two thatched wooden buildings stood just off the main street. Several men could be seen prowling back and forth. De Belem was obviously taking no chances with his precious saffron. Bartholomew tried to think. He would not be able to reach the storehouses without being seen by the guards. And even if he did reach them, he would be an easy target for the bows they carried: the same great longbows that had been used to devastate the French at the battle of Crécy.

He thought quickly. 'I need a bow,' he muttered to Lucius. He began to assess which of the guards he might be able to overpower without the others seeing.

'Will you shoot them?' Lucius asked fearfully. 'More killing?'

Bartholomew shook his head and clenched his fists to stop his hands from shaking. He could hear de Belem's voice raving from the church. He was running out of time.

'I will get you one,' said Lucius, suddenly decisive. He rose from where he had been crouching and slipped away.

Bartholomew took a flint from his bag and began to kindle a fire from some dry grass. He took rolled bandages and began to soak them with the concentrated spirits he used to treat corns and calluses. When Lucius returned, Bartholomew wrapped the bandages around the pointed ends of the arrows and packed it all with more grass. That should burn, he thought. Clumsily, he tried to fit the arrow to the bow, but it had been many years since Stanmore had taught him how to use the weapon, and he had not been good at it even then.

He almost jumped out of his skin as a hand fell on his shoulder. It was Cynric. 'Those men were difficult to lose,' he said. Bartholomew closed his eyes in relief.

'Michael and the others are captive in the church,' he said. 'We need to create a diversion. If de Belem sees his saffron burning, he will try to save it and we might be able to rescue them.'

Cynric nodded, and calmly took the bow from Bartholomew's shaking hands. 'A Welshman is better for this, boy.'

'When the arrow begins to burn, shoot it where you think it will catch light,' said Bartholomew.

Cynric, understanding, looked across at the storehouses. 'They thought to frighten us by making our College gate explode into flames as if by magic, and now we use their idea to burn the saffron!' he said in satisfaction.

Bartholomew nodded, knowing he would never have thought to use fire arrows on the saffron stores had he not seen them used on the gate a few nights earlier.

Cynric touched the arrow to the fire, and Bartholomew and Lucius ducked back as it exploded into flames. Cynric put it to the bow and aimed. They watched it soar through the air like a shooting star and land with a thump on one of the thatched roofs. Without waiting to see what happened, Bartholomew began preparing another. Their only hope of success was to loose as many arrows as possible before they were discovered. He gave Cynric a second, and then a third. He glanced up, his body aching with tension. He could see no flames leaping into the air, hear no cries of alarm from the guards.

'It's not working,' he said, his voice cracking in desperation.

'Give it time,' said Lucius calmly. 'It has been raining a good deal lately. The thatching is probably damp. Try another.'

Bartholomew used the last of the alcohol and handed another arrow to Cynric. They watched it sail clean through a gap between the roof and the wall, leaving a fiery trail behind it. Nothing happened. Bartholomew put his head in his hands in despair. What else could he do? He could do nothing with only Cynric against a band of mercenaries and an entire village. He took a deep breath. He would grab a handful of burning grass and run towards the storehouses with it himself. If he reached them and set them alight before the guards realised what was happening, the diversion would be caused; if they shot him, then that would also cause a diversion. Michael and Oswald would have to use it to fend for themselves.

'Look!' whispered Lucius in excitement. 'There is a fire inside!'

As Bartholomew looked up, he saw yellow flames leaping up inside the nearest of the storehouses, while the other began to ooze smoke from its roof.

'The dry saffron is going up like firewood!' said Lucius,

his eyes gleaming. 'Do you have any more of that stuff that burns?'

Bartholomew shook his head, but made two more fire arrows from bandages and grass alone. They did not burn as well, but there was no harm in trying.

There was a shout as one of the guards saw the flames and ran towards the building. He grasped at the door and pulled it open. As air flooded in, there was a dull roar, and the entire building was suddenly engulfed in flames. Of the guard there was no sign. The flames began to lick towards the other storehouse.

'Back to the church,' Bartholomew said urgently to Lucius. 'You must raise the alarm.'

Lucius nodded and they ran back to the main road. He began yelling as they reached the church, flinging open the doors to rush inside. The frightened villagers looked at their priest in confusion, while de Belem hesitated at the altar. Bartholomew and Cynric slipped into the church while attention was fixed on the apparently gibbering Lucius, and hid behind a stack of benches.

Bartholomew saw with relief that Stanmore and his men were unharmed. De Belem, however, had Michael in front of him, held securely by two of the mercenaries. The knife de Belem waved glittered in the torchlight.

Janetta stepped forward. 'Why do you disturb us, priest?'

'Fire!' shrieked Lucius. 'Fire in the saffron! Run to see to your houses, my children! Save what you can before the fire spreads!'

Bartholomew saw de Belem's jaw drop as he heard his precious saffron was burning, and he exchanged a look of horror with Janetta. Lucius, meanwhile, was exhorting his people to save their homes. Lucius was clever, Bartholomew thought, for if the villagers were scattered to see to their own property, they could not quickly be organised into groups to fight the fire in the saffron stores. In twos and threes, the people began to run away, the fear of losing what little they had greater than de Belem's hold over them.

Bartholomew expected that de Belem would drop everything and run to save his saffron, but the flickering light of the fires could be seen through the windows, and de Belem obviously knew that there was little he could do. In the turmoil, he turned his attention back to Michael, and Bartholomew saw the raised knife silhouetted against the wall behind. He closed his eyes in despair, before snapping them open again. Silhouetted!

He edged round the pillar, and raised his hands near the torch burning on a bracket. They were enormous on the blank wall opposite. He moved them around until he got them into something vaguely resembling an animal with two horns and waggled it about on the wall.

'*Caper* is here!' he yelled at the top of his voice, hoping de Belem would be taken off guard for the instant that might enable Michael to wriggle free. At the same time, Cynric unleashed one of his bloodcurdling Welsh battle-screams that ripped through the church like something from hell itself.

The few remaining villagers fled in terror, led by Father Lucius. Several of the mercenaries followed, while de Belem and Janetta looked at the shadow in horror. Janetta glanced at de Belem once and followed the mercenaries. As she ran past, Bartholomew dived from his pillar and caught her, wrapping his arms firmly around her so

356

she could not move. Meanwhile, Michael had seized his chance, and the two mercenaries lay stunned on the ground, their heads cracked together. Stanmore and his men appeared as dazed as the mercenaries, but a furious shout from Michael brought them to their senses.

'Any man who works for me will be paid twice what de Belem pays,' said Stanmore quickly, addressing the bewildered mercenaries. He plucked a purse from his belt and tossed it to one of them. 'Down payment. And I promise you will not have to do anything that is against the law or against God. The brave heroes of Crécy deserve better than this,' he cried, waving his hand at de Belem's satanic regalia.

For a moment, Bartholomew thought his speech had not had its desired effect, since the men merely stood and watched. Eventually, one of the men gestured impatiently at Stanmore. 'So what are your orders?' he asked.

'No,' yelled de Belem. 'I have power over you. You saw what I can bring into this world!' He pointed towards the wall where Bartholomew's goat silhouette had been.

Michael raised one of the hands and made the shape of a duck on the wall behind him.

'Children's tricks!' he said. 'Is that not so, Matt?'

De Belem looked in disbelief at Michael's duck and then down the church to where Bartholomew was holding a struggling Janetta, and sagged in defeat.

CHAPTER 11

AS DAWN BROKE, ALL THAT WAS LEFT OF DE BELEM'S store-houses was a smouldering heap of wood. Bartholomew turned to Father Lucius.

'What will happen to the people?' he said. 'How will they live without the saffron?'

Lucius smiled. 'I have some tucked away that I stole as we laboured in the fields. We will be able to sell it at the inflated price forced by de Belem. I hear the labourers can earn high wages these days for their toil, and now that we are free, some may well look elsewhere for work.'

'Were you at St Mary's Church about two weeks ago?' Bartholomew asked, wanting to get certain things clear in his mind.

The priest looked surprised. 'No. I have never been to Cambridge. I have heard it smells like a sewer in the hot months and have no wish to go there.'

'How long has de Belem been here?'

'He was buying land here before the Death, but I was foolish enough not to guess that it was he who came in the guise of this high priest later. After the Death took so many, it was easy for him to buy, or simply take, all the remaining stocks, and the few who resisted selling were threatened with demonic devices until they sold too.'

'Demonic devices?' asked Bartholomew.

'Goats' hooves left in their houses, black birds flying around at night. All things with a rational explanation,' said Lucius. He turned to Bartholomew. 'Not like that thing he called up in my church,' he added, shuddering.

Bartholomew smiled. 'I did that,' he said, and, seeing the priest's expression of horror, added quickly, 'with my hands against the light, like this.'

Lucius looked blankly at him for a moment and then roared with laughter. 'Is that what it was?' he said. 'Are you telling me that de Belem, who had fooled so many with tricks, was fooled by one himself?'

Bartholomew nodded and watched Lucius, still laughing, stride off to tell his parishioners. He went to join the group of soldiers who had Janetta, de Belem, and several others carefully guarded. Tulyet had arrived when all was still confusion. De Belem had underestimated him, and the Sheriff had not trusted the words of a conveniently alert villager to send him down the London road.

'I owe you an apology,' said Tulyet. 'But they had my son. After you came to see me, Brother, they sent me some of his hair, and said if I spoke to you again, they would send me one of his fingers. I had to be seen to be following their demands, which is why I threatened you so vociferously. One of the soldiers was watching my every move and reporting to de Belem.' He smiled grimly. 'He is now in the Castle prison awaiting the arrival of his high priest.'

'Did you have any idea de Belem was involved in all

this?' asked Michael, waving a hand at the smouldering storehouses.

Tulyet shook his head. 'I had only begun to suspect that the high priest was de Belem recently. After his daughter was killed, he told me that he had been the high priest of the Guild of Purification, but that he had given that up in grief. I now realise that there was never a Guild of Purification, that it was simply a ruse set up by de Belem to keep his other coven in fear.'

'That cannot be,' said Michael. 'Hesselwell and your father told us the new priest arrived only a month ago after Nicholas died.'

'But he had spies in the Guild of the Coming,' said Tulyet, 'right from the start. Nicholas's death was simply an opportune moment for de Belem to step in and control directly what he had been controlling indirectly for some time.'

'But why bother with the covens at all?' asked Stanmore. 'It all seems rather elaborate.'

'Because it gave him power over people,' said Bartholomew. 'Everyone who had become embroiled was terrified – like old Richard Tulyet and Piers Hesselwell. Once they were in, it was impossible to leave, and tricks, like the ones we saw used in All Saints', were employed to keep them frightened. The murders in the town, too, aided his purpose. He claimed they were committed by his satanic familiar, showing his presence to his followers.'

'But why did he need this power over people?' persisted Stanmore.

'Because all over the country, labourers are leaving their homes to seek better-paid work elsewhere. De

Belem had no intention of paying high wages to the villagers here, although he needed their labour. He realised that he could use tricks to make them too terrified to do anything other than bend to his will.'

'I had worked that out myself,' said Stanmore impatiently. 'But why bother with the likes of old Tulyet and Hesselwell? They did not labour for him.'

'In Hesselwell's case, de Belem wanted a contact in Michaelhouse where Michael and I were working for the Chancellor. Hesselwell said the high priest asked him many questions.'

'And my father?' asked Tulyet.

'De Belem had a monopoly on saffron and was the only dyer in the town. As Oswald will attest, he was sufficiently confident of his monopoly that he was even beginning to sell cloth, the prerogative of drapers, not dyers. De Belem would want to know of plans by cloth merchants and tailors to attempt to buy dyeing services from anyone else. Oswald arranged to buy coloured cloth from London, but his carts were attacked and the cloth stolen. That was because Oswald had mentioned it to your father, and your father told his high priest: de Belem.'

Stanmore nodded. 'The stolen cloth is in de Belem's storerooms in Milne Street if you have any doubts,' he said.

Tulyet sighed and looked at where his men were guarding de Belem and his helpers, waiting for full daylight. Tulyet was taking no chances by travelling too early, and running the risk of being attacked by outlaws.

'So that was it,' he said. 'The note I received said my

son had been taken to ensure I did not investigate the guilds, but what I was really being stopped from looking into were de Belem's business dealings. I should have thought harder: my son was taken when I began to investigate the theft of Sir Oswald's cloth. To me, the theft was far less important than the whore murders, but to de Belem, it was obviously paramount. Well, we have him now.'

Stanmore gazed about him. 'I am astonished this is all so well organised,' he said. 'You say Buckley overheard that half the mercenaries were garrisoned here and half in Primrose Alley?'

'Primrose Alley?' said Tulyet sharply. 'Where Froissart lived?'

'Froissart and his family were among the few people who survived the plague in Primrose Alley,' said Bartholomew. 'Because there were so many empty houses, and because no one wanted to live there if they could be somewhere better, de Belem used it to garrison his mercenaries. Poor Froissart probably discovered something incriminating. He ran to the church for sanctuary not for killing his wife, but to escape de Belem. That night, Gilbert hid in the crypt, to which he has the only set of keys, while the church was locked. He emerged from his hiding place, garrotted Froissart, and waited for "Father Lucius" to come to help him hide the body where it would not be found. Father Lucius, was, of course, de Belem, and he was let into the church by Gilbert, and not by Froissart, as the guards believed.'

'The guards saw de Belem, and described him as mean-looking with a big nose,' elaborated Michael.

'For de Belem, used to dealing with the trappings of witchcraft, it would not have been difficult to make himself unrecognisable to guards more interested in dice than in watching the church, especially a man wearing the hooded robe of a friar.'

'Gilbert is involved in all this?' asked Tulyet, amazed. 'The Chancellor's clerk? I will send a man for him before he realises something is amiss and escapes.'

'That is not necessary,' said Bartholomew. 'Have you noticed that you never see Janetta and Gilbert together? That is because they are one and the same.'

'What?' exclaimed Michael, Tulyet, and Stanmore simultaneously. Michael continued, 'That is outrageous, Matt! Gilbert has a beard for a start, and Janetta is a woman! That fall you had at de Belem's has addled your wits!'

'Go and see,' said Bartholomew. 'You will find that splendid head of hair will come clean off if you give it a tug.'

'You do it,' said Michael primly. 'Monks do not pull women's hair!'

Bartholomew went to where Janetta was being guarded with de Belem in the back of a small cart, followed closely by the others. Janetta smiled falsely at Bartholomew, and he smiled back as he reached out a hand towards her hair. Her smile faded, and she tried to move away.

'No! What are you doing?'

Bartholomew grabbed some of the hair and Janetta screamed. It was held in place firmly, so he pulled harder. Then the wig was off, and Gilbert's thin, fair hair emerged, plastered to his head. De Belem watched impassively, while Gilbert, barely recognisable without his beard, spat and struggled.

'How did you know?' asked Tulyet in astonishment.

'Because the wig may have fooled us, but it did not fool the town prostitutes,' said Bartholomew. 'Matilde told me the hair was a wig. I looked closely when I met Janetta in St Mary's churchyard, and I saw that she was right. And I was puzzled that a woman, obviously concerned with her appearance, would not take pains to hide her scarred face with the thick powders she wore on her cheeks on occasions.'

'That would not be easy to do,' mused Tulyet thoughtfully. 'My wife has a mark on her neck that she does not like to be seen. When she cannot cover it with her clothing, she applies powders. The whole business is very time-consuming. If Janetta had needed to make a sudden appearance, there would not be time to start such a lengthy process. Better to be open about the scars from the start than try to hide them and have them exposed at a point that might be inconvenient.'

'I also noticed that Janetta's hair partly hid her face when she spoke to me, but not when she spoke to the men. That was because I knew Gilbert, and he was taking precautions against being recognised. I was certain, however, when I grabbed him in the church earlier. It did not take a physician to know that the person I held was no woman!'

Michael continued. 'Cuthbert drew attention to the fact that the woman in Nicholas's grave had sparse hair. She died a month ago, at the precise time Janetta made her appearance with her luxurious black hair.'

'Nicholas's lover,' said Stanmore. 'Was she killed for her wigs, then?'

Bartholomew was stumped. It was a possibility he had not considered.

Michael answered instead. 'No, she was killed for something far more serious. The woman had thin, fair hair just like Gilbert's.'

He looked at Gilbert, who refused to look back. Bartholomew gave an exclamation as Janetta's relationship with Gilbert suddenly became clear.

'She was his sister!' he said. 'She was small like him, too. Tiny, in fact.'

'Yes, his sister,' said Michael, still looking at Gilbert. 'Janetta of Lincoln was no fictitious character, was she? She was your sister who was summoned from Lincoln to help with de Belem's plan. You knew Nicholas was working on a book, and that it might contain information dangerous or detrimental to you. Janetta came to insinuate herself into Nicholas's affections in order to discover exactly what he had learned. Cuthbert told us Nicholas was deeply in love, and that the woman seemed to reciprocate these feelings, so perhaps her affection turned her from her true purpose, and that was why she was murdered.'

'And why Gilbert stole her body away from the crypt,' said Bartholomew. 'I hope she lies somewhere peaceful now, without the desecration of that foul mask.'

Gilbert gave a half-smile. 'You will never prove anything other than the fact that I occasionally assumed another identity,' he said.

Tulyet shrugged. 'It does not matter. There is evidence enough to hang you already. Anything we learn now will make no difference to the outcome. We can prove two cases of kidnapping and the practice of witchcraft.'

'We have never practised witchcraft,' said de Belem. 'Everything we did had a rational explanation, and was only harmless fun. A joke. It is not my fault that people were afraid. We have killed no one, and all my property came to me perfectly legally. My lawyer, Piers Hesselwell, will attest to that. You have no proof, just a series of unfounded suppositions. I have powerful friends in the town and in Court. You will not hang me.'

Bartholomew had a cold feeling in the pit of his stomach that de Belem might well be right. They had strong evidence – Tulyet's baby in de Belem's house, Buckley's kidnapping, and Stanmore's stolen cloth – but it was so complex that he imagined a good lawyer could easily find alternative explanations that de Belem's powerful friends would choose to believe as the truth. He walked away, finding de Belem's confident gloating unbearable. He ached all over from his hard ride, and his head was beginning to throb from the hours of tension.

A small stream trickled behind one of the rows of houses, and he crouched at the edge of it to scoop handfuls of water over his face. He heard a sound behind him and spun round, thinking it might be one of de Belem's men still lurking free, but relaxed when he saw it was only Michael.

'Father Lucius has some potage for us,' he said. 'Come. We need something warm inside us if we are to face the rest of the day.'

Bartholomew followed him to the small priest's house next to the church. It was little more than a single room with a lean-to shack at the back for animals. But the rushes on the floor were clean and the crude wooden table in the middle of the room had been scrubbed almost white. Bartholomew sat on a bench with Michael next to him. Stanmore was already there, sipping broth from a blue-glazed bowl. Lucius set other bowls on the table, and Bartholomew closed his cold fingers around one, grateful for the warmth after the chill of the stream.

'De Belem is right, you know,' he said to the others. 'A good lawyer will be able to overturn the evidence we have, especially if the court is full of his powerful friends.'

Stanmore shook his head. 'There is no lawyer that good,' he said. 'And I too will hire one. It was my cloth he stole, and my man he murdered for it. For Will's sake, I will see he does not go free.'

'But we cannot prove he killed the prostitutes,' said Bartholomew. 'De Belem will claim he would not kill his own daughter, nor his woman.'

'But we know they killed Janetta,' said Michael. 'And all the women died of wounds to the throat, like she did. It is too much coincidence not to be true.'

'But the others had that circle on their feet, and we cannot show Janetta had one,' said Bartholomew. 'And we cannot really prove they killed Janetta. We have no witness, no firm, undeniable proof.'

'I am still confused by much of this,' said Stanmore. 'Pieces fit together, but I have a problem with the whole.'

'We should clarify it,' said Michael. 'We have deduced so much that has been proven wrong over the last week, that we need to see whether we agree now.'

Bartholomew grimaced. He was tired, and, like Stanmore, the complete picture still eluded him. There were pieces that still did not fit together, and he was not sure whether his mind was sharp enough to analyse them properly. He took a sip of the potage and almost choked as Michael slapped him encouragingly on the back.

'Let us begin at the beginning,' he said heartily, and Bartholomew wondered where the fat monk's energy came from. 'We need to go back a long way, before all this business started, to Lincoln from whence Gilbert and his kin hail. In Lincoln there was a judge who punished petty criminals by disfiguring their faces. Gilbert must have been punished, rightly or wrongly, for some crime while visiting his family.'

He paused, and Bartholomew recalled what Buckley had said to him as they sat in de Belem's yard waiting for Stanmore to come with the horses. 'Buckley remembered Gilbert's returning from Lincoln with the beard, because he wondered whether he might be able to grow one to hide the sores on his face. Buckley grew a beard, but was impressed that Gilbert's was so much fuller, while his own remained straggly. But Gilbert's scarred face could never sprout such luxurious growth, and the beard was false. He has worn it ever since, to hide the scars that betray him as a criminal.'

'Well, no one would suspect he and Janetta were one and the same, as long as Gilbert wore a beard,' said Stanmore.

'Then we come to the book,' said Michael, holding out his bowl to Lucius for more potage. 'Nicholas had been employed by the Chancellor to write a history of events concerning the University, so that there would be a record for future scholars. As the Chancellor told us, it contained information that could prove embarrassing in some quarters. It not only involved members of the University, but people from the town with whom scholars had had dealings. Nicholas appeared to have taken his task seriously. He joined the Guild of the Coming in order to see what he could learn, and was even elected their leader.'

Bartholomew took up the tale. 'When de Belem learned from Gilbert that Nicholas was writing the book, he became nervous. Gilbert's sister was drafted in from Lincoln to worm her way into his affections to discover what he had learned.'

'But Cuthbert thought that Janetta and Nicholas seemed happy together,' said Michael. 'She failed to tell de Belem and Gilbert what they wanted to know, and possibly even gave Nicholas information about them. And now we are stuck. What happened next?'

Bartholomew pondered, smiling up at Lucius as he filled his bowl again. Stanmore looked from one to the other in anticipation.

'Well, what *do* we know?' said Bartholomew. 'Cuthbert said that Nicholas felt he was in fear of his life, so he feigned his death. De Belem must have threatened him in some way. Nicholas, apparently, felt the only way he could be safe was if he were presumed dead. If he and Janetta were as fond of each other as Cuthbert believes, then the chances are that she helped him execute the plan.'

'And of course we know how!' exclaimed Michael suddenly. 'Gilbert was able to switch Nicholas's body for Janetta's in the crypt yesterday because he is the

369

only one with the keys. Janetta, who doubtless shared Gilbert's house, must have stolen his keys when Nicholas was sealed in his coffin and locked in the church for the night, and gone to let him out. How else would he have escaped the church and still kept secret the fact that he was alive?'

'Gilbert must have suspected, or perhaps he woke to see the keys gone,' mused Bartholomew. 'He followed her to the church and saw Nicholas alive.'

'But then what?' said Stanmore. 'A small man like Gilbert could not hope to overpower two people.'

'He must have fetched de Belem,' said Michael. 'Nicholas and Janetta had to make the coffin look as though there were still a body inside, and that would take a while. Gilbert would have had time. Then there must have been a skirmish in which Janetta was killed and Nicholas escaped.'

'And why the mask?' asked Stanmore. 'Why would Gilbert bury his sister with that?'

'Perhaps she had worn it to hide her face when she went to release Nicholas,' said Michael.

'No,' said Bartholomew slowly. 'I think de Belem probably wore it to frighten Nicholas when Gilbert fetched him. He probably meant to terrify Nicholas into revealing what was in the book before they killed him. The mask was huge, and perhaps dawn was coming by the time Janetta was killed and Nicholas had escaped. It was probably placed on Janetta merely to get rid of it so that de Belem would not have to carry it home through the streets, and Gilbert would not have to hide it in the church.'

Michael nodded. 'And de Belem must have gained

some information from Nicholas before he fled, because he knew there was something important in the book. De Belem then hired a professional thief to come to steal it for him. Gilbert could not steal it, because he had the keys to the church but not to the chest. And we know what happened to the friar.'

'I see,' said Stanmore. 'But why bother with poor old Buckley?'

'We know de Belem and some of the mercenaries went to kidnap Buckley at the same time that the friar went to steal the book,' said Bartholomew. 'They took everything from his room to make it look as if he had fled the town after some guilty deed – the theft of the book. But the plan misfired when the friar scratched his thumb on the lock and died.'

'We suspect Gilbert went to check on the friar, found him dead, and tipped him into the chest in a panic,' said Michael. 'The friar had been told to steal the whole book, because not only did de Belem want the information about himself, he liked to know the secrets of others. We know he asked questions of old Tulyet and Hesselwell: de Belem liked to gather information so that he could use it against others.

'Gilbert, panic-ridden because the plan had gone awry, did not steal the whole book as the friar would have done, he stole only the parts that involved him and de Belem. The Chancellor obviously did not deem these parts important because he did not miss them. But de Wetherset later removed sections he *did* deem important, thus muddying the evidence. Because Gilbert had taken the part that concerned de Belem, there was nothing left to shed light on the affair. Thus it seemed to us that Buckley lacked a motive for fleeing and taking all his belongings.'

'Buckley told me he thought something had gone wrong, and he was a problem to de Belem,' said Bartholomew. 'De Belem was keeping him prisoner until the opportunity arose to use him, or his death, to further his plans.'

'Now,' said Michael, leaning across to peer into Bartholomew's bowl to see if he had left any food. 'Janetta died from a throat injury, Froissart was garrotted, and Nicholas was garrotted. This is not a common method of execution, and we are sure all were killed by one and the same. We know Gilbert killed Froissart because he had the keys to the crypt and could hide there unseen while the church was locked.'

'Froissart's wife was garrotted,' said Stanmore. 'One of my men told me.'

The four men were silent, Lucius looking from one to the other in horror at such convoluted evil.

'So Gilbert killed his sister when he found out she was planning to run away with Nicholas; he killed Froissart when he discovered something amiss in Primrose Alley; he killed Froissart's wife to make it appear as if Froissart had fled into sanctuary for her murder; and he killed Nicholas when he mustered the courage to return to Cambridge to look for Janetta,' said Bartholomew.

'Gilbert must also be the killer of the whores,' said Stanmore. 'Because their throats were slashed.'

'Frances was not a whore,' said Bartholomew. 'Her last words that her killer was not a man must mean that it was Janetta. It was not a man in a mask at all, but the mysterious woman she had perhaps seen in and out of her father's house in the night. Oh, Lord!'

'What?' said Michael. 'What have you thought of?'

'Boniface,' said Bartholomew. The others looked at him uncomprehendingly. 'Frances asked Boniface to meet her in the orchard because she had something to tell him. He waited but she never arrived. I thought she was going to tell him something personal, but she must have been going to tell him about strange happenings at her father's house – the baby crying in the night, birds and bats in his attics, a room always locked where Buckley was captive. I imagine she thought that, as a friar, he might be able to secure the help of the other Franciscans and investigate. Perhaps she knew of her father's involvement with the guilds and considered he had become too deeply caught for his own safety. Gilbert guessed what she was about to do, followed her disguised as Janetta, and killed her in Michaelhouse.'

'That makes sense,' said Michael. 'Her father's involvement with the coven was probably something that became an increasing worry to her as time went on. Perhaps she reached the end of her tether with her other problem.'

'What problem?' asked Stanmore, interested.

'Nothing that will concern her now,' answered Michael quickly, catching Bartholomew's eye and wincing at his own near-indiscretion.

'The wounds on Janetta, Frances, Isobel, and Fritha were not the same,' said Bartholomew thoughtfully. 'Isobel's and Fritha's throats were slit; the others' were hacked.'

Stanmore looked at him distastefully. 'It is all much the

same,' he said. 'And anyway, they all had bloody circles on their feet. It stands to reason de Belem would not kill his own daughter and whore. I wonder if he knows Gilbert is their killer.'

'He cannot,' said Bartholomew, 'or he would not have asked us to investigate. It was Gilbert as Janetta that warned us away from investigating – once in Primrose Alley and once in the churchyard; it was Gilbert who instructed Hesselwell to leave the head in Michael's room claiming it was the will of the high priest; and it was Gilbert who ordered Hesselwell to prepare the back gate of Michaelhouse with a substance that would burn. He knew we used the gate at night, and planned to set it alight as we emerged. Even if we were not killed or injured, we would have received another warning. Meanwhile, de Belem discouraged us from looking into the guilds, but encouraged us to look elsewhere. He must believe the murders have nothing to do with his business.'

'But he is the high priest who said there would be another killing,' said Michael. 'He must know!'

Bartholomew was silent, trying to impose reason onto the muddle of facts. 'Well,' he began uncertainly, 'he knew Tulyet would not investigate Frances's death, because he was bound by de Belem's own blackmail note. If he wanted her killer found, he would have to ask others to investigate. He had Hesselwell walking the streets at night. He urged us to investigate, and then, at the meeting of the Guild of the Coming that night, he called on the murderer to strike again, hoping to draw him into the open. He received no note from the killer purporting to be from the Guild of the Holy Trinity.

That was a ruse to encourage us to help him, but to ensure we did not start by looking into the covens.'

'Perhaps he really does believe the killer is from the Guild of the Holy Trinity,' said Michael. 'If Gilbert had any sense he would encourage that belief to protect himself.' He shook himself. 'I am glad Gilbert and de Belem were lying to each other and misleading each other as they did to others,' he added.

Lucius scratched his head. 'All this makes sense, except for why Gilbert should assume his sister's identity.'

Bartholomew frowned. 'Buckley said de Belem was beginning to lose control of his mercenaries. He needed help. Gilbert could not risk entering Primrose Alley as himself, but he could control the mercenaries as Janetta, the mysterious woman who was the subject of so much speculation among the town's prostitutes.'

'And all so that de Belem could continue to maintain a monopoly over the dyeing business!' said Lucius, shaking his head.

Stanmore pursed his lips. 'That would be a most lucrative position to hold. He would have held sway over a vast region.' He twisted round to look out of the window. 'The sun shines,' he said, 'and we should be away before the day is gone.'

They thanked Lucius for his hospitality and went to where Tulyet was organising a convoy with the cart of prisoners in the middle. De Belem regarded them with a triumphant sneer, while Gilbert huddled in a corner looking frightened. Michael strode over to them.

'We have it reasoned out,' he said. 'We know Gilbert murdered his sister, then Froissart and his wife, and then Nicholas. We know that you hired the friar to steal the book. And we know that the covens were merely a front to hide the size of your business empire from prying eyes, and to ensure these poor people continued to work for you for pitiful wages.'

De Belem shrugged. 'You can think what you like, but you can prove nothing.'

'Taxes!' said Stanmore all of a sudden. 'Part of the reason you have kept the size of your business secret is that you are swindling the King out of his taxes!'

De Belem paled a little, but said nothing. Stanmore rubbed his hands together. 'Old Richard Tulyet has an eye for figures. We will petition the King that we be allowed to assess how much you have cheated him. I am sure he will be willing to let us look. Then the Sheriff will charge you with treason!'

'Why did you kill your sister, Gilbert?' asked Bartholomew gently, hoping to coax with kindness what they might never learn by force.

'Do not deign to answer,' said de Belem harshly. 'They can prove nothing.'

'We can prove Gilbert killed Froissart,' said Michael. 'And he will hang. Is that what you wish, Gilbert, for you to hang while de Belem goes free?'

'She betrayed me,' said Gilbert in a small voice. De Belem made a lunge for him, but was held by two of Tulyet's men.

'Say nothing, you fool! I can hire lawyers who will make a mockery of their feeble reasonings.'

'Now you have no saffron, you have nothing. Tricks and lies will not work now.'

De Belem tried to struggle to his feet, but was

held firmly by the soldiers. Gilbert ignored him and continued.

'I did not mean to kill her. The knife was in my hand. I was angrier than I have ever been before, and the next thing I knew was that she was lying at my feet. I regret it bitterly. Nicholas seized his opportunity and escaped.'

He gave Bartholomew a weak smile. 'I heard you say to Master de Wetherset that Nicholas's coffin had been desecrated because it was meant to be found. You could not have been more wrong. It was never intended to be found. I tried hard to dissuade the Chancellor from excavating the grave, and moved the marker so that you would dig up another. But all failed, and she was exposed to prying eyes in the end. I did not want her to be reburied where she had been so defiled by that mask,' he said, casting a defiant look at de Belem. 'I buried her elsewhere. I will never tell you where because I do not want her disturbed again.'

Bartholomew hoped no one would ask. He had no wish to conduct more exhumations.

'And Froissart and Nicholas?'

Gilbert nodded. 'Marius Froissart came barging into my house when I was removing my beard. It was obvious from his face he knew who I was. He fled to the church. I followed and told him I would kill his family unless he kept silent. I killed his wife, put about Froissart had murdered her, and killed him later that night. Nicholas was easier. He came to look at Janetta's body in the crypt, and I killed him there.'

'And why did you kill Frances?' Bartholomew asked.

'Frances?' whispered de Belem, the colour fleeing from his face.

'She knew too much,' said Gilbert. 'She was on her way to reveal all when I killed her.'

'You killed Frances?' whispered de Belem. 'My daughter?'

'Yes!' said Gilbert loudly. 'I killed her. I did it for the sake of the saffron. Believe me, Reginald, once that fox-faced friar knew about it, it would not have been a secret for long, and we would have lost everything.'

'How could you?' whispered de Belem. 'Why did you not tell me what she was doing? I could have spoken with her. She loved me!'

'Like Isobel?' asked Michael casually.

'Did you kill her too?' asked de Belem, his face grey.

'I did not,' said Gilbert. 'Although doubtless I will be accused of it. I did not touch the whores.'

'But you have already told us you killed Janetta and Frances!' said Stanmore.

Gilbert raised his manacled hands. 'But I did not kill the others. Perhaps de Belem did. It was he, who as high priest, called for another murder. How would he know if he were not the killer?'

De Belem looked away. 'Not I,' he said.

'Rubbish!' said Michael. 'Gilbert deliberately started the rumours that Froissart was the killer because the killer was him! He confessed to killing Frances, and she, like the others, had a circle on her foot.'

'I saw that mark on the others,' said Gilbert. 'I copied it. It was the high priest who killed the others.'

De Belem eyed him coldly. 'What anyone thinks matters nothing now that I know my daughter's murderer will hang.' He gave a soft laugh. 'I really thought it was the Guild of the Holy Trinity punishing me for my involvement with the covens. I did not imagine it would be a colleague! The reason I predicted another death was because it is time. Excluding Janetta, whom Gilbert killed, there has been a murder every ten days or so. The ten days since Isobel are almost up.'

'It does not matter which of you is the killer, you will both hang,' said Tulyet impatiently, and called to his men to start the journey back to the town. It was light, and time spent talking now was time wasted.

Bartholomew and Michael watched them go. 'Do you believe him?' asked Bartholomew.

Michael shook his head. 'I do not. De Belem is merely trying to confuse us. He lied to us in the garden of the Brazen George, so why should he not lie to us again? And Gilbert has confessed to killing Janetta and Frances. We know why the friar died and how; we have discovered who killed Froissart and Nicholas; and we have rescued Buckley. We have done all that de Wetherset has asked of us.' He rubbed his eyes tiredly. 'It is over for us, Matt.'

'You are wrong, Brother,' said Bartholomew softly. 'This business is not over yet.'

ChAPTER 12

STANMORE INSISTED THAT BARTHOLOMEW AND
Michael stop at Trumpington for breakfast.
Tulyet and his men, aided by Stanmore's new
recruits, rode on to Cambridge. Tulyet had a busy
day ahead of him. He would need to interview all his
prisoners, round up any others who were implicated,
and begin the documentation of the case. As they parted,
Tulyet made arrangements to call at Michaelhouse later
to go over the details once more. Cynric wanted to see
Rachel Atkin to let her know he was safe, and said he
would take word to de Wetherset.

'Shall I tell him that his clerk spent his spare time as
a woman?' Cynric asked guilelessly.

'Not unless you want to spend the rest of the day
in the custody of the Proctors,' said Bartholomew
mildly. Cynric grinned and sped off after Tulyet's
cavalcade.

Michael leaned back in one of Stanmore's best
chairs and stretched his feet towards the fire Edith
was stoking up. Stanmore sat opposite him, sipping
some wine. Michael's habit was still splashed with the
paint Bartholomew had flicked at him the night before.

Bartholomew wondered who would dye it now de Belem was gone.

They discussed details of the night's work. Edith sniffed dismissively when they told her how Gilbert had disguised himself, and claimed a woman would have been able to tell the difference.

'You are probably right,' said Bartholomew. 'Once I knew, it was very obvious. His walk was masculine and his cheeks were sometimes thickly coated in powders.'

'That would be to hide his whiskers,' said Edith. 'He would need to shave constantly, even though his beard was not adequate to hide the scars on his face.'

'No wonder Janetta was difficult to track down,' said Michael. 'And Gilbert fooled Tulyet, too. He went to interview "Janetta" when Froissart first claimed sanctuary, and she even told him she had witnessed the murder she had committed herself!'

'And then she denied ever meeting Tulyet to add to our growing concerns over Tulyet's involvement,' said Bartholomew. He thought for a moment, staring pensively at the wine in his cup. 'But I am still concerned about their claim that they did not kill the other women.'

'They are lying to confuse us,' said Stanmore. 'It was them. Gilbert confessed to killing Janetta and Frances. How much more evidence do you need? Think about Sybilla's description, Frances's last words, and the circles on their feet.'

'Sybilla gave no kind of description at all,' said Bartholomew impatiently. 'It could fit just about anyone. And, as you pointed out, they will hang anyway, so why bother to lie?'

'Because they have spent the last several months doing little else,' said Stanmore. 'They have perpetrated the most frightful fraud, terrifying people with false witchcraft, and pretending to be those they are not. Their whole lives have been a lie.' He reached for the jug of wine. 'It is over. We should look to the future, and I must decide whether I should employ a dyer until another comes to take de Belem's place.'

'What will you do with your private army?' asked Michael, beginning to laugh.

Stanmore regarded him coolly. 'I do not see why you find that prospect amusing,' he said. 'If there had been men like these with us tonight, we would not have been ambushed. We live in dangerous times, Brother. These men will guard my goods, and I will be able to trade much further afield.' He rubbed his hands. 'Ely is lacking in good drapers.'

Michael rubbed his eyes. 'I will have nightmares about this for weeks,' he said. 'I hate to confess this to you, Matt, but when I saw that shadow figure and heard that awful screech, I thought de Belem really had conjured something from hell. It was something to do with the atmosphere of that place, with the chanting and the torchlight. I can understand how de Belem was able to use people's imaginations to increase their fear.'

Bartholomew stretched, feeling his muscles stiffening from his unaccustomed ride. 'I did not imagine de Belem would give it a second glance, but I was desperate. I certainly did not think you would be fooled by it, especially in view of the fright you gave me last week.'

'But mine was only a goat!' said Michael, his eyes round. 'Lord knows what yours was meant to be, but

it looked like a demon from hell! It was horrible: all
gnarled and twisted!'

'It was meant to be a goat. And I am sure you will
appreciate there was little time for practice under the
circumstances,' Bartholomew added drily.

Michael gave a reluctant smile. They took their leave
of the Stanmores and walked back to Michaelhouse. De
Wetherset had posted a clerk at the Trumpington Gate
to bring them to him when they arrived. He was waiting
in his office with Buckley and Harling at his side.

Bartholomew smiled at the grammar master, pleased
to see that he had regained some colour in his face,
and his eyes had lost the dull, witless look they had
had the night before. De Wetherset, however, looked
grey with shock.

'I am sorry,' he said. He must be shaken indeed,
thought Bartholomew, to admit being wrong. 'When
did you begin to suspect Gilbert?'

'Only yesterday,' said Michael, 'although the clues
to Gilbert's other identity were there all along. It is
ironic that Gilbert heard us discussing the probability
that Master Buckley was the culprit, while all along, it
was he.'

De Wetherset put his face in his hands, while Buckley
patted him on the shoulder consolingly. Bartholomew
wondered how he could ever have considered the
possibility that this bumbling, gentle old man would
have hidden bodies in chests and stolen from the
University.

He stole a quick glance at Harling. He stood behind de
Wetherset, his face impassive, although his fingers picked
constantly at a loose thread on his gown. Now Buckley

was back, he would have to relinquish his position as Vice-Chancellor.

Michael tried to encourage the dejected Chancellor. 'It is over now. No one stole the book, so the University's secrets are safe. Even from me,' he added guilelessly, making de Wetherset favour him with a guilty glance. 'I must say that it has caused me to wonder whether such a book should exist at all, given that it could become a powerful tool in the hands of wicked men.'

De Wetherset pointed at a pile of grey ashes in the hearth, twitching gently in the draught from the door. 'There is Nicholas's book. You are right, Brother. Master Buckley and I decided that if the book were gone, no one will be able to use it for evil ends. But I am afraid you are wrong when you say it is over. There was another murder last night. A woman was killed near the Barnwell Gate.'

Bartholomew looked sharply at Harling, but his face betrayed nothing.

'But that is not possible!' said Michael. 'We knew where de Belem and Gilbert were all of last night.'

'De Belem and Gilbert do not know the identity of the killer,' said Buckley. 'I heard them talking about it.'

'Well, who is it then?' exploded Michael.

Bartholomew watched Harling intently.

'And of which guild were you a member, Master Harling?' he asked quietly.

Harling gazed at him in shock before he was able to answer. 'Guild? Membership of such organisations is not permitted by the University!'

'No more lies, Richard,' said de Wetherset wearily. 'Brother Michael and Doctor Bartholomew have served me well in this business. I will not have them deceived any longer.'

Harling pursed his lips in a thin, white line and looked away, so de Wetherset answered.

'Master Harling became a member of the Guild of the Coming when he took over as my deputy. I am ashamed to say that a Physwick Hostel scholar was a member, and Richard persuaded him to take him to one of the meetings. He joined to gather information to help you.'

Bartholomew looked sceptical, and Harling's eyes glittered in anger. 'My motives were purely honourable,' he said in a tight voice. 'As Vice-Chancellor, it was only a question of time before I took over from Master de Wetherset. I did not want to inherit a University riddled with corruption and wickedness, so I undertook to join the coven so that any University involvement in this business could be stamped out.'

'Only I knew of Harling's membership,' said de Wetherset. 'I considered it too dangerous even for Gilbert to know.'

'So what did you discover?' asked Bartholomew, looking at the still-angry Harling.

'Very little,' he said. 'Only that the high priest often had an enormous man with him, and there was the woman, whom I now understand was Gilbert.'

'Yes, I saw him at de Belem's house!' said Buckley. 'A great lumbering fellow that shuffled when he walked, and whose face was always covered by a mask.'

'There was something odd about him,' Harling continued. 'His movements were peculiar – uncoordinated

– but at the same time immensely strong. Frankly, he frightened me.'

'Are you suggesting that this man might be the killer?' asked Michael.

Bartholomew's mind raced. He remembered the huge man whom he had struggled with in the orchard, and who had probably knocked him off his feet in St Mary's churchyard when Janetta had wanted to speak with him. Hesselwell had mentioned a large man, too.

Harling shrugged. 'I can think of no other, now that it appears that Gilbert and de Belem cannot be responsible.'

Bartholomew and Michael took their leave and walked to the Barnwell Gate.

'Damn!' said Michael, banging his fist into his palm. 'The high priest claimed that another victim would be taken before new moon, and we were so convinced that it was de Belem that we did not consider the possibility of another.'

Bartholomew rubbed tiredly at his mud-splattered hair. 'We have been stupid,' he said. 'Logically, neither de Belem nor Gilbert could have killed Isobel. Gilbert was in the church waiting for the friar, and de Belem was off kidnapping Buckley. Of course this large man could be a ruse of Harling's to deflect suspicion from him.'

'What?' said Michael. 'Do you think Harling is the killer?'

Bartholomew spread his hands. 'Why not? We have little enough evidence, but it can be made to fit to him. First, he is a self-confessed member of a coven, whatever his motive for joining. Second, he would have had a good deal to gain if Buckley had not returned to reclaim his position, so why should he not be in league with de Belem to keep Buckley out of the way? Third, I do not like him!'

'Oh, Matt!' said Michael, exasperated. 'That is no evidence at all! I do not like him either, but he says he joined the guild after Buckley's disappearance, and I hardly think de Belem would be so foolish as to trust him immediately with the information that he had the previous Vice-Chancellor as prisoner in his house!'

They walked in silence until Bartholomew saw the large figure of Father Cuthbert puffing towards them. Although the day was not yet hot, Cuthbert's face was glistening with sweat and dark patches stained his gown from his exertions.

'Good morning,' said Cuthbert breathlessly, drawing up for a welcome pause. 'I have been out visiting before the sun gets too hot. Have you heard the news? Another murder at the Barnwell Gate, the same as the others.'

'How do you know it was the same as the others?' asked Bartholomew. He saw Michael's glance of disbelief and tried to pull himself together. Now he was suspecting everyone! There was no way the cumbersome Father Cuthbert would be able to catch a nimble prostitute.

'Master Jonstan told me,' said Cuthbert. 'I have been to visit him. He has not been himself since the death of his mother.'

'His mother died?' said Bartholomew. 'We had not heard. I am sorry to hear that. He talked about her a lot.'

'Yes, they were close,' said Cuthbert. 'But it was as well she died. She was bed-ridden for many years.'

He ambled off, waving cheerily, and Bartholomew

turned to watch him as he stopped to talk to a group of dirty children playing with an ancient hoop from a barrel.

'No,' said Michael, firmly taking his arm and pulling at him to resume walking. 'Not Father Cuthbert. He is too old and too fat, and you are clutching at straws.'

Bartholomew stopped abruptly and took a fistful of Michael's habit. 'Not Father Cuthbert,' he said, his mind whirling. 'Alric Jonstan.'

Michael stared at him, eyes narrowed, and pulled absently at a stray strand of hair. 'Jonstan told Cuthbert the murder was the same as the others, but how would he know?' he began slowly. He shook Bartholomew's hand from his robe impatiently. 'It does not fit, Matt! Jonstan lives near the Barnwell Gate and probably heard the alarm when the body was found and went to see. As Proctor, he probably saw the other victims.'

'His mother!' exclaimed Bartholomew suddenly. 'When Jonstan sprained his ankle, he said his mother would look after him. Cuthbert just said she was bed-ridden.'

'He probably said that so you would not worry about him,' said Michael.

'Father?' yelled Bartholomew, running after the fat priest. 'When did Master Jonstan's mother die?'

Cuthbert turned, surprised at Bartholomew's tense face and the question out of the blue. He scratched one of his chins and thought. 'Mistress Jonstan passed away . . . four, perhaps five weeks ago . . .'

Bartholomew sped back to Michael. 'Come on!' he cried.

Michael lunged at him. 'His mother died four weeks ago? So what?'

Bartholomew struggled to free his tabard from Michael's grip. 'He was talking about her as if she were still alive last week. The man is unhinged.'

'Grief does things to people other than make them into murderers,' said Michael, gently maintaining his hold on his friend's clothes. 'Matt, you cannot go charging into Jonstan's home and accuse him of committing these foul crimes with the evidence you have. It is all circumstantial.'

'Think!' said Bartholomew, exasperated. 'Tulyet's men patrolled the streets and so did the Proctors and their beadles. Jonstan was out in the dark quite legitimately about University business. He would become familiar with others who regularly stole around in the night – the prostitutes, over whom he had no jurisdiction because they are not members of the University. I am willing to wager anything that the murders were committed on days when it was Jonstan's turn to do night patrol. For heaven's sake, Michael!' he yelled, 'Sybilla saw the Proctor and his men the night of Isobel's murder.'

Michael began to waver. 'But what about the Guild of the Holy Trinity . . . ?'

Bartholomew shook his head dismissively. 'That is irrelevant. All the other murders were committed in churchyards of the High Street, and now this one is committed at the Barnwell Gate, near Jonstan's home, from which he cannot move because he has a sprained ankle.'

Michael relinquished his hold of Bartholomew's gown with a flourish. 'Have it your way. I remain sceptical. We will visit Master Jonstan. You can say you came to look at his foot, and that way, if we find you are wrong, we will at least have an excuse for being there.'

They walked the short distance to the Barnwell Gate. Tulyet was still there, looking exhausted. He indicated a sheeted body in despair.

'I thought we had it all worked out,' he said. 'And now this. Is there no bottom to this pit of wickedness?'

'Have you rounded up any more of de Belem's followers?' asked Michael.

'Oh, yes,' said Tulyet. 'My men started the moment we arrived. Primrose Alley had been used to garrison de Belem's mercenaries, and we discovered Gilbert's clothes and beard and a spare wig in one of the houses. There were red masks, too, and more black cloaks than you would believe. We also found him.'

They looked to where he pointed. Against the wall of a house, an enormous man sat smiling up at the sun with a vacant grin, guarded by one of Tulyet's soldiers. He saw a black cat slink past and gurgled at it. Bartholomew went over to him and knelt down. The man beamed at him with an open mouth of poorly-formed teeth and then began to prod at a spot of mud on Bartholomew's tabard.

'What's your name?' he asked.

The man continued to prod at Bartholomew's tabard.

'Be careful,' Tulyet warned. 'He is dangerous.'

Bartholomew snapped his fingers near the man's ear, but there was no reaction. He put a hand under his chin and gently tipped his head back so he could look at his face. It was flat, and his tongue was too large for his mouth and lolled out. Bartholomew looked at the faint marks still on his hand from when he had been bitten in the orchard, and saw that they matched the man's asymmetrical teeth. He had unquestionably found his attacker. The man gurgled in panic, and Bartholomew let him go.

'I think he is deaf, and I doubt he can speak. The poor man has the mind of a child. He was at Michaelhouse the night the gate burned, but I do not think he had the slightest idea what he was doing. Give him to the Austin Canons at the hospital, Master Tulyet. Perhaps they can find some simple tasks for him to do until he becomes too weak.'

'Weak?' said Tulyet. 'He is as strong as an ox, as my men can attest!'

'He is dying,' said Bartholomew. 'Listen to his breathing. I have seen this before in these people. Their chests do not develop normally and they are prone to infections. Perhaps he will recover this time, but I doubt he will the next. Let him go: he is a child.'

Tulyet grimaced, but gave a curt order to the guard to escort the man to St John's Hospital. 'When we found him, he was tethered to a door frame with a simple knot that any five-year-old could have untied. You are doubtless right in that he was unaware of what he was doing. But I hope he is not dangerous.'

Bartholomew shook his head. 'If he was violent to your men it was probably because they frightened him. Mistress Starre had such a son, but I assumed he had died when she did during the plague. He was probably cared for in Primrose Alley by neighbours, until de Belem and Gilbert came and used him for their own purposes.'

'Who was the victim?' asked Michael, nodding at the sheeted figure being loaded onto a cart.

'Sybilla, the ditcher's daughter,' said Tulyet. 'She was identified by that woman over there.'

Bartholomew stared in disbelief, and felt the blood pound in his head. He looked to where Matilde sat on the grass at the side of the road with her back to him. He walked over to her, feeling his legs turn weak from the shock, and sank down on the grass.

'Why?' he asked.

She turned a tear-stained face. 'She saw you ride off after de Belem and Janetta last night and heard Master Buckley telling the Sheriff's men that de Belem was the high priest. She thought she was safe. She said she was going to the Sheriff's house to tell him what she had seen so that she could be a witness for him. She was killed on her way there.'

Bartholomew rubbed a hand across his face and stared at the cart containing Sybilla's body. She had jumped to the same conclusions that he had done, but for her they had proved fatal. He suddenly felt sick, as the exertions of the previous night's activities caught up with him.

Matilde rested a hand on his arm. 'There was nothing you could do, Doctor. You were kind to her and I will never forget that.'

As he looked from Sybilla's body to Matilde's grieving face, Bartholomew's despair began to turn to anger. He stood slowly.

'Do you know which house belongs to Master Jonstan, the Proctor?' he asked softly.

Matilde stood with him. 'Yes. It is a two-storey house with a green door on Shoemaker Row. Why do you want to see him? He will not help you for our sakes. He was always calling us whores and bawds. Each morning, he would prop his bed-ridden mother near the window so that she could yell abuse at us as we walked past her house.'

'They did not like prostitutes?' asked Bartholomew. He thought of when they had drunk ale with Jonstan at the Fair and he had told them his belief that the plague would return if people did not amend their sinful ways.

'Few people do,' said Matilde. 'At least not openly. But Master Jonstan is perhaps one of our most hostile opponents.'

Bartholomew waited to hear no more. Leaving Matilde staring after him, startled, he raced across the road and made for Shoemaker Row. He ignored the shouts of Michael and Tulyet behind him and ran harder, almost falling as he collided with a cart carrying vegetables to the Fair. He leapt over the fence surrounding Holy Trinity Church and tore across the churchyard, bounding over tombstones and knocking over a pardoner selling his wares on the church steps. When he emerged in Shoemaker Row, he pulled up, shaking off the angry hands of the pardoner who had followed him.

Then he saw the house, near the lower end of the street. He set off again at a run and pounded on the door of Jonstan's house. There was no answer and the shutters were firmly closed. Bartholomew grabbed one and shook it as hard as he could, drawing the attention of several passers-by, who stopped to watch what he was doing.

'Try the back door, love,' said an elderly woman

kindly. 'He never uses the front door now his mother has gone.'

Bartholomew muttered his thanks and shot around the side of the house to where a wooden gate led into a small yard. Finding the gate locked, Bartholomew stood back and gave it a solid kick that almost took it off its hinges. He heard shouting in the lane and guessed that Michael and Tulyet had followed him.

The yard was deserted so Bartholomew went to the door at the back of the house. He grabbed the handle and pushed hard with his shoulder, expecting that to be locked too, and was surprised to find himself hurtle through it into Jonstan's kitchen. The Proctor was there, sitting at the table eating some oatmeal, his injured foot propped in front of him. He looked taken aback at Bartholomew's sudden entry, his blue eyes even more saucer-like than usual.

Behind Bartholomew, Michael elbowed his way in, his large face red with exertion and his breath coming in great gasps.

'Matt has come to see to your foot,' he said, his chest heaving.

'I have not!' retorted Bartholomew. He was across the kitchen in a single stride. 'So, you could not walk to the High Street last night!' he said, seizing the front of Jonstan's tabard and wrenching him from the chair. 'And you had to kill Sybilla here, where it was not so far for you to go. You were lucky, were you not, Jonstan? Most of the prostitutes have been off the streets for the past two days, but then Sybilla appeared.'

'I have no idea what you are talking about,' said

Jonstan. He appealed to Michael with Tulyet behind him. 'He has gone insane!'

Bartholomew dropped Jonstan back into his chair.

'Where are your bloodstained clothes, Jonstan?' he said. He began to look around the kitchen. 'I have seen the bodies of your victims. You must have been covered in blood when you came home. What were you wearing?' He grabbed a bucket and upended its contents onto the floor, and then began to open the doors to the cupboards.

Jonstan rose unsteadily to his feet, favouring his injured ankle. 'Stop him!' he said to Tulyet. 'He cannot barge into my home and start going through my possessions! Arrest him! Brother, he is your friend. Stop him before I decide to press charges!'

Tulyet took hold of Bartholomew's shoulder, but was shaken off angrily. Michael made a half-hearted attempt to stop his friend as he went towards the small scullery.

Jonstan limped across the floor after Bartholomew.

'Stop!' he almost screamed. 'You have no right!'

Bartholomew grabbed something and pushed it into Jonstan's face. It was a bloodstained hose. 'What is this?' he snarled.

Jonstan's face was an unhealthy colour. 'I cut myself,' he said. 'I was going to wash that this afternoon.'

'Show me where you cut yourself, Master Jonstan,' said Bartholomew, clenching his fists to stop them from grabbing the Proctor by the throat.

'I will do no such thing. I am a Proctor of the University and you are under my jurisdiction. Brother, take your colleague back to his College and lock him away where he can do no more harm,' said Jonstan, pushing Michael towards Bartholomew.

Bartholomew wrenched the doors open on another cupboard and rummaged inside. He held up an assortment of women's shoes. The victims Bartholomew had seen had their shoes removed so that the little circle could be painted on their feet.

'Where did you get these?' he demanded, hurling one at Jonstan.

'They belong to my mother, not that it is any of your business,' said Jonstan.

Bartholomew continued his prowling and bent to retrieve another article of clothing from where it had been hurled into a corner. He held it up so that Michael and Tulyet could see the huge dark blotches that stained Jonstan's tabard.

'I told you I cut myself,' said Jonstan. 'You go too far, Doctor. Leave my house at once!'

'Show me the cut that produced this much blood, and I will leave,' said Bartholomew.

Tulyet looked from the bloodstained tabard to Jonstan and began to move towards him. Jonstan made a sudden dive into the scullery, slamming the door closed, locking Michael and Tulyet in the kitchen. He turned to Bartholomew and brandished a knife coated thickly with clotting blood. He lunged towards Bartholomew, who countered his blow with a small stool he had grabbed. One of the legs bounced to the floor and Bartholomew began to back away.

'Harlot-lover!' Jonstan hissed. 'I know how you visit that filthy Matilde, and I know how you secreted the ditcher's daughter away, thinking to keep her from me!'

A great crash shook the kitchen door as Michael and Tulyet began to batter it down. Jonstan ignored it.

'My mother warned me about men who go with whores,' he said, limping closer to Bartholomew. 'And she told me the Death would come again as long as we did not learn from our sins and continued to allow the whores to roam.'

There was another crash from the kitchen door. Jonstan darted forward and made a feint to his right with the knife. Bartholomew swung wildly with the stool, and remembered that Jonstan was well trained in hand-to-hand fighting. He was not a Proctor, prowling the streets at night for miscreant scholars, for nothing. He had doubtless wrestled many a reluctant student back to his lodgings. Before he realised what was happening, Bartholomew felt one arm bent painfully behind him and saw the knife flash at the same time that there was a third crash from the locked door. He saw the hinges begin to give, as he squirmed sideways using every ounce of his strength. Jonstan's knife stabbed harmlessly into his bag. Jonstan wrenched it free but did not relinquish his hold on Bartholomew's arm.

As the door flung open, Jonstan calmly held the knife to Bartholomew's throat and smiled at Michael and Tulyet. They stopped dead. Bartholomew began to struggle, but Jonstan merely pressed the knife more firmly to his throat.

'This is a sharp knife, gentlemen,' he said. 'I have reason to know.'

'Let him go, Alric,' said Michael softly. 'You cannot escape now.'

'He is a lover of whores,' said Jonstan again. 'And that

is not appropriate behaviour for a scholar. I am a Proctor and it is my duty to see that he does not do it again. My mother would not be pleased to hear that I had let him escape.'

'Your mother is dead,' said Michael. He began to move towards Jonstan, but stopped as he lifted the knife, preparing to strike.

'Stay back! My mother is upstairs. She will come down soon to see what all this noise is about. She will not be pleased to see what you have done to her door.'

Bartholomew felt Jonstan grip him tighter still. He saw that Jonstan was sufficiently unbalanced that if Michael or Tulyet made a move towards him, he would not hesitate to kill. Gritting his teeth against the ache in his arm, Bartholomew began to undo the strap on his medical bag.

'Why did you kill all those women?' asked Tulyet, seeing what Bartholomew was doing and trying to buy him time.

'My mother told me to,' Jonstan replied.

'That is not possible,' said Tulyet. 'Your mother died before the first of your victims was killed.'

'I told you, she is upstairs,' said Jonstan with exaggerated patience.

Bartholomew had his hand inside the bag and began to feel around.

'Were you a member of one of the guilds?' asked Michael, keeping his eyes firmly fixed on Jonstan's face so he would not betray what Bartholomew was doing.

'It is against the University regulations to be in a guild,' said Jonstan. 'And I most certainly was not a member of a coven.'

'But what about the Guild of the Holy Trinity?' asked Michael. 'Men like Richard Harling believe as you do that continued sin will bring about a return of the Death.'

Bartholomew had what he wanted and was struggling to open the packet without making it rustle. Jonstan made a dismissive gesture at Michael, who licked dry lips.

'If you were not a member of the covens, why did you kill Sybilla before new moon as the high priest demanded?' he asked.

'I did nothing of the kind,' said Jonstan. 'It was time for another whore to die – one every ten days so they will all be gone before Christmas – and that is why she died, not because that raving maniac in the mask told me to do it.' He took the knife away from Bartholomew's throat but put it back again when Tulyet made a move forward.

Jonstan continued matter-of-factly. 'I killed them because my mother did not like whores patrolling the streets outside her home. You must appreciate that the Death will return if we do not take steps to eradicate evil from our land. We have been warned, and God will send another plague to destroy us if we continue to sin.'

'Why did you draw a circle on the feet of the victims?' asked Tulyet, seeing beads of sweat breaking out on Jonstan's face, and desperately trying to keep him talking.

'Because that was the sign one of the guilds used: a fallen halo. A sign that represented evil seemed an appropriate mark for evil women,' said Jonstan. He gave a short chuckle and began to move the knife.

'Matt!' yelled Michael, leaping forward. Bartholomew hurled the contents of his hand backwards into Jonstan's face, and struggled free as the Proctor fell back, choking and flailing wildly. As the powder began to burn Jonstan's eyes, he dropped the knife and began to cry out, covering his face with his hands. Bartholomew staggered back, while Tulyet kicked the knife out of reach and pushed Jonstan up against the wall.

'I cannot see!' Jonstan cried, struggling to wrench his arms from Tulyet to rub at his eyes.

'Neither can Sybilla!' said Bartholomew quietly, as he left the house.

Later that day, after they had spoken again to de Wetherset and had made formal statements to Tulyet, Bartholomew and Michael sat on the fallen tree next to the wall of the orchard, watching the sun sink down behind the trees. There was a haze of insects in the air, but it was quiet in the orchard, and Bartholomew did not want to answer any more questions that day.

He stretched his legs out in front of him and folded his arms across his chest. Next to him Michael fidgeted to get comfortable as he leaned back.

'So,' Michael said. 'Jonstan acted alone in the murder of the women. He claimed his first victim the day that his mother died, selected a prostitute randomly every ten days or so, and intended to continue so that the town would be free of them by Christmas. He was wholly unconnected with the guilds and selected one of their symbols only because it represented evil to him, in much the same way that the poor prostitutes did.'

Bartholomew was silent. Jonstan's mad claims had so unsettled him that he had asked Michael to return to Jonstan's house, just to make certain that there were no ancient mother still living upstairs as Jonstan had maintained. Michael had found no mother, but had found her room laid out as though she would return at any moment to use it.

He watched a blackbird hopping through the grass, eyeing them cautiously with beady, yellow-rimmed eyes. Michael cracked his knuckles and stretched his arms.

'So, we were called to investigate the possible death of a friar in the University chest, and we discover that the friar died because the Chancellor did not maintain his locks; that a man was killed and hidden in the bell tower because he saw the Chancellor's clerk changing his identity; that one of the town's best-known merchants was using witchcraft and kidnapping to terrify people into helping him gain a monopoly over the dyeing trade; and that the Senior Proctor was insane and was killing the town's prostitutes. Quite a feat of investigation considering how little we had to go on,' he said.

They sat for a while longer, watching the red fade from the sky as it grew dark and silent; black bats flitted between the trees. Bartholomew was tired, but did not want to move. The air was cool and pleasant after the long, hot day. His students' disputations were the next morning, and he did not want them pestering him trying to find out what questions they might be asked.

'What did you throw at Jonstan?' asked Michael after a while.

'Pepper,' said Bartholomew. He smiled suddenly. 'It is not a usual component of my medical supplies, but I was rash enough to ask Deynman to refill some of the bottles and packets that I wanted to replace after my bag was stolen in Primrose Alley. It is not a difficult task, and they are all clearly marked. I use ground mustard seeds for some treatments, but Deynman could not find any because it had all been used to make Walter sick. He gave me pepper instead. I meant to take it out and get the mustard, but never got around to it.'

'Would mustard have worked?'

Bartholomew shook his head. 'Not nearly as well as pepper.'

A shadow fell across them and Bartholomew looked up to see Boniface. In place of his habit he wore baggy homespun leggings and a dark green tunic. He sat next to them on the fallen tree and looked up to where the bats were feasting on the thousands of insects that hovered in the air.

'I assume you have decided what you wish to do,' said Bartholomew.

Boniface nodded. 'I made my confession to Master Kenyngham, and he agreed that I should go home. He said I need time to consider, and that I will be a better friar if I return than if I stay.'

'Wise advice,' said Bartholomew. 'And I imagine you do not wish to be a physician either?'

Boniface grimaced. 'Never!' he said. 'I only agreed to study medicine to follow in my father's footsteps.'

'Your father is a physician?' said Bartholomew in disbelief. How had a physician managed to sire the surly Boniface, with his rigid ideas about bleeding and treatments?

Boniface nodded. 'We seldom see eye to eye,' he added with a wry grin at Bartholomew. 'Perhaps we might do better now.'

'You live in Durham, I recall?' said Bartholomew.

Boniface nodded. 'Do you have enough money to travel?'

Boniface shook his head. 'I gave it all to Master Kenyngham for my College bill, but I will manage.'

'Take this,' said Bartholomew, rummaging in his bag and handing Boniface a package.

'What is it?' he asked, taking it warily.

'Saffron,' said Bartholomew. 'Friar Lucius gave it to me. You should be able to sell it for a high price, since it is apparently almost impossible to obtain these days. It should give you enough to get home.'

'Saffron!' exclaimed Boniface, turning the package over in his hands. 'I have not seen saffron since before the Death.' He thrust it back. 'I cannot take this from you.'

'You can,' said Bartholomew. 'And if you will not take a gift, you can send the money later. Go, Boniface, before Father William realises you are missing.'

The student turned to leave, and then came back.

'The Master was right,' he said, with a sudden smile that made him look young. 'You are a good man for a heretic!'

He sped off through the trees and they heard the gate slam behind him as he left.

'Father Lucius gave me some saffron too,' said Michael, standing stiffly and stretching.

'And what did you do with yours, Brother?' asked Bartholomew, rising and looping his battered bag over his shoulder.

'I gave half to Agatha and half to Lady Matilde,' said Michael. 'Agatha will now let me into the kitchen again, while Matilde has promised me a fine meal.'

Since it was a pleasant evening to be out, they decided to walk along the river and then cut back to Michaelhouse along the High Street. The paths and streets were full of people returning home after a day at the Fair. Bartholomew saw Stanmore's apprentices pulling a cart, and realised that his brother-in-law's already considerable fortune was still being made even when he was away chasing murderers and tricksters. Bartholomew stopped to buy some over-ripe pears from a scruffy child, and shared them with Michael as they walked. As they turned down St Michael's Lane, they met Master Kenyngham going in the opposite direction.

'The Chancellor told me he is very grateful for your help over these last few days,' he said, beaming benignly at them. 'He has asked me to read over his account of it to ensure that it is accurate.'

'His account? Why would he write an account?' said Bartholomew.

'For the book of the University history,' said the Master, surprised at his question.

'But de Wetherset burned the book,' said Michael. 'He showed us.'

'He burned the one in the University chest,' said Kenyngham, 'but there is a complete copy in the chest at the Carmelite Friary – one that is not missing the pages that Gilbert stole. Of course, there are duplicates of most documents there.'

'And he is keeping that book up to date?' asked Michael incredulously.

'Well, of course,' said Kenyngham. 'It would be of no use to anyone incomplete.' He suddenly stood back, putting his hands over his mouth like a child. 'I do hope

I have not been indiscreet. The Chancellor told me to keep its presence secret, but I assumed you would know, since you have been involved with the affair during the last two weeks. Oh, dear!'

'The Bishop told me there was a second chest,' said Michael. 'You have not told us anything we did not already guess.'

Kenyngham looked relieved, and his habitual gentle smile returned. He patted Michael on the arm and went on his way. When he had turned the corner, Bartholomew started to laugh.

'What is so funny?' said Michael. 'We have just learned that the Chancellor has deceived us yet again. He withheld important facts from us about members of the University; he hid vital pages when I was trying to discover a motive for the friar's death; and now he has claimed to have burned the book while all the time there is another!'

'Yes,' said Bartholomew. 'But how can you fail to admire his guile? He not only misleads us into believing that he had burned the only copy of the book, but he is using our own Master to check his facts!'

Michael laughed too, and took his arm. 'Come on, Matt. Let's go home.'

hISTORICAL NOTE

In 1350 Cambridge, like the rest of England, was still reeling under the impact of the Black Death. It is not known how many people died: social historians estimate that between one third and one half of the population of Europe perished between 1348 and 1350. The consequences of this high mortality rate have been argued for many years – some historians have suggested that the full impact of the massive population drop was not fully felt until the subsequent plagues in the 1360s and 1370s, while others argue that the effect was devastating and immediate.

Neither the University of Oxford nor the University of Cambridge left contemporary accounts of the Black Death, and so we cannot be certain how the academic communities dealt with the catastrophe and its aftermath.

Contemporary records tell that in Cambridge all members of the Dominican Friary died, while the monks at Barnwell Priory lost half their number. This abrupt decline in the number of clergy meant that there was a serious shortage of priests willing and able to work in the community. In 1349 the Bishop of Bath and Wells wrote to the clergy of his diocese to instruct them that confessions might be made to a layman if a priest was unavailable. In the same year the Archbishop of York wrote to his brother and bemoaned a lack of secular priests. Churches fell into disuse and were decommissioned, or closed up to await the time when they had a congregation again. And a few people, bereft of clergy, began to turn to other forms of worship.

In 1350 Thomas Kenyngham was the Master of Michaelhouse; Richard de Wetherset was Chancellor of the University of Cambridge (Richard Harling succeeded him in 1351); and Richard Tulyet was Mayor of Cambridge six times between 1337 and 1346. Guilds were an important part of medieval life, some taking the form of trade associations, while others were predominantly religious. The Guild of the Holy Trinity and the Guild of Purification existed in medieval Cambridge.

Important documents were kept in the tower of St Mary's Church until 1400. After 1400 Colleges began to build their own towers, and took responsibility for their own muniments. Some of these can still be seen today in Christ's College, where a narrow staircase leads to a chamber in the gate tower, where precious documents are still stored in heavy oak, iron-bound chests. The great chest at St Mary's was seized by rioting townspeople in 1381, and all the documents burned. A similar chest at the Carmelite Friary was also destroyed. Today, general University funding is still referred to as 'the University Chest', recalling a time when valuables really were kept in a strong-box.

Michaelhouse was founded in 1324 by Hervey de

Stanton, who was Edward II's Chancellor of the Exchequer. King's Hall was endowed in 1337, and was a powerful institution with 32 Fellows. Physwick Hostel was a small institution which was a dependency of Gonville Hall. In 1546, Henry VIII founded Trinity College, and the buildings and lands of Michaelhouse, King's Hall, and Physwick Hostel went to make up the new institution. No parts of Michaelhouse survive, but Trinity's Great Gate dates from 1520, and was part of King's Hall.

Finally, the Stourbridge Fair was one of the most important trade gatherings in medieval England, taking place each year between August and September. The licence to hold the Fair was granted by King John to the leper hospital of St Mary Magdalene. Although the hospital ceased to exist in 1279, the Fair continued to grow and is Bunyon's 'Vanity Fair' in *Pilgrim's Progress*. It began to decline at the end of the 19th century, and finally died away in the early 1930s.